AUNTIE CLEM'S BAKERY 19-21

AUNTIE CLEM'S BAKERY 19-21

AUNTIE CLEM'S BAKERY

P.D. WORKMAN

PD WORKMAN

ISBN: 9781774687581 (KDP Paperback)
ISBN: 9781774687574 (ePub)

ALSO BY P.D. WORKMAN

FIND MORE BOOKS AT PDWORKMAN.COM

MYSTERY/SUSPENSE:

Auntie Clem's Bakery

Culinary & Pet Cozy Mysteries

Gluten-Free Murder

Dairy-Free Death

Allergen-Free Assignation

Witch-Free Halloween (Halloween Short)

Dog-Free Dinner (Christmas Short)

Stirring Up Murder

Brewing Death

Coup de Glace

Sour Cherry Turnover

Apple-achian Treasure

Vegan Baked Alaska

Muffins Masks Murder

Tai Chi and Chai Tea

Santa Shortbread

Cold as Ice Cream

Changing Fortune Cookies

Hot on the Trail Mix

Fateful Plateful

Cut Out Cookie

On the Slab Pie

Wedding Cake Crush

A Waffle Death

Murder Meringue Pie

A Fowl Play on Christmas Day (Christmas crossover story)

Cinn-Full Secrets (Coming Soon)

Muffin to Lose (Coming Soon)

Custard Cream Conspiracy (Coming Soon

Recipes from Auntie Clem's Bakery

Parks Pat Mysteries

Police Procedural Set in Canada

Out with the Sunset

Long Climb to the Top

Dark Water Under the Bridge

Immersed in the View

Skimming Over the Lake

Hazard of the Hills

Knows the Hills

Spanning the Creek

Sanctuary in the Stream

Echoes of the Engine

Bench with a View

Beneath the Icy Depths

Stand Alone Suspense Novels

Looking Over Your Shoulder

Lion Within

Pursued by the Past

In the Tick of Time

Loose the Dogs

AND MORE AT PDWORKMAN.COM

WEDDING CAKE CRUSH

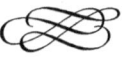

*For friends you can depend on
for anything*

CHAPTER 1

I'm getting cold feet!" Mrs. Peach said, clutching at Erin's arm. "I'm too old to be doing something like this. I should just go home. What was I thinking, leaving when I am just starting to renovate? That's when I need to be home the most."

Erin looked at the big red "Departures" sign on the outside of the airport.

"You'll be fine," Erin assured her, patting her hand comfortingly. "You don't want to be in the house while they're renovating, so you'd end up having to be in a hotel anyway, and, since there are no hotels in Bald Eagle Falls, you wouldn't even be able to be in town. Unless you took me up on my offer and used my guest room. Then you would be right next door."

"Oh, no, I couldn't impose on you like that. You're already doing far too much for me."

"All I'm doing is dropping you off at the airport and keeping an eye on things while you're gone. I'm sure nothing will happen that needs my attention, but I'll be there if something comes up. So you won't come home to... I don't know, orange tiles or something like that."

"Renovations are always more stressful than you think they should be and take longer..."

5

"All the more reason for you to be away enjoying yourself. Why put yourself through it?"

"And as far as cold feet go," Vic chimed in, "be glad you're going to Mexico instead of Alaska! I swear I was never warm on that whole cruise."

Erin remembered it well. She didn't think she would be going on another cruise ever again. Not even when she was Mrs. Peach's age. But if she did, it wouldn't be anywhere cold. It had been fun to see puffins and whales, but she'd rather go somewhere she could see a coral reef and colorful fish. If she ever went on another cruise. Which she wouldn't.

"You are going to have such a nice time," she told the older woman. Mrs. Peach would not have any of the experiences that Erin and Vic had with the seamy underbelly of the cruise industry. There would be no murders while she was aboard, and Erin was sure that what she had seen of the violence and human trafficking would not be duplicated for Mrs. Peach. Even if there were illegal practices going on aboard, Mrs. Peach would know nothing of them. She would be blissfully unaware as she played bingo and shuffleboard and ate at the endless buffets.

And she wouldn't get seasick as Erin had. Erin had been told more than once how rare it was for anyone on such a large ship to experience more than some minor vertigo or nausea.

"And when you get back, everything will be done," Vic agreed. "And it will be like you have a brand-new house."

Mrs. Peach finally released her grip on Erin's arm. "You must think me a very foolish old lady to be spending money like this. I should be more frugal."

"You've spent your whole life being frugal while your husband went off and did whatever he felt like," Erin chided. "Now that you have the money he left you, you should enjoy it while you still can. You don't have any children expecting to inherit it. It's yours to do with as you please."

"I know; I just feel so guilty about it. Think of all the good I could be doing with it; instead, I'm just spending it on myself. That big screen TV? What was I thinking? The old one was just fine. And a cruise? It's so frivolous, just throwing money away."

"And adding on to your house," Erin said. "That's an excellent investment. It will make things more enjoyable and comfortable for you and will improve the house's resale value. It's not really *spending*; you make all that money back when you sell the house. Then you can give it to charity or do whatever you want to with it."

"My estate will have to sell it. I plan to live there for the rest of my life."

Erin nodded. "You *should* enjoy it. It's your house."

"But do I really need a hot tub? And a greenhouse?"

"Think of how good it will feel on your muscles and joints at the end of the day. It is *therapy*, not excess."

"Exactly," Vic agreed. "You'll live a longer, happier life because of it. And plants and nature are supposed to be really good stress relievers and have all kinds of other benefits too."

"And you girls will come over?" Mrs. Peach asked. "You may as well enjoy it too. Whenever you want. You must get sore after being on your feet all day long at the bakery."

Erin saw a flash of doubt cross the face of her transgender employee, who might have some hesitation over wearing something as revealing as a swimsuit. She patted Mrs. Peach on the back. "You'd better be going in, you don't want to miss your flight, and you'll have to go through all those lineups and security first."

"Yes, I suppose you're right," Mrs. Peach agreed, turning toward the doors. She had a purse and a small carry-on bag on the shelf of her walker. Erin had been a little concerned about the management of Mrs. Peach's luggage on her trip, but the cruise had been planned with seniors and mobility issues in mind, and the cruise line had picked up all of her heavy luggage ahead of time so Mrs. Peach did not have more than she could carry with her.

"Have a great trip!" Erin and Vic chorused.

"Don't worry about anything," Erin called after her neighbor as she walked away. "We'll make sure that everything goes smoothly!"

CHAPTER 2

By the time Officer Terry Piper got off of his shift the next evening and they sat down to dinner, Erin had received confirmation that Mrs. Peach had made all of her connections and was on the cruise ship, unpacking and getting ready for a couple of weeks of relaxation and fun in the sun.

"I'm glad that she's not here for this," Erin said, rolling her eyes as they paused for another round of loud hammering and the whine of a power saw next door. Erin checked again to make sure the window was shut to muffle the noise, even though she already knew it was.

"Well…" Terry smiled, showing a dimple, "at least you can tell they're working. They should have lots of time to complete everything before she comes back. It won't end up lasting months and months like some renovation projects."

"They're motivated to get it done while she's gone. I'm sure they don't want her hovering over them supervising and asking questions while they're working."

"Exactly. So we shouldn't have to put up with the noise for very long."

Erin looked down at K9, lying by Terry's feet looking miserable. It must have been even worse for him with his sensitive hearing. Erin had been worried that Orange Blossom, her cat, had somehow gotten outside and run away because she hadn't been able to find him in any of his usual napping places. But then she had found him in the back of the closet, hiding from the noise of the renovations. Despite his long ears, Marshmallow the rabbit didn't seem bothered by all the racket.

"I should be glad it doesn't bother us as much as the animals. They can't go anywhere to get away from it, either. Well, you can take K9 on patrol with you so that he gets away from it, but if I tried to take Blossom somewhere to escape the noise, he would be miserable in an unfamiliar place."

"Yes. They'll weather the storm. They'll probably act like they don't even hear it in a couple of days. They'll adjust."

"I hope so. I'd hate for them to be miserable the whole time."

"Well, if there is anything you wanted to be able to do around here without a cat underfoot, now would be a good time."

Erin laughed. If it had been December instead of July, she could have used the time to wrap presents. What else did she wish she could do without the cat getting into everything? Now that she was thinking about Blossom hiding, all she could picture was how much she enjoyed the cat cuddling with her on the couch or in bed during the night.

"So…" She looked for something else to distract her from her pets' misery. "How did things go at work today? Any excitement?"

Terry shook his head and had a bite of his stew. "Nothing out of the ordinary. Just the normal, everyday crime of Bald Eagle Falls."

"I always thought there wouldn't be any crime in a little town like this. Or next to none. It's the kind of place where people don't bother to lock their doors. So that means it's safe, right?"

Terry shrugged with one shoulder. "It is relatively safe. Tennessee actually has a pretty high crime rate compared to the national average, but we'll blame that on Memphis and the big cities. I think you are still safer in these small mountain towns than in much of the rest of the country. But there is still crime." He hesitated, making a face like he was trying to decide whether to say something like "as you have discovered." But he closed his mouth and didn't add the observation that Erin had been too involved in too many murders and other crimes around Bald Eagle Falls.

"But we still have thefts and domestic violence," Erin agreed, steering away from murder and kidnapping, "Those things are always going to go along with poverty, and we have a lot of people around here who are just barely scraping by."

"And drugs. A way to escape and flush the money that you do make down the toilet." Terry sighed and shook his head. "As much as I would like to say that we don't have any 'big city' problems, I'm not sure that would bear examination."

"I do feel safe here most of the time," Erin said, pretending she could not see the back door burglar alarm panel from where she sat. There had been threats on her life, even attempts on her life. But everyone involved in those incidents was now in prison or dead. She didn't have anything to worry about.

Terry touched her hand briefly, smiling. "And most people here don't have their own private security force."

"It is nice having a law enforcement officer at my beck and call," Erin admitted. "I know I never need to worry."

"*Two* law enforcement officers," Terry said, which confused her for a moment, until he nodded at K9 on the floor beside him.

"Oh, right. K9 too."

K9 raised his head at the mention of his name but, when Erin didn't appear to be speaking to him directly, he put it down again.

"I thought you were talking about the sheriff or Stayner and I couldn't figure out why you would say that," she said with a laugh.

Terry chuckled. "Neither of them had better be showing up on *this* beat," he told her.

The contractors had worked far too late for Erin's schedule. As a baker, she went to bed early and got up before dawn to start the baking at Auntie Clem's Bakery so that it would be ready and on the display shelves by the time she opened the shop. The banging and power tools and equipment kept her tossing and turning long after her usual bedtime. By the time they left, she felt like it was nearly time to get up and was so wound up that it took still longer for her to get to sleep. She was headachy and foggy when she dragged herself out of bed and prepared a large cup of coffee, hoping it would help wake her up and keep her going for at least the morning shift. She might have to call in someone else for the afternoon, but it wasn't like she'd be able to go home and sleep if she did. The construction crew would be hard at work once more.

It was a relief to get to the familiar surroundings of her Main Street bakery. It was quiet when she and Vic got there, and they were used to working together to prepare the morning's breads and sweet treats, so not much conversation was required to keep them on track. Erin spotted Vic yawning a couple of times.

"Did the noise keep you up too? I thought you would just take a sleeping pill."

"I did, but they're not magic. Normally they work great but, apparently, they are less effective when there's a fr—an almighty jackhammer operating next to your head."

Vic's apartment was in the loft over the garage in the back of Erin's lot, so she was even farther away from Mrs. Peach's house where the work was being done than Erin was. But apparently, that space had not muffled the noise any better than Erin's walls. It had sounded to Erin like the jackhammer was operating two feet away from her.

"It was *somewhat* noisy," she agreed.

"It was as noisy as drunks doing karaoke," Vic countered sourly.

Erin smiled and kept working. As tempting as it was to spend the morning grousing about how noisy the construction was, it would just keep them both in a bad mood and they wouldn't be at their best for the customers.

"It will be so nice for Mrs. Peach when she comes back. I just keep thinking about how pleased she'll be with it when it's done."

"She'd better enjoy it," Vic said. "And use it too!"

"I'm sure she will."

"At least something good will come out of that no-good husband's shenanigans."

They had everything arranged in the display cases on time. Erin flipped the Closed sign to Open and unlocked the door for the before-work rush.

Erin was surprised that Melissa Lee was one of the first people through the door. She didn't usually get there until later in the morning, often buying donuts or muffins for the police department where she worked. Her dark, tightly spiraled curls were in disarray and bounced around her face as she looked around to see who else was there. She was beaming, bursting to share something.

While Melissa would never admit to gossiping, she was notorious for spreading details she learned while working as a part-time administrator for the police department. She was never as happy as when she was in the middle of a big drama with everyone's eager attention on her.

Erin exchanged glances with Vic, who also appeared to have noticed Melissa's excitement.

"Well, good morning, ladies," Vic greeted. "How are y'all this fine morning?"

There were various pleasant responses from the early-morning customers and a glower from Mr. Carlisle, the sole male customer so far.

"No offense, Mr. Carlisle," Vic said quickly. "Good morning to you, too."

He grunted and set down his cup of coffee on the top of the display case while he peered at the goods in the display case, eventually ordering a dozen assorted muffins. "It's a shame that you don't have any *normal* baking here," he told Erin with a scowl. "Since there is no other bakery here in town and the only other option is to go and get something prepackaged at the grocery store."

"I think you'll be happy with our gluten-free goods."

Erin kept a pleasant smile fixed on her face. People often disparaged gluten-free baking until they tested her products and admitted that Erin's gluten-free fare was just as good as "the real thing." If she let herself be offended by every customer who came into the shop grumbling about not being able to get conventional baking there, she would be miserable. She needed to keep her goal in front of her. People like Peter Foster or Carolyn whose choice was not "gluten or gluten-free," but "life or death." Those were the people she had set up the bakery for. Most of the Bald Eagle Falls population could choose whether they liked gluten-free or wanted to go to the city to get something else.

Mr. Carlisle muttered something indistinguishable and paid for the muffins. He was, Erin knew, on the construction crew working on Mrs. Peach's house, so the dozen donuts were probably breakfast for the workers. Or a midmorning snack for when they had burned off the calories from breakfast.

Erin watched him head for the door and turned her attention to

Melissa, watching her brightly, her generous mouth in what seemed to be an exaggerated smile. Erin blinked and cocked her head.

"You're looking… *cheerful* this morning."

Melissa's grin got even wider, which Erin would not have thought possible. She covered her mouth briefly as if embarrassed by this show of emotion. "I am," she admitted. She leaned closer to Erin, pressed right up against the display case. "I am getting married."

CHAPTER 3

*E*rin was sure that her jaw hit the floor. She stared at Melissa, gape-mouthed, trying to process this news.

The only romantic interest she knew Melissa had was Davis Plaint—currently incarcerated in the state penitentiary for killing his brother Trenton and Bertie Braceling and his attempt on Erin's life. If Melissa had been seeing anyone else, word of it had not gotten to Erin. And as far as she knew, most people didn't even know of Melissa's interest in Davis and the fact she had been going to the prison to visit with him several times a month.

"I—what? I can't believe it! You're getting married?"

The last thing Erin should do was ask Melissa, "to who?" Those details would be forthcoming, she was sure.

"Yes," Melissa agreed, grinning away. "I can hardly believe it myself. But… he talked me into it. Why should I care what people think? If we're in love with each other, then it shouldn't matter what anyone else says or does."

"Right," Erin agreed. She glanced around and saw that Vic was looking just as wide-eyed and floored as she herself felt. Vic knew of Melissa's interest in Davis, but the other customers probably didn't know anything about it. "You'll have to give me all of the details. Have you… picked a date? Are you sending out invitations?"

Melissa was nodding. "It's just going to be a quiet ceremony, of course, we can't do much at the prison. Just the chaplain and a couple of witnesses. Maybe someone will throw a handful of confetti. But I'm going to have a reception." She said this with determination, in a tone that told everyone else they would not be able to talk her out of it. "A big reception. With all of the normal stuff."

"Will they... but they won't allow him out for the reception, will they?" Erin asked in confusion. Davis had recently been part of a prison break, and she was sure he wasn't the type of offender they would allow out on a day pass.

"No," Melissa agreed. "But that doesn't mean I can't have my family and friends around me to celebrate, does it?"

"Of course not," Erin shook her head. Why couldn't Melissa have a party? Whatever kind of recognition she liked? She could have all of the traditional wedding reception things. Just not a groom who was present. That wouldn't stop her from having drinks, a cake, gifts, a toast—whatever she liked. "That will be really nice. I'm so excited for you."

Melissa's cheeks got rosy. "I'm glad. I thought... I was afraid you'd be upset, but you've been so good to me and Davis, so..."

"No, no, I don't hold anything against you for what he did. I want you to be happy, and if that's what makes you happy... who am I to stand in your way?"

She thought she should be proud of herself for her measured reaction. She could be happy for Melissa even if she disapproved of her choice of a husband. Melissa understood Davis and knew more of what he'd been through than Erin did and, if she could see someone worthy of redemption there, who was Erin to argue?

"You'll do it, then?" Melissa asked.

"I... what?"

"The wedding cake and organizing the catering? I know it is short notice, but..."

"Short notice. Did you say when you were holding it?" Erin asked, confused.

"On the fifteenth." Melissa watched Erin's face as she calculated how much time this would give her. Less than two weeks. That wasn't much time to organize a wedding, even if she didn't have to worry about things like Melissa's dress, a bridal shower, flowers, or hall rental. The wedding cake itself would take hours, not just to bake all of the layers, but to decorate them properly. She had some experience with fondant, but not enough to be comfortable with the job.

"You should get someone in the city to do the cake. Someone with more experience than me. And then you can get what kind of cake you want too…"

"I want a gluten-free cake. I want everyone to be able to eat it. Does that mean you won't do it? I really wanted you. I thought…"

Her liquid brown eyes were like K9's when he was begging for a cookie. Pleading. Vulnerable. Melissa was her friend, and Melissa had asked her to make the cake at this very important celebration of a life milestone. Erin needed to suck it up and proceed with confidence instead of acting like she would fail. Of course she could bake the cake. And she had plenty of experience with fondant. If it didn't work… She would just try again. She just needed to start far enough in advance. She could practice on some cupcakes. The ones that worked out could be used for the wedding and the ones that didn't could go in the freezer for her own desserts. Not that she didn't have a full freezer already. But that was mostly cookies. She was sure Terry would appreciate some cupcakes.

"Well… okay. But I will need to know exactly what you want right away. Because that doesn't leave any time for error or thinking about it."

Melissa's smile blossomed once more. "Oh, that's wonderful, Erin. I knew I could count on you!"

Erin sat at the kitchen table with a pen in one hand, looking at her planner and the lists that she had been making. Her other hand cradled her head, elbow planted on the table.

"Why did I say yes?" she demanded of Vic. She looked over the list of jobs and their tight margins, and moaned. "She ambushed me! How am I going to get this done with everything else I have on my plate?"

"You're going to need to clear some of the other things *off* of your plate," Vic said gently. "You're right. You can't do everything. You were already overbooked before you agreed to take this on. So unless you're going to go back to Melissa and tell her no, you realize now that you don't have the time to get this ready for the fifteenth, then you're going to have to find the time by dropping other things."

"I can't drop anything else."

"Yes, you can. If you're going to go ahead with this, you need to ask for help on some of those other things. Like covering most of your shifts at Auntie Clem's. You've got other employees who can pick up the slack. Just like when we had to go out of town when Pa was in the hospital. Just like when we went on *our* cruise. You can't work fourteen-hour days at the bakery and do all of this other stuff too."

"I can't do that on such short notice."

"You did before. I'll call Bella and Charley, and we'll work out a new schedule for the next two weeks."

Erin knew that it made sense, but she couldn't shake off the feeling that she was letting everyone down by not being at the bakery every day. Or almost every day. She had been trying to cut down on at least her weekend hours and at least once during the week so that she could run errands. Which ended up mostly being errands for bakery stuff anyway. Terry had been telling her for some time that she was doing too much and needed to scale back before she burned out. Rely on her employees more and not do everything herself. And Terry wasn't the only one who had told her that.

"That's really going to be hard on everyone else."

"No, it isn't," Vic said firmly. "We can spread it out enough that it won't be a hardship on any one person."

"Well…" Erin looked at her lists for the wedding and everything else she had planned to do over the next couple of weeks, and had to admit that it would be much more manageable if she didn't have to put in so much time at the bakery. She could still go in and work a few shifts but, if she just helped to cover the peak times a couple of times a week, she would have a lot more time to do Melissa's wedding cake, other desserts, and make arrangements for the other foods she wanted catered. "I guess. I can still put in a few shifts. I'll need the ovens at Auntie Clem's to get the baking done anyway. I can man the register while the wedding cake layers and other desserts are baking."

Vic nodded. "You leave Auntie Clem's to me. I'll make sure that all of the shifts are covered. That's off your plate."

Erin breathed out. She had to admit that it felt like a big burden off her shoulders. That made the wedding a lot more manageable.

"Now what about the rest?" Vic asked. "You still have the business management stuff to do. Sale flyers and accounting and all of that. Employee payroll. Some of that you can put off for a bit…"

"But not payroll."

"No," Vic agreed with a smile. "That might be a problem. But all you have to do is send the payroll company everyone's hours. What about the renovation work?" She tilted her head in the direction of the noise. "Mrs. Peach left you in charge. How much work does that involve?"

"It isn't much. Just checking in with the foreman every couple of days, making sure they are on track. Answering any questions they might have and inspecting what has been done."

"An hour a day?"

"I don't think it will take that much," Erin protested. "Just ten minutes here and there."

"I think you should put it down as an hour a day."

Erin looked at her book dubiously. It would *not* take that long to keep up with Mrs. Peach's renovations. But she didn't know how long it would take and, if she ended up spending ten minutes a couple of times a day, walking back and forth, interrupting her other jobs to check in on the construction, it could easily amount to an hour of productive time lost. "Okay, fine. An hour a day for that."

"And you're going to tell Officer Terry Piper to take over dinners a couple of times a week?"

Erin hadn't said any such thing. She looked at Vic. Vic raised her brows. "He's been living as a bachelor for years. He knows how to cook his own meals. You don't need to be the one to do it all the time."

"But… I can't just tell him to take over something that's been my responsibility until now."

"Did you ever agree that cooking was your responsibility and not his?"

"No."

"And he cooks sometimes, right? I've seen him do it."

Erin nodded.

"Then you tell him that the next couple of weeks you are really busy, and he can help out with the meals more often."

Erin rubbed her face. A tension headache was developing in the middle of her forehead. She should be able to relax now that she'd gotten some of the responsibilities cleared off of her calendar. But she didn't want to have an argument with Terry about cooking meals. He was tired when he got off from work.

But then, so was Erin.

"You really think he would push back on it?" Vic asked.

"No… I just think… I don't know. That I'm letting him down."

"You don't need to be superwoman. How many times has he told you that you're doing too much?"

Had Vic been listening to their pillow talk?

Terry had probably said it in front of Vic enough times, though.

"Maybe once or twice," Erin said dryly.

Vic chuckled. "Yeah. Once or twice that I've heard. So tell him yes this time. Yes, he can help you out by taking a couple of suppers a week. That's not too much to ask."

"Okay." Erin sighed. "Okay, I will."

CHAPTER 4

*E*rin looked down at the schedule she had drawn up for the upcoming week and her carefully color-coordinated and dated task list. Everything would fit. With the adjustments that Vic had discussed, she could meet all of the deadlines for the wedding reception, allowing herself enough time to practice her fondant decorating skills on the cupcakes and allowing for one major disaster with the cake. She had enough time for her business duties, including getting her advertisements into the Bald Eagle Falls weekly. She had time to relax with Terry when he got off his shifts, extra time to sleep if the construction work kept her up late, and some wiggle room built in for walks, meals, and other breaks to maintain her sanity.

It was a thing of beauty.

And just in time for Terry to get home. She could see his truck's headlights as he pulled in front of the house and, in a minute, could hear his footsteps on the sidewalk. She prepared to show him the schedule and inform him of his part.

He opened the door and smiled when he saw her waiting for him. It was a tired smile, happy to be at home at the end of a long shift. But she couldn't see any sign of tension around his eyes that would indicate that he had a headache or was particularly stressed about anything that had happened on his beat. K9 walked in with him and barely waited for the signal from Terry that he was off duty before letting out a sigh and trotting over to Erin for an ear scratch. In a moment, he was stretched out on the carpet on his side while Erin gave him a full belly scratch.

"That looks like it feels really good," Terry observed as he sat down on the couch beside her. "Do I get one too?"

Erin turned her attention from K9 and gave Terry a kiss, a tight hug, and held on to him for an extra few seconds to scratch his back. He was warm and eager in her arms, but his duty belt and equipment dug into her. She withdrew, shaking her head. "You'll have to divest your belt before you get any more."

"I'd be happy to divest more than my belt." He raised his eyebrows and gave her an inviting smile, the dimple showing on his cheek.

"Dinner before that," Erin told him. The smell of warm Chicken à la King had already been tempting her for too long. She could eat dinner on her own before Terry got home, but she preferred to eat with him if they could swing it. "I'm starved."

"I won't forget…"

"Good." Erin laughed and patted him on the knee. She looked at the schedule on her planner lying on the coffee table, not getting up immediately.

Terry's eyes moved to it as well. "This is… colorful."

Erin smiled proudly. "It's all color coded," she agreed. "I've worked everything out so I'll be able to help Melissa." She looked at his face, wondering whether Melissa had also announced her upcoming nuptials at the police department. And whether Terry had been at the office to hear about it or was still in the dark.

"That was quite the bombshell she dropped today," Terry observed.

"Yeah. I was floored. I knew she was visiting Davis at the penitentiary, but I didn't think… I never thought that she would actually marry him. She always said that they were just friends, that was all."

"I guess they're more now. I'm not surprised, to tell the truth. I think that once word got out after the prison break that she was… in a *special relationship* with him, it was probably a relief not to have to hide it anymore. And if she didn't have to hide it, why not… formalize it?"

"I was still surprised. I never thought that she would admit that there was more between them than just friendship. I've talked to her about Davis before, and she would never admit they were anything more, or ever could be. And once he went to prison, I didn't think she'd ever do anything like this."

"People can surprise you." Terry looked back at the schedule. "So what are you doing for Melissa? A bridal shower?"

Erin hadn't even thought about that and hoped that Melissa wasn't expecting her to pull together a shower as well. After all, Erin was not the maid of honor, just the baker.

"No. She wanted me to do the cake and the catering."

Terry's brows went up in surprise. "That sounds like a lot of work. Or is she just having a little celebration at the prison?"

"No. She's decided to go ahead and have a big wedding reception. It will just be her instead of her and Davis. So it's... a pretty big thing, and she hasn't left much time to get it all arranged."

"Is it right away? She could schedule it for a few weeks after the wedding..."

"No, right away." Erin nodded her confirmation at the look that he gave her. "Yeah. So it's a big deal."

"How can you take that on with everything else?"

Erin pointed at the schedule. "I've got it all worked out. Vic is going to see to it that all of my shifts at Auntie Clem's are covered. So that frees me up during the workday. I need to practice because, honestly, I'm not up to snuff on my fondant decorating skills. But this will give me enough time to make the main cake and some desserts and arrange for catering for the rest of the food. She's not doing a full dinner—thank goodness—but she does want canapés and drinks and all that."

"You're not going to be at Auntie Clem's?"

"Well, some of the time. That's the best place to bake, because I've got the commercial ovens and nothing will be contaminated with gluten ingredients. And I still need to do business stuff. But I won't be doing the main baking or waiting on customers. Just doing my own thing in the back during the quieter periods."

Terry nodded slowly, studying the schedule. Erin shifted uncomfortably, worrying that he would see the "Terry cooks dinner" before she had the chance to ease him into it gently.

"Looks like you've got it all figured out," Terry observed. "What do you need me to do?"

Erin's face warmed. His question made it easy for her. She felt embarrassed and pleased at the same time. "There's not much," she assured him. "I was hoping you could take over dinner prep for a few nights."

"I'm sure I can open a can of something," he assured her, cheekily echoing the way Willie teased Vic when it was his turn to cook or arrange a nice date night dinner. Willie liked to get Vic riled up. And Vic would oblige, telling him that opening a can of beans or soup did not constitute "making dinner" by her standards.

But Erin didn't care. Terry could open a can of beans; she didn't care as long as she didn't have to think about it. "Good," she pronounced. She pointed to the places on the schedule where she had hoped that Terry would be able to take care of their dinner.

He took out his phone and entered them on his electronic calendar. "As long as nothing comes up. If I get called to a major crime scene, you know I won't be able to."

Erin nodded. She understood that. It was part of the package. With such a small police department in Bald Eagle Falls, any major crime would require all hands on deck, and he would need to ensure that everything was taken care of before he could even think of making dinner.

"Deal," she agreed.

"All right." Terry nodded. "And now, I think you said you were starving? That chicken is driving me crazy. Speaking of which, where's Orange Blossom? I expected him to be out here crying for his dinner."

"Yeah. He doesn't like all of the noise over at Mrs. Peach's." Erin nodded in the direction of her neighbor's house, though Terry needed no further explanation. "So he's hiding until he knows that I'm in the kitchen."

They both got up from the couch and headed into the kitchen to eat. Erin waited for the familiar gallop of Blossom's feet as he tried to reach the kitchen, and the pantry in particular, ahead of her, but he didn't try to beat her there. She looked around.

"Blossom? You want a treat? Blossom?"

There was no raucous meow in response. Erin frowned, waiting. Eventually, she returned to the kitchen doorway and looked down the hall for the cat. He was not coming.

"You don't think he could have gotten out, do you?" she asked Terry worriedly.

"No, you and I are both pretty careful. If he manages to slip out, we always see."

Erin walked down the hall toward the bedrooms, first checking the spare room, looking under the bed and in the closet. "Blossom? Orange Blossom? Aren't you hungry? Come on. Treats."

K9 followed and nosed at Erin's hand, suggesting that he was ready for his treat, even if Orange Blossom was not.

"Just a minute, K9."

Erin continued, going to her bedroom. A tail stuck out from under the bed. Erin bent over and tickled it. The tail was quickly pulled in, and her cat turned around to face her, looking simultaneously angry and forlorn.

"Treat," Erin tempted him. "Come on. Come to the kitchen for a treat. Can't you smell the chicken?"

He didn't come immediately but, with a little more coaxing, finally slithered out from under the bed and meowed at her plaintively.

"I know. The noise bothers me too. You don't want to have to come out. But you'll come for a treat, won't you?"

He followed her to the kitchen, where he immediately began meowing and telling her how he had been starved all day, having to hide from the loud, disturbing noises next door.

"I know, I know," Erin told him.

"Looks like you found him," Terry commented.

"It's that quick cop's eye, isn't it? Doesn't miss a thing."

He grinned. Erin got out a couple of the commercial kitty treats she bought for Orange Blossom and sent them skating across the floor for him to chase. He sat and washed his face and didn't even look at them.

"Oh, is that how it is now?" Erin asked.

She put on her oven mitts to take the chicken out of the oven, and then Blossom was winding around her legs, begging for a portion.

"You're too good for kitty treats now?" Erin asked, "You'll only eat people food?"

She had cut human food out of his diet completely after he had been poisoned, worried about the many seemingly harmless ingredients that could harm a cat's digestive tract and make him very sick. Pet sites on the internet and books always warned about how chocolate could poison a dog, but they never seemed to get into the long list of things she should not feed her cat.

But she had set aside a little chicken without any added ingredients for Blossom and K9. She divided the pieces between two dishes and offered the first to Blossom, who was standing up on his hind legs, trying to swipe it out of her grip before she could put it down on the floor for him.

"Blossom! Get down. You don't need to be so aggressive."

She managed to get it to the floor without dropping it. Blossom tucked in immediately. K9 waited patiently for his portion and ate it like a gentleman.

"You need to teach that cat some manners," Terry said.

"It's not quite as easy to train a cat as a dog."

"Yeah…" Terry had a glint in his eye. "Dogs *are* smarter."

"They are not. Cats are just more independent. They don't want just to please their owner like a dog does."

Terry smirked and set the plates down on the table.

CHAPTER 5

They had just dished up and were ready to eat when there was a loud crash from next door, followed by swearing and shouting that was even louder. All of the machinery noises stopped. Erin didn't even think, she just dropped everything and ran out the back door.

Across her yard, out through the back gate, and through Mrs. Peach's gate into her yard.

Something was wrong. She didn't know what it was, but it was serious. Had someone been injured?

She knew some first aid, and Terry would be right behind her. He had first responder training and knew what to do in most emergencies.

"Erin!" She ignored Terry's call and kept going. They could talk once they knew what was going on. "Erin, wait—"

Erin ran through the backyard filled with tools and equipment, aiming for the group of workers clustered together at the back of the house.

"What is it? What happened?"

Several faces turned to look at her. Their mouths opened, but either they didn't know what to say to her or she wasn't able to hear their answers, so caught up in her anxiety. What if the construction project had been completely derailed? What if Mrs. Peach blamed whatever had happened on her? She hadn't done anything. She was trying to stay on top of the construction crew and what was going on and whether or not they had everything they needed, but she wasn't doing the renovation herself. She couldn't control it if they came in late or had a catastrophic failure along the way.

They moved back enough to admit her into the small semicircle around the hole in the wall.

She wasn't surprised to see a hole in the wall. They needed to cut a hole for the internal doorway from Mrs. Peach's kitchen area into the large greenhouse and hot tub room she was having constructed. No one wanted to go outside to get to and from the hot tub dressed in only a swimsuit or towel, especially not in the winter. Tennessee might not have the chilly winters she had experienced in the north, but it still got too cold to wander around in little more than one's altogether.

But, of course, no one had been expecting to find anything inside the wall.

Other than the usual, of course. Erin had read about construction workers finding old newspapers, coins, or bottles when doing a renovation or restoration. And sometimes other things.

But not bodies.

She had rarely heard of them discovering a body during a renovation like Mrs. Peach's.

Terry was right behind Erin, breathing heavily from the sprint across the yards. K9 panted at his side, ears alert, sniffing the breeze. It took a few more seconds before Terry could see past Erin or process what he was looking at.

He swore under his breath. "You've got to be kidding me."

Despite Erin's thoughts about first aid and Terry's higher first responder training as she had run over from her house to Mrs. Peach's, there was nothing they could do for the man in the wall. He was not just dead, but obviously *long* dead. And he would have to be. Erin had lived in her house for two years and, during that time, Mrs. Peach had not had any work done on the house. And certainly, the little old lady hadn't walled a man up there herself during that time. The very idea was ridiculous.

And Erin was no expert in such matters, but it looked to her like the man had been there much longer than a couple of years. He hardly even looked human, but like something from a haunted house or prop room. Stretched brown skin in some places, skeletonized in others. There were still clothes draped around the body but, from what Erin had glimpsed before Terry had hustled her away—along with the entire work crew—he had been dressed in modern clothing. Blue jeans and a t-shirt with a bird crest on it. A work belt similar to Terry's duty belt or the ones the construction workers wore, with loops and pockets for carrying equipment. Heavy work boots. How long had people been wearing blue jeans and t-shirts? Thirty years? Fifty? Not a hundred.

Terry had initially moved her and the work crew back, instructing them to stay out of the way and not to talk to each other while he called in to his dispatcher to get the rest of the police department on the scene. Erin didn't speak to any of the men, but she could see that they were murmuring to each other and thumbing their phones, probably texting each other or someone else who would appreciate the horror of their find. When the sheriff, Tom Banks, and Stayner arrived, they split everyone up the best they could so they could not talk to each other about what they had seen or knew about it.

"Why don't you go back to your house, Miss Price?" Sheriff Wilmot suggested. "We know where to find you. But please don't talk or communicate with anyone else about this until we've had a chance to talk to you."

Erin nodded. "Okay. I'll…" She looked back toward the house, thinking about the meal they had abandoned and the fact that Terry would now probably be stuck dealing with the discovery of the skeleton for several more hours. "I'll go home and have dinner. But Terry hasn't eaten yet. We were just about to sit down."

"We'll give him a break once we've got everything under control here."

"Okay." Erin licked her dry lips. "I can't believe this is happening. I mean… what are the chances…?" She remembered another grisly discovery not long ago, before she had built her new garage with the loft suite. Two bodies hidden so close together, but otherwise having nothing in common? The odds of that seemed astronomical.

"Don't you worry about it. I'm sure we'll be able to keep this one out of your hair. You go home and relax and don't think about it. Put something on the TV and try not to focus on what you saw."

Erin nodded.

"And don't talk to anyone." Wilmot pointed his finger at Erin's chest, almost touching her. "And I mean no one. That includes Miss Victoria."

"Okay." Erin let out a pent-up breath. She felt like she couldn't get enough oxygen. How could something like this have happened? And why did she have to be the one to see it?

But it wasn't like she had discovered the body. She had been next door. She hadn't known anything about it or even that the workmen would be knocking a hole in that wall today. It was all just a coincidence. She could just as easily have been at Auntie Clem's, a restaurant, or shopping. She could have been anywhere.

But she hadn't.

CHAPTER 6

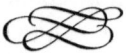

Of course, not talking to Vic about what had happened wasn't as easy as it sounded. As soon as Erin got back into the yard, Vic came clattering down the stairs from the loft apartment to meet her.

"Erin! What happened? What's going on?"

"Oh…" Erin kept walking, feeling as if she were fleeing from her friend. "I'll have to talk to you about it later."

"Later? I want to know what's going on now. Did something happen? Did someone get hurt?"

"No. Yes. I don't know how to answer that. I'm not supposed to say anything to you. I'm sorry."

"Why not? Erin?" Vic followed close behind her, not to be put off that easily.

"I'm not supposed to talk to you. I told you that. You'll have to wait until later. After I've talked to… Sheriff Wilmot or whoever, then I'll be able to talk to you."

"Then there's an investigation," Vic concluded. Though, of course, that should have been obvious. Why would all of the police cars in town come to one location if there were not something to investigate? "And no one was hurt? Or someone was? I didn't understand your answer."

"I can't tell you anything." Erin reached the door and stopped, turning to look at Vic. "Go back to your apartment, and I'll talk to you about it when I can."

Vic looked stubborn and mutinous. But there was nothing Erin could do about it. Vic could stay in the yard, waiting for someone to talk to her about what was going on, but Erin could not let her into the house and discuss it with her. Even if all she could do was speculate, Wilmot had told her explicitly not to talk to Vic. She didn't want there to be any suggestion that she had disobeyed his command.

Giving Vic a look that she hoped conveyed she was sorry and would have talked to her if she could, Erin entered the house and shut the door.

"Hey!" Erin shouted when she saw what was going on in the kitchen. "Get down! Off the table!"

Orange Blossom didn't immediately obey, enjoying his feast of Chicken à la King. Erin rushed at him, waving her hands. "Get down!"

He jumped down just before she could lay hands on him to push him off or pick him up, uttering a loud growl in protest.

"You are not allowed on the table! You know that!"

He slunk a few steps away but kept eyeing her as if trying to decide if she might turn her back again to allow him a second go at the chicken.

"Get out of the kitchen. Go on. Go to bed."

He grudgingly left the kitchen. Erin turned back and looked at the mess on the table, trying to decide what to do about it. She couldn't tell if the cat had only been into the chicken that was on their plates or whether he had also gotten into the serving dish. If she knew, she might have been able to just toss what was on their plates and re-serve them from the serving bowl but, since she didn't know, she couldn't serve possibly contaminated chicken.

She sighed and started to clear it all away.

Erin had just finished her bowl when Terry returned with Sheriff Wilmot. Terry frowned and looked at the table, eyeing the small bowl of baked beans that remained from the can Erin had opened.

"What happened to the chicken?"

"Orange Blossom."

He shook his head. "Darn cat." He sighed and sat down. Not bothering to get out a plate, he just picked up the bowl Erin had warmed the beans in, picked up the fork she had put down, and took a bite. "It's not Chicken à la King, but it will do."

Erin started to stand to get him a plate or to offer him a hot dog to cut up into it, but he waved her down.

"This is fine. Let's just get this done here."

"Okay…" Erin sat back down. Sheriff Wilmot pulled out a chair and sat down as well. Erin felt awkward not offering him something to eat, but She didn't have anything else prepared. "Do you want a cookie or muffin? We've got lots."

"No, I have to watch my figure." Wilmot put a hand on his slightly rounded stomach and shook his head. "My wife blames menopause for the weight she's put on. But all I can blame is sitting on my… behind all day. Too much, anyway."

Terry was still trim, spending much of his day on foot patrol rather than sitting in front of a computer. Though Erin knew that he had put on a few pounds in the last year and worried about how much they might slow him down. He worried that it was just the beginning of the end, that his physical fitness would just get worse as time went by.

Wilmot leaned forward. "To the matter at hand. I don't really need much from you. I know where you were at the time of discovery. I know that you weren't the one that killed that man or put him in a wall. But I still have to collect a statement from any witness when a dead body is discovered, so that means I need to talk to you."

Erin nodded her understanding. She looked at Terry, half hoping that he would take over the questions. But of course he wouldn't. Not when he was another of those witnesses and it was important for them not to let witness statements get tainted. Wilmot had obviously already asked Terry for his story, and he and Stayner would be questioning the entire work crew. Now it was Erin's turn.

"You are in charge of the construction crew while Mrs. Peach is away?" Wilmot asked.

That wasn't what she had been expecting him to lead with. She had been prepared to tell her story of the discovery of the body from the time they had heard the first crash and curse to the time that the rest of the cavalry had arrived. "Yes, that's right. Mrs. Peach is hoping that it will be done by the time she gets home. She doesn't want to live in the house while it's being worked on. The noise and the dust…" Erin made a motion that encompassed her kitchen. Though of course, the sounds of the construction had ceased and Wilmot probably couldn't see the fine layer of white dust that covered everything. The renovations weren't even being done on her house, and Erin still had to deal with the noise and the dust. She couldn't imagine trying to live in Mrs. Peach's house while the workmen were there.

"What exactly did Mrs. Peach say to you before she left?"

"I don't know." Erin thought back. "Just… thank you for looking after things while she's gone. I don't know."

"She never said anything to you about being worried about what might happen while she was gone? Any warnings about areas to stay away from? What to do if there was an emergency?"

"No. Nothing that could have been related to this. She did *not* give me a heads up that they might find a body while she was gone."

"And you're sure that she went on the cruise that you thought she was going on? She didn't just… leave town?"

"Yes, I'm sure. She's checked in to the cruise. Sent me some pictures of the boat and her ticket. She hasn't skipped town." Erin couldn't even believe that he would suggest such a thing. Of course Mrs. Peach hadn't skipped town. She wasn't a killer. She hadn't started the renovations on her house because she wanted someone to find the body. She had gone on vacation.

"How much do you know about the history of the house?"

"The history?"

"How long Mrs. Peach has lived there. If she's the only owner. If there has been any major work done on it."

"I think a long time… They were married about fifty years. And they lived in that house together before he left, which was thirty years ago. I don't know of any renovations she's done before. Not much, I don't think, because it's pretty much a mirror of this house. Dated. No new rooms or major upgrades."

"She hasn't mentioned anything to you. Any renovations done more recently?"

"No. I don't think she's ever had much money, you know. When Mr. Peach left, she had to make do on her own."

"He didn't pay her any spousal support?"

"No, I don't think so. The money that he left her, he accumulated over time. Money that he should have paid to her while he was still alive. Instead of indulging himself and building up his own bank account." Erin shook her head. "He seemed like a nice man when I met him, but I don't have much respect for him after finding out the way he treated his wife."

"That's understandable," Wilmot said neutrally.

"She certainly never told me anything about a man being left in the wall," Erin said, trying to make it sound lighthearted. "I think I would have remembered that."

"I imagine you would. Even though you may have become accustomed to running across corpses around here."

Erin bit her lip, trying to think of something slightly witty as a comeback, but she couldn't. Wilmot's face reddened.

"You have a way of reaching Mrs. Peach to discuss this with her?" Terry asked, changing the direction of the conversation.

"Yes, of course. I... I guess you have to call her about it..."

"I don't think this is something that we could just not happen to mention."

"It's just that she's on vacation. It is supposed to be her one big holiday, with everything perfect, and you're going to ruin that by calling her up and telling her that there was a body discovered in her wall. Nothing is going to change between now and when she gets back in a couple of weeks, so can't you just wait until she gets back?"

"I don't think so."

Erin sighed. She rubbed her forehead. "I just want her to have a nice time. I told her I would take care of everything while she was gone."

"I think that ship has sailed."

CHAPTER 7

*V*ic was eager to hear all the details as soon as Sheriff Wilmot and Terry walked out of the house. She allowed them to walk away, and then she was in the door, her eyes wide as she sought out Erin, who was putting the dinner dishes into the dishwasher. She let Nilla, her fluffy white dog, in with her, and he scampered off looking for K9. Or maybe for Orange Blossom, if he didn't know what was good for him.

"They found a body?" Vic demanded. "I can't believe what I'm hearing. Is that true?"

Erin nodded. "Yes." She tried to think of some way to soften the news, to make it sound less dramatic and worrisome. "But... at least it wasn't anyone we know."

"Well, we hope not," Vic said. "But I've been around here more than you have, and I know more about the families in these parts. It *could* be someone I know about from way back."

Erin looked away. Too many unpleasant memories. Her Aunt Clementine had died of natural causes after an illness. But the same was not true of her father and mother, and their deaths had left a lasting imprint on her, even though she had done her best to eradicate them from her memory and not to think about how they had died. It had happened so many years ago, but they still pained her. Maybe because she had only uncovered the details in the last couple of years.

"It isn't anyone we know," she repeated firmly.

"Okay," Vic said quietly, picking up on Erin's mood.

After loading the dishwasher, Erin turned it on, went into the living room, and sat on the couch. Vic followed her but did not sit down immediately. She paced restlessly, stopping to peer out the front window and then retracing her steps.

"I just can't believe this is happening all over again," Erin said. "I don't want to know what happened to that man. I don't want to know who he was or what happened to him. Everybody should just leave it alone. I don't want to hear his sad, tragic story."

"It was a man?" Vic asked. "You could tell?"

"Well, it wasn't a close physical exam or anything. But... men's clothes. The size of a man. I don't know. Looked male to me, but I'm not the medical examiner."

"So Mrs. Peach didn't kill her husband's mistress," Vic said with an ironic smile.

"If she did, she must be hidden in another part of the house."

Vic sat down in one of the easy chairs. "How do you hide a body in the walls of a house without anybody noticing? People must have known!"

Erin shook her head. "I don't know. I can't imagine."

She had experienced living somewhere where an animal had died inside the wall: a rodent or other small creature. The smell of the decomposing body was so bad that she could not stand to be in the house. Other people in the foster family only seemed to smell it when they were in close proximity, a room that shared that wall. And even then, they didn't seem to know what it was or where it was coming from, only that it was unpleasant. To Erin, it had been like trying to live in the same house as a dog that had just been sprayed by a skunk. Or nuclear waste. While her foster parents had scolded her for being overly dramatic and attention-seeking, they had not been able to deny that there was a bad smell. But they said there was nothing they could do except wait for it to fade. It had been weeks before Erin had been able to be in the house without suffering from the stench and, even then, she wouldn't go back to the room where it had originated.

She couldn't imagine what a man-sized body would smell like as it decomposed. How long would it take before the house would be livable again? She shuddered.

"Sorry," Vic apologized, thinking Erin was reliving what she had seen. "It must have been terrible for you. Did it… look terrible? Could you tell what had happened to him?"

"It was awful," Erin said, still thinking of the smell. She rubbed her forehead and considered Vic's question. "I don't want to think about it. Focusing on what I saw will burn it into my memory more. If I avoid thinking about it… it will be better."

Vic nodded sympathetically.

Erin was the one with experience in the area, after all. She knew how such a discovery could affect her. Could keep reappearing in her nightmares and occupy her thoughts during the day when she should be focusing on other things.

"At least this time, no one can suspect you of being involved," Vic pointed out, her tone light.

"No. It had to be there long before I ever moved back to Bald Eagle Falls."

"What about Clementine's journals? Did she ever write about… anything weird going on next door?"

Erin shook her head. "She was getting into family history and her journal twenty-five or thirty years ago… but I never read anything about her suspecting something was going on with the Peaches. She didn't even write about Mr. Peach leaving, which was quite a scandal. I think that must have been before she started to write. No clues there."

"What did the local law enforcement say?" Vic nodded in the direction Sheriff Wilmot and Terry had retreated to continue their investigation. "Do they know anything about who it is or how he died and ended up in that wall?"

"Neither of them remembers anything about any rumors of what might have happened there. Terry wouldn't have been old enough to be aware of anything. The sheriff is older, but still not old enough to remember any of the rumors that might have been going around at the time. He'll have to talk to some of the old-timers. Maybe look up old articles from the newspaper." Erin pondered how she would go about it if she were trying to solve the crime.

Not that she would.

She was going to stay well away from this investigation. Leave it to the local law enforcement. They would find out what had happened and Erin didn't need to get close to the case.

She had enough to do without throwing a murder investigation into the mix.

CHAPTER 8

*E*rin tried to pretend that everything was normal and she could follow her usual routine, going to bed at the same time, falling asleep, and getting up early as if she were going to Auntie Clem's to start on the morning baking, even though she would be staying home and doing other things instead. She would let Vic and Charley do the early-morning baking, as Vic had arranged, and would go in later when she wouldn't be in the way to spend some time in her office and putter around the kitchen to see what supplies she needed to pick up in the city in anticipation of the wedding.

But, of course, it didn't work out that way. Erin went to bed with Terry, just as they normally would, but Erin tossed and turned and was wide awake. There was no way that her brain was ready to settle down and go to sleep. Terry too seemed restless, either because of what he had on his own mind or because Erin was flip-flopping around like a landed fish and was keeping him awake. Since he worked shift, he was pretty good at being able to go to bed and go to sleep when he wanted to. But if he had something on his mind, or had a headache from his injury the previous year, or if Erin was too restless, he wouldn't be able to go to sleep so early in the evening. He would get up and watch TV or do something else until he was tired enough to sleep. Usually, that was when he would return to bed, but sometimes Erin found him asleep on the couch in some position that looked extremely awkward and painful.

That didn't happen as often as it had after the attack, but it still happened sometimes. And it always worried her when she knew that Terry was having a hard night or she was keeping him up.

Terry moved in to cuddle with Erin, despite her restless attempts to move around. He held her firmly, close to him, trying to help her to calm down.

"Everything is fine," he murmured in her ear. "You don't need to worry about anything. The police department will take care of it."

"I know, I know. It's not that. I'm sure it will all get sorted out. But I did want Mrs. Peach to have a nice vacation. I hope she doesn't come back early."

"You can't control that. Just like you couldn't control them finding a body in the house. In reality, there wasn't even much you could do if they were too slow and falling behind on their deadlines. You could talk to them, but that's all."

"I wish the sheriff would just let it go until she gets back. The body has already been there for years; what's the rush to talk to her about it before she gets home?"

"It's just protocol. You get things done as early as you can. The first few days of an investigation are crucial."

"With a cold case? Maybe the first few days after he died or disappeared, but that happened a long time ago." She wanted to say years or decades ago, but she didn't know how long it had been and didn't want to muddy the waters or make Terry think she knew more than she did. "What's the hurry now?"

"Well, for one thing, it will be all over town. And if the police sit back for a couple of weeks and don't do anything, how do you think the citizens of Bald Eagle Falls are going to react?"

Erin sighed. "They'll think that you're incompetent."

"If we're lucky, they'd think we're incompetent. Worse, they'd think that we were intentionally covering something up. That we knew what had happened all along but were hoping that people would just forget about it. It's our duty to investigate vigorously from the moment evidence of a crime crosses our radar."

"I suppose." She still thought that since it was a cold case, they didn't need to be quite *that* vigorous. Terry always told her that it took days or weeks, even months, to get back full lab results on an autopsy. Fingerprint and DNA processing were frequently backed up so much that they had to seek out independent laboratories in other states to get evidence processed in a timely manner. So why couldn't they just say that they were waiting for lab results before they could pursue the case any further?

Erin pressed her hands against her face and rubbed her eyes, snuggling into Terry at the same time. She was glad he was there. Despite worrying about his sleep and not wanting to cuddle initially, she was glad he was there, holding her, helping her stay focused on one thing at a time.

"Then there's the wedding."

"Are you worried about it?" Terry asked. "Have you taken on too much?"

"No. It's fine. I made sure that I had enough time to get things done. I even built in extra time for mistakes and time to go for a walk or do my tai chi. I'm making sure that everything is balanced."

Or trying to. She liked to think that if she wrote everything down in her notebook, she could keep it all under control and make things happen just the way she wanted them to. But of course, she couldn't. As much as she tried to anticipate everything that could go wrong and find ways to deal with it, there were always things she couldn't anticipate or control. Like the work crew at Mrs. Peach's house finding a dead body. Erin couldn't be blamed for not having foreseen that.

"But you're still worried about it," Terry said.

"Yeah, I guess. Not worried; just… thinking about it. Can't get it out of my mind. I'm constantly reviewing my checklists and what needs to be done, trying to see what I might have forgotten or how things could go wrong."

"Maybe you should take a sleeping pill."

He knew that she didn't like to, didn't like how dopey they made her. She wouldn't be able to wake up in the morning to get to Auntie Clem's to do the morning baking. But she didn't need to get up in the morning to do the baking this time. Vic and Charley were doing that.

"I don't know. I'm going to try to sleep for a little longer."

"Okay." Terry nestled his chin into the curve of her neck and shoulder and breathed, which was warm and comforting and tickled at the same time. Erin giggled. "Stop that!"

"Stop what?"

"Stop breathing."

"I'm kind of addicted to oxygen. Can't live without it."

"Stop breathing on my neck and in my ear."

He turned his head slightly so that he was still against her neck but no longer blowing it. Erin closed her eyes and sought sleep once more.

CHAPTER 9

*E*rin tried to sleep in the next morning. Something that other people made sound easy. But she kept having nightmares, developed a hangover-like headache, and was irritable and bad-tempered even once she was up and had a shower and her morning coffee. She felt like she'd had too little sleep instead of too much.

Terry slept like a log, snoring even after she got up and attended to the animals. She was happy that he was asleep and not happy at the same time. Happy for his sake that he was getting the sleep he needed and would be fresh for his next shift, and not happy for herself because she wanted company, even though she wasn't in any mood to get along with anyone. It was an irritating place to be in, all because she'd tried to sleep past her normal alarm time.

After a second cup of coffee—normally she didn't have more than one —she took a few deep breaths and headed to Mrs. Peach's yard. She'd seen the foreman and a few workers show up, but they were standing around talking, and it wasn't a full crew.

They looked as if they needed some direction.

When she opened the gate to the backyard, the foreman looked in her direction, and his mouth settled into a long, thin line that pointed down at both ends.

"Miss Price."

"Hi. I just thought I would check in and see how things were going."

He looked at her sourly. "Things are not going anywhere, which I am sure you are aware of. We can't exactly work on what has been declared a crime scene until it has been released."

"It's not a crime scene," Erin protested. The murder, if it had been a murder, had occurred years earlier. Did the police department think that they would be able to get any evidence from it? They had already taken the body and presumably anything else they could see that looked like it might be related to the case. They should have released the scene at that point, and the foreman was just being stupidly cautious. "Whatever happened here happened decades ago. There isn't any evidence left."

"Well, we're agreed on that matter." The man pulled a pack of cigarettes out of his pocket, removed one from the box, and lit up without asking whether it would bother her or not. "There's no reason to stop what we are doing just because an old body was found. Bodies show up on reno sites all the time. It's nothing new. You take the body out and keep going. If you and that boyfriend of yours hadn't run over and stuck your noses into things, we could have disposed of it ourselves without any interference from the police."

He gave her a gap-toothed smile totally devoid of humor, and Erin didn't know if it was supposed to be a joke or whether he was serious. Would they have just moved the body somewhere else? Buried it in the woods or taken it to the nearest landfill? If they had done that and no one ever found out, would there be any consequences? It wasn't like anyone had missed the man, or they would have at least known who he was when they uncovered him. So far, as far as she knew, no one had laid claim to him or even knew who he was.

"Sorry to have spoiled your plan," Erin returned, keeping her voice just as stoic as his. "What are you planning to do today?" They would need to get right back to work to keep everything on schedule.

"I just told you, it's a crime scene. We can't do anything."

"The whole place?" Erin looked around. "If it's just that one little spot in the wall…"

"They told us to hold off work until they release the scene."

"Everything?" She tried to think of something they might still be able to do without technically breaching the police department's order.

"Everything, honey. What do you expect me to do about it?"

"Well, you're here. You must have intended to do something."

"I was hoping the sheriff would be here, or your boyfriend, telling us that we could go ahead and get started." The foreman looked around at his sparse crew. "I told everyone to be here, but it looks like we're down a couple of men."

"They said it's haunted," a younger man contributed, not looking his boss in the eyes. "They don't want to work on it."

"Haunted?" The foreman swore. "They were working on it before and nothing bad happened. It's not haunted."

"They say they had bad luck because it is haunted," an older Hispanic man advised. "They not want to work on it any more."

The foreman rolled his eyes heavenward and shook his head. "Then not only do I need to get the scene released, I also need more workers. Ones who will not be scared off by rumors of spooks."

"Couldn't you talk these other guys into coming back?" Erin pressed. "If you tell them they're not going to get any money if they don't finish the job they started..." She wasn't someone used to making threats herself. She would feel terrible telling one of the construction workers that she wouldn't pay him. But she knew that other people would be more assertive about it than she would. The foreman must be used to firing people or threatening to fire them. It was that kind of industry.

"These guys?" he shook his head. "No. They're as superstitious as they come. If they say there's a ghost or some other kind of mojo on a site, that's it. They won't be coming back. We need more men."

"I'll see if I can find someone," Erin promised.

He looked at her with bloodshot eyes and shook his head. "You're going to find someone? It will take a couple of weeks to do interviews, see who has their certifications, check references, and hire someone. You might think we can just pick people up off the street like they do in the big city, but we do things the right way here. No untrained illegals are going to get on my crew."

"What certifications do you need? What do you need people to do?"

He smoked his cigarette, looking at her. He closed his eyes for a moment and drew in a long drag of smoke, then blew it over Erin's head. "I need at least one who can do electrical. The other one can be a general hand and I'll show him what to do. But he needs at least basic safety training and to know how to put in a hard day's work. You think you can fill two positions for me like that?"

"I'll sure try," Erin agreed.

He shook his head, doubting her abilities. Or maybe doubting the availability of any workers that would fit the bill. He'd been in the industry long enough to know what kind of workers were available.

"Before you do that, talk your boyfriend into releasing the scene. Won't do any good to get more workers if we can't work."

Erin nodded. "Okay. I'll see what I can do."

She wasn't going to wake Terry up to get him to release the scene. It wouldn't be up to him. Erin would go directly to the sheriff. She didn't think it would be too hard to get him to release the scene, since there wasn't any evidence to preserve there.

But getting a couple more workers would not be quite as easy.

CHAPTER 10

*E*rin could hear the foreman muttering something as she walked
back to her own yard. Nothing very flattering, she was sure. Men
like him did not tend to like assertive women. No one who challenged
their ideas or tried to boss them around. But she had promised Mrs.
Peach that she would do everything in her power to get the renovation
done while she was on vacation. And Erin believed she could still do that,
even with this new wrench in the works.

She sat down in the kitchen and considered how best to approach the
sheriff. She could talk to Terry first, of course, but if he tried to block her
and she went around him, he would be offended. She could call the sheriff, or she could go over to the police department offices in the Town Hall
building to talk to him face-to-face. She suspected he would be less likely
to turn her down if he had to look into her eyes when he did so. And she
could bribe him with sweets, even if he did say he was trying to cut back
and lose a few pounds. He still always accepted something when she
brought him a box of freshly baked muffins or cookies. A phone call
would be easier, but more likely to fail, and she couldn't afford to fail.
Mrs. Peach's house needed to be opened up again for construction.

So it was cookies and an in-person visit.

Erin would normally not even consider taking the police department
anything but fresh cookies or muffins. It really didn't take long to whip up

a batch, and she was always proud to bear something that had just come out of the oven. But she didn't want the construction crew to have to wait any longer than they already had. So she filled a box with cookies from the freezer and warmed them gently in the microwave before heading to the Town Hall.

Clara Jones was the gatekeeper for the police department, making sure that curious civilians like Erin could not just walk into the police department offices. Not again. But Erin had been very careful not to sneak by Clara lately, which would have gotten her in trouble, and had very politely stayed in the reception area or whatever room she was led to rather than giving rein to her curiosity and walking around, possibly overhearing discussions of current cases.

Clara raised her brows questioningly at Erin as she walked in. She had brassy red hair and large moon-shaped earrings with a matching chunky necklace. She was always nicely turned out and, as far as Erin could tell, was efficient at her job.

"Is Sheriff Wilmot available?" Erin asked.

Clara eyed the cookie box. "If you want to just leave that for him, I'll ensure he gets it."

"No... I really need to talk to him. Sorry. I know he's got this new case, but do you think he could spare just a few minutes for me?"

"Have a seat and I'll see," Clara conceded.

Erin sat in one of the visitor chairs and pretended that she wasn't trying to overhear Clara's phone conversation with Sheriff Wilmot. But Clara turned her face away and spoke quietly, and Erin couldn't make out their conversation. Clara hung up the phone.

"He'll be out in a moment."

"Oh, thank you. I really appreciate that."

Clara nodded and looked back at her computer to continue with her work.

"You should grab a couple of these before they're gone." Erin stood up and offered the open box to Clara.

It wasn't like there were that many people in the office. There were plenty of cookies to go around. But Clara had never turned down any baking Erin had brought to the office and, at her encouragement, helped herself to a couple of cookies, which she put on a napkin next to her cup of coffee.

"Thank you. Those look delicious."

Erin bit back the honest answer that she had just pulled them out of the freezer. That wasn't what Clara wanted to hear. She wanted to know that she was special and that Erin always made baked goods especially for the police department and walked them over while they were still warm from the oven.

And they were—just from the *microwave* oven this time.

"I figured you would like those ginger snaps," she said instead, having watched to see which cookies Clara had selected.

"You know my weakness for ginger," Clara said with a chuckle.

Erin did now.

Sheriff Wilmot came out of his office and down the hall to greet Erin. "You had something you wanted to discuss, Miss Price?"

Erin nodded. "I'll only take two minutes of your time...."

He sighed and led her back to his office, where he removed a stack of files from the visitor's chair and motioned for her to sit down. Erin knew from experience that the chair was not comfortable. Wilmot didn't want anyone parking there for any longer than necessary. Erin offered the cookies, putting the open box on his desk. Wilmot hesitated, but Erin was right; with the cookies in front of him, he could not resist the temptation. He selected a chocolate chip cookie and sank his teeth into the soft, warm cookie with a moan of pleasure.

"I don't know how you do it, Miss Price. Everyone says that gluten-free baking is like cardboard. But your baking is always top of the line."

Erin smiled her thanks.

"I am sorry to bother you. I know you must have a ton to do, especially with the discovery at Mrs. Peach's yesterday."

"Finding bodies always means more work, whether they're old or new," he agreed.

"I was over there this morning to talk to the construction crew—"

"Are they over there?" he demanded, "They're not supposed to be working today."

"That's what they said. But I need them to be able to work so that everything will be done for Mrs. Peach when she gets home from her vacation."

"You'll have to be patient. If you lose a day or two of work, that's nothing in the grand scheme of things."

"But... I don't see the need to keep them from working. You've already taken the body, and there can't be any more evidence than that lying around."

"There could be fingerprints, DNA, or other trace evidence. We've got some techs coming in from the city to take a look."

"Can't you do that? Or Terry? He collects evidence all the time."

"This is an unusual case. We don't have a lot to go on. I figured we could use the help of the experts. See what they're able to find."

Erin was dismayed. "And when are they supposed to be coming?"

Wilmot shrugged. "As soon as they can, but I don't know when that will be. Hopefully sometime today." He grimaced at Erin's expression. "Hopefully, this morning, but I can't guarantee anything. I'm sorry."

"And as soon as they're done, you'll release the scene so that the construction crew can get back to work?"

"As long as there is nothing left to do." Erin opened her mouth to speak, but Wilmot beat her to it. "And no, you can't have the name of the guys we contracted to see if you can light a fire under them. They'll get here when they get here, and we don't need anyone putting a strain on relations between our department and them."

"I wouldn't..."

Sheriff Wilmot grinned and shook his head. "I've seen you work. You don't fool me."

"I'm just trying to get the construction crew back to work. So that they'll be done in time for Mrs. Peach."

"Mrs. Peach knows why they are being held up. She's going to have to be okay with that. There's nothing that you could have done differently. Nothing she could have done if she had been here. That's just the way..." Wilmot took a large bite of his cookie, and the remainder broke into a couple of pieces in his hand, "...the cookie crumbles."

"You've talked to her?"

"I have."

Erin sighed. "How was she?"

"She is in good spirits. Enjoying herself. She was disappointed that the construction would be held up for a day or two, but she understands."

Of course, how Mrs. Peach felt when she was away and couldn't do anything about it, and how she would feel when she got home and the work wasn't done, were two very different things.

"Did she…" Erin shook her head, thinking of how to pose the question. "Did she know anything about the man in the wall?"

Wilmot sat back in his chair, making it creak in protest. "Didn't have a clue, according to her."

"So… it's been in there since before they bought the house? There wasn't any time that someone could have… hidden it there without her realizing it?"

Even though Mrs. Peach said that it was the first time she had taken a vacation, she might very well have forgotten about one that she took when she was younger. Something with her husband, in the first blush of their marriage. Or maybe she'd had to go away to take care of a sick sister. There were other reasons she might have been out of town for a few weeks or months. She was an old lady. They forgot things sometimes.

"According to Mrs. Peach, she has never been away from the house for more than a day or two at a time. She's not a wealthy woman and couldn't travel to take vacations. There was *one* time when some work was done on the house. A tree blew down in a storm and damaged the roof and wall. We are looking for information on what happened around that time. Trying to figure out who it is and who put him there."

"How could they not know there was a decomposing body in the house?" Erin was thinking again of the stench of the dead mouse. She couldn't even imagine how much a man's body would stink, how long it would last. She got nauseated just thinking about it.

"That is a good question. I'm not sure we have an answer yet. But before we're done with this case… we'll be able to answer all of those questions. Who it was, how he died, why he was put there, and how no one could know or no one came forward at the time. We will get the answers to all of those questions eventually."

There was a pause while he let Erin think about this.

"But you, Miss Price, are not the one who is going to be answering them."

CHAPTER 11

*E*rin looked at the clock and decided to head over to Auntie Clem's. Even though she wasn't supposed to be on shift, she could still check in to ensure everything was going all right and get started on the preparations to make Melissa's wedding cake and other goodies. Even if Mrs. Peach's renovations were not going ahead, that didn't mean Erin couldn't keep the rest of her projects moving forward. A dead body wouldn't keep her from creating a beautiful wedding cake for Melissa.

Talking to the work crew and the sheriff hadn't taken very long, so she arrived at Auntie Clem's just before opening.

"What are you doing here?" Vic demanded when she saw Erin's arrival through the back door. "You're supposed to be at home. We've got everything covered."

"I know you do." Erin tried not to give away the fact that she *had* been checking up on them, even though it wasn't what she was there for. "I'm here as part of my second job."

Vic looked at her blankly. Charley paused in her work to squint at Erin, trying to figure out what she was talking about.

"As caterer for the wedding reception. And the cake designer."

Cake designer sounded way different from baker. She wasn't just baking a cake.

"Oh!" Vic nodded. "Well, okay, but stay out from underfoot." She grinned at her own cheeky answer.

"I'll do my best," Erin assured her. "How has everything gone this morning? No problems?"

"You're not here as the boss," Charley reminded her. She'd never had a problem being just as cheeky as Vic. "We can manage things."

"I know. I just wanted to make sure." Erin glanced at the big clock on the wall and bit her tongue to keep from pointing out that it was opening time.

"We know," Vic said and hurried out to the front to unlock the door and flip over the Open sign. Charley followed. Erin could hear the usual morning customers entering the front of the shop, chattering away to one another and each other. She was tempted to go out and start the day as she normally would, serving up muffins and bread and other baked good to the ladies—and a few gentlemen—of Bald Eagle Falls. But she schooled herself and instead went to work in the kitchen and office, making sure that she had all of the pans she would need for a wedding cake that would delight Melissa. There was a lot to be done. She needed to get started even if she had built extra time into her schedule. One never knew what unexpected events might crop up and cause delays.

Charley returned to the kitchen after a few minutes to take some muffins out of the ovens just as the timers started to ring. She wiped her forehead with the back of her arm and grinned at Erin. "Lots of questions about your latest body," she advised. "People want to know all the details."

A murder or other big news always brought people to the bakery in droves. They wanted all of the latest gossip and, if Erin or one of her employees was involved, a chance to ask her everything they could think of. There was nothing like the grapevine in a small town on the Bible belt for spreading news, whether it was true or not. At least they were doing their best to go to the source and get all of the details right.

Erin shook her head. "We don't know anything yet. It isn't like any of us have special insight into who the victim was or why his body was hidden in the wall."

"It's shocking. That's all they care about. Things like this just don't happen in Bald Eagle Falls."

Actually, they happened far more commonly than Erin liked to admit.

It would be one thing if this were her first body, but it wasn't. Not by a long shot.

"Well, murder means extra business. Make them buy more baking if they want more questions answered."

Charley chuckled. After placing the muffins on cooling racks, she returned to the front of the store.

Erin was just checking the cupboards for ingredients when she heard a burst of activity from the storefront that she recognized. Children's voices. Unless she was mistaken, it was her favorite customers, the Fosters. And her particular favorite, Peter Foster, the oldest boy in the family. The only boy until the recent birth of Alan, who Peter adored.

She wasn't there to work at the bakery, but that didn't mean that she couldn't take a short break to say hello. She put down her planner and walked out to the front, where Mrs. Foster stood looking at the baked goods on display and negotiated with Peter about what she would buy him today. The little girls were picking out their kid's club cookies, chattering happily and getting fingerprints on the display case as they discussed their choices. Little Traci didn't let herself be pushed around and would, Erin knew, get increasingly louder until she got the exact cookie she wanted.

"Good morning," Erin greeted cheerily. "How is the family this morning?"

Mrs. Foster sighed, swaying to rock the baby in her sling. "We're getting along just fine, Miss Erin. Thank you for asking. The children are growing like weeds, as you can see. They'll eat me out of house and home, I swear."

Erin nodded, smiling. Mrs. Foster bent over to address the little girls, trying to get them to lower their voices and stop touching the glass of the display case. Peter wandered around the end of the counter, meeting Erin's eyes. She made her way over to him and leaned closer to see what he wanted.

"Will you help my dad?" Peter asked solemnly.

"Help your dad? Well, yes, if I can," Erin agreed. What could Mr. Foster need help with? Peter had celiac disease, and maybe Mr. Foster had figured out that it came from him, and he also needed to eat gluten-free. It could be a daunting task for an adult to overhaul his whole diet.

"He needs work," Peter explained. Unlike the girls, he kept his voice low, and Erin suspected he didn't want his mother to hear what he was saying over their requests. "We don't have much money and Mom wants to stay home with the little ones. It's hard to make ends meet with a single income," he said with authority, obviously having overheard this, or even been told it directly when he had asked for more than his family could afford.

"I didn't know that," Erin said. Though she had sensed that the Fosters were having a difficult time. She had provided several boxes of baking for them when Mrs. Foster had been on bed rest and recovering from Alan's delivery. But despite the fact that Erin offered day-old baked goods at no cost to families who needed them, few people took her up on the offer. They were proud and didn't want to take "charity." The Foster children looked well-nourished and cared for, but some of the other children that Erin had seen camped out near Bald Eagle Falls were skinny and ragged, and it hurt Erin's heart to see them and not be able to help. "What kind of work is your dad looking for?"

"Anything. He's not too proud to do any honest work," Peter again parroted what he had heard from his parents. "If you know of anyone who is looking for someone…"

"Actually," Erin thought about it. "I might know of someone…"

"Peter, what kind of cookie did you want?" Mrs. Foster called over to him.

"Uh—chocolate chip," Peter said quickly.

"Which kind?"

He stretched his neck out to look at the display case. "The two colors. Chocolate and white chocolate."

Mrs. Foster nodded to Vic, who was getting the kid's club cookies out for each of the children. "Now come over here and help with the girls."

"Okay," Peter called back to her, but he didn't move from his place at the end of the counter. "You might know someone he could do some work for?" he asked Erin eagerly.

"My neighbor is doing some house renovations and the crew working on it recently lost a couple of workers because they—because they couldn't work on it anymore. Can your dad do construction work? Or electrical?"

"He can build. He's good with tools."

"Peter, now!" Mrs. Foster insisted in frustration.

"Mom!" Peter drew the word out into two syllables, expressing his own frustration at being interrupted. "Miss Erin might know of a job for Dad."

Mrs. Foster, Vic, Charley, and the other ladies waiting to be served all stopped talking and only the girls' whispered comments filled the silence.

"Your dad already has a job," Mrs. Foster said firmly, her face red.

"But he needs something else. You *said* he does. You said that he's underemployed and needs a second job to make ends meet."

Erin tried to get Peter to lower his voice, making a downward motion with her hands, but he paid her no attention. He didn't recognize his mother's embarrassment at their family trouble being announced to everyone in the bakery.

Mrs. Foster's mouth was a tight, worried line, but she looked at Erin, not wanting to brush off the opportunity despite her embarrassment.

Erin tousled Peter's hair. "Peter, do you think you could help me take some garbage out to the dumpster? There's a lot and it would save me an extra trip back and forth. Your mom could just drive around and pick you up in the parking lot."

Peter looked over at Mrs. Foster and she nodded her agreement. Erin lifted up the hinged counter to let Peter walk through and join her, and they went into the kitchen. He looked around with interest. "I've never been back here before. Whew, it's hot!"

"Yes, even with our fans and air conditioners going, the ovens and the Tennessee summer keep things pretty warm back here." She motioned to him. "Let's get together everything that needs to go back to the trash bin and cardboard recycling."

He nodded seriously and let Erin direct him what to do. In a few minutes, they both had armfuls of garbage to be taken out to the bins in the back alley and, while they put everything in, Mrs. Foster drove around with the rest of the family in the van. She left the van running and stepped out so that she could walk over to Erin instead of yelling at her through the window. She gave Peter a stern look, then look back at Erin.

"I don't know what Peter told you, Miss Erin, but..."

"He just said that his dad was looking for a second job," Erin said, brushing it aside. "You know my neighbor Mrs. Peach? She went on vacation and left me in charge of the crew doing renovations on her house."

"I heard something about that," Mrs. Foster agreed cautiously, glancing at Peter. She had clearly heard something about the body, but didn't want anything said about it in front of Peter. Erin knew from past experience that she tried to shelter the children from any talk of violence or death.

"A couple of the men on the crew had to leave yesterday and won't be coming back, so they are going to need someone else if they are going to get done before Mrs. Peach comes back. It's only a short-term project, but maybe if your husband can get in on it, the foreman would see that he's a good worker and would give him other jobs when it is done. I don't know Mr. Foster's hours. Would he be able to fit something like that in?"

"The job he's working right now is a lot of evening hours. The company he was working for before closed down. He didn't get fired."

Erin nodded. "So maybe he would be able to do work during the day? It's not a lot of heavy construction, it's just a house renovation. They need an electrician and a general hand. He just needs safety certification."

Mrs. Foster clutched at Peter's shoulder, giving it a squeeze. Erin didn't know whether it was thanks for getting Erin's help or censure for talking "out of school." Peter squirmed and put his hand over hers, but didn't try to pull it away. "He has safety training," Mrs. Foster said. "Who should he talk to?"

"Howard Monroe is the foreman. I'll give you his number." Erin pulled her phone out and found the foreman's phone number. She recited it slowly to Mrs. Foster while she tapped it into her own phone.

"Thank you. I... really appreciate the help. I hope you don't think that we're being presumptuous asking for help," she looked at Peter, "but he really could use another job..."

"Anytime," Erin said. "I'm glad you asked. And if you ever need anything to tide you over, I've got all of this day-old baking that I have to take into the city to get rid of. I'd sooner give it to someone here in town, save me an extra trip."

Mrs. Foster shook her head. "We've already taken enough from you. Thank you again. Peter, time to get in, or you'll all be late for school."

Erin touched Peter on the shoulder. He obeyed his mother and got into the car.

CHAPTER 12

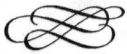

*E*rin returned to the bakery and continued with her inventory of the kitchen and setting aside the pans and ingredients that she would need for the cakes. Vic was busy out front for the morning rush but, eventually, she returned to the kitchen to get some more product in the ovens.

"So… everything settled with the Fosters?" she asked.

"For now. I hope we can help them. And I was wondering… do you know what Willie is up to today?"

"I'm not sure. He doesn't share much about what job he is going to or what he's working on. He knows where to find me, and I guess that's good enough."

Erin gazed at her for a moment. "And it doesn't bother you not to know where he is? What if something happened to him, like before? When he got hit on the head and was wandering around disoriented and no one knew where he was? I mean… he works alone all the time; anything could happen."

Vic shrugged. "I can't control the man. He's been working that way longer than I've been alive. What am I supposed to do about it? He's survived this long. I think he'll be fine."

"I'm sure he will. It just scares me sometimes when I think about it. That he's out there all alone. There could be some claim jumper after one of his mines or a problem with one of the clans. Or he could fall and break something. And we wouldn't know."

Vic nodded. "Did you need him for something?" She redirected the conversation. "You should be able to get him on his cell. If not, leave a message and he'll pick it up when he's back in the calling area. That's the best way to reach him."

"Sorry, I didn't mean to be so negative…"

"You want to see if he has something for Mr. Foster to do?" Vic asked. "Willie likes to work alone. I'm not sure he has anything that he'd be willing to subcontract for."

"I hadn't thought about that." It might actually be a good option if Willie could be talked into letting someone help with something. If Howard Monroe couldn't take Mr. Foster on or keep him employed past Mrs. Peach's job, then maybe Willie would have some suggestions. Some portion of his work that he was not so secretive about. "Actually, I was wondering whether Willie would be able to help out with Mrs. Peach's renovation. They lost a couple of men from the work crew who think that the site is haunted now and won't work on it. Mr. Foster can help with general labor, but he doesn't have any electrical. I think Willie has done some of that kind of thing, hasn't he?"

Vic nodded. "He can do house wiring. I don't imagine there will be anything too challenging or out of the ordinary at Mrs. Peach's. Unless there's another dead body."

"Don't even suggest that!"

Vic laughed. "It isn't like me suggesting it will make any difference to whether there is another body or not. The one that they found was how many years old? Too long ago for my saying anything to have any effect on it."

Erin shrugged uncomfortably. "I just don't like you saying that… we've already run into one glitch with the renovation. I don't want to jinx it."

"You don't believe in jinxes."

"No… not really… but still don't say anything." Erin laughed at herself. "I'm just really paranoid about getting everything done on time. Never mind. I'll call Willie and ask him whether he would be able to help out with the work crew for a week or two."

Vic nodded. "He might be able to; he doesn't mind working for someone else so much if it's just for a few days. But don't think that he's going to stay on permanently. He likes to do his own thing."

"Yes, of course. I know that."

"Okay." Vic headed back for the front of the store. "Talk to you later."

~

Erin didn't like to interrupt Willie from whatever he was doing, but there wasn't really any way to contact him without doing so, unless she just waited for him to come to the house to visit Vic. And there was no guarantee that he would be there tonight. He didn't come over every night and Vic hadn't suggested that he would, so maybe she knew he had other plans.

She sat down at her desk and dialed his number. Maybe she would just get his voicemail and could leave a message for him as Vic had suggested. She never liked the way she sounded on a recording. Too many hesitations. She sounded too young and tentative.

"Uh… hi, Willie. It's Erin. I guess you probably know that from the caller ID. Listen, I was wondering whether you had any free time in the next couple of weeks. The crew working on Mrs. Peach's renovation is a couple of men short and I told her I would do whatever I could to make sure that it got done on time. Before she gets back. It's Howard Monroe, and he's looking for someone who can work on the electrical. Vic said you do that sometimes. Could you give me a call back and let me know? Okay? I'd really appreciate it. I told Mrs. Peach that it would be done when she gets home. Okay. Thanks."

She pressed the End button before she could tell Willie again how she had promised Mrs. Peach that it would be all done when she got home. If Willie were free and wanted to take it on, he would let her know. If he didn't call back before the end of the day, then she would have to see who else she could think of that might be able to help out with the reno. She wasn't sure who else had the electrical skills. There couldn't be anything too complex in the wiring for just one room, could there?

~

She immersed herself in the accounting and marketing work that needed to be done for the week. She couldn't let that slide just because she had taken on the wedding on top of her usual projects. It needed to be done and people needed to know what was on sale or new at Auntie Clem's when they put together their shopping lists and meal plans after receiving the weekly.

Math had never been her strong suit, but luckily the program did most of the work and she just had to enter the appropriate numbers every day or week. Even though she didn't like doing it, she knew better than to put it off. Then it was that much harder when she finally got around to working on it and there was a huge pile of work rather than just a handful of entries.

There was a knock at the back door. Erin left it for Vic to handle. Maybe a delivery. Or Adele coming by for some day-old baking. Adele helped to take care of a family or two in the area who wanted to stay anonymous. Erin wasn't sure how Adele had talked them into it, when Erin had only met with brick walls when she'd offered anyone "charity."

Vic was in Erin's doorway, looking uncertain. "It's Joshua Cox. Do you want to talk to him?"

"Joshua?" Erin closed her file and put it to the side. "Sure, of course."

"In here?"

"Yeah." Erin looked around. The room was the size of a closet and there wasn't really space for a visitor. Nor was there a chair for a visitor to sit in. "Well... maybe not. Where...? I guess I should take him out for coffee."

Vic shrugged. "It depends what he wants."

"What did he say?"

"That he wanted to talk to you. That it's personal. It doesn't sound like it's anything to do with Auntie Clem's."

Erin decided that she should meet with him somewhere that was public, but where they could talk without being overheard. She looked at the system time on her computer screen. "Coffee, I guess," she decided.

Vic backed out of the doorway to let Erin exit. Joshua was waiting at the back door, outside, holding it open.

"Hi, Joshua," Erin greeted, smiling. "Do you want to go for coffee? Over to the family restaurant?"

If he just wanted something quick, it was his opportunity to say so. But he didn't. He considered her suggestion and nodded. "Yeah, that sounds good, thanks."

CHAPTER 13

ald Eagle Falls was not a big place, and the family restaurant was only a few minutes away. It was after the lunch rush, and the waitress seated them in a booth and promised to be back with coffee shortly. Erin sat back.

"How are you doing?" she asked the teenager sitting across from her. Joshua had been through a lot of tough stuff in his teenage years, but he looked pretty good. Not pale and drawn as he had. He looked healthy and determined. Back on track, Erin hoped.

"I'm… feeling better," Joshua said. "I'm feeling pretty good. How about you? Everything going okay with Auntie Clem's?"

"It's doing pretty well. I've been lucky when you consider how many start-up businesses fail, even with experienced businesspeople running them. I'm a better baker than a businessperson, but I've been able to keep it afloat. It's making enough to pay my employees and let me support myself. I never really asked for anything more than that."

"That's good. I know how hard it is for Mom to make ends meet." He pressed his lips together, probably thinking about what his mother would say if she knew he had said such a thing, even to a family friend. Much like Mrs. Foster chiding Peter for asking for help. "But we manage okay. And I've been able to make a little by writing for the newspaper. Not a lot, but they pay me when they run one of my articles."

"That's great. I wasn't sure whether they were paying you or whether it was just for 'exposure.' Sometimes people don't seem to think that they should have to pay for artists and creatives. I guess it's because you can't hold or eat what they produce. It just... came out of your head."

Joshua gave a little smile at this. "Yeah. Well, they've been pretty good to me. I can't complain."

"And how is Cam? Do you hear much from him?"

Like Joshua, his older brother Cam had been subjected to a lot of pressure and trauma, but his response had been to withdraw and rebel. He had dropped out of school, quit all of the sports that he had been so good at, and moved into the city, where he supported himself mostly by crashing on friends' couches or flophouses, as far as Erin could tell. She didn't know how much he was into the drinking and drug culture. Not too much, she hoped, but he had already been the target of one police investigation when he had been caught with drugs in his car. Not his, as it had turned out, but that wasn't much of an excuse as far as the law was concerned.

"He was home for Easter. Seemed like he'd kind of cleaned up a bit since Thanksgiving. I hope. I think he's settling down..."

"That's good. I was worried about him." She met Joshua's eyes. "And you."

"I'm still here." He spread his hands to indicate Bald Eagle Falls. Or maybe just his existence on earth. It had been touch and go for a while there. They had not known what his fate would be. "I wouldn't leave Mom. I couldn't do what Cam did; I saw how much it hurt her."

"What about school? Are you going back in the fall?"

Bella, one of Erin's employees, went to high school with Joshua, and Erin knew she had been encouraging him to return. Maybe now he could see how much Cam was limiting himself by dropping out of school and would have the courage and mental strength to go back and finish getting his diploma.

Joshua sighed. "I don't know yet. I don't really want to. That whole thing... just wasn't good for me, and I couldn't see the point in staying. But I know... people expect you to have a high school diploma. And if I want to go into journalism, people will expect it, and I won't be able to get a degree if I don't have it. I just... I really don't want to go back to school. It was just so much pressure... and in a small town where everyone knows who you are… everything about your family… everything about Cam. Probably more than I know about him. They look at me, and I know they're wondering if I will turn out like him. And if they're not comparing what happened to him with me taking a break from school to consider my options… then they're comparing my athletic ability with his, wondering why I can't do what he could on the court. Why I never measured up."

"You measure up. You're not the same person as Cam and you don't need to be like him in any way you don't want to. You pursue what you're interested in and the future you want to have. It doesn't have to be anything to do with your family."

"Yeah… maybe it's easier for you to say that because you don't have a family. You didn't have to live up to anyone's expectations. The way that Mom expects me to… represent the family. To always look like I'm doing better than I am." He gave a little shrug, drawing his shoulders forward and together like he was cold. "It's pretty tough to live up to generations of Coxes."

"I had a lot of parents with a lot of different expectations," Erin said. "Different expectations everywhere I went. But the ones where people just expected me to fail and be a loser, those were the hardest. Not the ones that expected me to stretch and grow."

Joshua scratched the back of his neck, thinking about this. "Different perspectives. A reporter should always be looking at things from different perspectives."

"That's right," Erin agreed. "That's how you learn. Putting yourself in someone else's shoes."

"I guess I'd rather have a family of my own, even if they are as messed up as mine, than not to have anyone. Or to belong anywhere." He raised his eyes to her again. "But you do belong here now. Maybe you didn't have anywhere permanent as a kid, but now you're one of us. Right?"

"That's right." Erin often felt like an outsider in Bald Eagle Falls. She didn't exactly fit in with the church ladies. She respected their right to believe whatever they wanted to, but they didn't extend the same courtesy to her right to think what she wanted to. They tried to correct and convert her.

But she didn't need to get into that with Joshua.

"I hope your mom knows that I'm her friend and if she ever wants to talk to anyone…"

Mary Lou was self-sufficient. A proud woman. She was pretty hard on herself and unwilling to go to others for help, even when circumstances were dire. Erin hoped that Mary Lou *was* making ends meet and wouldn't have a breakdown over everything that had happened to her family.

"Dad's home," Joshua said, surprising her.

Erin tried not to look too astonished by this. She knew Roger had been allowed a visitor's pass a couple of times to spend the holiday or weekend with his family. But she hadn't expected him to be released from the facility where he had been living since he had been found to be a danger to others. Mary Lou and Joshua could not be expected to look after him alone. They had done their best before, but Roger had been too much for them to handle without outside help.

"They say he's stable on these new medications," Joshua explained. "And it seems like he's better than he was. He hasn't been wandering, and a care worker comes to see him twice a day to ensure there aren't any problems."

"And you and Mary Lou are okay with it? He isn't… violent; he hasn't done anything to worry you?"

"He's been good. And we have emergency medication if something happens; if he gets upset and won't settle down. We haven't had to use it. It's been nice to have him at home, even if he isn't the same as he used to be."

"Wow. That's really good news, then. I'm happy that you can be together as a family again."

"Yeah. Things aren't ever going to be the same again." Joshua swallowed. "But it's something."

CHAPTER 14

*E*rin touched Joshua's hand briefly. Roger's case was tragic. He had invested all of the family's money in a sure thing, which had, of course, gone south. His subsequent suicide attempt had failed, leaving him with brain damage. The doctors or institutions that had evaluated him had said that he was capable of living at home with his family's assistance and had ignored Mary Lou's repeated requests for help as his behavior had deteriorated. That had led to the death of Joelle Plaint and Erin narrowly escaping two murder attempts. At that point, the authorities had finally decided that Roger did, in fact, need more than just the helping hands of his family, who had worn themselves to the bone trying to look after him.

If he was back home and doing well, that was good news. But it did make Erin anxious about what could happen if his violent behavior recurred. Not so much because she was worried for herself, but because Mary Lou and Joshua were vulnerable, living in the same house with him. And there were other neighbors to worry about; people who lived closer to him than Erin.

"He stays in the house," Joshua said, maybe reading some of Erin's concerns in her face. "He has a tracker, so we will know right away if he leaves and we can find him. Right now... nobody really knows he's back, so I probably shouldn't have told you. If you could... you know... keep it under your hat."

"Of course." Erin gave his hand a squeeze and then let go. She leaned back to give him some breathing room. "I'm glad things are working out."

He nodded. "So far. It's almost like being a family again."

Except that Roger would never be the father he had been, and Campbell would probably never live with them again. But they could still be a family even if they didn't all live in the same house. Cam was still part of their family and was at least spending holidays with them and keeping in touch. He was doing better than he had been.

Joshua took a long swig of coffee and wiped his mouth with the back of his hand. "Well... I didn't really come here to talk about my family."

Erin had hoped that he was just touching base. Reaching out to a friend for a listening ear.

But that wasn't how this was going to go.

"I heard about your newest body," Joshua said, giving Erin a lopsided grin. "I guess everybody has by now."

"There seemed to be a lot of active discussion at the bakery," Erin admitted. "Seems people are a mite curious to find out what happened. Get all of the details." She shook her head in amusement. "At least it keeps people coming back to the bakery."

"It's more than gossip that keeps people coming back to Auntie Clem's. But I was hoping to get an exclusive interview with the woman who discovered the body."

"I wasn't the person who discovered it. That was the work crew. I just happened to be next door. And to be supervising the crew. It wasn't in my house, and I wasn't the one who found him."

"Him," Joshua repeated, and pulled out one of his spiral reporter's notepads to start taking notes. "You're sure it was a man?"

"It looked like a man. I'm not the medical examiner. He's the one that will have to confirm all of those details."

"How did it look like a man? I understand that the body was in pretty bad shape after being there for so long. You couldn't tell from his face."

"No. But he was wearing blue jeans, a t-shirt with a bird on it, and a heavy belt. Like one that you use to hold different tools and pieces of equipment. He was broad-shouldered and tall. I wouldn't have ever taken him for a woman, though I could be wrong. There are plenty of big women out there. Maybe who work construction."

"You're sure it was a construction worker? Not someone else who might have that kind of belt? A cop? Roofer? Gardener?"

"It didn't look like a policeman's belt. Those are quite different."

"And you've seen one close up," Joshua teased.

"Well… yes," Erin agreed, her cheeks getting hot. She'd seen it close up, unbuckled it, held it in her hands… "But it could have been some other kind of laborer. A roofer or a gardener, sure. I assume they all wear the same kind of thing. Not a black, polished duty belt like Terry's. Officer Piper's, I mean. But that yellow kind of leather, rough, with big rivets."

Joshua nodded eagerly, writing down these details.

Erin didn't really want to do an interview. She didn't know anything about that man who had died and didn't want to. But she hated to turn Joshua away. And it wasn't like she was telling him anything confidential or that was part of the police investigation. The police hadn't told her anything. All she could tell Joshua was what she had seen with her own eyes.

"Was there anything else you could tell about him?" Joshua asked. "Boots? Hair? Was there anything left of… anything that would tell you his race or what he looked like?"

"Uh… heavy work boots. Probably steel-toed. I don't…" Erin had tried not to take in any details and, in the intervening time, had tried to forget what she had seen, taking care not to replay it over and over again in her mind. She didn't want to look at the mental picture now to answer Joshua's questions. She didn't want that man's desiccated face to appear in her nightmares. "I don't know about his hair. I guess there was hair. And… glasses. There were glasses."

"Could you tell the shape of his face? Anything about his face? Or his skin?"

Erin shook her head. "I don't know, Joshua. It was… not recognizable." She shuddered. "I don't want to think about it."

"Sorry. Just getting what I can. Most of the people who were there don't want to talk about it. There's like… a wall. Like they've been told not to talk to me."

"They probably were." Erin shrugged. "Probably the sheriff told them to keep it to themselves and not spread around any speculation."

"I don't know. Maybe they think I'm just some stupid kid. They don't know that I'm actually a published reporter."

"They probably don't read the paper." Erin didn't get the idea that any of the men she had seen on the crew would be that interested in current events, other than maybe sports scores. They were immigrants, or too busy, or just weren't the reading type. She had heard a lot of statistics about how people didn't even read books after they left high school.

Not that Erin read a lot of books. But she wasn't one of those people who hadn't ever read another book after graduating. And she did read the newspaper. Especially Joshua's articles.

"I guess," Joshua agreed with a nod. "A lot of people don't read anything they don't have to."

"That's true."

"Did anyone have any idea who it might be in the wall? Any of the guys on the construction crew? Officer Piper or the sheriff?"

"No, not that anyone is telling me. I don't think he has been identified yet."

"And Mrs. Peach didn't know who it was. Or said that she didn't." Joshua's tone seemed to indicate that it was a statement rather than a question. Erin hadn't asked Mrs. Peach anything about the man. She had left it to the sheriff to contact her and ask his questions. Erin wasn't an investigator. She would leave all of that to the police.

"You talked to Mrs. Peach?" she asked.

"Yeah. I didn't know if I'd be able to get ahold of her, but I did," Joshua smiled, pleased with himself. Since Erin hadn't given him any details of Mrs. Peach's travel plans, he must have gleaned what he could from the community—maybe his mother—and then called travel agents or cruise lines until he'd been able to pinpoint what cruise she was on. And had managed to get a call through to the boat and get through to her. That took a lot of work and persistence.

"I'm sure if she had known something about who he was, she would have told the sheriff."

"Yeah. But she didn't know anything about it. She was just as shocked as anyone to find out she'd been living with a dead body in the house for all of these years."

"But no one knows how long yet, do they? I mean, it looked like he'd been there for a long time, but I'm not an expert in that kind of thing."

"Well… working off the theory that no one could have just busted open her wall, put a body in there and closed it all back up again without a trace of what he had done without anyone noticing…" Joshua chuckled. "If we go with that assumption, and the assumption that she didn't actually have anything to do with it, then it must have been put there when she had work done on the house before."

"Repairing the damage from the tree."

He raised one brow. "She told you about that too, huh? That's the only other time that wall has been touched since she moved into the house more than forty years ago. Maybe it could have been left there before they moved into the house, but then why wasn't it discovered when the previous work was done on that wall? I think it pretty much had to be left there when the repairs were made after the storm."

Erin conceded that sounded most likely. "That makes sense to me."

"So who would do that?" Joshua asked meditatively. "Was it the men who did that repair job? Mr. Peach? Someone else who just took advantage of an opportunity?"

While Erin might have previously scoffed at the idea of someone other than the construction workers using a reno site to hide a body, she had seen it happen once before, so she couldn't discount it as a possibility. Unlikely, maybe. Two such similar incidents happening so close together felt even more impossible.

"I would guess one of the construction workers," she admitted. "But anything is possible. Was Mr. Peach still living at home when the damage from the tree was repaired?"

"Mrs. Peach says no. She was on her own at the time; it was the first time she had to deal with the insurance company by herself, to arrange for all of the work to be done. An old lady like her doing that by herself thirty years ago…"

"Thirty years ago, she wasn't that old a lady."

"Well, no," Joshua admitted, shifting uncomfortably. "She would have been what? Forty? Fifty? Like, Mom's age?"

"You'd have to fact-check. I'm not sure how old Mrs. Peach is. You never ask a lady. Did *you* ask her?"

"No. I didn't think I'd need it. But I still think… doing that thirty years ago, when she wasn't used to dealing with companies like that, it would have been pretty challenging, right?"

"Yes. Mr. Peach really left her with a lot of things to deal with that she shouldn't have had to. I have a hard time understanding why he just left her. After twenty years together. Apparently happy, from what Mrs. Peach says."

"Guess he wasn't as happy as Mrs. Peach thought. Or she's forgotten what it was like. We color our memories. Remember them the way we would like to. After someone dies or… leaves our life. We can rewrite things to be just the way we want them to be." He looked wistful. Like maybe there were some things in his past that he would have liked to have rewritten. Erin was sure there were probably plenty of things he would have changed. Even if it were just to have spent more time shooting hoops with his father.

"The thing that I don't get is how she could have ignored the smell of a decomposing body," Erin confided. "I mean… they smell really bad."

Joshua's eyes danced. "Can I quote you on that?"

"I didn't mean that I have smelled a decomposing *human* body. Just that… I've lived in houses where a mouse or something had died in the walls, and it was really bad. You couldn't just not notice it unless you had no sense of smell. And that's just something small. A human, especially one the size of that man…" Erin shook her head. Her eyes were practically tearing up just imagining the smell. She had to suppress a gag.

"I didn't ask her about that," Joshua said. "I guess I'll have to call her back."

"I wish you wouldn't interrupt her on her vacation. She's supposed to be having a nice quiet holiday. She's never had one before."

"If she wanted to have a quiet vacation, then she shouldn't have left a body in the wall for the construction workers to find," he teased.

"Do you want me to talk to your mother about that attitude?"

He suppressed his smile. But it wasn't like he was worried she would really follow through on the threat. "I have a deadline to meet," he said apologetically. "I'll need to call Mrs. Peach to get some more details before we go to print."

CHAPTER 15

*E*rin emailed a few pictures to Melissa to see how she liked the ideas Erin had for the cake and checked the time to see how long it would be before Terry got home. It was later than she thought, and he should be arriving any minute. Erin hadn't even started anything for supper, and it wasn't one of the days that she had assigned to Terry, so she couldn't really put it on him either. She ran through a list of possibilities as she heard his truck pull in front of the house. She called Orange Blossom and Marshmallow to the kitchen. It had been a nice quiet day, so Orange Blossom wasn't holed up in a closet this time, but trotted to her quickly, starting to yowl. Terry entered the house and Erin fed the cat and rabbit.

He looked around the kitchen, undoubtedly noting the lack of food. "Hi, honey." He bent down to kiss her. "How was your day?"

"It went by fast. I thought I could get done more than I did since I wasn't working. But stuff just piled up."

She hadn't been planning on visiting the sheriff or having an interview with Joshua when she had made her list and blocked in her schedule. The unfortunate discovery of the body had thrown a wrench into the works.

Terry nodded. "Work expands to fill the space allotted."

"That's stupid. I should be able to do *more* when I have more time."

"Not always the way that it works, unfortunately."

"Huh. So as you can see, I don't have anything on the table. Not even on the stove. How about we go out to eat today?"

She was prepared for him to push back, saying that he had just gotten home and didn't want to go out again. That he was tired and just wanted to relax at home. But he didn't.

"Sure, if you want to. Do you have the time?"

It would take more time to go out and eat at a restaurant than to open a can of soup or make some sandwiches. But Erin had been through a lot over the past couple of days, and she didn't want soup or a sandwich. She wanted real food.

"If work expands to fill the space allotted, then I can take all of the time I need for supper, because I'll be able to fit the work into a smaller space."

"Unfortunately, it doesn't always compress to fit into a smaller space. But you've got lots of time before the wedding. So let's go ahead. If you're okay with that."

Erin looked at the other animals. "Do you want to feed K9 before we go?"

"Just give him a cookie to bring with him. That will hold him until we get back home."

Erin got one of the Auntie Clem's gluten-free dog biscuits from the cookie jar on the counter and handed it to K9. "You can eat that in the truck."

K9 seemed confused about being given a cookie and immediately leaving, but he carried it in his mouth back to the truck and, once they got in, he lay down in the back seat of the extended cab and munched on his treat.

"What do you feel like today?"

"Chinese?" Erin suggested, having already visited the family restaurant with Joshua.

"Chinese it is," he agreed.

When they reached the Chinese restaurant and looked around, waiting to be seated, Erin saw Vic and Willie were also there. Erin gave a little wave. Vic waved back and said something to Willie. After a moment of discussion, Vic waved Erin and Terry over. There was space at their table. Vic motioned for them to sit down.

"Come and join us. The more, the merrier. We haven't even ordered yet so, if you want, we can order dishes to share or order dinner for four?"

Erin looked at Terry to ensure he was okay eating with Vic and Willie, and he nodded. "Sure. Works for me."

They sat down and looked at the menu to discuss what they wanted so that everyone got one of their favorite dishes.

After flagging down the waitress to order and handing their menus back, Erin looked around the restaurant, then back at her dinner companions.

"This is nice. It's a while since we've done something all together."

Vic and Terry nodded their agreement.

"I'm surprised you want to be seen with me," Willie said, looking at Terry. "I would think you wouldn't want to be seen fraternizing with a known criminal."

Erin's face got hot. She studied Willie, trying to read his face. As always, his skin was stained dark by the mining and processing he did on his own, making him look dirty and unkempt, even though Erin knew that he was a habitually clean person. He washed off the dirt, but his skin remained stained. It made it harder to read his expression. Or maybe she didn't want to see any negative emotions there. She didn't want Terry and Willie fighting. Willie was normally a pretty laid-back guy, but Terry had suspected him of being involved in more than one crime around Bald Eagle Falls, maybe even still involved with the Dyson organized crime family he'd been a part of when he was younger. Even though Willie had made it clear that he didn't move in those circles anymore.

"Let's just have a nice evening," Terry said, sighing.

They all looked at each other for a moment. Erin was surprised that Terry hadn't risen to the bait, at least engaging in discussion with Willie on the matter of his alleged illegal activities.

"You're not going to bust my chops over everything you think I should or shouldn't be doing?" Willie asked.

Terry shook his head. "There are times in this job when things become very isolating. Right now... I don't feel like I have much of an opportunity to do anything with a friend in this town, so if you don't mind, let's just eat and have a pleasant conversation."

Erin put her hand on Terry's arm, trying to express sympathy with her touch. "Had a bad day?"

"No. The day went fine. It's just that people don't see police the same way anymore. There was a time when they were heroes. People looked up to cops. Appreciated them keeping the peace. Children played cops and robbers, and most of the kids wanted to be cops. Not the robbers." He took a sip of his water. "Now... police are the villains. Whenever anything is reported in the media, no matter what city or state is involved, that shows the police in a bad light, then suddenly, we're all painted with the same brush. Violent, racist, crooked... people to be feared and avoided. Not admired or trusted. And sometimes, I'm just not sure if it is all worth it."

They were all quiet for a few minutes, unsure how to respond to this revelation.

"I don't think you're bad," Vic said. "I don't think that you're any of those things."

"I appreciate that, Vic. But there are still things you wouldn't say in front of me. Things you don't want to reveal about your past. The operations of the Jackson and Dyson clans. Your family. Maybe even parts of your life now. Because you're afraid of what I would do as a law enforcement officer."

"Well, maybe," Vic admitted. "It isn't like you clock out at the end of the day. You're always a cop. Always on. Listening and judging."

And there had been times when each of them had been suspects. Erin herself. Vic and Willie had both been suspects just recently in crazy Theresa's death. And not just because they might have had motives to kill her. Erin suspected that Terry, like the rest of the town, still thought Willie had been the one to kill Theresa, even though the feds had told the police department to stay out of it. And she was sure that the recent revelation that Willie was somehow still involved with Nelson Dyson, a member of the Dyson family, had not served to soothe any of his suspicions about what criminal activities Willie might be involved in.

"We're not going to talk about any of that over dinner," Erin said decisively. "This is just a group of friends getting together to enjoy some good Chinese food. I'm really looking forward to the General Tso's Chicken."

"Always a good choice," Willie agreed. His eyes were softer when he looked at Erin than when he looked at Terry. Erin considered Willie a good friend, someone who had protected her in the past and would do anything to keep Vic safe and happy. He was a good guy, no matter what his business scruples were.

"And don't forget the fortune cookies," Vic agreed. "Just watch out for those gluten-free ones."

Erin rolled her eyes. The fortune cookie fiasco was not far enough in the past for her to laugh it off. She still regretted the pain that her carelessness had caused Mary Lou.

CHAPTER 16

*L*ook here." Willie leaned forward. He had downed several beers with his dinner and was waxing loquacious. "You can't worry what other people think," he told Terry. "Do you think I spend my time worrying about what other people think of me?"

They all looked at each other, not sure what to say to this.

"I know how people talk about me. What they think of me. Willie, the deadbeat. The dirty, shiftless no-good who even washed out of the clan. What kind of criminal can't even make his place in the Dyson family? You think I don't see how women pull their children closer when I enter a room? How people cross to the other side of the road? Everyone is sure that I killed Theresa Franklin. Even you." He pointed at Terry. "You'll take any opportunity to saddle me with another suspected crime. Not because you can prove it. Just because you know that I must be doing something. I must be up to no good."

Terry shrugged, leaning back in his seat. He hadn't had as much to drink as Willie, and didn't take any offense at his words. "I follow the evidence, Willie. Wherever it leads me."

"Oh, yeah? Funny how it leads to me more often than it does to anyone else."

"Yeah. It is, isn't it?"

They both stared at each other for a few seconds. But there wasn't really any hostility between them. Just comfortable old arguments.

"You can't worry about it," Willie reiterated. "Just like I don't worry about what *you* think."

"That's good. Wouldn't want you worrying about what I think."

Erin rolled her eyes at Vic, shaking her head. "Maybe we should all be heading home."

"You've got more friends here than you think." Willie ignored Erin and continued to address Terry. "I may not appreciate your opinion or the way you come after me when you think I might have stepped over the line, but you're still a friend."

Erin looked at Terry to see what his reaction to this announcement was. There had always been a strange relationship between Terry and Willie. Terry called on Willie to help him out, especially if he needed to run search and rescue or navigate the cave systems in the area. He trusted Willie implicitly in these areas. But he still couldn't trust him in others. He still didn't believe that Willie was no longer in the Dyson clan and that his activities were above-board. And while Willie might not like the suspicion Terry cast in his direction, he did seem to respect Terry and had helped to rescue him in the past. They were like polar opposites. The ends of two magnets that pulled together.

Terry's lips pressed together slightly as he tried to come up with something to say to this. Willie reached across the table and slapped him on the shoulder.

"You're okay, Piper. Don't waste your time thinking that no one in this town cares about you, because they do."

Vic drove Willie back. Erin had been watching Terry's alcohol consumption level and behavior and deemed him fit to drive, so she didn't have to wrestle the keys away from him. At home, they fed K9, and Erin started her evening routine.

"You should do more with the others in the police department," Erin told Terry as she opened her planner and sat down on the couch next to him.

"What?"

"If you feel like you don't have any friends outside of the police department, then you should do more things with the other law enforcement officers. Even Beaver. We could do things with her and Jeremy, too."

Jeremy was one of Vic's older brothers and was in a relationship with Rohilda Beaven, an agent with an unnamed federal law enforcement agency. She was nothing like Terry, but had worked with him on several cases and, while Erin knew that Beaver aggravated Terry sometimes, they got along okay. There was no reason they couldn't do things with Beaver and Jeremy now and then as well as Vic and Willie. And the men that Terry worked with in the police department—Sheriff Wilmot, Stayner, and Tom Banks. Maybe even Clara and her husband, though Erin knew nothing about him. Or with Melissa. Clearly not with Davis Plaint, who would be a guest of the penitentiary for many years to come. Maybe the police dispatcher who worked from her own home. Erin couldn't remember her name.

"What about a police department party? We could get together for a barbecue. A Christmas party in December. Why don't you guys ever get together for anything?"

"Because we work with each other all the time. The point is to get away from work to relax."

"But you get along with each other. And you can understand each other's perspectives; you won't automatically misjudge them and think that they're bad cops because of something you heard on the news. Like you said outsiders do."

"Well, no. I'm not going to do that."

"Then maybe give them a chance. Why don't you pick a day, and we can set something up?"

"Don't you think that you have enough to do already with the wedding?"

"Well, it would have to be after the wedding, of course," Erin admitted. "But that's so soon. As long as we pick a date that's a month or so out, we should be just fine."

Terry put his arm around Erin and leaned into her. "We'll see. It's a nice offer, but I don't know if anyone would want to get together. Like I said, we spend so much time together during the workday."

"You really don't, though," Erin countered. "Not like people who work at an office together. How much time do you spend with the sheriff during the day? You don't. You go on patrol while he works at the office, go out to separate calls. Have some meetings together. But it isn't like you're on top of each other all day. Not like people who work office jobs. And you and Stayner are usually on opposite shifts, so you don't spend a lot of time together. Vic and I spend a lot of the day together, but we still do other things together too."

"Well… maybe you're right. I don't know. We can talk about it another time, when you're not also trying to organize this wedding stuff."

"I'm only doing the cake and the catering. Nothing else."

"Well, that seems to be a pretty significant piece of the action."

"I just think you should think about it. If you're feeling isolated, then we should reach out to some of the others."

CHAPTER 17

*E*rin had been up for some time when she heard Terry's phone ring. She paused and listened to see if it would wake him up. Usually it did, of course, but sometimes if he were really deeply under, he would sleep right through it.

Apparently, he'd gotten enough sleep that waking up was not a problem, and Erin heard him clear his throat and answer the phone, sounding clear, as if they hadn't woken him up.

"Piper. Yeah. Uh-huh. We have a name?" He paused and listened for a few minutes without saying anything. "Okay. Good. I'll see what I can find out. Ask some questions."

If he said anything else after that, Erin didn't hear it. She waited in the kitchen and, after using the bathroom, he made his way out in bare feet and pajama pants. He rubbed his eyes and blinked in the sun.

"Morning."

"There's coffee," Erin offered, nodding to the machine.

He helped himself to a cup and watched Erin. "What are you doing?"

"Sourcing out some ingredients and cake decorations." Erin scrolled down the list of search results on her tablet. She wasn't using a full computer at home, but was finding a tablet to be handy. She still didn't use her phone as a computer. Vic and the younger kids seemed to be able to do anything on their phones, but she had grown up without cell phones. Even if she'd had one, at a couple of foster homes, they were just cheap pay-as-you-go flip phones, and she had to give them back when she moved to the next home. So she didn't see them as an appendage like so many of the other people her age. She liked her planner notebook, and she was getting to like the tablet. Maybe someday she would turn into a smartphone user.

Terry sipped his coffee and didn't say anything.

"Did I hear your phone?" Erin asked.

He looked at her over the rim of the cup, amusement in his eyes. It wasn't like she was fooling him. She knew she had heard his phone and part of his conversation. He knew it. There was really no need to be so circumspect about it.

"Yes. A call from the sheriff. I guess they have made a preliminary identification on your newest corpse."

"It's not *my* corpse."

He smiled. "That's good."

"So you know who he is? Or was?"

"Yes."

Erin waited as if he might actually tell her. But he didn't.

"You're going to be asking the public for help, aren't you? Trying to find out who knew him and when he was seen last? If anyone had any motive to kill him?"

Terry shook his head, his cheek dimpling. "You'd think that you were a cop or something."

"I have been around a couple of investigations now."

"Yes, I suppose we'll be reaching out to members of the public to try to trace his movements." He paused, watching Erin's face. "But since you were not around at the time he apparently died, you won't have any useful information for us."

"You can't tell the public his name and not me!" Erin protested. "It will be in the paper. I'm going to know."

He sat down at the kitchen table. "You have any of those cinnamon muffins? I really liked those."

Erin folded her arms and made no movement toward the freezer. "No."

"All gone? I'm not surprised. Blueberry?"

"No."

Frown lines creased his forehead. "Chocolate chip?"

"No."

He leaned back in his chair. "Why do I get the idea that the answer to everything I ask for will be no?"

Erin shrugged, her arms still folded, staring him in the eye. "If the answer to what *I* want is no…"

"Oh, I see." Terry chuckled. "But you know I can't give you classified police information."

"It's not classified. You're going public with it. You've already talked to Sheriff Wilmot about it and are going to start asking around. As soon as you're finished eating your breakfast."

"Which apparently I am not getting today…"

"Nope, I guess not," Erin agreed. "So there's no point in waiting. You might as well start asking your questions now."

"I know that *you* don't know anything. So I guess I'll head into the office."

Erin pretended to be uninterested. "Okay. I'll see you later."

He continued to gaze at her. "Jack Perry."

"What?"

"That's the name of the victim. Jack Perry. Are you satisfied?"

Erin sat down at the table with him. "And who was he? What do you know about him?"

"Nothing, yet. I haven't begun my investigation."

"The sheriff must know something. If he was ever charged with anything. Who his family is. Where he lived. His background."

"That's a bit much to expect when we've just barely gotten his name."

"You'd at least do a computer records check and DMV."

"Listen to the expert," Terry teased.

Erin went to the freezer and got out one of the cinnamon muffins. She warmed it in the microwave for just long enough. She sat back down at the table, placing the muffin on a plate in front of herself, as if it were her breakfast. Terry eyed it.

"Did he live in Bald Eagle Falls?" Erin asked.

"About thirty years ago," Terry admitted. "After that… we don't know yet. We haven't had a chance to find anything else yet."

"About the time that Mrs. Peach had the damage to her house fixed. After the big storm that blew the tree into her house."

"I would guess that must be about when he disappeared," Terry agreed.

"What did he do?" Erin picked the muffin up, studying it.

"You are a very good interrogator."

She nodded.

"He was a laborer. Construction, casual labor, sometimes unemployed. Sometimes working here and sometimes in the city or one of the nearby towns, depending on where the work was."

Erin put the muffin back on the plate and slid it across the table to him. Terry picked it up and took a bite, chuckling again. He closed his eyes and savored it. "Those really are the best muffins I think you've ever made."

"They turned out nice, didn't they?" Erin agreed. "The great thing about gluten-free muffins is that you don't have to worry about over-mixing them like regular muffins. So you can get away with some things you can't with wheat muffins."

Terry licked his lips. "They are outstanding."

"So, who are you going to talk to? Who would know Jack Perry?"

"That's a good question. I will have to see if we have anything on file, if anyone in the office or our regular sources knows who his friends were. Failing that, I can check his school yearbooks to get an idea of who knew him and whether he was in any clubs with anyone still around here."

"You really don't know yet?"

"Not yet. We're good, but not that good. We just got the name. Haven't been able to do anything but check the police records and a few public databases yet."

"Jack Perry." Erin wondered whether she had heard of his name anywhere before. In one of Clementine's old journals? He would have been younger than she, but he would have been around when Mrs. Peach's repairs were being done, and Clementine had lived next door.

There were, she thought, some Perrys in the genealogical records she had gone through. No one closely related to her, but it was one of the families that had lived on the mountain for generations.

"I don't think I've heard of Jack before."

"I wouldn't expect so."

"In any of Clementine's books, I mean. I don't think she ever mentioned him."

Terry nodded his understanding and took another bite of the muffin. "We'll have to ask around to get a fix on him. I'm too young to remember him. But there are plenty of older folks around who will remember."

"Sheriff Wilmot didn't?"

"No. Said the name is familiar, but he couldn't put a face or any specific memory to it."

"Have they determined the cause of death yet?"

"Autopsies take time. Especially when you have to ship the bodies off to the city and wait until they have a space in their queue to perform it. Their cases will always take precedence. Unless you've got a child or a public figure."

Erin didn't want to think about that. Cases involving children were tragic, even if they were accidents rather than homicides. Even if it was a child who died of natural causes in his sleep. It was still a terrible tragedy for the family, left to grieve the tiny new life.

She would have told Terry to let her know what he found out but, of course, he wouldn't. Even when they got the report back from the medical examiner, she would hear it from gossip or the newspaper rather than from Terry. The same was true of anything he discovered in his interviews with the old-timers around Bald Eagle Falls. Erin might hear gossip from the ladies at the bakery, but she wouldn't hear it from Terry.

CHAPTER 18

$\mathcal{E}$rin heard a saw powering up next door. She looked at Terry.

"Has the crime scene been released?" she asked eagerly.

"Yes. As you can hear, it has been released and the crew is ready to start working again this morning."

"Oh, thank goodness. I'm going to go over and talk to Mr. Monroe!"

"You might want to stay out of the way," Terry cautioned.

"I'm not going to get in the way. I want to make sure that they have everything they need. They needed a couple more men for the crew, and I suggested Mr. Foster and Willie, but I don't know if that all worked out or if they need someone else." Erin threw open the back door and was gone before Terry could call her back. Luckily, he chose not to follow her. She didn't want to give Mr. Monroe the impression that she needed male supervision. She needed him to respect her because she had been left in charge by Mrs. Peach and knew what she was doing.

She flitted out of her gate and into Mrs. Peach's, and approached the work crew. The one with the saw spotted her coming and turned it off so that she and Mr. Monroe wouldn't have to shout over it. The foreman looked at Erin and shook his head with a "Heaven help me" eye roll. She ignored it and spoke to him crisply, one professional to another.

"Officer Piper tells me that the scene has been released so that you will be able to get back to work today."

"Yeah, that's why we're here," he pointed out. "We're on top of it."

"That's great. I really appreciate it. And Mrs. Peach does too. She'll be pleased to hear that everything is back on track again."

"Uh-huh."

"And you said you needed a couple of new workers to replace the ones who didn't show up after the… body was found." She didn't like to mention it in front of any other workers, as if one of them might quit just because she had brought it up again. "I talked to a couple of men and gave them your name…" Erin looked around at the crew and saw Mr. Foster there. She hadn't recognized him in a hard hat. He nodded to Erin and gave her a small thumbs-up, trying not to attract everyone else's attention. Erin didn't see Willie. Her heart sank. She heard the gate open and closed again behind her and turned to look, catching sight of Willie Andrews sauntering toward her, also with a hard hat on, the appropriate safety measures in place.

The foreman nodded at Willie. He looked back at Erin. "Yeah," he said grudgingly. "You did good finding what I needed in such a short time. Provided they work out, we should still be able to get everything done before Mrs. Peach gets home."

"That's great. I appreciate that." Erin hesitated, not liking the "Provided they work out." But she supposed that he hadn't worked with either Willie or Mr. Foster before and didn't know whether they would be able to do everything they said they could, show up on time every day, and all of the other things that were required of a worker, but that no one knew until they were actually put to the test. "Is there anything else you need? Anything that you have questions about or…?" Erin shrugged. "Anything?" She was aware that her voice had gone higher, nervous as she was about talking to the foreman.

"I think we're all set here," Mr. Monroe assured her.

"Okay. Well, good. I'm glad you've got everything under control. Let me know if anything comes up that you need someone to make a decision on. I'm not even working at Auntie Clem's right now, so I'm right next door…" She gestured. Her offer was met with another eye roll. The lady couldn't even trust them to work without direct supervision. "Sorry, that's not because of you. I didn't mean that. I've taken time off to work on my friend's wedding. But if you're looking for me, I'll be close by. I won't be underfoot, I promise."

"Okay, lady," Monroe said. "I'm gonna take you at your word. Clear out and let us get to work."

Erin's cheeks flamed. She nodded and headed for the gate. Willie stood to the side and nodded to her.

"I really appreciate you coming," Erin told him. "You're a lifesaver."

He jerked his head toward her yard. "You'd better get out of here."

Erin did as she was told.

CHAPTER 19

*E*rin had decided to bake the layers for the cake ahead of time and freeze them. The actual decorating of the cake had to wait until they were closer to the reception date, but she would do everything else she could ahead of time. Baking the layers. Forming the sugar roses and other decorations that she was not buying premade. The other desserts that she was providing for the reception. And she would make cupcakes to practice her technique. Those could be frozen until the wedding as well.

She worked in the kitchen at Auntie Clem's, keeping an ear on what was happening in the front of the store, even though Bella and Vic were covering it and she didn't need to do anything. She liked being a part of the rhythms of the store that she'd grown accustomed to over the last couple of years. The familiar sounds and routines were comforting.

As she loaded up the ovens with the layers needed for the wedding cake, Erin heard Betty Thompson's voice as she exchanged pleasantries with Vic. One of their elderly customers. Erin put the last layer in and set the timer, then went out to the front to talk to Betty.

"Oh, Miss Price is here," Betty observed. "I thought you were working on the wedding for you-know-who."

Erin smiled. "I don't think it's a secret who's getting married," she said with a laugh. "Is it bad luck to say her name before the wedding?"

Betty smiled. "I wouldn't want to be accused of spilling the beans to anyone she hadn't told yet."

Erin looked at Vic and Bella. "I don't think you need to worry about that. We all know. Anyway—I am working on the wedding. I just put the layers for the cake in the ovens."

"Oh, how exciting!" Betty clapped her hands together. "I've never worked on a wedding cake. It must be thrilling."

Erin wasn't sure about *thrilling*. "I'm nervous about it," she admitted. "I don't want to do anything wrong. The last thing I want to do is wreck Melissa's special day."

"Yes, you want it to look just perfect, just the way that she pictured it."

That made Erin more nervous. She and Melissa had exchanged pictures and talked about what Melissa wanted, but what if Erin didn't actually share her vision? What if what she made was different from what Melissa had pictured? Even if it was beautiful, if it wasn't what Melissa wanted...

"I hope it will work out. I've never made a wedding cake before."

"It can't be all that different than the other cakes that you've made. You make birthday cakes. Some of those are elaborate."

And Erin couldn't count the number of times she'd had to scrape the icing off of a cake and start over.

"Yes. I'm sure it will be just fine."

Betty leaned forward on her walker. "How is Gladys? Have you heard?"

"Last time I talked to Mrs. Peach, she was doing very well. She's enjoying the cruise, trying to participate in everything they offer. She'll exhaust herself before they even get to Mexico."

"Well, then she can lie on the beach and not worry about anything."

"That's right."

Erin hoped that Mrs. Peach wouldn't be worrying about anything. But if Erin had been in that position, she would have had a hard time focusing on the fun activities, thinking about what was happening with her home and the man who had been found in the wall.

"Isn't it terrible," Betty said in a low voice. "I couldn't believe it when I heard that a body had been found."

"No. It was quite a shock."

"I heard a rumor that it was the Perry boy. Do you know from your policeman if that is true?"

"Uh… yes. Jack Perry. That's what I heard too." Erin didn't know about "the Perry boy," but she supposed that anyone more than twenty years Betty's junior was just a boy in her mind.

Betty shook her head. "He always was a wild one. His daddy could not do anything with him."

"Really?"

"I always figured he would come to no good. We'd see him at the law office sooner or later."

"Did the firm ever represent him?"

"I couldn't tell you if they did!" Betty chided. "That would be confidential information."

"Oh, yeah, I guess it would."

"We didn't," Betty told her in a low voice. "That's *not* confidential information. There's nothing wrong with saying that you didn't represent someone."

Erin chuckled. "You had me going there."

"We never did, but I would not have been surprised. He was always into something. He was a bad sort."

"How old would he have been when he died?"

"Well, let's see. Thirty years ago. His mother was my music teacher when I was a young lady, and I remember him hanging around. He must have been… forty years old thirty years ago? Early forties. Somewhere in there."

So he hadn't still been a kid. Not even when one extended the appellation to include young people into their thirties. He'd been a full-grown man, independent, with a place of his own, probably.

"Was he married? Did he have a family?"

"Jack Perry? No, no. He was so ornery. No woman would ever marry him. And I'm sure he didn't want anything to do with kids, even if he did father any. None of their mothers would have wanted him in their lives, either."

Erin knew plenty of mean and abusive men who had convinced women to marry them. Somehow, meanness did not seem to be an impediment to getting married.

"He doesn't sound like a very nice person."

"No, he was not. Hard drinking. A brawler. A nasty mouth on him. Even as a child, he was so disrespectful. He would secretly call me names when I went for my music lessons and his mother wasn't in the room. Heaven only knows where he learned them all. I didn't know some of them myself, and I was a good ten years older than him!"

"Do you think *his* father was abusive toward him?"

Betty looked at Erin, frowning. She cocked her head to the side. "Well, I declare... I never even thought of that, to tell the truth." She considered about it for a moment, brow furrowed. "His pa was always getting on his case, yelling and threatening and telling him to mind his manners. But that's how folks used to be. I always just thought that he yelled so loud because Jack was such a little... hoodlum. That he was trying as hard as he could to keep him on the straight and narrow. But I suppose... nowadays, they'd call that emotional abuse. I don't know whether he beat him or not. I wasn't around the house except for my lessons. I didn't have any desire to be there the rest of the time."

But by the time he was killed, Perry had certainly had plenty of time to learn how to behave himself in polite company. He might have learned inappropriate behavior and language from his own father but, by forty, he was responsible for his own behavior. Erin felt bad if he was the product of abuse; she had seen too many people who bore the scars of childhood abuse, both while she was in foster care and in a number of the cases she had looked into in Bald Eagle Falls. Even Vic. It didn't seem to be a problem that was only confined to one part of the country or one social class. It was everywhere.

"Could I get you anything else?" asked Vic, who had been patiently standing by with Betty's order as she and Erin talked.

"Oh, no, that should be plenty. I didn't mean to talk your ear off, dear," she told Erin. "I don't know what I was thinking."

"Not at all," Erin murmured.

Betty paid her bill, loaded the shopping bag onto her walker, and left Auntie Clem's. Vic looked at Erin.

"Even when you're not working, you're still here talking with the customers."

Erin shrugged. "I know. I just heard Betty's voice and had to say hello."

"Well, you'd better stick to your wedding baking. You know what Terry would have to say about you investigating…"

"I'm not," Erin said immediately. "Did I bring anything up? I just came out to say hello to Betty Thompson. She's the one who brought Jack Perry up."

"Uh-huh," Vic agreed, "and butter wouldn't melt in your mouth."

"I never did understand that saying."

CHAPTER 20

*E*rin was surprised when, a couple of days later, Terry returned home with Officer Stayner, a junior law enforcement officer who Erin tolerated, but didn't really like. He was young and hotheaded and hadn't yet learned how to handle people and avoid putting his foot in his mouth. At least, that had been the case when the Bald Eagle Falls police department had first hired him to take over Terry's position while he had been out for medical reasons. They had managed to find the space in the budget to keep him on, so he hadn't gone back to the city once Terry had recovered enough to go back to work full-time. They really did need Stayner, but Erin still resented him for having taken over from Terry, even though it had been necessary and had nothing to do with Erin. The police department was too small to handle things without him. It hadn't been because of any personal failing of Terry's. But she had been worried that he had waltzed in thinking that he would have Terry's job permanently.

But now Terry was back at work and Stayner was still there and had, Erin hoped, had a few of his rough edges smoothed away. She had learned that he had his good points, just like anyone else. But she still hadn't learned to like the guy.

"Rod came over for the game," Terry advised Erin. "You don't mind, do you?"

She couldn't very well say that she minded, since she had encouraged him to bring work colleagues home in the first place. She had thought that they would plan it all out ahead of time, but Terry had understood it differently. He and Erin didn't have anything special planned. He was just going to have a bite to eat and watch the game for a little while, so why not bring Stayner home to do it with him?

"Of course not." Erin swallowed and smiled. "Who's on tonight, then? You guys usually work opposite shifts."

"Tom was looking for some more hours this month. So he's taking a few more shifts. He's on tonight. We've been putting in extra time trying to get somewhere on the Jack Perry case, so Sheriff Wilmot thought it was okay if we both took the night off." Terry looked Erin in the eye. "Is it okay?" he asked again. "We could go to the bar and watch on the big screen. If we're in the way here or you had other plans…"

"No. No, that's fine; I'd rather have a bit of company. It's nice you could come, Officer Stayner."

He nodded politely. "Thank you, ma'am."

"I thought we would order in," Terry offered. "You haven't started on dinner, have you? It was supposed to be my night." He glanced at Stayner, and Erin wondered if he was worried about looking henpecked in front of the junior officer. "If you don't mind, we could get some hot chicken. It's been a while since we had any, and I know you like it."

"That sounds good," Erin agreed. She had thought Terry would make something to eat the night he was in charge. But she supposed it was a bit much to expect him to make anything when he was just coming off a shift. Especially with how busy they had been this week with the newly discovered body. But she had told herself that she'd be happy with anything he made, even if he just opened a can of soup. If a can of soup was okay, then a hot chicken dinner certainly had to be. "That's, uh… that's good. I'll feed the animals now so they won't be in the way when we eat."

"They're going to be in the way anyway," Terry said with a laugh. "Or the cat will be, anyway."

Of course he would. Any time anyone was in the kitchen, Orange Blossom wanted to know why he wasn't being fed. And with the smell of chicken wafting through the house, he would be mightily offended that she had chosen to eat something he wasn't allowed to have any of.

"I'll feed them now," Erin repeated, and she stepped into the kitchen to do so.

"It's okay?" Stayner asked Terry once she was out of the room. "You're not going to have to pay for it later?"

"No, it's fine," Terry assured him. "You heard her. We'll have a nice dinner that she didn't have to make. She told me to invite someone over. She doesn't mind."

Erin got the animals' food out. Orange Blossom did not come running. He was again hiding in a closet with his face turned away from the loud noises next door. Erin had to coax and drag him out before he would come eat dinner. With that ordeal, she had barely finished getting all of the animals settled when the doorbell rang, and it was the delivery boy with their hot chicken dinner.

"Why don't you eat yours in the living room?" Erin suggested. "Then you're not missing any of your game."

"Are you going to eat with us?"

"No, I'm just going to eat in here," Erin indicated her seat. "I have a book to read. And then I need to get back to work. I'm going to do some cupcakes tonight."

"Are you sure, Erin?" Terry asked, apparently not liking this development.

"Yes, I'm sure. Go enjoy the game. Just don't spill."

They dished up and took their meals into the living room. Erin waited until they were gone before getting hers.

The book she wanted to read was not a novel, but a cookbook. *Traditional Tennessee Treats and Weddings.* She'd managed to get it from the library. It seemed like just the thing to help her prepare for Melissa's wedding. Everyone would assume she knew all of the traditional stuff to bake or do at a Tennessee wedding, but there were probably a lot of cultural things that she didn't know. She wanted everything to go well for Melissa's wedding, even if it was a rush.

With the men settled in the living room, Erin ate her chicken slowly, wiping her fingers before touching the pages of the library book. Terry and Stayner watched the game, their conversation sporadic, between cheers or jeers at the players on the screen.

"It was probably an accident," Stayner said. "He was working on the roof and fell between the walls and died there. I heard of another case where that happened. They didn't find him again until decades later when the building was being demolished. Kind of like this. No one ever knew what happened to him."

Terry shouted at a player's mistake and didn't answer immediately.

"I don't think this was an accident," he said. "Yeah, it could happen like that, obviously, since it has before, but it's not likely. When you find a guy buried in concrete or entombed in a wall, he didn't usually get there by himself."

"You think it's mafia? Organized crime?"

"It isn't like we're free of organized crime around Bald Eagle Falls. The clans may not seem like a big deal to an outsider, someone without experience with them, but for us… we know that they are involved in a lot of crime, a lot of violence in this area. Tennessee is not a crime-free area by any measurement. We have more violent crime per capita here than in New York or California. A lot more."

"Not in a sleepy little town like this. I know we've had an unusual spike in crime lately, but that's just an anomaly. A clump of crimes. They don't get evenly distributed throughout the year."

"I think if you look at our statistics, you'll find that it isn't an anomaly. This is a poor state, and we are in a poor part of the state. People are struggling. And when you have poverty, you see an increase in crime. Not just property crime. Not just theft. Violent crime."

Their following comments were on the game rather than on the investigation. Erin went back to reading her book. She was almost finished eating her dinner, and then she would need to put the book aside and work on the cupcakes. She wanted to ensure her skills were polished to perfection before tackling the decoration of the wedding cake.

CHAPTER 21

 ut what does that have to do with our victim?" Stayner asked.
"He was killed decades ago. You don't know what the crime
rate was like back then or what he might have been involved with. They
didn't have the same safety standards back then as they do now. He could
have been working on the roof alone, with no one else with him, no
tether or any way to call for help if he fell."

"Maybe the medical examiner will be able to give us a better idea of
whether or not it was an accident or murder," Terry said gravely. "But I'm
betting on murder. I don't think this was an accident. It just... doesn't feel
like it."

"He was never reported missing."

"No," Terry agreed. "Sounds like everyone assumed he had left town.
Maybe he'd been talking about going somewhere else. We need to find
people he might have talked to about his plans or dreams."

Stayner grunted his acknowledgment. "You don't realize how much
you rely on the internet and modern technology until you don't have it.
Not being able to search through digitized records of the crimes he'd been
investigated or arrested for." He snorted. "It's like the dark ages."

Terry chuckled. "Well, from what we have so far, it does not look like
he was well-liked. Nobody has been particularly surprised by the fact that
he came to harm."

~

Erin was working on the cupcakes and keeping half an ear on Terry's and Stayner's conversation when Vic tapped at the back door and let herself in. Nilla ran in ahead of her and made several wild circles around the kitchen, his toenails clicking over the floor. Erin laughed.

"Looks like someone needs to burn off some energy."

"He's already been on a walk," Vic said, rolling her eyes. "I think that's what got him so wild. He can't chase the birds and squirrels, so he goes nuts when he gets into the house and I let him off the leash. I think he imagines the chase."

Erin watched Nilla, giggling. "Is that what you're doing, boy? Reliving everything you would have done if you had been off leash?"

Eventually, Nilla settled down and went over to Erin, nose in the air as he investigated what she was doing.

"You can get him a cookie," Erin suggested.

Vic got one of the dog biscuits out of the cookie jar and gave it to Nilla. K9 padded into the kitchen. "He's got ears like a bat," Vic said. "I didn't make that much noise opening the cookie jar!"

"They hear everything."

Vic looked at the cupcakes Erin was working on. "Those are cute. You're doing a really good job."

Erin sat back to survey them. They were pretty, and she was testing and practicing all the techniques on them that she would need on the big wedding cake, so they had a wide variety of textures and decorations instead of all looking identical. "It's pretty fun. My wrist is getting tired, which probably means my technique is terrible, but I'm enjoying myself. And I'm getting better."

Vic looked up and down the rows. "I don't see any mistakes. They all look pretty good to me."

"Well, a few I've had to scrape and start over. But it's pretty easy to wipe out your mistakes on a cupcake. It won't be so easy if I make a mistake on the wedding cake."

"Melissa is going to be delighted with it. I'm glad you're doing it for her. She's going to have a very nice reception."

Vic sat down and reconsidered what she had said.

"Actually, I think it's going to be a pretty weird reception, with only the bride and no groom. And people will be talking about her and asking her awkward questions. So I'm glad that you're there to support her and make a beautiful cake for her even if she doesn't have a groom on hand. And I know that *you* won't be asking her awkward questions and making her feel bad about Davis not being there."

"Maybe she'll start a new trend. Bride-only or groom-only receptions. You could each have a separate one and not have to mix your weird friends and relatives with someone else's weird friends and relatives. You get drunk Uncle Mike dancing with someone else's married Aunt Bertha, and fireworks ensue. This way, you only have your own people to keep under control."

"I'll have to suggest it to Willie," Vic laughed.

Erin raised her brows. "Are the two of you talking about getting married?"

"No. Not really. Only in the most general 'maybe someday' terms. It's not like either of us has families who would want to be there, and I can't get my birth certificate fixed. If we were ready to get married—and neither of us is—I would want to be married under my own gender and name, not what's on my birth certificate."

Erin nodded. Tennessee was one of the hold-out states that would not allow gender markers to be changed on birth certificates and driver's licenses. Maybe someday. Maybe when Vic and Willie were ready, the laws would have changed.

Vic cocked her head, listening to Terry and Stayner talking in the living room. "I didn't realize you had company. Who's with Terry?"

"Rod Stayner."

"Oh, him. Well, I understand why you're in here doing cupcakes."

"Besides the fact that I *need* to be making cupcakes and practicing my technique."

"Well, besides that, yes. Have you found anything out?"

Erin didn't look up from the cupcake she was decorating. "About what?"

"About Jack Perry," Vic said in a low voice.

Erin glanced at her, smiled, and looked back down at the cupcakes. "What would I have found out about Jack Perry?"

"Are you telling me they haven't been talking about him?"

"Well, yes. Actually, they have."

"Spill! What have you found out?"

Erin looked over her shoulder toward the living room. "Now is probably not the best time to discuss it. If I can hear them, they can hear us."

"Oh, we are far quieter and more discreet than they are. Tell me, what did you find out?"

"He had a record. Neither of them has said what it was for. I'm hoping they'll mention it."

Vic nodded eagerly.

"Stayner thinks it was an accident, but Terry doesn't."

"What does Stayner think? That he drywalled himself into that wall?"

"No, that he was working on the roof and fell into the space inside the wall. He's heard of a case where that happened once, so that is what he thought happened to Perry. But Terry says no. He figures someone killed him and put him there."

"Well, of course they did," Vic agreed. "Anything else is ridiculous."

"And you were there when Betty was talking about him. He wasn't a very nice person, even when he was young. That kind of person could attract a lot of enemies."

Vic nodded seriously. "Willie said that too, that not many people liked him. He was a rough kind of guy, chased after women, and maybe was into drugs. I don't know if that means dealing drugs or just using them. Willie was pretty closed mouthed about the whole thing. I don't know why he wouldn't want to tell me everything. I mean, it isn't like the guy is going to come after me. He's already dead."

"Willie knew him?"

"Not really. But some of the construction guys remembered him because he was in construction and they worked with him back then."

Erin pictured the older men on the work crew. She didn't really know any of them. She supposed she had seen them around Bald Eagle Falls, but she generally knew the women who came to the bakery. Not their husbands or the single men who didn't come to the bakery. People mostly followed traditional roles in Bald Eagle Falls, with the wives doing the shopping and cooking, even though most of them worked just as hard as their husbands at jobs outside the home during the day. A few men came in occasionally but were not regulars.

"Willie thinks he might have been into drugs? Addicted?"

"Maybe."

Erin picked up the next cupcake to be decorated, thinking about that. A guy who was mean and nasty to start with, maybe abused as a child and exposed to violence in his home. Add addiction into the mix and perhaps a jealous husband or two. A pretty explosive formula. It sounded like they would not lack for suspects. But would those suspects all still be in Bald Eagle Falls? A lot of people left because of the lack of work or to live closer to schools with better opportunities. And if Erin had killed a man, then even if he were well-hidden, she would probably have found an excuse to move away. Why stay somewhere she was in danger of being found out? She would rather hit the road and avoid arrest.

She had always found it easiest just to move on and leave trouble behind. Until Clementine had given her the opportunity to settle down in Bald Eagle Falls and have a go at making a life for herself. Without Clementine's estate, who knew what dead-end job she would be in now, living out of a suitcase in some dive, waiting for things to fall apart yet again? Instead, she was a well-regarded baker who had made a home and friends for herself in Bald Eagle Falls.

"Where are you?" Vic asked softly.

"Oh. Trip down memory lane, I guess."

Vic seemed to sense that these were thoughts Erin was not ready to share and didn't ask for details. She clicked her tongue at Nilla to call him over to her and scratched his fluffy white ears.

"Maybe the question isn't who killed Perry and why, but why anyone didn't kill him any earlier," Erin said, shaking her head. "Was he friends with anyone?"

"Some of the women around town, it sounds like."

"They'd be old now. Do you think they'd be more or less likely to talk about him?"

"*I* wouldn't. I think that's the kind of thing I would close up and leave behind."

Erin nodded her agreement. Vic stopped scratching Nilla's ears and sat up.

"You don't think that Mrs. Peach was involved with him, do you?"

Erin wrinkled her nose. It was hard to imagine an old woman like Mrs. Peach being involved with a philanderer, especially one who was so rough and abusive. But she hadn't been an old woman thirty years ago. A mature woman. One who had been abandoned by her husband and was suddenly on her own for the first time in her life. That would be scary. Had she reached out to the wrong person for help? Someone who offered to help but really only wanted one thing from her?

"I don't know... I just think of her as this proper old lady, but then she'll say something to remind me that she was young once too and that she wasn't necessarily always sedate and proper. She teases me about Terry. Laughs when she embarrasses me."

"Well, you're such a good target. I love the shade of red that your cheeks turn."

Erin rolled her eyes and focused on the cupcakes, trying to keep her body's systems under control so that she wouldn't blush at Vic's comment. She added rows of little dots to the top of the cupcake, evenly sized and spaced.

Maybe she'd better have a longer discussion with Mrs. Peach about what had happened thirty years before.

CHAPTER 22

$\mathcal{B}$etween Erin's work on the wedding and the time difference and Mrs. Peach's busy cruise schedule, it was a couple more days before Erin could get ahold of Mrs. Peach on the phone. They kept missing each other.

At least Erin knew she was still enjoying herself, not locked in her cabin worrying or weeping about everything happening at home, regretting having left Erin in charge.

"Oh, Erin," Mrs. Peach greeted, sounding far away. "I finally reached you. I am sorry that things have not worked out the last few days. Things have been so busy here. I'm booked for a lot of activities, and they like you to be at the things you have signed up for. They come looking for you if you don't show up." She laughed merrily. "I guess they're used to dealing with forgetful old folks and assume that if you didn't come, you must have forgotten about it, not decided you had something better to do. They are a little... what's the word... paternalistic?"

"Mmm." Erin made a noncommittal noise. "I'm sure they're just trying to be helpful." She had dealt with enough forgetful old folks in her life to know what it was like to have to remind someone of what their plans were for the day, even if you had reviewed them together just five minutes before.

"Oh yes. They are certainly pleasant about it. It's just that whole attitude… you know I'm an independent woman. I'm used to taking care of myself. I don't want to be treated like a child or a demented old woman."

"You're certainly not that."

"That's right," Mrs. Peach agreed, sounding reassured. "Now, you have been trying to reach me and I'm sure it's not just to check my social calendar or to remind me what day I'm supposed to be getting back home."

"No. It isn't anything, really. I just… I wanted to talk to you about this man who was found in your wall."

"I've already talked to the police about that. I told you I don't know anything about that odious man or what he was doing in my wall. All these years, I had no idea that he was in there. That may sound strange to the police, but would *you* know if there was someone sealed up inside of your walls?"

"Uh… no, I guess I wouldn't."

"No, you wouldn't," Mrs. Peach agreed. "I don't have x-ray vision. I have no idea how he got there, except it must have been when the repairs were done after the storm. Everything was so frazzled during that time. You can understand why I never knew anything about it."

"Did you know him? Jack Perry?"

"*Know* him would be a bit strong," Mrs. Peach said tartly. "He was on the work crew that did the repairs to my house. I might have taken them a jug of lemonade at some point. I might have known their faces, but that was a long time ago; I wouldn't still remember him."

"I understand that he… got on with the ladies. He never reached out to you? Tried to get you to let him in at night, never stayed late to work on something by himself?"

"Certainly not. I wouldn't have had anything to do with a character like him."

"Like him. You did know him, then, and something about his reputation or personality."

"I didn't say that. I wouldn't be hanging around with the type of character to get killed and sealed into a wall, if that's what you're asking. No, thank you."

"Do you know anyone who was seeing him?"

"No, I doubt it. And if they were, they wouldn't be telling me about it. People weren't as free with gossip back then as they are now. If any of my girl friends had taken up with the likes of Jack Perry, they would not be telling me about it."

"You knew that he hooked up with women? Married women?"

"I really don't know anything about the man," Mrs. Peach said dismissively.

Erin figured that was as far as she was going to get on the matter of whether Mrs. Peach knew Jack Perry personally. If she didn't close that topic, Mrs. Peach would hang up on her before long. But Mrs. Peach definitely knew more than she was saying. Her clear disdain for Jack Perry had not sprouted up in just a few days, finding out that he had been killed and secreted in her wall.

"I'm sorry to keep harping on it. I guess I'm just curious. Not my best personality trait."

"It's fine to be curious," Mrs. Peach said, "that's how you learn and discover things. But I've already talked to the police about this. They know everything I do. I've told them everything I could remember, and that wasn't much at this point. Remembering my next massage appointment is one thing, but remembering what I ate for dinner thirty years ago is another."

"The thing that I don't understand is, how did you not know there was a body decomposing in the wall? The stench must have been awful."

"Well, yes, it was."

"You remember that?"

"Ugh. How could I not? For weeks I was trying to get the construction crew to figure out where the smell was coming from. Dealing with the municipality about whether it was something in the sewers. My insurance company. I wasn't used to having to take care of things like that. Mr. Peach had just recently… departed. I didn't know who to talk to or how to talk to these different companies and professionals on the phone. I was a total innocent about how to manage such a large project. You are very competent, Erin. You have been very good at getting your business set up, right from the start, and I didn't have any qualms about leaving my renovations in your hands when you offered. But I wasn't like that. I didn't grow up learning how to do those things."

"So, tell me, what happened? When did you notice and what did they check? Obviously, they never tore apart that wall again."

"No. They said it was probably a raccoon. That the smell would fade in a few days. Do you know how long it took? It was not just a few days."

"Even just a mouse can stink for weeks."

"You know what it's like then, trying to cover up the smell. To go along with your life as usual while trying to deal with a horrible stench…"

"It's terrible," Erin agreed. "I don't know how anyone can stand it. I know that not everyone is as sensitive to smell as I am, but…"

"It was within a few days of them finishing the work," Mrs. Peach answered Erin's previous question. "I had signed off on everything, said that it was good. How was I supposed to know that they had done something like that? Walled a man in? Everything looked fine. Everything *was* fine until it started to smell."

"And you went back to the construction crew about it?"

"Yes. I started with them. They looked around, could smell it, but they said it wasn't coming from the wall, but that it had just come up through the sewers and it was actually coming up through the toilets and vents. They said to call the town. It took so many calls to get someone out to look at it. They inspected the sewers, then said there was nothing wrong with them. It must have passed through the system. In a few days, the smell would be all cleared away."

Mrs. Peach stopped for a moment. Then began again.

"But of course, it wasn't. The smell was still there. I talked to the insurers, and they said nothing could be done because it wasn't caused by the accident, but something that had happened after the accident. After a while, an exterminator came and looked at it, and he said that it was definitely from an animal decomposing in the wall, maybe a raccoon. To do anything about it, they would have to cut a hole in the wall and then repair it again. And without the insurance money to do that, I just couldn't afford it. I had started working, but I was barely making enough to make ends meet. I didn't even have a car. Bald Eagle Falls is small, so I could walk around wherever I needed to go, and if I needed to go into the city, I could usually find someone to take me along when they were running errands."

"So you just had to live with it."

"I taped up plastic sheets to try to isolate it to that area and burned incense and scented candles. Used air freshener. Fans. Everything I could think of that I could afford or borrow. I could get used to it when I was there, but I had to go to work every day, and when I got back, it would be awful again. I don't know how coroners can stand it."

So that explained how Mrs. Peach had lived for thirty years with a dead man in her wall and not known about it. But it didn't answer the question as to who had put it in the wall to begin with. Had it been intentional? Had the murderer been one of the people who inspected the house and told her there was nothing she could do about it? Or was there a chance it had been an accident like Stayner had suggested, and Perry had fallen down into the wall? Didn't they have crossbars in walls? He wouldn't be able to fall from the top of the house to the bottom, would he? Wouldn't there be an obstruction that would block his descent somewhere along the way?

"I'm so sorry that all this stuff has happened while you are away," Erin apologized. "I wish I could have prevented it."

"I'll be glad to have him out of my house. Can you imagine living with a corpse for thirty years? It can't be very sanitary. Have I been breathing horrible bacteria all that time? Could it give me cancer or a disease? I've always been very healthy. Hardly ever missed a day of work."

Erin supposed it probably was better for Mrs. Peach that the discovery of the body and its removal had happened while she was gone. She didn't have to see it or have nightmares about it. When she returned home, she would have her new room and hot tub and would be able to enjoy it, knowing that she was alone in the house.

CHAPTER 23

It was after closing time at Auntie Clem's, and Erin was decorating the wedding cake layers. She had read everything she could on the best way to decorate and assemble a wedding cake and knew that transporting it while assembled was a bad idea. She would need to put it together once she got to the hall where Melissa's reception was being held.

After all the cupcakes she had decorated, she hoped her skills were up to snuff. It was time to jump in and find out. If she really screwed it up and couldn't fix her errors, she had enough time to make additional layers and try again. Just enough time. The murder investigation seemed to be taking up more time than she expected. Or maybe just distracting her so much that she was slower than she had expected. Perhaps she had just overestimated her skills from the beginning.

Not that she was investigating the death of Jack Perry. Because she wasn't. The questions that she had asked were just to ease her own mind, to understand what was going on. The police department was fully capable of investigating Perry's death on its own.

A knock on the back door made Erin jump. She carefully wiped away a stray squirt of icing and turned to look at the door. There was no security camera outside, so looking in that direction was not at all enlightening. Erin approached the door, which she had locked after the departure of the bakery employees.

"Hello?"

"It's Beaver."

Erin paused for a moment before opening the door, wondering what Beaver was there for. Not that it mattered. She trusted Beaver. She didn't have to worry that the woman was there for nefarious purposes. Beaver was safe. A federal agent. Someone who had protected Erin's or others' interests in the past, even when it pushed the boundaries of legality.

But what was she coming to the bakery for?

Erin opened the door. Beaver greeted her with a wide grin, chomping industriously on her ever-present wad of gum. She was not the most attractive person; her nose and mouth too big, no makeup, little care put into her appearance. She had beautiful fine blond hair, but she simply swept that back into a ponytail so that it was out of the way, or occasionally tucked it under a hat so that it wasn't immediately obvious from a distance that she was a woman. Despite the heat of the day, she had on her usual outfit of camo cargo pants, a halter top, and a hunting jacket with lots of pockets and hiding places. She nodded to Erin and walked in.

"Working on the wedding," she observed, looking at the slabs of cake laid out on the counters.

Erin looked around at it all. She had been focusing on one step at a time, and hadn't stepped back to look at the whole picture since getting out all of the layers for the cake. It was pretty impressive. "Yeah. Going to decorate the layers today, and then at the reception, I just have to assemble them. Put it all together. And hope that no one trips over the table or anything like that."

"Melissa will be pleased. This will be very nice."

"Is it strange, her getting married to Davis? I keep going back and forth on it. I mean, on the one hand, why not? Why shouldn't they get married? They've been friends for a lot of years. Melissa doesn't have anyone else in her life, and she doesn't want to be an old maid. Who else is Davis going to get at this point?"

"Some cons have very active romantic lives. You would be surprised at the number of women who write to prisoners."

"I know it happens. But I don't understand why women would do that. Why would you start a correspondence with someone you don't even know? Especially someone you have been told is a violent criminal? Doesn't that fly in the face of all reason?"

"I suppose women feel like it is safe. What could be safer than having a boyfriend in a maximum-security prison? He's not going to get in the way of anything at home. When she visits him, there's plenty of supervision, so he can't get away with attacking or abusing her."

"Are they just lonely hearts, or is there more to it than that?"

Beaver shrugged and chewed her gum, considering. "A lot of the groups I know are Christian women's groups. I'm not sure why they think they should write to convicts. It's some kind of outreach thing."

"For I was in prison and ye visited me," Erin muttered. "Is that it?"

"I thought you were an atheist."

"That doesn't mean that I don't know anything about Christianity. Most of the foster families I grew up with were some kind of Christian."

"I suppose they've taken it literally," Beaver agreed with a shrug. "So they visit prisoners."

"Looking for Jesus?"

"Just doing what he said to do."

"Hmm." Erin shook her head. "Still not sure I get why."

"It seems to have made Melissa happy."

"Yeah, but she knew Davis back when they were kids. Long before he was ever in any trouble. She wasn't someone who just started a random correspondence."

"So that's what makes them happy."

Erin nodded. "I accept it. Just like I accept that having a wedding reception on her own is what will make Melissa happy. I don't have to understand it, just support her."

Beaver nodded, chewing her gum vigorously.

Erin knew that she hadn't come to make small talk about Melissa's wedding. Beaver wasn't that kind of person. She was intense and intelligent, always watching and learning from everything around her. She was passionate about her job and though she came across as relaxed and even lazy, there was always much more going on behind that bland expression than anyone could guess. Erin continued working on the cake layers, waiting to hear what the visit was about.

"You want a seat?" she asked, gesturing to one of the other stools. "A cookie and some tea?"

Beaver dragged a stool closer to where Erin was sitting and sat down. She looked leonine, like she could slide off that chair and move into action in half a second. Which she could, Erin knew from experience. She was powerful and athletic under the bulk of her jacket and cargo pants. Someone who took care of her body to keep it in prime shape.

She didn't follow up on the offer of a cookie and tea.

"How is your neighbor, Mrs. Peach?" Beaver asked eventually.

Erin didn't look at her, but kept working on the cake. "She seems good. She's very busy on her cruise, taking advantage of everything the ship has to offer. It's hard for me to get through to her because she's always doing something or other and doesn't bother to call me back."

"How does she feel about what has been going on here? You've talked to her about the body, I would assume?"

"I've talked to her, but… I don't know. I think it isn't really real to her, because she isn't here. She can talk about it logically; she understands in her head what is going on, but I think there will be a bigger impact when she returns and she is living where there was a dead body."

"Did she know Perry?"

"I don't know. She says she didn't, but then she describes him in a way that makes it sound like she did, not that she's just quoting what someone else has said about him."

"That's very perceptive."

"Maybe. Or maybe I'm just seeing what I expect to or want to. Maybe I want it to be a big mystery when it was just an accident. Someone who worked for Mrs. Peach, that she didn't know, just happened to be drunk one day and fell down into the space inside the wall. It could all be innocent, just an accident, like Stayner says."

"Is that what he thinks?"

Erin was caught out. Stayner hadn't told *her* that. And if questioned, he would know she had been eavesdropping on him.

"Uh… well… I might have overheard something to that effect."

Beaver gave Erin a slow, wide smile, her eyes laughing. "Might have overheard."

"He was over at my house the other day for supper. I can't help overhearing something when he's right in the next room. He isn't exactly soft-spoken."

"No, he's not," Beaver agreed. "What do you think? Do you think it was just an accident?"

"I think… I don't know. It isn't like I'm a trained investigator. All I know is what I've heard from others. I saw the body, but I don't know how it got there or how the house or the wall was constructed. It seems like a really small space for a full-grown man to fall into, but I know that kind of thing happens sometimes. Stayner was talking about a specific case where it happened just like that, and they didn't find *that* body until the building was being demolished. So it does happen."

"But you don't think that's what happened in this case."

"The more I hear about Perry and the kind of guy he was… the more people seem likely to have wanted him dead."

Beaver chuckled. "Lots of motive, is there?"

"Seems to be. It doesn't seem like anyone was really fond of him, and he was a rough guy who fooled around with other people's women. Not the kind of guy who happens to get into an accident and disappear for thirty years. Although…" she amended her answer, "if he also had addiction issues, like people say, then they do tend to have accidents or end up in bizarre situations." She thought about some of the drunks that she had known. You never knew what a drunk was going to do.

"I think we can be pretty sure that it wasn't just a drunken accident," Beaver advised.

"Oh? You don't think so?"

"The medical examiner says that he was shot."

"Oh." Erin nodded. "Well, he probably didn't shoot himself and wall himself in there, then. I mean, you'd have to combine him working on the roof, possibly drunk, with him carrying a gun that just happened to go off, killing him and making him fall down between the wallboards." She rolled her eyes. "And I still don't see how he could have fallen all the way from the roof to the ground level without getting stopped by a crossbeam or snagging on something on the way down."

"I'm not a house builder, but it doesn't seem all that likely, does it?" Beaver asked, agreeing. She chewed her gum, staring off into the distance. Was she expecting Erin to speculate more based on this new information?

Or was Erin supposed to ask more questions and get details on exactly how Perry had been killed and ended up in the house?

"So there was a bullet in him?" Erin asked. "One that would have caused his death?"

"So it would appear."

"And where…" She wasn't sure she wanted to know any of the details. It was hard enough to remember looking into the dead eyes of a corpse without picturing whether he was shot in the head execution-style, in the heart or belly, or the face. Each possibility brought a host of other gruesome images to Erin's mind. "I mean… was it instantaneous? Could it have been accidental? What kind of a gun?"

"It would have been very quick if not instantaneous. A forty-five. Something you could carry in your pocket or under your shirt."

Not someone running him off of their farm in the middle of the night with a shotgun. Not an accident. Someone had deliberately killed him.

"So it's murder."

Beaver gave a brief nod. "That is the medical examiner's finding. Death by gunshot, murder."

Erin silently worked on the edging on one of the layers, thinking it through. Thinking about why Beaver was even there.

"How did you find out about this before anyone else? And why do you care? You're not exactly part of the Bald Eagle Falls cold case squad."

Beaver chewed, smiling. "No, that's true. But I like to know what's going on in my jurisdiction. Even if it isn't any of my business."

"What's *going* on?" Erin repeated. "This happened thirty years ago. It isn't going on in your jurisdiction. It happened years ago."

"It all connects, don't you think?" Beaver asked. "Everything is connected with everything else. Just because it happened thirty years ago, that doesn't mean it isn't connected with any modern crime. The person who murders another man by deliberately shooting him isn't usually the kind who only breaks the law once. He's likely to have committed other crimes. To keep committing other crimes until he's stopped. By someone like me."

"But it was thirty years ago. Someone who committed a crime thirty years ago… he'd be old now. Not as likely to be committing more crimes. Not likely to be part of the drug scene. And if it was over someone's wife… that could be just a one-off. Done in the heat of the moment. He wouldn't *keep* killing for his wife. He would… try to keep it hidden and return to a normal life. Cover it up and let everyone forget about it."

"Not in my experience. If he were impulsive enough to shoot a man for messing around with his wife, he would probably kill in other circumstances too. Or steal something on the spur of the moment. If it was someone who was involved in the drug scene, then there are all kinds of other crimes he could be involved in. Stuff that I would want to pull him in on. If he hasn't already been put away."

"If he was involved in the drug scene thirty years ago, he wouldn't still be today, would he? He'd be too old. And if he was an addict, he'd either be dead or in recovery. Thirty years of drug abuse…"

"It does happen. I think you are underestimating how much someone would age in thirty years. He could have been twenty when he killed Mr. Perry. He would only be fifty now. Young enough to still be involved in any number of things. And believe me, I have met seventy- and eighty-year-olds who were active criminals. Age won't necessarily stop a person."

"If he was still killing people and stuffing their bodies into walls, I think we would probably have heard something about it," Erin said, trying to lighten the mood. She didn't want to think about old men who were still violent criminals. It made her think of Vic's father, still in the Jackson crime syndicate. Still violent and the target of violence himself. And she didn't want to think of all of the lives that might have been destroyed over the past thirty years by someone who had never been caught. She shook her head. "If it was someone that violent, he probably would be in the penitentiary by now. Someone would have caught him."

"Or he might have gone quiet, thinking that he was safe as long as the crime was covered up," Beaver suggested. "But now that the body has been discovered, he is in danger again. I think… you've had some experience in that kind of thing."

Beaver knew about Erin's experiences since moving back to Bald Eagle Falls. Erin had not been there since she was a little girl and her parents had been killed in a car accident. Or she thought they had been killed in a car accident. It turned out that she didn't know as much as she thought, and the discovery of what had happened to Erin's father had triggered a series of events that she didn't want to think about. She had nearly been killed herself, and further violence had been done that could not be reversed. Not ever.

"Yeah, I guess I do," she admitted. A crime that had occurred thirty years before could still trigger violent crime today. Maybe that was what had made her so uneasy about the discovery of Jack Perry's body. The parallels to her own father's case. Perhaps unconsciously, she had associated the two. But Perry's death had nothing to do with Erin's father's death. The man responsible for that had already been put behind bars.

CHAPTER 24

*V*ic sat on the steps to her loft apartment to visit with Erin at the end of the day. Erin was going through her tai chi forms, stretching her muscles and releasing the day's tension. She breathed carefully between comments to Vic. She had spent another evening at Auntie Clem's after closing. The layers of the cake were complete. The following evening she would take them over to the hall and assemble them so the cake would be ready for Melissa's wedding reception. The preparations had gone remarkably smoothly, other than the distraction of the body found in Mrs. Peach's house. It had taken longer than Erin had expected, but that was why she had built extra time into the schedule. One never knew what was going to go wrong in a project. It was wise to assume something would and plan for it accordingly.

"Now you can add wedding cakes to your offerings at Auntie Clem's," Vic said. "You can charge a premium for them. And if it's something you enjoy doing, then why not? You can do specialty decorating while we're managing the day-to-day stuff."

"I don't know. I'll have to think about it. I never really thought that I was good enough to make a wedding cake."

"But you've done a gorgeous job on this one. You can't use that as an excuse anymore."

Erin smiled, her cheeks warming a little. "It's not an excuse, I just didn't have very much experience, so I wasn't sure I could do it."

"Now you know."

"I miss talking to everyone, though. I didn't realize how much satisfaction I get from interacting with customers daily. I've been kind of lonely the last week."

"Most wedding cakes won't be last-minute like this one. You can build some time into the schedule—shifts where you can interact with the customers. Decorate cakes every second day. If it's something you like doing. If you find it stressful and mind-numbingly boring, then don't."

"No, I enjoy doing it. It's good thinking time. And the results are… really beautiful."

"You should be proud of yourself. You did a great job."

There was shouting next door. Not just one worker calling to another at the other side of the yard or in the house, but a clamor. A fight, Erin thought, as she ran to the back gate and then into Mrs. Peach's yard to see what was going on. Had someone gotten hurt? Were they just cheering on a play in whatever game they had playing on the radio as they worked? It couldn't actually be a fight…

But it was.

Erin couldn't tell who was involved as she hurried up to the fighters. There were several men, arms swinging, shouting at each other, the noise of blows falling, thumping on bodies and faces.

"Stop!" she shouted. "What's going on? Make them stop this!"

One of the workers, taller and heavier than Erin and rank with sweat, put a hand on her, stopping her from getting any closer. "You try to interfere, you're going to get hurt."

"What's going on? Why isn't anyone stopping them?"

"They are." He shook his head at her, frowning. "Just stay back and out of the way. What are you doing over here at this time of day?"

"I heard the fighting."

"Go back home. Let us take care of this."

The fighters broke apart. Erin saw that, despite what she had first assumed on seeing the group of men involved in the fracas, only two of them had been fighting, and the others had been trying to pull the fighters apart. They were wrenched away from each other and kept several feet apart. The rest of the crew continued to hold on to them to keep them from starting the fight again. They were both swearing and angry.

Looking at their faces, Erin realized that one of them was Mr. Foster. His boyish, handsome face was a mess, bleeding from a split lip, a tear beside his eye, and a flattened nose. She barely recognized him. And probably when everything swelled up and changed color, there was no way she would recognize him anymore.

"What happened? What is this all about?" Erin demanded.

Mr. Foster's face turned in her direction, but she wasn't sure if he could see her through the blood and lids that were puffing up.

"Miss... Miss Price." His S's were sibilant, whistling and drawn out as if he were trying to act the part of a snake in a children's show. "Please..."

The other fighter was yelling a mixture of English and Spanish phrases, a number of them that Erin had never heard before. Her cheeks burned just at hearing him rave.

"Miss Price, you're not needed here," a man's voice told her. Erin looked around and realized it was the foreman, Mr. Monroe. He folded his beefy forearms and jerked his head to indicate that she should return to her own yard. "Let us take care of this."

"This is terrible! Mr. Foster is badly hurt. Are you going to take him to the hospital? What were they fighting about?"

"That is not any of your business. We don't need you interfering here."

"It is too my business! Anything that affects your ability to do the work and complete it on schedule is my business. I don't know what's going on here, but it looks like another member of your crew is not going to continue." She looked at the man who had been swearing in Spanish. He was not as badly hurt, but he was still dripping blood. And both of them had bloody hands. If that was any indicator of their unfitness to work, then Monroe had lost not just one man but two from his work crew.

"They look worse than they are. This won't impact our ability to complete the job by the time Mrs. Peach returns. We're nearly done now."

Looking at the house, Erin had to admit that it was looking pretty good. The glass of the new greenhouse room was all in place, gleaming like a jewel. The little bit of siding that had to be replaced was in position and just needed to be prepped and painted. She could not see inside, but she knew from the previous days when she had looked through the house that the interior work was also nearly complete.

"What was this all about?" No one had given her any indication of how the fight had started. The other men, both holding the fighters and standing back watching, didn't answer. They just looked at each other, silently agreeing to block Erin out. Erin turned and looked at Vic, who had followed her into the yard. "Can you believe this behavior? What could cause this much contention?"

Vic shook her head and didn't offer anything.

It had to be a woman. Nothing but a fight over a woman would have produced that much anger and blood so fast.

"Get out of here and let me deal with my crew," Monroe told Erin irritably.

"They need medical care."

"I'll be the one to determine what they need. Or to sack them both. I don't need your help with this."

He continued to glare at her and, eventually, Erin obeyed, backing off and returning to her own yard.

She didn't know what had started the fight. Maybe it was just the pressure of a deadline and the stress of dealing with the unexpected discovery of a body on the work site. Maybe all work crews were equally explosive. She had to give the foreman the space he needed to deal with them.

She led the way back into her yard.

After she shut the gate, she looked at Vic. "Just what do you suppose that was all about?"

CHAPTER 25

I'm so excited," Melissa whispered. "I can't believe that I'm actually getting married today. I can't wait to see the cake."

Erin couldn't help being caught up in Melissa's excitement. As much as she questioned the wisdom of Melissa getting married to someone who was in prison, especially when that someone was Davis Plaint, she couldn't help being happy for her friend. She was doing what she wanted to, ignoring the disapproval of the church ladies. Pursuing her own bliss despite what anyone else might think. Erin hoped that she could be that strong in going after the things that she wanted. She was often critical of herself for being tentative and not speaking up for herself.

That was what came of growing up in foster homes where she was constantly told to keep quiet and not make waves. She hadn't stopped making waves, but she had stopped being vocal about it, finding other ways to go about getting what she wanted.

Erin unlocked and opened the side door to the hall and let Melissa enter ahead of her.

Melissa had obviously been to other events in the hall and knew the layout of the building and where the sometimes difficult-to-find light switches were. She moved ahead of Erin confidently, one hand stretched out to touch the wall as she moved down to the end where the bank of switches was. Erin trailed along a distance behind her, not wanting to trip over any chairs or decorations that had been set up since she had been there to assemble the cake.

The lights went on. Erin squinted and held her hand over her eyes at the sudden onslaught of light. Melissa shrieked.

It didn't sound like the happy shriek of a woman who had just seen her wedding cake for the first time.

Erin rubbed her eyes and forced them open.

It was immediately obvious why Melissa was upset. Someone had been there since Erin had left. A number of the tables and chairs had been broken or thrown to the floor. The little arbor that the decorator had been setting up when Erin had left was a pile of kindling and leaves. Who had been rampaging through the hall? Why would anyone want to destroy Melissa's wedding reception preparations? It didn't make any sense.

Erin looked over at Melissa, looking for some comforting words to impart. There was still plenty of time to get everything cleaned up and arranged again. They might have to forego the arbor, but ribbons and flower arrangements and other decorations were still intact. They could pull it off. No one would be any the wiser.

Melissa was staring, not at the chairs and the broken arbor, but at something Erin couldn't see, because Melissa was standing in the way. Erin took a few steps to get to her side and her eyes were drawn to the horror that Melissa had seen first and which still held her bound.

It was the wedding cake.

Erin had given herself enough time to make, decorate, and assemble the cake. She had given herself enough time to cover for things that took longer than she expected, accounted for disasters, and delivered her creation on time.

She no longer had time to replace it.

Erin's mind ticked off the problems one at a time.

The table the cake was on had been smashed and was flat on the floor. The cake had been remarkably stable, apparently landing, still on the tabletop, with the layers relatively intact. The main problem was the man whose face was firmly planted in the bottom layer, after smashing through the two layers above that.

CHAPTER 26

ho is it?" Melissa demanded. "What happened? I don't understand what happened here!"

"I don't know," Erin said, drawing a blank. It was like a trick—someone pulling a prank on her. Knowing Erin's history with bodies in Bald Eagle Falls, they thought they would be funny and prank her. It wasn't real, of course, but someone's idea of a joke.

Erin took a few steps closer. She tried to get a better look at the man, but his face was completely hidden in the cake. And he didn't come up for air. He didn't sit up, laughing, cackling about the looks on their faces. Did they think it was *real?* Of course it wasn't real. It was just someone's idea of a harmless joke.

The real wedding cake was somewhere else, safe and sound. The man was just an actor. Everything else that had been done could be easily put back into position and Melissa's wedding and reception could go on just as planned.

"Should we call the police?" Melissa asked in a quavering voice.

"If you think we should."

Melissa gave Erin a wide-eyed look of disbelief. She dug around in her purse, looking for her phone. Erin's was close at hand, but she seemed to be frozen like a statue, waiting for everything to go back to normal.

Waiting for the cry of "Surprise!" and their friends laughing and coming into the room from wherever they were hiding in the corridor.

Melissa found her phone and dialed the number of the police dispatcher. Erin could make out a few words here and there, but it seemed like Melissa was far away and her voice was muffled. She would need to speak up if she wanted the dispatcher to understand what she was saying.

"Don't know who it is," Melissa was saying. "I can't tell." And then, after another pause. "He's dead. I'm not touching him. I just do. He's dead."

Erin thought that she should probably go over and check to make sure that the man with his face in the cake was, in fact, dead. She could check his radial pulse. She didn't have to get close to his face and neck. Then they could verify to the dispatcher that he was actually dead so that she wouldn't send out an ambulance. Bald Eagle Falls had very limited emergency resources, and she didn't want to tie up the paramedics for a dead man when they were needed more for someone who could be treated.

She remembered giving CPR to Trenton Plaint. She didn't want to be in that position again. Once you started, you were not supposed to stop until medical staff told you to. She and Terry had taken turns for what seemed like hours before someone had arrived to examine Trenton and tell them to stop.

She didn't want to do that again. Melissa was right; the man in the cake looked dead. She was sure Melissa was right. Erin didn't move.

They didn't talk to each other.

In a few minutes, they could hear the sirens approaching. Erin swallowed hard and waited. Would Terry be the first to arrive? He would probably realize that she was at the hall. He had known that she was going to go there. He would want to get there immediately to see and comfort her.

"It will be okay," Erin murmured, to herself more than to Melissa.

"I know."

Neither of them moved a muscle. Maybe Erin should have gone outside to wave the police car down and direct them into the hall. But they probably all knew better than she did where they were supposed to go. They had been to weddings, funerals, birthday parties, and charitable lunches in the hall. They had grown up knowing it and thinking that it was perfectly safe.

Little did they know…

"Police," a male voice called as the first law enforcement officer arrived on the scene.

Not Terry.

Erin swallowed her disappointment and waited. Terry would be there. Unless he had been sent out of town for a call, he would be there soon. Even though he wasn't on shift, he would hear the call go out, get the notice on his phone, and realize that Erin was involved.

Not *involved*. She hadn't been *involved* in this death or even in the discovery of the body. That had been Melissa. They couldn't tease her this time.

"In here," Melissa called back after a moment.

Erin didn't make a sound.

Rod Stayner was there a few minutes later, his gun out, carefully approaching, clearing the corridor and maybe the small rooms and closets along the corridor as he went. His eyes flicked around the hall, and he holstered his weapon.

"Are you both okay?"

Melissa nodded. "We're not the ones who are hurt."

Stayner's eyes were on the man in the wedding cake. "How did this happen?"

"We just found him like that," Melissa said impatiently. "How would we know what happened?"

"It's your rental, isn't it? Who had access to the hall? Who was here last?"

"I don't know. Everybody was in and out, getting set up for the reception."

"We need to establish a timeline. Narrow down the time of death."

"I set up the cake last night," Erin said. "I left here at about nine."

"Nine o'clock last night?"

"Yes."

"Twenty-one hundred hours?"

"What? Yes, I guess so." Erin was impatient. She had never cared to learn military time. Surely Stayner understood what nine o'clock at night was without having it converted into military time.

Stayner approached the man, circling him at a distance before getting close enough to reach out and touch him. He touched the man's arm and immediately withdrew.

"You didn't check for a pulse," Erin pointed out.

"I don't need to."

He seemed uncertain as to what to do next. He'd gained a lot more experience since the first time she'd had to call him about a body, but he still acted as if he'd never been at a crime scene before. Erin knew he should be backing up and ensuring that no one touched anything. Establishing a perimeter. Putting up crime scene tape. Not standing there or continuing to circle as if trying to make sense of the whole thing. He wouldn't solve a murder by standing there looking at the body.

There were more sirens. The next person into the building was Terry. Erin's body sagged with relief when she heard his voice.

"Rod?" Terry called.

"All clear," Stayner called back. "In the main hall."

Terry arrived at a quick clip. K9 trotted at his side, looking around with interest, ears pricked. Terry's eyes went to Erin, and he nodded at her reassuringly.

"We'll just check things out here," he told her. He looked at Melissa. "You okay?"

"I'm fine," Melissa said in a remarkably calm voice.

Terry approached the body. "Did you check for signs of life?"

"Touched him. He's waxy," Stayner advised.

Terry nodded and didn't ask for more details. "Let's get the ladies out of here. Did either of you touch him?"

"No," Melissa assured him. "We stayed back. Only Rod did."

"Did you see anyone else here? Any sign of anyone else?"

"No."

"What did you touch?"

Melissa looked around. "The light switch. Maybe the wall."

"Erin, you?"

"Nothing today. But I was here last night. I touched a lot of things last night."

"Okay. Looks like he made a mess of your cake," Terry said lightly.

Erin felt nauseated at his humor. She shook her head, unable to reply.

"Sorry. Like I said, let's get you out. Back the way you came, please, and don't touch anything on the way out."

Terry walked them back out of the building, putting his hand on Erin's back as they walked down the corridor. K9 trotted close to his side, alert to everything.

The last couple of law enforcement officers were pulling up outside the building when they stepped out into the parking lot. Sheriff Wilmot and Tom Banks got out of their cars quickly, faces grim. Terry made a downward motion, indicating that they could relax.

"Scene is secure. Stayner can coordinate the investigation. Someone other than me should interview these two ladies." Terry indicated Erin and Melissa. "I'll assist wherever Stayner needs me."

It was probably difficult for Terry to let Stayner be in charge of the scene and the investigation when he was the senior officer and the one who had been in Bald Eagle Falls the longest. But there was no obvious strain or disappointment in Terry's voice. Erin was proud of him for being able to put aside his feelings, whatever they were, and handle it so professionally.

"What have we got?" Wilmot asked.

"Why don't you go in, have a look, talk to Stayner about it. I'll keep an eye on things out here until you're ready to talk to the witnesses."

"We didn't see anything," Melissa said faintly.

"We'll need your statements anyway. You may have seen something important without realizing it. Just because you didn't see whoever did this, that doesn't mean that you don't have any information that would be helpful to the investigation. Whoever was on the scene earliest could have vital information. And you were here last night too," Terry focused on Erin. "You may also have seen or heard things that are relevant."

"All I did—"

Terry held up his hand to stop her. "Don't talk to me or Melissa about it. Wait until your interview."

Erin looked at him for a moment, mouth open, then conceded, realizing he was right. She couldn't taint Melissa's testimony, and there couldn't be any question of her talking to her intimate partner about it before speaking to the authorities. She closed her eyes and tried to think of her next step.

"Are you still going to get married today?" she asked Melissa.

"What?"

"I mean…" Erin jerked her head toward the hall. "We're not going to be able to use this venue today. It might be a few days before we can get in there. You could still get married today and put off the reception a few days. Or move it somewhere else. But you should probably decide pretty soon, so we can let people know and start making the alternate arrangements."

Melissa rubbed the space between her eyes. Her usual cheerful, bouncy demeanor was gone, and Erin wasn't sure how to deal with her. Did she need comfort? Someone to take charge? Was asking her to think about the rest of the day exactly the wrong thing to do?

"I don't know," Melissa said faintly. "How long is this going to take? The interview, I mean. If I can't even get to the penitentiary…"

"We'll conduct the interviews as efficiently as possible," Terry told her. "But it may take a couple of hours. What time are you supposed to be over there?"

"Not until this afternoon. Three o'clock."

"That shouldn't be a problem. You can still get there in good time. But Erin's right, you're not going to be able to use the hall today."

"Even tonight? You won't be done by seven or eight?"

"Can't guarantee it. You know that we have to get transport from the city. If there's no one available, it might be twenty-four hours or more."

Melissa nodded, familiar with the difficulties of operating a police force in Bald Eagle Falls. She worked with the police department on a part-time basis and, although she was not in charge of arranging things like the transportation of bodies, she had probably read and filed enough reports to be more familiar with the issues than anyone else in town who wasn't a full-time cop.

"I'll call and see if the church hall is available," she told Erin. "Then we'd have to call out for decorations. I could pick up a few things here in town, and there are some things stored at the church that I could use. I'm sure the church ladies would help to get things set up over there." She shook her head. "It wouldn't be exactly what I had planned, but I could still go ahead with just the venue changed."

But what was she going to do for a cake?

CHAPTER 27

*B*efore Erin and Melissa had a chance to discuss what alternate arrangements could be made, Sheriff Wilmot was back from the hall. He nodded at Terry, who went back into the building. Tom Baker was assigned to keep an eye on Erin while Sheriff Wilmot took Melissa into one of the smaller classrooms in the hall to get her initial statement. Erin suspected they would also be re-interviewed back at the police department offices. It seemed like any time there was a murder investigation, she had to deal with multiple interviews, going over the same thing again and again. And today was not a good day for that to happen. It was a really inconvenient time for anyone to be murdered.

She had her planner in her purse so, with Tom's permission, she sat down in her car, pulled out the planner, and started making lists to figure out how she would get done everything she needed to while working around the police investigation. Especially since she didn't yet know what Melissa was going to decide. Melissa's initial reaction was to go ahead with everything and just change the venue but, as she saw the difficulties that would present, she might change her mind. So Erin needed to make two plans, one in case Melissa just moved the venue and one if she moved the date. Moving the date would make things much easier for Erin. She might even have enough time to pull together another wedding cake, though it would probably have to be smaller than the first.

Focusing on her lists helped her not to think so much about what had happened to bump the wedding arrangements. She had not recognized the man with his face in the cake. Who had it been? Someone she knew or a stranger?

Eventually, Sheriff Wilmot came looking for her.

"If you would come with me, Miss Price?" he asked politely.

Always polite. But Erin wouldn't say no to his request. Not because he was mean, but because she didn't want to look guilty. They'd already had enough reason to suspect her in other cases. She didn't want to go through that again. She didn't want to do anything that might suggest to someone that she was guilty. She had nothing to hide. At least, nothing to do with the case.

Erin tucked her planner away, still thinking of the wedding plans and what she could do to make things work to the best possible results for Melissa as she followed Wilmot back into the building to the small room he had borrowed.

The room was bare. Scarred concrete walls and an old blackboard. A couple of metal chairs that had seen better days. She could imagine a little group of Cub Scouts meeting there forty or fifty years ago. Gathering to salute the flag, recite the motto, and talk about the activity they were going to do before going out. Maybe practicing their knot-tying.

She had always envied the kids who had clubs, sports, or Scouts to go to. Not because she had particularly enjoyed athletics or tying knots. Just because the grass was always greener on the other side. She was rarely with a family who could afford such things. And there was no guarantee that she would be there all the way through the year. She probably would have hated the uniforms the girls had to wear and been bored with badge requirements. But to *belong* to something. To be an official part of a group. She imagined that she would feel the love and approval of the leaders and the other kids in the group. She would fit in as if she were the missing piece completing a puzzle.

Looking back now, she knew that she would never have actually felt that way. Kids always felt out of place, and there were several reasons she would not have fit in.

"Have a seat, Erin."

She reluctantly took one of the metal chairs. It was still warm from Melissa having sat in it for her interview.

"Okay, I have Melissa's description of what happened today, and I'm going to get the same information from you, but first, I wonder if you can tell me about what happened last night. You were here setting up?"

Erin nodded. "Yes, I came over after an early dinner. I had the wedding cake to assemble. That was the biggest thing. But I also had other treats to put in the kitchen fridge and freezer. So that they would be ready to put out tomorrow—today."

"You were here alone?"

"Mostly." Erin shrugged. "Some of the time, someone else was here. Putting up decorations or dealing with some other aspect of the reception. The AV equipment. When I left, someone was setting up the chairs. Everybody was working on making it a nice party for Melissa and—for Melissa."

"What time was the reception supposed to be today?"

"Seven o'clock."

She waited to see if Wilmot would tell her to use military time, but he did not. She relaxed back against her chair.

"So what time do you think you got here and left last night?"

"Maybe… seven to nine. Something like that."

He wrote it down in his notebook.

"And Miss Lee was not here?"

"No. We were setting up for her. So she could get the full effect once everything was pulled together."

"I see. Who was setting up chairs when you left?"

"Uh, Mr. Foster. I guess I don't know his first name. Peter's father."

Wilmot nodded. He wrote this down as well. "So he was still in the building when you left?"

"Yes."

"Did you lock up?"

"As far as I know, the doors were still unlocked when I left. I wasn't in charge of opening or closing the building. I didn't have a key."

"Whose job was that?"

"One of the church ladies. I'm not sure who. Just that it wasn't one of the items on my list."

"Your list was probably quite long enough already."

Erin nodded, rolling her eyes. "Yes. It was… busy."

"I can imagine. Melissa—Miss Lee didn't exactly give you a lot of advanced warning."

"No. And I was doing more than just the cake. So… not a lot of wiggle room. It took longer than I thought it would. But I got everything done on time!" Then Erin's heart sank, thinking about the destroyed wedding cake. It had been so beautiful. And now it was useless. Part of a crime scene.

Wilmot looked sympathetic for a second or two, then was back to his professional policeman persona. "Can you tell me who else was in and out of the building and who was expected?"

"Melissa could tell you better than I could. I was only in charge of the catering. As I said, Mr. Foster was here to set up chairs. The decorations were mostly done when I got here. I saw Cindy Prost and Naomi. There might have been others here earlier. It was pretty quiet by the time I got here. I didn't want to be in the way of the decorators. The more people walked by the table carrying stuff, the higher the chances the cake would get knocked over."

Or that someone would do a face-plant into it. How had it happened? Had he been pushed? Tripped? And what had killed him? Erin hoped it wasn't because he had inhaled a chunk of cake. She could just see the comments she would get if people thought that the cake had killed him, even if it was something completely out of her control.

Wilmot was writing something in his notepad.

"Do you know who he is?" Erin asked, not too hopeful that he would tell her, "Or how he died?"

Wilmot looked up. He considered his answer for a moment before opening his mouth. "His name is Miguel Ortiz. Probably not someone you have run into around town. Not the kind of guy to hang around the bakery or ladies' tea. That hasn't been released yet, so keep it under your hat. Chances are it will leak out before we make the official announcement, but I don't want the leak to trace back to you."

Erin nodded. Melissa was the one who was best known for her liberal release of information gleaned from her work in the police department. But there were others too. Gossip spread like the proverbial wildfire in Bald Eagle Falls.

"As far as how he was killed… that will be determined by the medical examiner. There are no obvious signs of a fatal wound. No gunshot wound that would clearly identify the cause of death. Although it is obvious from his face that he was in a fight recently, that was clearly before whatever altercation occurred here. Wounds already sealed, not bleeding at the time of death."

Maybe something had happened during that fight. A slow brain bleed that would eventually prove fatal. Nothing to do with Erin's cake or the wedding.

"You didn't know Miguel Ortiz, did you?" Wilmot checked.

"No. I don't think I've heard that name before. Certainly not someone I would recognize on the street."

"I think he was on the construction crew working on your neighbor's house."

CHAPTER 28

*E*rin found it suddenly more difficult to breathe.

"What?"

Wilmot looked at her, his brows drawing down. "Your neighbor. Mrs. Peach."

"This guy was working on her house?"

"Yes, he was one of the men on the crew, as far as I know. You may have seen him sometime when you were over there."

Erin didn't know very many of the men on the crew by name. She knew that the foreman was Mr. Monroe, and she knew Mr. Foster because she had introduced him. And Willie, of course. But the others were little more than placeholders in her mind. Other men who were there to do the work, nameless faces.

The name Miguel Ortiz suggested that the victim was Hispanic. A few Hispanic men were on the crew, but most of them were not heavyset like the victim. They were slender, more recent immigrants, not yet filled out by eating the local fare, rich and plenteous. But the heavier one, Erin had paid attention to.

"You know him?" Sheriff Wilmot asked, watching Erin's face.

"I... no, I didn't know him, not to talk to him, but... he had been in a fight recently? Like... twenty-four hours before he died?"

Wilmot raised his brows. "Yes. Like that."

"Oh, dear. I think I know which one he was."

"Because he had been in a fight?"

"Yes."

"With who?"

Erin hesitated, not wanting to answer the question. "I don't want to get anyone into any trouble."

"I'm afraid you'll have to tell me what you know, even if you want to protect someone. People who withhold information impede our investigation."

"I know, but... I know it has nothing to do with this man's death..."

"You don't know that. You are only guessing. Let's hear it."

Erin rubbed her temples. She supposed the information would come out sooner or later anyway. The fact that Miguel Ortiz had been in a fight wouldn't stay a secret, nor would the information about who he had been fighting with.

"It was Mr. Foster. He's... I got him a place on the work crew. They were short a couple of men, and I knew that Mr. Foster was looking for something, so I connected them."

"And Mr. Foster was in a fight with Miguel Ortiz?" Wilmot's voice gave away his surprise at this fact. "I never would have pictured him the type. He's always been a quiet, peaceful sort of chap."

Erin nodded. "I don't know what it was about. I asked but was told that it was none of my business. And I guess it wasn't. Maybe they'll tell you."

"Oh, they'll tell me," Wilmot agreed.

"Mr. Foster would never do something like this," Erin motioned in the direction of the main hall.

"You know him well, do you?"

"Well, no. But I know his family, and they're very sweet. I've met him a couple of times and he never struck me as..." Erin hesitated, trailing off. She tried to think of the right way to finish her sentence. "He seems like a really nice guy. Not violent. And his family has never sent up any red flags about being abused. No bruises or avoidant behaviors. I've seen all the kids regularly, and I think if there was any domestic violence, I would have picked up on the red flags."

"What was it you were going to say and then you stopped?"

"I don't remember."

He raised one eyebrow and waited. Erin had never felt bullied or pressured by him, but his waiting in silence for her to come clean was unnerving. A nice cop, but still a cop, and one who intended to get answers out of her.

"I don't know exactly what I was going to say. I lost track of the words I wanted to use."

"He never struck you as what?"

Erin grimaced, trying to come up with words that wouldn't sound accusatory. "I just thought... maybe he's a little weird. A little... *off* from what I expected him to be like. Every now and then, Mrs. Foster strikes me that way too. Umm... old fashioned? Kind of... overly religious? Judgy?"

"I know that you're not religious, so a lot of people might come across that way."

"Yeah, it's just a little bit different with them. Yes, the other church women who come to buy at the bakery and visit for the ladies' tea are a little bit the same way. They'd kind of like to push you—me—into being like them. Buying into their religion and using that filter for everything. And yeah, they judge me for stuff that is only important to them because their church tells them it is. But the Fosters just sometimes act a little bit... radical. Super-religious. Like... being extra critical about what people can talk about around the kids. For a while, Mrs. Foster didn't want me to talk to Peter at all."

"Uh-huh."

"And having so many kids. Even though sometimes Mrs. Foster looks like she could drop. Most people now are okay with birth control. With just having one or two kids. But the Fosters have five, real close together, and I don't know if they plan to stop. It has to be hard, supporting a family that big, but they don't want Mrs. Foster to work. Just to stay home with the kids. I guess... they're old school. It's not bad, I'm not being critical. I'm just saying... they're a bit weird. And Mr. Foster being in that fight... the other guy must have started it. I really can't see him ever starting any kind of argument, let alone a fist fight. Well, maybe not true," she admitted. "I could see Mr. Foster having an argument about right and wrong, about some religious point he's stuck on. Just not... things most people would argue about."

Sheriff Wilmot nodded and jotted down a few notes. "We have a few families like that. Raised stricter. They find each other and raise their kids strict like they were and won't mix with other folks because of their rigid views."

Erin nodded. "I don't think it means anything. Some folks like that can get violent or can be abusive if their kids don't follow the rules, but I never got that feeling from Mr. or Mrs. Foster. Or from the kids. They don't act like they have to behave perfectly or they might get hit. They just fool around like regular kids, whine, argue. You know what I mean?"

"Sure," Wilmot agreed. "So, you were a witness to this fight?"

"Not when it started. We heard them and went over to Mrs. Peach's to see what was going on. And they didn't stop fighting right away, they were still going at it while we were there, until the other men managed to separate them."

"Had you ever seen Mr. Ortiz before that?"

"I saw him, I guess," Erin said slowly. "But I don't think I ever talked to him directly. He was just one of the laborers that Mr. Monroe hired. I was never actually introduced to any of them."

She did know that he was one of the grumblers. Whenever Erin talked to Mr. Monroe or had anything to say about the way things were being done with Mrs. Peach's renovation, Miguel Ortiz was one of the men who whispered and jeered behind her back. Acting like she couldn't hear or understand what he said. Erin chose to ignore it and never brought it up with the foreman. As long as he was listening to her and responding to what she had to say, what did it matter what the grumblers were saying behind her back? She couldn't address them all. If she tried to stop the grumbles, she would never get anything else done. She just had to put up with their undercurrent of dissatisfaction and pretend that she didn't hear it.

"You didn't like him?" Wilmot asked.

"I don't think he liked me. I never talked to him."

"How do you think he got in here without a key?"

"I guess... someone let him in. Or he snuck in while the doors were open and people were carrying stuff in and out. Or he picked the lock."

Wilmot nodded. "You didn't see him hanging around the building?"

"No."

"No one mentioned his name, said he was coming to work on something?"

"You'd have to ask Melissa. I was only in charge of the cake and catering. And he didn't have anything to do with the food."

CHAPTER 29

*I*t seemed like it should be time for bed by the time they were finished with their police interviews but, of course, they had gone to the hall first thing in the morning, and it was not even noon. Erin knew that Melissa had made an appointment to have her hair and nails done for the wedding, and it was probably too late to cancel or reschedule, so she might as well still go.

"Would you go with me?" Melissa asked, suddenly clingy. "I just want… I don't have any close 'girlfriends,' you know? I want to be pampered and do something with 'the girls,' but I don't have a clique that I hang out with."

Erin was surprised. "I thought you and Mary Lou and some of the church ladies…"

"We go together for the church stuff," Melissa admitted. "We're close in that way. But it isn't like I went to school with many of them or that we hang out and talk outside of church functions. If I'm on my own… well, I'm on my own. And I don't want to be today."

"Uh… okay. Let me just tell Terry so he doesn't worry."

Melissa nodded, her dark curls bouncing around her head. She withdrew a step or two away and looked the other direction as if that would give Erin any privacy she needed for the phone call.

Terry was still inside the building and answered after a couple of rings. "Erin? Everything okay? I really can't talk to you about the investigation."

"I know," Erin agreed, shaking her head at his assumption that she would try to pump him for information on the case. "I just wanted you to know that I'm going to be keeping Melissa company. She has some appointments to go to and doesn't want to be alone."

"What kind of appointments?"

Erin didn't know why this should matter. "Uh, hairdresser, manicure, things like that."

"Oh," he sounded relieved, as if he'd suspected they would go see the killer. "That sounds good, Erin. That's just what both of you need. A bit of pampering."

"Well, I'm not—"

"Take whatever time you need. I don't know how long I'm going to be tangled up with this today. I'll get home when I can but, if Melissa needs you, don't worry about getting back at a specific time. If you're not there, I can look after myself and the animals."

"I'm not going to be that late. Just a couple of hours."

"Okay. That sounds good. I'll see you later."

Erin hung up and looked at Melissa, forcing a smile.

"Is he harassing you?" Melissa demanded, "telling you not to take too long?"

"No, it wasn't that."

"Uh-huh." Melissa was unconvinced.

"He said it was fine, to take as long as I needed."

But Melissa remained skeptical. She had heard Erin protest that she would only be a couple of hours, and assumed that meant that Terry had told her he didn't want her taking that long. Erin shrugged this off. "Let's get you to your appointment before they decide you're not coming."

"I'm not late."

"Then we should get there early."

Melissa looked confused but didn't argue this logic.

There were a couple of older ladies at Serena's, the hairdresser's storefront. Erin had expected it to be a busier place and had been prepared for everyone there to know about the body found in the hall and be ready with a list of questions to interrogate Melissa and Erin about what they had seen, what they knew, and what they speculated. It had always been that way at the bakery, and the familiar expectation was that hairdressers were hotbeds of gossip.

Erin waited until Melissa had had her shampoo and comb-out and was waiting for the hairdresser to begin arranging her curls for the wedding. Hopefully, Melissa was nice and relaxed after the warm water and scalp massage.

"So, did you decide where and when you want to do the reception? If we're going to do it today, my afternoon is going to be pretty busy."

Melissa sighed. She sat with her eyes closed, deep in thought or trying to hold on to the mellow feeling the shampoo had left her with.

"I think... there's really no way we can do it all today. If we wait a couple of days, they'll either release the hall, or they'll let us go get our stuff so that we can set up at the church hall. Today... it would be too bare and boring. I want it to be nice. I want... a fairy-tale experience. Not just a bunch of people sitting around in metal chairs gossiping about me."

"So we need to make phone calls today and let everyone know not to come to the hall, that we'll let them know when it's rescheduled for as soon as we've worked it out."

"Yeah. I guess so. I mean, most people will hear through the grapevine, but we should let people know. I'll put it up on my social media, but not everyone will check there before going to the hall. We can do a phone tree like we do for an emergency evacuation."

"Oh... okay." Erin wasn't sure how a phone tree worked, but it sounded like a good plan.

"I'll show you when we get done here. We only have to call a couple of people at the trunk, and then each person calls other people and it all fans out until everyone has been told. I have a copy of the police department's protocol."

"Am I even on the phone list? No one has ever said anything to me about it before."

"You'll be near the top somewhere. By the time the calls get to you, most people will have been notified. But the person who calls you would tell you who you are supposed to call next since you're new."

Erin wondered whether the Bald Eagle Falls gossip ran through a phone tree. It would explain how information got disseminated so quickly.

Melissa continued to sit with her eyes closed while the hairdresser gathered her damp hair into sections and worked quickly through each section to form Melissa's curly hair into long spiraling curls arranged around her face.

"I can't believe someone was killed in my reception hall," Melissa said.

The hairdresser clucked and didn't ask any questions as she trimmed ends and shaped Melissa's hair.

"And in my wedding cake," Melissa said. "It must have been so beautiful. It looked really good… other than half of it being crushed by that Ortiz guy."

"It was really pretty," Erin confirmed. "I'm afraid if I try to replicate it, I'll never get it right a second time. It's too bad he had to choose that place to die."

"He wasn't even an invited guest or there to set up for it," Melissa complained. "If you're going to die at someone's wedding… at least make it a wedding you were invited to!"

"Yes. How rude," Erin agreed with a grin. "Don't they know that's a major faux pas?"

Melissa giggled. She was probably still feeling pretty shocked about the day's events.

"He probably couldn't get himself invited to a wedding," Erin said in a more conciliatory tone. "I'm not sure his bride would even want him to be at theirs."

"Yes. She should do like me and insist on the reception being only for the bride and her guests. Let the groom do his own somewhere else."

CHAPTER 30

The bell over the door rang and Erin turned her head to see the new arrival. But it wasn't the type of clientele she expected to see. Not an older woman who needed a trim or her nails done. Instead, it was Willie Andrews. He didn't say anything to Erin; he just sat down in one of the waiting area chairs and picked up a magazine. He sat there with the fashion magazine in front of his face as if no one would notice him that way.

"Uh, Willie…?"

He closed the magazine partway to look past it at Erin. "Yes?"

"What are you doing here?"

He looked around. "Just… keeping an eye on things."

"Why are you doing that?" Erin's forehead creased. She was starting to get a tension headache. "You think something is going to happen in here? To who?"

"You can never be sure," he said obliquely.

"You think something could happen to me? Or Melissa?"

"The two of you *did* discover a dead body this morning."

"Yes… but that doesn't mean we're in danger, does it?"

"I don't know. You've gotten yourself into some… situations… before. Probably better to be safe."

"Did Terry send you?"

"I don't need anyone to send me."

"What about Vic? Shouldn't you be keeping an eye on her?" He was Vic's boyfriend, after all. Not Erin's. They were friends, but she wouldn't want Willie giving her attention when he should be focused on Vic.

Willie looked bemused. "Vic is at Auntie Clem's. She's not the one who found the body this morning."

"But Melissa and I didn't have any more to do with that body than Vic. And it's not like we can tell who killed him just by seeing the body. I mean... I couldn't even see his face. Sheriff Wilmot had to tell me who it was."

"You think it's just by chance that the man was killed there? Where you were setting up for the reception?"

"Well..." Erin hadn't stopped to think about why Ortiz had been there. As she had told Sheriff Wilmot, he could have slipped in at any time while they were setting up. But why would he be there in the first place? Supervising the decorating? Because he wanted to see someone there? If he'd wanted to talk to someone, why didn't he just do that? Walk up and talk to one of them?

It wasn't like there was anything expensive to steal from the hall. Maybe the DJ equipment, but would Ortiz want to cart all that heavy equipment out of there? Erin couldn't remember seeing a car in the parking lot. He couldn't have just walked away with the massive speakers or other equipment. That didn't make any sense. And what else was there to steal? The wedding cake?

"I guess I don't know. It didn't have anything to do with the wedding."

Willie looked over at Melissa, sitting comfortably in her chair. "How do you know that? It isn't your wedding."

"Melissa didn't even know him. Did you, Melissa?"

Melissa made an inquiring sound. "Hmm?"

"Miguel Ortiz. Did you know him?"

"The man was a Neanderthal. How would I know him?"

Erin laughed. "Well, I guess you know who he was, anyway. But you don't have any connection with him, do you? You don't really know him?"

"I didn't have any dealings with him. He wasn't part of any of my circles."

Erin looked at Willie. "See? It was just a coincidence that he was killed at the reception hall. It could have happened anywhere."

"Why was he at the hall?"

"I don't know. He was curious. He wanted to see how we were decorating. How many people we were expecting. What the wedding cake looked like. I don't know."

Willie grunted. "I doubt he was there to find out anything about the wedding. And if you don't know why he was there, then you don't know if you saw anything important and could be in any danger."

"We're not in any danger," Erin reiterated. "There wasn't anyone else at the hall when we got there. If whoever killed Ortiz didn't want the body to be discovered, then they would have to move him somewhere else. They can't just leave him at the hall where a reception is booked and not expect him to be found."

"Doesn't mean that they didn't make a mistake and leave something incriminating behind. Or they could be paranoid and think you know something just because you talked to the cops. You don't know unless you know who did it."

Erin sighed. Willie was there to stay. But he wasn't getting in the way or telling her that she had to go home or that the reception had to be canceled. He was just sitting there pretending to read a magazine and letting them do their thing. If he wanted to spend his time sitting at the hairdresser, thumbing a fashion magazine, that was his own business.

"Wait," Erin had a sudden thought. "Why aren't you on the work crew? Aren't you supposed to be helping to get Mrs. Peach's work done on time?"

If Mr. Foster and Ortiz had been kicked off the work crew because of their fight, then Monroe needed all the hands he could get.

"I've done the wiring. They don't need me for painting and finishing work."

"It's going to be done on time, right? Mrs. Peach gets back in just a couple of days."

"It will be done. It's just the cosmetics now. Everything is in place."

Erin was silent for a few minutes, thinking about what else she needed to do. The phone calls would presumably only take a few minutes if they employed a phone tree. If Melissa was keeping the reception at the hall and just delaying it, then the chairs and tables were already mostly set up, the decorations were up, the AV equipment was ready to go, and the catering other than the wedding cake was already in the fridge.

It would be good if they could find an arbor to replace the one that had been broken. And Erin needed to design a new, smaller wedding cake that she could get done in a day. Two at the most. It could be done, of course, as long as it wasn't too elaborate. The cake layers would need a chance to cool before being decorated. She would need to get them baked tonight, and then they would be ready to be decorated in the morning.

"What were Mr. Foster and Ortiz fighting about?" Erin asked. "You were there when it happened. What was that all about?"

Willie looked around his magazine at her. "If they didn't feel like sharing it with you, I don't see that it's any of your business."

"Oh, come on, Willie. Tell me what it was about! I never thought that Mr. Foster was the type to get into a fight. So why did he?"

"Your Mr. Foster can be a bit of a pain."

Erin shifted uncomfortably. She didn't like Willie calling him *her* Mr. Foster. Yes, she'd helped him to get the job, but that didn't make him her responsibility or some kind of pet project. Except that he was. She loved Peter Foster and the little girls and wanted to do whatever she could to help them out. It pained her to hear anything negative said about Mr. Foster.

"What do you mean he can be a bit of a pain? You guys only worked together for a few days. What could he have done in that length of time to bother you?"

"Do you know anything about him?"

"I've met him a couple of times. I know his family better; they come to the bakery a couple of times a week."

"And they never struck you as oddballs?"

Erin was offended by his suggestion, even though she had just told Sheriff Wilmot that Mr. Foster was a bit weird. She hadn't meant it in a mean way. She had just been trying to explain herself and her experience with Mr. Foster clearly to the sheriff.

"Oddballs?" she repeated.

Willie raised his brows. "Would you prefer religious nuts?"

"Oh. Well, as far as I'm concerned, you're all religious nuts." Erin smiled.

"He drove the whole crew crazy proselyting. Talking about God all the time, when it didn't have anything to do with what we were doing. Saying prayers. Getting offended when men on the crew 'blasphemed.' He was a pain in the neck. If we hadn't had a deadline, he would have been off the crew the first day."

Erin's heart sank. "Really?"

"Really."

She sighed. "Somebody needs to tell him to stop doing that, or he's not going to be able to keep a job anywhere."

"I nominate you. But don't expect him to listen. He sees it as his responsibility to warn everyone else. Keep them from fire and brimstone."

"And that's what the fight was over? Ortiz just got tired of it?"

"He did more than get tired of it and tell Foster to stop. A few of us had already told him to stop, including the foreman. Ortiz took it a step further."

"He tried to shut him up physically?"

"He... insulted Foster's wife and children."

"Oh no... he didn't."

Willie nodded. "He did. And even a namby-pamby pacifist like Foster will react when you insult his wife."

"Oh, dear." Erin felt terrible for being the one who had suggested Mr. Foster join the work crew. He and his family had been looking for help, and she had put him into a situation where his beliefs and his family had been insulted. Where he'd been pushed into a physical fight with a man who was far stronger and more skilled than he was. "Oh, I feel so bad for him."

"He got a few good licks in. He can be proud of himself for that."

"And now he's a suspect in Ortiz's murder."

Willie raised his brows. "Do you really think that he is a serious suspect? Foster got beaten once. He's not the type to choose a physical fight. Do you really see him meeting with Miguel Ortiz in an isolated area where there is no one to help? And do you think that he would win in a physical fight?"

Erin had been about to respond that he could have won if he'd taken a gun or a knife to the fight. But Wilmot had said that there were no obvious fatal wounds. Even a small caliber bullet should have been fairly obvious.

She had to admit to the truth of Willie's words. She couldn't see Mr.

Foster agreeing to meet the man he had just fought with alone and beating him. He had probably been home with his family. He would have an alibi. Even without one, she had to agree that he didn't make a very good suspect. Willie himself would be a better one, if he'd had any reason to dislike Ortiz.

CHAPTER 31

*A*fter Melissa's hair and nails were done, she was on her way to the penitentiary. Her cheeks were flushed and her eyes sparkled. Erin knew that it would be a very simple ceremony, and none of Melissa's friends would be there to see it, but Melissa was still excited to be getting married to Davis. There must be something more to their relationship than Melissa feeling sorry for an old friend who'd had hard breaks and made bad decisions. More than her settling because she didn't have any other prospects and was afraid of becoming an old maid. She really did want to get married to Davis and was looking forward to it.

She gave Melissa a tight hug. "Good luck and congratulations," she said. "Davis is one lucky guy."

"Yes, he is," Melissa giggled. "Thanks for everything. I needed to be with someone this afternoon. Especially after *that.*"

"Are you going to tell Davis about it?"

Melissa considered for only an instant before shaking her head. "There's no reason for him to know that anything didn't go as planned. By the time I see him again, we will have had the reception and I can tell him all about it. He doesn't need to know it happened on a different day than we had first planned."

"The wedding is going ahead, and that's the important thing."

Melissa nodded her agreement.

Erin wondered fleetingly whether Ortiz being at the reception hall or being killed had anything to do with Melissa and Davis's planned nuptials. Was someone trying to stop them from getting married? Ortiz or whoever had killed him? Maybe they had thought that if something terrible happened to prevent Melissa's reception, that she wouldn't go ahead with it. She would be spooked or think it was bad luck or an omen.

"Did you know Miguel Ortiz?" Erin asked.

Melissa stopped, looking at her for a moment. "I already told you I don't," she said flatly.

But she hadn't. She had deflected the question before. Even now, she wasn't answering directly, maybe suspecting that she would not be able to fool Erin with a direct lie.

Melissa gave Erin a brief hug and a broad smile. "I'm getting married!"

"You're getting married! I hope you're really happy with Davis."

She nodded, giggled, and climbed into her car. "Thank you, Erin. Next time you see me, I'll be Mrs. Melissa Plaint."

Was she really going to take Davis's name? Erin hadn't even considered the idea before. Even though Melissa was marrying a convicted felon, and everyone knew it, she hadn't thought that Melissa would want to carry the Plaint name with her the rest of her life. Like a scarlet letter.

Erin forced an excited smile and waved at Melissa until she was out of sight. There was no "Just Married" painted across her back window, nor were there tin cans trailing behind the car. Did people even do that anymore? Even if they did, she knew that the prison wouldn't allow it. Nothing showy or dramatic would be happening at the penitentiary. It would all be quiet and understated. Melissa wasn't even allowed a wedding dress, just the nice sedate skirt suit that she was wearing, with black flats. Would they let Davis give her a simple wedding band? Or had Melissa already arranged for it herself? Davis wouldn't be allowed to wear a matching band.

Erin returned home. She looked through wedding websites for inspiration, making a plan for the replacement cake. After a while, she heard Terry's truck arrive and he let himself in. She stood up to greet him.

"Erin." Terry took her into his arms and hugged her. Erin reveled in it, feeling his strength and safety and knowing he would take care of everything. Even though she wasn't really afraid that something would happen to her, she felt better knowing that he would never *let* anything happen to her.

He pushed her back slightly and kissed her. "How are you? Are you okay?"

He had seen her after the discovery, so he knew she had not gone into hysterics over what she had seen. But it had still been a shock, and she had probably been a bit distant when he had arrived.

"Yes. I'm fine. Had a nice time with Melissa, getting ready for her wedding and then I've just been on my tablet."

He looked around, noting that there was no dinner on the table. It was still early for dinner, but Erin usually at least had something started by then.

"I am just taking a short break, and then I need to go back in to continue the investigation," Terry said. "There are still a few leads to chase down, which are time sensitive. I want to get everything done that I can early on."

Erin nodded. "I haven't gotten anything started. Do you want a sandwich?"

"Toast and jam would be fine."

"I think we can find something a bit more substantial to put in it. Something higher in protein will get you through the evening better."

"Peanut butter?"

Erin smiled. "If you really want peanut butter and jam. But I thought I would get some of that nice chicken out…"

"Chicken is good."

"Good. Have a seat. Take a load off for a few minutes."

He spent most of his day on his feet, and Erin was sure that this day had been no different. Maybe when he went back to continue the investigation, he would sit down with his phone and computer and get a bit of rest. While sitting all day wasn't good for the body, being on his feet all the time came with its own issues.

Terry shifted his duty belt and sat down, motioning K9 to lie down beside him. Not yet released from duty, K9 gave a little grumble as he lay down as instructed. Erin got him a cookie and then had to deal with Orange Blossom wailing like a banshee that someone else had just gotten a treat and he hadn't. It was close enough to the usual dinner hour that Marshmallow followed Orange Blossom into the kitchen to get his supper too.

Once the animals were all served, Erin washed her hands and began to prepare Terry's sandwich. She decided she'd better have one too. She wasn't hungry, but she would need something to fuel her for the rest of the evening.

"I'll be going over to Auntie Clem's," she informed Terry. "Need to get started on a replacement wedding cake."

"That can wait, can't it? I don't like you being over there alone when I can't check in on you."

"So give me a call later. But I need to get the layers baked tonight, or I won't have anything to decorate tomorrow."

"Melissa is really going ahead and getting married and having the reception?"

Erin looked at her watch. "Already married, unless something happened to stop her. They can't have the reception tonight as planned, but as soon as you release the scene, she will be ramping up for the reception."

"I want Melissa to be happy as much as anyone but, under the circumstances, I'm surprised she didn't reconsider. At least about the reception."

"Why would she let something like this change her mind?" Erin asked, even though she had been the one asking Melissa just a couple of hours before.

"I would just think that everything that has happened might have made her think twice about whether she wanted to go ahead with the wedding, or whether she should wait and make sure it is what she really wants and that she's ready to go ahead with it."

"I asked her," Erin conceded, "but it doesn't have anything to do with her. She was just unlucky to have someone killed in the reception hall while her stuff was being set up."

Terry said nothing, and Erin turned to look at him. The look on his face told her that he didn't think Melissa had just been unlucky. What, then? Surely he didn't think that Melissa getting married and Ortiz's death had anything to do with each other.

"None of this has anything to do with Melissa," Erin said tentatively.

He didn't argue, but he didn't agree, either.

"You think this was something to do with Melissa?" No response. "With Davis?"

"I don't think it is anything to do with Davis."

That surprised Erin. Davis was the one with the criminal record, after all. Wasn't a death on his wedding day more likely to be something to do with him than it was to do with Melissa?

"Melissa said that she doesn't know Ortiz," she asserted.

"That may be what she said."

"How would she know Ortiz? He's older than her. More like the age of her father. And she's not in the construction field and doesn't need anything done. So how would she know him?"

"There are events that occurred in the past that you are unaware of."

Erin considered this. "You think that Ortiz's death and Perry's are related?"

"I don't think the possibility can be ruled out. When two such extraordinary events happen close together—the discovery of a thirty-year-old murder and a brand-new murder—you have to consider the possibility that they are related."

"Ortiz and Perry? Did they know each other? Thirty years ago? Melissa would have been what, eight? She wouldn't even remember anything that happened that far back. She certainly couldn't be involved."

"I don't think she was involved with Perry's murder."

"But you think she knows Ortiz?"

"I think the two are related and, therefore, that she knows something about it."

The only logical conclusion, then, was that Melissa knew Perry. But if she had only been eight years old when he had died, then she couldn't have had anything to do with his murder and covering it up. She hadn't handled the gun that had killed him or been involved in boarding him up inside Mrs. Peach's wall.

Erin cut the sandwiches in half and placed them on plates. She took them to the table and sat down, sliding one across to Terry.

She knew that Terry couldn't tell her what he knew. He was doing his best to give her oblique hints without actually telling her anything about the case or what he knew about what had happened.

If Melissa had been too young to have had anything to do with Perry and Ortiz, then it had to be someone else in her family. *Her father.* Erin had discovered that her own father had an unsavory past in Bald Eagle Falls. Maybe Melissa's father did too. Melissa had never talked about it, but she had attached to Erin, been her friend. Perhaps it was because she too had dealt with the secrets of her father's past.

"Her father," Erin suggested to Terry.

He shrugged and spread his hands apart. He couldn't tell her anything, but Erin was free to speculate.

"Melissa's father knew Ortiz."

"Maybe," Terry acknowledged, but that wasn't the piece of the puzzle Erin was missing. Then…

"Melissa's father knew Perry," Erin suggested.

The dimple appeared in Terry's cheek, even though he was doing his best to suppress a smile.

"Melissa's father knew Perry," Erin repeated. "Perry's body was discovered before Melissa's wedding. Purely by chance, because Mrs. Peach didn't know he was there and she's the one who hired the work done. But then, Ortiz is killed in the hall set up for Melissa's wedding. Two deaths tangentially related to Melissa. And it's not just a coincidence?"

"You'd need a crystal ball to answer that question right now, with the information we've got. But you know how I feel about coincidences. Do *you* think that two murders being connected with Melissa are a coincidence?"

"Maybe. Sometimes things look bad when they're completely innocent. People are wrongly accused of crimes all the time, and we're not even making any accusations right now. There's nothing that says that Melissa *killed* either man. In fact, she could not have killed the first."

He raised one eyebrow.

"But her father could have," Erin said. "It's a possibility. And then, what, she killed Ortiz because he knew about it? He's trying to blackmail her? Trying to stop the wedding?"

"I doubt he cared about the wedding. I don't think that's why he was in the building."

"You think he was there to talk to Melissa."

"Seems logical."

"You don't think it was anything to do with Mr. Foster?"

"The sheriff told me about that... but I'm with you, I don't see him as the type. I think that he could be prodded into a fight with slurs against his wife and children, but I don't see him as the type who would intentionally kill a guy. I don't think he lured Ortiz there to kill him."

"Or that Ortiz lured Mr. Foster there?"

"Why would he do that? Because he wanted to check out the decorations? He wanted to feel like a part of it? He wanted the body to be found right away? No, there are a lot of better places to kill someone and dispose of the body. Ortiz wouldn't be that clumsy."

He said it as if he knew Ortiz well. As if he knew that Ortiz had plenty of practice getting rid of bodies and that he wouldn't make such an amateur mistake.

"Does Ortiz have a record?"

"He might."

"For murder? Has he served time?"

"I can't talk to you about his criminal record. You could do a public records search, but I couldn't tell you anything discovered in the course of our investigation."

He had a record, or Terry wouldn't have phrased it that way. But what for? Erin wasn't about to run to the courthouse to request a public record search on Ortiz's name.

"It's not really what he's been caught for that's of interest," Terry said slowly. "It's more what he *hasn't* been caught for."

He had been suspected of crimes that he couldn't be prosecuted or convicted of. The police suspected him of something but hadn't been able to get enough evidence for him to be put away for it. Maybe he was really good at getting rid of bodies. Not the kind of guy who would have asked to meet Mr. Foster or anyone else at the hall. That wasn't why he had been there.

Erin looked down at her plate. She didn't remember eating her sandwich, but it was gone. Her head was pounding. She would need to take some Tylenol if she were to keep going. She sighed.

"We are going to have to talk about this—or not talk about it—some more later. I need to get to the bakery to get some cakes in the oven."

Terry nodded and pushed his chair back from the table. His plate had also been cleaned. Had he been any more aware of what he had been eating than she had? Erin shook her head.

"Melissa is safe, right? I don't understand how she's connected to all of this, but you guys have got her back, right? She's one of you. Is someone watching her?"

Terry nodded. "Don't worry about Melissa, she's fine."

CHAPTER 32

*E*rin got to Auntie Clem's before it closed for the day. She planned to arrive there just before closing so she could start her work as soon as the kitchen was free. She didn't want to get in the way of the day's baking, but she also didn't want to be up half the night getting the layers of the new cake baked.

There was an animated conversation going on in the storefront. Erin walked through from the back to say hello to the day's last few customers, recognizing their voices.

As soon as she walked in the door, everyone stopped talking. Erin looked at Vic, giving her a questioning look. Were they talking about Erin? Or had something else stopped them from talking? Maybe she had just startled them or arrived at a natural break in the conversation. The women looked at each other, slightly awkward.

"Hi, Mary Lou," Erin said, nodding to Joshua Cox's mother. "Clara," the administrator for the police department, "Cindy." Cindy Prost was Bella's mother and had been helping decorate for Melissa the evening before. Erin didn't particularly like the woman, but she got along the best she could. They didn't have to be friends for Erin to sell her baked goods. Or for Bella to work there. They got along with each other as much as they could, and Erin tried to ignore any mean-spirited comments Cindy made. For a Christian lady, she could say the most unladylike, unchristian things.

"It was poisoning," Clara said eventually, obviously picking up the conversation that had stopped when Erin walked in. "That's what they're thinking to start with, anyway. It might be a few days before the medical examiner can make his preliminary finding. And longer to prove exactly what poison it was, if he can figure out what it is most likely to have been and have the lab test for it. But they think it was poisoning."

"Erin's cakes kill again," declared Cindy. "First Angela Plaint, then Trenton, and now Miguel Ortiz."

"My cakes haven't killed anyone," Erin shot back, jumping in to defend herself. "And if you're going to start spreading stuff like that around, I'll sue you for defamation."

"There's no need to be so *sensitive*," Cindy said with a laugh. "I'm only joking."

"That's a joke you'd better not repeat," Erin warned. She looked Cindy in the eye, holding her gaze, making sure she understood. Erin wasn't going to be pushed around. She wasn't going to lose customers because Cindy "joked" that her baked goods were poisoned. Angela Plaint and her son had both died of allergies, not from being poisoned, and Erin's baking hadn't had anything to do with it. Except in Trenton's case, but then he had been fed something that his killer knew he was allergic to. There hadn't been anything wrong with the cupcakes that he'd consumed. She had warned the killer that they contained dairy. It had been murder, not an accident or anything Erin had done wrong.

Cindy rolled her eyes and pretended to be offended by Erin's warning to stop spreading any lies about her food. "How do I know what's in your baking? I'm no expert. What's just fine for me could kill someone else."

"Exactly, and that's why I'm so careful about cooking food that's completely gluten-free and doesn't contain any major allergens. And why I offer dairy-free or vegan alternatives. Because different people have different needs, and I want people to be able to enjoy baking from Auntie Clem's, no matter what their dietary restrictions."

"Well, you can never please everyone. There's always going to be someone who gets sick because of some ingredient or cross-contamination."

"Miguel Ortiz did not die from eating the wedding cake. He landed on the wedding cake when he died!"

"We don't know. He might have had a slice of it first. That could have been what killed him."

"If you repeat that—"

"I know, I know, you'll sue me," Cindy said in a bored tone. "I'm not going to say anything about you or your baking."

Erin held her stare for a few more seconds. "You'd better not."

Cindy paid for her order. "Of course, Erin isn't the only one who has been accused of poisoning in this town." She glanced around at her audience, giving a self-satisfied smile. Her eyes skittered away from Erin and she headed for the door, figuring out that she'd better get out of there before Erin blew her top or banned her from ever shopping there again. It was a good thing that Bella wasn't there to see how her mother had behaved. It was better for their domestic harmony that she hadn't.

Mary Lou, next in line, was as white as a ghost. Erin wanted to rush around the counter to give her a hug, but she had a feeling that would not be appreciated. Mary Lou was not the affectionate type.

"I'm so sorry," Erin apologized. "There is no excuse for that kind of behavior. Cindy knows better." She shook her head. "I don't know how she can say things like that and still consider herself a—a good person. She knows she's hurting people. She enjoys it."

"I don't know," Mary Lou said faintly, apparently focused on smoothing invisible wrinkles in her pantsuit. Her attire was impeccable, just as it always was. But Erin could see her hands shaking as she transferred her attention to her gray bob, making sure that not a hair was out of place. "I imagine it's something to do with her childhood. The way she was raised." She shrugged. "We never know what goes on behind closed doors. A family that seems perfectly normal and kind can be completely different when they are away from prying eyes."

"That's kind of you," Vic drawled, "but she still has a choice about how she behaves. And that's not acceptable."

"She didn't name any names." Mary Lou swallowed. "And even if she did, it's only a statement of fact." She stood as straight and stiff as a statue. "Roger wasn't only accused of poisoning. He did it. He was ill at the time, but that doesn't change the facts."

"A kind person would never say something like that."

"And you girls are very kind," Mary Lou acknowledged. "Now, I need to get a couple of things for the weekend. As you may have heard, Roger is home, and Cam may stop by for a visit. So I need to be prepared. Four eat a lot more than two."

She picked the various rolls and loaves of bread she wanted, her eyes calculating. She moved down to the register and carefully counted out the money to pay her bill, down to the last penny.

"Can I interest you in any day-old?" Erin asked. "My freezer is over-flowing and I don't think I'm going to have any time to get to the city shelter this weekend. Could you take any off my hands? Joshua likes those pizza pretzels, and I know I've got a bag of those."

Mary Lou automatically shook her head, looking away from Erin. "That's very thoughtful of you, but no. We're fine."

"You'd be doing me a favor. With Melissa's wedding, I haven't been able to take care of it, and now I need to bake a new cake, so it's not going to happen in the next few days. If I don't make some room in my freezer, I'm going to have to throw out the day-old, and I hate to waste food."

"Well…"

Erin was sure that Mary Lou was going to say no again. As much as she was struggling, she was not willing to take charity. Her family wouldn't starve—she had enough baked goods to last a few days—but Erin knew things were tight.

"I suppose if you have to get rid of them," Mary Lou said finally, with a sigh. "I'm sure Joshua would love the pizza pretzels. Cam too."

"Great." Erin moved toward the kitchen to fetch them. "Can I get you some brownies and chocolate chip squares too? They'd be a nice dessert on Sunday. Just something light."

"Fine," Mary Lou agreed. She looked at her change purse. "Can I give you something for them? I don't like to take anything for free."

"No. I need to get them out of here." Erin went to the freezer and pulled out the bags of pretzels and brownies. She returned to the front and added them to Mary Lou's purchase. "There you go. I appreciate you taking them off my hands."

Mary Lou's face was pink as she picked up the bags and retreated. "Thank you, ladies. Have a nice weekend."

They watched her go. Clara turned her attention to the display case.

"You are kind," she echoed Mary Lou's sentiment. "I appreciate you looking out for her."

"Freezer's full to bursting," Vic said. "I don't suppose I could get you to take anything? Cheese buns? Cookies?"

Clara shook her head. She pointed to the baking she wanted, choosing to pay for the fresh goods over the free day-old offerings. "Cindy is right about Roger, though," she said. "He has been back home for a few weeks. If Ortiz was poisoned, suspicion will fall on him at some point. They've kept his return home pretty quiet, but people will talk."

"He's on an electronic monitor," Erin said. "That will prove that he wasn't anywhere near the hall or Ortiz. And how would he get Ortiz to eat anything anyway?"

"Poisoners can be very sneaky. He could have offered him a drink from a flask. Or put it on the end of a cigarette. Or maybe they were friends before Roger's... accident. He thought they would get together for old time's sake, maybe put a game on the TV and have some pizza and beer..."

"At the reception hall?"

"There's nothing to say that's where he was poisoned. Poisons can take hours, even days. He could have been with Roger Cox before he went to the hall."

Erin shook her head. "Mary Lou would have said something. She wouldn't just let it happen again."

Clara shrugged. "You never know what could happen. They were all similar ages. Roger, Ortiz, Jack Perry. I don't know if they were friends. But they certainly knew each other."

"What reason would Roger have to poison Ortiz?"

"None that I know of," Clara said. She tugged at the colorful scarf draped around her neck. "But the man is off his rocker. Does he really need a reason that would make sense to you or me?"

Erin heard the back door open and shut. Charley returning from her smoke break, no doubt. Erin looked at the time on the electronic register. Charley should be running through the close-of-day routine in the kitchen, and then Erin would be able to use the mixers and ovens.

"I can't understand why Ortiz was at the hall in the first place," Vic said. "I mean... it wasn't like there was anything there to steal. He wasn't helping with the set-up. He wasn't an invited guest. So why was he hanging out there to begin with?"

Erin looked at Clara. "Did Melissa's father know Ortiz too?"

"Too?" Vic echoed.

"From what I can gather, he knew Perry."

"He was a cop," Clara said. "He knew all the major players in town."

Vic and Erin looked at her. "Who was a cop?" Erin asked.

"Melissa's father."

"Melissa's father was a cop?"

"That's why she works at the police department offices," Clara said as if they should know that. "She started working there in high school when her dad was on the job. Has worked there ever since."

"Why hasn't anyone ever mentioned him?" Erin demanded. "It's not like we don't talk with any other law enforcement officers in town! What happened to him? He wasn't killed on duty, was he?"

"He... took early retirement," Clara said carefully. She looked from Erin to Vic and back. "There were rumors. He would have been investigated. It was better if he just retired quietly."

"He was crooked?" Vic asked.

"There were rumors," Clara repeated. "Nothing was ever proven. Or even investigated. But people talked."

"Is he still around?"

"No." Clara shook her head. "It's been a long time. A high percentage of law enforcement officers die within two years of retirement. Too many years of stress and hard living. Or they don't do well settling down. The demons take over."

"How did he die?"

"I heard it was a heart attack or stroke."

"You *heard*?" Erin studied her.

"Don't know if it was true. If it was suicide, his widow wouldn't get his insurance or death benefit. So... better if it was natural causes."

"You think he committed suicide?"

"That was sort of the understanding around the police department. I don't know if he did or not. Maybe it really was natural causes. Or maybe he helped nature on its way a little. Either way... he's been gone for years, but Melissa has kept working for the police department. Ever since she was sixteen."

Erin had no idea that either Melissa or Clara had been working there for that long. That was a lot of institutional knowledge. Terry and Stayner hadn't been working there for more than a few years. She didn't know how long Sheriff Wilmot or Tom Baker had been working there. They could have been there for twenty or thirty years. She hadn't ever thought to ask.

It was no wonder no one wanted to fire Melissa, despite her propensity to leak information like a fire hose. With her dad being a cop and Melissa having been there for decades, no one wanted to upset the balance. Let her stay there until she was ready to go on to other things. Maybe they hoped that with her getting married, she would be making other changes in her life. She was finally coming out of her shell. Perhaps that would carry through to other things.

CHAPTER 33

Once Clara was on her way, Erin helped Vic and Charley to close, getting out the cake pans she needed while putting away other things and getting ready for the next morning. While Vic prepared their bank deposit and balanced the till, Erin mixed the cake batter in a couple of industrial mixers. By the time Charley was finished wiping down and sweeping, Vic was ready for the bank run and dinner, and Erin was filling the cake tins.

"Enjoy the quiet," Vic said, having already offered more than once to stay and keep Erin company. "And don't stay up too late! You'll want to be fresh to start decorating the cake in the morning. Clara said that the city had sent an ambulance to pick up Ortiz's body, so the police might have the scene cleared early tomorrow."

"Would you give Melissa a call after dinner? I just want to make sure everything went okay and we have a good idea of her plans tomorrow, but I don't have time to chat with her. I need to focus on this job, and she'll want to stay on the phone talking for hours."

"So you're pushing her off to me to talk to for hours?"

"You'll get her off the phone faster than me."

"Because I'm not as nice as you?"

"Because you're more… assertive. Even when I tell her I have to go, she doesn't believe me and keeps me talking forever. I can't just hang up, but I can't think of any other way to convince her that I mean what I say when I have to go."

"Hanging up may be your only recourse," Vic agreed.

"Will you call her?"

"Of course."

"Great. Okay, I'll see you tomorrow."

"You won't be too late tonight?"

Erin looked at the baking she had to do. "No, I shouldn't be too long. About all I can do tonight is get these baked. I can't start decorating until they're completely cool and settled. Although, I have some more fondant to make too. And maybe color and roll it tonight. And make the roses…" The more she could do ahead, the more smoothly things would go tomorrow.

Vic rolled her eyes. "Don't stay too late!" she repeated.

"I won't."

Charley waved from the doorway, already lighting up another cigarette. Vic followed her out, waving her hand to prevent any smoke from blowing back into the kitchen. She pulled the door shut behind her.

Erin turned back to her cakes to tap the air bubbles out of the poured batter before putting them into the oven. There was a rapid knock on the back door. Erin glanced around at the counters to see if Vic had left her purse or something else behind. She opened the door far enough to realize it wasn't Vic, and paused, unsure what to do.

"Yes?" she asked uncertainly. "What can I do for you?"

CHAPTER 34

There was a knock at Vic's door. She opened it tentatively, not used to anyone knocking on her door at night. She didn't usually have evening visitors. Willie would let himself in, and Erin would text before she came over. Anyone else would usually call before showing up on her doorstep.

When she saw Joshua Cox's young, earnest face, she opened the door the rest of the way.

"Joshua. Hi, it's nice to see you. Come in." She showed him into the small loft apartment and shut the door. "How are things going?"

"Okay," Joshua nodded. "And how are things with you, Miss Victoria?"

Always polite, as he'd been trained to be.

"Good. Saw your mom earlier today. Did you get those pizza pretzels?"

"Yes! I love those. I'd like to thank Miss Erin for them."

Vic looked out her window toward the house. There were only a couple of lights on. Meant to look occupied, but obviously not. Terry would probably be working late on the Ortiz case, and Vic hadn't seen or heard Erin return from the bakery yet.

"She had some work to do at Auntie Clem's. Since Melissa's cake got smashed, she has to make another one on an emergency basis. I don't know how long she'll be. I told her not to take too long!"

"Oh." Joshua looked disappointed. He looked back toward the house. "I tried calling her, but she didn't pick up. I had some questions I need to ask her about a case."

The Perry or Ortiz cases, no doubt. Or maybe he had managed to find some thread to tie them together.

"It might have to wait until tomorrow. She's as busy as a one-legged cat in a sandbox with the wedding arrangements. Everything went south with Miguel Ortiz doing a face plant in the wedding cake."

Joshua grinned, whether at the image of the cat in the sandbox or Ortiz landing in the wedding cake, Vic wasn't sure. "I really do need to talk to her. Do you think…" he looked around uncertainly. "Do you think I could hang out here for a few minutes to see if she shows up?"

Vic hesitated, then nodded. "For a bit," she agreed. "If it gets too late, I'll need to get to bed. I'm in charge while Erin is busy with the wedding, so I can't afford to sleep in!"

Joshua nodded. He looked around and tentatively sat down on the couch. Nilla, lying in his doggie bed on the other end of the couch, started to growl.

"Nilla!" Vic chided. "Be a good boy."

The little white dog eyed Joshua suspiciously, not liking this new development. He wasn't used to having to share the space and Vic with anyone but Willie. Willie didn't hesitate to correct him if he wasn't behaving, but Joshua wasn't sure how to respond. He looked like he might get up, abandoning the couch to the dog.

"You stay put," Vic told him. "Nilla is going to have to get used to the fact that the couch is not his territory and visitors might want to sit there. He has plenty of room. And a nice soft bed."

"I don't want to upset him…"

"Don't be silly. Can I get you some tea? Cookies?"

Joshua looked out the window toward the house as if hoping that Erin had returned in the last thirty seconds. "Uh… I don't want to put you out. I didn't mean to crash your evening. I just need a minute to talk to Erin."

"Well, give her some time. Her phone is probably set to Do Not

Disturb, since she's usually in bed by now. I doubt she'll be out too much longer. Her body is used to an early schedule."

Joshua nodded.

"Tea?" Vic repeated.

"Uh, sure. Yes, please, I mean. That would be very nice."

Vic put the kettle on to boil and removed a few cookies from the freezer. She and Erin always had plenty of leftover baking in the freezer.

"Erin said that your dad is at home."

Joshua nodded. "Yes. It's been nice to have him home again." He looked wistful. "Not the same… but nice to have him there, anyway. To know where he is and that he's safe."

"I'm sure the poor man is happy to be back home again. After all he's been through."

Joshua's shoulders lowered as he let out a breath, apparently relaxing as he realized that Vic was sympathetic about Roger rather than blaming him for what had happened when he was sick. Vic was all for holding people responsible for their choices, no matter what kind of a crappy childhood they had, or addictions, or other excuses for making poor choices. But with Roger, she had seen for herself. She knew that it was his brain injury and mental illness that had resulted in the things he had done. He really didn't have an understanding of the consequences of his actions and didn't have control over his mental processes.

"The doctors say he's doing better at home than he was in that place," Joshua agreed. He took the teacup from Vic when she offered it and picked one of the teabags from the tray Vic had placed on the coffee table. "Being more relaxed and in surroundings where he feels comfortable, he doesn't need as much medication."

"And it hasn't been too much for you and Mary Lou? I know that before, it was hard for the three of you to look after him, and now it's just you and Mary Lou."

"We have care workers as well, twice a day, and with the electronic monitoring, we don't need to worry about him leaving the house. He mostly watches TV or plays his handheld game. It keeps him calm."

"That's good." Vic was happy that he was at home again, but was not a danger to his family or the community. It was the best that any of them could have hoped for. Vic had certainly never expected him to be able to live at home again.

They sipped their tea and talked about TV shows and gossip around town, watching for any sign of Erin returning home. Vic was getting a little concerned. Erin was going to be pretty tired if she didn't get to bed soon. her body would still wake her up at the usual time. But if she had decided to prep all of the fondant and make roses and ribbons so that they'd be ready to go in the morning, it might take her a little longer than either of them had expected.

~

Terry's phone rang. He knew it was probably Erin wondering when he was going to get home. She would have to go to bed and liked him to be home if he wasn't on shift. It wasn't a scheduled shift, but he had told her that he might be working late, trying to get a handle on the Ortiz murder. The first few hours after a homicide or other major crime were critical to getting it cleared. Chances were that even if a crime took years to solve, the critical clues had been gathered during those first forty-eight hours.

But his eyes were getting gritty and he had a headache. He needed to get some sleep too, or he would make mistakes.

He reached for the phone but saw the screen right before he picked it up. Not Erin, but Vic.

"Vic?" Terry held the phone to his ear, his stomach tightening. Why was she calling him? What had happened? "What's up?" he asked as casually as possible.

"Have you heard from Erin, Terry?"

"No. She's working at the bakery. Should have been there before you left, right?"

"Yes. She was. But she's not picking up her phone and she isn't home yet."

"It's probably on Do Not Disturb."

"I know. But I did that trick where you call a few times in rapid succession, so it breaks through the Do Not Disturb as an urgent call. And I still can't get through."

"If it's on silent, she might still not have noticed."

"Yeah. I think I'm going to pop back over to Auntie Clem's. I'm getting worried."

"She had lots to do for the wedding. It probably took her longer than she expected."

"I know. I told her not to do too much tonight, but I knew she would. I'm going to check anyway."

Terry stood up from his desk, not bothering to gather his paperwork and sort it and lock it away at the end of the day as he should.

"I'll meet you over there."

K9, snoozing at Terry's side, was instantly on his feet, ears pricked alertly, looking around. Ready for business.

"Come on, boy," Terry murmured. "Let's go find Erin."

CHAPTER 35

erry drove into the parking lot at the same time as Vic pulled in with Willie's truck. He brushed away his annoyance over her driving Willie's truck when he knew very well that she didn't have a driver's license. That would have to wait for another time. If Vic was worried enough about Erin that she'd taken Willie's truck, knowing that Terry was on his way over there too, then there was a lot more to be concerned about than an unlicensed driver.

They both climbed out of their respective vehicles simultaneously, practically running to the back door of Auntie Clem's. Vic had a key, and Terry didn't. She fit it into the lock, and Terry motioned her briskly back, pulling his gun. Vic reached forward to open the door, staying behind him so that he could get in cleanly without anything blocking his view of the room.

The kitchen was still and silent. Terry moved in, cleared the room quickly, checked Erin's closet-sized office and the front of the store—lights turned off, door locked, and sign turned to Closed.

"Stay here while I check downstairs," Terry ordered. He descended to the basement and looked around. No sign of an intruder. No Erin lying at the bottom of the stairs with a broken leg or concussion. The secret passage that had once led out of the storage room had been closed up. There was nowhere else to go. Terry moved briskly back up the stairs. K9's claws clicked on the hard tiles. Terry looked around the kitchen.

Vic was shutting off the ovens. The room was hot and close. The air conditioner was only programmed to run during the day, so the ovens and the summer heat had driven the temperature up to unbearable levels.

Which meant that Erin had not been there for some time. She would have manually turned on the air conditioner and fans. Even if she had been baking for hours, it would not have been that hot.

Vic pointed to the cake pans on the counters, filled with batter, ready to be put in the oven.

"She had just poured these when I left. She never got them into the oven. That means she's been gone since we finished closing."

Terry looked at his watch. Between three and four hours.

She had been focused on getting the cake done for Melissa's reception. Nothing would have distracted her from that. No call or request would have been as important as getting those cake layers in the oven so that she could make Melissa's cake. Terry swallowed and looked at Vic.

She was bone white, her skin almost as pale as her hair. She understood it every bit as well as he did.

Erin was missing. And she had not gone voluntarily.

Everybody was already tired. They had been working on the murder file all day and everyone was ready for a good night's sleep so that they would be able to do something in the morning. Tom Banks was the only one who'd had any rest, going home to sleep in anticipation of covering the night shift while everyone else got caught up.

Terry's heart was pounding. He didn't need coffee to wake him up. With Erin's disappearance, all sleepiness was gone. But he was aware that his body was exhausted. His reflexes were slow. His movements felt clumsy. He had to focus to keep his thoughts on track. Stayner's and Wilmot's eyes were bloodshot, and his probably were too. No one complained. No one suggested waiting until morning to see if Erin turned up on her own.

Vic filled them in on all of the details she could think of, from Erin's arrival at Auntie Clem's just before closing, to what she had been doing in the kitchen as Vic left, to Joshua showing up and asking after her, asking if he could wait at Vic's until Erin got back.

"Where is Joshua?" Terry demanded, looking at Willie's truck, but not seeing him inside the cab.

"He went back home. I told him I needed to get to bed and he'd have to catch up with Erin tomorrow."

"Why did he want to talk to her?"

"About finding Ortiz's body, I assume. He'd want all of the details to write a piece for the paper."

"How long did he stay?"

"About an hour."

"And he went home?"

"I didn't follow him to see."

Terry didn't have Joshua's phone number on his cell, but he had Mary Lou's. He tapped her name and waited impatiently while it rang.

"Hello?"

"Piper," Terry said curtly, getting the words out as quickly as he could. "Is Joshua at home?"

"No." Mary Lou's voice was hesitant. "No, he went out... he hasn't come back."

"Did he say where he was going?"

"To do interviews. To talk to Erin, Melissa, I don't know who else."

"And he hasn't called you or returned home."

"No. What's going on? What's wrong?"

"Erin isn't here. He was looking for her. I want to know where he went after that."

"Have you tried him?"

"I need his number."

Mary Lou gave it to him slowly. Terry repeated the number aloud, then hung up and dialed it. It rang two times. Three. Seven, eight, nine. It went to voicemail. Terry hung up and tried it again.

"Are you sure you got the number right?" Vic asked, watching him with wide eyes.

"It's Joshua's voice on the recording."

The second time it went to voicemail, just as it had the first. Terry hung up. He went to his contacts and searched for Melissa's name. He tapped it and put his phone back to his ear.

"Hello?" Melissa's voice sounded mellow and full, not like someone who had been worrying all day or knew that one of her friends was in trouble. "Terry?"

"Have you talked to Erin?"

"No. Not since the wedding."

She sounded so happy when she said "the wedding." Despite how Terry pictured a jailhouse wedding—small and plain with little ceremony or sentiment—Melissa sounded satisfied. Like it had filled a need in her that had been empty for a long time.

"Have you talked to anyone? Did Joshua Cox come to see you?"

"No. Why would Joshua come? Oh, is he doing an article for the paper? About the wedding?"

A lot of people would be very interested in the details, Terry was sure. They would want to read all about what it had been like to marry someone convicted of murder.

"Erin is missing. Joshua was looking for her earlier. I need to know why he wanted to talk to her. If he knows what happened to her."

"What?" Melissa didn't screech, but was immediately concerned. "Erin is missing? She must be at the hall. Setting things up for the reception."

"No, she's not." Though Terry had not gone there to look for her. It was one of the first places they would put on the list when Willie got there.

Willie was good at search and rescue. He could organize a search like nobody's business and knew the area around Bald Eagle Falls like the back of his hand. Even the caves that ran through the mountain like Swiss cheese.

"Has anyone spoken to you?" Terry asked Melissa. "Has anyone asked you about Perry and Ortiz? Tried to connect you with them or connect them with each other?"

"No." Melissa was anxious. "Only Sheriff Wilmot. He's the only one I talked to. I don't think anyone else... remembers anything from back then."

"Has anyone made any threats? Told you to stay out of their business? Not to ask questions?"

"No. I wasn't asking any questions. I just talked to the Sheriff and then went to the prison."

Terry knew that wasn't quite true. She had stopped at the salon between the discovery of Ortiz's body and going to the prison. But he didn't think Melissa was trying to hide anything. She was just summing up. Giving him the most salient points.

"What did you and Erin talk about when you were getting your hair done?"

"I don't know. This and that."

"Ortiz? The murder?"

"A little. But I didn't really want to focus on that. I didn't want to dwell on negative stuff. I wanted to be excited about the wedding."

"Who was there?"

"I don't know. Serena. A couple of the older ladies. Erin. Willie."

"Willie?"

"Yeah. He said he wanted to keep an eye on things. Make sure that Erin and I were okay. It was sweet."

"Why did he want to make sure you were okay?"

She didn't answer for a minute. "You don't think he would want to keep Erin and I safe?"

"No, of course I do. But what made him think that you might be in danger in the first place?"

"Oh… just because we had found the body, I guess. He thought that whoever the killer was, he might come after one of us."

"Why?"

"I don't know. Because we might have seen something. We didn't. Whoever killed that man, he was long gone by the time Erin and I got there. There was no one else in the building."

Terry thought about Mr. Foster. About anyone else who had been coming and going with deliveries and decorations and things that needed to be set up in the hall. Had Melissa and Erin seen something incriminating without realizing it? Had the killer seen them or been afraid that they would guess who he was?

"Thank you, Melissa. That's… helpful."

"Will Erin be okay? You're going to find her, right? Everything will be okay."

"Yes. I'm sure it will be fine. She can't have gone far."

He hung up the phone.

Whether or not Erin had gone far had nothing to do with whether she would be okay. She hadn't left under her own power. If the killer had thought that she could identify him, then he could have taken care of her just as easily as Miguel Ortiz. The only positive sign Terry could point to was that her body had not been left in the kitchen. He hadn't killed her on the spot. So he must have had something else in mind. Maybe she was still okay.

CHAPTER 36

Terry walked over to Vic, who was talking to Sheriff Wilmot, telling him what she had already told Terry.

"Where is Willie?" he demanded.

Vic and the sheriff stared at Terry as if they couldn't believe he would be so rude as to walk up and interrupt their conversation. Terry was not concerned about whether he was being polite or not. There was work to do if they were going to have any hope of finding Erin unharmed.

"I called him. I'm not sure."

"You have his truck. He must be in town, within walking distance."

"Yes… but he didn't say where he was. Having a drink with friends. I don't know."

Terry looked at his watch again, calculating every minute that had ticked by since they had walked in and discovered Erin missing. "You called him ten minutes ago. Where is he?"

Vic swallowed. "I don't know. I'm sure he'll be here soon."

Wilmot was looking at Terry. He jerked his head to the side. "Should we talk?"

"Willie may know something. I want to know what."

"What makes you think Willie knows anything about this?" Vic demanded, her voice getting louder and higher.

"Because he was at Serena's to look after Erin and Melissa this afternoon. To make sure nothing happened to them."

Vic opened her mouth, but nothing came out. She looked at Terry and then at the sheriff.

"He knows something," Terry reiterated. "Why would he go over there if he didn't know something? He wasn't there to get a shampoo and rinse."

"No," Wilmot agreed. "I'll give him another call. See if I can light a fire under him. If I need to, I'll send someone to pick him up."

As it turned out, there was no need to send anyone to find Willie. He walked out of the darkness into the pale light of the parking lot, his stained face even darker and more ominous than usual in the shadows cast by the security lighting.

"Willie." Terry knew his voice was loud and gruff. He pressed his hand against Vic, pushing her back when she moved to go to Willie. It wasn't time for a tearful reunion. He needed answers. "Where is Erin?"

Willie shook his head. "I have no idea. Tell me what you know."

"She was supposed to be here making Melissa's replacement wedding cake. When Vic left after closing, she had just finished pouring the batter into the pans. The pans never made it to the ovens."

He could see Willie calculating this. Thinking about means of entry, how long Erin had been gone, and exactly how she had been taken. He knew as well as Terry that Erin hadn't just walked out. She hadn't left Auntie Clem's with the layers of the wedding cake unbaked to run an errand or because she had been distracted by some other more important job. Willie already had his own concerns about Erin and Terry wanted to know what they were.

"You were at Serena's earlier to keep an eye on Erin and Melissa. Why?"

"I was concerned... with them having found the body."

"Why?"

"They could be in danger. Someone might think that they knew something."

"Why? If the killer left Ortiz's body there, he knew someone would find it. He didn't make any attempt to hide it or take it away. Why would the person who found his body be in danger?"

Willie gazed at Terry, his expression masked. He was a good poker player. He kept his cards close to the vest and didn't give anything away.

"Why were they in danger? Something has happened to Erin, and you know what."

"I don't know." Willie shook his head slowly. "All I know is… first Perry's body was found, and then Ortiz was killed."

"You think they are both connected?"

"I don't like coincidences."

"Neither do I. But what is the connection?"

Willie looked away. "I don't know. Assuming there is a connection, Erin was there when both bodies were discovered. Maybe she drew a line between them? Maybe someone was afraid she saw a connection between them. I thought… she would be safe here."

The back door to the bakery was solid, and the doorframe was reinforced—a good, secure door. The front wasn't as strong, but it was visible to anyone on Main Street, and a burglar or attacker who used that door would be seen almost immediately. It wasn't yet late enough that everyone was asleep. People were still around, walking to the restaurants, going for an evening stroll, stopping to gossip.

She should have been safe there. But she had let her kidnapper in.

"Who would she have let in?" Willie asked. "Why would she let someone in who intended her harm?"

"I don't know. Obviously… she didn't think that he would do anything to hurt her."

And she'd been wrong. Despite her background, Erin was too trusting,

Another car pulled up to the entrance of the parking lot and was forced to stop there. They weren't letting anyone close to the scene. There might be evidence to process. Though from what Terry could see, there was little physical evidence left behind. Maybe the kidnapper had left behind a stray fingerprint, but there was no sign of violence. Nothing knocked over. No blood or hair. Nothing that they could use to point at who had entered the kitchen and taken Erin away.

He watched Mary Lou get out of the driver's side and another figure out of the passenger's seat. Joshua? That was good; Terry wanted to talk to Joshua.

Tom Baker was keeping any lookie-loos outside the perimeter, but Terry motioned for him to let Mary Lou and Joshua through.

Only it wasn't Joshua. Terry had not been able to see clearly under the shadows cast by the lights. It was Joshua's father, Roger. A man Terry had arrested for murder once before. His stomach tied in a knot and he tried to remain objective.

Mary Lou's expression was anxious. "Where is Joshua?" she asked. "Tell me what's going on."

"Erin is missing. Joshua was looking for her earlier. His phone goes to voicemail. So does hers. I don't know where either one of them is."

"Joshua is missing?"

"I wouldn't jump to that conclusion. He was at Vic's earlier, waiting for Erin. But Erin disappeared from here at least an hour before that. So he was safe when she was… already gone."

"Do you think he came back here? And someone was still here, waiting for him?"

Terry shook his head. "No. I don't think so. I think whoever took Erin was long gone by then. I don't think it was done by more than one person. I think that if Joshua came back here, all he would have found was an empty kitchen. Maybe he had somewhere else to go."

"I tried to get him. His phone is supposed to ring when I call, no matter what. He promised me that he wouldn't ignore my calls. Ever." Her jaw clenched. Terry could understand why they had made the pact. Joshua had been kidnapped. Mary Lou probably freaked out any time he didn't answer his phone. She needed to know that he was safe. And he wouldn't get any peace as long as she thought something might have happened to him again.

"He might be out of service." Terry looked around, trying to imagine where Joshua had gone. There were plenty of wooded areas around Bald Eagle Falls that didn't have proper cell service. Even on the highway. Joshua could be close by and not have intended for anyone to worry about him.

"Maybe," Mary Lou agreed, her voice measured. "But let's piece this together. He was looking for Erin. He wanted to interview her."

"He waited at Vic's. When Erin didn't show up and Vic wanted to head to bed, he left there."

"Did he talk to Melissa?"

"No. He never got there."

"Then he must have..." She shook her head. "He must have gone somewhere else to look for Erin."

"Maybe. Or he had someone else to talk to. Or he went to get something to eat. Or went into the city to see Cam. We don't know."

Roger was plucking at Mary Lou's arm. She put her opposite hand over his. "It's okay, Roger. We'll figure it out. I'm sure he wouldn't go into something dangerous." Her eyes were on Terry, pleading. "He knows better now. He knows to be careful."

"Something dangerous," Roger echoed.

"He'll be careful. He won't go into something he knows is dangerous," Mary Lou repeated.

She wanted it to be true. She wanted Terry's reassurance. She had nearly lost Joshua once; she couldn't face having to go through that again.

"No," Roger said. "Has to be careful."

Terry wasn't sure what to expect from Roger. The last couple of times he had seen Roger before he had gone away, he'd been agitated. He had been growing more violent at home, was wandering off, and had attacked others. He had been able to speak clearly, but had skipped unexpectedly from one thought to another and had been very impulsive. Now, under the med cocktail they had him on, he seemed to have slowed down to the point where it was difficult for him to get the words out. It was sad to see him so impaired but, of course, they couldn't take the chance that he would hurt anyone else.

"If he knew something, why didn't he come to the police?" Terry asked, frustrated.

"Because he wants the story," Mary Lou said. "That's the most important thing for him. Maybe he thought that what he knew wasn't that important."

"He was practicing," Roger said, the words coming out more easily this time and not obviously echoing someone else.

Mary Lou looked at him. "Practicing what?" She shook her head slightly as if to say that Joshua hadn't been practicing anything and Roger was just confused.

"Protecting himself. From dangerous." He blew his breath out hard as if he knew he wasn't making any sense, but couldn't find a way to formulate the thought. He looked around and pointed to Vic.

"Vic is not dangerous," Mary Lou dismissed.

"No. He was practicing."

His eyes stayed on Vic. Something about the situation involved Vic. Terry didn't think that any of it was anything to do with Erin's disappearance, but he wasn't going to be accused of not listening to every clue he was given. If they were going to find Erin, he needed more information than he had.

"Vic, can you come here?"

Vic hesitated, then approached Terry, Mary Lou, and Roger. She and Mary Lou were not the best of friends. There had been quite a lot of friction between them to begin with. They had settled into a somewhat awkward friendship but were obviously still not that comfortable with each other.

"Miss Victoria," Terry addressed her more formally. "Do you know what Roger is talking about?"

Vic turned her eyes reluctantly to Roger. A lot of people were awkward around those with disabilities.

"What was Joshua practicing?" Terry prompted Roger.

Roger brightened a little and leaned forward eagerly. He was happy to know that someone was listening to him and trying to understand him. He probably dealt mostly with people who were not willing to take the time with him to understand that there was still a brain in there, even if he was impaired in many ways.

"Protecting himself," Roger said once more, his eyes intent on Vic.

Even in the dimness of the parking lot, Terry could see the red flush that crept into her cheeks and throat. *Not* a good poker player. Not in a high stakes game like this, anyway.

"Oh." She looked down, swallowed, and then looked back up at Mary Lou. Her cheeks got still redder, and she looked away. "I was, uh, giving him some pointers."

"In self-defense?" Mary Lou asked, frown lines between her eyes.

"Y-yes…"

Clearly something more than just self-defense instruction.

Roger raised his hand from his side to the horizontal, index finger out, and made a little jerking motion. Terry understood this gesture even if it wasn't quite the way they had done it as kids. No trigger-pulling or hammer-cocking gesture, just the jerk of the barrel as it fired.

Shooting. Joshua had been taking shooting lessons from Vic.

CHAPTER 37

*E*rin pressed her wrists outward, again testing the confines of the flexicuffs. She could hear her captor snoring away nearby. She was surprised and slightly insulted that he could sleep now, when he had just kidnapped someone. There had to be something wrong with the man. Who could just drop off to sleep and saw wood like that after kidnapping a woman?

Maybe the same man who had killed not just once but multiple times. Maybe kidnapping was so tame compared to what he usually did that it didn't bother his conscience at all.

Or maybe she was misjudging him, and he was asleep not because he was relaxed and unconcerned by his crime, but because he was overwhelmed by what he had done. She had seen that response before. Faced with a daunting situation, Erin's natural reaction was to make lists. To at least convince herself that she had some level of control over the situation, and if she just played her cards right, she could make everything turn out.

Of course, her other response was just the opposite—to cut and run, as fast and as far as possible.

And maybe sleep was his version of running away. If he were conscious, he would have to think about what he had done and what he would do next and how he would get himself out of this situation. But asleep, he didn't have to. He could close his eyes and be somewhere else altogether.

Maybe he'd been awake, anxiously trying to get things worked out, ever since he had killed Miguel Ortiz, and his body was taking over now, making him sleep even if it was something he knew he couldn't afford to do.

But apparently, he *could* afford to do it, because Erin wasn't going anywhere. She wasn't having any luck escaping the flexicuffs or figuring out another way to get out of the room he had left her in.

At first, she had been afraid that there was someone else on guard. That there was a whole gang of them and that any move she made would be monitored. If she did anything wrong, they would be angry and would beat or kill her. There would be no way for her to fight back against all of them.

But she hadn't seen any sign of anyone else—no one watching her or standing outside her door. No one went out for food so her kidnapper didn't have to show his face outside or do anything that might be out of the ordinary or suspicious. It seemed just to be him. And that meant he would have to go at some point, leaving her alone. Assuming he wasn't just going to kill her. She couldn't understand why he hadn't. He had killed others. Why had he balked at killing her? Because she was a woman? Because he could see it continuing like a line of dominoes and needed to stop it while he still could? Because he'd been too tired?

Considering the noise he made as he slept, it was entirely possible that he'd just been too exhausted to kill her yet. But he'd get around to it sooner or later.

In the movies, there was always a way to escape. Some brave or MacGyver-esque approach that would allow her to get out of the flexicuffs or to get out of the house without harm—or at least without a fatal injury —so that she could run to safety. She wasn't even sure that escaping the house would allow her to run to safety. They were some distance away from Bald Eagle Falls itself. She would need to steal a car or other trans- portation or run a half marathon. And considering she'd never even run a 5K, she couldn't see that happening. People did amazing things when they were desperate, but Erin felt sapped rather than adrenalized by her misad- venture.

The wind blew a branch against a window. It tapped, stopped for a minute or two, and tapped again. Like something that wanted into the house rather than something that needed space to grow outside. Erin closed her eyes and imagined that it was someone who had come to rescue her rather than just an inanimate tree that couldn't care less whether she lived or died, escaped or remained captive.

"Erin!"

Erin's eyes flew open. She looked around. Nothing had changed. The man was still snoring in the other bedroom, sawing logs like there was no tomorrow. She blinked and looked around some more, trying to find the source of the voice.

"Erin. The window."

She looked at the window. It was dark outside and, out in the woods, there were no light sources other than the moon to see by. The light inside the room kept her from seeing anything but blackness or her own reflection when looking at the window. She shuffled along on the bed, moving her feet a bit, and then sliding her butt, an awkward inchworm movement that was probably hilarious to watch. But it did the job, at least. Eventually, she was at the point where the window was directly behind her.

"Who's there?" she asked in a low voice. Her breath caught at the sound of her own words, worried that the kidnapper would wake up and come to find out what was going on.

"It's Joshua."

Joshua? Erin's mind went back to the time when he had been kidnapped. When she hadn't been able to convince anyone that he was in danger and hadn't just left home voluntarily. It had taken her forever to find him. How could he have found her in just a couple of hours?

Erin tried to get her bound arms around to a position where she would be able to work the mechanism on the window to open it. How that was going to help, she wasn't sure. But it seemed like the only logical next step. Joshua was at the window, so she needed to open the window.

With her wrists in the flexicuffs, however, it was difficult to do anything. Her shoulders hurt when she tried to raise her hands to a level where she could work the window lock. She leaned forward, which helped a little, but she still couldn't get them up far enough, and straining for it was very painful.

"Try getting up on your knees," Joshua suggested.

Erin worked her legs around and managed to get into a kneeling position, which was higher than just sitting on her butt. And when she leaned forward, she could bend down farther, which lifted her hands up higher. She kept looking behind her to get a picture of the lock in her mind, then turning away from the window and just trying to use her sense of touch. It was one of those systems that required several actions in sequence. Unlocking the window with two different levers, one at the left and one at the right, and then flipping a handle and turning it around to wind the window open. Except the handle was stuck, and she couldn't figure out which way it needed to be turned to open the window. She didn't know whether she was trying to wind it more tightly shut or to open it. The handle didn't want to budge in either direction.

"You've got it," Joshua urged. "Keep going. It's just a little stiff."

It was more than a little stiff. It was a lot stiff. As if the owner had never opened it since he'd had the window installed, and it had seized up.

"It's too hard."

"You can do it. You're doing great."

"Call for help. Call Terry. The police department dispatcher."

"My phone won't work out here."

Erin suspected hers wouldn't either. It hadn't rung in all of the time she'd been there. She was sure that Terry would be calling her. He was bound to have noticed that she had not returned home. Assuming he was at home himself and hadn't decided to work through the night on the case.

"Do you have a car? Go for help."

She wasn't sure how he would have gotten out there without a car. She felt like she was losing her mind.

"Can I try breaking the window?"

"You'll wake him up. We'll never get away from here."

"I've got a gun."

Erin turned to look out the window at him in disbelief, even though she couldn't see through the dark glass. "What are you doing with a gun? Your mother would kill me!"

"It doesn't have anything to do with you," he pointed out.

"Oh, yes it does. If you shoot a gun rescuing me, then it will be my fault. Go back to Bald Eagle Falls and get help. Now, while he's still asleep. Because I don't know what he's going to do when he wakes up."

"I could shoot the lock on the front door. I've seen them do that in the movies."

"This is not the movies."

"I know…"

"Listen to what I'm telling you, Joshua. You need to go get help. It's not that far back to Bald Eagle Falls if you're driving. Fifteen minutes there, and another fifteen back. Less, because you'll have a police escort. Half an hour. I'm sure he'll sleep another half hour."

He would, wouldn't he? He didn't sound like he was getting up any time soon.

"Stay there," Joshua warned her worriedly. "Don't try to get away or go anywhere. Don't do anything that might wake him up."

"I won't."

"I'll be right back. I promise."

CHAPTER 38

*J*oshua climbed back onto his bike, his stomach a tight knot. He didn't have the heart to tell Miss Erin it would take at least twice as long as she thought to get help. Assuming he was successful and nothing happened to prevent him.

No flat tires.

He'd been worried about the way the gravel had crunched and popped on the way in. He'd thought for sure he was going to pop a tire. He was very quiet and kept an eye open for sentries. It was possible that he'd only been lucky on the way in, and someone was keeping watch while the kidnapper slept. He might have just been relieving himself behind a tree when Joshua had shown up.

He made his way slowly down the gravel driveway until he was sure he was past the property line and any possible guards. When he hit the highway, he turned on his headlamp and pedaled as fast as possible.

He would be faster getting back to town than he had been finding Erin. He'd had an address, but rural addresses could be challenging to find, and he'd had to go slowly in the dark, searching for numbers on fenceposts and poorly signed crossroads. He'd made a mistake in not telling anyone where he was going. He'd been after the scoop to begin with, and it had taken time to get out of that mindset and realize that there were lives at stake and he couldn't afford to be selfish with the information that he had.

By that time, he had been out of cell service.

Just before reaching the town limits, his phone started ringing, startling him so badly that he nearly fell off his bike. He stopped and dug out his earbuds, shoving them in his ears and into the phone jack so he could continue talking while he pedaled. The caller ID said, "Mom."

"Hi, Mom."

"Joshua!" He knew *that* voice. She was tired and angry and upset, all mixed together. She had heard him use that tone with Cam, and she'd heard him use it with their father. Joshua tried not to make her worry. He tried to do everything right so that she didn't have to worry about him like she did about everyone else, but now he'd gone and done it. He'd failed her.

"It's okay, Mom. I know I'm late getting home. I'm sorry, I didn't mean to be so long. I just have to do one more thing, and then I'll be back."

"You need to talk to Officer Piper."

Joshua swallowed. He wondered how much she knew and how much she had guessed.

"Yeah, I was going to see him now. I just got back into cell range."

"He's been trying to reach you and so have I."

"I'm sorry. I didn't mean to be out of touch."

"Do you know where Erin Price is?"

"Yes. I'm going to talk to Officer Piper right now. Is he—"

"He's in the parking lot behind Auntie Clem's. That's where we all are. Why didn't you talk to someone before you took off?"

"I wasn't sure... I didn't know if I knew anything or could find anything out. And I didn't know for sure that anything had happened to her. Vic—Miss Victoria—said that Erin was working at Auntie Clem's, that she just had to focus on Melissa Lee's wedding cake, and that's why she wasn't answering. But I was worried..."

"Where are you now?"

"I'm just into town. I'll be there within five minutes."

"Okay..." Joshua could tell she wanted to stay on the phone with him, but didn't know what else to say. "I'll see you soon, then."

He could see that all the police cars in town were at the bakery when he was a few blocks away. Everybody was there waiting for him. He was the only one who knew where Erin was. She was depending on him.

Joshua nearly wiped out when he pulled into the parking lot, trying to slow down and avoid hitting any of the vehicles or people gathered around. Mary Lou, Roger, Terry Piper, and Sheriff Wilmot all surrounded him, asking questions at the same time.

"I found her," Joshua said, ignoring all of the questions and panting with the exertion of his high-speed bike ride. "But I couldn't get to her, and she couldn't get the window open or get out. He's asleep, so she's safe for a few minutes, but I told her I wouldn't be long getting her help. She'll be wondering what's taking me so long because I didn't tell her I only had my bike."

"Where is she?" Terry Piper demanded.

Joshua turned his phone around to show him the address and GPS map. Piper started to copy down the information.

"Whose place is this? Who has her?"

"Monroe. Howard Monroe, the foreman."

Terry blinked, assimilating this information. "The foreman," he repeated. He shook his head. "When we get back, you and I will sit down and discuss what information you have and where you got it. Describe the situation. Is it just Monroe, or are others involved? You said that you saw Erin?"

Joshua nodded. He leaned back in his bike seat. Roger was tapping him on the arm, and Joshua turned to look at him and saw he was handing him a water bottle. He smiled. "Thanks, Dad."

Roger smiled back. Mary Lou had her arm through Roger's like he was escorting her, keeping him close so he couldn't wander off or get into any trouble. Her smile was more strained, but she didn't censure Joshua for what he had done.

Joshua cracked open the water bottle, took a sip, and answered Officer Piper. "He's sleeping in one bedroom and Erin is in another. She's hand-cuffed with those plastic zip ties. It doesn't look like she's hurt. She's on a bed right by the window, but she couldn't get it open. She told me to come back and get help. I didn't see anyone else there. I was looking for anyone keeping guard outside, but I never saw anyone else."

"What's the layout of the property and the house? Can you draw it for me?"

Joshua pulled out his reporter notepad and pencil. Officer Piper shone a flashlight on the paper so that Joshua could see, and watched carefully as he sketched out first the access road and the house, and then the doors and bedrooms so that they would know where to find Erin. Of course, they could have cased the house out themselves, but Joshua supposed it was better if they knew what they were going into ahead of time. It would save time in the long run.

"I want to come with you."

Mary Lou shook her head. "I don't think that's a good idea." She didn't say what she was thinking—that she wanted him to go home to where he was safe and nothing bad could happen to him. But, of course, bad things *had* happened to him there. Joshua preferred to be in control of the situation himself and to see what was coming. And the situation with Erin Price was exciting and was going to make a great story. He couldn't possibly go home and watch TV when something was going down.

"I'm an investigative reporter," Joshua told Officer Piper. "This is my story. I've given you the information, but I still want to be there. How can I write about it if I don't see what happens with my own eyes?"

He could interview the police and anyone else involved after the fact, but he assumed that Officer Piper and the others would not want to be interviewed. They would have procedures to follow, paperwork to file, and, at some point, would want to go home to their families and bed. Especially Officer Piper. He wouldn't want to spend time with Joshua going over it, especially not tonight when it was still fresh in his mind.

"I'll stay where you tell me to," he promised, "as long as it's some-where I can see what's going on. I won't get in anyone's way or try to 'help.' I just want to be there so I can report on it."

Officer Piper's frown said he wasn't very likely to give a positive answer. He looked over at Sheriff Wilmot, who shrugged.

"Why not? It's good press for the police department. The paper will want to run the story either way; it may as well be an eyewitness account."

Joshua nodded, keeping his mouth shut and waiting for Piper's response. Of course, the sheriff was in charge and, if he told Piper that they were doing it, he couldn't really argue. But Joshua hoped he would buy in himself so there wouldn't be any problems. He wanted to be able to see and he didn't want to have issues dealing with Terry Piper in the future because he had done something to tick him off. If they left without him, he would follow on his bike. He would arrive late, possibly after Erin was already safe and sound. But if the police took their time scoping out the situation and getting established, he might still see part of the rescue.

"All right," Piper said eventually, probably reading Joshua's intentions in his eyes. "But you have to do what you're told. You don't want to do anything that will endanger Erin."

"No. I came here for your help. I didn't go in guns blazing and try to get her out myself. That should count for something."

"Speaking of which…" Piper's eyes were stern. "Do you have a gun?"

Joshua swallowed. He wondered whether he dared deny it. Someone had obviously already told Piper that Joshua had been practicing his shooting. Vic?

He saw Mary Lou's grip on Roger's arm tighten. *Roger.* His dad had given him up. He had never liked the idea of Joshua training with a firearm.

"It's okay, Dad," Joshua assured him, not wanting Roger to think he was angry about it. He turned to the side slightly and pulled up his shirt so that Piper could see the handgun secured in the holster in the small of his back. Not the best place to put it, Vic had told him. Awkward to get at if he needed it in a hurry. But leaning forward riding a bike, he couldn't have it in front where it would dig into his hip or belly. He couldn't carry it somewhere visible, leaving the small of his back as the best solution for him.

"Leave it in the holster and take it off," Piper told him. "We can't have you carrying that into a dangerous situation."

Joshua obeyed, unbuckling the holster belt. Piper nodded toward Roger. "Give it to your parents to hang on to."

Joshua was pretty sure Piper knew that he didn't have a gun permit, especially considering the fact that he had to be twenty-one to hold one, and he was a few years shy of that. Piper was giving him a pass on that one, probably because Joshua had gone to him voluntarily with the information about Erin. But he wouldn't do it again. Joshua handed it over, and Roger took it. Everyone's eyes were on him for an instant. Handing a gun to a man known to be mentally impaired and who had harmed someone before? But Roger simply folded the belt over a few times to make it into a small, neat package and did not give any sign of an intention to remove the gun from the holster. If they knew Roger like Joshua, they would know how opposed he was to firearms. He had said nothing to Joshua about owning a gun and training with Vic, probably because he knew that Joshua had been the victim of violent crime and just wanted to protect himself. But that didn't mean that he condoned it.

"Hop in," Piper nodded to his truck. Then he turned to the other cops to give them all instructions. Joshua climbed up into the cab of the truck, his heart still pounding hard. He was glad to have everyone's eyes on Piper so no one could see how much Joshua's legs were shaking.

CHAPTER 39

*E*rin was finding it impossible to remain vigilant. She wanted to be awake and alert when Joshua returned, but the minutes dragged by and he wasn't back yet. Her body was used to being asleep at that time of night and, despite everything that had happened, she was getting drowsy and finding herself drifting off. The adrenaline that had pumped through her veins for the first few hours had waned, leaving her exhausted.

At first, she didn't pay any attention to the night sounds. Everything was muffled through the window that she was still unable to open. She was frustrated by her inability to do something so simple. If she'd been a TV heroine, she wouldn't have even had to open the window; she could have just kicked it out or run and jumped through it. As it was, she felt utterly ineffective. What kind of kidnappee could do nothing but lie on the bed and let her kidnapper do whatever he liked? She was lucky he hadn't seemed to have any personal or physical interest in her. She was repulsed by the idea of his putting his hands on her.

So far, he hadn't killed her and hadn't assaulted her. So what exactly was his plan?

She gradually became aware of noises outside, even through the closed window. The crunch and pop of vehicles traveling over gravel roads. A truck engine that sounded familiar. A single dog bark that seemed to be closer than the nearest farm. She hadn't seen or heard a dog on Monroe's property. But maybe he had one and it was simply tied up behind the house or somewhere else out of the way where Erin hadn't seen it. Or it was the bark of a fox or the yip of a coyote.

Erin wanted to rub her eyes. They were sticky and gritty. But that probably wasn't good for them, and her hands were still fastened behind her back, so she couldn't even get them close to her face. Her shoulders were aching from having them pulled behind her in that unnatural position.

She heard a door open and tensed. Was Monroe up? Ready to take the next step in his ill-advised plan? But she could still hear him snoring away. So what was the noise? Just one of the noises that houses made? She'd been spooked by empty houses before, especially when she'd been young and her foster sister Reg had been there to tease her and egg her on. Everything always seemed a little bit crazier when Reg was around. With Reg there, the noises in the house escalated to the chains and moans of ghosts, the scratching of rats and goblins, and the fearful tap-tap-tapping of some undead creature outside who wanted to be let in.

She struggled to sit back up. She had let herself fall onto her side to close her eyes and get some rest, but now she regretted that. She wanted to be fully upright for whatever was coming. There were more noises she couldn't identify. Footsteps? Whispered voices? She was sure it was just the creaking of the floorboards and the wind outside. She was imagining things, freaking herself out. She needed to just stay calm and wait. Monroe was still sleeping and Joshua had gone to get help. All she needed was patience.

But then Erin smelled something. Sounds might be able to trick her. She might imagine things in the dark. But she could not be fooled by her nose. The thread of scent that she caught was the aftershave Terry wore. But not just his aftershave. That was not unique and might be worn by dozens of men in Bald Eagle Falls. But there was also Terry's sweat, individual and unique to him, and a hint of dog and the shampoo she had used on K9 just the day before. She clenched her hands into fists, waiting. She wanted to call out to him but didn't dare. He needed to do his job, and it was more important for him to secure Monroe than to enter her room and reassure her that everything was okay.

Then a light going on in the room across the hall blinded her, and Stayner's voice rang out like a megaphone.

"Police, Monroe! Stay where you are! Lace your hands behind your head!"

Erin jumped at the shout, even though she had been expecting it and she knew it was not aimed at her. There was an angry bellow of protest from Monroe, but they had him surrounded and overcome before he even knew they were there. Erin listened to the sounds of them putting him on the floor and locking the handcuffs over his wrists, her eyes closed against the blinding light.

"Erin. I'm here. It's okay."

Erin let a smile grow across her face. "I could smell you."

He moved in close to her and hugged her. "Of course you could."

K9 was whining. Erin wanted to scratch his ears and reassure him, but her hands were tied. Literally.

"I'm going to cut those off," Terry told her, examining the flexicuffs. She waited while he got a tool out of his duty belt and slid the blade behind the plastic ties to snip them, one at a time, releasing Erin from her prison. She brought her hands in front of her body and rubbed her wrists.

"Thank you." She opened her eyes enough to see K9, though still squinting against the assault of the light, waiting for them to adjust. "Hey, boy, did you come to rescue me?" She scratched K9's ears and then put her arms around Terry for a full hug this time, ignoring the uncomfortable bits of the equipment on his duty belt. "Thank you."

He hugged her tightly and rubbed her back. He stroked her hair away from her face, studying her for any injuries or what she was feeling.

"Is Josh okay?" Erin asked him. "He was here, but I couldn't get the window open."

"Yes, he's fine. He's in my truck. Best to allow us to rescue you rather than a sixteen-year-old boy. You couldn't expect him to arrest Monroe, even if he did get you out of here."

"That's true," Erin admitted. She had wanted desperately to get out when she'd realized that Joshua was there and been bitterly disappointed by her inability to open the window, but what Terry said was true. Of course it was better for him to be able to arrest Monroe. Who knew what might have happened if he had awakened while Joshua had been there or after Erin's escape? He might never have been seen in Bald Eagle Falls again. While that was fine with Erin, she didn't want to be responsible for other deaths or kidnappings in the future when Monroe ran into new difficulties that he decided to solve with violence.

"I was so stupid," Erin confessed, putting her head into the hollow of Terry's shoulder. "I opened the door to him. I thought he wanted to talk to me about Mrs. Peach's renovation. That there was a problem or a question he needed to ask, or to tell me that it was all done, on time and under budget, and they would be submitting their final bill."

"That's a little unbelievable." Terry's dimple appeared on his cheek. "On time and under budget?"

Erin laughed. "Yeah, I know. I live in a dream world. A renovation project could never come in on time and under budget."

"You're right about that."

"I'm sorry."

"Sorry?" He stroked her hair, cuddling her against himself. "You don't have anything to be sorry for."

"If I hadn't answered the door… this wouldn't have happened."

"I think that if he was intent on taking you, it wouldn't have mattered whether you answered the door or not. He could have waited until you left Auntie Clem's and bagged you in the parking lot. Or he could have waited a day or two and picked you up somewhere else. It would appear that Howard Monroe is not a person who lets a whim like this blow over. And he isn't someone who plays by the rules."

"I guess not."

"All secure in here, Piper?" Stayner asked from the doorway.

"All secure. Thanks. Take our guest out to the car and his new accommodations."

Stayner nodded. He had one hand on Monroe, in the hallway out of sight, and pushed him on.

"This is a violation of my rights!" Monroe growled in protest, "You don't have the right to break into my house in the middle of the night! Where is your warrant? Show me your warrant! I'll have your badges, you Podunk backwoods cops!"

Stayner took him out of the house, and Erin could still hear him outside, though his voice was now muffled. Terry shook his head. He leaned past Erin to examine the window. He grabbed hold of the crank to open it and gave it a hefty tug. There was a cracking noise around the window, but it didn't move. He got closer to it to see what was going on, then pointed at it.

"There's a screw there to prevent it from being opened."

"That's why I couldn't open it?"

He nodded. "There's no way you could have gotten it open. Not without a screwdriver to take the screw out first, and I don't see how you could do that with your hands behind your back."

Erin rested her head against him. "That makes me feel a little better."

"The best thing to do was to send Joshua back for help. That was the right choice."

"He asked if he should break the window or shoot the lock of the door."

Terry made a noise like something was caught in his throat. "Ack! I'm glad you didn't let him do that."

Erin nodded. He looked at her again and pushed her hair back from her face, studying her expression. "Are you okay?"

"Yes."

"Did he hurt you? Do you want to go to the hospital?"

"No. He didn't do anything. He just… he came to the door and I let him in. He grabbed me, told me not to scream or fight him… I didn't know if he had a gun or other weapon." She closed her eyes. "I just froze."

"That's perfectly natural. Nobody would expect you to fight him. You're a baker."

"I could have escaped. Maybe. If I'd just fought back and pulled away from him. I'm strong."

"Not as strong as a man who works construction every day. With a lot more fighting experience. And not against someone who wouldn't hesitate to hurt you."

Erin still felt guilty, like she had let him down. She tried to put herself in Terry's shoes, to understand how he saw her. She was afraid that he saw her as a helpless woman, which wasn't how she wanted him to see her. She thought about when Joshua had been kidnapped. She had not blamed him. She knew that there was nothing he could have done to prevent it. It wasn't his fault. It was the fault of the person who had kidnapped him. And it was Monroe's fault, and not Erin's, that she had been taken.

It was just hard to convince herself of the fact.

CHAPTER 40

"Do you think you could tell me why he took you? What he said?" Terry prompted.

Erin shivered and looked around. "I'm cold. Do you think we could go somewhere else?"

"Of course. Let's get you to the truck. I can turn the heater on."

He put his arm around her shoulders and helped her off the bed as if she was a frail old woman who might fall down if she weren't supported. But she didn't push him away. She let him hold on to her as he took her out of the house, warm and safe in his grasp.

He escorted her out to the truck. The other members of the police department were there, but there was apparently not a lot to be done now that they had her back and had Monroe in their custody. Erin had expected them to search the house, but they did not go back inside.

"We'll need to get a warrant to search the place," Terry said, following her eyes. "He was right about that part. We can go in to rescue you under exigent circumstances, but to do a full search, we'll need paperwork."

Erin nodded her understanding.

Terry helped her to climb up into the king cab of the truck, although Erin had done it on her own many times. She had to admit she was a little wobbly and didn't mind the assistance. She saw that Joshua was already in the truck waiting. He helped her up from above.

"Miss Erin, are you okay?"

"Thanks to you, yes," she told him, giving him a quick hug.

"I'm sorry I took so long. I only had my bike."

"Oh!" Erin laughed. "I suppose that makes sense. I don't know why I thought you had a car."

Terry slid into the driver's seat. He reached down behind the seat and found a blanket, which he helped Erin to wrap around herself. "There. And we'll put on the heat, too," he worked the controls on the dash.

"Well, don't cook me!" Erin cuddled up in the blanket. "Oh, this is nice. I'm so sore from lying in the same position for so long. I could move around, but I couldn't move my arms and shoulders." She rolled them carefully, working out the stiffness.

Terry looked from Erin to Joshua. "So which one of you wants to tell me how we got here? How is Monroe related to the murders, and how did one or both of you make the connection?"

Erin looked at Joshua, then back at Terry. She shook her head. "I didn't make the connection at all. He showed up at the bakery and I had no idea he was involved with either death. I thought he was there to talk to me about Mrs. Peach's renovation project."

"And you?" Terry nodded to Joshua.

"It was something Miss Erin said when I interviewed her about the first murder. About Perry, the man who was found in the wall."

As if they needed him to clarify which murder they were talking about. There might be more crime than one would expect in Bald Eagle Falls, but there weren't so many murders that they wouldn't know which one Joshua meant.

"Something I said?"

Joshua nodded. "When you were describing the man who was found. His clothing."

Erin thought about it. He'd been wearing blue jeans and a t-shirt. And work boots. She couldn't think of anything unusual or telling that would have connected that body to Monroe. "What about them?"

Terry had been there right after the body was discovered too. He shook his head, mystified as to what Erin had told Joshua that had connected him to Monroe.

"You said that there was a crest on his shirt. The shape of a flying bird."

"Oh, yeah. That's right." Erin shrugged. "I thought it was just a branding thing. How would that lead you to Monroe?"

"I thought it sounded like a company crest. Not just a fashion brand. I didn't know of a brand that was just a flying bird."

"And you managed to find one, obviously," Terry said.

"Yeah. I tried to find something on the internet, but I wasn't finding anything. It was thirty years old, so I guess it wasn't digitized. It wasn't still in use. But I drew it out like Miss Erin described, and Dad said it was Blackbird Construction. So I looked up the old corporate records. The man who was president wasn't around anymore, but his wife was, and I asked her about who had worked with the company. Who might have been on the crew. I didn't tell her it was anything to do with the guy they found in the wall, just that I was doing some Bald Eagle Falls historical stuff."

Terry nodded. "You should have come to us with what you knew."

"I was investigating. Seeing what I could find out for my story."

"That's no excuse. You could still write the story, but maybe you could have avoided other people getting killed or kidnapped if you had come forward with what you knew sooner."

Joshua's mouth twitched. Erin thought he was trying not to look worried or guilty at this accusation. Could anything he did have stopped Monroe? How long had it been since he had made the connection?

"So his wife gave you some names," Erin asked.

"Yeah. I still didn't know which one of them it was. Miguel Ortiz had worked with him. And Howard Monroe. And some other guys I knew were still around town but not in construction anymore. I didn't know which one of them it was. Or if it was any of them. Just because he was working in construction, that didn't mean that his killer was someone he worked with."

"Considering he was entombed in a wall rather than buried in a shallow grave or thrown in a river or down a mine shaft, it's probably a fair guess that whoever killed him had a working knowledge of construction."

Joshua's face was red in the dim light of the truck. "Yeah," he agreed. "That's what I was counting on. But I didn't have any proof, anything that could actually connect them for sure. I didn't know which of the guys working at the company might have been involved. Or if the owner's wife even remembered everyone who had been on the crew at the time. She probably didn't. People forget things in that length of time."

Terry conceded that point. "It would have been nice to have had that information. You going around town asking questions stirs things up. It makes it worse. Maybe he thought it was Erin who was asking questions."

"I don't think it was because of anything Joshua did," Erin interjected. "Monroe thought that Ortiz might have talked to me."

"Why would he have talked to you?"

"I don't know. He was at the reception hall and I was at the reception hall. Or because I was over at the construction site a few times while the men worked, and I might have talked to Ortiz or said something to him that made Monroe think that I knew something. Or maybe because you and I are *together*, he thought Ortiz might come to me for help because it was easier than going to you directly."

"And why would Ortiz want to talk to the police? You think he knew details of Perry's murder?"

"If they were all on the same work crew together? Yes. They knew things about each other. Maybe Ortiz suspected that Monroe had been involved, but he couldn't prove it. I don't know."

"What about Willie?"

Erin shook her head, not understanding. "What about Willie?"

"What does he have to do with all of this?"

"Nothing that I know of. Why? How could he be involved?"

"He went to talk to you when Melissa was having her hair done. Went specifically to keep an eye on the two of you to ensure you were safe. I want to know why."

"I don't know. You'd have to ask him."

"Did he talk to you about Perry or Ortiz?"

Erin massaged her temples, thinking about it. "Uh... I don't know. I don't remember a lot of that conversation. He wondered about a connection between Melissa's dad and Perry. I don't know why. I didn't know that Melissa's dad was a cop."

"Well... he was," Terry admitted. "But he didn't exactly go out on a good note. There were a lot of suspicions about him being on the take. That was before my time. All I've heard are the rumors, and those were pretty quiet because of Melissa. No one wanted to upset her by talking about him being crooked."

"Poor Melissa. It must have been really hard for her."

Terry rolled his eyes. "And then she goes and marries a convict? It obviously didn't damage her too deeply."

But Erin wasn't so sure.

CHAPTER 41

$\mathcal{E}$rin ended up spending much of the day sleeping. She had been exhausted when she got home but couldn't settle in. She had taken a long, hot shower, sat with Orange Blossom going over her planner to try to sort out the upcoming week, and had made cookies. All things that should have calmed her down enough that she could sleep. But it wasn't until mid-afternoon that she had been able to fall asleep. Once she had decided that she wouldn't be able to sleep, of course. Wasn't that always the way it worked?

Then she couldn't wake up. She tried a few times to get up and get out of bed, knowing that there were things she should be doing. But she couldn't rouse herself enough to get out of bed. She just kept lying down to close her eyes for two more minutes, then waking up thirty or forty minutes later, realizing she was running late and there was no way she would be able to get anything done for the day.

Eventually, Terry tapped quietly on the door and spoke to her. "I know you're tired. I didn't know whether I should wake you up for the wedding reception."

"Oh…" Erin rubbed her eyes. "Is Melissa going ahead with it today?" She looked around as if she might have misplaced something. "Wait—how can she have the reception? I didn't have a chance to make a new cake yet!"

"Maybe she decided she could go ahead without one. Everything else was still set up. Maybe she just bought a cake already made from a bakery in the city. I don't know. But she hasn't been hanging around here waiting for you to make one."

Erin couldn't help the guilt that washed over her. But also relief. She didn't want to make another cake. Too much had happened and she didn't want to try it again so soon. Sometime, maybe; she didn't want to throw away the idea of Auntie Clem's making custom wedding cakes. But it was too soon.

"I don't know. I probably shouldn't go, since I didn't get one made. If people think that I'm perfectly well and should have been able to make it…"

"Why are you worrying about what anyone thinks? You have exhausted yourself preparing for the wedding for the past two weeks, and then today, recovering from the…" Terry hesitated, clearly not wanting to call it a kidnapping in case Erin found the word triggering or didn't want to think of it that way. "The way things turned out. You needed to sleep and let your body recover, no matter what anyone else thinks you could have or should have done."

Erin nodded, rubbing her eyes and her face. She would need to get up, have some coffee or something to get her engine running, then get dressed and made up so that she didn't look like something that had crawled out of the black lagoon.

"Melissa will miss you if you don't go," Terry told her. "She thinks the two of you are best friends."

"I'm going," Erin told him. "It's just going to take me a few minutes to get ready." She looked at the time on her phone. "We might be a bit late getting there, but she'll be okay with that. It can't be helped."

"Do you want me to let her know you might be late?"

Erin nodded. "Just send her a text. Don't interrupt her photos or whatever she is doing with a call."

"Is she doing photos?" Terry asked, frowning. "Just of herself?"

"Yeah. She wants pictures of her dress and the decorations. Maybe some extended family or friends in them. I don't know. But she wanted the whole wedding experience. Just… that the groom wouldn't be able to be there for the reception."

Terry rolled his eyes. "Only Melissa would do something like that."

"I think it's very brave of her. And good for her to do what she wants and not worry about how other people judge her. What does it matter to anyone else whether what she does is traditional or 'appropriate'?"

"You're right, of course. I'm just surprised she would dare go against conventions. Most of the time, she's very... careful of what people will think. Maybe you've had an effect on her."

"I don't think it's me. Davis, maybe. Once she was brave enough to let it be known that she was seeing him... everything else has just kind of followed."

Erin arrived at the reception on Terry's arm. Even though she had seen the decorations being set up, she hadn't seen the full effect they would have with the party lighting, Melissa in her dress, and the crowds of well-wishers there to congratulate her on her new path in life. Even if most of them did not approve of her choice, they were at least putting on a good show.

The hall was beautiful with white twinkle lights, gauzy fabric, and fake ivy, as well as cut flowers and table decorations. It was lovely and festive, and Erin would not have guessed that it had been the scene of a murder and police investigation just a day earlier. Erin focused on the present, keeping her mind from wandering to how things had looked when they walked into the hall the previous morning.

And there would be no cake. Or if there was, it would not be the one that Erin had taken so much time and care to create. She looked to where her cake had previously been set up, and there was a multi-tiered display there, so she moved closer to have a look and admire whatever new cake had been provided.

But when she got closer, she saw it was not a cake. It was a dessert display stand with several levels of plates in graduated sizes filled with cupcakes. Erin's eyes teared up when she realized that the beautiful white cupcakes decorated with various techniques were her practice cupcakes. And they were decorated with the roses she had either made for the original cake or that she had made as she was preparing to bake the cakes the night before. Satin ribbons of pink and white with clusters of pearls curled around the cupcakes and were tied to the display's pinnacle.

There was a light touch on Erin's back, and she turned to see Vic smiling down at her. Vic's fine blond hair was pulled away from her face in a French braid decorated with pearls. She looked like a model.

"Did you do this?" Erin asked, looking in her purse for a tissue to dab her eyes before her makeup started to run.

"No, *you* did this. I just assembled them."

Erin found a tissue just as the tears overflowed. She wiped at them and sniffled. "Thank you! I thought I had failed. I didn't have time to make a replacement cake. I slept the day away today. I thought Melissa had to buy one or go without. But this is…"

"So simple and beautiful," Vic finished. "No point in hiding all of these lovely cakes in your freezer. Melissa was delighted."

Erin gave Vic a sideways hug, careful not to rumple her sleek blue dress.

"Thank you so much. What a great idea."

Melissa was circulating the room and headed toward Erin. She was glowing, her dark curls bouncing around her face, a beautiful white satin gown just skimming the floor.

"Erin! I'm so glad you could come." She hugged Erin and brushed both cheeks with a kiss. "Isn't this beautiful? I can't believe everything turned out so well with how quickly you pulled it all together. And your cupcakes! So cute! I just love them."

"I meant to bake and decorate another cake after the other one… got smushed. But I… I ended up not being able to."

"And this was the perfect solution. I just love them. And no need to slice and hand out the cake. People can just take one when the time comes. I'm so glad we didn't let that awful man ruin everything."

"Monroe?" Erin asked, not sure who she meant.

"Ortiz! He should never have been here."

Erin glanced around to make sure that no one was hovering close by. The other guests seemed satisfied with gossiping and eating the hors d'oeuvres that Erin had arranged for, at least for the moment.

"You knew him, didn't you?"

Melissa raised her brows and looked around as if she'd been distracted by something else and hadn't heard her. "Everything just turned out so beautifully."

"It did. Did Miguel Ortiz know your dad?"

Melissa's smile disappeared. "Why would you say that?"

"I didn't know your dad was a cop before. I just thought… maybe Ortiz had a record. Maybe your dad had arrested him before."

"Probably," Melissa conceded. "Being a cop in Bald Eagle Falls, he pretty much knew everyone's record, even if he hadn't arrested them himself. I'm sure Terry would tell you that."

Erin nodded. "Yes. You're probably right. So when he came here… it must have been to talk to you."

"Why?"

"Because he'd known your dad. Maybe he… was trying to talk to you about him. Maybe… to congratulate you on your wedding," Erin finished lamely, knowing that was ridiculous. But was she really going to suggest that Ortiz might have been trying to blackmail Melissa about her father? At her wedding? 'Congratulations, and by the way was your dad crooked and Ortiz trying to extort money from you?' She could not even hint at such a thing, especially on Melissa's big day.

Melissa hadn't been the one to kill Ortiz, so what did it matter why Ortiz had been there?

Melissa gave Erin a long, puzzled look, then apparently decided to take the comment at face value and not pursue what Erin had actually been about to say. She put on a bright smile and squeezed Erin around the shoulders. "I'm so glad that you were well enough to come tonight. I was worried that you wouldn't be able to after everything that happened last night. Get some munchies and enjoy yourself. We'll 'cut the cake' and start the dance in about an hour."

She steered Erin toward the tables that were filling with chattering guests. Erin glanced around for Terry, but he seemed to have disappeared, off talking with one of his friends or on the phone with Sheriff Wilmot, probably. Erin and Vic drifted over to the goodie table and picked out a few canapés. Erin looked around for Mary Lou but didn't see anyone from her family there. They had probably decided to lie low after being out so late the night before. She and Vic selected an empty table.

CHAPTER 42

*I*n a few minutes, Willie joined them with a plate loaded with considerably more food than Erin's and Vic's. He grinned and set down a plastic cup of wine as well.

"It's a party. You wouldn't want Melissa to think that her efforts were unappreciated. And I know that Erin was in charge of the food, so it's bound to be good."

Erin's face warmed. "I didn't actually *make* the food, except for the baking, so I can't speak to how it turned out... but it was highly recommended, and everything I've had so far has been very nice."

Willie nodded, digging into some hot wings immediately. He must have worked up a good appetite on the crew working on Mrs. Peach's house. Or else he had been catching up on his work, having left it while working on the crew.

"Were you back to your own work today?" Erin asked tentatively.

"Yeah. Everything is done at Mrs. Peach's. All of the finishing too. When I left for work this morning, the crew was clearing all of the equipment and refuse out of the yard. It should be in pristine condition for Mrs. Peach's return."

"Oh, good. I didn't know... well, I couldn't exactly go to Mr. Monroe to ask him if everything was done, could I?"

Willie laughed loudly. "Are you telling me that you didn't ask him that last night? I would think that would have been the most burning question on your mind."

Erin shook her head, her cheeks getting even hotter. People were looking at them, curious about Willie's laugh.

"It didn't come up," she told Willie as dryly as possible. "And I didn't have my planner with me to check my to-do list."

Willie snickered appreciatively and Vic smiled.

People started attending to their own conversations again. Erin studied Willie. "I still haven't figured out why you checked up on Melissa and me after we found Mr. Ortiz. Did you know it was Mr. Monroe?"

Willie had a sip of wine, considering the answer. He looked around to make sure no one was listening in. Probably looking for Terry in particular.

"You wearing a wire?" Willie asked, giving Erin another smile and selecting a bacon-wrapped scallop from his plate.

"It's just me and Vic."

It still took him a few more seconds to decide how to answer her. He spoke slowly. "I didn't know it was Monroe. He was one of the possibilities, but not the only one. And I didn't know who else was around. The few men I was aware of were not necessarily the only suspects in the case."

"Which case?"

"Jack Perry's murder. It's been many years, and a lot can change in that time. People move. Change their names. Pretend that they have put it behind them. And then... something like this happens. You realize that..." He stared off into space, considering. "The dead are not gone after all."

"How could you know anything about the Perry murder?" Vic demanded. "You would have just been a kid when he was killed. How old, seven or eight?"

Willie nodded his agreement. "Yeah. Something like that. When I was a kid... I was interested in everything—building and figuring out how things work. I liked to do things with my hands. I was very mechanically minded. Not so good about school stuff. I was too active. Didn't like to sit down and be quiet for my teachers. I was okay at the three R's, just not the social or behavioral stuff."

None of this came as a surprise to Erin. He had been good with his hands as long as she had known him, but he also couldn't stick to one thing. He had his mines, which he visited in some kind of rotation, and not only did he mine the minerals, but he did processing by himself as well, something few people did. And he did search and rescue around Bald Eagle Falls and knew a lot about first aid and emergency medical care. He helped out with smaller jobs, was involved in some security and computer network stuff with Nelson Dyson, and who knew what else. He never told anyone exactly what he was up to from one day to the next, not even Vic. While they could have lived together, he preferred to keep a separate residence and was not at Vic's loft every day. He was the kind of person who was constantly moving from one thing to the next.

"So, what, you hung around construction sites?"

Willie shrugged. "Yeah. I mean, they weren't big construction sites like in the city. More like the stuff that we were doing for Mrs. Peach. Renovations and small building projects. Repairs. Rebuilding fences, upgrading wiring, stopping a leak, replacing a toilet. I wanted to be in on all of it. My dad figured if it kept me out of his hair, why not? He didn't have a problem with me hanging around watching stuff."

"But what about the workers? They didn't mind a seven-year-old underfoot?"

"As long as it was something I was interested in, I could be as quiet and still as a mouse. I stayed out of the way, but if I could help with something—even just handing a worker his tools—then I got involved. Learned from the ground up, a little bit at a time. Sometimes they gave me a responsibility. Run a message. Go to the store, pick up something on their account, and bring it back. Free labor; why not take advantage of it?"

"Did you work on Mrs. Peach's house back then?"

"I don't remember if I specifically hung out at her house. Probably. But I worked with Blackbird enough. I knew all of the guys who were on the crew back then."

"So when Jack Perry was found, you remembered him."

"Yeah. He worked for Blackbird. He wasn't one of the guys who let me do stuff with him; he'd only let me watch, and only if I stayed out of the way. But I remembered him. And I figured if he was entombed in the wall like that... then it was one of the construction workers. If it had been someone else... Melissa's father," he nodded to her visiting with a couple that Erin didn't recognize, "or a bookie or a drug deal gone bad... it would be different. No one like that would wall him in. That had to be someone in construction."

Erin nibbled on a mini quiche, nodding. That made sense to her. She had come to the same conclusion. Not just anyone would bury him in a wall.

"I knew that some of the guys who had been with Blackbird back then were still in town, but a lot of them had moved out of town or retired or gone into something else. And I was just a kid; I didn't even know everyone's last names."

"Did you tell Terry that you thought it was someone from the construction crew?"

"From the *Blackbird* construction crew," Willie corrected. "No, I didn't." His eyes moved around the room, seeking Terry out and ensuring he was well out of earshot. "He had the same clues as I did. He knew Perry had been in construction and had been walled in. Nothing else made sense. It had to be another construction worker."

And Willie didn't like talking to the police, despite claiming he wasn't doing anything illegal. He said he didn't have anything else to do with the Dyson family, but Erin believed he did. At least with Nelson Dyson. Maybe Nelson wasn't working with his clan anymore. He had said that he was building his own network. But he was still dangerous and Erin didn't like the thought of Willie being mixed in with his organization.

"And then you heard that Erin and Melissa had found Ortiz's body here," Vic said, indicating the hall with a movement of her head. "And you knew Ortiz had worked with the construction crew too."

"Right." Willie had made good headway on his meal and was already looking back at the buffet table again, eyeing what food remained. "I figured that the only reason Ortiz would be killed was if he had confronted Perry's killer. Said he knew him and knew what had happened. Or something along those lines. And the only reason for Ortiz to tell the killer that he could identify him was to blackmail him."

Confronting a killer was a dangerous move. Wasn't he more likely to be killed than paid for his trouble?

"So you came to Serena's to keep an eye on us." Erin shook her head.

"Why? Why would we be targets? We didn't know anything about the killer. We didn't see anything. He was long gone by the time we found the body. Stayner said Ortiz had been dead for hours."

"I had to make sure you didn't know anything. Or say anything to make the killer think you knew anything. Melissa's dad was a cop. He might have known who Perry's rivals were. He might have made notes that she still had, or have said something to her mother long ago when Melissa was within hearing distance. People keep or remember things from their childhood. Even if they don't seem like sentimental people. Melissa… likes to talk about things. And if Perry's body being found or finding Ortiz like that triggered a memory, something she wanted to discuss…"

"That gal's tongue wags at both ends," Vic proclaimed.

"To put it charitably."

"And you…" Willie looked at Erin and shook his head slowly, as if she'd failed a medical test. "You had them working right next door. You saw both bodies. You were talking to Monroe and the work crew nearly every day. You got me and Foster onto the crew, and either one of us could have been a spy. You live with a cop. Were making wedding plans with Melissa. Do you know how many people might have said something to you that pointed you out to the killer?"

"Uh…" Erin scratched the back of her neck. "I guess not. I was pretty oblivious. I just wanted to get the cake made for Melissa's wedding and have Mrs. Peach's renovation done by the time she got back."

"But it was Joshua who figured out who it was," Vic said. "How did he?"

Erin told him about Joshua realizing that the crest on his shirt was the logo for the old construction company and then tracing the ownership and employees of the company.

"Not bad," Willie said admiringly. "The boy's got a good head on his shoulders. Other than possibly alerting Monroe to the fact that someone was asking all of the right questions."

"It wasn't Joshua's fault," Erin said firmly. "And he's the one who found where I was being held hostage. He's the one responsible for saving me."

"How did he know it was Monroe and not one of the others?"

"He didn't. He just started with someone whose property was more remote. Figured that a killer wouldn't want to hold anyone right here in the middle of town. If he hadn't found me there, he had a list. He was going to start with the farthest one away and work his way to the closest."

"He's a smart cookie," Vic declared. "And *you* were lucky. I was so scared that we wouldn't find you alive."

CHAPTER 43

*P*eter Foster climbed up on one of the empty chairs at Erin's table. His face shone with excitement. Erin had seen him helping to take care of his siblings earlier, but he seemed to have managed to rid himself of that responsibility for a few minutes in order to talk to her.

"Miss Melissa said I can have one of the little wedding cakes," Peter declared, grinning widely. "She says since you made them, she knows they're safe for me to eat."

"Well, she's right. When I said she might want to get someone from the city, someone with more experience with wedding cakes, she said that she wanted it to be gluten-free so that you and everyone else could eat it. She was looking out for you."

"She's nice. I like her... but not as much as you."

"Well, Melissa doesn't make you cupcakes, does she?"

"No," Peter agreed. "And I *like* cupcakes."

He knelt on the chair, looking around in satisfaction as if he'd organized everything himself.

"How's your mom doing?" Erin asked. "I didn't see your dad here tonight."

"She said she could look after the kids for a few minutes so I could talk to you." His lips pressed together and he looked very solemn. "Dad was in a fight."

"I know. I was almost there when it happened. I'm sorry he got hurt."

"Mom said it is *reprehensible*, him fighting like that. He can't go back there, but Mom said he couldn't go back anyway; she'd be too ashamed of how he behaved."

"Oh… well, does your mom know that he was fighting because of the things the other man said about her and you kids? That he was defending you?"

Peter's eyes widened. "Really?"

"Yeah. That's what I heard from Willie Andrews," Erin nodded to Willie, who was back at the serving table again. "He was there when it happened."

"Why would he say things about Mom?"

"He wasn't very nice. He was irritated with some things that your dad said, so he decided to be mean about it, hurt your dad or get him angry."

"That's not very mature."

"No," Erin agreed. "It's something that bullies do. But… that man died, so he's not going to bug your dad anymore."

Peter accepted this. "I wish he could get a job he could keep. So he could make enough money."

"I know. It's tough. What about… something through your church? I get the feeling he likes to talk about church stuff a lot, and some people don't like that. But maybe if he had a church job, it would be a better fit."

"We don't exactly have a church. Mom and Dad teach us at home. And we watch meetings on the computer. But we don't go to a church here."

"Oh." Erin didn't want to suggest they go to one of the established churches in Bald Eagle Falls, since their teachings might contradict what the Fosters believed. She'd have to think about other suggestions. It was hard to find employment for someone who preached religion on the job. She couldn't exactly tell Mr. Foster that he was wrong to proselytize on the job. Some churches pushed for their members to do that kind of thing. "Well, I hope he can find something that works for him."

"Me too," Peter agreed.

At that point, Melissa called for everyone's attention and brandished a knife at the cupcake display table. "It's time for the ceremonial cutting of the cake!" she announced. She didn't point out that they didn't have a big cake because of what had happened the day before. She thanked Erin for making the cupcakes and seeing to the other catering. Then she pointed her knife at several different cupcakes as if threatening to slice each, evoking laughter. Eventually, she picked one and sliced it neatly in half. She picked it up. "Normally, this is the point where the bride and groom shove cake into each other's mouths and make a big mess." She wrinkled her nose. "I never did like that tradition. Since it's just me, and I'd look weird shoving cake messily into my own mouth, I'm just going to have a dainty bite!"

She picked one of the cupcake halves and did just that. She lifted the remaining bite of cupcake and raised it as if to toast her guests. "Please help yourself to a cupcake. When they are all gone, there will also be some sheet cakes on the serving table. But make sure anyone who eats gluten-free gets first choice at the cupcakes."

She put the knife down. "And now, cue the band. It's time to dance."

The DJ started his playlist. There was a smattering of applause and then a rush for the cupcake table.

There were lights on in Mrs. Peach's house when Erin got home. Willie had said all the work had been completed, so Erin wasn't sure who would still be there.

"I'm just going to take a look and make sure everything is okay," she told Terry, climbing down from the truck.

"You know, I'm the cop; it's kind of my job to check out trouble."

"I don't think there's any trouble. I just want to make sure it isn't anyone who shouldn't be there."

"Like I said… I am trained…"

"You can watch me over," Erin conceded. "But you don't need to come."

She walked confidently over to Mrs. Peach's house, trying not to think about the things that must be running through Terry's mind about intruders and kidnappers and everything else that a cop knew could go wrong because he saw them every day. She was just walking next door. Nothing bad was going to happen.

Erin stood on the front step and knocked. In a few minutes, Mrs. Peach herself opened the door. Erin waved to Terry to let him know that everything was okay.

"You're back! I hope everything looks good and they got all the junk cleaned up," Erin said worriedly, trying to look past Mrs. Peach. But the work that had been done was beyond another wall, so she couldn't see even if she could get a clear line of sight behind Mrs. Peach.

"Yes, it's perfect," Mrs. Peach assured her. "Come in for a moment and see."

Erin followed Mrs. Peach's slow footsteps into the house, to the back where the additional room had been built. Erin looked around. The hot tub was filled with clear blue water, the scent of chlorine in the air. The potted trees and plants purchased for the greenhouse were scattered throughout the room, making it look like a forest clearing if she used her imagination.

No sign of any dead bodies. No holes in the wall or work left undone.

"Would you like to join me for a soak in the hot tub?" Mrs. Peach asked. "After traveling today, I can't think of anything better."

"Thank you… I would, but I'm beat. I'd fall asleep in there. Maybe another day."

"Well, you feel free any time. There's a standing invitation."

Erin walked over to her house. Terry had released K9 from duty and the dog was nosing around the back of the couch looking for Marshmallow, the rabbit.

"Mrs. Peach is back?" Terry asked.

"Yes. Everything is all finished… it looks good."

"No bodies?"

Erin *had* been half expecting to find someone floating in the hot tub.

"No bodies."

"Good." Terry pulled her in for a hug. "Now everything can go back to normal."

A WAFFLE DEATH

For those who stand firm
when something waffle happens

CHAPTER 1

The warm morning sunshine spilled into the bakery and glinted off the glass of the display case at the front of Auntie Clem's Bakery. Erin studied it to make sure that everything was in order. And of course, it was. She and Vic had been doing this long enough to know how to arrange everything quickly and efficiently before opening the store in the morning. The baked goods she loved filled the case: muffins with fat blueberries bursting out of the tops, breads sprinkled with sugar, cinnamon rolls glinting with icing. The smells of yeast and spices perfumed the air. Erin walked through the front of the shop to turn the sign to Open and unlock the door. A few morning customers were already waiting outside with their piping hot coffees, ready to pick up a morning muffin or the baked goods they would require for the day or the week.

"Good morning!" Erin greeted cheerfully.

It was still early for the rest of the townspeople, so she didn't get enthusiastic smiles in response. A few muted greetings. People would be more cheerful once they finished waking up.

Vic stood behind the counter, her long blond hair pinned back in a bun and hidden by her baker's cap. Erin's young transgender employee always succeeded in looking more polished five minutes after rolling out of bed than Erin felt after an hour of preening and trying to pin her dark hair back so that no locks would escape. She never even reached the door without a few strands managing to spring free.

"What can I get y'all today?" Vic asked the ladies.

Mary Lou moved forward and made a few selections. Her baking for the week. Erin knew that things were tight for the Coxes. Mary Lou struggled to make ends meet. Her husband, Roger, had lost their life savings and house in a bad investment a few years previous and, since then, the family had experienced a number of serious setbacks. Roger had been hospitalized for most of the past year but was back home again, which was an extra burden on Mary Lou financially, as well as physically and emotionally. She had one teenage son still at home to help with Roger's care, and health care workers that checked in a couple of times a day, but the lion's share of making sure that he was kept calm and happy and didn't wander still fell to her.

Erin wanted to offer Mary Lou more of the day-old baking they gave to needy families for free, but knew that she couldn't say anything about it in front of the other ladies. Mary Lou knew she could come to the back of the store to pick up day-old privately, but she was a proud woman and would not accept Erin's "charity" unless Erin managed to frame it as a favor to her, something that she couldn't get away with very often.

Mary Lou smoothed her wrinkle-free pantsuit over her hips as she waited for Vic to package up her order and put it through at the till. Erin slipped behind Vic to take up her position behind the counter to help the next customer. She smiled at Mary Lou.

"How is everyone in your home today? Everyone okay?"

Mary Lou gave a brief nod. "Yes, fine, thank you, Erin. And you? Have you recovered from your..." Mary Lou trailed off and didn't say "kidnapping" or "abduction." She probably would have preferred something more generic, like "incident," but she just let the sentence hang. Erin could fill it in as she liked.

"Oh, yes," Erin told her cheerfully. "I'm just fine. Thanks to Joshua, I'm perfectly well."

She kept a smile on her face, not letting Mary Lou see any cracks. Mary Lou didn't need anything else on her plate to worry about. Her son, Joshua, was the one who had rescued Erin—or at least found her so that the police could rescue her—and Erin knew that she couldn't say too much about what he had done. Mary Lou wanted to keep him safe. She didn't want him running around into dangerous situations, rescuing people. Let the police do the footwork. Joshua needed to be in school, earning his high school diploma, rather than pursuing a career as an investigative journalist before he was even an adult.

But Joshua had other ideas about the matter. He would, Erin hoped, go back to school in the fall with Bella Prost and the other teens. Bella was one of Erin's part-time employees and for months had been gently encouraging Joshua to return to school. Erin hoped she succeeded.

Mary Lou didn't need anything else to worry about, least of all the increased anxiety and nightmares that had plagued Erin since her abduction. It wasn't like she'd been the best sleeper before. It was a struggle to get the sleep that she needed to get to the bakery in the small hours of the morning in order to have the fresh breads and muffins ready to go when they opened.

"Now that the wedding is over, you can go back to normal," Vic told Erin. "No more wedding cake. Until the next one." She smiled cheekily. Melissa's wedding cake had been a one-off, a favor for a friend. Erin had not planned on taking on more. But Vic thought it would make a good addition to the bakery's offerings if Erin were willing to take them on.

Erin hadn't decided yet. There had been too much else going on at the same time as decorating Melissa's cake. She hadn't yet sorted out her feelings and separated the negative emotions about certain other events from that of preparing Melissa's beautiful wedding cake, which had ended up being crushed. At least Vic's creativity had saved the day so that they had still been able to pull off the fairy-tale wedding reception that Melissa had dreamed of.

"Did you get a thank you card yet?" Lottie Sturm asked the others in the bakery. "I haven't gotten a thank you for my wedding gift yet. When I was a young person, there were certain expectations…"

Erin actually had received a very nice thank you card from Melissa the week before, but she wasn't about to announce the fact to Lottie, as it would just encourage her complaints that Melissa hadn't sent her a card yet. Erin imagined that Melissa had sent notes to those who had helped with the reception before those who had given her a gift. It had been a big reception, so there would be a lot of cards to send out. Melissa was probably attacking the process in small batches. Lottie would receive hers in the mail in the next few days.

"It isn't like it was a *real* wedding," Cindy Prost contributed. Of course she would say something like that. Cindy was Bella's mother, and her natural disposition was the opposite of her daughter's cheerful, helpful attitude. Cindy was as negative as Bella was positive.

"Of course it was a real wedding," Vic objected. "How can you say that?"

"Well, there was no groom at the reception, was there?" Cindy pointed out the obvious. Davis, Melissa's new husband, was a guest of the Tennessee penal system and would not be going to any community events in the next few years.

"But they still got married," Erin said, removing the bread and buns Lottie pointed to from the display case. "Davis doesn't have to attend the reception for the marriage to be legal."

"I'm not talking about *legal*." Cindy wrinkled her nose. "And it isn't like any of us witnessed the actual marriage, *if* there even was one. All you have is her own word on that."

"Why would she pretend to be getting married?"

"Because she wants certain benefits of being married." Lottie tittered. "But without all of the responsibilities of a wife."

Erin opened her mouth to ask what benefits Lottie was talking about, then closed it again. As far as the church ladies were concerned, any extracurricular activities outside of marriage were a sin so, as far as Lottie was concerned, Melissa had to be married to Davis for her friendly visits to the prison to progress to conjugal visits. As far as Erin knew, Melissa probably believed this too, but they had never discussed it. Why would they? Such a thing was none of Erin's business.

But it was, apparently, the business of the rest of the members of Melissa's congregation in Bald Eagle Falls. Lottie and Cindy immediately fell into a spirited debate about whether Melissa was really married in the eyes of God if she wasn't living with Davis and keeping house for him. There was more to marriage than just "visiting" with Davis at the prison.

Erin looked at Mary Lou to see what her opinion of the discussion was, but her mind appeared to be somewhere else. Erin wasn't sure she had heard a word of Lottie's and Cindy's discussion. Erin wished that she could have blocked it out herself. She didn't look at Vic. All she would need was Vic rolling her eyes expressively, and she would not be able to keep a straight face and would have to excuse herself to the kitchen to check on a batch of cookies.

"Did you hear about the waffle contest?" Erin asked in an effort to distract the ladies from the discussion about Melissa's intimate affairs.

Lottie stopped talking and looked at Erin. There was silence in the bakery.

"What waffle contest?" Vic answered obligingly, even though she knew very well what waffle contest Erin was asking about.

"Yes, what contest?" Lottie asked. She didn't actually look at all interested.

"There is a waffle recipe contest being run by The Kitchen Crew commercial bakeware company. The grand prize is a restaurant-sized waffle maker that makes twenty Belgian waffles in one go."

"Twenty waffles?"

"Yes, it has the molds for twenty waffles. You fill them all with batter, close the lid, and wait five minutes for them to cook. Open the lid, and presto—twenty perfectly cooked waffles."

"Are you planning to open a waffle house?" Cindy asked dryly. "Don't you have enough to keep you going with the ownership of the bakery?"

"I think waffles would be a great offering for Auntie Clem's. Fresh or frozen. Wouldn't you rather buy waffles made right here in the bakery than those frozen ones at the grocery?" Vic asked. "Sometimes those have been sitting in the grocer's freezer for months, and they're just mass-produced and churned out. Nothing like a handcrafted waffle made from one of Erin's special recipes."

Cindy looked as if she didn't know whether to agree or to find some-thing nasty to say about Erin's recipes. If she didn't want to get thrown out of the bakery, she should probably keep her mouth shut.

"Have you already submitted a recipe to this contest?" she asked Erin stiffly. "I suppose you already have a dozen waffle recipes ready to go when you win that big waffle iron."

"Not yet." Erin handed Lottie's order to Vic to ring up on the register. "You're only allowed to enter one recipe into the contest, and I'm still trying to design the *perfect* gluten-free waffle recipe. It has to be just right if I want to have any hope of winning the waffle iron."

"It's never going to be exactly like a normal waffle." Cindy was not afraid to rain on Erin's parade. She never complained about the gluten-free baked goods she bought from Erin every week. They were delicious, and no one would ever have guessed they were gluten-free unless they were told so. But Cindy was right; they would never have the exact same flavor and consistency as a traditional Belgian waffle. A lot of kitchen chemistry and experimentation went into getting the recipe for each of the baked goods that Erin sold *just right*. So that they were not only as good as the regular gluten goods offered at the grocery store, but much better.

"I'm thinking of a pumpkin-based recipe," Erin told them, ignoring Cindy's jab and pretending she had asked in a nice way what Erin had in mind for the contest. "Pumpkin and spices, nutmeg and cinnamon. Nice and light and crisp, but with a hearty, rich flavor. Something that will remind people of Thanksgiving and Christmas and all of the good feelings surrounding those holidays and could be used for sweet or savory toppings."

"Mmm. I love pumpkin spice," Lottie confessed. "*Anything* pumpkin spice." She beamed at Erin as if she were a child who had just pulled off a perfect math score. "Great idea!"

"That sounds really good," Vic agreed. "Drizzled with a little syrup and topped with whipped cream…"

Someone else moaned in agreement. Erin smiled, pleased. Not everyone liked pumpkin spice or the idea of waffles that could be savory or sweet, so she was happy to hear the approvals of her plan.

"I hope you win," Lottie said. "Then you can start including those waffles in your regular offerings."

"What about chocolate chip waffles?" Cindy suggested. "Or blueberry."

"If she had that big waffle iron, she could make any kind you liked." Lottie licked her lips. "Blueberry or raspberry, cinnamon swirl, chocolate chip, *white* chocolate chip…"

"M&M," Lottie took up the list of candies that could be added to the batter.

"M&M?" Cindy repeated, sounding shocked.

"If you can put them in cookies, why not in waffles? Or gumdrops!"

CHAPTER 2

The ladies finished their purchases and left, still discussing what additives were or were not appropriate for waffles.

When the early morning rush was finished and they were tidying up and preparing cookies and pizza pretzels, Vic looked over at Erin. "So, you don't have any concerns about entering this waffle contest?"

"Concerns?" Erin shook her head. "No, what kind of concerns? It's a big company, I'm sure it's legit. And they say you retain the ownership of your recipe. So many of these contests are actually scams to get your recipes. You transfer rights to them whether you win or not. With this contest... the worst that could happen is that I develop a really good waffle recipe and don't win the prize."

"No, I was thinking more along the lines of... the other contests we've been involved with the last couple of years."

There was the Fall Fair contest where Erin had entered a gluten-free stack cake. She had won the contest, which had been very exciting. The cruise that she had won, however, had been another story. Things had gone off the rails surprisingly quickly—if a boat could be said to go off the rails.

And then there was the CO2 contest she had judged, where entrants used CO2 to make fizzy drinks or ice cream. She should have known when she found Beryl in the walk-in freezer at the restaurant that things were not going to end well.

Erin grimaced back at Vic. "Well, I wasn't thinking about any of that stuff. I'm sure that… everything will be just fine. Nothing will go wrong this time."

Erin's sweetheart, Terry Piper or, as Vic liked to call him, "Officer Handsome," stopped by during the afternoon lull to refill his water bottle and get a gluten-free doggie biscuit for his furry partner, K9. He sat down for a moment while Erin went into the kitchen to fill the bottle, and smiled at her when she returned, a dimple appearing on his cheek. Boyishly handsome with a five o'clock shadow and a dimple. Erin's heart did a flip when she looked at him. She handed him the water bottle, looking away and hoping he wouldn't see her blush. It was rather silly that she should have such a physical reaction to his good looks when they were living together and the magic should have worn off. After all of the challenges that they had been through, they were like a comfortable old married couple.

Sometimes.

But there were still those sparks.

When she looked back at Terry, his eyes were dancing, and she knew he was thinking the same thing. He scratched K9's ears and looked to see if he was finished eating his cookie.

"Well, buddy, I guess we'd better hit the pavement again."

K9 got to his feet and shook himself off as if he were wet. Then he was ready for them to be on their way again.

Erin looked at the clock on the wall, frowning. It was nearly time to close, and she had expected Naomi to stop by with a couple of platters. Erin had taken treats over to The Book Nook for their book club meeting, and Naomi had said that she would return the platters when they were done. She was usually very good about it, but The Book Nook closed earlier than Auntie Clem's Bakery on Tuesdays, and Erin was expecting her to have returned them by now.

"What's up?" Vic asked, noticing Erin's look at the clock.

"I think I'll just pop over to The Book Nook to see if I can get those platters back."

"They're probably closed by now."

"Maybe. I'll just see. If they are, I guess I'll get them back tomorrow."

Vic nodded. The bakery was not busy; she could certainly handle things by herself for the five minutes it would take Erin to duck into The Book Nook and retrieve the platters. Even if she stopped to talk to Naomi for a few minutes.

Erin didn't bother to take off her apron. It would only be a minute and she wouldn't spill anything on it at the bookstore.

It was hot and muggy outside. The bright sun reflected off the colorful storefronts and awnings of Main Street, dazzling Erin. She wasn't sure she would ever get used to Tennessee summers. She should be able to handle them; after all, she had been born in Tennessee, but she had spent most of her years in Maine and other places in the north and had apparently lost any tolerance for the southern sun. She was sweating by the time she got into The Book Nook, which didn't seem like it should be possible. The bells over the door jingled as she walked in, just like they did at Auntie Clem's Bakery. A friendly little sound that announced the possibility of a sale. Erin looked around for Naomi but didn't see her immediately.

That wasn't unusual. With all of the shelves blocking her line of sight, Naomi could be a few feet away from her and Erin wouldn't know it. Especially if she were crouching down to shelve a book. Erin walked farther into the store, looking around, peeking between bookshelves, expecting to see the store owner at any moment. The front door had been unlocked, so Naomi couldn't have closed and gone home already.

"Naomi?"

Erin stood on her tiptoes and spun in a slow circle. "Are you here?"

She was probably taking a bag of trash out to the dumpster behind the building. Erin held herself still and waited. Naomi would only be gone from the store for a minute or two.

The seconds ticked by. Erin looked at her phone several times, but that didn't help the time go any faster. She walked through the employee-only area in the back and pushed the crash bar on the back door to open it. She looked around, but Naomi wasn't in the parking lot. Neither was her car. Had she really left and forgotten to lock the front door? Maybe there had been an emergency and she had been too distracted, forgetting everything she had to do before leaving. It was understandable. Things like that happened sometimes.

As Erin walked back toward the front door, trying to decide the right thing to do, she saw that the door to the stairs was cracked open. What if Naomi had fallen and broken her leg, or worse? What if she was lying hurt or unconscious in the basement in need of rescue? Erin opened the door farther. The hinges creaked noisily, making her wince and put her shoulders up as if to brace herself against what was coming next.

"Naomi? Naomi, are you down there?"

She thought she could hear someone moving around, but there was no answer.

"Naomi?"

Was she hurt and unable to answer? Or maybe she was moving around the basement stockroom with earbuds in and couldn't hear Erin. Erin waited a few more seconds, each one ticking by with several beats of her thumping heart. She stepped down to the first step.

"Naomi?" she called again, as if being one step closer would make all the difference.

There were noises. The shuffling of shoes or books? Or someone lying on the floor writhing in distress? Erin tilted her head, trying to see into the basement before she was all the way down the stairs, but it was impossible to see through the walls and shelving units.

Erin tiptoed. She wasn't sure why; she had called out to Naomi already and wanted her to hear her. She didn't like intruding on Naomi's "employees only" space. A stair creaked, and she winced. But she was down to the bottom of the stairs in a few more seconds. She looked around. She could say that she was looking for her platters. Or for Naomi. But she felt like she was trespassing. She hesitated, deciding whether to complete her search or just run upstairs and pretend that she hadn't ever been down there.

But she was just there to make sure that Naomi was okay and to figure out what to do about locking the store up for her. It was the neighborly thing to do when you discovered that another store owner had accidentally left the place unlocked.

Erin didn't call out again, but made a swift circuit. She could go through the stockroom once and then go upstairs, knowing she had checked everything out and done the right thing.

It was creepy. She loved libraries and bookstores, but the basement of The Book Nook seemed hollow and ominous. She was sure Naomi wasn't down there. She wasn't listening to her headphones and just hadn't been able to hear Erin calling her. She wasn't restocking shelves or unpacking a box of new books. There was no one there. Maybe she had misheard the sounds. She'd always had a vivid imagination.

There was a hint of cologne in the air, a smell that a man she had once known had worn. It sent a shiver over her. One of Naomi's employees must wear the same scent. She didn't know the part-timers very well, just Naomi herself.

Erin rounded the corner of the shelves and saw a crumpled form at the end of the aisle.

CHAPTER 3

*E*rin ran forward. It was only a few strides sprinting, and she knew it wasn't Naomi by the time she got there. The shape was bigger and bulkier than Naomi. The shiny black shoes on the legs lying akimbo were men's shoes, not ladies'.

"Are you okay?" Erin asked breathlessly. The words came out as barely a whisper, even though she had meant to be loud and authoritative. She could take charge, give the person some medical assistance, and everything would be okay. It was just someone who had tripped or fainted—easily fixed.

The figure didn't move, even when Erin reached down and shook him by the arm.

"Sir? Are you all right?" she whispered.

He wasn't all right. Something was very wrong with him. There was no resistance in the muscles and joints. No resistance to her shaking. She pulled him up slightly to look at his face and assess what kind of medical help he needed.

She saw the hilt of a knife sticking out of his chest, but ignored it, looking at his still, gray face. This was bad. Worse than she could have imagined.

Erin felt for a pulse on his neck, breathing loudly through her mouth. She had a sense of urgency and, at the same time, felt like she was pushing her way through concrete. She felt for her phone and eventually found it in one of her apron pockets. She pushed the button to wake it up. They would need a stretcher or gurney of some kind to get him out of there. They needed to be prepared for a trauma, and she wasn't sure if anyone in Bald Eagle Falls had the required training. There was only one ambulance in town, assuming it hadn't been called out somewhere. Was it stocked with blood? Enough to get this man to the city for treatment before he bled out?

She couldn't seem to get her fingers to push the right buttons on the screen to initiate a phone call. Eventually, there was a series of beeps and Call Failed popped up on the screen. Erin tried Terry's phone number instead of the emergency dispatcher's number. At least she would be able to get through to him. He would sort things out and ensure everything was taken care of.

Despite her best efforts, she wasn't able to avoid looking at the hilt of the knife. She remembered Jack Ward, a knife hilt sticking out of his back, talking and complaining to her about getting stabbed. He had miraculously survived until they could get him to the hospital and surgery. He recovered from the stab wounds faster than Terry had recovered from his head injury. Maybe this victim would be lucky too. Maybe he could still be saved if she could get help.

She looked at her phone, but the call to Terry had also failed.

She didn't want to touch the man. Her flesh crawled and she could hardly bring herself to look at him, but she forced herself to put a finger to his neck, looking for his carotid pulse. Or maybe she would be able to feel him breathing. But she couldn't find any sign of life.

That didn't mean he couldn't be saved. She'd seen things on crime TV that were unbelievable. People that police thought were murder victims when they arrived at a scene but who had survived to name their attacker and recover and live for years. She didn't know how long or what their quality of life was, but just the fact that they had survived when the cops thought they were dead was miraculous.

She took a deep breath and let it out. She tapped Terry's name once more on her phone, and it again failed. The basement was blocking her signal—too much concrete. Or maybe there was radon or something that interfered with the signal. But she wasn't going to be able to get through while she remained downstairs.

Erin abandoned the man crumpled on the floor and hurried up the stairs. She was back at Auntie Clem's in a minute, the phone to her ear, breathing heavily. It shouldn't have taken so much out of her to go up the stairs and back to the bakery. It must have been the adrenaline. She couldn't be that out of shape.

"Erin?" Vic looked at her with wide eyes. "What's wrong? What happened?"

Erin imagined she must be pale and wide-eyed. Or Vic had been startled by her dashing back into Auntie Clem's as if she were being chased. She waved a hand at Vic to indicate that she would explain when she could, waiting for Terry to pick up the phone.

"Erin," Terry's voice was calm and pleasant, "are you off already?"

"Need help—someone in the basement of The Book Nook. Hurt. Stabbed." Erin's sentences were short because of her breathing. And maybe because she was having trouble putting coherent sentences together. It seemed like it took way too many words to explain what was happening. And the longer she took explaining, the longer it was going to take for help to arrive.

"What?" Terry's voice was now urgent. But he didn't make her repeat herself or calm down and take longer to explain. "I'll be over there right away. Are you there now?"

"No. Auntie Clem's. No signal."

"Stay put until someone comes to get you."

"Okay."

He hung up. She knew he had to hang up on her to call the dispatcher and get an ambulance and the rest of the police department over to The Book Nook, but she still felt hurt that he had disconnected without even saying goodbye. Or that she had done a good job and he was proud of her.

There would be questions.

She knew there were going to be a lot of questions.

CHAPTER 4

*B*ald Eagle Falls was a small town. It didn't take long before Erin
heard the sirens. The sounds grew louder and louder until they
were piercing. Then Terry was there. He pulled his car in front of The
Book Nook. The red and blue lights danced across the front wall of the
bookstore. Terry didn't come to Auntie Clem's first, but waited for Stayner
to arrive. Stayner left his cruiser and walked over to join Terry. Terry
moved cautiously into The Book Nook with his gun drawn, K9 at his
side, and Stayner just behind him and to the other side. They were graceful, like dancers or synchronized swimmers. Or like an air show with
planes moving in tandem. Their movements were neat and precise. Then
they were out of her view, and she could only imagine them proceeding
through the store and down the stairs to the basement.

They were back out before Erin expected them to be. Terry had put
his gun back in its holster. There was no one else in The Book Nook, of
course. No one he had to protect himself or his partner from. He entered
the store, looking at Erin with concern.

"Erin, what—" He stopped short, the words dying away as he stared
at her. Erin looked at Vic, then followed Terry's eyes and looked down at
her apron, which was smeared with red. She wiped at it but, of course, it
didn't come out. She might have some chance if she soaked it in cold
water right away. And being white, it could be bleached.

"Tell me that's cherry pie filling," Terry choked out.

That brought back unwelcome memories. Erin shook her head. "No. Not pie filling."

But he'd seen the body. He knew.

"Sit down," Terry told her. "Take off the apron and give it to me first. Then sit down." He motioned to one of the chairs at the front of the bakery, which they used for the ladies' tea on Sundays.

Erin fumbled behind her back for the string to pull it loose, but her fingers were numb and clumsy. She looked back toward The Book Nook. Stayner must be the one preserving the scene. The sheriff would want a look at it, and then they would collect what evidence they could and call the city about getting the body transported to their morgue. Hopefully, that wouldn't take more than a few hours, because bodies that sat out in the Tennessee summer heat quickly began to break down, which wouldn't be nice. Erin could smell it already.

Terry reached for her and, putting a hand on her waist to still her, reached around her to pull the string and help her to remove the apron.

"What did you see down there? Tell me slowly."

The same thing that *he* had seen down there, Erin imagined. She tried to keep her thoughts slow and orderly.

"I thought Naomi would be there, but she wasn't. I went downstairs. The door was open and I thought she must be downstairs in the stock room. I needed to pick up my platters. She always returns them when she says she is going to."

"From the book club treats?"

Erin nodded. "Yes. Right. I went over looking for them. And Naomi wasn't there. I went downstairs to look for her, but then…"

Terry waited. Erin waited for him to fill it in himself. She didn't want to have to describe the body or the scene. He had seen it for himself.

He didn't say anything. Erin made a little gesture of impatience.

"Well, *you* saw it."

"You need to tell me what you saw."

"I saw his shoes, and then his legs, and then his whole body. I tried to call the dispatcher. I tried to call you. The call wouldn't go through."

"So then, what did you do?"

"I tried…" She grimaced, squinching her eyes closed. "Tried to take his pulse, see if he was still alive. Couldn't get a pulse, so I left him and came back here to call you."

"How long between when you found the body and you called me?"

"I don't know. Thirty seconds."

He frowned. "Longer than that."

Erin didn't know how he could be so confident about that. But he was probably right. She had probably misjudged the amount of time during those adrenaline-filled minutes.

"Maybe a minute."

"And you couldn't find a pulse."

"No."

"So he couldn't have gotten up and walked away."

Erin stared at him. "No."

"There was no one down there, Erin."

Erin shook her head in disbelief. "What are you talking about? I saw him. I wasn't just hallucinating. I touched him. He was there. And he *was* dead."

"You don't think... that it could have been a prank of some kind? Someone who was trying to scare or fool you?"

"No. I think I've seen enough—" Erin broke off. She didn't want to talk about how many dead bodies she had seen since coming to Bald Eagle Falls. That was sort of a sensitive topic, and she didn't want to think about it. "I know the difference between someone dead and someone who is just playing a prank."

Though she had argued with herself that maybe he could still be revived, Erin doubted that was true. That was just her brain looking for a way out of the situation she found herself in. She was just trying to rationalize. The man had been dead. There could be no doubt of that fact.

"Was he..." Terry looked uncomfortable. He sat in the chair across from her and put his hand over hers. "When you touched him, you couldn't find a pulse."

"No."

"What did the body feel like?"

"I don't want to think about that!"

"I need to know. How warm or cool it was. How stiff. Any details you can tell me to help get this sorted out."

"He was warm. His skin didn't feel... it felt normal. Not stiff."

"So, if he was dead, he hadn't been that way very long."

"He was dead!"

He just continued to look at her, waiting for her to consider his statement.

"Yes. He hadn't been that way for very long," Erin agreed. "I thought that if I got help… they might still be able to do something for him. Like they did for Jack."

"Jack?" Terry looked blank. "What does Jack have to do with this? Jack Ward?"

"Because he was stabbed. Like Jack. I was hoping that… if they treated him… they could save him, like Jack."

"But Jack was conscious when you found him. He wasn't dead."

"I know. But… he had the knife in him. Buried to the hilt."

"Jack did? Or the body in The Book Nook."

"Both. That's why… I thought maybe if they repaired the damage, they could get his heart going, and he would be okay. I mean…" Erin looked away from Terry, knowing that her thoughts had not been logical, "I know that's crazy. I know there's no one in Bald Eagle Falls who could do that, and it would take too long to get him to the city. But that's just what my brain was doing… trying to find a way that he might still be okay. I know that… they wouldn't actually be able to do anything for him."

Terry nodded sympathetically. "I understand. Tell me about this knife. Where was he stabbed? What kind of a knife was it?"

"It was in his chest. I don't know what kind…" Erin tried to picture it again in her mind. She had not taken much in, but she had stared at the knife handle for long enough that she should be able to give him some description. "I think… similar to the one that Jack was stabbed with. It wasn't a folding knife, like a pocketknife. Or a kitchen knife. But… something meant for fighting."

"A combat knife."

"I guess so, yes."

"Can you describe the handle?"

"Black… with indentations on it, for grip, you know? Shaped for your hand?"

Terry nodded, writing it down. "Okay. And can you describe the man?"

Erin didn't want to. She wanted to forget what she had seen. She didn't want to talk about it and cement it into her memory. She wanted to forget she had ever seen his face. She shook her head and covered her eyes with both hands.

"I'm sorry, Erin." Terry squeezed her hand. "I'm sorry that you saw this and that it happened to you. But I need to get as many details as possible about what happened and who this man was. Without a body, it's pretty hard to identify him, but maybe if there is a missing person report, we'll be able to figure it out. For that, I need a physical description."

She shook her head again, hands still over her eyes. "He was... a man, white, brown eyes and hair. Going a little bit gray, I guess. Forties, I think, but looked older... dressed in a t-shirt."

"Hair was long or short?"

"Short... thinning a bit in front, longer in the back, down to his collar or a little below it."

"I know height and weight would be pretty difficult to describe when you only saw him lying on the floor..."

"A little overweight. He was a— he was a little heavy in the face, if you know what I mean? Bags under his eyes, a bit jowly, sagging." She touched her throat, then shrugged. "Past his prime."

"It wouldn't be easy to move him."

Erin knew he wasn't trying to criticize her or say that he doubted her story, but the statement still angered her.

"Are you saying that he wasn't there? Or that I must not be telling you everything? That I helped to move him?"

"No. None of that. We're just trying to figure out what happened."

"I'm telling you what I saw."

"You saw a man who had been stabbed to death lying in The Book Nook basement. And five minutes later, when we got here, he was gone."

"I don't know the second part. But if *you* say so."

She could play the doubt game too. Maybe he was the one who was lying or mistaken about what he had found at the bookstore. Erin rubbed her forehead and folded her hands on the table. She didn't understand how any of this could be happening.

"Maybe you don't think that I found anyone there at all. Maybe you think it was just a hallucination or I am looking for attention."

"No. I don't. Even if I did, there's the state of your apron."

Erin looked down and realized she wasn't wearing it anymore. Of course not. Terry had taken it away. Because it had been smeared with red. "Right. I forgot."

"I know that you saw something, that you were down there and got blood on your apron. But I'm telling you, there's no one down there now. So, something about your story doesn't square. There wasn't long enough for someone to get a body out of the basement. Bodies are not easy to move. And it means that someone was in the bookstore when you were there. Probably more than one person, to be able to get it out so quickly."

Erin shook her head. "There wasn't anyone else there."

"How do you know that?"

"I didn't see anyone," Erin insisted. "I looked through the store before I went down to the basement. If there had been anyone there, I would have seen them."

"They could have ducked behind a shelf so that you couldn't see them. Or hidden in the bathroom. Did you check? And there is a back room on the main floor, just a small one, with a coffee service counter. And the loading dock. Did you go in there?"

Erin nodded. "I looked out the back door because I thought Naomi might be taking her trash to the bins. So I had to walk through the back room."

"And there was no one there? No one could have been hiding anywhere?"

Erin shook her head. She didn't want to think that there could have been anyone in the store with her. Watching her. Maybe wondering if he were going to have to stab her to death too. She shuddered. "I didn't see anyone. I walked through the whole store. If someone else had been there, I would have known it."

Terry made a couple more notes in his notepad. But Erin was afraid that he wasn't writing down what she said, that there couldn't have been anyone else in the store. Instead, he was writing down how she was wrong. How there must have been someone else in The Book Nook just waiting for her to leave again so he could remove the body from the scene.

"Vic, maybe you could get Erin a cup of coffee?" Terry said, raising his voice slightly. "Hot and sweet. For shock."

"I don't need anything. I'm fine."

"I can see you shaking. You should have something to calm your nerves and keep you focused."

She wasn't shaking because of fear, but shuddering at the thought of someone else being in the bookstore. Over what she had seen in the basement. Over the idea that the killer had probably stood just a few feet away from her, watching and waiting to see what she would do.

"Have something to warm you up," Terry insisted. "I really think you need it."

"In this heat? I need something to cool me down, not warm me up. I was soaking wet when I got back here." Erin plucked at the sleeve of her limp blouse. "I don't even remember my feet touching the stairs."

"Well, they must have," Terry gave her a smile. No dimple this time. He was too serious, too concerned about her. "I'm pretty sure you didn't learn to fly overnight."

"I wish I could. That would be really convenient." Erin's mind wandered, thinking of all of the things she could get done more efficiently if she could fly from one place to another instead of having to drive or walk. Zip here, zip there. Quick as a wink.

Vic brought two cups of coffee over to the table, setting them down gently in front of Terry and Erin. Erin picked hers up and took a tiny sip. It was too hot. She didn't want to scald her throat.

"There's really no one in the basement?" she asked Terry, not sure she believed it.

"Well, Stayner is over there now. Whoever else has arrived since I left. But a body... no, I'm afraid not."

CHAPTER 5

$\mathcal{E}$rin had answered all of the questions she could, posed first by Terry and then by Sheriff Wilmot as they tried to sort out what had happened to the body between the time Erin had abandoned it and the time that Terry and Stayner went down the stairs to look for it. And what had happened before that—how the man had gotten into the basement in the first place and been stabbed, and by whom. None of it made any sense. So after having answered everything she possibly could, Erin went home. Terry asked Vic to keep an eye on her, which wouldn't be hard, since Vic lived in the loft above Erin's garage and spent much of her time in the house. She wouldn't have left Erin alone anyway. She didn't need anyone telling her to make sure Erin was okay.

"This is crazy," Vic said, putting the kettle on to boil. "How could a body just disappear like that? And what was it doing down there in the first place? It isn't like Naomi killed someone! There's no way."

"No," Erin agreed. It was true that anyone could be a killer if pushed far enough, if the stakes were high enough, but if someone had been pushing Naomi like that, they would have known about it. They would have seen the stress in her life, how she was becoming increasingly desperate. But Naomi was always pleasant, relaxed, and laid back. When things when wrong for a library event, she always made lemons into lemonade and came out on top, smiling away and not even breaking a sweat. Erin admired her for her poise.

They would have known if something was wrong.

"Do you know who it was?" Vic asked.

Erin looked at her, not following the question. "That killed him?"

"No, who the victim was. You didn't say. Just that there was a man, a body, it wasn't anyone you knew?"

"No one from Bald Eagle Falls," Erin confirmed, shaking her head.

"Yeah. That's really weird. What would some out-of-towner be doing in the basement of The Book Nook to begin with? He just walked into the bookstore and went downstairs? No one noticed him come in or sneak off?"

"I don't know… Naomi wasn't there. No one was there. Why would the door be left unlocked with no one there to mind the store?"

Vic picked up the whistling teapot and poured water into a couple of mugs. She was frowning. "You don't think something happened to her, do you? To Naomi? Is she missing? Was she abducted by whoever killed the man?" She placed one mug on the table in front of Erin.

"No." Erin picked a teabag and dangled it into her cup. "Terry called her and she was okay. She just had an appointment this afternoon. She wasn't planning to be there. She said that Dave was supposed to lock up."

"And was Terry able to get ahold of him?"

"He was trying. He didn't answer, but people don't always answer right away. He might have turned it off for dinner or a movie, or be out of the calling area."

"Terry doesn't think that anything happened to him?"

"There wasn't any other sign of violence. No sign that there'd been a fight or burglary or abduction."

"Just a dead guy in the basement," Vic summarized, shaking her head.

"Yeah. Perfectly normal, right?"

Vic rolled her eyes. "For Bald Eagle Falls? I'm beginning to think so."

They sipped their tea in silence for a few minutes.

Orange Blossom finished eating his dinner and, seeing as Erin was still in the kitchen, he rubbed against her legs and yowled, waiting for her to realize that she hadn't given him enough food. Erin shushed him and scratched his ears. "You've had plenty. It's time to curl up and have a nap."

But he kept getting progressively louder. Erin winced. She hated it when he got so loud and she had to start worrying about neighbor complaints. Besides the fact that she couldn't hold a conversation in the same room with him or hear herself think.

"Blossom. Blossom!"

The cat quieted slightly to see what she had to say.

"Be quiet! You're finished eating. No more."

He gave a long, low, drawn-out meow that was almost a growl. Erin shook her finger at him. "That's enough! Go find Marshmallow. Have a nap."

Marshmallow, the rabbit, never begged for more. He was always placidly happy with whatever she gave him and would lollop back into the living room when he was done, to lie down on his side in front of the couch. Or behind it, if there were too many people around or he didn't want any attention.

Orange Blossom started to yowl again, and Erin pushed him away with the side of her foot. "No more. Be quiet now."

Each time he started to make noise, she pushed him away, until he finally withdrew into the living room in a huff, leaving Vic and Erin to their tea.

"Do you think Dave forgot to lock up?" Vic asked. "Could he have just walked away without locking the front door?"

"I guess anything is possible. Some people are forgetful or easily distracted."

Erin had never known Dave to be absent-minded, but anyone could be distracted by bad news, or excitement over his evening plans, or could be on a medication that made him forget things he would otherwise have remembered.

"Someone could have picked the lock," Erin said. "It wasn't very secure."

"Who would know how to do that? And wouldn't the police be able to tell if the lock was picked?"

"More people than you think. On TV, the police can always tell, but if a person is careful, he can pick a lock without scratching it. Or if it is old, it already has a bunch of scratches and nicks. They can tell if it was forced with a crowbar—but it wasn't. But if an expert picked it, they wouldn't know the difference."

"Could you have picked the lock?"

Erin shrugged. "It wasn't very secure," she repeated.

Vic gave a knowing smile and chuckled. She sipped her tea. "So it was unlocked when you got there, right? You didn't decide to pick the lock instead of waiting until tomorrow to get the trays back?"

"Why would I do that? They weren't that important. And why would I go poking through the rest of the store? I would just grab the platters and lock the door again. Naomi had already washed them and put them to the side for me."

Vic sighed dramatically. "Well then, why do you think someone broke in?"

"Maybe they didn't break in. Maybe the victim let them in. Maybe he had hidden out in the basement just so he could let his accomplice in. And then..." Erin tried to think of the next step. "Then they met..."

"And the victim's accomplice stabbed him? For no reason?"

"I'm sure he had a reason. I just... don't know what. They were fighting over something of value. Maybe... a rare book. A first edition or a misprint, or something that just came out and he had to get his hands on it." Erin knew that none of her ideas made any sense. Naomi didn't sell used books or antiques. She sold new books. Popular stuff that would sell well. If she had to special order something obscure, she demanded upfront payment, so that the person couldn't change their mind when it got there. Naomi might complain about the skyrocketing prices of books with the pulp shortage, but she didn't have a bunch of really valuable books lying around or a lot of cash in the till any more than Erin did.

CHAPTER 6

"So..." Erin stared through the kitchen window behind Vic, which looked from the kitchen into the backyard, eyes lingering on the gravel parking pad on the other side of the fence where Willie's truck would have been parked if he were home. She wanted to talk about something other than the man who had been stabbed in the basement of the bookstore. Really, anything other than that. "Where's Willie tonight?"

Vic looked over her shoulder as if she, too had to check to see if Willie's truck might be there. "I don't know. He didn't say what he was doing tonight."

"You're not expecting him?"

"No. He said he probably wouldn't be around. Working late or going on a trip, I guess. I don't know."

Erin would have found it challenging to live with a man who was as secretive as Willie. Private was probably a better word. It wasn't that he had anything to hide, just that he saw his business matters as his own business. And when someone worked in mining precious minerals, he had to keep things to himself to keep anyone else from jumping his claim. Did people still jump claims like in the westerns? Or was that a thing of the past with modern land title registries?

She liked Willie and had once considered pursuing a deeper relationship with him, but Erin had backed off when it had become clear that Vic was interested in him. Erin had also been interested in Terry, so it seemed like the gracious thing to leave Willie to Vic. On reflection, she was glad that she had. Vic's temperament was better suited to someone as independent as Willie. She wasn't concerned that he wasn't home every night and didn't tell her everything he was doing. Erin was afraid she would have given up on the relationship long ago.

"What?" Vic asked, looking at Erin. "I don't need to know where he is every minute of the day."

"I didn't say that you did."

"No, but you get that look."

"What look?" Erin shrugged and tried to blank her face, to keep any "look" from settling there.

"That look that says I'm being naive or should be worried about it. I'm not worried. He can do what he likes."

But Vic sounded like she did care. She sounded like she was trying to cover up what she was really feeling. Normally it was okay if Willie wasn't going to be back overnight, but maybe something was going on this time that made Vic anxious.

"So... it's okay?" Erin asked. "Everything is okay?"

"Of course."

"You didn't have a fight?"

Vic opened her mouth to deny it, then stopped, saying nothing, her mouth still open. Maybe Erin had hit on it. They had fought and Vic was concerned that Willie was still mad, which was why he wasn't there tonight.

"We had a *discussion*," Vic said finally.

"The kind where you don't both agree with each other?"

"The kind where... you are each calmly laying out your differences of opinion."

"Calmly?"

Vic sipped her tea, hiding her face behind the mug. "Initially, yes."

"What about?"

"Nothing." Vic's shoulders rose and fell. "Personal stuff."

"Okay." Erin accepted this and tried to redirect the conversation as if she weren't worried about whether her friend was happy or not. "What's he been working on lately, anyway? He always has so many projects on the go. But always at least one really good one."

"Mining. Some odd jobs around the house. A few things to finish up home renovation jobs where Mr. Monroe had left people in the lurch. Some computer stuff." Vic's voice trailed off.

Some of the *computer stuff* Willie had been working on a year before had been for Nelson Dyson, one of the members of the Dyson clan, though Nelson said that he had split off his own organization. Erin didn't know whether that was good or bad. Was his new organization still organized crime? Was Willie involved in anything illegal or unethical in his dealings with Nelson? Was there any personal danger? Not just of being arrested, but being caught in the middle of some kind of violence?

"He's good at search and rescue. Maybe we could get him involved in the search for the dead man," Erin suggested with a short laugh.

"I don't think it counts as search and rescue if they're already dead. I think then it becomes recovery."

"Or zombie hunting." Erin giggled.

"What kind of tea did you have?" Vic asked, pretending to be serious as she looked at the tag on Erin's tea. "What did they put in there? Jimson weed?"

"No weed," Erin assured her. "Just nice, calming lavender."

Vic shook her head. "Even if someone did pick the lock or break into The Book Nook," she returned to the previous topic as if there had been no intervening conversation, "how would they get a body out of there so fast? You would need at least two people to get a body up the stairs, wouldn't you? Unless he was a giant, and then I don't think he'd fit on the staircase. That stairway is pretty narrow."

Erin had been thinking about that herself and, at first, she had not been able to come up with the answer, but then she had remembered how Naomi normally got cases of books—which could also be very heavy—down to and up from the basement.

"The elevator."

"The elevator?" Vic repeated. "The Book Nook doesn't have an elevator."

Erin nodded. "It does. From just inside the loading dock down to the stock room. Can you imagine if Naomi had to take every case of books up and down the stairs one at a time? Or a partial box at a time if it was too heavy for her?"

"She has an elevator?" Vic repeated.

"Yes. It's not big. But big enough for a couple of stacks of delivery boxes. If she gets a delivery of six cases of books, she can just put them all straight on the elevator, send the elevator downstairs, and unload them in the stock room."

"That's very smart. I wish we had an elevator at Auntie Clem's. I hate having to take those big bags of flour down the stairs. Or back up again. It would be so much easier if you could throw the bags on an elevator and then unload them at the bottom."

Erin had envied Naomi her elevator more than once, and agreed with Vic. She really hated carrying heavy things on the stairs, going up or down. She was always afraid she would overbalance and topple down to the bottom, ending up in a heap at the bottom.

In her mind's eye, she again saw the splayed limbs of the man's body. She rubbed her eyes.

"I guess I should be going to bed soon."

"Probably," Vic admitted, covering a yawn. "Have you had anything to eat? You really should have some supper before you knock off for the night."

"I don't like going to bed on a full stomach." Erin looked toward the fridge. "I'll find a light snack." She stood and gathered up their teacups and the other tea things. The meaning of the gesture could not be mistaken. It was time for Vic to go home. They both needed to be up early in the morning.

CHAPTER 7

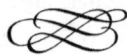

*E*rin slept restlessly, but the visions of the man crumpled in The Book Nook's stock room with a knife in his chest kept repeating in Erin's head, over and over again. She knew that Terry hadn't returned home, and she really wanted him to be there. He would probably work through the night if there were things he could do. Maybe not interviewing witnesses, but organizing a search for the body, looking into the backgrounds of each of the employees of The Book Nook, and trying to identify the man who had been killed.

At some point, Orange Blossom came into the bedroom and jumped up on the bed to snuggle against Erin. She couldn't keep tossing and turning with him against her, so it forced her to be still for long enough for her body to start settling into sleep, even though her brain was still whirling with thoughts and problems.

She tried to redirect them, thinking instead of the waffle contest. The different blends of flours that might work best for waffles. She wanted a flour that was light and would crisp up properly in the waffle iron. She might use superfine rice flour as the base, which would provide the crispness. Rice flour was hard, though, and would need to soak overnight for the best finished product. It would require a starch like tapioca to keep it light and provide flexibility. And a gum to hold it all together and retain moisture. Xanthan gum and guar gum were falling out of favor, with less processed ingredients like flax or chia seed taking their place. Psyllium powder, maybe?

Pumpkin pulp would provide a lot of moisture and the hearty flavor she wanted. If she did it right, she could avoid eggs, which many gluten-free products relied upon for a protein lattice structure. But eggs were a top-ten allergen and were also shunned by those following a vegan diet. She wanted the waffles to be a good choice for the widest variety of people as possible. Her business plan hinged on not only serving the gluten-free community, but other special diets and conventional diets as well. Products that were good for the whole family, no matter what their varied restrictions.

She remembered Bertie Braceling fondly. He had been such a challenge to bake for, and she often evaluated a new recipe by how many ingredients it contained that Bertie would not have been able to eat. A Bertie allergen rating scale. He would not have been able to have the rice flour or tapioca starch she intended to try for the waffle recipe. Choosing psyllium over the processed gums was a good choice. He would have been able to have that. But she couldn't remember if she had ever discussed pumpkin with him. Had he been able to eat pumpkin or was he allergic? He was okay with most vegetables, so they were a good idea to use as the base in a recipe. Pumpkin, sweet potato, white potatoes, zucchini—they could all be used successfully in baking.

Before she even knew that she had fallen asleep, Erin was roused by the ringing of her alarm. She turned on her lamp and looked around blearily. She felt like the bed should be scattered with papers, with the notes of the various ingredients and recipes she had thought about the night before, trying to escape the visions of the man in The Book Nook and to trick her brain into slowing down and going to sleep.

But the bed was clear, occupied by just her and Orange Blossom, who stretched all of his toes out, then got to his feet and arched his back, sending shivers all the way from his neck to his tail. He gave a couple of trills of greeting and sat back to have a bath, starting by licking his back toes. Leaving him to his ablutions, Erin got started on her own.

She didn't like how empty the house felt without Terry and K9 there overnight. But Terry often took the night shift, so it wasn't like she was used to his being there every night. Sometimes their schedules did not mesh together well for a few days or weeks.

But that didn't mean she couldn't miss him.

She showered and did her hair, then pulled on some clothes and went to the kitchen to turn on the kettle and throw a slice of bread in the toaster. As soon as she was in the kitchen, Orange Blossom began singing for his breakfast, rubbing against her legs and wondering why she was taking so long. He never could seem to understand that she needed to eat as well, and her food did not come ready to eat from a can. As far as he was concerned, his needs came before hers.

She carefully measured out his food for the day. He was now eating "weight control" formula, having grown too heavy for Doc's liking. And when Erin picked him up, she had to admit he was getting to be quite an armful.

Marshmallow hopped into the kitchen and waited patiently for his pellets and fresh vegetables.

"You see how nice he is?" Erin asked Orange Blossom, "Marshmallow doesn't need to make a racket and trip me up all over the kitchen before he gets his food. He just waits until he gets it, and he still gets it just as fast as he would if he was harassing me."

Orange Blossom looked up from his dish and glowered at her. He obviously didn't believe a word of it. He knew that if he didn't yowl like the world was ending, she would never remember to give him his food. Or she would wait until it was convenient for her, and who knew when that would be?

She knew that things would be crazy at Auntie Clem's Bakery that morning. It always was when there was shocking news or gossip, and Erin finding a body definitely qualified. She and Vic had joked many times about how a murder always improved the bottom line at Auntie Clem's. It was sad but true.

As expected, when she opened the door first thing in the morning, there was a larger-than-usual morning crowd waiting with their coffee cups outside. They filed in, already chattering with each other about the latest news.

"I don't know how you do it," Betty Thompson declared. "If there is a dead body in Bald Eagle Falls, we know exactly who will find it!"

"It's all so mysterious." Melissa's dark curls bounced as she moved her head around to make sure that everyone was paying attention to her. She worked part-time at the police department, so she often had important tidbits to share at Auntie Clem's. Information that she was not exactly authorized to release. "How could a body appear in The Book Nook and then disappear before the police could get there to investigate? I mean, it was like magic. There one minute, gone the next."

Erin shook her head and kept a smile pinned to her face, trying not to show any irritation to Melissa. Melissa seemed to consider Erin her best friend, and Erin didn't want to make her feel bad by showing her irritation at the comment. "There's nothing magical about it. Someone—or more than one someone—just managed to move the body in the time it took me to get back here, make a call, talk to the dispatcher, and for the police to get here and enter the building. That's not exactly instant."

"When you're talking about moving a dead body, it is. They're heavy! And awkward. It isn't like picking up a box with handles. It's a two-person job, unless you're really big or they are very small."

"But it isn't impossible," Erin repeated. "There's nothing mysterious or paranormal about it."

She could just imagine what story her foster sister Reg would have come up with to explain the body's disappearance. She always told the best ghost stories but, when they had been growing up together, her paranoia about conspiracies and wildly imaginative explanations for the most mundane things had been aggravating.

"Maybe there wasn't a body," Lottie suggested, looking sideways at Erin to watch for her reaction. Lottie wasn't usually at Auntie Clem's two mornings in a row. Erin suspected she was there just for the gossip. Auntie Clem's was the place to go to discuss the latest tragedy.

Erin wasn't sure where they had gone before she had opened the bakery. Had they gone to Angela Plaint's bakery to discuss such things before Erin had come to town? Or had they just gotten into the habit of coming to Auntie Clem's because she was so often involved in the investigation on one end or the other? Or maybe it was just because she was with Terry, and they figured she could get information about the police investigation from him and pass it on to them.

"What do you mean, 'maybe there wasn't a body'?" Vic demanded. "You think that Erin just made it up? Looking for attention?"

Lottie shrugged. "I'm just considering all of the possibilities. What proof is there, after all, that there was a body there in the first place?"

"Well, there was the blood," Melissa pointed out.

"Blood isn't the same as a body. Someone could have cut themself. Erin could have seen the blood and made up the rest."

"It wasn't just a little bit of blood," Melissa told her, shaking her head. "There was too much for it to have just been a little accident—someone stabbing themself with a box cutter or getting a paper cut from one of the cardboard boxes. Someone was badly hurt down there; that was obvious."

Lottie was smiling like the cat who caught the canary. Maybe she hadn't really doubted that Erin had found a body and was trying to get more information about the crime scene. If so, she was sneakier than Erin had ever thought. She always believed that Lottie said everything she thought without a filter. But maybe she did hold some things back. Maybe she just liked to aggravate people but had other thoughts that she kept to herself.

There were murmurs among the women about this detail of the crime scene. Even though Erin was trying not to keep picturing what had happened, she tried to visualize what the crime scene had looked like after the body had been removed. She hadn't seen a lot of blood, but it had probably pooled under the body. A stab to the chest could be expected to bleed a lot, unless it was directly to the heart and stopped it from pumping.

She was glad she hadn't seen how much blood there was.

"Who do you think it was?" Melissa asked. "You must know pretty much everyone in town now. It wasn't anyone you had ever seen before?"

Erin shook her head. "It wasn't anyone I've ever seen around Bald Eagle Falls. I don't know everyone, but I think he must have been an out-of-towner. If it was someone associated with the bookstore, I think I would have seen him going into or coming out of there sometime."

"If he was from out of town, how are the police ever going to figure out who he was?" Betty asked Melissa. "It isn't like Erin saw his identification. They can't check his fingerprints."

"They took fingerprints at the scene," Melissa said. "He may have left prints while he was there if he wasn't wearing gloves. And he wasn't, was he, Erin?"

"No. I don't think... no," Erin agreed. Her stomach was tight. If they managed to find the man's fingerprints in The Book Nook's stockroom, it wouldn't take long to identify him. Even without a body, they would know who he was. The investigation would move forward.

"Or there could be a missing person report," Vic offered.

"He could have come from anywhere," Betty pointed out. "Can they check for missing person reports all over the country? Or even Canada? It isn't impossible that he came here from Canada, you know."

"I'm sure if there's a fingerprint record or missing person report from Canada, we'll find it," Melissa said firmly, but the frown on her face indicated otherwise. An international investigation would take on all kinds of new complexities.

CHAPTER 8

"What can I get for you today?" Erin asked Lottie.

Normally, she would have served Betty first, since she was the oldest and used a walker. Erin didn't like to keep her waiting on her feet for too long. But if Lottie was going to come to Auntie Clem's just to gossip or make more trouble for Erin, she wouldn't get away with sneaking out of the store when no one was looking and not buying anything.

Lottie met Erin's eyes and seemed to understand what she was doing. She shrugged and chuckled. "Well, something decadent," she suggested. "Something like 'Death by Chocolate'?"

Erin reviewed the selections to see what might qualify. "I have double fudge brownies. You could warm them slightly in the microwave and top them with ice cream or whipped cream and chocolate sauce. Or I have a nice Black Forest cake," she pointed to the chocolate cake under glass, with plenty of creamy icing, cherries, and curls of bittersweet chocolate.

Lottie pondered the two possibilities, finger to her chin. She took a deep breath and sighed. "I guess it had better be the double fudge brownies. I don't think I can eat a whole cake before it begins to go off. Two double fudge brownies."

Erin nodded and got them out for Lottie, making sure they were generous portions. As far as she knew, Lottie lived alone, which might explain why she came to Auntie Clem's to gossip so often.

~

It was a while before the flow of traffic into the bakery slowed and Erin and Vic could take a breather. They took a few trays of cooled cookies from the kitchen and restocked the display case, enjoying the momentary quiet.

The bell on the door jingled. Erin looked up and saw that it was Dave Wolfe, one of Naomi's part-time employees. He was around her age, maybe a little younger. In his late twenties or early thirties. He was a nice-looking young man with a preppy style that fit with the bookstore, and he had always been pleasant with Erin when she stopped by The Book Nook and he was there. She had conversed with him once or twice when she'd had to wait for Naomi but, usually, a wave and nod of greeting was about as far as their interactions went.

"Oh, Dave. How are you?" Erin searched his face for any sign of distress. He would have had to talk to Terry or someone else in the police department after Erin discovered the body the day before, and Erin already knew from Naomi that he was the one who had neglected to lock up after closing. Or he had remembered to lock up and someone had come along and picked the lock.

But the lights had been on, and Erin assumed he would have turned the lights off when he closed up, and a burglar would not want to turn them on and draw attention to the store.

Dave's expression was serious, but he didn't look too upset about whatever had transpired during his interview with the police. And he was in the bakery, after all. He had not left town or crawled under his covers to hide for the next week. His clothes were neatly pressed as usual. A good sign that he was taking care of himself and had not, at least, slept in his clothes or been up all night.

"Um... I'm okay, I guess." Dave swallowed and shook his head. "I can't believe that all of this really happened. It seems like it should be the plot of some TV movie, not my real life."

"Or maybe you're dreaming or someone is pulling a prank on you?" Erin suggested.

He laughed and nodded. "Yeah, exactly; how did you know?"

"Been there," Erin assured him. Had she ever. Been there, done that, got the t-shirt *and* the mug. Even with all of the unusual deaths she had dealt with in the past couple of years, it was still a shock. She was better at dealing with it than she had been. Things had been bad there for a while, but she was learning to adjust and be more resilient.

For poor Dave, this was probably the first time he'd had to deal with an unexpected death. At least he hadn't had to see the body. Everything might feel slightly unreal for him because he hadn't actually seen it, but it was better that way. Better than having to deal with nightmares about what he *had* seen.

"I guess you have," Dave admitted. He had moved to town shortly before Erin, so he would have heard about everything she had been involved with while she'd lived in Bald Eagle Falls. He should have known not to take a job so close to her bakery. Things happened around Erin.

"I guess you've talked to Terry by now. Or one of the others."

"Yeah." Dave's voice was low. He glanced at Vic, unsure about talking in front of her.

Vic raised her brows. She turned toward the kitchen. "There's the timer; I'd better take care of the next batch of cookies." She stepped through the doorway into the kitchen and out of sight. Dave took another step toward Erin, looking intently into the display case as if he were one of the children in the Kid's Club trying to pick out the best cookie. Erin leaned forward on the edge of the display case on the other side so that they were close together and Dave could talk to her quietly without worrying that anyone else might overhear him.

"I can't believe this all happened," Dave said. "And I'm so sorry… Naomi said I must have left the door open, but I'm sure I didn't. I would never have put you through something like this on purpose. I'm so sorry."

"I know you didn't set it up," Erin assured him, laughing at the ridiculousness of the thought. "If you had known what was going to happen, you would have done anything you could to prevent it."

He nodded, giving a heavy exhale in his relief. "Yeah. That's right. I would never have allowed something like this to happen." His shoulders were hunched and he tried to relax into a less tense posture. "I'm just afraid that you won't be able to come to The Book Nook anymore. Because of what happened there."

"Well… I've still been able to come to my own bakery, and things have happened here too. I'll be fine, Dave. I might not ever go down to the stock room again, but I don't exactly need to. Naomi can get me whatever I need. And if she ever needs someone to go down there to help her rearrange boxes or something… well, she can find someone else."

They both laughed awkwardly. Erin was doing her best to put Dave at ease, but wasn't sure it was helping.

The door opened, the bell jingling loudly, and Dave and Erin both jumped. Dave whirled around to see who it was and looked stricken when he saw his boss standing there.

"Dave," Naomi said, impatience in her tone.

"I was just returning Miss Price's platters," Dave protested. Then he looked down at his empty hands. He looked at Erin as if he might have already given her the platters. But he hadn't had anything in his hands when he entered the bakery. "That is, I…"

Naomi held up the trays. "These platters?"

"Uh…" A red flush was creeping up Dave's tanned neck. Erin felt bad for him, wishing there was something she could do about his embarrassment. But the more she focused on it, the worse it would be. "I guess… I forgot them. I don't know where my head is today."

Naomi nodded. She swept her long hair away from her face with her forearm, then strode forward to place the platters on the top of the display case. "Thank you, as always, for putting together such a nice treat for the book club."

Erin nodded. "Always glad to help. Is there a theme for the next meeting?"

"I think maybe we're going to do a back-to-school theme. Talk about young adult books, explore the genre a bit, make some suggestions for books they might want to read to better understand what kids these days have to deal with at school and at home."

"Hmm." Erin thought about what she could bake with a back-to-school theme. She didn't want to do cliched items that were found in school lunches. Jell-O cups. Twinkies. That was too depressing. "How about 'an apple for the teacher'? I can put together some apple tarts and bars."

"That would be wonderful! You always have such great ideas."

Erin smiled. She enjoyed the creativity of finding a food that would fit with the book that the book club was reading or the theme they were discussing. Sometimes she would pick a food that a character in the book had eaten, something traditional from their culture, or something historically accurate. It was fun. "I enjoy doing it."

"Well, you should. You do such a good job of it."

They both looked at each other for a minute, unsure what to say. There was a big pink elephant in the room.

"So... are you okay?" Erin asked. "With everything that happened over there? You've probably had police all over the place all night and interviews and everything..."

Naomi nodded. "It's been pretty crazy. I've never been at the center of a murder investigation before. It's... kind of surreal. Like it's happening to someone else. I've only ever seen this kind of thing on TV before."

"I was just talking to Dave about that. How it seems so unreal. Your brain tries to rationalize it."

"Yeah. Because if it's real..." Naomi shuddered. "It's just too much. How do you go on if it was all real?"

"You find a way."

"I hope so. But..." Naomi squared her shoulders. "Luckily, I wasn't there when it happened. That could have been me. I could have been killed. Or been the one to find the body. It was only dumb luck that I wasn't there. My own mistake."

Erin raised her brows, not understanding. "What do you mean?"

"I had to go into the city to see my lawyer. Just for some business stuff, nothing to be concerned about," Naomi waved away any questions about legal trouble she might be in. "But I got the date and time of the appointment wrong. The meeting isn't until next week, but I wrote it down wrong, and I ended up being away when all of this happened. I was in shock when I got the call from Terry Piper, I'll tell you!"

"I'll bet," Erin agreed. "That was lucky. I'm glad you weren't there. That you didn't get hurt."

"Yes, me too. Though I'll bet you wish that it was someone else who found him."

Erin wasn't sure what to say about that. It was true that she didn't want to stumble across any more dead bodies. She hated the anxiety and nightmares as well as the reputation she got from always being the one who seemed to be magically drawn toward the bodies of the dead. But she wouldn't wish that on Naomi either. Erin had been through enough that she could hold it at a bit of a distance. Though it was a shock to her system, she was sure that it would have been much harder on Naomi if she had been the one to find the dead body. She might have gone into hysterics. It might have changed her forever. She might have been sick and depressed and traumatized for weeks, months, or even longer.

But she hadn't had to go through that because Erin had been there and found the body instead. As much as she didn't enjoy that part of life in Bald Eagle Falls, she didn't wish it on someone else.

"It's hard," she admitted. "But it does get easier. You get more... not *used* to it, exactly but find ways to handle it better. Usually. I've had my problems."

"Well, thank you for finding this one for me." She started to turn toward the door. "Except, maybe neither of us was supposed to find it. If you hadn't been there exactly when you were, you would have missed it. It would have been gone."

"Oh... I guess so." Erin hadn't thought about it from that perspective. She'd had a half-formed belief that the body had disappeared *because* she had found it and called the police, and that if she hadn't been there, it would have just lain there until it was discovered during the ordinary course of events. But that wasn't necessarily true. The body hadn't disappeared because she had seen it. And if she hadn't seen it, no one would have been the wiser. No one would know that someone had died in the basement of The Book Nook.

CHAPTER 9

*E*rin had only been booked for the opening shift at Auntie Clem's Bakery and had given herself the afternoon off to work on other things. She could have stayed at the bakery to do the books, which she was getting a little behind on, but she didn't really want to stay there. She wanted to be home where she could relax and maybe catch a nap to make up for the poor sleep she'd had the night before. She might even be able to catch Terry napping, if he had finally decided to take a break from the case and catch some shut eye. Either way, she knew she needed to rest for a while and get recharged.

Terry was not home, but had left a sticky note on the fridge indicating that he had been home while she'd been on her morning shift, had caught a few hours of sleep and had a bite to eat, and had headed out again. Heading off all of the questions she would ask him to make sure he was taking care of himself. Erin read the note through again, folded it in half, and threw it in the garbage.

She made herself a sandwich. She needed to follow Terry's example and take care of herself too. Though she was already doing that by coming home to rest instead of staying at the bakery to do her accounting or pitch in on the next shift because she couldn't keep her fingers out of the pie. Her employees were fully capable of looking after the regular shifts without her there to supervise them all the time.

She sat on the couch to read—which she knew she shouldn't do because she would get crumbs on it, and then complain later about certain people eating in front of the TV and getting crumbs on the furniture. But she would be sure to clean up after herself so that wouldn't happen. She wanted to be somewhere comfortable to eat and read through her email on her tablet.

Erin yawned, rubbed her eyes, and put down the half sandwich that remained, scrolling through the emails to look for anything important. But she knew that what she was looking for wasn't in her inbox anymore. It was in the trash. And she wasn't looking for it; she was trying to avoid it, pretending to herself that she wasn't looking for it, but just scrolling for anything new.

Orange Blossom got up from his spot on the easy chair, yawned widely and stretched, then jumped up on the couch beside Erin and curled up against her leg. He didn't even show any interest in the half sandwich, though he might have been trying to lull Erin into believing that he wasn't going to go after the people food the first opportunity he got.

"Hi, sweetie," Erin greeted him, and scratched his ears and neck. "You're very cuddly today."

He purred. Erin closed her eyes, enjoying his warmth against her leg and the rumbling purr that made her feel at home.

She looked at her email again. She couldn't help herself. She clicked on the email trash and scrolled down. She should empty the trash. That was what it was there for, after all. A place to put things that you never wanted to see again. To destroy them forever.

But there she was, scrolling down and skimming for the familiar string of characters.

She missed it the first time. She could feel that she had gone down too far and scrolled back up more slowly, eyes fixed on the screen. And there it was.

Meet me at Canyon Park Wednesday afternoon at 2:00

She knew better than to do it. She had said that she never wanted to see him again, and that hadn't changed. She really didn't want to see him again. Or talk to him, or respond to his emails. She had assumed that if she never responded, he would eventually give up.

That was what the foster moms and dads had always said about bullies, wasn't it? Just ignore them and they will eventually go away.

But it never worked that way. At least, it hadn't for Erin. Maybe she was just a target, like Reg had told her. She looked too vulnerable, acted too tentative, and people thought that meant they could take advantage of her. If she were tougher, if she showed people that she wasn't the type of girl who could be pushed around, they would respect her.

But that had never worked either.

She wasn't going to the park. There wasn't any point because she knew he wouldn't be there. It was a pointless gesture and would just prove that she had never managed to get him completely out of her life, no matter how far away she had moved.

Instead, Erin would lie down and have a nap, get caught back up on the sleep she had been short on the night before. She would take care of herself and get the rest and relaxation that she needed so that she would be able to bounce back from her gruesome find quickly and move on with her life. She didn't need to dwell on it. Life went on despite damaging and traumatic experiences. If she'd learned anything in life, it was that.

But she knew she wouldn't be able to sleep when she lay down in her bed. As much as she wanted to, it just wasn't going to happen. Her mind was going like a hamster wheel. Between replaying the discovery of the murdered man in the basement of The Book Nook and the email requesting her presence, there was no quieting it. The hamster was determined to keep running, even if he wasn't actually getting anywhere. What made them keep running, anyway?

Erin tried for twenty minutes, and probably tossed and turned at least twenty times in the process. She couldn't stop twitching, let alone lie in the same position for more than thirty seconds at a time. She looked like some jumped-up meth freak.

She decided to go for a walk. That would help to calm her down. A walk in the woods was always calming and refreshing. It was the hottest part of the day, in the hottest part of the Tennessee summer, but the woods were shady and it was time she got acclimatized to the weather conditions in Tennessee. She was never going back to Maine.

Vic wasn't home yet, or Erin would have invited Vic and her fluffy white dog, Nilla, to go along with her. The dog's need to sniff every leaf and tree trunk along the way would keep them moving slowly, even if she felt like she always needed to be productive and keep things moving as quickly as possible. With her tai chi practice, she was learning just to breathe and let the rest of the world flow around her. A person needed more than productivity. She needed rest and meditation as well.

Erin began to walk. The woods behind the house were quiet, as they always were. A buffer between Erin and the rest of the world. Her own little piece of paradise. Bugs buzzed and whirred, but the rest of the animals were quiet, resting during the heat of the day just as she had planned to.

In a few minutes, she was passing Adele's cabin. Adele, a practicing witch, was Erin's gamekeeper, keeping trespassers out of the woods where they could harm others or themselves. And then sue her because she had allowed it to happen. She liked to sit and visit with Adele, who sometimes seemed wise beyond her years. But Erin wasn't going to knock on her door in the afternoon. Adele was usually up late at night to perform her gamekeeper duties or religious rituals, so she would probably be asleep in the afternoon. Maybe on the way back to the house, it would be late enough to see if she were up and around.

Erin had looked up the address of Canyon Park. Just in case she ever wanted to go there someday. Through online satellite and street-level photography, Erin could see that it was a small park, out of the way, without any playground equipment for the children. A little place to enjoy nature, maybe have a picnic, maybe take dogs for a walk, but there wasn't really anything to do there.

Which was probably why there was no one there now. And likely why her email correspondent had picked such an isolated spot in the first place. With nobody around to eavesdrop, he could talk to her about whatever he wanted to talk about, and no one would overhear, and he could persuade Erin to his way of thinking. The secluded location provided a perfect opportunity for the two of them to talk without inter-ruption.

But she knew he wasn't going to be there. That would be impossible.

CHAPTER 10

*E*rin suppressed a shudder. Goosebumps popped up all over her arms, and she rubbed them as if she were cold, despite the oppressive heat. Her shirt was nearly drenched with sweat, and she wished she hadn't walked so far from home and was back there so she could shower and change without having to walk all the way back.

It was familiar from the satellite pictures but a little larger than Erin had thought. Some walking paths where people could go to enjoy nature, much like the paths through Erin's own woods.

She looked around. There was no one waiting there for her. She had known there would not be. But she'd needed to reassure herself. Nothing but trees, with the songs of birds that seemed far away and cheerful, as if it were a perfectly normal day. She walked around the small clearing. There was a large sandstone rock with the words Canyon Park chiseled into it. There was a single bench for someone who wanted to take a break to sit down.

She sat. She looked around at the trees and the blue sky and the brilliant green grass. It was all so beautiful. So peaceful. So quiet. Like nothing bad could ever happen there.

She heard a rustling in the trees. She turned her head watched a deer walk into the clearing.

It looked at her with liquid brown eyes for a long moment, then it turned and disappeared in a flash, back into the shadows of the trees. Erin let out her breath.

She knew she couldn't stay there forever. It was only a matter of time before someone would be looking for her. Terry would call her, or someone from the bakery, or someone who hadn't been able to make it to the bakery and still wanted to ask her about the body in the basement of the bookstore.

Erin stood with a sigh.

Approaching the rock from the other side, she could see a shoe lying beside it. Who would leave a shoe in the park? It wasn't a hiking or walking shoe. Maybe someone had changed before they went for a walk.

And had just left it lying there?

Then she realized it looked familiar. She'd seen that shoe before. A shiny black shoe like she had seen in the basement of The Book Nook.

Her stomach knotted tightly, Erin got closer and pushed back the bushes that obscured the rest of the shape behind the big rock.

A startled noise escaped her mouth. Not quite a scream, but a little yelp that she couldn't stifle.

The face was obscured by the bushes, but she knew who it was.

She reached for her phone with nerveless fingers and pulled it out, searching for the buttons she knew so well. The phone felt hard and cold in her hands instead of responsive, every tap taking several tries before she managed to get it to do what she wanted. She was afraid that it would be just like before—that she wouldn't be able to get a signal, wouldn't be able to reach out for help and would have to go somewhere else to place the call.

And then what would happen? Would it still be there when the police arrived? She knew it was irrational, but she couldn't take her eyes off of the form lying in the shadows of the brush and the rock. If she looked away, it could disappear. Just like before.

She finally managed to tap Terry's name enough times that the call started to go through. Then was canceled because she'd also managed to hit the hang-up icon. Erin swore under her breath, tried to hold the phone steady, and tried again.

"Erin?" Terry's voice finally sounded in her ear. "Everything okay?"

Erin stifled a sob. She took a deep breath, let it out, and tried to sound as calm and collected as possible. "Well... *I'm* okay."

"What's going on?"

"I'm at Canyon Park. Do you know where that is?"

"What are you doing at Canyon Park?"

"I… went for a walk."

He didn't answer, probably considering the fact that he'd never known her to go walking to random parks before. She usually stayed in the woods behind her property when she went for a walk. Or walked between Auntie Clem's and the house.

"Terry, I found him."

"You found who?"

"The… man who was in the basement. At The Book Nook."

"You found him. Does that mean he is alive?" Terry's voice was cautious, not accusatory, but he must have thought she was crazy. Either she thought that a live man had been dead, or that a dead man was wandering around the neighborhood.

"No… he was dead. I mean, he was dead when I found him in the bookstore, and he's dead now, but he's here. In Canyon Park."

"How did you—" he started to interrogate her, then broke off. "No, never mind. I'm going to hang up and call the dispatcher. You'll stay there?"

"Yes."

"I'll be five minutes. Don't…"

"Don't take my eyes off of the body?"

"Well…" In her mind's eye she could see his helpless shrug. "Yeah. One of us will be there in a few minutes. I don't know who is closest."

"Okay." Erin hung up so he wouldn't feel guilty about disconnecting her when she might be distressed.

She stood there, staring down at the body, not taking her eyes off of it despite her instinct to look away. She didn't want this moment impressed on her memory. But like Terry, she also couldn't dismiss the fear that it would be gone by the time he arrived.

A siren sounded in the distance. She hoped that Terry would be the first to arrive, but, of course, it didn't matter. All of the Bald Eagle Falls police department would be on their way, whether they were on shift or not. They would all be there within a few minutes.

As the siren drew closer, she could also hear a truck engine. The truck that sped into sight was Terry's. She sighed in relief and looked back down at the body, realizing in an instant that she had looked away from it. But it was still there.

Terry jumped out of the car and hurried over to her, K9 running at his side. He got in close where he could see the body and seemed to relax. He put a warm hand on Erin's back, which felt incredibly comforting.

"Are you sure it is the same body?" he asked, studying it closely from top to toe. The hilt of the knife still stuck out of the chest and looked like Erin had described it. The shoes she had recognized from The Book Nook were on his feet. Or at least, one of them was. She didn't see the other nearby, but she wasn't about to start poking around the bushes or under the body to find it. Some things she didn't mind leaving with the police.

"Yes. It's the same one."

"Good. Always nice to find what you have misplaced."

Erin knew he was trying to be lighthearted and distract her from the gravity of the situation, but it didn't seem funny to her.

"You don't have to keep looking at him," Terry said. "If you want to sit down for a while until one of us can interview you…"

Erin sighed and walked back over to the park bench and sat down. Her sweat-damp clothes stuck to her. She didn't want to sit and wait to be interrogated again. She wanted to go home and pretend that nothing had happened.

Why had she insisted on coming to the park? She had known that she shouldn't, and she had anyway.

CHAPTER 11

*E*rin felt Terry's gaze on her, and she glanced at him. However, he didn't say anything to her. He, the sheriff, and Stayner cordoned off the area and started the initial processing of the scene. When someone came to sit on the bench and talk to her, it wasn't Terry, but Sheriff Wilmot.

"Miss Price. How are you doing?"

"I'm hot and sticky and want to go home."

He took the opportunity to remove his hat, wipe his sweaty brow, and put the hat back on again. "It is a warm one," he admitted.

"When can I go? You can come to the house to talk to me."

"Soon. We'll cover the preliminaries here before we let you go anywhere so that everything is still fresh in your mind and you haven't had a chance to be influenced by anything else."

"There isn't really anything to tell. I just came here, out for a walk, and I saw the shoe…" She pointed to the shoe of the corpse, which extended just beyond the big rock. "I went over for a closer look and saw him there."

"Did you touch the body?"

"Why would I?" Erin shuddered. "No."

"Maybe to turn it to get a better look at his face. Or to make sure that he was dead."

"I already saw his face when he was in the basement of the bookstore, and I already checked to make sure he was dead then. I didn't need to check again today."

"You were sure it was the same man."

"Yes. I was sure. I could see him. Same clothes, same knife. Same body."

"You didn't need to see his face."

"No."

"Are you sure you don't want to take a look so that you can confirm one hundred percent that this is the same man as you found in The Book Nook? There isn't anyone else who can confirm it is the same body. You were the only one who saw him."

"And whoever took him away."

"Well, I suppose so, but whoever that is, they aren't going to tell us anything. They didn't want anything to do with the police in the first place, so why would they now? If they were inclined to go to the police, they would have done it in the first place, like you did, not take the body away." He shook his head. "I don't know what they intended to hide, moving him from there to here. Exactly what does moving him accomplish?"

Erin shook her head. Nothing that she could see. Other than to make everyone think she was going crazy. If they were going to leave him somewhere that he would be discovered anyway, why do such a thing? If it had been Erin, she would have dumped him down a mine shaft or left him somewhere deep in the woods where no one would ever find him. It was ridiculous to remove him from the bookstore just to dump him in a public, easily accessible park where anyone could see him and he would be found within hours or days, depending on how much foot traffic went through the park.

Wilmot grunted. "I don't know either. But not all killers are very bright. It isn't like on TV, where they are all criminal masterminds. Actual criminals tend to be pretty stupid. They have poor impulse control and never think they will get caught. But of course they do."

"You'll figure out who killed… whoever this is."

Wilmot looked at Erin sidelong. "Do you know who he is?"

"Not anyone I've ever seen in Bald Eagle Falls before."

He grunted again. "Me either. Out-of-towner. Someone looking for trouble."

"Didn't he... have a wallet? Identification?"

"No. No wallet, no phone, nothing to identify him. We'll have to check missing person reports to see if we can figure out who he is. Maybe he'll have a criminal record and his fingerprints will pop something."

Erin stared off into the trees. "Maybe."

And when they did manage to identify him... what then? "Do you think that who he is has something to do with why he was killed?"

"What do you mean?" Deep wrinkles formed between Wilmot's eyes.

"I mean... do you think it was just random, like any victim would do? Or do you think that he was targeted because of what he did or who he was?"

"Oh... well, that's a good question. I'm not sure I can answer it." Wilmot considered the question for a minute. "He has no wallet, so it could have just been theft, a mugging. Except for the fact that he was found in the basement of the bookstore. Not out on the street or in an alley, where it might conceivably be a mugging. He was in the basement, and no one knows why; what he was doing down there, who let him in, or why his body was removed. That says something about it being personal. Someone knew he was going to be there and intentionally followed or met him. It couldn't just be some random person who happened to wander by."

Erin nodded slowly. Who could have known the out-of-towner? Had he come to case out The Book Nook, thinking they had something valuable on-site? Who had known that he was coming or why he had shown up?

It was disturbing. There were too many questions.

"Then whoever killed him had some kind of connection with him."

"Yes, that's what I'm thinking. And as soon as we can identify him, hopefully we will be able to identify who the connection was. Through phone or text records, an email trail, something from his past. When we find out the connection, we'll know the *why* and the *who*. It will just be a matter of getting enough evidence to prove it."

Erin rubbed her forehead. She swallowed, but her mouth and throat were so dry. "Do you have any water? I sweated so much on the way over. I think I'm getting dehydrated."

"I surely do." Wilmot smiled at her. "Be back in a tick."

Erin watched him walk over to his car. She took a quick look at Terry, but he was occupied with whatever evidence he was cataloging. He didn't give her another of *those* looks.

Wilmot opened his trunk and pulled out a bottle of water. He brought it back to Erin, cracking the top open on his way.

"It ain't cold," he warned, "but it's wet."

The water was lukewarm and tasted flat and stale from sitting in the warm trunk of Wilmot's car, but Erin didn't complain. It felt good going down. She swished a mouthful around and swallowed again. She poured a small amount into the hollow of her hand and then wiped it over her face and neck to cool down a bit. She should have known to bring a water bottle when going for a walk in the Tennessee summer heat.

"What possessed you to venture out for a walk in the middle of the afternoon in this heat?" Wilmot asked, his mind obviously following the same track.

Erin took a deep breath. "I just… needed to get out and clear my head. I was thinking a lot about finding the body in the bookstore, you know… I needed some exercise and fresh air."

He looked around, thinking. "Do you come here often? It's sort of off the beaten path."

"No. Someone mentioned it the other day and I thought I would check it out. Give myself something to do."

"Uh-huh. Who was it that mentioned it?"

"Umm… I don't know. Someone at the bakery, I guess. I don't remember what we were talking about. But I hadn't been here before, so today, when I was looking for something to do to keep my mind occupied, I thought why not check it out?"

He nodded slowly. Erin shifted. "Is that everything? Can I head back home now?"

"I suppose so. You should probably get a ride, if you're already dehydrated. No point in trying for heatstroke."

"I guess." She looked at Terry's truck. Was Wilmot suggesting that Terry could take her home, or was he expecting her to call someone to be picked up?

"Maybe Miss Victoria could pick you up?" Wilmot suggested.

"Well… I could try Willie." Erin knew Vic did not have a driver's license, although she sometimes borrowed a vehicle to get where she needed to go. It was probably best not to let Terry see her driving. Just because he had overlooked it once before, that didn't mean he'd give her a break again. And even though the sheriff had been the one to suggest it, he might remember later on that Vic didn't have a driver's license and decide to give her a ticket.

Wilmot nodded. "See if you can get someone. I know it isn't far, but I'd feel better knowing you weren't trying to make the hike back when you're already feeling poorly."

"Okay."

Wilmot stood up and went back to the other law enforcement officers to help with the investigation. Erin toyed with her phone for a moment and then tried Vic's number. It rang a number of times, which told Erin that she was probably serving a customer. She had tried to train her employees not to answer phone calls when they were on shift, but particularly not when actually in the middle of serving a customer.

"Hello, boss," Vic answered eventually, sounding slightly breathless. "What do you need?"

"I just wondered what Willie is doing today. I need a short ride, and if he's in town…?"

"You need a ride?" Vic sounded confused. "Did your car break down?"

"No. I went out for a walk, but I went too far and I'm tired and overheated. I was hoping I could get a ride back home from somebody."

"Well… you'd better take Willie off your list. I think he's out of town today. Sorry."

"It's okay. He's the first one I tried. I'm sure someone else will be able to help out."

"Do you want me to leave Charley to mind the store and I'll come and get you?"

"No, you'd better stay there," Erin said immediately. Charley, her long-lost biological sister, was older than Vic, but Vic was more dependable. Erin wasn't comfortable leaving Charley without some kind of supervision. Vic might only be nineteen, but she was more responsible than many thirty-year-olds. "I'll call around to see if anyone else is available. Or I'll walk. It's not really that bad; I've had a rest and a drink."

"Don't do anything stupid. You didn't grow up around here, and heatstroke is a real thing. You don't want to end up dead in the middle of the woods."

"I'm not going to do that."

"Call me back if you can't find anyone else. Where are you?"

"Canyon Park."

"Where is that?"

"Just a little park a couple of miles from home." Erin was going to describe it as peaceful or undisturbed or something else to indicate that it was isolated and not a busy place but, looking around at the busy cops, she decided that peaceful was not the word.

"Okay. I'll look it up. Just promise me you won't walk home alone."

"I won't."

"Good. Text me when you get back home, because I'm going to be worrying about you now."

That had not been Erin's intention. She looked through the other names on her favorites list. Most people worked or had other commitments during the day. She didn't like disturbing anyone.

Beaver? Adele? Adele might be asleep. Rohilda Beaven worked, but she wasn't on a nine-to-five schedule like an office worker. She was an agent for a federal agency, and Erin thought she had a lot of control over the hours she worked. Depending on what she was investigating at the time, of course.

Beaver might be a good choice. She was a down-to-earth, savvy woman who wouldn't mince words and could give Erin advice on what she should do, stuck in the middle of this investigation.

CHAPTER 12

*B*eaver answered after just one ring.

"Erin?"

Erin could hear her chewing her gum. Beaver was constantly chewing a wad of gum. Erin sometimes wondered what it did to her jaw. Would it make it stronger because she was always chewing, or break the joint down because it never got a rest? Erin suspected that the reason Beaver chewed was not that she'd had an addiction to chewing tobacco in the past, but because she needed something to keep her busy, or because she ground her teeth when she had to be still. Beaver moved languidly, as if she were calm and relaxed and nothing could affect her but, underneath that, Erin knew she was coiled like a viper just waiting to strike. Chewing gum made her appear casual and unconcerned, but she knew that Beaver was anything but.

"Hi, am I interrupting you from anything important?"

Beaver might have answered right away because she was awaiting a call. It might mean it was a bad time for her to talk.

"No, everything is quiet. What can I do for you? I hear you've been out tripping over bodies again."

"Again?" Erin repeated. Had word of the body in the park spread that far already? She supposed Beaver might be listening to a police scanner and know what was going on the instant she had called Terry for help.

"I heard something about a body in the basement of the bookstore? Or have you found too many lately to remember such an insignificant thing?"

"Yes, that's right. I did find one there. And then again..."

"Again?" It was Beaver who repeated the word this time.

"Yes. You heard that the body I found in the bookstore disappeared before the police could get there?"

Beaver chuckled. "I did hear something about that. Sounds like something from an old *Three Stooges* flick. Or *Keystone Cops*."

Erin was gratified that Beaver was blaming the police department rather than her. "Well, as it turns out, I found him... again."

"In the bookstore?"

Erin laughed. "No. In the park this time. Canyon Park."

"Don't know it. Is it close?"

"It's in Bald Eagle Falls." Erin suddenly wondered whether Beaver was even in town. She was often in the city or elsewhere in the state for an investigation. Though she spent a lot of time in Bald Eagle Falls with her boyfriend Jeremy—Vic's brother—she didn't actually have a residence in town. "Are you... around?"

"I haven't been called in by the boys in blue to consult. Do they need my expertise for something?"

"No. I just need a ride home from the park and was wondering whether you were even in town."

"Ah. I could do that. Though I would need to harass the locals first," Beaver warned, laughing. "They need someone keeping them on their toes."

"I think you could say I have been doing that already."

"So you have. Two bodies in two days. Or one body in two different locations in two days. Now, why did you find him and not them? They should have been all over it today."

"I'm just lucky, I guess."

"Will Canyon Park show up on my GPS, or is it too small of a place to matter to the GPS gods?"

"It should show up, I think. I looked it up on the internet, and it was on their map with all the access roads and satellite imagery. Even street-level pictures."

"It should be on the GPS then," Beaver agreed. "I'll see you in a few minutes."

When Beaver showed up in her clunker a few minutes later, Erin heard Terry swear and ask, "What is *she* doing here?"

He had worked together with Beaver plenty of times in the past. But Erin supposed he still didn't like to find that she was on a case he had thought his, or that a seemingly innocuous death was something bigger that the feds were already interested in.

Erin stood up to walk to the car and get in, but Beaver had already warned that she intended to harass the local police department about the case, and she hadn't just been joking. After getting out of the car, she loped over to the cordon taped off with a slow, lazy gait.

"What's up, Beaver?" Sheriff Wilmot asked. "Haven't been told you have any involvement in this case."

"When have the higher-ups ever told you I was involved in a case before I showed up at the scene?"

"Well... not very often," Wilmot admitted.

"Probably never. What've we got?"

"DB. No identification yet, so I don't see how you could be involved. Unless you already knew who it was when Erin found him in the bookstore."

"It's not anything to do with any of my cases." Beaver shrugged and chewed her gum, mouth partially open. "I'm just rubbernecking."

"Well, don't be asking questions about the case if you're not involved. You can get it from the newspaper like everyone else."

"Will this even make the news?"

Wilmot laughed sharply, like a cough. Had Erin been finding so many bodies in Bald Eagle Falls that it wasn't even noteworthy anymore?

"I'm sure there will at least be a footnote," he said. "Maybe a letter to the editor."

"About how you need to be keeping the parks clean?" Beaver suggested. "Free of trash like this." She gestured toward the dead body.

"Trash?" Wilmot repeated, looking at the shiny shoe that was visible from where they were standing. "Doesn't seem to me like you are in a position to be making that kind of judgment."

"Just a joke, Sheriff."

"Hmm. What are you here for, if you don't have any involvement in the case?"

Beaver nodded toward Erin.

"Ah. Good." Wilmot nodded. "Glad she's got someone to take her home. Now don't you go putting any ideas in her head. We don't want her contaminated or biased by anything you might have to say."

"Would I do that? I told you it isn't my case."

But Wilmot's suspicious look suggested that he was not convinced of the fact. Just because Beaver said she didn't have any interest, or didn't *yet* when the body had not yet been identified, that didn't mean that she didn't know something that he didn't, or that it wouldn't become a case that she was officially interested in in the future.

Beaver gave a nod of acknowledgment or farewell. "See you later, Sheriff."

He nodded and turned back to the body. Beaver strode over to the bench and Erin stood up. Despite the fact that it was hot and she had warmed up her body with the walk, her knees and back protested at having to get up from the bench after sitting there for a while. Erin straightened and stretched.

"Thanks for coming to pick me up."

"No bother at all, Miss Erin."

"I appreciate it."

"Always good to see what's going on in the neighborhood."

"I didn't interrupt you from anything important?"

Beaver didn't answer as she led the way to the car and climbed in. She looked over at Erin as she slid into the passenger seat.

"If I couldn't get away from what I was doing, I wouldn't say yes. I would tell you no, and you could go to the next person on your list."

Erin nodded, feeling a little better. She didn't like to impose on anyone and didn't want Beaver to help her out just because she felt obligated by her relationship with Jeremy or because of something Erin had done to help her out in the past. But Beaver was one of those people who was upfront about how she felt and didn't make her guess.

"Okay."

Beaver pulled out. "What's your relationship with this guy?"

"What? With Terry?"

Beaver snorted. She chewed her gum and her eyes roved back and forth when she drove, as if she were waiting for something to happen. A sniper, maybe, or a drive-by.

"Your relationship with the guy with the knife in his chest."

"I didn't put it there. I've never even seen the guy around Bald Eagle Falls before."

"That's not what I asked."

Erin shrugged and stared out the window. It was quiet. Despite Beaver's vigilance, there wasn't anything going on outside to distract Erin's attention or explain why she wasn't answering Beaver.

"You just happened to find this guy in the park," Beaver said, in a tone that told Erin she knew it wasn't true.

"I wasn't expecting to find him there. There's no way I could have known that someone would dump his body there."

"Yes. Makes you wonder, doesn't it?"

"I didn't put him there. I'm the one who called the police, remember? If I had something to do with it, do you think I would have called the police? I especially wouldn't have called the police to an empty basement, telling them that there *used* to be a body there. And then dump it somewhere else and call the police again to tell them that I'd found it *again*! You think I want to end up in this kind of situation?"

"Nope. Which is why I'd be interested in finding out exactly what is going on."

"Nothing is going on. This doesn't have anything to do with me. I appreciate the ride home, but I really don't want to talk about it all. I already talked to the sheriff about it, and I know he's going to want to talk to me again, and I know Terry is going to want to talk to me about it when he gets home. Whenever that is. I don't want to have to discuss it with you, too."

"You're not going to be able to mislead everyone."

"I'm not trying to."

"No? Huh. Could have fooled me."

Erin looked at her sharply and almost repeated that she didn't want to talk about it with Beaver. But then she didn't. That would be denying it too much. Beaver would want to know why she was so resistant if she hadn't had anything to do with the death. If Erin just kept it casual, and shrugged off any of Beaver's theories, she would be in a much better position.

It only took a few minutes for Beaver to drive her home. Erin climbed out of the car. "Thanks again. I really appreciate it. Now I'm going for a cool shower and fresh clothes. And maybe a nap."

Beaver chewed. "Sounds like a plan." She shifted the car into drive. "You know how to reach me if you want to talk."

CHAPTER 13

Of course, Erin was right about Terry wanting to talk to her about the case when he got home. She wouldn't have expected him to be home early, but he finished in plenty of time to make it home to dinner, leaving the others in the police department with whatever other processing and paperwork needed to be done. Terry had, Erin supposed, been elected as the person most likely to be able to get the full story out of Erin.

She had been thinking of what to say to him but still hadn't come to any decision. She couldn't lie to Terry, and she couldn't tell him the full story, and that left her in a difficult position. It had been the same since she moved to Bald Eagle Falls. Terry knew that Erin didn't want to talk to him about her past, that she had things she didn't want to be part of their relationship, and he'd had to accept that. But he never really had. He'd kept quiet about it, played along with her, and pretended he was happy with her, but she knew all along that he had doubts. He wanted to know the whole story, no matter how unhappy he might be to hear it.

And when he found out, how was he going to react? Would he dump her? Tell her that things weren't working out? Say that he just couldn't live with her, but it was his own fault and not hers? She would be alone again. Just she and the animals. And she would miss K9.

But maybe it was better to be alone than in a relationship that wasn't open and equal. She'd been deluding herself into thinking they could be happy together.

Terry walked in the door and saw her in the kitchen, putting the finishing touches on dinner.

"I'm going to have a shower," he told her, pinching his uniform shirt between his fingers and making a face. "Change into something more comfortable. I'll only be a few minutes. You can keep it warm?"

"It will keep," Erin agreed.

He was true to his promise and didn't take long to shower off the day's sweat and dust and change into a light t-shirt and shorts to keep cool. Erin fed K9 and the other animals while he washed up, so she was ready to eat once he sat down at the table.

Terry ate without any comment. He probably couldn't even have told her what he was eating. He shoveled the food in steadily and didn't seem to enjoy it or even notice that he was eating.

"Is everything okay?" Erin asked.

She meant the food, but he didn't take it that way.

"Is everything okay? No, I don't think everything is okay. I keep trying to figure out how it happened and how everything fits together, but I can't. Of course you didn't have anything to do with this man's death, but... what's going on? How did you find him? Not just once, but twice? What were you doing in the basement? What were you doing in the park? You shouldn't have been in either place. Are you trying to cover for someone? Are you trying to mislead us? It just doesn't make any sense."

Erin took a few more bites of her dinner, chewing carefully and pretending to give the food all of her attention.

"I told you what happened," she said finally. "If you don't believe me..."

"How can I believe you? You just happened to go over to The Book Nook when it was supposed to be closed but someone had left the door open, happened to go down the stairs where you shouldn't have been, and happened to find a body. And then lost it. You walk to a park that you've never been to before just out of curiosity or an impulse, and you come across the same body again. You don't have a good explanation for why you were in either place."

"I went to The Book Nook to get my platters," Erin said evenly.

"But you didn't get them. They were on the kitchen counter waiting for you, if that was what you really wanted. There was no reason to go downstairs. If you didn't want to wait around for Naomi or another employee, you could have just gone back to Auntie Clem's."

"I thought I heard a noise."

"But you didn't. By your own account, the man was dead and no one else was down there. So you didn't hear anything. You didn't have a reason to go down there."

"I *thought* I heard a noise. You can *think* you hear a noise when there isn't anyone else there to make it. The house makes all kinds of noises when there is no one else there. Creaking and tapping and all kinds of other noises. Sometimes I think I hear someone on the stairs going up to the attic. But there isn't anyone else at home and no one has pulled down the stairs. It's just the house making noises. Or ghosts, if you want to believe in a supernatural explanation. It's the same thing with The Book Nook. I thought I heard a noise. Maybe it was just the pipes or the ventilation."

He stopped eating for a moment and stared at her. Then his eyes dropped to his plate again. It was obvious that he was trying to avoid seeming confrontational. He was trying to act casual about the whole thing. Like it was just a conversation between couples, not a custodial interview.

"Maybe that's true. But then explain to me what you were doing in the park today. Exactly what you were doing there, in a park you had never been to, where someone just happened to have dumped the same body again."

"Bald Eagle Falls is a small place."

"Not that small. I patrol this town regularly, and I can't think of the last time I walked around that park looking for any trouble. I've never found a body over there."

"Well, I hadn't either. Until today."

"You'd never been there before. You just happen to hit the jackpot the first time?"

"It wasn't exactly the jackpot. That would imply that it was something I wanted to find. Trust me—it was not. That was the last thing I wanted to find in the park today."

Almost the last thing. The second-to-last thing.

"Why were you there? What possessed you to go there today on this little walk? A walk that took you out of the way in the heat of the day, so far from the house that you couldn't make it back safely."

"I could have made it back. I just... didn't think it was a good idea to push myself too hard."

"Why, Erin?"

"I just wanted to check it out. I wanted to see what kind of a park it was. If it was nice. Someone mentioned it when we were talking about places to go and things to do around town. I thought I would go have a look."

"Places to go and things to do in Bald Eagle Falls? I have never heard anyone put Canyon Park on that list. There is nothing to do there. Literally nothing. It is some grass and a pathway through some trees. You have more wildlife in your backyard."

"There was a deer," Erin argued.

"What?" Terry was momentarily derailed.

"In the park. I saw a deer. It didn't stay long, but... there is wildlife there. I don't usually see deer in the woods here." She pointed toward the woods beyond the back fence.

She was too noisy when she walked through the woods. She was clumsy and always seemed to put her feet in the wrong places, rustling the leaves, breaking dry sticks, rustling through the bushes. The deer didn't stay long enough to see who was there. Only when Erin stopped and was quiet and still like she had been sitting in Canyon Park.

"I'm not talking about the wildlife." Terry shook his head irritably. "I'm talking about you going there for no reason and finding a body. Like you knew it was there. Like you went there looking for it. How are you involved in this? How did you know that's where the body had been dumped? Who told you?"

"Reg would tell you that I just happen to stumble across these things," Erin said. "I attract trouble. Like... karma or something. I don't know. My psychic energy."

"Reg? Reg Rawlins? You think I want to hear what some scam psychic has to say about it? That would settle things for me?"

Erin shrugged. She nibbled at her meal. "No. But sometimes there are coincidences. You can't explain why something happens; it just does. You believe in miracles, don't you? I know you're not very religious, but you believe that those stories in the Bible really happened. And you believe in people in modern times being healed, or guided to do something, or protected."

He'd never said much to her about it. She was an atheist, so why would he share those things? But Erin had heard him talk to others. She had gone to church with him once for a Christmas Eve service and had seen the look on his face when they talked about the Christmas story and faith and miracles.

Terry scowled. "This wasn't a miracle. You didn't pray to be guided to his body. Nothing... *spiritual* led you there."

Of course he wouldn't believe that. Even if he were an ardent church-goer, he wouldn't think that God could guide an unbeliever, would he?

"I can't explain it to you," Erin said finally, shaking her head. "You know me. You're just going to have to trust me when I say I didn't have anything to do with that body being dumped in Canyon Park."

The look he gave her was not reassuring.

CHAPTER 14

*E*rin was studiously avoiding discussing anything that had happened the afternoon before as she and Vic worked together in the kitchen to prepare the day's morning breads and muffins. Erin really didn't want to spend any more time answering questions about the body that had now reappeared or how she had just happened to be the one to find it.

Instead, she was talking waffles.

"I have a few new recipes to try out. Some different flour combinations to see how they will hold up. I really think that the pumpkin spice idea is a good one. If I totally liquefy the pumpkin in a blender, it can act as most of the liquid for the waffles and shouldn't make them too heavy. Maybe I'll add a bit more baking soda or cream of tartar to make sure it has enough rise."

"You always need a bit extra for gluten-free recipes anyway," Vic agreed.

Erin smiled and nodded. Vic was picking up on some of the nuances of gluten-free baking. She wasn't making any of her own recipes yet but, like all of the Auntie Clem's employees, she made plenty of suggestions as to things they could make in the future, variations on favorites, and holiday or promotional treats that would keep people coming back again and again, interested in the variety rather than being bored with brown rice bread and chocolate chip cookies. Erin often discussed the possibilities with Vic, talking about what things she might have to tweak in a new variation to make it work. And Vic was clearly picking up on and remembering the details.

"You're getting the hang of it," she commented. "How you need to adjust for different flours and ingredients, I mean."

"Well, not like you, but I'm getting more of the basics."

"One day you'll be coming up with new recipes all on your own."

"As long as I document them." Vic nodded to the recipe binder on the counter.

They couldn't be casual about the recipes. They needed to replicate it exactly every time, and customers needed to know exactly what ingredients were in each baked good. Some people were only following a gluten-free diet and could have anything in the bakery, since no gluten-containing ingredients were allowed in the kitchen. And the majority of the bakery customers weren't actually following a gluten-free diet. Because Erin's was the only bakery in town, they chose to go there rather than to drive all the way into the city to get to a regular bakery or settle for the mass-produced loaves of bread and boxes of cookies at the grocery store.

But more often than not, those who had a problem with gluten also had other allergies or intolerances and needed to be very careful about what they ate. A single purchase could involve a careful review of half a dozen different recipes to find a product that was suitable.

"I don't think I'll ever be as good as you," Vic said. "You really have a knack for it. And there aren't a lot of people around who know how to bake for gluten-free diets like you can."

Erin shrugged modestly, feeling a flush creep up her throat. "Not in a small town like this. I know Mrs. Foster did some gluten-free baking before I opened up Auntie Clem's, for little Peter, but she must be so busy with all those kids. I don't think she makes much anymore, and it was just the bare basics when she did."

"Aunt Angela never got the hang of it," Vic referred to Angela Plaint, who had died shortly after Erin had moved into town. "Even though she was a baker and ended up with a wheat allergy. She mostly just bought that awful stuff off the shelf."

"Most of the commercial stuff isn't that awful anymore," Erin said generously. "You can hardly even tell that some of it is gluten-free."

"Hmm. Not to hear Aunt Angela tell it. She was miserable when she started reacting to wheat."

It had affected Angela's living—being the owner of The Bake Shoppe at the time Erin moved into town—as well as her health and ability to enjoy the foods she loved, so Erin could understand it. She knew other people who had reacted that way. Who were so miserable eating a special diet that every meal was a chore and a cause for distress. It was no wonder Angela Plaint had been such a grouch, so miserable to everyone else around her.

Though from what Erin understood, Angela had always been a hard woman. Tough on her kids, maybe even abusive. She had been accepted into the church ladies' group that met at Auntie Clem's every Sunday after the Baptist services but, as Erin had discovered after Angela's death, no one had really liked her. It was hard to embrace someone who was so prickly.

"There is Lacey," Vic said, "Lacey Moore."

Erin looked toward the door but didn't see anyone waiting outside yet. "Lacey Moore?" Erin repeated.

"Not actually *here*. I just meant that she had a knack for special recipes, like you."

"And who is Lacey Moore?" Erin knew she'd heard the name before but didn't know where. One of the older ladies, she thought. Not a regular customer. Of course, if she were a good baker herself, there wouldn't be any reason for her to patronize the bakery.

Vic raised her brows in surprise. "Bertie's sister."

"Bertie Braceling?"

Vic nodded as she started one of the big mixers running. "You know how challenging *he* was to cook for."

"I didn't even realize he had a sister." Erin had been at Bertie's funeral, but she couldn't remember much about it. She had probably still been in shock at the time, after Davis Plaint had tried to run them down. But Bertie had pushed Erin away and he was the only one who had ended up being hit. Bertie had been coming to Auntie Clem's in the weeks preceding his death. Erin wouldn't have guessed that he had someone cooking for him at home. "Why did he come to the bakery if she cooked for him?"

"I don't remember. Something was going on at the time. She had to go look after their ailing mother or something like that. She was away for a few months. Came back after Bertie and her mother died."

"Oh, the poor woman. That's too bad."

"Yeah. I don't imagine she has anyone to cook for now. No one who needs her special touch, anyway. She's getting on in years, though, and probably isn't sorry not to have to do that anymore."

"It can be a big job, especially with someone like Bertie who had *so* many allergies. He wouldn't be able to have anything packaged or off the shelf. Everything had to be made from scratch."

"She must be in her eighties now. She's probably happy for a break. Though… of course, she wouldn't see it that way." Vic gave a little grimace.

"I know." Erin kept her eyes on the cupcake batter she was pouring rather than on the images that sprang into her head.

CHAPTER 15

The door burst open, sending the bells swinging and jingling madly. Melissa swept in like a tornado. Dark spirals of hair bounced around her face.

Erin pressed her hand to her heart. "You want to give us a heart attack? What's going on out there? Are you being chased by a bear?"

Melissa laughed. "No... nothing like that. I was just... really eager to get here."

The only time that Melissa was that eager to get in the door at Auntie Clem's was when she had some bombshell news she wanted to share. She loved the drama and basked in everyone's reactions to good, bad, or shocking news.

Since she worked part-time with the police department, the information she had to share was often not the kind of things she was supposed to be telling anyone, but some little tidbit she had learned of an investigation while she was filing reports, reading or perhaps overhearing something that was going on in the office.

"Well..." Erin pretended not to know that Melissa was only there because she wanted to burst whatever bombshell she had and watch the destruction. "What are you looking for today?" She looked down studiously at the contents of the display case, bringing up Melissa's personal baked good preferences from her brain's filing cabinet. "These double chocolate brownies have been very popular this week. Or maybe some salted caramel fudge?"

"Oooh." Melissa was distracted at least momentarily from her news as she considered the possibilities. "Have you ever considered selling the two together in some kind of package? Or maybe adding a layer of salted caramel on top of the brownies?"

"Two very good ideas!" Erin approved. She would have to remember them the next time she was working on a new variation. "Would you like one of each, then?"

Melissa nodded, her lips slightly parted. At least she wasn't actually drooling. Not down her chin, anyway.

"Anything else?" Erin raised her brows and looked over the rest. "Some crusty bread to have with soup for a simple lunch or dinner? Rosemary herb breadsticks?"

"Maybe half a dozen of the breadsticks," Melissa decided. "Do you have garlic oil to go with them?"

"Of course." Erin packaged up the breadsticks and added a small condiment container of garlic oil for dipping. "Just put them on parchment and heat them gently for a few minutes."

Melissa knew that, of course. It wasn't the first time she had purchased Erin's breadsticks in one of their many variations. Maybe sun-dried tomato next time…

As Vic tapped the register's keys, Melissa's eyes slid back over to Erin.

"Did you hear," she asked in a low, confidential tone, "that they have identified your dead body?"

Erin swallowed. This was not welcome news. She kept her face blank. "It's not *my* dead body," she pointed out.

"You've found him twice." Melissa laughed, her generous mouth a wide grin showing off plenty of teeth, "I think that makes him yours."

"I don't have anything to do with him. That was just… a weird coincidence."

"Mind your manners, Miss Melissa," Vic warned. "You wouldn't want to bite the hand that feeds you." She passed Melissa her bag of baking, raising her brows significantly at the word "feeds."

Melissa laughed again, but more repressed this time.

"Well, whether you want to call him yours or not, we have a name for him now."

Erin nodded and didn't ask the obvious question.

"Well?" Vic took up the opportunity instead. "What is it? He was an out-of-towner, right?"

"His name is Brandon Quayle. And he is from Maine." Melissa looked at Erin expectantly.

Vic's eyes turned to Erin as well, surprised by this news.

"Huh." Erin shrugged. "Do they know anything else about him?"

"He's from Maine," Melissa repeated.

"Yes... do you know everyone who lives in Tennessee?"

"No," Melissa laughed. "Of course not. But Maine is much smaller."

"Well then... do you know everyone who lives in Bald Eagle Falls? Would you know everyone's names? Anything about them?"

Melissa frowned. "No. But I thought... since he came to Bald Eagle Falls from Maine, and you came to Bald Eagle Falls from Maine, that you probably knew each other. We don't get a lot of people here from New England. Maybe you were brought here by the same thing."

"He was brought here by his aunt leaving him a bakery or storefront?" Erin asked dryly. "I'm sure there are other people in town who come from Maine or New England. It's just a coincidence."

"That you kept finding him *and* he was from Maine?" Melissa looked doubtful. She had obviously been expecting Erin to immediately volunteer that she knew the man and was disappointed by the lack of response.

Erin looked from Melissa to Vic and back at Melissa again, waiting for her to recognize that it was time to leave. She had purchased her baked goods, dropped her bomb, and there was nothing else for her to do.

The silence drew out awkwardly. Erin could have made things easier on Melissa by asking her how she was doing now that she was married. If she had been happy with the way the wedding and reception went, if Davis was happy, if she felt any different being married instead of single— which Erin thought was unlikely since none of their living arrangements had changed. Davis remained in the penitentiary; it wasn't like he was going to move in with Melissa any time soon. Or within the next decade or two.

But she didn't want to make things easier on Melissa or help her to make a graceful exit. She just wanted Melissa to leave.

"Well... thank you for these," Melissa said, holding up her shopping bag. "I'm really looking forward to dinner tonight."

"Enjoy." Erin gave her a genuine smile. She was happy to see a customer enjoying her wares.

Vic gave a little wave, and Melissa left the bakery, the bells jangling more sedately as she left than they had upon her arrival.

Vic glanced toward Erin after Melissa was gone. "You don't think there's anything significant about him being from Maine? You don't think it's anyone you know… or who knows you?"

"That man and his death have nothing to do with me," Erin said firmly. "It doesn't matter how many points of similarity you find between us or how many lines you draw connecting us, his death didn't have anything to do with me. I wish everyone would just drop it." She tried not to think about the man in the bookstore basement or let the memory of his face and the knife seep back into her thoughts.

Vic pressed her lips together and nodded.

"Sorry. I wasn't thinking about how annoying it probably is for everyone to be asking you about him like you should know him. I know you didn't have anything to do with his death. I saw you when you came back here to report it. You were as white as a ghost."

Erin gave a small smile. "Thanks. I really just want to put this behind me. But…" She looked toward the door, "I know that's not going to happen now. If they know that he was from Maine, then it's just a matter of time before they come to ask me more questions."

CHAPTER 16

*A*s Erin had expected, it was not long before the police department wanted to speak to her about her possible connection with Brandon Quayle. Sheriff Wilmot wanted her to come in but, when she arrived, it was not Wilmot who was waiting to interview her, but Rod Stayner.

Erin had never been particularly comfortable around Stayner. Her first few experiences with him had not been positive, and she knew that had colored her opinions of him. She was sure he was a fine law enforcement officer and was well-trained and had what it would take to be great at what he did one day. But from the beginning, she had seen only his flaws.

He covered up his shortcomings with a bold, brash attitude that said he couldn't do anything wrong, and anyone who suggested it didn't know what they were talking about. If he missed taking fingerprints, touched something before it had been processed for evidence, or made a wrong assumption, that wasn't his fault and he wasn't responsible for the consequences. He made sexist or racist comments without any indication that he understood it was wrong and could hurt someone.

On the other hand, she knew that he did show some compassion toward crime victims, and still treated Erin with respect although she had been a suspect in the past.

But now she was facing him again. He had grown and matured since his first arrival in Bald Eagle Falls to cover Terry's position while he was recovering from an assault. He was no longer brand new. His overconfidence had been replaced with real knowledge and experience, and he would probably be more insufferable than ever—a bully with experience and training in how to intimidate and interrogate.

"Uh, I thought I was supposed to talk to Sheriff Wilmot," Erin told him. "I think I'll just wait for him."

"No, you're here to talk to me," Stayner told her firmly. "Just come in here and have a seat, and we'll have a little chat."

Erin shook her head again. "Maybe Terry, then, if the sheriff isn't free."

"Miss Price. You're here to talk to me, and I'm the one you are going to talk to. Please come in and don't waste my time."

His square jaw clenched. He apparently did not appreciate her attempts to get out of the interview or to see someone else in his place. Now she had insulted him or hurt his feelings, but hadn't gotten out of talking with him, so he would hold that against her.

Erin reluctantly followed Stayner into the interview room, her stomach tied in knots. She knew that she could refuse and go home. She wasn't under arrest and if she didn't want to talk to him, she didn't have to. But she didn't want to look guilty and didn't want them to think they had to investigate her further because she was trying to hide something. She wanted them to be satisfied that there was nothing in the coincidence that both she and Brandon Quayle came from Maine. It was not that big of a deal. There could be hundreds of people in Bald Eagle Falls who had come from Maine. Or dozens, anyway.

"Thank you for coming in," Stayner said formally as he sat down across from Erin. He turned on a digital recorder on the table and dictated the date, time, and persons present. Erin looked at the security camera in the corner of the ceiling and wondered whether Terry was watching on his computer or in another room with a monitor in it.

"I don't think there's really anything to say to you," Erin told him. "I told you guys before that I didn't have anything to do with this guy's death. It's just one of those random things. Just a weird coincidence. Things like that happen, you know. Like when two twins do the same thing at the same time even when they're a whole world apart and haven't coordinated it. Sometimes you run into the same person twice in two different places, two days in a row. You might think they're stalking you, but it's just a coincidence."

"How did you know Brandon Quayle?"

Erin closed her eyes and shook her head. "I don't think we've established that I did," she pointed out. "Just because we both came from Maine, that doesn't prove anything."

"You said that you had never seen him before you found his body in the basement of The Book Nook."

Erin was pretty sure she hadn't said that. She waited for him to actually ask her a question. He was fishing, that was all. Trying to get information from her by twisting what she had said. She had been pretty careful of what she had told them previously.

"Did you know Mr. Quayle in Maine?"

"We might have met. I lived there for a lot of years."

"You didn't know him well?"

Erin shook her head. She looked over his head, trying to keep her expression blank. Stayner studied her, his eyes narrowed.

"Were the two of you in a relationship?"

Erin opened her mouth to answer him, but Stayner cut her off. "*Any kind* of relationship."

She closed her mouth again. She took a deep breath and let it out again. "I never told you I didn't know him at all."

He blinked at her.

"I've read through Sheriff Wilmot's and Officer Piper's notes… and I'm pretty sure you did."

"They may have misunderstood me."

"If they misunderstood, it was because you deliberately misled them."

Erin couldn't exactly argue that, so she just kept her mouth shut.

"What was your relationship with Mr. Quayle?"

"We were… it was never really formalized. I was with him for a while, but we were… it was more casual. It wasn't like there was a *defined* relationship."

"You were 'with' him."

Erin tried to find a way to clarify what she had meant or take it back, but couldn't think of a way.

"Uh, we knew each other."

"Casually."

She shrugged.

"What does that mean? That you had friends in common?"

"Some, yes."

"Did you ever date?"

"We never…"

"Never *defined* that," Stayner guessed. "If you didn't call it dating, then what was it?"

"Just… going out with friends. Or later, we went together because…" Erin foundered, trying to find an explanation that wouldn't make it sound like she and Brandon had been what they were.

"Because you knew each other casually."

She nodded.

"But then after a while, if you were seeing each other alone, you got to the point where you weren't just going out with each other as casual friends."

"Uh…"

"You were intimate partners?"

"Sometimes."

"Did you live together?"

"Not… exactly…"

"You had separate residences? But you slept over?"

"No… I crashed with him… because I lost my place. But it wasn't like… *that*."

"You just slept on the couch," Stayner said sarcastically.

"Sometimes, yeah."

"And sometimes with him."

Erin swallowed hard. "When I had to."

Stayner cocked his head slightly, considering that. "What do you mean, when you *had* to?"

"If I had to… in order to stay there. Or if he was… drunk or violent."

There was a long silence.

"Why would you stay with someone who treated you like that?"

He was so young. He had seen so little of how the world worked, sheltered in rural Tennessee. She was sure it happened there too, but he hadn't been exposed to it as a boy. If he had, he wouldn't have sounded so surprised.

"Survival." Erin shrugged. She couldn't explain it all to him in detail.

The way that the world worked for people who didn't have families, money, or homes. People who did their best to make it in the world without relying on homeless shelters, stripping, or selling drugs. American society was not set up for people who had to make it on their own without anything.

"Survival," Stayner repeated.

"If you want a roof over your head, a warm place to sleep, maybe even food or companionship, you do what you have to. Guys like Brandon... depend on that. That you won't leave because you don't have anywhere else to go."

"So. Despite what you told me, you did know him well."

"No. I…"

"Lived with him."

"Not like… a couple."

"How was it not like a couple?"

"We didn't… we weren't friends. We didn't share interests or spend time talking with each other. I never considered him a boyfriend."

"But you went out together, shared friends, and slept together."

"Some of the time."

"Some of the time," Stayner repeated.

Erin nodded and shrugged, looking down at the table. Stayner considered this in silence. After a few minutes, he stood up and walked out of the interview room. He shut the door behind him, and the latch clicked loudly in the emptiness of the space. Erin blew out her breath. She had done everything she could to avoid having to tell them about Brandon, but she had known from the time she first saw him in the basement of The Book Nook that she was in trouble. They would find out and would immediately jump to the conclusion that she had been the one who killed him.

CHAPTER 17

$\mathcal{I}$t seemed like a long time before Stayner returned to the room. It probably wasn't as long as it seemed—just a short conversation with Sheriff Wilmot or someone else to figure out what he should do next. Erin half expected him to return with a pair of handcuffs and inform her that someone would be coming to take her to the penitentiary and lock her up.

The same place as Davis Plaint and other men she had been instrumental in having arrested were incarcerated. But they wouldn't be allowed in the women's wing. Still, she might have to face women like Kim Brandon, who she did know.

When Stayner finally returned, he held a card in his hand, which he read to her. The Miranda warning. She'd heard versions of it so many times in cheesy TV mysteries and dramas, she was tempted to look around for a movie camera and the audience. It seemed unreal to hear it here, in safe, sleepy Bald Eagle Falls.

Terry had walked in the door behind Stayner, and he listened to Stayner's recitation of the warnings on the card. He nodded when Stayner was done, approving it.

He sat down at the side of the table, around the corner to her right rather than directly across from her like Stayner was. K9 sniffed at Erin and lay down between them. Terry reached for Erin's hand, but she pulled it back with a jerk.

"Erin, do you understand what is happening?" he asked.

"Am I under arrest? You don't have any evidence that I had anything to do with Brandon's death."

"No, we don't. You're not under arrest. But this is what we would call a custodial interview. Rod is interviewing you about a crime you might have played some part in, and you need to understand your rights."

Erin nodded.

"I'm not here as a law enforcement officer," Terry assured her. "I'm here for you. I'm here to make sure that Rod does everything by the book and that your rights are not compromised. I'm here to support you."

Try as he might to divide the two roles, he couldn't turn off what he heard in the interrogation room and not use it at home, or turn off his cop's brain and not see the things she did at home that might implicate or clear her in the case. He was still a cop. Like he'd been ever since they met that first day and had confronted her in Auntie Clem's Bakery, demanding to know what she was doing there.

"Do you understand that?" Terry repeated.

Erin shrugged. "I heard you."

Terry looked at her for a minute, then decided it was okay for Stayner to go on. He nodded at his fellow officer.

"Did you know that Quayle was in Bald Eagle Falls?" Stayner asked.

"No."

The two cops looked at each other. Erin pretended she hadn't seen them exchange looks. Terry was there for her? Communicating nonverbally with Stayner? Analyzing whether Erin was telling the truth or not, whether she could be trusted?

"He had not been in contact with you?"

Erin didn't answer.

"Had Quayle been in contact with you?"

"No."

Another look passed between the men.

"When you went into The Book Nook, was it to meet with Quayle?"

Erin was taken aback by the question. She shook her head. "I didn't know he was going to be there. Why would I expect him to be in The Book Nook basement?"

"You don't know why he was there?"

"How would I?"

"I'd like a straight answer. You don't know why he was in the bookstore?"

"No. I was shocked to find him there. As shocked to see it was him as I was to find a dead body there. I had no idea that he would be there."

"He was right down the street from you. And you didn't know he was there?"

"No."

"He didn't tell you he was going to be there?"

"I don't know. Not as far as I know."

"What do you mean you don't know?"

"I don't know what he might have *tried* to tell me. Some message he might have tried to get to me. I didn't know he was going to be there. I don't know if he tried to tell me that or not."

"What does that mean?"

Erin turned her face away from Stayner to look at Terry. "How hard is that to understand?"

"What Rod is asking is, how would Quayle have tried to contact you? How would he have gotten you that message?"

"I don't know. Calling, texting, emailing, getting someone to give a message to me. Sending it by carrier pigeon. I don't know, since I didn't get it."

"He had your phone number?" Terry asked. Funny how quickly he had gone from observing and being there by her side to protect her from Stayner to being the one asking her questions.

"I don't know."

"Did he ever phone you?"

"I don't know. He could have. I don't answer... anything with a 207 area code."

"In case it could be him."

"In case it is anyone from my past. I don't have anyone there I want to keep in touch with."

And if she did, if someone from her past reached out to her that she wanted to be in contact with, they could leave her a voicemail. There was no need for Erin to answer an unrecognized number.

"You never talked to Quayle about meeting him at The Book Nook?"

Erin shook her head. "No."

"Or why he might be going there?"

"No."

She gave Terry a long look, and then looked at Stayner. She shifted in her seat. "I want to go home."

The two cops exchanged glances. But Terry had said that she wasn't under arrest, and she didn't have to stay there and talk to them and give them more details that might incriminate her. She had already done enough damage to herself and her reputation in Bald Eagle Falls.

It had taken the church ladies a long time to get over the fact that she was an atheist, without even the slightest inclination to join one of their churches. And that she had ensnared one of the town's most eligible bachelors, who was at least Christian in name. And had taken a transgender runaway into her home and employed her in the bakery. A gluten-free bakery, at that, where a family couldn't even get a normal loaf of bread. It had taken time for them to come around and accept her as she was, with all of her quirks and shortcomings.

How were they going to feel about her when they found out that she had been involved with someone like Brandon Quayle up north and was a suspect in his death? It wasn't just a shocking story of discovering a body in The Book Nook basement anymore, or the fact that it had disappeared and reappeared. Now they would hear the rest of the story, as far as the police knew it. Her business at Auntie Clem's Bakery might not survive the blow. If they boycotted her and went into the city or to the grocery store for their baked goods, Auntie Clem's would fold.

Neither of the cops told her that she couldn't leave. Erin pushed herself to her feet. "I'm going to go home. Have some supper. I need to get to bed."

She didn't know what time it was. But she was completely wrung out and didn't want to deal with the world. If she could sleep, at least she could turn it all off for a few hours and maybe recover her equilibrium.

"I'll take you home," Terry said, also standing up.

Erin looked at him for a moment. Did he really think that he could swap roles like that? Go from being one of the cops interrogating her to being her boyfriend?

But maybe he didn't mean he was going to drive her home as her friend and partner. Maybe he was just offering to drive her home like he would any other suspect who was at their offices without a car. A courtesy.

"Fine," she said eventually, "you can drive me home."

CHAPTER 18

They went out to Terry's truck in silence. Maybe Terry just didn't want anyone else in the office—Clara or Melissa—to hear the discussion between them. Or perhaps he wanted to say something to her that he couldn't say in front of Stayner. Whatever his reason was, it was fine with Erin. She didn't want to talk to him either. Both because she didn't want to spread her business all over the town grapevine and because she was upset with him.

She tried to decide as they walked out to the truck and got in whether she was justified in being upset with him. Did she just feel like that because she was tired? Having an emotional reaction that was not rational? She didn't think so. Terry had excused himself from investigations that involved her in the past. That was what he was supposed to do, even if her connection to a case was only tenuous. If he didn't pull himself off, the sheriff would do it for him.

But this time, he had pretended to be on her side and not involved in the case and then had participated in the interrogation, trying to pry extra details out of her. He hadn't been doing that as a supportive partner trying to help her.

They didn't speak on the drive home. When Terry pulled up in front of the house, Erin had her door open before he was even fully stopped. She got out without a word and headed up to the front door without pausing to look at him or speak to him. He could pull back out and go straight back to the police department offices to continue investigating her background and anything that tied her and Brandon together. He could verify what she had said, start making phone calls to track down Brandon's friends to ask them about his relationship with Erin. He could dig deep and turn over as many of her secrets as he could, exposing them to the light of day.

She was nearly to the front door when she heard Terry's truck door open. He didn't call out to her, but followed her up the sidewalk into the house. Erin went into the house, shutting the door behind her, not waiting for him and holding it open as she normally would.

There wasn't anywhere she could go to escape him. She couldn't lock him out of the house when he lived there with her. It wouldn't be morally right or legal. If she tried, he could just call the sheriff, who would force her to let him in to at least remove his possessions from the house. And Erin didn't want to involve anyone else in their drama.

The door opened and closed quietly. Erin could hear K9 panting and, in a moment, he galloped across the house to catch up with her in the kitchen, which meant that Terry had released him from duty and was planning to stay rather than going back to the police department to continue the investigation. He needed his sleep too.

Erin talked to Orange Blossom and K9 as she got out their treats. Nothing that was going on was their fault. She tried not to treat them any differently from when she'd had a good day.

She opened the fridge and looked for something appetizing. Terry stood in the doorway of the kitchen, watching her.

"Erin."

She bent down to open a couple of containers of leftovers to see if there was anything she felt like eating, keeping the fridge door as a barrier between them.

"What?"

"We need to talk."

Erin shook her head. "I don't think so."

"I don't want things to be tense between us. We need to talk it out."

"I don't think that's the best solution."

He continued to stand there, waiting until Erin straightened up and closed the fridge door. "What do you think we should do, then?"

"Pretend that nothing happened. You can go back to work if you want. I'm going to bed."

She attempted to go into the walk-in pantry. He caught her by the arm, stopping her. His grip was not tight, but Erin stopped, her heart rate speeding up, just waiting for it to escalate.

"I don't want to go to work. I want to stay here and support you. But you need to let me do that."

"You can do what you want." Erin shrugged and tugged away from him, pulling out of his grip. "I didn't say you had to go back to work. It's up to you."

She looked at the various cans lining the shelves of the pantry. Eventually, she settled on a can of peaches. They would be sweet, go down easily, and be gentle on her stomach. She wouldn't eat much. She didn't want a full stomach keeping her awake. But she didn't want to lie awake hungry or wake up after a couple of hours needing something either.

Of course, all of that assumed that she would be able to sleep at all. She might not.

Terry watched her open the can and spoon some peach slices into a bowl. He helped himself to a few after she sat down at the table. He opened the freezer and added a small scoop of vanilla ice cream to the peaches. "You want some?"

It looked good, but Erin shook her head. "No."

He looked at her for a minute as if she were just being difficult and would change her mind if he waited her out. But Erin started to eat her peaches, and he put the ice cream back away. He put the remaining peaches into a plastic bowl with a lid and put them in the fridge before sitting down to eat his snack.

Hopefully, he would eat more later. He would order a pizza after Erin went to sleep or settle in front of the TV with a couple of beers and a bag of chips. But she wasn't going to offer to cook him anything or insist that he had to eat more, because that would just bounce back to her, with him suggesting that she had to eat more too. Erin didn't have the energy to argue that her stomach simply wasn't prepared for anything heavier.

"You never told me about Quayle," Terry said after the room had been filled with nothing but their clinking spoons for a few minutes.

Erin didn't look at his face. "We haven't discussed our previous relationships."

She didn't know all the details of who he had dated in Bald Eagle Falls, either. She'd heard some rumors and knew some of the women he had dated in high school or since then. But they'd never discussed details with each other. Maybe he figured it would be too awkward for her to deal with those women as customers at the bakery and community events.

"I would think that you would have told me about something like that. About... the difficulties that you'd had before. It might have come up."

"Why?"

She glanced up at Terry's face for a moment. His brow crinkled and the corners of his mouth turned down. He was clearly upset; she had never seen him like this before. Usually, when he was upset, he kept a blank, stoic expression, giving nothing away. The revelation of her past relationship with Brandon had obviously bothered him significantly.

"Because... it sounds like a pretty traumatic experience. You might have wanted to talk about it. Or to work through it with a counselor. Or... to let me know if anything in our relationship... bothered you. Triggered a traumatic memory."

Erin ran her spoon through the leftover syrup in the bottom of her bowl, swirling it in circles and figure eights.

"I don't see why I would do that."

"When you're in a relationship... you share things."

"About past relationships? Why?"

He couldn't seem to come up with a reasonable explanation, demonstrating to Erin that it wasn't something that a normal couple would have discussed. He was just trying to get more information out of her as a suspect.

"I didn't know that things had gotten quite that bad for you," Terry said, approaching it from another angle. "I know you said that things were tight when you aged out of foster care. You had to start working immediately and couldn't always get something stable."

Erin nodded her agreement.

"But you didn't say... that you had moved in with someone like that in order to survive."

"I wouldn't share that."

She could feel his eyes on her. "No. You don't share much from your past."

Erin rubbed her forehead uncomfortably. "You've known that from the start. You knew... that I'd had trouble. You ran background on me when you were investigating Angela Plaint's death."

He had to admit this was true. "I knew that you'd faced charges a couple of times. That you had gone by other names. I guess once we got to know each other I thought that if it was anything big, you would talk to me about it. You said you'd had trouble with families thinking that you had stolen things from home care patients you had worked with, or the patients themselves thinking that. And kids in foster care often go by several different names. I just... didn't anticipate anything like this."

"Like what?" Erin challenged. K9, lying on the floor next to Terry raised his head at her sharp tone. "I didn't do anything wrong. This isn't... you make it sound like I broke the law by being with him. I didn't. I just needed somewhere to live."

"No... I didn't mean that you did something wrong. Just that you went through something a lot worse than I thought. You only talked about trying to keep a steady job, having to move when a client died, because your job had included board. You never said that you had lived with anyone else. I thought... maybe a shelter for a few days to get back on your feet, or sleeping in your car until you could find an apartment."

"And that would have been okay?" she demanded.

At least living in a shelter or car would not have resulted in her being suspected of murder. Did Terry and the others really think that she'd had something to do with Brandon's death? That she had coldheartedly set up a meeting with him and then stabbed him in the chest? Did he really think she was that kind of a person?

"You're taking this the wrong way. I'm not accusing you of doing anything wrong. I'm just... a little hurt that you would not share something so important with me."

"That's a part of my life that I would rather forget."

Though she wasn't looking at him directly, she could see him nod his head. "I can understand that. I'm sorry if you think that I'm being intrusive or asking about something that's none of my business. But couples who live together usually share. They have more... emotional intimacy."

"They don't tell each other everything. Do you think that Willie tells Vic everything? She doesn't even know where he is half the time. Or that she tells him everything about her past? Or Beaver tells Jeremy about her previous relationships or stings?"

"Sorry," Terry muttered. He was silent as he ate his last few slices of peaches.

When he was finished, he ran his hand over his face, a fatigued gesture. He'd been short on sleep while he'd been investigating Brandon's murder. Or the disappearance of his body. He needed to get to sleep and not to be up another night.

"What do you want me to do?" Terry asked tiredly.

"About what?"

"Do you want me to sleep in the guest bedroom? Or leave?"

He looked at her, waiting for her response.

CHAPTER 19

"No, you don't need to leave," Erin said quickly, as if she would never think such a thing. As if she hadn't already been thinking about whether she could keep him out of her house, now that she was a suspect and Terry was being a cop instead of her boyfriend.

"The spare room, then?"

Erin didn't know what to say. It was good of him to suggest that he sleep somewhere else. There was a rift between them, and she didn't know if it could be repaired. He chose to be a cop over being there for her in a supportive role like he had first suggested. She had turned out not to be the person he thought she was. Someone who had sunk lower than he had ever imagined. Who might have killed a man to hide her past.

She wanted him to be there in her bed and to hold her tight and to say that it didn't matter and that he forgave her and didn't think she had killed Brandon Quayle. She wanted his warmth beside her, anchoring her. But that was a dream. It wasn't going to happen. They couldn't just erase what had been said over the last hour or two.

"Yeah, I guess," she conceded. "There are fresh sheets—"

"I know where everything is. I'll get out of your way."

He stood up and took his bowl to the dishwasher. Then headed out of the kitchen and down the hall to the spare room. He shut the door with a soft click, and Erin heard K9 whine in confusion. Terry opened the door again, and K9 exited, running back out to Erin and then heading toward her bedroom, where his kennel was.

But then he looked around and ran back to Terry in the spare room.

"Sorry," Terry apologized from within the room. "He's confused. I can move the kennel in here so he knows where to sleep."

Erin's heart gave a tug. Not only was she keeping Terry from her bed, but she was also upsetting K9. It wasn't his fault that his master had chosen the investigation over his relationship. Erin wanted to tell Terry that K9 could sleep in her bedroom, but she suspected that still wouldn't be a good solution. K9 would want to be in his kennel and near Terry. He wasn't used to sleeping in a different room.

"Yeah, I guess."

Terry came back out of the guest room and went down the hall to retrieve K9's kennel from Erin's room. He looked at her face for a moment when he returned. Was he wondering, as she was, whether this would be a permanent separation? He was probably running through his options, figuring out how quickly he could get his own place again if he needed to. Or maybe things would settle down and go back to normal and he would only be sleeping in the guest room for a day or two. K9 still ran back and forth between Terry and Erin, whining. Terry called him into the room, ordered him into the kennel, and shut the bedroom door.

K9 was a well-trained dog, and he would stay there, but Erin was afraid he would be unhappy all night, wondering why things had changed and he couldn't sleep with both Terry and Erin like usual.

K9 wasn't Erin's dog. She had known him for a much shorter time than Terry had. His loyalties were clearly to Terry rather than to Erin. She had never considered him her dog, but couldn't help the feeling that he was being torn away from her. She was attached to all of the animals in the household and would miss K9 if she and Terry did not work things out. And the other animals would miss him too. Orange Blossom took hissing and growling at K9 to a high art, but Erin suspected that he enjoyed the rivalry with K9 as much as his friendship with Marshmallow and would not be a happy kitty if his enemy no longer came around.

∼

"I take it you didn't sleep too well last night?" Vic asked as she watched Erin pour coffee into her tall travel mug. Erin didn't normally consume that much caffeine.

"No. Not very well. I was tossing and turning all night, don't feel like I got a wink of sleep, though I know I must have gotten some."

"You should just stay home," Vic urged. "I can start the morning routine and call Charley to see if she's still up. Then one of the others to help out with the afternoon shift. No point in you being miserable all morning instead of just staying home and having a rest."

"I need to work. I need to throw myself into something and keep my mind off of... things."

"I heard that you knew Brandon Quayle," Vic said, her voice quiet, eyes down and away from Erin. She didn't ask for details, though it was pretty evident from her manner she was curious.

"Yeah. I'm sure that will all come out now. We can talk about it later. We'd better hit the road."

Erin grabbed her purse, heavy with her stuffed planner and tall travel mug, and headed out the door. Vic followed her out the door without complaint. They probably should have walked, but Erin chose to take the yellow VW bug instead. When they were on the way, Vic looked sideways at Erin.

"So, Brandon Quayle?" she prompted.

Erin looked back at her. "What about him?"

"I just wondered. You said before that you didn't know everyone in Maine, so you didn't know him. But... there are rumors that you did know him. The police department was questioning you about it yesterday."

"Someone needs to learn to keep her mouth shut."

Vic nodded philosophically. "Yeah. She does. So... they were asking you about him? And things went south?"

"I didn't kill him."

"Well, of course not!" Vic exclaimed. "I was there! Well, not right there in the basement, but I was there when you left Auntie Clem's and when you came back. I know you didn't have anything to do with it."

A huge weight lifted from Erin's shoulders. The police could suspect her all she liked, even Terry, but *Vic* knew that Erin hadn't had anything to do with Brandon's murder. She would stand up for Erin no matter what. And maybe others would too. Surely the residents of Bald Eagle Falls that she had rubbed shoulders with the past two years knew something about her by now. They knew that she wouldn't have done something like that.

If she had, she would have done a much better job at covering it up, and would not have moved the body, called the police, and then done it all a second time just for her own entertainment. Who did something like that? She had a hard time understanding why Brandon's body had been moved in the first place. And she was baffled at why it had been left in Canyon Park.

"I know you didn't kill the guy, Erin," Vic assured her. "There's no way. You didn't have enough time and, even if you did, why would you kill him? What motive did you have?"

"I don't know. I left him..." Erin shook her head, "before I ever came to Bald Eagle Falls. I haven't had anything to do with him since I left. So why would I do something now? All of that stuff, anything that happened between us, is way in the past."

"It doesn't make any sense," Vic agreed. "You didn't even know he was in town."

"No." Erin studied Vic. "I didn't."

"I knew it. If he was an ex, there is no way you would have gone over to The Book Nook to meet with him."

"Of course not."

Were there other exes that she would have met up with? Erin went through them in her mind and shook her head. She couldn't think of one of them that she would have agreed to meet with. Or one who would have wanted to meet with her. Who would come to Bald Eagle Falls to see her? It wasn't like she was a lottery winner and everyone wanted a piece of her. She was comfortable for the first time in her life but didn't have money to burn. Or to give away to anyone.

They reached the back door of Auntie Clem's Bakery, and Vic stepped aside to wait as Erin unlocked it and opened the door.

"Melissa said that Quayle was writing a memoir."

CHAPTER 20

*E*rin turned to look at Vic as they walked into the kitchen and turned on the lights.

"What?"

"Brandon Quayle was writing a memoir."

"A memoir?" Erin let out a laugh. "Why would he do that? Who would read it?"

"He didn't lead a very interesting life?" Vic asked. "I gather he wasn't anyone famous."

"An interesting life?" Erin echoed.

She didn't say anything while she pulled the bowls of batter out of the fridge and lined them up on the counter. Vic started turning on the ovens.

An interesting life? She supposed Brandon's life had been interesting. Certainly more interesting than she had liked. He certainly wasn't someone to hold up as an inspiration to others. He had been an addict, a liar, someone who was frequently in trouble with the police, and abusive.

He was a charmer. He had a way of making people think he was something he wasn't. But that only lasted for so long, as eventually people came to realize the truth about what he was—someone who manipulated others for his own gain. He got jobs and money from unsuspecting folks, used women for his own pleasure, and convinced people that his clothes were designer names and that his car was actually his. Yet in reality, he was not only behind on rent—but had been taken to court three times by his landlord to have him removed.

"Why would he write a memoir?" she asked aloud. "What exactly was it supposed to be about? A life he made up?"

"I don't know anything. Just that Melissa said that's what he was doing. Maybe that's why he was at The Book Nook."

Erin couldn't figure that one out. "Why?"

"To… read other memoirs or a book about writing memoirs. Or meet an agent or publisher."

Erin couldn't remember Brandon ever reading a book while she had known him. Not even a comic book. And he thought he could write one?

There was a knock at the door, which made both of them jump.

CHAPTER 21

*I*t was so rare for anyone to knock on the back door while they were open. And even more rare so early in the morning, before they had opened. One day, Beaver had dropped by early in the morning looking for something to eat after an unexpectedly long stakeout. She had not planned to be overnight and had not been prepared with the food she needed.

That had ended up being a pretty stressful day for anyone at Auntie Clem's or any of the businesses along Main Street, so Erin's heart was in her stomach as she walked over to the door to answer it.

"Who's there?"

"My name is Adrienne. I don't know if you remember me."

Erin opened the door slowly, trying to sort through her memories to find someone named Adrienne. She remembered as she opened the door and saw the woman standing there—one of the rural homeless around Bald Eagle Falls. There were families who squatted in the woods, trying to make enough to provide for their needs. People who couldn't afford the rental cost of an apartment or basement suite. Who maybe couldn't manage more than a tent over their heads, or living out of a car, as Terry had suggested the day before.

Erin knew what it was like not to have a proper place of her own.

Maybe that was why she had felt so strongly the need to help and support the poor in and around Bald Eagle Falls when other successful business owners in the town did not.

"Adrienne. Come in." Erin let her step inside the door. "What can I do for you?"

Adrienne looked nervously in Vic's direction, but Vic didn't stare at her or ask questions. She just went back to her work.

"It's okay," Erin assured her. "Do you want a coffee? Warm you up inside?"

Even though it wasn't cold outside, people who were malnourished often didn't have the fat to keep their body temperatures up and were constantly cold. Adrienne was thin. Her children were as skinny as sticks, but still seemed to have the energy to play all day, so they must be getting enough to eat. Adrienne probably skipped meals herself to put food on the table for them.

Adrienne shook her head, still looking around as if someone might attack her or might have seen her and followed her there.

"I just wondered… I know about your day-old bread program."

"Of course," Erin agreed. "I have so much in the freezer right now; I'd really be grateful if you could take some of it off my hands. We try not to make too much more than we need in a day but, of course, you have to keep food in the display case right up until closing time, so there has to be extra each day."

Adrienne nodded as Erin explained this and followed Erin over to the large chest freezer along one wall. Erin opened it up, and Adrienne's eyes popped at the variety of goods stored there. She had probably thought that Erin was kidding about needing someone to give the excess food to.

"Some bread and muffins, first of all," Erin said briskly, taking out several bags of frozen goods. "And what else do the children like? Some cookies? Chocolate, oatmeal, gumdrop, gingersnaps…"

Adrienne's eyes went over the possibilities. "Chocolate chip." She pointed at one of the bags. Erin pulled them out.

"And maybe some pizza shells? Bagels? The pizza pretzels are popular, so we always keep them well-stocked throughout the day and have a few left over after closing."

"That sounds nice."

"Let me get a shopping bag for you." Erin took a couple of bags of pizza pretzels out of the freezer and took a few shopping bags off of a shelf. She started loading the baked goods into bags. "Now, what else?"

Adrienne's eyes were big. She shook her head. "It's too much. I can't take all of this."

"Do you see anyone else taking it?" Erin motioned to the kitchen, occupied only by the three of them. "I take more home than I can eat with Terry—Officer Piper. Only a little bit of our day-old gets claimed, and I have to take the rest into the city for the shelters there or throw it in the garbage. And I hate throwing anything in the garbage."

Adrienne nodded, her eyes still big and skin pale. Erin would have expected her to be tanned or sunburned, with the amount of time she must spend outside but, if she wasn't getting enough to eat, starvation might have caused her pallor. "Of course. You can't throw good food away."

"Exactly. Are you sure I can't get you anything else?"

"No, this is plenty. We can afford to go to the grocery store." She said it defensively as if Erin had accused her of being unable to feed her family.

"Okay. Well, when you've used this up, just stop by. Or if you know someone else who could use it. It's so much easier for me if someone will take it off my hands."

Adrienne took the bags from her slowly. Her fingers were long and thin. For a moment, their eyes met.

"You are a nice woman," Adrienne said softly. "Most people don't understand."

"I think there are others who would… but they don't have as much to give as I do."

"*They* don't know what it's like to have nothing." Adrienne tossed another glance in Vic's direction, unsure of speaking in front of her.

"Vic understands," Erin countered. "When I first came to Bald Eagle Falls, she was living in the basement of the bakery. Hiding. She didn't have anywhere to go."

"Oh?" Adrienne looked at Vic for longer this time, and her shoulders lowered as she relaxed. "I didn't know."

"How would you? It was a couple of years ago, probably before you moved here."

The woman nodded, her lips pursed. She put her hand briefly on Erin's arm. "*We* know what it's like. Vic and I." She glanced over at Vic to elicit a nod. "Living how you can. Surviving. It isn't like people think it is. I wouldn't take my kids to one of those places. Catching fleas, getting molested, never being able to get a good night's sleep. You want a *home*. A place of your own." Her hand fluttered to indicate the direction of her camp. "Even if you have to start out living in a tent. Or with someone who…" Her eyes went to her feet, away from Erin. "Someone willing to help you out."

For Vic, that had been Erin. She had taken the younger woman in and invited her into her home. Vic was now more independent with her loft room over the garage, paying Erin a small amount in rent out of her earnings at Auntie Clem's. Erin didn't expect anything from her. But it had been different when Erin had been left with no job, no income, and no roof over her head. There were no savings to fall back on. No Clementine back then, before Alton Summers had come looking for her to tell her of her inheritance.

She'd had to survive somehow. It had been Brandon who had given her a hand, letting her crash with him while she tried to get back on her feet. Living in his apartment, eating his food, and trying to find another job when her last employer couldn't give her a reference and his family had refused to. Managing to find casual labor for a day or two, or saving nickels and dimes from panhandling. It took a long time working that way to put away enough money for a down payment on an apartment. And then she would need a job that paid enough to maintain it.

That's why it was better to find a job caring for someone who needed a companion, a position where she could board. Until that job ended, and the bottom fell out, and she was left again with no place to go.

"You did what you could at the time," Adrienne said, reminding Erin she was there, drawing her back from the memories.

Erin realized with a start that Adrienne wasn't just there for herself. She wasn't just there because of Erin's day-old baking program, though she appreciated the donation. She was there for Erin, to tell her that there were people who understood. It was hard for people like Terry and Stayner, who had always had a home, always had a roof over their heads, men with good jobs to support themselves. They'd had the stability, family support, and education needed to move into their chosen professions. They couldn't understand why she had stayed with Brandon and appreciated him despite his emotional instability and abuse.

"Thank you," Erin said softly, and put her hand over Adrienne's. She didn't know how word had gotten to Adrienne so quickly and still resented Melissa gossiping about the personal, private details of Erin's past. But she was thankful for Adrienne's empathy, even when everyone else only saw her as the prime suspect in a murder.

CHAPTER 22

Erin had known that it would be a busy day at the bakery, as it always was after a murder or other tragedy. Initially, they had been curious about the disappearing body—the shock of first discovering it and then its disappearance. Then there had been the rediscovery of the body in the park. Now, they were even more titillated by the fact that the victim was an ex-boyfriend—what else were they going to call him?—of Erin's. They wanted to see Erin and her red-rimmed, baggy eyes to speculate on how she felt about Brandon and his death and whether she might be his killer.

They hoped she would give them some salacious details to feed the Bald Eagle Falls grapevine and keep it chattering away. And if she didn't give them any, they would make it up.

There was a moment of startled silence when Dave Wolfe walked in the door, and then the whispers and giggles started. Erin found herself looking questioningly in Dave's direction to find out why he was there, even though there were several ladies ahead of him in line.

"I just thought I'd get a muffin," Dave offered. "And... Naomi had some questions about the next book club theme...?"

"Oh." Erin shook her head. "Things are pretty busy here today."

"Go ahead," Vic told her. "You look like you need a break. I can handle things here for twenty minutes."

"Are you sure? It's been so..."

"Go," Vic repeated firmly.

Things would probably quiet down once Erin left and they didn't have anyone to direct their curiosity at. Maybe they would follow her to The Book Nook and give Naomi some business. Had she been getting more customers since Erin had discovered Brandon's body in the basement? People had probably started their back-to-school shopping early. Any excuse to scout out a murder scene, even if they couldn't go down to the basement.

The Book Nook had just barely opened. Booksellers did not need to be up as early as bakers. There were no cars parked out in front of the store yet, even though Auntie Clem's had been buzzing with activity for several hours.

The door was unlocked and the Open sign up, so Erin walked in. The tinkling bell drew Naomi's attention, and she smiled at Erin, raising her brows as if surprised to see her.

"Oh, hi, Erin. What can I find for you today? Some more breakfast recipe books?"

Erin laughed. "I think I've already got a copy of everything you have. And a couple you don't. Dave said you wanted to talk to me about the next book club theme? We were going to do 'an apple for teacher,' right?"

Naomi walked across the floor to her. "I think it was probably more that he's just been concerned about you and wanted me to make sure you were okay. We've *both* been concerned about you since... you know. I just wanted to make sure that... things weren't going to be awkward between us. And you coming here... sometimes people can get kind of a phobia about going back somewhere that something bad or scary happened. And I thought... finding a body in the basement is *kind of* traumatic and you might feel... anxious about coming back here."

Erin had been distracted by wondering what Naomi's concern over the book club theme was and hadn't even thought about the bookstore being the location where she had found Brandon's body the first time. Now she looked around, actually thinking about it, testing out how she felt about being there.

She had been at The Book Nook many times before and had always had good experiences there and positive feelings associated with it. The fact that she had found Brandon in the basement, a place she had never been before and would probably never be again, made it a little bit easier. She could imagine it was some other world, someplace far away rather than right under her feet. A sort of a nightmare world that she had been dropped into once, but would never dream of again.

"No, I think I'm okay with it, actually. As long as I don't have to go down to the basement."

Naomi smiled, her face lighting up like the sun had just broken over the horizon. "Oh, I'm so glad, Erin. I wouldn't want to lose your friendship or your help with the book club just because… something unfortunate happened."

"It's not your fault." Erin gave a shrug. "I don't think you invited him over here or killed him in the basement. Why would you? You didn't even know the guy. Now if you had known him…" Erin tried to keep a teasing tone and not let her voice get serious or malicious. What *would* Erin have done if she had seen Brandon again? She had never been violent toward him. She couldn't see herself ever trying to hurt him.

And she would never have the opportunity to find out. Brandon Quayle was gone.

And good riddance.

Erin visited with Naomi for a few minutes, made sure they were both onside with the plans for the next book club meeting, and then Erin headed back to the bakery. She could see when she reached the door that the crowd had thinned out and only a couple of customers were at the counter waiting to be served. Vic had things well under control. There were a number of coffee cups, wrappers, and disposable plates on the little tables at the front of the store, where the women had gathered to gossip or catch up with one another's lives.

She figured her time would best be spent tidying up so that it didn't look like a pigsty for the next group of customers. She picked up the various detritus and threw it into the nearby garbage. It shouldn't be that hard for customers to take two steps over to the garbage to throw their own trash away instead of leaving it on the tables. That was just common courtesy.

Erin picked up a folded piece of lined paper that looked like it might be a school assignment and unfolded it to see what it was. If one of the students who stopped in for a quick treat had left it behind, they might be looking for it by the end of the day. Finding out that Erin had thrown it away—and having to dig through the garbage to find it and see if it were salvageable—would not be a good experience.

It was not a school assignment, but a recipe. Interested, Erin skimmed through it to see if she could figure out who had left it behind. She read through it a second time, more slowly, her heart racing.

"Vicky... do you know who left this here?"

"What is it?" Vic studied the paper in Erin's hand and shook her head. "No, I didn't see. Where was it?"

"On one of the tables. I was just clearing up."

"No. There were a lot of people over there in the past hour. It could belong to anyone."

Erin walked slowly over to the section of the counter that folded back on a hinge and let herself back into the "employees only" section.

"What is it?" Vic asked.

"It's a recipe."

"One of yours?"

"No. Not one of mine. I don't know whose it is."

"Well, if it's important, I guess they'll come back for it. Probably not anything you can use, huh? It would be nice if it was. A nice little gift from the gluten-free fairies..." She giggled. "Or brownies!"

"It actually is."

"What?"

"Gluten-free. It uses buckwheat. You don't know of anyone else in Bald Eagle Falls who was entering the waffle contest, do you?"

"No, not that I've heard."

Erin had been talking about the waffle contest to customers for a week. She thought that if anyone else had been interested in entering the contest, they would have mentioned it. Or asked her how to submit an entry to the contest. But no one else had expressed any interest in it, other than to ask her what she would be submitting.

"It's a waffle recipe?" Vic asked. She counted Mary Lou's change out loud and handed it over. "A gluten-free waffle recipe?"

"Yes." Erin looked toward the table again as if the person who had left it there might have materialized.

"Maybe it is the gluten-free fairy," Vic laughed. "She heard you wishing for a gluten-free waffle that would win the contest, and *behold!* There it is."

"That's weird." Erin shook her head. "Weird that someone would just leave something like that here."

"You're not going to use it, are you?"

"No. Not without knowing where it came from. I don't want to jeopardize someone else's chances of winning the prize."

"Though why anyone else would want to make twenty waffles at once, I don't know," Vic shook her head. "Who but a restaurant or bakery owner would want to win one?"

"Well… someone who wants to save time and put a bunch in the freezer for the kids to use for breakfasts and lunches. Someone with a big family. You know, if you've got six kids, twenty waffles don't really go far. Especially if a couple of them are teenagers. Sometimes it would be convenient to make a whole bunch of waffles all at once."

"Okay, you got me there. Maybe it was someone who is entering the contest. But why would they leave the recipe here? It seems to me that if I wanted to enter a contest, I wouldn't leave my recipe in my rival's house or place of business."

"No. It's probably not that. Just… a coincidence."

"Or the waffle fairy," Vic joked. She sobered up. "Or… someone who wanted to give you a chance at winning the contest. Maybe it isn't for someone else's entry, maybe it's for you."

"Then… why not give it to me? Or leave a note saying that it's for me to use? Just leaving it here like this…"

"I hope you solve your mystery," Mary Lou said with a smile, turning to leave the shop.

"Oh, I didn't even say hello to you," Erin realized. "I just barreled in here and completely ignored you. How are you, Mary Lou?"

"We are getting along fine, thank you," Mary Lou said with a small nod, pausing in the doorway. "I think you can be forgiven for ignoring a customer when you discover that the gluten-free fairy has left you a gift." She gave a small chuckle at their conversation.

Vic turned pink, grinning. "It isn't every day that the gluten-free fairy comes by." She wiped tears from the corner of her eyes as she tried to keep from laughing. "Although if there is any place in town that she should bless with her offerings, it would have to be Auntie Clem's."

"Of course," Mary Lou agreed. "It's only fitting." She shook her head and pushed the bar on the door to leave. "Have a nice day, ladies."

CHAPTER 23

*E*rin was left to puzzle over the serendipitous appearance of the waffle recipe for the rest of the day. At home, she and Terry came and went without much comment to each other, did not eat dinner together and, as evening drew on, Terry retreated to the guest bedroom again. It was earlier than he usually went to bed, so Erin could only assume it was a declaration of his intentions. He would continue to sleep separately until she talked to him about it and indicated she wanted the situation to return to normal. He wouldn't push her, wouldn't get in her way; he would wait until she told him she didn't like the status quo. Either to invite him to return to her room and her bed, or to tell him that she didn't want him in the house anymore.

She hated to think of him leaving and didn't intend to kick him out. Not yet, anyway. She felt the situation could be salvaged. She hoped that it could be. The two of them were not incompatible. They had just run into a speed bump in one area. When it was resolved, they could move on together again.

At least, that was what Erin hoped.

She heard K9 whining, and then the dog gave two sharp barks. She hovered outside of the guest room door uncertainly.

"Do you want me to take him out?"

There was a pause before Terry answered from the other side of the door. "I can take him outside, Erin. You don't need to do that."

"He's probably confused about why I'm not doing anything with him. I don't mind taking him outside for a few minutes. Let him know that I'm not mad at him or something."

"Well… if you want to, of course."

After a moment, Terry opened the door. He clicked his tongue at K9 to call him to the door.

"Come on, K9," Erin invited. "Let's go outside."

K9 bounded over to her and rubbed against her leg, his head repeatedly pressing into Erin's hand so that she would give him pets and scratches.

"Okay, okay," Erin laughed. "I'm right here. I'm not going anywhere. Let's go outside for a run."

He ran to the back door. Erin nodded at Terry. "We'll just be a few minutes."

"Sure. I'll leave the door open until you're back."

That way, she didn't have to knock to get him to open the door again to let K9 in. He was trying to make things convenient for her and not cause extra awkwardness, which made Erin feel more awkward about the whole thing.

Erin let K9 into the backyard. To begin with, he went straight to the dog run on the other side of the house. He and Nilla were trained to use the area so that they didn't have to worry about cleaning up after them in the rest of the yard. Erin kicked off her sandals and started practicing her tai chi forms. After a few minutes, K9 ran over to her with a ball in his mouth and deposited it at her feet. Erin picked it up and threw it for him. K9 chased after the ball and brought it back again. Erin continued to alternate tai chi forms with throwing the ball while K9 bounded around excitedly.

She was glad she had offered to take him outside for a while.

"Miss Price. I wonder if we could talk."

Erin turned her head, startled, and saw Sheriff Wilmot standing at the gate between the front and back yards. She often visited in the yard with Vic, Willie, or Adele, but she hadn't been expecting Wilmot.

"Uh… I don't know. It isn't really a good time."

"I think it's important. You probably want to get this case solved as quickly as possible."

Erin hesitated. Even though she recognized he was trying to manipulate her, she *did* want it all to be over. The sooner they could figure out who it was that had killed Brandon Quayle, the sooner she could go on with her life and she and Terry could get back on track if that was possible. K9 brought Erin the ball back again. He glanced over at Sheriff Wilmot, but didn't tense or act worried about his being in the yard. He saw Wilmot at work every day, so he knew he was not a threat.

Erin threw the ball again. K9 jumped up to catch it, but it was just a little beyond his reach. He snapped at it again once his feet hit the ground and managed to catch it on a bounce. He brought it back to Erin, his pointed ears and wagging tail showing that he was proud of himself.

"What do you want to know?"

"Could you come down to the police department?" At Erin's look, he changed his mind. "Or maybe we could sit down inside? I don't think *this* is conducive to a conversation." He indicated K9 and the yard and Erin starting another tai chi pose.

"Could it wait until tomorrow?"

"Are you able to come by in the morning?"

"Well..." Erin stretched her arms out, eyes on a distant spot on the fence. "No, I work in the morning."

"You work long hours. And I don't want to disrupt your schedule. That's why I thought that maybe now... you could take a few minutes with me."

Erin sighed. "Okay. Fine. I guess we can talk inside." Erin motioned to K9 to return to the house and started in that direction herself. K9's tail drooped, and he reluctantly followed her into the house. Erin gestured for Sheriff Wilmot to sit down at the kitchen table. She got K9 a cookie. "Good boy. Go see Terry."

K9 obeyed, taking the cookie in his lips and bounding off to the guest room. Erin turned her attention to Wilmot, but she didn't want to have to sit there with him at the table with no choice but to either look him in the face so that she seemed engaged, or not look at him and make him think that she was hiding something. Instead, she went to the counter and put on the kettle to boil.

"Have you heard that Quayle was writing a memoir?" Wilmot asked, watching her work and apparently deciding he might as well start on his questions rather than waiting until she was done.

"Heard that today."

"Yes, a lot seems to have gotten out today," he admitted.

"You really should do something about that leak."

He shrugged with one shoulder. Erin knew that Melissa had worked with the police department since she was sixteen, long before Sheriff Wilmot had started there, and before that her dad had been a cop. So she got a certain amount of leeway just because of her long history with the department. But Wilmot didn't seem too worried about the leaked information. Erin had her suspicions that he sometimes wanted information to be leaked. Maybe it was his way of shaking the tree to see what would fall out of it.

He didn't say anything, and Erin went back to his comment. Brandon was writing a memoir. She had been shocked when Vic had revealed that information. It certainly wasn't something that the old Brandon would have done. She couldn't imagine him taking on anything as serious as writing a memoir. Jumping off a bridge while drunk to get his name in the paper, maybe, but a memoir? A whole book? She couldn't imagine what he had been planning to put in it. What accomplishments did he have to tell about? It wasn't like he was a famous musician or actor. He hadn't discovered a scientific principle or new planet. Brandon had been much like Erin. Undereducated. Working class. He could make ends meet and pay the rent most months, but he wasn't the type who was getting ahead. He'd never achieved anything really big, so far as Erin knew. And she thought she would have heard if he had. Brandon had never been very motivated to do anything more than get out of bed in the morning, sometimes not even that.

"What was he writing a memoir about?" she asked Wilmot finally. "What did he ever do that he would write about?"

"It was a tell-all," Wilmot explained slowly. "All about his life before he sobered up and turned things around."

Who would care about his life before he sobered up? Erin shook her head.

Wilmot studied her. "Can you think of anything you wouldn't want him to write about you?"

CHAPTER 24

$\mathcal{E}$rin felt the blood drain from her face.

Stuff about her? What could Brandon write about her?

It wasn't like she had been involved in any criminal behavior that she was afraid he would reveal. They hadn't been knocking off liquor stores or doing drug deals together. Brandon had done a lot of crazy things, but Erin hadn't been a part of that. If he said that she had, he would be lying. But when had the truth ever been the barrier to a good story?

Despite her thought that he didn't have enough material in him for a memoir, Brandon had been a good storyteller. He had an endless supply of stories, mostly things that had happened to other people with some extra embellishments. It wasn't unusual for him to have the whole room on the edges of their seats or in stitches. He reveled in the spotlight.

"I have no idea what he might have written," Erin told Wilmot, shaking her head. "What makes you think it would be the truth?"

If the police already had Brandon's manuscript and were reading through it, she didn't want there to be any doubt that every word in there was probably a lie.

"Brandon liked to get people's attention. He liked to tell stories. I'm sure that's all he's done if he's really written something that he called a memoir. He's made up a bunch of stories and put them together like it really happened."

"And does that worry you?"

Erin swallowed and kept her face blank and unconcerned. "No. Why should it? Anyone who knows Brandon will know that it isn't true. And it's not like he's some famous person or bestselling author. Why would anyone care about the stuff he did when he was drunk? That's not literature."

Sheriff Wilmot nodded slowly. He wrote a few notes in his pad. "You wouldn't be concerned if he got a big book deal?"

"A *big* book deal?" Erin repeated. "I doubt he'd get any book deal. A *big* book deal? How would he get that? No one knows him. You can't get into those big publishers just because you send them your manuscript. You have to have an agent and... something really good. Not some no-name telling all of his favorite drunk stories."

"We haven't heard the details of the deal yet. We are following up on that. It's slow going because we don't have the name of his agent or who the deal is with. Just that he had been telling people he got a big deal."

Erin poured boiling water into cups and took them to the table with the rest of the tea things. "I'd take that with a grain of salt. The guy isn't known for his honesty."

"Wasn't."

"What?" Erin sat down and picked out a teabag for herself. Something herbal that wouldn't keep her awake.

"He *wasn't* known for his honesty. You said isn't."

"Oh." Erin shook her head, thinking about it. "I guess maybe I haven't accepted that he's dead. I mean, I know he is, but... talking about the way things used to be... I guess it hasn't really sunk in."

Erin heard the guest room door open and knew Terry was listening, trying to catch their conversation. She didn't know what she should do. Invite him to join them? Pretend she didn't know he was there? Wilmot didn't give any sign that he knew anyone was listening in on the conversation.

"So it didn't concern you. That Quayle might publish a tell-all book that included information about you. Or stories about you that weren't true."

"No. Nobody who reads it is going to know me, and anyone who really knows me will know what's true and what's not. Besides, when they publish stuff like that, don't they change the names and say it's been fictionalized? I mean, I heard that they merge several different people together to make one character or change things about people to make them more interesting or to fit with the story better."

"I've heard that."

"Then why would I care? He can say whatever he likes. And if it was a big publishing company, their lawyers wouldn't let them publish anything libelous. Nothing that they could be sued for."

Wilmot sipped his tea, a ginger orange blend with some notes of nutmeg. He seemed to have stalled in his questions. Maybe he was just regrouping or figuring out what to ask her next. Had he really thought she would be concerned about what Brandon might be threatening to publish about her?

"Did Brandon tell you that he was publishing a book?"

Erin shrugged. "No. I didn't know anything about it. I didn't talk to him."

"When was the last time you talked to him?"

"I don't know. More than two years. Not since I moved to Tennessee. And before that, I was doing the best I could to avoid him. I didn't move in those circles anymore."

"Why not?"

"I just... didn't. I wasn't interested in being part of that group. They did a lot of stupid stuff. Once I could get a job that would let me leave... I did."

"We would like to access your computer. Do you think I could have a look at that now?"

Erin stared at him. Did he think he could just walk in and get a look at whatever he wanted? She shook her head. "I don't have a computer at home. Just the one at the bakery that I do my bookkeeping on."

"That's your only computer?"

"Yes."

"You must have another way to pick up your email and communicate with people. Your phone?"

"Yes, sure. Of course."

"Could I see that?" Wilmot put his hand out as if he expected Erin to hand it over.

She didn't move. "No."

"You said that you haven't had anything to do with Quayle, so you don't have anything to hide," he reasoned.

"No. You don't need to see my email or my phone. There's nothing on there to do with the case. I have my right to privacy."

"If we are going to figure out who killed Quayle, we are going to need access to these things."

"No," she told him again. "That's private."

"I will come back with a warrant."

"We'll see."

He would need to go into the city for that, or at least to call a judge in the city. They didn't have one in Bald Eagle Falls. And he would need to prove that he needed access to it. That she was a good suspect in Brandon's murder. She didn't think that the facts supported him. Yes, she had known Brandon, and she had been the one to find his body, but it wasn't like she'd been caught hanging over him with the murder weapon in her hand or that her fingerprints were on the knife that had killed him. She had called the police about finding the body—twice—and that was what good citizens did, not murderers. Wilmot didn't have any evidence that she had been in contact with Brandon since moving to Bald Eagle Falls. That was what he was looking for. It was a fishing expedition.

"I think you're done here."

Erin and Wilmot both startled slightly and turned to look at Terry, standing in the kitchen doorway. Erin was torn between being grateful for his intervention and irritated that he had stepped in to take control of the conversation. She was handling it just fine, and she was going to get rid of Sheriff Wilmot herself. She didn't need him interfering.

Wilmot looked at Terry, scowling. "Why don't you see if you can talk her into letting us have a look at her emails? If she has nothing to hide…"

"She's not going to give you access to her email."

Sheriff Wilmot took another long sip of his tea and put the cup down. "I'll be back, Miss Price. You can count on that. This won't end until we figure out who killed Mr. Quayle."

"That's fine with me," Erin said flatly. "But that doesn't mean you're getting access to my personal property."

He nodded to her and Terry and slipped out the back door. Erin stood up and began gathering the tea things and putting dishes into the dishwasher.

"You shouldn't have invited him in," Terry said from the doorway.

"I didn't exactly. He said that he needed to talk. Kind of invited himself."

"You shouldn't have let him in. Don't talk to him voluntarily anymore. He doesn't have enough evidence to arrest you. And if he does, you still don't talk to him. You only talk to your lawyer."

"You think I did it?" Erin asked. "You think I killed Brandon?"

"No. I don't think you did," he scoffed. "No matter what he did to you years ago, why would you kill him now? You didn't invite him to meet with you in the basement of The Book Nook. You just told Wilmot that you don't care what he put in his memoir. That's not a motive. But you need to protect yourself. Don't talk to him. Don't give him anything to use against you. If he gets that warrant, you have to comply, but you don't have to talk to him. Get a lawyer and keep your mouth shut."

"You think he would railroad me?"

"I think it's been done many times. Not by Wilmot," he hastened to add. "He's a straight shooter. But that doesn't mean he couldn't be misled or make a wrong judgment. I don't want anything to happen to you. You need to protect yourself."

Erin nodded. "I will."

He stood there for a moment longer, then went back to the guest bedroom.

Erin waited a few minutes, puttering around the kitchen but not really getting anything done. She armed the burglar alarm and shut off the lights. Orange Blossom rubbed against her legs and chatted with her in low meows. After getting ready for bed, Erin pulled out her tablet and opened her email.

CHAPTER 25

*A*untie Clem's was closed on Sunday, as were the rest of the shops in town. But it opened for a couple of hours for the ladies' tea after services. Women came over to chat and gossip and relax with coffee, tea, and cookies. It was a low-key affair. There was nothing to do on Sunday but open, serve food and drink, and clean up after the ladies were gone. And while Erin frequently did this herself so she could keep up with the local news and visit with the women in a relaxed environment, it was a duty that any one of her employees could easily handle, and today Bella was taking the shift.

Erin slept in as much as she was able. It was later than she normally would have been able to sleep, which told her that she had not been getting enough sleep lately. She needed to make sure that she got to bed in plenty of time and was nice and relaxed, so she could get enough hours of good quality sleep to keep going. She made herself a slice of toast and cup of tea and sat at the kitchen table, reviewing her planner and working on her schedule and tasks for the next week.

Vic tapped at the back door and entered. Erin had already unlocked it for her and disarmed the burglar alarm.

"Morning, sunshine!" Vic greeted.

She was still in a pair of pajamas, with her fine blond hair pulled back into a ponytail, brushed but not styled.

"Hi. Grab yourself a cup of tea," Erin invited. She motioned to the teapot. "It's still hot."

Vic made herself at home and sat down across from Erin. "How is next week looking?"

"Not too bad. I hope to have the time to try a few waffle recipes."

Vic licked her lips. "I love waffles."

"Well, you should get your chance to test several varieties!"

"Did you find out anything about that waffle recipe you found on the table at Auntie Clem's?"

"No." Erin frowned, thinking back to her investigations so far. She had asked a few people she knew had been at the bakery that afternoon, but no one claimed the recipe or knew who had left it there. No one had come back looking for it. "It's all really weird. I don't know... why anyone would have left it there. I mean, it's one thing when the kids come for a snack and leave their homework on the table. That's understandable. But who brings a waffle recipe to a bakery? And then just leaves it there? Why did they bring it? Why did they forget it there? Why are they even making gluten-free waffles?"

Vic laughed. "It's a mystery, all right."

"It is," Erin agreed. And a much better one than trying to figure out who had killed Brandon Quayle. Of course she wanted to clear her name, but she didn't want anything to do with the investigation or Brandon. He was a part of her life long past, and she had not expected to ever see him again. Now she had, twice, but she would never see him again. She would much rather solve the mystery of the unknown waffle recipe owner than anything else. Except maybe making waffles.

"You should try out the recipe. See whether it is any good."

"Well... I thought of that. Just because I'm curious to see how it turns out. But I don't want anyone accusing me of stealing their mee-maw's old recipe without permission. Or competing against someone who enters the same recipe into the contest. What would they do if they got two identical recipes?"

"It probably happens all the time. Some guy thinks his mom's pie crust recipe was her own invention, without knowing that she just got it from the back of the shortening package. Or the Toll House cookie recipe was on the chocolate chip bag. Or in the Better Homes and Gardens recipe book for like, a hundred years."

"I suppose," Erin agreed. "Well, if I ended up using it, I'd have to rewrite it. Make sure the instructions are my own and maybe even adjust the number of servings so that the ingredient amounts change."

"Double it," Vic agreed with a nod. "Triple it. Or ten-times it so you can use it on that fantastic new waffle maker."

Erin sighed, picturing the waffle maker and how quickly she could turn out dozens of fragrant waffles. "I might just have to buy one if I don't win it."

"You're a sucker for new kitchen equipment."

"I know. But wouldn't it make it so easy... making ten waffles at a time..."

"Much easier than waiting five minutes for each one," Vic admitted.

Erin had folded the recipe and put it in the back of her planner with several other pieces of paper that she wasn't sure why she was still carrying around with her. She thumbed through the pages to find it, unfolded it, and smoothed it out on the table in front of her.

"Is that it?" Vic asked.

She nodded. "This is it."

"Can I see?"

Erin handed it over. Vic started to read the ingredients aloud. Erin closed her eyes, visualizing how the ingredients would work together.

"Wait... that's not gluten-free."

Vic's eyes dropped back to the page. "What?"

"Malt vinegar. That's barley. It isn't gluten-free."

"Oh." Vic considered. "Maybe whoever wrote the recipe didn't know that. You could use another kind of vinegar. I think it is just to react with the baking soda to make the batter lighter."

"And a little bit of deeper flavor." Erin pondered on this. "Maybe some caramel flavor... though it can be difficult to find caramel that isn't derived from corn or dairy."

"You could make your own caramel with sugar and non-dairy milk. Coconut, maybe?"

"Coconut can trigger people with tree nut allergies. I'll have to think about it. It's probably fine without the malt flavor. I can bump up the amount of vanilla."

"Okay. So then you can try this one next week. Or are you going to do it today?"

Vic was pretty good at reading Erin. Erin couldn't help the flush of embarrassment that spread from her neck to her face. "Well... I was wondering if I could swing it today."

"If you don't have a bunch of errands that you have to go into the city for, you should have time. Unless you've got a bunch of stuff to do that you didn't tell me about."

Erin's life was pretty much an open book for Vic. They were around each other for so much of their time, Vic probably knew Erin's schedule better than she did herself.

Erin took the recipe back from Vic and looked it over. Being a baker had its advantages. She could be reasonably sure she would have all the ingredients she needed on hand, either at home or at Auntie Clem's.

The recipe called for a commercial pumpkin pie spice mix that she wasn't familiar with. Erin pulled out her phone and tapped the description in along with the keyword "ingredients" to find a listing of the ingredients and guess at the proportions of the various spices. She would make it from scratch rather than relying on someone else's mix.

"That's weird."

Vic sipped her tea. "What's weird?"

"This pumpkin spice mix." Erin moved the paper over so Vic could look at it with her.

"Grandma Jo's Pumpkin Spice."

"Yeah. I just looked it up, and it's not gluten-free either."

Vic shook her head. "People just forget that they have to look at all of the ingredients in everything. If you're adding something from a box or a bottle, you have to see what's in it too."

"Yeah. Plenty of spice mixes have flour in them to bulk them up, thicken the dish, or make the spices flow better. Lots of people think they have to look for the word 'wheat' on the ingredients for it to have gluten in it, but that's not nearly enough. I can even remember people trying to tell my foster sister Carolyn that she could have white bread, just not whole wheat bread. As if the white bread you get at the store wasn't made of wheat too."

"You don't know about all of the other things to look for until you start cooking for someone who is strictly gluten-free. You want to avoid poisoning them."

344

Erin nodded her agreement. Anyone who thought following a special diet was easy was in for a big shock when they tried it.

The back door opened, and Willie walked in. Erin was startled. She looked at his black-stained face and smiled. "Morning Willie! I didn't know you were even around."

He smiled and bent down to give Vic a kiss. "You were already gone when I woke up."

"Baker's hours," Vic said with a shrug. "My body doesn't think it's possible to sleep past six."

"You could have woken me." He winked.

It was Vic's turn to blush. She looked away from Willie, shaking her head. "We're just in here talking baking. Grab a cup of tea or make some coffee."

Willie proceeded to do exactly that.

Even though it was Erin's kitchen, they were all so used to being there to visit or share a meal together that she didn't feel the need to make Willie's coffee or even invite him to do so herself. They were all comfortable looking after themselves.

Erin frowned as she studied the recipe again. Vic raised her brows. "Another bad ingredient?"

"No. There's just something about this recipe."

"Something about it?"

"Something... not wrong, exactly, but..." Erin tried to tap into the feeling at the back of her brain. "Something... familiar..."

Willie leaned against the kitchen counter, waiting for the machine to brew. "You think you've seen the recipe somewhere before?"

"I don't think so. I think I would remember if I had seen this one before. Especially with the malt vinegar and spice mix in it. But even if someone who didn't know about those containing gluten added them later, I don't remember ever seeing waffles with this combination of..."

Then it all came together.

CHAPTER 26

"Oh." Erin looked at the recipe with fresh eyes, suddenly seeing clearly what she had missed before. "That's it."

"What's it?" Vic and Willie asked in unison.

They all looked at each other and laughed. Erin let the recipe lay on the table, tapping it with her forefinger.

"Bertie."

"What?" Vic and Willie exchanged glances and then looked back at Erin, none the wiser.

"Bertie Braceling. This combination of flours is what we used for Bertie's tortilla and pancake mixes. Because he was allergic to or intolerant of so many different ingredients. Buckwheat, arrowroot, and psyllium."

"Really?" Vic looked down at the recipe and glanced through the ingredients. "How would you remember that?"

Erin laughed. "I know my customers. Bertie was really hard to bake for, but I enjoy a challenge. I was always trying to find combinations of ingredients that would work for him. And I remember that being the flour blend we used for most of the stuff I made for him. No grains of any kind, so no rice, cornstarch, sorghum, or oats. Tapioca starch caused him neurological issues. He couldn't tolerate xanthan gum or guar gum."

"So, buckwheat, arrowroot, and psyllium."

346

"Just like this recipe," Erin tapped it again. "I haven't seen that particular blend in anyone else's recipes."

None of them said anything for a few minutes.

"But Bertie is dead," Vic pointed out finally. "So whose recipe is it? And if it was for Bertie, it wouldn't have had malt vinegar or a spice blend that included flour in it."

"Maybe it's a recipe that started out as Bertie's," Willie suggested slowly, "but then someone else adapted it to their tastes and they didn't have the same restrictions as he did."

"Yes, that could be it. Cooks are always adapting other recipes, putting their own spin on them. What about his sister?" Erin looked at Vic. "Tracey…"

"Lacey Moore." Vic shook her head. "She's out of town. Mrs. Peach mentioned she's been feeding Mrs. Moore's cat."

"Does it matter where the recipe came from?" Willie asked.

"No, I guess not. I'd like to know, but it doesn't really make any difference. Unless I want to submit it to the contest. Then I should know where it came from and get permission before I submit it. And make sure that whoever left it at Auntie Clem's isn't submitting it themselves."

Vic nodded. "Right. It's really weird that it just showed up at Auntie Clem's."

"It is, isn't it? But it could have just been a coincidence. Or maybe someone wanted to show it to me because they knew I was developing a recipe to submit to the contest. And then… I wasn't there, so they left it behind. Or they had to go somewhere and forgot that they had put it down… maybe they haven't realized yet that they lost it, or maybe they're planning to come back and ask for it later."

"Or they don't even need it because they already have a copy," Vic suggested.

"Yeah. Would they have left it in Auntie Clem's if it was their only copy? You're right; it probably isn't. They wanted to share it, and I wasn't around, so they just left it there."

"They should have said something. I was there. They could have handed it to me. Told me to give it to you."

"It was probably still busy and they had to go. Didn't want to interrupt you. Maybe they'll be back next week and ask if I got it."

"Yeah. Maybe."

"Do you want me to see if I can find out who it came from?" Willie asked. He had poured himself a cup of coffee and took a tentative sip.

"Well… sure. But how are you going to do that? I've already been asking around, and no one has said anything. You don't even know who was in the bakery that day."

"But if it was originally a recipe for Bertie, I knew him. And some of his friends and family. I can ask around about his waffle recipe."

"Oh! Yeah, that's a good idea. Thanks."

Willie nodded. He glanced toward the living room and then back at Erin. "So… Piper around? What's going on with you guys?" he asked bluntly.

Vic reddened and made a motion for him to shut up. She had undoubtedly been aware of the tension between Erin and Terry and had mentioned it to Willie. But she hadn't meant for Willie to bring it up to Erin.

Erin sighed. She ran her finger over the crease in the paper the recipe was written on, smoothing it out. "Well, you know what it's like. When he suspects you of something, it doesn't really matter who you are. That's his first priority."

"Is that why you're fighting? Because you're a suspect? He doesn't believe your story?"

"He says he believes me. He says that he won't be involved in the case or question me about it. But he does. And he's upset that I never told him about Brandon."

Willie approached the table and sat down. "What about Brandon? That's the dead guy?"

Vic leaned forward, her eyes bright with interest.

Erin didn't know what to say. "I never talked about Brandon to Terry, and I guess he thinks that I should have. That I should share everything about anybody that I've been with in the past. But… he doesn't go out of his way to tell me about every person in Bald Eagle Falls that he ever dated. He'll say something every now and then, but I don't really know anything about any serious relationships that he's had. He hasn't told me all of that stuff either. I didn't think… that it was required."

"But now he's acting like it is."

"Terry knew about my life before I came here. He knew that I was in foster care and that I'd been in a lot of different places doing a lot of different jobs since then. He knows that... I'm a private person. So why would I tell him everything about Brandon? You wouldn't tell Vic everything about everyone you were ever with, would you?" Erin raised her brows. Willie too was a private person and it had caused a definite hiccup in their relationship when Vic had found out from someone else that Willie had been a member of the Dyson clan. Even though he knew that Vic was from a rival clan, Willie had not bothered to fill her in on that little detail and the five years that he had spent as a soldier for the family.

Willie looked at Vic and then back at Erin. "Are you trying to get me in trouble? Is that my punishment for opening my mouth?"

"You haven't sat her down and told her about everyone you've ever dated, have you?"

"No... I don't think that's the way it's usually done. You tell a little bit here and a little bit there. Casually. Building on it as you get to know each other better."

"You know everyone I've been with," Vic declared.

Willie shrugged. "Considering you weren't even legally an adult when you came to Bald Eagle Falls, it's not a very long list. I've been a bachelor for as long as you've been alive."

"Old man," Vic teased.

"That's right. And I honestly don't think it would be good form to make a list of everyone I've ever had an interest in and go through the circumstances of each one at a time."

"No. I suppose not." Vic looked sober, maybe considering for the first time the long history that Willie had had before the two of them had gotten together. It was one thing to acknowledge that he was older than she was. It was another to think about what that actually meant in terms of life experiences.

"So..." Erin brought the conversation back around. "He thinks I'm obstructing the investigation *and* keeping important secrets from him. And since I don't trust him..."

"You're not sharing a room anymore?" Willie filled in.

Erin looked reproachfully at Vic. She wasn't even sure how Vic had figured it out so quickly. It wasn't like Vic went snooping in the bedrooms when she was over. Her visits were usually confined to the kitchen and living room, and Erin didn't see how she could have figured out that Erin and Terry were no longer sleeping in the same bed together so quickly.

Vic held up her hands. "I'm sorry. I didn't mean to pry. I just used the facilities the other day, and I noticed when I went down the hall that K9's kennel and Terry's things were in the second bedroom, not in yours where they usually are. I haven't said anything to anyone else, I promise."

"I don't know. I can't really explain all of what happened. We were both tired and frustrated. It wasn't a fight. I wasn't happy with him, but it wasn't a fight. But if he doesn't trust me, if he puts the investigation before our relationship... maybe we're not supposed to be together. He offered to move to the guest room and I said yes. I didn't kick him out. He asked."

"He's just being a gentleman. If you ask him to come back to your room, he will,"

"I know."

They were all quiet.

"But you're not ready to do that," Vic said finally.

"No."

"Where is he now?" Willie asked. "On shift? At work?"

"No." Erin swallowed. "He went to church."

"What?" Vic's voice climbed up several notes. She made an effort to keep it calm and lower it again. "I know Terry's Christian, but he goes to church what, twice a year? Easter and Christmas?"

"And apparently... when he's having problems with me."

"You think he's being passive-aggressive? This is... getting back at you somehow? You're an atheist, and the two of you are on the outs, so he starts going to church again?"

"It's only once. Maybe he needed to say a prayer that... I'll come around and start behaving more like a Christian wife."

"Or praying for understanding," Willie said, his tone serious. "To be able to understand what you went through with this guy, and why you didn't share it, and what he needs to do next if he wants to keep you."

Erin sipped her tea, pondering this. Was that why Terry had gone to the church he barely ever frequented? Not to punish her somehow, or alienate her, but to find a way to get closer to her?

"I don't know. I never heard anything like that at any of the churches that I went to as a kid."

"Would you have? If you were in a children's Sunday School, they would not have been talking about intimate relationships. And if you were with a general congregation, would you really have listened to it and understood what they were talking about?"

"I probably wasn't the best listener at church."

Willie chuckled. "Few kids are. You go to hear the exciting stories like Noah and the Ark or Daniel in the Lion's Den, but most of the stuff that you really go to learn… you don't get until you're much older."

CHAPTER 27

$\mathcal{E}$rin enjoyed her day off from Auntie Clem's Bakery but, after a day, she was ready to go back to work. She really did love her work, and it was paying the bills. What more could she ask? Maybe there were things going on in other parts of her life that were difficult, but she still loved baking at Auntie Clem's and talking to her customers.

Willie dropped them off in the parking lot behind the bakery and Erin strode up to the door, her key out, to let them in. It wasn't until she was right up to the door that she could see that the door was hanging open an inch in the dim lighting from the streetlights. It had been forced, Erin could immediately see by the marks on the doorframe and the edge of the door. A pry bar and a good yank, and out it had popped.

Vic ran into Erin from behind because she had stopped so abruptly.

"What's going on—" Vic saw the door and turned back toward Willie's truck. He was pulling away, but she managed to bang on the side of the truck and stop him before he got out of the parking lot. Erin could hear Vic talking to Willie in urgent tones, but they seemed like they were far away or underwater. She used one finger to push the door open wider. No movement on the other side. Not a sound.

Erin's heart was pounding and her legs were so weak she had to hold on to the doorframe for support. Who would have done such a thing? She thought that she was well-liked and respected in Bald Eagle Falls. That no one would ever do anything like this.

But that hadn't always been the case. And she was afraid that there might be more than one person still harboring a grudge against her for her hand in exposing the students in the burglary ring at the school, or for someone else who had been put behind bars at the penitentiary. She had been in too many cases to really believe that no one resented her for what she had done.

And then there was Vic. It could be a hate crime. There might be all kinds of slurs against trans people painted on the walls of the kitchen or even the public space out front. She didn't smell any paint but, if there was something like that, she needed to see it first and keep Vic from seeing it.

She had to know. The bakery was dark and she needed to find the light switch, which didn't seem to fall right under her hand like it usually did as she walked in the door. She inched her way along, one hand on the wall, her eyes wide open and searching, her heart pounding in her chest as if it would jump right out of her body.

"Erin!" Willie's sharp whisper behind her made her jump. "You shouldn't go in there. Someone could still be inside. You stay out here until the cops get here."

"I have to see," Erin insisted. "There isn't anyone here."

She finally touched the light switch and flicked it on.

Erin squinted in the sudden brightness, blinded for a moment. She forced her eyes open, though tears started to run down her cheeks from the light. There wasn't a mark on the walls. No vandalism was apparent. No damage. No one was there. The appliances gleamed. The long counters were clear and clean, waiting for them to begin their morning work. She would have thought she was being paranoid and that the shop had been left unlocked, rather than being broken into. But she couldn't ignore the pry marks on the door.

"Erin." Willie was tugging her from behind. "Come on. Wait outside until the police get here."

Erin let herself be pulled back out of the kitchen into the parking lot. Vic was there, pale and anxious.

"It was broken into? Who would break into the bakery? It isn't like we leave money in the till overnight."

"Maybe they heard there was a lot of dough there," Willie offered, deadpan.

Vic stared at him for a moment without smiling. Then she shook her head, the corners of her mouth twitching. "Do you really think this is an appropriate time to joke around?"

"Well, you asked. I can't help that. The joke is going to be pretty lame if I use it on a day when the bakery *hasn't* been broken into."

They could hear an approaching siren.

"If someone was looking for a lot of bread..." Willie tried again. Erin turned her head to glare at him. He grinned and shut up.

"Did everything look okay?" Vic wanted to know. "I mean... it isn't all smashed up or anything, is it? We'll still be able to open today?"

Erin nodded. "It looked fine... didn't look like anything had been touched."

Vic let out a breath. "Good. Glad to hear it. We'll just wait for the boys in blue to clear it and confirm that there isn't anyone else still around, and then we can get to work."

Erin remembered having the police check out the first iteration of Auntie Clem's Bakery, which had been across the street from her current location. Looking for the "ghost" that had moved things around in her office and smashed a coffee mug that had been left on the counter. And the burglar who had pried open a cabinet in the basement. Because there had been a murder in her basement, her reports were taken seriously.

The ghost, it turned out, had been Vic. Sleeping in the bakery overnight. Somewhere safe and warm and sheltered. Though she hadn't been the one to pry open the cabinet. Erin smiled at Vic, remembering her discovery of the slim young woman in her shop.

Vic raised her brows questioningly, probably wondering if Erin was in shock. Why would she be smiling like that after a break-in? She didn't see the parallel like Erin did. She had been on the other side of the equation, the burglar who was trying to avoid detection.

A police car pulled into the parking lot. Not Terry's truck. Stayner stepped out, releasing his sidearm as he strode across the parking lot toward the door. "Have you been inside?"

"Just into the kitchen," Erin said. "No one in there."

"Stay out here. Don't come in behind me unless you want to get shot."

It seemed like a good idea to do what he said. Erin and the others waited after he disappeared into the bakery, waiting for him to clear the building and confirm that it was safe to go in. Erin felt a little silly about the police being called to the scene when there had apparently not been a theft or vandalism. Someone had pried the door. Maybe kids thinking that they could get something out of the till, not realizing that they cleared it out and made a bank deposit every night.

Or maybe on a dare. Kids did stupid stuff.

Erin had always been a goody-two-shoes, according to Reg. She had tried to follow all of the rules in order to stay out of trouble and have the best possible chance of achieving success when she finished school and was out on her own.

Some kids ended up with foster families that agreed to keep them on after they aged out of foster care, helping them to get through college or getting them to pay rent to contribute to the household expenses. But Erin had not ended up with one of those families. When she aged out of foster care, that was the end of anyone taking care of her. She had to take care of herself, and she wasn't always able to do that.

Kids did stupid things. So did young adults like Brandon had been when she knew him. She wondered what he had written in his memoir. Had he really "told all" about the stupid things he had done while they had been together? The drinking and doping and partying? The abuse, dishonesty, stealing, bar fights, and everything else? Had he ever broken into a bakery on a dare? The record store down the block from them? One of the other little businesses run by hardworking folks trying to make ends meet?

Stayner walked back out of the bakery at a relaxed pace, his sidearm properly secured in the holster. He nodded to Erin. "All clear, Miss Price. No one in there. Would you like to take a walk-through and point out anything that might have been damaged or stolen?"

"Yeah. Thanks."

Her knees were still a little shaky, but it felt better to be walking than standing still. Erin led the way back into the bakery, followed by Stayner, with Willie and Vic behind them. Nothing appeared to have been touched in the kitchen. Everything was as clean and pristine as it should have been. Erin was really glad that they hadn't painted slurs all over the walls. Glad that it wasn't a hate crime.

She went out to the front. The register did not appear to have been touched. Erin pressed a few buttons to pop open the drawer, which was empty, as expected. The mechanism still worked, which she assumed meant it had not been pried open with the crowbar. Everything appeared to be functioning. There was no sign that the burglar had even gone out to the front of the store.

Erin was beginning to think she was right and that it had just been some kids on a dare. She walked back through the kitchen to the stairs and went down to the storage room to see if anything appeared to have been touched or stolen. For a moment, she flashed back to descending the stairs at The Book Nook and finding Brandon in the basement, dead. Having found his body twice already, she half-expected to find it lying in the basement of the bakery. But of course Stayner had already been down there and would have noticed if there were a body. And he certainly hadn't dragged one in there to plant it there himself.

The basement was well-lit, not spooky and shadowy. All modern and bright, with finished walls and floor and gleaming shelves to hold all of their bulk goods. Erin glanced over the goods on the shelves but couldn't see anything that was missing initially. She would have to go through the inventory sheet to be sure, but nothing appeared to have been touched. She shrugged at Stayner, who had stopped partway down the stairs to wait for her response.

"Everything looks fine."

She climbed back up the stairs and returned to the kitchen.

"Your office," Vic prompted, nodding to the tiny room off the kitchen where Erin kept her files and the computer. It was barely big enough for a desk with an integrated file cabinet and had probably been a closet in its previous life, but it was large enough for Erin to get done what she needed to.

She glanced around the room and nodded. Again, nothing appeared to have been broken or messed with. The keyboard and monitor were exactly where they always were. Pencil jar. In box. Writing pad.

Except... taking a closer look, she saw that the computer CPU itself, which sat in the kneehole under the desk, was missing.

CHAPTER 28

The sheriff had arrived to help with the investigation of the burglary. Stayner had agreed that Erin and Vic could begin work on the day's baking as long as they stayed out of the office, which was just fine. They weren't normally in there during their morning baking session anyway. Other than to drop off their purses where they were a little more secure.

Stayner took a cursory look around the tiny room, then guarded the door to prevent anyone from entering until Wilmot arrived.

"The computer was the only thing stolen?" Wilmot demanded.

He looked at the office and took a walk through the rest of the bakery and basement, as if Stayner and Erin might have missed something of importance.

"Well, that's convenient, isn't it?" he asked, brows drawn down in a scowl. "You knew I was getting a warrant for your computer, so it conveniently disappeared."

"Are you kidding?" Vic demanded. "You think that Erin set this all up? She wouldn't damage the door so that she could make it look like a burglary. Who do you think has to fix that door? Who has to work here and worry about whether it is secure until it gets fixed? Erin didn't do this to keep you from looking at her computer."

"Miss Victoria," Wilmot said gravely, "I don't think I was addressing you."

"Well, I still heard and I still had something to say about it. I can't believe you would throw around accusations like that. Erin could sue the department for slander."

Erin wasn't going to sue anyone, and Wilmot would know that. Erin wasn't the type of person who would make waves over something like that being said. It would be far more trouble than it was worth.

"No, it isn't convenient," Erin told him. "That computer has all of my bookkeeping on it. All of my promotional graphics and files for the next few months. Recipes that I've been collecting or developing. This is..." She shook her head hopelessly, her eyes filling with tears. "This is terrible. I don't know how I'm going to replace it."

"Computers aren't that expensive anymore," Wilmot assured her. "You have a backup, right?"

Erin kneaded her forehead. When was the last time she had made a backup? It was always one of the last things on her list. Something she knew she had to get to sooner or later. The backup drives were in the desk, but she worried they would not be much help. She walked into the office, ignoring Wilmot's grunt of protest. He was too far across the kitchen to stop her. She opened the top drawer of the desk to look at the dates written on notes stuck to the backup drives. How much work would she have to redo because she hadn't been doing her backups as often as she should?

But there were no backup drives in the drawer. Erin stared at the odds and ends for several long seconds. She even opened the next drawer, a file drawer, and looked through it as if she might have accidentally filed the backup drives in one of her folders. She swallowed hard and looked at Wilmot.

"My backups are gone too."

"Well, that's conven—" He cut himself off before finishing the statement. "Don't you have any offsite backup? A cloud drive? Safety deposit box? Safe at home?"

Erin wiped at the corners of her eyes. "No."

She fell into her desk chair, helpless to stop the tears. She put both of her hands over her face. Vic moved in, pushing past Sheriff Wilmot in the doorway, to rub Erin's back and murmur comforting words to her.

"Your accountant has last year's financial files. You can start with that. You have all of the paper files. You can hire someone to enter the bookkeeping for the first half of the year. Email is all online."

That helped a little. It was a lot of work, but it was manageable if she could hire someone to do all of the inputting instead of doing it herself.

"The promos," she said, swallowing. "All of my swipe files and graphics and plans for holiday promotions this year."

Vic stroked her hair and rubbed her back soothingly. "The newspaper office and printer will have all the graphics for what you've done over the last couple of years. We can reuse them. And the paper will have all of your copy for what you've advertised in the weekly. And your promos, we talked about stuff and you wrote notes in your planner. We can reconstruct from there."

The tears started to slow. Vic was right. Erin had been worried that the business would collapse without everything she had on her computer. But they could start with what they had done in the last two years. No one would notice if the promotion graphics were reused. And there was time to start rebuilding her plans for upcoming holiday promotions.

"What about... employee paychecks and shifts, and our client list?"

"Uh... you use a human resources company for the paychecks and withholdings. There won't be any break in that. We'll reconstruct what we remember of the shifts and ask everyone what they remember for hours worked last week and shifts in the next couple of weeks. No one is going to abandon you because your computer got stolen. They know you'll treat them fairly."

Erin nodded. She grabbed a tissue from the box on her desk, blotted her eyes, and blew her nose. "And the client list is online."

"That's right, it is," Vic agreed. "In your CRM manager. You haven't lost that."

"I'll have to reset passwords." Erin sniffled. "I never could remember all of them."

"Resetting passwords is easy."

"Yeah. But my recipes?" Erin tried to avert another flood of tears, but was not successful. She swore. "What is a bakery without recipes?"

"All of the ones that we use are in the binder." Vic referred to the reference binder they kept in the kitchen, with all the recipes in plastic page protectors in case they got spattered with batters. "We can scan them so you have them on your new computer. The ones that you haven't used or are still experimenting with..." She shrugged. "You can start over. You got most of them online to start with. So find them again. We'll try to remember what we can for the ones you've been experimenting with. But everything we make regularly, we've got. You're not going to go under because you don't have any recipes."

"Okay." Erin swallowed and nodded. "Okay, we can do this. We can recover."

"Right now, it's time to get to work," Vic said sternly, looking at the clock on the wall. "We open in half an hour."

That was exactly what Erin needed to galvanize herself and throw herself back into the morning's work. There was no time to cry over spilled milk. She could recover from the lost computer. In the meantime, she needed to get back to work.

CHAPTER 29

"Uh, Miss Price…?" Wilmot was standing outside Erin's office door when she exited, intent on getting the morning's baking done and everything ready to open for the day. "We still need to talk."

"I don't have time right now. I have a bakery to get open."

"The sooner we can get onto this, the better the chances are that we'll be able to recover your stolen property. Can you talk while you get ready?"

"Uh… I guess I can try." Erin went back to the muffin batter she had been in the midst of and started pouring it into cups.

"Do you have any idea who would have broken in here to do this?"

"No. I guess someone wanted a computer."

"I think this was targeted. I don't think it was just 'a computer.' I think it was *your* computer."

She glanced over at him. "Does that mean you don't think that I did it myself? I didn't just ditch my computer so you couldn't find whatever incriminating evidence I have saved on it?"

"Well, there's no need to be snippy about it," he grumbled. "Yes, I'm coming around to your way of thinking. But I still need your cooperation if we're going to figure out who it was and recover it. If you aren't going to help me out, then I have to wonder why."

"I didn't say I wouldn't help."

"Is there anything on that computer that someone might want? Or want to destroy? In particular, anything to do with this case?"

"No. I don't have anything to do with this case on my computer. And you just heard what valuable stuff I have on it—my financial records and recipes. Not... I don't know what you're looking for. Pictures of me and Brandon together? I don't even know what you think you're going to find on it."

"Well, I was hoping to find evidence of whether you were in touch with Brandon or not. But if someone stole it, I would think that it has more than that on it. Something that this case hinges on."

"There isn't anything on my computer to do with Brandon."

"Nothing at all?"

"Why would there be? If I was threatening to kill Brandon, or whatever it is you're implying, why would I have it on my work computer?"

"Does anyone else have access to what's on that computer?"

"No!"

"Victoria, maybe?"

Erin looked over at Vic and shook her head. "She doesn't have my password. I'm the only one who touches the financial files and who sets up the advertising and everything. Vic bakes and works the till. She doesn't run the business."

Vic nodded her agreement. "And happy as a hound dog with two tails that I don't have to do all of that stuff," she affirmed.

Wilmot's mouth twitched.

"If it isn't anything to do with Brandon, then can you think of anyone else who would want your computer for any reason? Someone who is upset with you and might have targeted you? Someone who you told you have something on your computer and they want it? Anything?"

"No. It was just a crappy old computer, Sheriff. Nothing fancy on it. It wasn't a system you could have used for gaming or anything like that. Anyone who needed a computer wouldn't go after a dinosaur like that. They'd want the latest and greatest with lots of memory and a fast graphics card and all that. That one could barely keep up with putting together text and graphics for a flyer."

He smiled. "Maybe I should look into insurance fraud, then. Maybe you're angling to get a new one."

"I wouldn't go through all of this rigmarole for that. I'd just go out and buy one. Take this one home to do email or family history stuff."

He nodded at this.

"And you don't have any clue who might have broken in? You didn't see anyone hanging around the last few days? Smell someone's cologne when you came into the store after the break-in? See that something was moved or taken that might have been connected with someone you know?"

"No… I don't think so."

His mention of cologne got her thinking. *Had* there been a trace of a scent as she had entered Auntie Clem's to turn the light on? Any smells were quickly wiped out by other people moving in and out of the kitchen and by the smells of the batters and baking bread that soon permeated the bakery. Had there been a smell when she had entered The Book Nook? It was all so fleeting, she couldn't be sure. Her other senses had quickly been overwhelmed and she had forgotten anything else.

"Do you know anything about Brandon's manuscript?"

Erin looked up from her muffins, frowning at Wilmot's question. "Brandon's manuscript? What about it?"

"Did he show it to you? Email you a copy?"

"No."

"You haven't seen it."

"No. I can't see why I would have wanted to."

"Maybe so that you could see what he had written about you. How he had portrayed you. The only reason I can think about that he would have come to Bald Eagle Falls is to talk to you."

Erin was baffled as to what other reason he would have had to be there. But whatever it was, it had nothing to do with her.

"I don't care what he wrote in his book. I don't even care if it got a big New York literary deal. So what? It's not about me. If I'm in it, he'd have to spice it up to make it anything interesting. Because nobody cares about the girl who crashed on his couch."

"There was more to it than that, from what you said."

"In your mind, maybe. But that's all it ever was to him. Or to me. Somewhere to live while I found something else."

"It is missing."

"What's missing?"

"His manuscript."

"Because he didn't have it on him? He wouldn't carry it around with him, would he? It's not like a phone."

"We've been in contact with the authorities in Maine. They've searched his apartment there and have his computer. If he had a hard copy, he must have brought it with him."

"Why would he?"

"To show the person who was in it."

"Well, he didn't. I never saw him or his manuscript."

"Until he was dead."

"What?" Erin asked in irritation.

"You didn't see him until he was dead. If I am to believe you. You *did* see him. At least twice."

"Okay." Erin rolled her eyes. "Not alive. So he obviously couldn't show it to me when he was dead."

"Unless it was on his body when you found it."

"Again, why would he be carrying it around?"

"Again—to show you."

"I had no idea he was in town until I found him there. I had no way of knowing he was in The Book Nook."

"We'll see if your email history bears that out."

Erin put trays of muffins in the oven and turned to look at him, wiping her hands on a towel. "My email? My computer was just stolen."

"Yes. But your email is still available in the cloud. Like you and Miss Victoria were just saying."

Erin rolled her eyes and shrugged. She didn't think there was any way for him to get access to it. And if there was, she'd already done what she could to eliminate any trail. He could look all he liked and not be able to prove her wrong.

"How do you know there even *was* a manuscript?" Erin asked. "Had anyone seen it? Brandon didn't exactly tell the truth all the time, you know."

Wilmot considered this, his eyes rolling upward. "Well, that is something I can inquire about. I'm sure someone must have seen it. He wouldn't get a book deal without someone reading the manuscript, right?"

"How do you know he had a book deal?"

"That's what he told everyone."

Erin nodded. "But did anyone see this book deal? Talk to his agent? To the publisher? It could all just be made up out of thin air."

CHAPTER 30

*E*rin didn't feel up to making supper after a long day at Auntie Clem's. She hadn't realized how much energy the burglary and seemingly endless questions by Sheriff Wilmot would take out of her. She also knew that Terry would be getting off work and didn't want to be home with him, tiptoeing awkwardly around each other, trying to decide if she was still obligated to make supper for him, or if she wanted to have him messing around in the kitchen without her. There really wasn't a winning answer.

Sooner or later things would have to either settle down with Terry or come to a head. She hoped that things would work out, but she recognized that she wasn't putting much effort into it, waiting to see what he would do and how he felt. He was the one who had decided she was not trustworthy. She hadn't done anything wrong. She figured he should be the one making the first move.

A meal at the restaurant seemed like the best bet. Erin decided she was in the mood for Chinese and avoided the family restaurant, which was Terry's favorite. If he decided to go out to dinner too, in order to avoid her and having to make his own meal, she didn't want to run into him there.

Erin only had to wait for a few minutes to be seated and was given an empty booth in the back. Too close to the kitchen to be considered a prime spot, but she was happy to be out of the way and have some relative privacy instead of being at one of the round tables out in the open.

She was perusing the menu, deciding what she wanted to order since she was there by herself and usually ordered a combination of meals to share with Terry, when she was interrupted.

"Miss Erin...?"

She looked up from her menu. "Oh, Dave. Hey, how are you?"

"Good." He looked around. "Are you here by yourself?"

"Yes." Erin hesitated a moment, then motioned to the opposite bench seat. "Do you want to join me?"

"Oh, I don't want to interrupt anything. You look like you wanted some alone time."

"No, it's okay. I'll have plenty of that when I go home tonight." That sounded pretty pathetic. "Well, except for the cat and the rabbit, of course." She laughed. That sounded even more pathetic.

"I thought..." He trailed off and took the seat that she had indicated. Maybe deciding that it was better not to dig into her personal affairs.

"That I would be with Officer Piper?" Erin suggested.

He nodded, getting red around his throat.

"Well, we're not exactly seeing eye to eye right now. So I'm... taking a bit of a break."

"Oh. I'm sorry. Is that because of... the investigation? Brandon Quayle, I mean?"

"Yes. I can't thank the guy enough for dying on my watch. Why did he have to come here and screw everything up for me?"

"Are you getting a lot of flak from the police department? They think you had something to do with it?"

"I don't know. I don't think they believe I did it, but they have to follow the evidence and show that I didn't do it and someone else did. It's very annoying. I want them to be finished with their investigation and not bother me about it anymore. I didn't kill him, and I think it's highly unlikely that anyone would kill a person and then call the police about it. And then hide the body. And then call the police about it again..."

Dave chuckled. "That does seem like a bit of a stretch," he agreed.

"But cops don't like coincidences. They want answers to all of their questions and... I can't give them the answers to everything."

"Yeah. If you could, you probably *would* be the killer. They're the ones who always have the best alibis, aren't they?"

"On TV, maybe. Not in real life. Not in my experience."

And she'd had way too much experience in Bald Eagle Falls. Maybe she should have stayed in Maine and never accepted her inheritance from Clementine. Alton Summers would probably have eventually found Erin's half-sister, Charley, and given it to her instead. If Erin hadn't come to Bald Eagle Falls, she wouldn't have gotten involved in that first murder. She wouldn't have been a suspect. She wouldn't have discovered all of the stuff she did later about her family and what really happened to her parents. She wouldn't have had to worry about drug cartels or kidnappers or cooking contests gone bad. She could have just kept living the way that she had in Maine. Nothing would have changed.

"Do you want to order together?" Dave asked, indicating the menu Erin held in her hands but was not focused on. "It's kind of fun to order a few dishes and have a bit of everything."

"Yeah. That's what we usually do. What do you like?"

Erin managed to bring her focus back to the meal and, for a few minutes, she and Dave were occupied with seeing what they both liked best and wanted to share. After giving their order to the waitress, they both sat back, quiet and trying to think of a conversational topic.

"I was sorry to hear about your break-in today," Dave offered. "Did they catch whoever did it?"

"No." Erin shook her head. "And I doubt they ever will. It isn't like he left fingerprints or DNA all over the place or that the police even care about catching him. Sheriff Wilmot kept saying that I needed to cooperate with his questioning so that they could find my computer and get it back to me, but... I don't think they will put too much effort into trying. It isn't even like it's valuable. I just got the cheapest machine that I could when I was starting off. It isn't fast enough to do anything special. Not like gaming or anything that takes a special graphics card. Or speakers. I don't think it even had speakers."

"Usually they have a built-in speaker, even if you don't have an external sound system."

Erin nodded. "So okay, it probably had sound. But I don't see why anyone would want that computer. Or why they would target me."

"I guess the police have been asking you a lot of questions about Brandon?"

Erin nodded. "But it's been years since I saw the guy; it's not like I knew anything about this tell-all memoir he was working on. Or had a deal for, if you're to believe anything he said to anyone else. And you shouldn't."

Dave laughed. "Not the most honest guy?"

"No. You could never believe anything coming out of Brandon's mouth. He told a lot of whoppers."

"I've known people like that. It can be pretty disconcerting when you realize that none of the stuff they're telling you is the truth."

"Yeah. I kind of start from the position of not trusting anyone, and then if you prove that you are trustworthy, that's great. If not, I'm not disappointed, at least."

"Smart… but maybe a little dysfunctional."

"That's me."

When the waitress brought their order, Dave leaned forward to dish up some of each item onto his plate. "So," he said conspiratorially, "Was Brandon ever involved in anything criminal? Or was he just a liar?"

"Oh…" Erin dished up some General Tso's chicken. "He wasn't just a liar." She thought about the drugs. The abuse. Other things that he did if he thought he could get away with it. There had been run-ins with the police, but Brandon could be very charming and talk his way out of just about anything. He was one of those guys, Erin thought, who would have chatted amiably with a cop while he had a body in the trunk of the car or apparently snoozing in the passenger seat next to him. A guy like Dahmer, who kept escaping by the skin of his teeth because he was so skilled at talking himself out of trouble.

But criminal? He *hadn't* been a serial killer like Dahmer. Just a guy who did whatever he could get away with. Who served himself and his own interests without concern for anyone else.

CHAPTER 31

*E*rin poked at her food, thinking about how much she wanted to tell Dave. She couldn't talk to Terry about anything that had happened back then. He was already upset that she hadn't told him about her previous relationship with Brandon, and he was all mixed up in the investigation. They were barely speaking to each other, aside from a few polite comments as they got breakfast ready or navigated around each other at the house, pretending there wasn't any awkwardness.

She could talk to Vic. Vic even had some relevant experience, with her relationship with Crazy Theresa, and having lived on the street for a short time in Bald Eagle Falls. She understood it better than most people in Bald Eagle Falls. But she also talked to Willie, and Erin wasn't sure she wanted Willie to know about anything. Who knew what kind of reaction he might have to her stories? He *had* gone hunting for Crazy Theresa, even if he wasn't the one who had killed her. It was too late for him to go after Brandon, but who knows what else he might do. And she didn't want him looking at her differently, as Terry now did.

Dave was safe. He had only been in Bald Eagle Falls for a little longer than Erin had been, so he wasn't woven into the fabric of the town like those who had been born and raised there. He wasn't necessarily connected to any of the branches of the grapevine. He had always seemed to her to be a bit of a loner. He didn't hang out with a bunch of other people. Didn't go drinking with the boys after work. He was just a nice guy living a quiet life in quiet little Bald Eagle Falls. He had a steady job at The Book Nook, which was enough to support himself. He was lucky, when she thought about the inadequately housed poor living in and around Bald Eagle Falls. He didn't have half a dozen mouths to feed and have to be constantly worried that he would be kicked out and have to find somewhere new to live. He made enough to rent an apartment somewhere, get internet, and entertain himself with cable or streaming video service.

"How long have you been in Bald Eagle Falls now?" she asked.

Dave slurped a noodle and wiped his face, laughing at himself. "Just over two years. A bit longer than you. I think I'd been here about three months before you moved in."

"And you moved here because of your aunt? Is that right?" Erin tried to remember any details of his arrival and what people had told her about him.

"Aunt Jane. Yes, it's been nice to be able to spend time with her. She's kind of cut off from everyone else."

Erin had heard about his Aunt Jane once or twice, but couldn't remember the woman's last name. She was a bit of a recluse. It was good that he'd been able to move close to her and be allowed into her life. At least she wouldn't be completely alone when she died, with nobody to look after her affairs.

"Where did you come from?"

"I've been all over." He shrugged. "Mostly north."

"Me too." Erin cut up more chicken with the side of her fork. It was a bit tough, and she might need to resort to a knife instead. "Mostly in the north. I tell people Maine because that's where I spent the most time the last few years before moving here, but it wasn't the only place I lived. It's just easier. When you tell people you come from 'all over,' they don't know what to say. How to ask after your people or find out what you were doing when you were living there. There's no reference point."

Dave gave a nod. "People like a reference point. Something to anchor to."

"Yes. Exactly."

She and Dave actually had a lot in common. Both were quiet people, tending toward being alone, arriving in Bald Eagle Falls around the same time, after a semi-nomadic life in the northern states. Working practically next door to each other. It was surprising that she hadn't eaten a meal or had a one-on-one conversation with Dave before. But it was probably because of Terry. It wasn't proper to approach a woman who was seeing someone else. Even for just a casual conversation.

That was the South—lots of rules about what was proper.

Erin took a sip of water, considering how to approach the subject of Brandon and what he had been involved in.

"Brandon took care of me, so I don't want to say anything bad about him. He helped me out when nobody else did."

"I get that. Need can bond people together who wouldn't have normally had anything to do with each other."

"It's true." Erin nodded slowly at the wisdom of this statement. She sometimes wondered how she had gotten involved with some of the people she had over the years. Whether there was something wrong with her. But she had turned to those people because she needed them, or they had needed her. And that had brought them together in solidarity, if not in friendship. "I had lost my job, and it came with board, so when I lost my job, I lost my room too. I hadn't been able to save anything while I was working there. Or not enough, anyway. I couldn't put a down payment on an apartment. Didn't want to go to a shelter. There weren't a lot of other options, other than finding someone who would take me in until I could get back on my feet."

"And you and Brandon got together somehow."

"Yeah. I don't even remember how. We ran into each other at a bar or had friends in common, one of those things. And… he said I could crash on his couch." Erin shrugged.

How long had *that* lasted? A few days? A week? Had it even lasted one night? It was all a bit muddled in Erin's memory. There had been alcohol involved, and she had been stressed out by losing her job. He had been friendly, invited her to crash at his place, comforted her. She knew when she accepted the offer to crash on his couch that she would end up in bed with him. It was inevitable. She didn't have any other way to show her appreciation or earn her keep.

"That was nice of him," Dave said neutrally. How much had he guessed about her relationship with Brandon? Maybe everything. Maybe nothing. Maybe she was reading too much into his carefully smooth, nonjudgmental expression. Maybe he really didn't think that there had been anything else between them.

"It was longer than I thought it would be. It wasn't so easy finding another job. I was always looking, but it isn't easy, as a young woman, to get something stable. Especially in that economy."

"What was he like? Other than what you said—him being a liar."

Erin looked up at the ceiling, thinking back. "He was fun. I thought at first that he was really nice, but he wasn't. I don't mean he was really mean, either, just that... he looked out for himself, and the things that he did, like inviting me to stay with him, or buying a round of drinks, or things like that... were calculated. Things that he did to get what he wanted. I don't know if he thought that's the way the rest of the world operates too or if he knew he was different that way."

"Like a psychopath?"

"No... I don't know. Calculating. Self-centered. What's the word when you do things for money? Mercenary. He'd do you a favor if he thought it would get him something he wanted. Something that was more valuable to him."

"A situation like that could get bad pretty fast."

"Yeah. I guess so. And it did. I was naive in a lot of ways. I was okay having some fun with him. But then I'd find myself at the other end of his fun the next time... the brunt of a joke or his temper. A punching bag because he'd had a bad day or was drunk and couldn't handle himself. I kind of pretended that it wasn't happening. Because what else was I going to do? Where else was I going to go? I was already doing everything I could to find another situation, a job and a place to rent once I had some money. No one else had offered to help me. Any other 'friends' were relieved not to have to. Nice guy Brandon had stepped in and saved the day."

"But he abused you."

Erin shrugged. She didn't want to focus on that. Didn't want to remember or recount the details. "It was a long time ago now. That's all in the past."

"But he did. He wasn't such a nice guy at all."

"Yeah, that's what I found out. But it was too late to back out. I was already there. And I didn't have anywhere else to go. Until I had lined something else up, I was stuck there."

"So, you can see how someone would want to kill him," Dave suggested.

CHAPTER 32

*E*rin's heart thumped harder. She looked at him, studying his face for some sign of what he was going to do about it. Had this whole conversation just been a way of eliciting information that the police wanted from her? She wasn't going to turn herself in to them. She wasn't going to confess to anything she hadn't done. She wasn't going to let them railroad her into anything just because they couldn't find anyone else with a motive.

"There were probably a lot of people who would have wanted to… get back at him other than me," Erin said carefully.

"Because you aren't the only one he treated that way. He took advantage of other people too. Found ways to use them."

"Yeah. I remember one guy…"

Erin stopped short. Dave looked at her, waiting for her to continue. Erin looked away.

"I don't know. I probably shouldn't say. I'm sure he messed up a lot of people. Like you say, he found ways to use people. Especially people dumb enough to think they could trust him."

"Uh-huh."

"He got a call in the middle of the night," Erin said, deciding to go ahead and give him some of the details. Show him what kind of a guy Brandon was, in case he didn't already understand. It wasn't like Dave would ever know who she was talking about. Erin didn't have to share his identity. And if his story was included in Brandon's tell-all, that wasn't Erin's problem. As she had told the sheriff, she was sure that they would have had to change his name. To protect his publishing house against a liability claim, if nothing else. "This guy… Kyle."

It had been the wee hours of the morning, and Erin hated being dragged out of sleep by something like that. The irritating jangle of Brandon's phone. Him shouting into it to be heard over whatever background noise was going on on the other end. Erin's head hurt and her body hurt, and she just wanted to sleep… knowing that it would start all over the next day. The pointless searching for a job. The claustrophobic feeling of being trapped with Brandon. Whatever demands Brandon put on her for the day.

"Something had happened. Kyle had been driving drunk. Had hit someone. I didn't talk to him directly, so I don't know all of the details. Brandon was shouting at him to settle down. Said that he would take care of things. Kyle didn't need to worry about anything. Go home and settle down, have another drink and just be calm. If anyone came looking for him, Brandon would say that Kyle had been with him. He couldn't have been the one to hit anyone, because the two of them had been together. There would be witnesses. He'd arrange everything, as long as Kyle cleaned up the car and stayed calm."

Dave had forgotten about his dinner, leaning forward with his mouth slightly open, his face a white glow in the dimness of the restaurant.

Erin didn't reveal the whole conversation to Dave. How Erin had lain there and listened to him, her teeth clenched.

"I'll tell them you were here until four. Erin will say whatever I tell her to. Don't you worry about that. We'll all tell the same story, and the cops won't be able to get anything on you. You weren't ever there."

After apparently getting Kyle settled down enough to follow his instructions, Brandon had hung up.

"He laughed about it," Erin told Dave. "He wasn't the least bit concerned for his friend. About what he was going through emotionally or about the person he'd hit. He wasn't worried about seeing that justice was done or that his friend was protected. You know why he said he'd cover for him? What he wanted?"

Dave shook his head wordlessly.

"He said that Kyle would owe him. That from then on, Kyle would do anything he wanted, because if he didn't, Brandon could go to the police and tell them that he knew what had happened that night and that he knew who it was."

"That's… horrible. And you thought he meant it?"

"Of course he meant it. That's the kind of guy he was. He would be more than willing to let Kyle dangle for the rest of his life, doing one favor after another for him. If Kyle ever refused him something, Brandon would remind him, 'You owe me for covering for you. If you don't, I'll go to the cops.' He was delighted to have something to hold over his 'friend.'"

"I wonder how many people he did something like that to."

Erin nodded. She ate a few pieces of her chicken, which was starting to get cold. How many people were there like Kyle, who would be relieved to find out that Brandon was dead and no longer a threat to them? Had one of them followed him to Bald Eagle Falls and killed him? After holding something over Kyle for years, had he threatened to reveal the story of the hit and run to the world in his tell-all memoir? There could be a dozen Kyles out there, each with a motive to kill Brandon and make sure that the memoir never hit the shelves.

The rest of the meeting was somewhat subdued. Erin supposed they were both thinking about Brandon and his false friendship, the people he had used and abused over the years. Erin knew that she should feel sorry that he was dead. He had helped her. He had kept her from whatever fate might have awaited her on the streets. He had made her life more bearable, much of the time. But she wasn't sad for him. She was relieved.

Relieved that he couldn't pop up in her life again. Emailing or messaging her or, worse, walking in the front door at Auntie Clem's. He couldn't ruin her relationships, remind her of what she had been, try to coerce her into doing something else for him. They were done, and she didn't have to worry about him stalking her to Bald Eagle Falls or any other place. She could finally stop holding her breath.

It was while they were each paying their individual portions of the bill that Sheriff Wilmot showed up.

Erin supposed she should have been expecting it. He had told her, after all.

"When you're done here, we would like to talk to you at the office," Wilmot informed her.

Had he been watching her for some time, waiting until she was paying her bill rather than interrupting her dinner? Had he been close enough to listen in on any of their conversation? Had Dave been instructed to see if he could get the story out of her?

She flashed him a look, but he seemed just as surprised as Erin was to see Wilmot there. So maybe it wasn't a setup.

Would Wilmot tell Terry that Erin had been having dinner with Dave? Make something out of it, like it had been a date instead of just a casual discussion between two people who had ended up at the restaurant alone? Erin stood slowly, handing the point-of-sale machine to the waitress, who looked confused by what was going on.

Erin looked once more at Dave. What did she even want to say to him? "Talk to you later"? "See you at the bookstore"?

"This way, please," Wilmot encouraged, nudging Erin's arm.

The other restaurant patrons stared at Erin as she was escorted out of the room by the police. By the time she got to the police department offices, they would already be speculating about what she had done.

CHAPTER 33

"What's going on?" Erin asked as Wilmot opened the door of his squad car for her. He didn't put her in the back seat, pushing down her head so that she wouldn't bump it on the way in. He just allowed her in the passenger side in the front. She could see his onboard computer and equipment and all of the little knobs that she didn't know how to use. "Why do you want me to come in?"

She had a feeling that she already knew. But she didn't want to give anything away. Maybe he didn't have anything more. Maybe it was all just a bluff like they did on TV. If you don't have anything, pretend that you do and make the suspect fall for it.

"We'll go over the details once we get there."

"I'm not sure... I don't really want to go in today. We could arrange to talk sometime tomorrow instead..."

"Are you not working tomorrow?"

"Well... yes, I am."

"Then it's easier for me to just get you while I can today. Otherwise, I won't get you until this time tomorrow, and will have wasted another day of the investigation for nothing."

"I'm not sure that I'm up to any questions right now."

"You seemed fine in the restaurant. At any rate, you've had a little chance to relax, you should be fine for a little longer. We won't keep you up late."

They knew that she went to bed pretty early, so they must not be planning on the questioning taking very long. If Erin insisted on waiting, she would just have another twenty-four hours of worrying and wondering what they had, if anything.

Erin waited, watching out the window. Hopefully, it was just a bluff. She didn't want to end up sleeping in one of the temporary holding rooms in the police department offices, waiting until they could transfer her to the pen.

"Is Terry there?"

"No, I don't believe so. Do you want him there?"

"No… I don't know. Maybe."

"Think about it and let me know. If you want him to be there, I'm sure we can make arrangements. It won't take him long to drive over."

If he even *wanted* to be there for her. But Erin knew that was unfair. Terry wanted to help her. He wanted to support her. He just couldn't stop his cop side from taking over and analyzing the situation, demanding answers. He couldn't seem to control his suspicions about what she was hiding from him. And the fact was, after dealing with a guy like Brandon, it was unlikely Erin would ever share all of her secrets with anyone. It would leave her too vulnerable. And without an escape route if she ever needed to get out of the relationship. If he knew all of her friends and past history, he would know where to look for her. He would be able to track her down.

Of course, as a cop, he could probably track her down whether he knew anything about who her friends outside of Bald Eagle Falls were or not.

Sheriff Wilmot pulled into his reserved spot in the parking lot of the town hall and shut off the engine. "Follow me."

Erin appreciated that he wasn't taking her there in handcuffs, and didn't see the need to keep his hand on her arm to ensure that she followed him in. She didn't feel quite as much like a criminal.

It was after hours, so Clara was not at the reception desk and Melissa was not there doing any filing or other administrative work. The public-facing doors were shut and locked, and it was just official personnel there now. Erin knew Sheriff Wilmot and wasn't particularly worried about being there with him alone. People had seen them leave the restaurant together, after all, so it wasn't like Wilmot could do something to her and then pretend that she had never been there. But she was still relieved to see Stayner working in the office he shared with Terry, tapping away at the computer. He looked up and nodded at Erin as she walked by.

Wilmot escorted Erin to one of the interview rooms and motioned for her to sit down.

"Do you want coffee? No muffins today, I'm afraid."

"I just ate. I don't need any food. But coffee… sure."

He nodded and left the door to the room open while he went to the nearby alcove to pour them each a mug of coffee. He returned and placed Erin's in front of her. He placed his cup slightly to his right and squared a yellow letter-size pad in front of him, lining it up with the edge of the table. He tapped a pen on it and looked at her.

"You haven't been open and honest with us in answering our questions about Brandon Quayle."

"I told you that I don't want to discuss him."

"You said that you haven't been in contact with him."

"I haven't."

"We have recovered a number of emails sent to you from Quayle over the past few weeks."

Erin had been hoping that there was no way they would be able to recover them once they had been deleted from her deleted mail folder. But she knew the axiom. How anything that had been on the internet was still there, somewhere.

"I never wrote to him."

Wilmot sipped his coffee. He put it down and wrote something on the notepad. "You admit that you received emails from him."

Erin shrugged. "I told you that he might have messaged me or tried to reach me."

"You didn't say that you had received emails from him."

"You asked if I was in contact with him. I wasn't. Just because he emailed me, that doesn't mean I had anything to do with him. *Anybody* can email you. Some Prince in Jordan who wants your bank account information. You just junk it and go on."

"Is that what you did?"

"Did you find any emails from me to him?" Erin challenged.

He apparently had not. "Quayle did email you telling you about the memoir he was writing. You acted as if you had no idea he was writing a book."

"I only glanced at the emails long enough to see what they were. I didn't read them through. And if I had, I wouldn't have believed him anyway."

"You wouldn't have believed what?"

"Anything he said. I certainly don't think he ever wrote a book."

"We now have witnesses that confirm that he did."

"They saw it? Read it?"

"Saw it. Read portions of it."

"Do they have copies?"

He shook his head. "It was only shown to them in hard copy format, and he kept the only copy with him. No one has a copy in any format. And we don't know what happened to his printout. I would really like to know what happened to it."

"He probably didn't write a whole book. Probably only enough to make people think there was a full book."

Wilmot grinned suddenly. "You're pretty skeptical, aren't you? You don't believe he could write a book?"

"Not the Brandon I knew."

"From what I understand, he had sobered up. Straightened his life around. Was trying to make things right with the people he had harmed in the past."

Erin shook her head. "I didn't believe it when he said it. I don't believe it from you either."

Remembering the story about Kyle had helped to cement it in her mind. Brandon might look like he was doing the right thing. He might have acted like he was being generous and only wanted the best for his friends. But he was just getting more ammunition. Brandon making sincere amends was the very definition of a leopard changing its spots.

"He told you he was trying to straighten things out with people from his past?"

"He might have. Something along those lines. But how exactly does that align with writing a tell-all book? Isn't he... telling everyone's secrets and worst moments?"

"I think that the point is he is telling all of the things *he* did wrong, not revealing secrets about his friends. Sort of 'all of the stupid stuff I did before I sobered up.'"

"But that would have included stuff he did with friends. Stupid stuff they did or mistakes that they made. People he humiliated. He can't tell about all of the stuff he did when I was living with him and not include me in the story."

"You know that gives you a motive, rather than taking it away."

"If I believed he was going to write something like that. But I don't. And even if he did, it's like I said before. Anyone who knew him would know that he can't tell the truth. And anyone who doesn't know him won't know me."

"So, you had absolutely no reason to want him dead."

No reason to want him dead? Erin wished that he had died years before. But she hadn't been the one who killed him. All she did was leave.

"I didn't kill him."

"Why did you go to Canyon Park?"

Erin had been afraid he would get to that. She looked away from Wilmot. "I told you; I was just out for a walk."

"He told you he would meet you there. At just about the time that you found his body."

"The second time."

He tilted his head slightly. "The second time," he agreed, as if he didn't understand why that part was significant.

"I already knew he was dead. I didn't go there to meet him."

Wilmot sat back in his chair. He pursed his lips and nodded. "Yes. You already knew he was dead. Unless you had any doubts about it. Maybe you thought that since the body disappeared, he had gotten up and walked away. That you were mistaken and he wasn't really dead."

Erin had considered that. But she had known absolutely when she saw him and when she touched him that he was dead. There was no doubt about it. She immediately discarded the idea that he could still be alive after seeing him that first time.

But she had still gone to the park.

"I felt... compelled," she confessed eventually. "I knew he was dead. I knew I wasn't going there to meet him. But I felt like I needed to go there to... close a chapter in my life. I needed to go there and *not* meet him to convince myself that he was dead and would never be coming back into my life again."

"Who put him there?"

"I have no idea. I was… as shocked as could be by him being there. I really was. I have no idea how he got there."

"Were you supposed to meet him there with someone else? His agent? A lawyer?"

"No. Nobody."

"Who else would he have told he was going to meet you there?"

"I don't know. I haven't been in his life for a couple of years. I don't know what happened between then and now."

"Someone knew that you and Quayle were supposed to meet there."

"I don't know who. Did he have a girlfriend? A sponsor? A priest? I don't know who he would tell about any of this. I wasn't supposed to meet anyone else there. Maybe someone hacked my email."

"That's a possibility, I suppose," Wilmot conceded. "Or someone happened to see it while you had it open. Someone shoulder surfing while you were at work or somewhere else? Your computer left on at the bakery with his email on the screen? Your phone put down on the table or counter at home where someone could see it?"

"Do you mean Terry? He never said anything about it. He would have asked me what it was all about."

"Maybe. You have other people in and out of your house too. Vic and Willie. Other friends, family members."

"Vic or Willie? Charley? You don't think that any of those people would have set up a meeting with Brandon in The Book Nook basement and killed him?"

"It seems like a stretch, that's true. Could have been several people in on it, though. You, one of them, one of The Book Nook employees. It could have been a conspiracy."

"A conspiracy. Are you serious? There wasn't any conspiracy to kill Brandon Quayle. If there was, I would not have called the police. We would have just gotten rid of the body our own way, and no one would ever have seen him again."

They kept coming back to that. Why would Erin have called the police if she had been the one to kill Brandon? And if she did, why wouldn't she call it in as self-defense? Say that he had attacked her? What would be the point of making the body disappear between the time she called the police and when they got there?

"I don't think you did this," Wilmot said. "I don't think it was a conspiracy. But I can't make it fit. I can't find any explanation for what happened. And you can't deny anymore that you knew him and lied to me about the fact. You knew from the start who he was and why he was here. You pretended you didn't and waited for us to figure it out on our own. Because you were hoping not to be part of this investigation."

Erin nodded. "That's exactly why."

"Well, it didn't work, did it? I don't know why you would think that it would. Did you really think that you could keep us from finding out who Brandon was or that he had a connection with you? Or that you went to Canyon Park to meet him—or where you had arranged to meet him? You must have known that it would all come out in the end."

"I could hope it wouldn't. Maybe no one would be able to identify him and it would just go away. He would be buried as a John Doe and I wouldn't ever have to think about him again." Erin had known that this was highly unlikely, but such things happened. If there wasn't anything to connect Brandon with his identity in Maine and no one stepped forward, Erin could have gotten lucky.

But she hadn't been lucky.

The police knew who he was. They knew she and Brandon were connected. And they knew that he had told her to be at Canyon Park, and she had gone, even though she had known that he was dead.

She couldn't explain that. Not because her reasons for going to the park would incriminate her, but because she couldn't even explain them herself. She had felt compelled. So she had gone. She had never imagined that the killer would dump Brandon's body there.

CHAPTER 34

"That's what I don't get," Erin mused, shaking her head. "Why kill him and then make him disappear from The Book Nook? And why dump him in Canyon Park, where he had planned to be? How did whoever killed him know that? And if they made him disappear from The Book Nook, then why dump him there instead of just disposing of the body down a well or in a mining tunnel somewhere? Why make it reappear instead of disappearing forever?"

"To throw suspicion back on you. I think that you are the key here, Erin. I just don't know how."

"How could I be the key?"

"You know something. Maybe you don't even know you know something. Maybe Quayle said something in one of his emails that you didn't even read."

Erin rubbed her forehead. "Then how can I figure it out? Someone must have hacked my emails."

"Or maybe Quayle told them something. Maybe he was in contact with someone else in Bald Eagle Falls. Or near here. And *they* decided that him publishing his memoir was too dangerous for them."

"No one else in Bald Eagle Falls knew him."

"You don't know that."

"He would have said something. Or I would have known them from

Maine. If Brandon knew someone here, then he would have known that *I* was here a long time ago."

"He didn't know where you were?"

"I never told him where I was going. I just hopped in my car and left. And I didn't go straight from his place here, either. I had a couple of jobs in between. Different places… different names. I didn't want to leave a trail that he could follow."

Wilmot pondered this. "Then how did he? And when did he?"

Erin shook her head. "I don't know. I guess… I'm on social media now and have a website, and it's all in my real name. The same name that I was using when I was with him. I thought I was safe, being here, in another state, in a small town away from the big cities. I didn't think it would be a problem to use my own name." She shrugged. "I'm not the only Erin Price in the world. Or in the USA."

"He didn't get in contact with you until recently?"

"He didn't *get in contact* at all. He started sending emails. I didn't respond. As far as he knew, I was a totally different Erin Price who didn't know who the heck he was."

"But he persisted, so he must have been pretty sure. You don't have your picture on any of your social media or your website?"

Erin considered this. She had gotten careless over time. Brandon hadn't been a part of her life anymore, and the fear of his tracking her down had faded. She had gone on with her life. She thought that he had gone on with his. That he didn't care where she was anymore. She had probably posted pictures of herself without ever thinking about him, once the danger seemed to be past.

"Maybe, yes. I guess so."

"Then he could know that it was you and not another Erin Price. And he came to Bald Eagle Falls to talk to you. To tell you about his book and that you were in it."

"Why? Why bother telling me I was in it? Why would I care?"

"He must have thought that there was something in there that you *would* care about. If he didn't want to make amends, then maybe he wanted to blackmail you. Or to try to resurrect the old relationship. He doesn't say much in his emails, just that he wants to see you, get together."

"Yeah."

Wilmot sat looking at Erin. "You can't help me out at all."

"I have no idea. I'm sorry, I can't help you. I don't know what's going on any more than you do."

There was a tap at the door, and Erin turned, expecting to see Stayner with a note in his hand to ask Wilmot something. Or maybe Clara back from dinner and checking in to see if he needed anything else before she left for the day. But it wasn't either of them. It was Terry. K9 stood at attention at his side, panting, watching Erin and Terry and waiting for a command.

Terry wasn't smiling. He didn't look happy to be there. Erin supposed he had more questions for her. Why she didn't tell *him* about the emails.

"Sheriff," Terry said gruffly. "I think Erin's ready to go home."

Erin was surprised by this. He'd heard that Wilmot was questioning her and had flown to her side to be her protector now? She expected him to be on the same side as Wilmot, wanting answers from her. The answers that would solve the case.

Wilmot nodded and sighed. "I think we're done here anyway. I wish you had been more forthcoming with me, Miss Price. I think we could have shortcut a lot of this investigation if you had told us who Quayle was and what you knew about him."

Erin stood slowly. "Now that you know... has it gotten you anywhere? Working on your own, you might have found something I couldn't have told you. Something you wouldn't have looked for if you thought it was all about me. I just didn't want to be involved."

Wilmot shook his head slowly. "Take care of yourself, and if you think of anything that might be helpful... please pass it on."

Erin didn't agree or disagree. She went to the doorway to join Terry. He stepped back to give her space to exit, and they walked in silence out to his truck.

Erin climbed up into the seat. She pulled on her seatbelt and buckled it as Terry walked around the vehicle to his side. "Thank you," she told him as he slid behind the wheel.

Terry looked at her for a moment, waiting for her to say something else, but Erin didn't have anything else to say to him.

"You're welcome. It looks like he was ready to wind things up anyway. I'm not sure I saved you anything."

"Still... I appreciate you looking after me."

He started the engine and spent a moment adjusting the airflow to the perfect temperature.

"I do want to help you, Erin. You may not believe that, but I have your best interests at heart. I don't want anything to happen to you. I don't want you to be arrested or even investigated. But sometimes, I am conflicted. I wish I wasn't, but I am. I'm sorry about before... that you felt like I was more interested in being a cop than in protecting you." He hesitated. "Not that you *felt* I was. I don't mean you misinterpreted something or were too sensitive. I *did* make a mistake. I know that you are your own person and you have a hard time sharing. It shouldn't surprise me. And I should wait until you're ready to tell me things and not to share just because I say so."

Erin was quiet, thinking about that for the few minutes it took them to drive to the house.

"You won't ask me to tell you more about Brandon?" she asked before he had cut the engine.

Terry shook his head. "I won't ask you anything else about Brandon."

"Or anyone else I might have had a relationship with?"

"Or anyone else."

"Or anything else I'm not ready to talk about?"

He swallowed and looked at her, trying to meet her eyes and convince her of his sincerity. "I will try not to ask sensitive questions or ask things about the past that you haven't offered to share. But I'm a cop and I care about you, and I might ask something that you aren't ready for. But... you don't have to answer. Just tell me. And I won't make you feel bad for not answering."

It had been a pretty tall order. Erin would have been satisfied if all he would agree to was not to ask her anything else about her life with Brandon Quayle.

"Okay," she said, and popped the truck door open. She heard Terry scrambling to get out of the truck and catch up with her before she could get to the door. K9 hurried along at his side.

"Okay?" Terry demanded as he and Erin reached the door. "Okay, what?"

"Okay," Erin fit her key into the lock. "I accept your apology."

"You do?"

"Yes."

Erin got the door unlocked and stepped into the house. Terry followed Erin into the house, not stopping to make sure the burglar alarm was disarmed. He was always diligent about arming and disarming it.

"Wait! You do?" Terry's voice was full of relief. Erin intended to beat him to the kitchen, but he was too intent on catching her, and she only got a step or two away from the door before he snatched her up in his arms and whirled her in a wide circle, feet off the ground. Like her father had spun her when she was a little girl. Erin let out a sound that was between a shriek and a whoop. She didn't know how to respond to his enthusiasm.

She didn't have to come up with words, because as Terry bent down to set her feet back on the floor safely, he first kissed her on the forehead, and then grasped her face with both hands and held her still to kiss her again, on the lips this time.

Erin's heart was pounding as she leaned into his embrace. She longed for the closeness and warmth of her partner, a feeling that had been absent for far too long. It had been a lonely week. She didn't like the awkwardness and the solitude, with him spending his time in the spare room instead of with her. She hated the rift and would do anything within her power to heal it. She hated Brandon for being the one to cause trouble between them, even if he was dead. How many times was Brandon going to screw things up for her?

No more. He was out of her life, he was dead, and no matter what happened in the investigation, she and Terry were okay again. For sure.

Terry released her from the kiss when the burglar alarm started to whoop. He swore and dashed over to the panel to shut it off.

"You'd better call the police department to tell them they don't need to respond," Erin advised.

Terry swore again and pulled out his phone to do so. Erin couldn't help laughing at him and at his embarrassment over forgetting to disarm the burglar alarm because he had been too busy with other things.

CHAPTER 35

*E*rin moved into the kitchen to make tea while Terry called the police dispatcher to assure them they didn't need to send someone to deal with the burglar alarm. There was a flurry of noise at the back door, and Erin could see both Vic and Willie trying to get the door open. They had a key, but might have forgotten it when they heard the alarm or hadn't managed to fit it into the lock in their hurry to see what was wrong.

Erin turned the deadbolt to unlock the door and they both pushed their way into the kitchen.

"Is everything okay?" Willie demanded, keeping Vic behind him until he could assess the situation.

"Yes. It's fine. It was an accident. There's no intruder."

Willie pushed past Erin to check the rest of the house to ensure that she was telling the truth and not just saying that because someone was holding a gun on her or something equally terrifying. He heard Terry apologizing to the police dispatcher and quickly checked out the other rooms to make sure there wasn't anyone else there.

Vic moved forward, red-faced with anger or embarrassment at being forced into the secondary position by her boyfriend. She had her gun out, a small handgun she kept in a holster under her bra. She hugged Erin around the shoulders with her free arm.

"Are you okay? Are you sure everything is fine?"

Erin nodded. "Yes. You can put the gun away. I don't want anyone getting hurt by accident."

Vic stayed there, on the alert, ready for any trouble, while she waited for Willie to finish looking around the house and return to confirm that Erin was telling the truth and everything was, in fact, safe and sound. Terry put his phone away, having finished talking with the dispatcher. Erin wondered whether they would send a car by anyway, just to ensure that the call from Terry hadn't been coerced by whoever had set the alarm off, an intruder who could be holding Erin hostage if it weren't for the fact that the house was now filled with protectors.

Erin's phone began to ring, and she knew who it would be before she reached down and found it in her pocket.

"Hi, Mrs. Peach. It's okay; false alarm. Terry and I were just occupied when we came in the door and both forgot to turn it off."

She listened to Mrs. Peach's worried tone, waiting for the words to run out again and leave her space to answer.

"I promise everything is alright. I'll tell you about it later."

She made a few more noises to assuage Mrs. Peach's worries and then hung up the phone.

"You're going to tell her about it later?" Terry repeated, his face already flushed red with embarrassment. "Explain to her why we didn't disarm the alarm?"

"Yes." Erin grinned. She looked at Willie and Vic, who had now both put their guns back in their holsters. "I'm going to explain to her why we were too... busy in conversation to disarm it."

Vic and Willie looked blank at first, but then Vic started grinning. Willie looked at her and then at Terry.

"You were... engaged in conversation?"

"Deeply engaged," Erin agreed. She hadn't thought that Terry could get any redder, but his ears were a brilliant scarlet. His cheek dimpled.

They all started chuckling.

The kettle started to whistle, and Erin motioned everyone to the table as she went to get it. "Everybody sit down and get out of the way," she told them with mock severity.

"I guess that means that the two of you made out," Vic said. "I mean —made up."

Erin giggled loudly and tried to cover it up with a cough. She took the tea things over to the table and gave everyone their favorite mugs. Of course, K9 lay beside Terry to wait for his cookie and Orange Blossom started to yowl. Apparently, Terry hadn't remembered to feed him while Erin had been at the restaurant and then at the police department office.

"Don't you believe a single meow," Terry warned. "He's been fed."

"I'll just give him a little treat, then."

Erin fed K9 one of the gluten-free dog biscuits and skittered several small kitty treats across the floor for Blossom to chase and gobble up. Marshmallow hopped into the kitchen and got a carrot from Erin before she opened the freezer to find some people treats for the rest of them. Some cookies to go with their tea. She sighed as she sat down at the table. Everyone else had already started on their drinks.

"What a day!" Erin declared.

She didn't need to fill everyone in on all of the details. The major points had already made their way around town so that everyone knew that Erin had been questioned by Sheriff Wilmot as part of the ongoing investigation into the murder of Brandon Quayle. They chatted about non-murder-related stuff, keeping the conversation casual and relaxed.

It was amazing to Erin how right everything felt. The four of them around the kitchen table with their tea and cookies. Erin reconciled with Terry. Terry and Willie talking as if they were buddies, despite the way that Willie always seemed to fall under suspicion when some crime had been committed in Bald Eagle Falls. Everything seemed to have fallen back into place. Tonight, she would be able to sleep. Brandon and his death and the repercussions of it would not keep her awake again.

"Oh, that recipe," Willie said, pointing a finger at Erin as he remembered. "You should talk to Jane Pooler."

Erin pulled out her phone to make a note of the name, and any contact information Willie might have. "And who is Jane Pooler?"

"She was a friend of Bertie's and apparently did some cooking and baking for him when his sister was out of town. So she would know all of his allergies and the flours that could be used in his baking."

"Great. Do you have any information on where she lives or her phone number?"

"I gather she is quite protective of her phone number. It is unlisted and no one is supposed to give it out. I think it's a landline. I don't think she even has a cell phone. But I do have her address."

"That will work."

Erin took down the information that Willie gave her.

It was just a little thing, but maybe it was a sign that things were going to change now and flow in her favor instead of landing one catastrophe after another in Erin's lap. If she could find out if the waffle recipe belonged to Jane Pooler and get her permission, she could try it out and see if it would work for her contest entry. She liked the ingredients and, if it turned out like she imagined it… it could be a winning entry.

CHAPTER 36

*E*rin didn't have to sleep alone that night. Everything was back as it should be. She stayed in Terry's arms for a long time, snuggling back into him if he tried to move away. His arm was probably asleep all night, but Erin wasn't giving up her grip on him.

She felt refreshed and energetic, ready for her morning at Auntie Clem's when her wake-up alarm went off. She was convinced that everything was going to go right for her. No more bodies, no more burglaries, no more mysterious recipes. She would leave the crimes to the police department to solve, and they would. She didn't need to worry about anything except how her baking turned out.

The morning at Auntie Clem's went by quickly. Of course, everyone wanted to know the scoop on Erin having been called in to the police department offices the previous day. Even if they were too polite to ask, they still wanted to listen in on any details they might be able to overhear.

She had arranged for Charley to come in for the afternoon shift—Charley was a night owl, so it was best to schedule her for afternoons—so that Erin could pop over to Jane Pooler's house to find out if the waffle recipe was hers, and then run a few other errands. There were always things to do for a business like the bakery. Something that needed to be fixed or picked up.

Erin put the address into her phone GPS, but it wasn't hard to find.

Bald Eagle Falls was a small town laid out on a fairly regular grid. After double-checking the address against what Willie had given her, Erin got out of the car.

She hadn't thought to ask whether Jane worked during the day or if she would be likely to be found at home. She had pictured her as a grand-motherly lady making bread for Bertie Braceling. Bertie had been a contemporary of Erin's mother, so she pictured Jane as being a generation or two older. In her sixties? Her eighties? She would be at home, wouldn't she?

There wasn't any way to find out now except to try. Erin strode up the sidewalk and knocked politely on the door. People in Bald Eagle Falls knocked before ringing the doorbell. She waited, listening for any stirring from within. If Jane was an older lady, she might use a walker or be slow.

Of course, she might also be half deaf and not hear Erin's knock. Erin eventually knocked again, as loudly as she could and, ten seconds after that, rang the doorbell. There was no answer, no stirring from within. Maybe she was out running errands or, despite what Erin had assumed about her age, might be at work. She should have asked Willie what he knew of her schedule.

Erin walked slowly back to her car. As she turned to look back at the house, a movement caught her eye. Not at Jane's house, but next door. A curtain twitched—someone looking out to see who was knocking on Jane's door. Maybe a nosy neighbor who knew Jane's comings and goings and could tell Erin her expected schedule.

After a moment of consideration, Erin walked up the neighbor's side-walk, mentally composing what she would say about needing information about Jane. By the time she reached the front door, the occupant had opened it. No need for extended knocking and ringing there.

"Who are you?" the woman asked, looking Erin up and down. "Wait... aren't you the baker?"

Erin nodded. "Yes, that's right. I own Auntie Clem's Bakery and do the baking there."

"What are you doing over here? Shouldn't you still be at the bakery?"

"My staff is covering it this afternoon so I can do a bit of visiting and running errands." Erin made a small gesture toward the house she had come from. "Do you know when Jane will be home?"

"She's home."

"Oh, is she? She didn't answer the door. I wondered if maybe she couldn't hear me knock or ring the bell."

"She's not deaf. I'm sure she would have been able to hear you."

"Oh. Then maybe she's out. Maybe she snuck away while you were doing something and didn't notice."

"She doesn't go out a lot. And…" The neighbor hesitated. Erin leaned closer, cocking her head.

"And?"

"I haven't seen her out at all lately. I've been worried that something might be wrong. Because she has to go out *sometimes*."

Erin could hear the concern in her voice. "Do you know when the last time was? Should we call the police? Make sure she's okay?"

"No, she wouldn't like that…"

"If she fell down or anything, she could be hurt and need help."

"I don't think she fell down. She's pretty sprightly. You wouldn't guess she's as old as she is. But it does worry me."

"Does she have a car?" There wasn't one parked at the curb in front of the house. Other than Erin's yellow Volkswagen.

"Yes, but it's in the garage in back."

"Maybe we should make sure it's still there. That she hasn't gone somewhere out of town."

"Well, I suppose so…"

Erin motioned to the side gate of the neighbor's house. "Do you mind if I cut through so I can check?"

"Yes, yes, go ahead. But she hasn't gone out of town. If she goes out of town, she leaves a key with me and tells me where she is going to be. You can't be too careful."

Erin's uneasiness grew at the evidence of the care Jane took to let people know where she was going to be. Would someone like that just ignore the door? What if she *had* fallen?

Erin walked quickly through the neighbor's yard to her back fence and the gate to the alley. Then she moved over a house to try to see in the windows of the garage to see if Jane's car was still parked there as suspected. She couldn't see in the windows on the big garage door because they were too high but, in the yard, she pressed her face to the window to peer in. She could see the dark form of a car parked inside. So, Jane

Pooler had not gone anywhere, but was still in her house. Not answering the door.

Erin walked to the back door of the house. She would try one more time and, if she could still not raise any answer from Jane, she would call Terry. Someone who was too nervous to open the door to a stranger might still answer to a uniformed police officer.

She knocked again, hard, trying to be loud enough that Jane would be able to hear it throughout the house. Unlike many houses, Jane's was equipped with a back doorbell, a rare find that Erin took advantage of by immediately pressing it after her initial knock. Not leaving anything to chance, she followed up with another firm knock, ensuring that Jane couldn't possibly miss her arrival. There was no answer. Erin looked at the house on the other side. Maybe the neighbor there would know something. Maybe it was someone Jane talked to more than she did the nosy neighbor? If the neighbor were too intrusive and Jane didn't want to share anything with her, she might go to someone else instead.

Erin stepped down from the doorstep, deciding to go over and check, just to be sure. Then, if the other neighbor didn't know anything either, she would call Terry.

CHAPTER 37

There was a soft click and the door behind her opened. Erin turned back around. She smiled at the older woman peeking out from behind the door. She had gray hair and was dressed in a yellow sundress. The smell of freshly brewed coffee wafted out from the house. She smiled tentatively, wrinkles fanning out around her eyes.

"Hello?"

"Oh, Mrs. Pooler…? You don't know me, but I'm Erin Price, and I—"

"Come inside, come inside," Jane said quickly, opening the door farther and motioning Erin in. "Don't stand out there attracting the attention of the whole neighborhood." After Erin stepped into the house, Jane stuck her head out the door and looked quickly around before shutting it again. Maybe she had been staying inside, out of sight, because of paranoia? It could go along with dementia or even be triggered by something as simple as a bladder infection.

She looked around the house for other signs that the woman might be having mental challenges. The front entryway and the living room were neat and tidy. No growing piles of garbage that she couldn't keep up with or collections that indicated she was hoarding. Erin got the feeling that the room had just been dusted and the cushions on the furniture shaken out in anticipation of company.

"I don't mean to intrude. If you're expecting someone…"

There was the coffee, too. Jane had just put it on. Was she planning to drink it all herself? Maybe she had a Keurig or similar machine and had only made one cup.

"No, no, dear. Have a seat. I'll get the coffee."

A cozy fireplace and a few chairs made up the living room. The furniture was well-worn but comfortable looking, with a floral printed sofa decorated with colorful throw pillows on one wall and a matching armchair on the other side of the room. A cabinet crammed full of knick-knacks and photos sat beside a birch bookshelf lined with Reader's Digest condensed books. A crocheted afghan covered the back of one chair and a basket of yarn and knitting needles sat on the coffee table. The overall effect was homey and welcoming, making Erin feel comfortable and at ease.

She sat on the sofa and waited for Mrs. Pooler to return. There was the sound of clinking dishes in the kitchen and, in a few minutes, the woman was back, carrying a tray. Erin repressed her instinct to jump up and take it from her and serve the coffee herself. She was the guest here and Mrs. Pooler appeared to be perfectly capable of carrying the tray and setting things out herself.

"These are gorgeous," Erin admired the delicate coffee cups with accents of pink roses. "You must love getting them out and having a tea party."

Mrs. Pooler's face crinkled up in a smile. "You know, you're absolutely right. They are an absolute joy to use and take me back to when I was a little girl, playing with my friends or my dolls."

Erin stirred her coffee for a moment before taking a sip. "I work at Auntie Clem's Bakery, and I... well, I found a waffle recipe that someone had left behind, and I've been trying to find out where it came from. I thought I recognized the flour blend; it's similar to what I used when I was doing some baking for Bertie Braceling."

Mrs. Pooler nodded. "Bertie was always a challenge to cook for! And just when you found something that would work, he would start reacting to an ingredient he hadn't before. The buckwheat-arrowroot-psyllium combination was pretty stable for a couple of years, but I always worried about what would happen when he started reacting to buckwheat!"

"He was always so cheerful about it. I couldn't understand how he could be so... accepting of his dietary limitations. Some people can't comply with even one restriction, and he was so limited, but so upbeat about it."

"That was just his nature." Mrs. Pooler shrugged. "I do miss him."

"So... this is your recipe, right?" Erin got out the paper and smoothed it out on her lap. "I can't figure out how it even got into the bakery, because I don't think I've ever seen you there. Did you... drop it? Did someone else have it?"

"Dave had it," the older woman admitted. She was looking down at her coffee rather than at Erin. "He wanted to do something that would distract you from... well, you know, what you found over there, in the bookstore."

Erin felt a warm rush of gratitude toward Dave. He had been worried about what she had seen and how it would affect her, and he had come up with something that would distract her from the nastiness of it. The perfect solution—a mysterious new waffle recipe of unknown origin.

"Well... I would never have guessed that in a million years. How thoughtful of Dave. I guess it worked because I have definitely been engaged in trying to figure out where the recipe came from." She laughed. "I guess the question is, do you need this back? Or do you mind me keeping it? I've been working on a recipe to submit to the waffle contest. You probably know that. If this one works out, would you mind if I submitted it? I don't want to put any pressure on you if it is an old family recipe or something you wouldn't want to be circulated."

Of course, she knew it wasn't an old family recipe. It was a recipe carefully formulated for Bertie Braceling, using only ingredients that he could tolerate. Minus the malt vinegar and the pumpkin spice mix, of course.

"Dave doesn't know anything about gluten-free baking," Mrs. Pooler said, setting her coffee down and finally looking at Erin. She looked child-like. As if she were afraid she was going to be punished for doing something wrong. "He knows that the recipe can't have wheat in it, but that's about all he knows about gluten-free cooking."

Erin nodded. "I would say the same is true of most people. If it's not something you do, then you don't know all of the little tricks, what other ingredients you need to watch for, how someone could have a bad reaction from the smallest bit of gluten exposure."

"But I knew that you do. I knew that you would look at every single ingredient before deciding to make it."

Erin frowned, trying to follow Mrs. Pooler's train of thought. Again, it seemed like the woman was exhibiting symptoms of some kind of dementia.

"Then why would you put malt vinegar and the spice pack in the recipe?" Erin asked. "I know you didn't make it that way for Bertie. And you know that I couldn't bake it that way. Why would you change the recipe to include those ingredients?"

"It was so nice when Dave moved to Bald Eagle Falls," Mrs. Pooler wandered off on a tangent, not answering the question. "Having such a nice young man move in close by. Someone who offered to help, who wanted to do everything he could for me. He was so very sweet and doted on me. He offered to go out and buy my groceries so I didn't have to go to the store, to mow the lawn and do other maintenance around here…"

"Oh! I didn't even put it together." Erin shook her head. Even when Mrs. Pooler had said that it had been Dave who had wanted the recipe to give to Erin, the tumblers had not clicked into place. "You're Dave's Aunt Jane."

"Yes," she agreed. "That's what he calls me. But I'm not really his auntie."

Erin had run into the same situation dozens of times. Younger people were taught to call older relatives aunt or uncle even though they were related another way. First cousins once removed. Second cousins. Married to a relative. They didn't even technically have to be related, though most probably were once they got down to it. Erin had also discovered from Clementine's genealogy files that pretty much everyone in Bald Eagle Falls was related. The old families had intermarried many times. As Mary Lou had once told Erin, "If you're kin to Clementine, you're kin to half the mountain."

"I know how it is with these old Tennessee families," Erin agreed. "Everyone is related somehow."

"He's not from Tennessee."

But he was from a Tennessee family. He had come to Bald Eagle Falls to help care for his aunt. Erin supposed many of the older, established family members would see someone like Dave as an outsider. Sometimes even someone like Willie, who had been raised in Bald Eagle Falls, was seen as an outsider because of how he had decided to live his life.

"I know that," Erin agreed.

"He is from the north."

"Yes, like me."

"From Maine."

Erin nodded. "That's right. That's where I'm from." She was a bit surprised that Mrs. Pooler would know that much about her, but she supposed that even if she was usually at home and didn't come to the bakery, she could still be hooked into the grapevine. And she had one source, in particular, Dave Wolfe, working out of The Book Nook, which Erin was in and out of all the time.

"He does things for me," Mrs. Pooler said, reverting to the previous topic. "Looks after me. Makes sure I have everything I need and don't have to go out."

"That's very nice of him."

"He gets upset if I go out. He wants me to stay here all the time and not to go out and talk to people."

If she had the beginnings of dementia, as Erin supposed she did, then she might not be able to judge who it was safe to talk to and what she could say to them. Dave might have had to be quite stern with her, telling her not to go out or talk to anyone. Erin had seen how frustrated family members and caregivers could become, trying to help their loved ones to live at home for as long as they could, but getting more and more strict about what the family member could do. As they slipped into what had once been called a second childhood, their children became the parents, having to make rules and stay on top of them as they slid further and further out of reach.

Dave was doing a good job. Nothing in that room hinted at any loss of mental faculties. It did not feel institutional or like a prison.

Erin supposed that was why Mrs. Pooler hadn't answered the door right away. Dave had drilled it into her that she wasn't allowed to open the door to strangers. She wasn't allowed to go out or to let anyone in.

"That's why I put those ingredients in the waffles," Mrs. Pooler said, fixing Erin with a bright stare. "So that you would know that something dangerous can be hidden. That something that is apparently so sweet... can kill."

CHAPTER 38

Sheriff Wilmot had been in a meeting for the last couple of hours, dealing with the feds on another case. When he opened his office door, he waved a stack of papers at Terry and motioned for him to come in.

"We need to talk."

Terry followed Wilmot back into his office. K9 kept close at his side. Wilmot sat down behind the desk and settled himself into the chair.

"The background checks didn't all check out," he told Terry. "I got an alert last night about Dave Wolfe's ID and social security number not matching up properly."

Terry raised his brows. "His ID doesn't check out?"

"No. Something is wonky. I'm not sure who he is or why he is using a false name and ID, but we need to get this sorted out."

Terry nodded. "Yes. As soon as possible."

Dave Wolfe worked right next door to Erin. He had casually met her for dinner the night before. He was the one who was supposed to have locked the bookstore the night Brandon Quayle had been killed.

"Have you questioned him?" Terry asked.

Wilmot looked at him over the top of the paper he was holding. "Not yet. I want to see what we can find out first. I've got to get caught back up here. It would help if you could find a way to get his picture to Quayle's family and friends back north. See if anyone recognizes him."

"I'm on it," Terry said, getting up. He paused at the door, having second thoughts about leaving. "Do you think it was him?"

"I don't know. It could just be a coincidence." Wilmot put the paper he was holding down on his desk. "We're not sure yet. We have to be careful."

"Of course." Terry nodded.

"Don't say or do anything that will tip him off. He could bolt, and we have no idea where he would go at this point. Who he really is."

Terry sighed. "I'm on it, but why would someone fake his identity and hide in a town like Bald Eagle Falls?"

"Who knows what he was hiding from." Wilmot shrugged. "I wish I had the answers, but it takes time to follow up on all of the leads."

"I'll get to work on it right away," Terry said.

"Thanks." Wilmot nodded and turned back to his desk.

Terry turned and left the office, distracted.

He'd thought that they had eliminated Dave as a suspect. The man had been so shocked when Terry had described to him how Erin had stumbled upon the body in The Book Nook. The body that had then disappeared before the police could get there. Terry could clearly remember the shocked expression on his face: he had been as white as a ghost, his eyes wide and his mouth hanging open. He didn't see how that reaction could have been faked.

Terry hurried down the hallway and back to his office. He needed to find out just who Dave was.

Erin stared at Mrs. Pooler. She felt like she was losing *her* mind. She'd thought that the older woman was the one who was going senile, but Jane Pooler had just pulled the rug out from under her. Erin was the one who had been stupid, who had not seen what was in front of her own face. She was the one who had been too dense to see what Mrs. Pooler was warning her about.

She hadn't understood the secret language of the recipe. The warning it contained. It had led her to Mrs. Pooler, which was a start, but Erin should have seen that it was more than just an unexpected gift. The red flags were there, but she had chosen not to see them.

She hadn't understood Mrs. Pooler's words as they had begun their conversation.

I'm not really his aunt.

He gets mad if I talk to anyone or go out.

He's from the north. From Maine.

"Who is Dave?" Erin asked in a hoarse whisper, suddenly unable to find her voice.

"I don't know," Mrs. Pooler confided. "He's never told me… his real name or what his story is. I didn't realize what he was doing at first. That he was using me as his cover. Pretending he belonged in Bald Eagle Falls because I was his auntie and he was taking care of me. He was using me to explain why he had just shown up here one day."

Erin heard a car door slam. She and Jane Pooler looked at each other, startled and worried. Erin turned to look out the window and saw that the truck was not in front of Mrs. Pooler's house like Erin's was. It had pulled into the neighbor's driveway. The opposite side of the house from the nosy neighbor.

"It's just the neighbor," Erin said, laughing at them both for being so jumpy.

"No." Mrs. Pooler's eyes were on the window, not reassured as Erin was. "We need to hide."

Erin looked back out at the truck as the driver walked across the driveway and came into view. Dave.

"Don't answer the door," she told Mrs. Pooler.

"He has a key."

Of course he did.

"Come on," Mrs. Pooler insisted. "Hurry."

Erin felt like *she* was the old woman as she struggled to get her body to listen to her. Standing up, hurrying after Mrs. Pooler, feeling like she was pushing her way through concrete. Dave would see Erin's car and know who was there. Maybe he even had a monitoring camera pointed at Mrs. Pooler's house, and that was what had made him return home.

Nice and close. He had met the old lady and helped her, providing her with all of the help she could want before starting to close the net around her. His help gave him a legitimate reason for being there, and she, in turn, had someone to run her errands and mow her lawn, and eventually keep her there, a prisoner in her own home.

Mrs. Pooler had picked up the coffee things and bustled into the kitchen. Erin still had her cup in hand as she entered the homey, breezy kitchen. The curtain over the sink rippled in front of an open window. Mrs. Pooler grabbed Erin's cup from her and quickly rinsed it under the tap and set it on the drying rack. She left her own half-finished cup on the tray.

She looked around, face pale, eyes wide. There wasn't anywhere to hide.

"Do you have a basement or attic?" Erin suggested. "Even… something close by, like a shed."

"The attic," Mrs. Pooler echoed.

She led Erin to the mud room at the back door. Even the mud room was immaculate. There was an enclosed porch or sunroom beside it, and warm sunshine streamed in the windows. Mrs. Pooler pointed up.

A faint rectangle in the ceiling. An eye loop at the edge to pull down. Erin looked around for a stick with a hook on the end to pull it down but couldn't find one. And when they found one, how were they going to get up into the attic? Jump up through the hole? There was no ladder, and Dave was already knocking briskly on the front door, then fitting his key into the lock.

"Here." Mrs. Pooler, rummaging through a slim utility cupboard, managed to find a long broomstick with a hook on the end. Erin reached up with it and tried to fit it through the little eyelet in the ceiling. She failed several times, her hands too shaky, the eyelet too small and too far away. She looked desperately toward the front door. Dave was going to walk in and find them there. It was time to come up with an excuse. An explanation for being there with Dave's "Aunt Jane."

The best thing would be to tell him the truth, that she was following up on the recipe that he himself had dropped into her lap.

But then what?

He would know from their faces that Aunt Jane had told Erin what she knew and that Erin was no longer distracted by the new waffle recipe.

CHAPTER 39

*P*olice work was so much faster than it used to be. Before Terry's time, fax machines took a long time to transmit a detailed image and it wasn't a great likeness once it got through. And before that, actually having to carry or courier pictures from one place to another. Cops canvassed with hard-copy photos in hand.

So he really couldn't complain about how long it took to find a couple of pictures of Dave Wolfe on social media and to start emailing them out to everyone they had been able to find with connections to Quayle. Even if people didn't like him that much, they were still intrigued by the story and excited to be able to assist in solving a homicide case. The fact that Quayle's body had been discovered, disappeared, and showed up again intrigued people, and they wanted to be a part of the case. It wasn't hard to get people to look at the photos he messaged to them, but it still took time to find anyone who actually knew him and could put a name to the face. Then he started working background on the name that they gave him, trying to figure out why Dave would have left Maine and come to Bald Eagle Falls.

Terry couldn't help but wonder what the connection was. Dave had arrived in Bald Eagle Falls before Erin. Had she followed him there? It wasn't possible. He knew Erin had come to Bald Eagle Falls to receive the inheritance that her Aunt Clementine had left her. She hadn't come looking for Dave. And if the two of them had wanted to run away together, they could have sold the properties and taken off whenever they wanted to.

If Erin had not come to Bald Eagle Falls because of Dave, then had he come because of her? That didn't make sense either because his arrival preceded hers by several months.

Terry rubbed his forehead, trying to loosen the knot of muscles and relax. He needed someone to brainstorm with. To try to come up with the connections that they were missing. Who was Dave Wolfe? Did he have a friend in Bald Eagle Falls that he had come to visit, and then decided to stay there? Had he been on the run?

It would be a while for the name he had input into the computer to come up with anything. There were a lot of databases to search through, and not-Dave could show up in any of them.

"Terry?"

Terry pulled his hand away from his head and focused on the form in the doorway. Clara, looking tentative. "Sorry, I don't mean to interrupt you, but…"

"No, it's okay. I'm trying to figure everything out here, but I'm not getting far. I could use an interruption about now."

"Well… it's Naomi from The Book Nook. She wondered if she could see you."

"Of course I'll see her." Terry glanced around his office. It wasn't messy, exactly, but it was… busy. His desk was piled high with files, reports, and mail. "Uh, just hand me that stack of files." He indicated the chair. Clara picked them up and Terry put them on the credenza behind him. He held his hand over them for a moment, making sure they weren't going to immediately slide to the floor, taking everything else with them in an avalanche. He turned back around to face Clara. "Okay. Show her in."

Clara nodded and withdrew. She was back a minute later with Naomi. Naomi swept back her straight, blonde hair and sat in the chair when Terry indicated it. She had a stack of papers in her hands and, by the time they were finished with small talk, he was burning to find out what they were.

"What have you got there?"

Naomi looked down at the thick bundle of papers. "I found this… in a box in the basement."

Terry's heart quickened in excitement. He kept his voice even and his face as expressionless as he could manage, trying not to influence her answer.

"It wasn't there before. I ordered in some books that the freshman English class needs in the fall, so they were just set to the side. I didn't look at them again until today."

Terry nodded his understanding.

"I guess… well, it isn't anything that *I* put there. I think… it must have been put there by Brandon Quayle." She swallowed and licked her lips, clearly dry from talking to him. "His name is on the front page." She lifted the bundle and turned it away from her so that he could see the front page.

It certainly looked genuine. He'd never held a manuscript in his hands before, but it looked like he would have expected a manuscript to look like. A thick stack held together by a black fold-back clip. Somewhat dog-eared, with sticky notes protruding here and there. It looked like it had been read and re-read several times.

"Let's see." He held out his hand for the papers. Naomi handed them over. Terry placed the manuscript squarely on the desk in front of him. He opened it to a random page halfway through.

It was blank.

Terry turned it over and looked at the next. It was also blank. He thumbed his way through several at once. There were a few random photocopies. Like Brandon had emptied the recycling bin at the library and just thrown a bunch of completely disparate topics together. Terry picked a few of the pages with flags or sticky notes at the edge to see if the notes made any more sense than the random pages he had picked out. Several of them were blank. Others were random topics, again.

Terry looked at Naomi. "This is supposed to be his manuscript? But what would he do when he had to show it to someone?"

"I don't know. Maybe there are a few actual pages from his memoir in there… Or maybe he would email them something, and this was only a prop."

Terry fanned the pages a few times, looking for anything that was not so random.

No luck. Terry pushed it away. He looked at Naomi. "When Dave came to work for you, did you check references?"

"Uh…" Naomi took off her black-framed glasses and considered the question. "I always do, so I must have."

"But you don't remember?"

"I'm sure I called his references. I don't remember any specifics."

"Nothing out of the ordinary? Just what you were expecting?"

"I guess so, yes. If there had been something wrong, I wouldn't have hired him. He's been an excellent employee. Never late. Learned the systems quickly. Was diligent in his job."

"Didn't murder anyone in the basement until now," Terry contributed.

Naomi's mouth dropped open. "You don't think Dave had anything to do with the murder!"

"We know that he didn't close and lock the store like he was supposed to."

"But that doesn't mean he had anything to do with the murder. That was just an oversight."

"Which happened the exact day of the murder. You said he was diligent. He'd never forgotten anything like that before?"

"No. It was just a one-time mistake."

"On the day of a murder."

Naomi shook her head. "It doesn't have anything to do with the murder. You know that. He was just as shocked as anyone."

"You never had any issues with his social security number?"

"Why would I?"

"Because Dave Wolfe isn't his real name."

Naomi frowned. "But it was… that was the name I used when I talked to his references. They all knew him. There weren't any issues."

"There weren't any issues because the references didn't actually exist. They were set up. People telling you what Dave had told them to tell you."

"I can't believe that. He's been such a good employee. I've never had any trouble with him."

"He had to keep his head down and stay out of trouble if he didn't want to be caught."

"No," Naomi continued to shake her head. "I can't believe that."

Terry's phone rang. He looked at the number on the caller ID. "Do you mind if I take this?"

"Sure, of course." Naomi looked around. "I should go. Give you some privacy. I guess…" She motioned to the faux manuscript, "You'll keep that."

"Yes, thank you for bringing it in," Terry told her, reaching for his phone before the call could go to voicemail. "It was enlightening."

Naomi nodded and left the office as Terry picked up the phone.

"Piper here."

"Officer Piper." The voice on the other end of the call was low and gravelly, sounding like the owner of it had stayed up half the night drinking and wasn't quite ready for the day, even though it was mid-afternoon. "Detective Percival Jones here."

The caller ID already told Terry what police force Jones was calling from, and Jones didn't bother to supplement or repeat that information, driving straight to the topic of his call. "You are looking for information on a subject surnamed Pinckney."

"Yes. That's the name I was given. It may be an alias. I'm not sure yet; this is very early stages."

"We are also looking for information on Pinckney. Am I to understand that you know where he is?"

Terry's heart started to beat harder in anticipation. "He's a murder suspect in Tennessee."

"So he's there? You know where he is?"

"Yes. Do you have an active warrant on him?"

"He is wanted for questioning in connection with a felony murder. Owner of a convenience store who was shot during a hold-up."

"And wanted for questioning means he is your prime suspect?" Terry double-checked.

"Our investigation led us back to Pinckney but, by the time we had identified him, he had disappeared. In fact, it would appear that the hold-up was part of his departure from Maine. He was on the road at the time. Needed money. By the time we had identified him, any trace of where he had gone from there was gone. Though indications are," Jones paused for effect, "that he was headed south at the time."

Terry thought about that. "Just over two years ago?"

"Yes."

"Sounds like he came straight here."

"If you're investigating him for murder, chances are you're on the money. You'll want to keep eyes on him until you have enough to arrest. Make sure he doesn't slip through your fingers like he slipped through ours."

"Do you have enough for an arrest?"

"We have fingerprint and DNA evidence, but they need to be verified as being his. If you happen to have either on file, that would be most helpful."

"No. But I'll see what I can do about getting them to you."

"If they are his, we have enough for an arrest. The rest of what we have is circumstantial. Surveillance videos are grainy and he doesn't look directly at the camera. Eyewitnesses were shaky and aren't likely to have gotten any better with a two-year hiatus. But fingerprints and DNA would confirm his presence at the scene."

"Okay. I'll see what I can do. If we can make an arrest based on your evidence, then we can hold him while we pursue the investigation here. See if we can get him for both."

"Good. Anything else you need from me?"

"Anything you have on file that you would like to share. Contacts who knew him before he changed his identity. I've managed to track down a couple through a mutual acquaintance but, the more we can get, the easier it will be to make our case."

"I'll go through the file. Pull up any family or friends."

"Great. Appreciate that. I'll be in touch."

After Terry hung up, he stared at the phone for a few minutes, not seeing it, just working through everything in his head. It was hard to see Dave as a possible murderer instead of the polite and earnest young man who had worked at the bookstore for two years, respectful and hardworking, never causing any trouble. Most criminals gave themselves away eventually. Went to the bar and started a fight or got talking too much. Couldn't resist pulling a scam that they had done before. Did something to attract attention to themselves.

But Dave had been good. He had been very good.

CHAPTER 40

Terry drove to Dave's place of residence, but parked around the corner where the man would not be able to see his police truck when he looked out the window or door. Best to keep it all on the lowdown until they had a way to get a sample of Dave's fingerprints or DNA. A garbage search was the obvious route. Dave was unlikely to be wiping everything down before he threw it out. Even if he'd thought to do that two years ago, the chances that he would still be doing it two years later were pretty low.

But Terry wanted to get the lay of the land before moving in. He had called Naomi to ask what Dave's work schedule was, but hadn't been able to get through to her and had to be content with leaving a message. Terry checked out the back of the house first, peeking in the garbage bin to see if there was anything he could grab. Unfortunately, garbage pick-up day had been just a couple of days before, and Dave hadn't thrown anything out since then. Or else he burned his garbage or buried it somewhere out in the woods. Some people did that, but it was too much trouble for most. Since Bald Eagle Falls had started a municipal garbage collection program, all but the oldsters who were too set in their ways to change had adopted it.

In a few days, he would come by again and, if there were a fresh bag of garbage, he would throw it into the back of his truck and search through it in the parking lot behind the town hall.

K9 sniffed with interest around the base of the bin, and Terry let him for a few minutes, then gave his collar a little tug and ordered him to heel. K9 fell into place and they walked around the block to the front of the house.

Terry stopped and stared at the yellow VW bug in front of the house next door. Erin could not have driven anything much more recognizable. Her bright yellow bug stood out like a sore thumb wherever she parked it. He looked along the street for any sign of her. Had she come over to see Dave about something? Had Dave decided that she was too much of a liability and he needed to get her out of the way? Erin had been right in the thick of things from the time she had discovered Brandon Quayle's body. Dave couldn't let that go on forever.

Terry ducked back as a truck pulled into Dave's driveway. It was moving quickly, and he was worried at first that he might have tripped a burglar alarm or some other kind of early warning system that Dave had in place to let him know if someone started nosing around his property. But he saw Dave hop out of the truck and cross in front of his house to the neighbor's house.

The one Erin's car was parked in front of.

Terry hesitated, hanging back to see what Dave would do and whether there was any reason to interfere. Dave might have a completely innocent reason for visiting his neighbor at the same time as Erin. Dave might, for that matter, be completely innocent and have nothing to do with Brandon's murder or the robbery case gone bad.

But where there was smoke, there was fire. The chances that Dave was involved increased dramatically with every crime that he was suspected of.

Dave went to the door and pounded on it several times. There was no answer. He was already jangling a ring of keys and, in a moment, fitting one key into the lock.

There were a lot of reasons that Dave might be visiting his neighbor. The fact that he had keys and would go in the front door in broad daylight suggested that he had a legitimate reason to be there. A reason that did not involve Erin.

K9 whined at his side. Terry should have been reassured by the fact that Dave had keys to the house, but he was not. It didn't matter to him that Dave's neighbor trusted him.

They had all trusted him.

Naomi, Erin, Terry.

They all thought that he was a nice young man, an upright citizen, a nice guy working at the bookstore, not getting in any trouble.

But he thought K9's instincts were right. There was still reason to be concerned about what was going on. Why was Dave going into the house? Why hadn't the homeowner answered the door? He would have assumed that the house was empty or Dave was house-sitting while his neighbor was away, except for Erin's car parked in front of the house and the fact that Dave had knocked on the door.

Erin could be visiting with another neighbor on the block. She could be across the street and just hadn't turned around to park on the correct side. The odds that she and Dave would just be in the same place coincidentally was about as likely as the chances that Erin had randomly stumbled across Brandon Quayle's body after he had died.

Twice.

He waited until Dave stepped into the house and then followed, moving quickly, wishing his shoes were quieter when they clicked on the concrete sidewalk blocks. He slowed down when he reached the doorstep, unsnapped his holster, and eased his gun out. Somewhere in the house were Erin and the homeowner. And a suspected killer. A man who may have killed multiple times.

He moved silently, K9 at his side, on high alert.

⁓

"Jane?"

Erin heard Dave's voice. He was inside the house already. She wished she'd had more time to piece the clues together and figure out what was going on, but it was too late now. He was there and there was no time to call the police or bluff. Atheist though she was, Erin begged the universe that Dave wouldn't discover their hiding place. He could come in, look around, and then decide that Aunt Jane had just gone out for a walk or something equally innocuous. Erin had not left any sign of her presence.

Except, of course, there was the bright yellow bug parked in front of the house. Erin swore in her head. He was too close for her even to whisper it aloud.

"Aunt Jane, it's Dave. Where are you?" There was a pause as he looked around, taking the time to check each of the bedrooms as he walked by them. It would have made sense to hide in one of them. In the closet or behind the door, and then when he made his initial pass, jump out and run away.

"Is there someone here? A visitor?" Dave asked. "I thought I saw Erin Price's car out front."

His voice was calm and conversational—no reason for Jane and Erin not to show their faces.

Except that they knew he was a killer.

Dave made his way steadily toward them, his feet progressing quietly down the hall as he checked each room on the way to the back of the house.

"Jane, Erin, where are you hiding?" Dave asked in a pleasant, good-humored voice. "What kind of game is this?"

Neither of them moved. Neither breathed more than they had to. Dave came out of the hallway. He checked the kitchen and then the mud room.

The long red broomstick handle with the hook on the end was still leaning against the wall, not put away in the broom closet where it had been. Dave stepped over to it and picked it up. She could hear the gears turning in his head. Though she couldn't see him, she imagined him looking up at the rectangular patch in the ceiling. He was taller than either of the women and would find it easier to reach the attic door.

It only took him one try to get the hook through the eyelet. He gave the trapdoor a little tug, and the hatch opened slowly and noiselessly. The ladder unfolded and touched down right in front of Dave's feet.

Erin's heart was racing so fast she could barely breathe. But she suppressed the urge to gasp or draw in any more air than usual. If he couldn't see or hear her, maybe he would just give up and go home.

"In the attic?" Dave asked as he mounted the steps. "What are you ladies doing hiding in the attic? Did you really think that I wouldn't find you up here?"

Erin listened to him climb the ladder, step by step. She pictured his head and shoulders protruding into the attic and squeezed her eyes shut tightly, trying not to give their position away.

"Hold it right there, Dave."

CHAPTER 41

*E*rin swallowed a gasp. She knew that voice! Terry!

She did nothing that would distract him from his task at hand. Screaming and attracting attention to herself would not do any of them any good. She stayed still, though a shiver ran through her body that had nothing to do with how warm or cold she was.

"Who's that?" Dave demanded.

"I said to hold it there. Don't move. Drop the gun, Dave."

A gun? Dave had come after them with a gun? His dear old Aunt Jane?

"Officer Piper?"

"Yes. Let's see the gun. Just drop it through the hatch to the floor."

"I'm afraid it might go off if I do that," Dave said, wheedling, looking for a way to put himself back on the same level as Terry, to get an advantage over him.

Normally, the high ground won out as the best position. But with his head above the ceiling, Dave couldn't see Terry, but Terry could see him.

"I'll take that chance," Terry countered. "I said drop it. I'm not going to tell you again."

Still, Dave hesitated. Erin swallowed. Her eyes were still tightly shut as if Dave wouldn't be able to see her if she couldn't see him.

Then Erin heard the clunk of Dave's gun hitting the floor. Another noise that sounded like Terry had slid it along the floor. Away from Dave, Erin supposed, so that Dave wouldn't be able to get it again, like the criminals did so often on TV dramas.

"Come down slowly. Keep your back to me. Put your hands behind your head before you take the last step down."

She could hear Dave moving slowly and carefully, looking for a way out of the situation as he came down to Terry's level.

"What's this all about, Officer Piper? I was just looking for an intruder..."

"You're under arrest for breaking and entering," Terry told him firmly, handcuffing him and then feeling his pockets for any other weapons.

"Breaking and entering?" Dave laughed. "I have a key."

"When I hear that you had permission to come in here with a gun to check for intruders, then I will reconsider. Sit down cross-legged."

Erin could hear Terry lowering Dave to the floor. K9's collar jangled.

"Erin? Are you here?" Terry called.

For a moment, Erin couldn't respond. She had been doing everything she could to keep quiet, and her brain and her body didn't want to release and take the chance that something could happen to her if she were discovered. She forced her eyes open and tried to take deeper breaths.

"Erin?"

"We're here."

As Erin emerged, she saw Terry looking around in confusion. He looked up at the attic hatch and then at Erin and Mrs. Pooler.

"What?"

Erin giggled as she stepped out from the coat she had been hiding behind in the mudroom. She stepped out of the boots that had been hiding her feet and legs below the coat. Mrs. Pooler did the same, straightening the coat neatly on the peg and stepping out of a pair of gardening boots.

"I thought..." Terry looked up at the attic.

Erin shook her head. "I couldn't get it open. We didn't have enough time."

He chuckled and looked over at Dave, sitting on the floor. Dave's face was red, embarrassed that he had fallen for their trick, that he hadn't seen them standing right there in front of him. Not that it would have made any difference with Terry coming in right behind him.

"Erin, I think you know Kyle Pinckney," Terry said, looking down at Dave.

Erin felt like she'd been slapped in the face. "What? Kyle?"

"That's not my name," Dave protested. "I'm Dave Wolfe."

"You're not," Terry said firmly. "You have been identified as Kyle Pinckney. Who, by the way, is a person of interest in at least one other criminal investigation at this time."

"Kyle," Erin repeated breathlessly.

Terry looked at her curiously.

Dave's—Kyle's—eyes were dark and angry as he stared at Erin, threatening her without words. Warning her that he would come after her if she opened her mouth and spilled what she knew.

"I know Kyle," Erin explained. "That is... I know his name. I never knew his last name or met him. I just... heard him on the phone one night. Heard Brandon talking to him."

Dave tried to jump to his feet, but Terry knocked him down again easily and didn't let him get up. "You want me to shackle your ankles too?"

"I don't know what she's talking about. I didn't have anything to do with... Brandon. I never met him. She's the one who killed him. She's the one who kept saying that she'd just *happened* to find him. You really believe that? She's the one who knew him; of course it was her!"

Terry stared at Dave for a moment, then shrugged. "It probably doesn't make any difference what Erin says at this point. Detective Jones in Maine wants you for felony murder. We'll get enough evidence to prove that you killed Brandon when he confronted you with his fake manuscript. Anything else is icing on the cake."

"Fake manuscript?" Dave repeated, blood draining from his face.

Terry nodded. "The one he had with him when he met with you was fake, anyway. I don't know if that means there is no real manuscript or he just had the sense not to bring it with him."

"I told you he didn't really write a memoir," Erin pointed out, feeling vindicated.

"He might still have written one. We just don't have a copy of it. People in Maine said that he had written one."

"But no one ever read it," Erin suggested.

Terry nodded. "No one ever read it."

"That's what I figured."

"So, what exactly did you know about Kyle?" Terry asked curiously. He looked at Dave to ensure he stayed down and didn't try to attack anyone.

"He called Brandon one night. He'd hit someone while driving drunk. Brandon covered for him, gave him an alibi." A wave of nausea washed over Erin as she remembered how she had told Dave the story at dinner the night before. It was no wonder he'd been so pale. If Sheriff Wilmot hadn't come to get Erin when he did, and it had been up to Dave to walk her out to her car... alone, in the dark parking lot...

Dave didn't volunteer that Brandon had told him that Erin would cover for him too, would do whatever Brandon told her to. He had no way of knowing whether Erin had ever been faced with making that decision.

Terry looked at Mrs. Pooler. "And... I apologize for intruding in your house, Mrs...."

"Jane Pooler," she introduced herself with a bright smile. "And I think I can forgive the intrusion this once."

"This is Dave's 'Aunt Jane,'" Erin explained. "Only, they're not really related. Dave kind of... adopted her."

"More like took me hostage," Mrs. Pooler said. "Maybe now I can start going out again. If it's not too dangerous out there. Dave always told me..."

"It's safe. Officer Piper and the others keep Bald Eagle Falls safe," Erin assured her, putting aside any thoughts of the murders and violence she had been exposed to since moving to Bald Eagle Falls.

That was an anomaly.

Mrs. Pooler would be safe leaving her house to go to the grocery store, church, or bakery. She didn't need to live like the recluse Dave had forced her to be.

CHAPTER 42

"I don't really understand what happened," Vic said, shaking her head. "I mean... I thought that Dave had been eliminated as a suspect. How could he have had anything to do with Brandon's death? And how did he end up here, of all places? How could he and Erin both have ended up in the same small town by coincidence?"

"It wasn't a coincidence," Terry said. He'd explained it to Erin once already. Well, maybe twice. It was taking a lot of time and effort to unwind Dave's story, which was pretty convoluted. "Brandon Quayle *sent* Kyle Pinckney here to keep an eye on Erin. He held this hit-and-run accident over him and used it to blackmail him, to get him to do whatever Quayle wanted. It was a serious threat—Pinckney had killed a child in that accident. So he's been... *observing* Erin ever since she arrived in Bald Eagle Falls."

Erin shuddered. "Working at The Book Nook, watching me coming and going... I can't believe that none of us knew what kind of a guy he really was. That he was a criminal. He must have never let down his guard, never let anyone see him doing something out of character. It must have been really hard."

"Maybe he got to play at being the kind of guy he wanted to be," Vic suggested. "Not some egomaniac spy, I don't mean that, but... a nice guy.

Always pleasant, helping out the old lady next door. Just an honest, strait-laced, quiet kind of guy."

"Maybe." Erin shook her head. "I don't know." She sipped her tea, thinking about it. What she knew about him or had learned from Terry's investigation. Someone who wanted to be good and enjoyed playing that role? Or someone who hated it and had exploded when Brandon showed his face in Bald Eagle Falls, letting out all of the built-up pressure from the last two years.

"But Dave—or Kyle—came to Bald Eagle Falls before Erin," Willie pointed out. "How did he swing that?"

"Even *I* didn't know I was coming to Bald Eagle Falls yet," Erin agreed. She could almost believe that he had psychic powers, like Reg pretended to. She'd seen some things when Reg had been around. Strange, inexplicable stuff. But she had never believed Reg was psychic.

"How did you find out about your inheritance?" Terry prompted with a smile. "When did you learn that Clementine had left you her tea shop?"

"Right before I came here. From Alton Summers."

"A private investigator."

"Yes."

"Who had been tracking you from one place to another and asking questions about you."

"Yes! Oh…" It became blindingly obvious to Erin. "He found Brandon. He asked about me after I had left Brandon, telling him about Clementine leaving me the house and the shop."

So Brandon had installed Kyle in Bald Eagle Falls to keep an eye on Erin and report back on what she was doing. Had Brandon known about her relationship with Terry? How the bakery was doing? For two years, he hadn't come to Bald Eagle Falls. He hadn't tried to take her away from Terry or to get in on the success of the bakery. He hadn't decided that he wanted to live in Bald Eagle Falls or that she should come back home to him.

And then, two years later, the emails. The claims of recovery from alcoholism. A memoir being published. A date to meet her in the park.

"Was he really sober?" she asked Terry. "When you talked to people back home… did he really give up drinking? Was he trying to make amends? Or was this just some big conspiracy to get me back? I don't understand what this was all about."

"According to friends back in Maine, yes. He had stopped drinking. As for the rest of it, I don't know. I think... saying he was going to publish a tell-all book and showing up to talk to Dave... that sounds like more blackmail. Not amends."

"Did Dave say what happened? That Brandon confronted him...?"

"He has a story. I can't get into the details of an ongoing investigation. And of course, his story is designed to make himself look good. He says he was... protecting others from Brandon's predatory behavior."

"Me?" Erin squeaked.

Terry shrugged. It was as good as acknowledging that was Dave's story.

Had Dave tried to protect her? Or just to protect himself and his own reputation? The life that he had built in Bald Eagle Falls while he had been following Brandon's directions. She wasn't sure she believed it had anything to do with her.

"The thing I want to know..." Vic put her teacup down on the table and leaned forward. "Is how and why did he move the body? How did he make it disappear so fast?"

Erin had been thinking about that. She had worked through several different scenarios, trying to find one that fit. Knowing that the killer had been Dave, who knew his way around the bookstore, helped. He hadn't had to carry the body up the stairs, past Erin or following her up when she had fled.

She'd heard noises when she had stepped into the building. She had thought that Naomi was downstairs because she'd heard movements.

"I think... he cleared boxes out of the elevator or loading dock and then went downstairs to get Brandon's body. Maybe he was even in the elevator when I saw Brandon. I couldn't do anything for him or get a cellphone signal, so I left. Dave got off the elevator and used it to take Brandon's body upstairs. Used a dolly, took him right out from the loading dock to his truck and was out of there when he heard the sirens."

"At that point," Terry chimed in, nodding his agreement, "he had no idea that Erin had been in the store, gone to the basement, and seen the body while he was getting ready to move it. He thought he was alone the whole time. So, the shock he showed when we told him that Erin had found a body in the basement of The Book Nook and then it had disappeared was real. He had no idea anyone else had been there and seen the body."

"And in the meantime, he'd already dumped it in Canyon Park because that was where Erin was supposed to meet Brandon? So it would make her look guilty if the police ever got access to her email," Vic suggested.

It was strange how clear it seemed once they knew Dave's relationship with Brandon.

"But how did he know that Brandon had emailed me to meet him there?" Erin asked.

"Brandon told him," Vic said. "Or emailed him about it too. Maybe it was supposed to be all three of you. But first, Brandon wanted to meet with Dave for some kind of debriefing."

"It's just all so bizarre." Erin shook her head. "I thought I had left all of this back in Maine when I moved to Bald Eagle Falls. That life was behind me. But all the time, Dave was watching me. Brandon knew exactly where I was and what I was doing. Sheriff Wilmot said that he thought I was the key to solving Brandon's murder. I thought he was way off base. But…"

"But there you were, right in the center of it," Terry finished.

Now that Brandon was gone and they knew who Dave was and he had been sent to the penitentiary pending trial, maybe now Erin's life could finally get back to normal. She could just be a baker and not worry about the past catching up with her.

Vic put her hand on Erin's shoulder and squeezed it lightly. She didn't say anything.

CHAPTER 43

*E*rin took the platter filled with waffles, cut into small wedge-shaped pieces and condiment cups of real maple syrup for dipping out to the front of the bakery, filled with the usual morning crowd.

"Okay! Here they are!"

"Are those the waffles you are going to enter in the contest?" little Peter Foster asked, his eyes wide.

"Yup. This is the big day. I want to see what people think of them before I enter the recipe into the contest."

"And you win a big waffle iron."

"Well, I'd sure like to. I don't know if I will or not! I'd have to have a pretty big ego to be sure that I could win it. But I've won some other contests, and I think these are really good. They have a chance, anyway."

"How big are the waffles that the big waffle iron makes?"

"Just regular sized," Erin made a circle with her hands to demonstrate. "But you can cook twenty waffles at once!"

"Oh, wow."

Erin passed the platter around to her customers, encouraging them to have a piece or two of the waffles and see what they thought. There were full mouths and *mmmm*'s of pleasure and nods that it was a good recipe. Erin stopped in front of Mrs. Pooler and held the platter before her.

"These are 'Aunt Jane's Waffles,'" she said, "I hope they live up to their name."

"They look lovely. I'm sure they taste just as good as any I ever made," Mrs. Pooler said as she took a wedge of waffle and cup of maple syrup to test it herself.

Joshua had come with Mary Lou to the bakery, which was unusual. Roger was not with them, so Erin assumed that the care worker who visited twice a day was probably still with him. They each took a piece of waffle. Mary Lou did not help herself to the maple syrup, but took a bite of the plain waffle. She watched her diet very carefully, which Erin suspected was why she was so slim when most of the other women in Bald Eagle Falls of her age were thickening around the middle.

Joshua took both the waffle and the syrup. "I was wondering if we could get together, Miss Erin," he said politely. "So I could talk to you about Brandon Quayle and Dave Wolfe."

So that he could include her thoughts and background in whatever story he would be submitting to the Bald Eagle Falls weekly newspaper. Erin grimaced and looked around. "I'm pretty busy with things right now, the contest and everything. And getting ready for the next book club meeting. I don't really... I don't really want to talk about Brandon and our history."

"People will want to know. And maybe if it's in the paper, they won't have to come around here to bug you about it," Joshua coaxed.

"No. I don't think... I really don't want to, Josh. I'm sorry."

Mary Lou looked at Joshua and raised one brow, looking stern. Joshua shrugged. "Okay. I guess if you don't want to talk about it, you don't want to talk about it."

Mary Lou nodded her agreement.

"Cookie!" Traci Foster's high toddler voice rose over the chatter of the bakery customers. "Want cookie! Dat one!"

"It isn't cookie day," Mrs. Foster tried to explain to her. "We're here to try out Miss Erin's waffles. Come have a piece of waffle."

"No!" Traci shrieked and pounded on the glass of the display case. "Cookie!"

"If the kids don't want a waffle, they can have a cookie," Erin was quick to offer. She directed her words at Vic. "Go ahead and give her a cookie, if that's what she wants."

Vic nodded and followed Traci's directions to the exact cookie that she had to have.

"Dat one… dat one… no! Dat one! Yes!" She started to jump up and down. Vic handed the cookie over the counter to Mrs. Foster. "And the rest of you? Do you want a cookie or a waffle?"

Jodi also wanted a cookie, but Karen went with a waffle, like the grown-ups. Peter looked worried, trying to decide which he wanted.

"You don't really like pumpkin spice," Erin told him, remembering his reaction to pumpkin pie and gingerbread the previous Christmas. "So maybe you want to pick a cookie like the girls instead."

Peter looked around at the adults, shaking his head. He clearly didn't want to be one of the little kids. He wanted to do what the adults were doing. "I'll try a waffle."

"Are you sure? You don't have to. You can pick out something else."

"No, I'll try."

Erin lowered the platter so that he could reach it. He took a wedge of waffle and cup of maple syrup, and carefully dunked the corner of the waffle into the syrup. He bit off the corner he had dunked, and chewed and swallowed. Erin waited for his verdict. "I like it!"

"You do? Wow! I really do have to enter it into the contest."

Peter nodded. "You'll win. I know you will."

"Well, thank you for your confidence!"

The bells over the door jingled, and Erin looked over to see who it was. It was Naomi, looking somewhat harried, even though The Book Nook was not due to open for a couple more hours. She pushed a stray lock of hair back over her ear.

"I just had to come over to try your new recipe."

"That's so sweet! You look like you're pretty busy over there at the bookstore."

"Yes! It's kind of crazy with Dave being gone. I thought we would have plenty of staff to cover his shifts for a while, but I didn't realize how much time he was putting in. I'll need to fill his position soon, because I can't cover it all without him."

Erin nodded. She looked over at Mrs. Foster. "Is Mr. Foster still looking for something? Maybe he could put in an application."

"Well, yes. He is," Mrs. Foster agreed, bouncing baby Allan in his sling. She looked over at Naomi. "Do you think that you would consider him? He doesn't have any experience in a bookstore."

"I can train, if he is willing to learn."

"Okay! I'll tell him to bring his resume by."

Naomi nodded her agreement. "I need someone in there pretty quickly, so the sooner, the better!"

Naomi only stayed long enough to try a piece of waffle and render her opinion that, as Peter had said, the waffles should be entered into the contest. Then she headed back over to her own store.

Peter had a huge, Cheshire cat grin, and he helped his mother to get the girls rounded up. Erin laughed at his expression. "What's that about?"

"If Dad worked at the bookstore, he'd be able to come over to the bakery all the time," Peter observed.

Erin laughed. Mrs. Foster ruffled Peter's hair. "Your father is *not* spending his entire paycheck on gluten-free cookies!"

Peter just smiled. "And waffles."

MURDER MERINGUE PIE

*For the protectors
and those on the outside*

CHAPTER 1

$\mathcal{I}$t was Sunday morning, so Erin was having a relaxed breakfast with Terry rather than having to be at the bakery in the wee hours of the morning to bake bread and get everything ready for the day.

When she had first moved to Bald Eagle Falls, she had been surprised and taken aback by the insistence of the women in the community that the bakery could not be open on Sunday, because that would be breaking the Sabbath. It didn't matter that Erin was an atheist—that was a whole other problem—she was still expected to comply with the unofficial town by-law on the matter.

But that wasn't the most confusing part. They had been excited when she inherited the storefront from her Aunt Clementine, who had run it as a tea shop until her health began to fail. They hoped Erin would reinstate the ladies' tea after church services. She couldn't open the bakery to sell her gluten-free goods that day, but she was expected to open for a couple of hours and supply tea and treats for the church ladies.

She'd been not only confused, but a little resentful of the idea to begin with. But now, a couple of years in, she enjoyed the tradition. It meant that she did not have to get up early on Sunday, even on the days she took the Sunday shift, and she enjoyed meeting with the ladies of the community in something other than a baker/customer relationship.

Today, Bella was taking the shift for the ladies' tea, so Erin and Vic did not have to be there. And it was one of those rare days when Erin and Terry were both home all day—or could go out and spend the whole day together.

"Do you want to go into the city?" Terry asked. "We could go to a movie, dinner, run some errands…?"

Erin was trying to run her errands during the week so that she could have Sunday to relax instead of chasing after bakery supplies and getting caught up on grocery shopping and anything else she needed to do, ending up more exhausted by the end of her "day of rest" than if she had gone to work.

But a movie and dinner with her "Officer Handsome" sounded nice.

"Maybe," she agreed. "But no shopping."

"That's fine with me," Terry agreed with a smile that brought out the dimple on his stubbly cheek. He washed his toast down with a sip of coffee. "I'm quite happy to avoid malls and line-ups."

Erin and Terry heard a bang from the backyard and, looking out the kitchen window, saw Willie storming down the steps from Vic's loft apartment over the garage. Without another word, he hopped into his truck, slammed the door shut, and drove away with his tires spinning in the gravel. Erin watched with concern as he left.

"Uh-oh. That doesn't look good," Terry observed.

Erin looked away from the window, embarrassed. She didn't want to pry into Vic's private life. She didn't want to be that nosy neighbor who was always craning her neck to see what was happening.

"None of our business."

Terry gave a nod of agreement. As a law enforcement officer in Bald Eagle Falls, he knew which relationships were most likely to be volatile. He'd never been called to Vic's or Willie's residences to deal with a domestic dispute. They might shout, argue, or slam doors, but it had never escalated to violence as far as Erin knew. She'd never seen any indication of physical abuse in the relationship. They were just two very passionate people who didn't hold anything back.

The door to Vic's apartment opened again, and this time it was Vic's tall, willowy figure. She let Nilla out and locked the door behind her, then came down the stairs at a more sedate pace than Willie had. She let Nilla into the dog run to do his business, and then joined Erin and Terry in the kitchen.

"Mornin' ya'll."

"Good morning." Erin scratched Nilla's ears and chin when the fluffy white dog ran over to her. K9, Terry's partner, heard the little dog running around the kitchen and came to investigate. The shepherd and the small dog sniffed each other and ran to the back door to be let out. Vic let them out to play. She sighed and sat down at the table. She ran a hand through her long blond hair, hanging loose instead of in a bun like she wore it when baking at Auntie Clem's. It was the opposite of Erin's short, dark hair that never stayed in place like it was supposed to. Erin poured hot water from the teapot into Vic's cup and Vic chose a teabag from the selection on the table.

"That man." She shook her head. "I love him dearly, but he does have a temper."

"Mmm." Erin didn't ask for the details of their argument.

"What's going on?" Terry apparently didn't have the same compunctions. And Erin supposed that if Vic didn't want to talk about it, she wouldn't have brought it up or would just tell Terry it was none of his business.

"I don't rightly know. He's been on edge all weekend. But it isn't anything to do with us. It's just… probably work, I guess. The mines would be my best guess. But he hasn't said. He doesn't want to talk about it, but then he gets a call or text and just goes off like that." She motioned toward the backyard.

So it wasn't an argument. It was something different, an outside irritant. "Well, I hope he doesn't take it out on you. I always feel like slamming doors are aimed at me, even if they aren't. It's hard not to take your partner's anger personally."

Vic nodded. "It gets my back up," she admitted. "I get it; I know he's mad at something else, but I'm the only one there to hear him complaining or slamming doors. So I can't help feeling like he's aiming the gun in the wrong direction."

"You don't know what's going on with work that's bothering him?"

"He doesn't share that stuff. Never has. The closest I get to his mining operations is when we go spelunking together."

Erin's transgender employee was far more adventurous than Erin was. Caves and tunnels underground were *not* Erin's thing. She wouldn't have expected Vic to still be interested in spelunking after being caught in a tunnel collapse, but Vic and Willie had been right back at it as soon as they had their casts off. It wasn't like it had been a natural collapse. But the fact that there were people out there who would intentionally set explosives to trap or kill someone else did not reassure Erin. That was just one more good reason to stay away from caves. It had been a long time before she could even look into a cave, let alone walk a few steps into one. And a tunnel or shaft where she would have to crawl... no way. No, thank you.

"Well, whatever bee Willie has got in his bonnet, I hope he deals with it soon," she told Vic.

"Me too, sister." Vic sipped her tea. "Me too."

CHAPTER 2

onday afternoon, Vic and Charley, Erin's half-sister, helped Erin carefully pack several pies for a catering order.

"Lemon meringue does not travel well," Vic worried. "All you need to do is go over one bump, and the tops will all be sticking to the boxes."

"I'll go slowly," Charley promised. "No potholes."

Erin had seen Charley drive before. She wasn't sure the woman knew the meaning of "slowly" or "carefully." She could just see Charley unloading the boxes at their destination and finding that all of the meringues were pasted to the tops of the boxes.

"I really don't want these to be wrecked when you get there," she fussed. "I should have told them no. Made them go with apple pie or something with a top crust that would travel better."

"I'll get them there in one piece," Charley assured her. "You don't have to worry about it. Clive William Fontainebleau III shall have his pies."

"If he's happy with the results, he could be a profitable client. I don't know how many of these fancy parties he holds, but if we can supply him with desserts regularly, it could be lucrative."

"Don't pin your hopes on it," Charley warned. "I know guys like this. They're not loyal to one supplier. He'll go wherever he can get the best deal. And he'll keep asking for a lower price until you're not making anything."

Erin frowned. She hoped it wasn't true. But she hadn't heard many good things about Mr. Fontainebleau, so she couldn't argue with Charley's assessment.

"So you don't think it will be worth it?"

"I'll tell you what you do," Charley said. "You raise your prices next time. Tell him that they are *artisanal* pies. That he won't get quality product like that from anyone else. Especially not gluten-free. If he wants high-quality, gluten-free pies, you are the only game in town. Anywhere in the state, in fact."

Erin's cheeks warmed. "I couldn't do that."

"That's what you've got to do. Make him respect you. Make him want pies from Auntie Clem's Bakery and nowhere else, because no one else even compares. Why do you think guys like him buy Rolexes and Cartier's? It isn't because they tell the time better than any department store wristwatch. He wants people to see that he is willing to pay for the very best."

"I don't know." Erin slowly boxed another pie. "I'll think about it."

"Whatever you do, *don't* lower your prices. No matter where he says he is going to go instead."

Erin pressed her lips together, thinking about it. Charley was probably right. Charley was the one who had experience in dealing with big shots like Fontainebleau. She should take Charley's advice.

"You do your part and get them there in one piece. Then… maybe I'll get you to help with any negotiations too. I'm not sure I can stand up to a guy like that. Or his office manager, since I never talked to Mr. Fontainebleau directly."

"I'll take care of it," Charley agreed. "You can count on me."

Peter Foster showed up at Auntie Clem's Bakery after school had let out, without his mother and siblings. Erin had rarely seen him by himself, though she knew that he had sometimes been allowed to go to the store to pick up something his mother needed when she had been pregnant and on bed rest. The young boy looked at the cookies in the display case, standing tall and looking important.

"Hi, Peter. How's it going?"

He smiled, showing off the gaps in his teeth. "Good."

"Are you here for a Kid's Club cookie, or are you buying something? I have something in the back for you if you need it…"

The Foster family didn't normally take advantage of Erin's offer of free day-old bread. But they'd been struggling lately, and Erin hoped they would take what they needed.

"I'm just looking," Peter told her archly. "I'm going to visit my dad at the bookstore."

"Oh, I see. How is he enjoying working there?"

"He says that Mrs. Naomi is a good boss. And mom is glad that he *finally* has something stable since they cut back his hours at the other job."

"I'm sure it's a big relief for her. Especially since she wanted to be able to stay home with the little ones."

Peter nodded his agreement. "It's a good thing that you told Mrs. Naomi that Dad was looking for something. You're a good friend."

"Thank you. I'm glad I could help. Are you sure you don't want your Kid's Club cookie?"

"No. I'll get mine one day when I bring the girls."

"Oh, okay. That sounds good, then. Can I walk with you over to The Book Nook?"

"I don't need you to. I know where it is."

"I know, but I need to talk to Naomi about the book club."

Peter shrugged. "Okay. You can come over with me."

Erin trailed Peter down the street to The Book Nook and followed him in. The bells over the door jingled to announce their arrival. Both Naomi and Mr. Foster looked up from shelving books to greet them.

"Well, there's my son," Mr. Foster said, smiling. "School's out already?"

"Yes. You know I wouldn't skip!"

"That's what they all say. And Miss Erin. How are you?"

"Good. Peter just stopped to say hello to me at Auntie Clem's, and I needed to talk to Naomi about the book club, so we came over together."

Mr. Foster nodded, looking calm and relaxed about this. Erin was glad she hadn't gotten Peter into trouble, but she wanted to ensure that his parents knew where he was and were okay with it. They were strict about some things and lenient about others, and Erin hadn't quite figured out where the line was. She didn't want to be accused of encouraging Peter to do anything he wasn't supposed to.

Erin felt her phone vibrating, so the next time she went into the kitchen to take a tray of cookies out of the oven, she pulled her phone out and looked at it. Charley had texted her. Opening the text, Erin saw the pies that she had sent over for the party all laid out on a black granite counter, with Charley's comment that they had gotten there safe and sound, with no breakage or meringue stuck to the top of the boxes they had transported them in. The golden peaks on the white meringue looked picture-perfect.

Mr. Fontainebleau can eat pie to his heart's content

Erin was relieved. She texted Charley a heartfelt thank you and returned to the front of the shop to let Vic know they had arrived safely.

"See?" Vic said. "All that worry for nothing. Everything went smoothly. He's sure to call you back for another job."

CHAPTER 3

*E*rin had already turned the sign on the front door over to Closed and locked the door, so she was annoyed to hear someone rapping on the glass a few minutes later. Once the bakery was closed, it was closed. She couldn't keep serving people who showed up after closing or she would be there all night. There had to be a hard cut-off.

But the man standing on the other side of the door did not appear to be a customer. Not someone she had served before. Erin stood there looking at him for a moment, trying to figure out what to do. He could see her through the glass and indicated a package in his hands. A delivery? Bakery deliveries normally came to the back door, and she wasn't expecting anything. Especially not a small, light package like the delivery man had.

"Vic?"

Vic came out of the kitchen, wiping her hands on a towel. "What's up, boss?"

"You weren't expecting a delivery, were you?"

Vic shook her head. "No. I haven't ordered anything. Maybe it's a wrong address."

"Can you just stay here for a minute to make sure…?"

It hadn't been that long ago that she'd opened the door to the wrong person, and she didn't want to take any chances. Someone with nefarious purposes would not be as likely to try anything with Vic standing there. And Vic was armed if he did. Though Erin wouldn't want any gunplay under any circumstances.

With Vic stationed there watching, Erin unlocked the door and opened it just a crack.

"Yes? I'm not expecting anything."

"Are you Erin Price?"

"Yes," Erin admitted, her anxiety growing. Should she call Terry or the emergency dispatcher?

"This is for you."

Erin reluctantly opened the door far enough to take the small package from him. It was lightweight. He didn't try to grab her wrist or push his way into the bakery. He just nodded, gave her a pleasant smile and walked away.

Erin locked the door again, blowing out a breath of relief. Nothing to worry about unless it was a bomb, and she assumed by how light it was that it wasn't a bomb.

"What is it?" Vic asked curiously, leaning against the doorframe.

Erin unwrapped the brown paper and found a small bouquet of flowers.

"Oh, how sweet," Vic gushed. "Is it an anniversary?"

Erin shook her head. "No… nothing that I can think of."

They had already passed the anniversary of Erin's arrival in Bald Eagle Falls. Could it be the anniversary of when she and Terry had started dating? Another significant event along the path?

"Is there a card?"

Erin extended two fingers to grasp it and pull it from the bouquet. It wasn't in Terry's hand, but it had probably been written by the florist on Terry's instructions.

For the sweetest lady in town

Being a baker, Erin supposed it was apt. But not something Terry had ever said to her. Wouldn't he put something on the card that was meaningful to them both? Something they had shared?

He had also never thought to send her flowers before, even on Valentine's Day.

She read it to Vic, who seemed to think it was swoon-worthy, but

Erin was increasingly uncomfortable with the delivery. She looked through the flowers to ensure there was no other message or something she hadn't seen. It seemed to be just what it was at first glance—a small bouquet of flowers. No threat. No bomb. No hidden meaning.

Erin put it down on one of the small tables at the front of the bakery and pulled out her phone to call Terry. Vic watched, looking perplexed that Erin wasn't over the moon about getting flowers from her guy.

The phone rang a few times before Terry answered.

"Piper. Oh, hi Erin."

"I just got a special delivery."

There was a second of silence. "Okay... what was it?"

Erin's heart sank. She had been hoping he would confirm that he had sent her the flowers. "You didn't send me something?"

"No. What are you talking about? What did you get?"

"I got... flowers."

"Flowers." Terry sounded taken aback. "No, I didn't send you any flowers."

Erin didn't say anything, considering.

"Do they have my name on them?" Terry asked.

"No. No name."

"Maybe they were for Vic. Or a wrong address."

"No. He said they were for Erin Price."

"Well... I guess you have a secret admirer." Terry gave a laugh that sounded forced. "Is this the first time you've gotten something like that?"

Did he think she regularly got gifts from anonymous senders that she didn't bother to tell him about? Then why start now?

"No. This is the first time."

"Huh. Well, I'm sure it's nothing to worry about, but do you want me to pick you up? Make sure you get home safely?"

"I've got my car here. You don't need to come."

"I can if you want. I can drop you off in the morning and you can pick up your car tomorrow."

What would make her any safer tomorrow than today? If the secret admirer had malicious thoughts toward her, he would just wait for his opportunity. She couldn't have a bodyguard with her all the time. Sooner or later, she would be by herself, an open target.

"No. We'll just take my car home tonight. It will be fine."

"If you're worried…"

"I'm not worried. It's just a sweet gesture. Someone who didn't stop to think about whether I already had someone else in my life. Or an appreciative customer."

She thought about Fontainebleau, but was sure that he would never extend a gesture like that. He dealt with her on a business basis and wouldn't be sending her flowers no matter how impressed he was with the lemon meringue pies. But maybe someone else? Someone she had done something nice for recently?

Maybe even Peter Foster or his father. Something to say thank you for helping find Mr. Foster a job.

That was probably it. It was the kind of thing she could see Peter doing. He was very thoughtful and mature for his years. He could have suggested to his mother that they should get something for Erin, and they decided to make it anonymous to keep her guessing and give her a little thrill. Make her look at all her customers differently, wondering which of them had done such a nice thing. Maybe that was why he had stopped by the bakery earlier. Not to visit with her on the way to seeing his father, but to see if the flowers had been delivered yet.

"Okay," Terry said, a note of relief in his voice. "As long as you're not upset by it."

"No. It's very sweet of whoever sent them. I'll take them home and put them on the table."

"Maybe you should keep them at the bakery. You wouldn't want Orange Blossom to get into them. He still jumps up on the table sometimes and, if you put something that smells so interesting up there, he'll be knocking them over before the night is out."

"You're probably right. Do we have a little vase here?" Erin asked Vic. "Just a glass would work."

Vic disappeared into the kitchen to get her one. She could put the flowers out in the customer area to brighten everyone's day tomorrow.

Of course, she would have to explain where they came from, but she didn't think there was anything wrong with getting flowers from a secret admirer. It wasn't like she was cheating on Terry or had any thought of doing so. It was just an appreciative customer or friend. Maybe even a thank you from Melissa for doing the catering for her wedding, though she had already received a formal thank you for that.

She arranged the flowers in the glass Vic brought out to her and put them on one of the tables.

"There. That will brighten things up tomorrow."

Vic nodded. They both returned to the kitchen to continue cleaning up and prep for the next day.

CHAPTER 4

erry got home not long after Erin. She watched him enter through the front door and re-arm the burglar alarm immediately. Then he turned to her and gave her a firm hug.

"So what's this about someone else sending my girl flowers?"

Erin raised one brow. "Looks like you're going to have to up your game."

He chuckled. "I guess so. Can't have someone else showing me up."

"That's right."

Orange Blossom was immediately underfoot, meowing urgently. He knew that Terry getting home meant that it was time for supper, and he wanted his right away.

"You know, I'm not going to forget to feed you," Erin told him sternly. "Have I ever forgotten to feed you even once?"

He rubbed against her leg, yowling still louder. Erin laughed and led the way into the kitchen, with the animals following her like the Pied Piper. Orange Blossom, and then K9, and then Marshmallow, the rabbit. Blossom was the only one who made any noise. He was the only one who ever made any noise. But he made up for the others.

Erin got them each their dinners, and soon they had peace. Erin transferred the casserole she had left to cook in the slow cooker to the table.

"Mmm, smells great," Terry approved, sitting down at the table.

They dished up and began to eat, asking each other about their days.

"Any more drama over there?" Terry asked, nodding toward Vic's loft across the backyard.

"No. Haven't seen or heard anything from them. Willie's truck is here, so I guess he is too, but I haven't seen him."

Terry nodded. "Glad there are no ongoing problems."

"Yeah, me too. I know I might be oversensitive, but I hate it when other people are fighting."

"You are sensitive, but I don't think *over*sensitive. You just care about other people."

Terry's phone buzzed. He pulled it out of his pocket and laid it on the table. "No phones at the table" might be a good rule for most couples but, because Terry was one of the few law enforcement officers in Bald Eagle Falls, he couldn't just ignore any calls or messages that he got. She saw his eyes skim over the message on his screen, and his brows bunched together in a frown. He took a couple more bites of the dinner, then pushed his plate away, sighing.

"You have to go?"

He nodded. "There's been a suspicious death."

"Oh, dear. Who is it?"

His eyes flicked over to her for an instant, then away. He knew there was no point in keeping it from her. In a few minutes, the gossip would be spreading around Bald Eagle Falls, and Erin would find out.

"A mining magnate with a big property and house out in the bush."

Erin blinked several times as she processed this. "Mr. Fontainebleau?"

Terry's head jerked back toward her. "What?" he demanded sharply.

"Was it Clive Fontainebleau? The Third?"

"How do you know him?"

"I sent some pies out there for his party."

"Really." Terry scowled, shaking his head. "How did you get involved with that?"

"His assistant called me. They were looking for someone who could cater the desserts, and I'm the closest one unless they want to go into the city, so…"

She took in Terry's disapproval. "What happened to him?"

Terry sighed. "They think he was poisoned."

CHAPTER 5

*E*rin's stomach plummeted. "What?"

"He died after the party. And there are suspicions it could be poisoning."

"I didn't poison him!" Erin immediately protested.

That was what everyone was going to think. Once again, Erin's baking was going to be called into question. The lemon meringue pies had been perfectly good. Some people worried about salmonella in meringue because it wasn't cooked for long enough to kill the bacteria, but Erin had never heard of an actual case of food poisoning from meringue. And salmonella would not kill that fast, she was sure.

"There was nothing wrong with those pies," she insisted.

"I'm sure there was not, Erin," Terry soothed. "I don't think that you had anything to do with it. What reason would you have to kill someone like Fontainebleau? You've never even met him—have you?"

Erin shook her head.

"You haven't, right?" Terry persisted. "If you did know him or have some beef with him, now is the time to tell me, not later when we figure it out on our own."

"No. I don't know the guy. Never met him. Never had anything to do with him until his assistant called me about the dessert."

He stared at her for a moment longer, trying to discern the truth.

Then he nodded. Which Erin hoped meant that he believed her. She had kind of messed things up before by implying she didn't know a victim when she actually did. Terry wasn't going to forget that any time soon.

"All the food he ate will probably have to be tested," Terry told her. "Now, *I* know that you didn't have anything to do with this, but we'll need to make sure that we act in an unbiased way. So I'm going to ask you not to use any of the ingredients you put into those pies. Anything that is left over, just put to the side. Open up new bags. So that we can test all of the ingredients that came out of the bakery if we have to."

Erin supposed she was lucky that he wasn't shutting down Auntie Clem's Bakery altogether until they'd had a chance to do their testing. "Fine. I'll make sure that all of those ingredients get put to the side."

"Thanks. I appreciate that. I'll get back to you when I know something. Maybe they didn't even get to the dessert course."

"Okay. Thanks."

Erin walked him to the door and didn't know what else to say. Terry paused with his hand on the doorknob.

"This is going to be a big deal," he warned. "Fontainebleau was a very important person in these parts. He employed a lot of people in his mines and factories. He was not well-liked, but he was well-known."

"So it's going to blow up. It's going to be in all of the news outlets."

He nodded. "Newspaper, TV, internet. We're not going to be able to keep it quiet, and there will be a lot of scrutiny. A lot of people watching to make sure that we don't make a misstep."

"You don't think reporters will come here, do you?"

"It's possible. Since I'm going out there as law enforcement, and you catered the dessert for the event, I think it's actually quite likely. Sorry."

He kissed her goodbye, let K9 out ahead of him, and left to deal with the investigation.

Erin looked at the clock. How long did she have before people started to call to ask her about the murder?

With someone as influential as Fontainebleau, it wouldn't be long before word leaked out. Bald Eagle Falls had a very efficient grapevine. And there had been a lot of people at the party. Erin had provided eight pies, which, if cut into six slices each, would mean forty-eight guests. And each one of them a potential leak. Not to mention however many servers or domestic staff Fontainebleau had in his employ to make sure that the evening ran smoothly. There was no way to keep the sixty or so people who were on the Fontainebleau Homestead quiet. And with the call going out to the police in Bald Eagle Falls, each of the law enforcement officers and administrative staff knew about it too, and one of them in particular…

The phone rang.

Erin sighed and pulled it out of her pocket. Was there any chance it was just a call from Vic or a friend wanting to come over for a visit or to place a special order at Auntie Clem's?

She immediately put that thought to rest. The caller ID said Melissa Lee.

Melissa worked part-time for the police department and was the fount of all knowledge, eager to spread whatever news she picked up while filing or doing administrative duties at the police department offices in the town hall. Erin would not expect her to have been there when the call went out on Fontainebleau's suspicious death. But maybe Melissa had gotten herself onto the message distribution list when bulletins went out to all of the Bald Eagle Falls law enforcement officers.

Erin took a deep breath before answering the call. "Hi, Melissa."

"Erin! I just wanted to call and see how you are doing. It's been a while since we talked."

"Yes, it has." Erin sat back down at the table and had another bite of the casserole. "I'm actually just sitting down to eat."

"I don't know how you could eat at a time like this! I would be at my wit's end if I were you. Terry told you what happened, didn't he?"

"I know he got a call out," Erin told her, feigning ignorance. "I don't know what that has to do with me."

"Didn't he tell you who it was for? Clive Fontainebleau? You just filled a catering order for him, didn't you? And now he's dead under suspicious circumstances. I would be in a panic. What if there was something in your pies? What if… rat poison got mixed in with the flour or something like that?"

"It wasn't the pies. There was nothing wrong with them. Nobody knows what happened yet, so don't spread that around. We don't know what he ate or if it even was something he ate. They might not have even eaten the dessert; it is still early in the evening. People like him usually eat late."

Melissa *tsked*. "I don't know. I certainly wouldn't be so calm if I were in your shoes!"

Erin took another deep breath and let it out slowly. Melissa liked drama. She liked to stir things up and was probably disappointed that Erin wasn't panicking like Melissa thought she should. Erin took a few bites of her dinner. She'd already told Melissa that she was sitting down for dinner, so if Melissa heard her eating, she would assume that was why she wasn't responding to Melissa's prodding.

"Right now, we don't know anything," Erin told her. "So there is no point in getting all worked up over it. I doubt it was anything to do with my pies or anything he had at dinner tonight. Most poisons don't work that fast."

Though she remembered how quickly she had been affected when she'd been poisoned with belladonna. She had been lucky to get to the hospital in time for them to counteract the poison. If something like *that* had been administered to Fontainebleau without him or someone close to him figuring out what was wrong, it could have been very quick.

"Well, you're taking it all very well," Melissa said, disapproving.

"Maybe it just hasn't hit me yet."

"That's probably it," Melissa agreed.

CHAPTER 6

*E*rin was able to get off of the call with Melissa—she never seemed to be able to talk to the woman for less than an hour when she called—put away the leftovers, and put the dishes into the dishwasher, when there was a tap at the back door, and Vic stuck her head in.

"Yoo-hoo. You up for visitors?"

Erin shrugged. "Sure. Let's take some tea in the living room."

Vic entered, and Willie behind her. Erin looked him over. As always, his skin was stained dark by the processing he did of whatever minerals he got out of his mines. So he looked dirty, even though she knew he was not. Whatever mood had taken him the day before when he had been slamming doors and racing off in the truck seemed long gone. If anything, he seemed cheerful.

"Terry got called out?" Vic asked.

Erin suspected that she knew very well what had happened. Melissa's gossip was burning up the lines in Bald Eagle Falls.

"Yes. Something to do with Mr. Fontainebleau," she said vaguely.

"That's what I heard." Vic helped to get the tea things ready and took a tray out to the living room.

"It wasn't the pies," Erin told her firmly.

"Of course not!" Vic agreed. "That's what I told M—that's what I said. There was nothing wrong with those pies. They were a work of art.

454

And it isn't like there is any poison in the kitchen at Auntie Clem's. Nothing got accidentally spilled into the flour."

"No," Erin agreed. They both knew that the suggestion was ridiculous. And Melissa undoubtedly knew that too. It wasn't the dark ages. Erin kept a very clean kitchen and was scrupulously careful of cross-contamination, cooking for people with allergies and other health issues as she did. They followed very strict protocols and, even if there had been poison in the kitchen to deal with vermin, it would never have been on the counter at the same time as baking ingredients.

"Terry doesn't think it was anything to do with you, does he?" Vic asked.

"He knows I didn't have anything to do with it."

Not that his supposed faith in her had ever stopped him from investigating her before.

They all sat down in the living room.

"I don't even know anything about this guy," Erin said. "I hadn't really heard of him until I got the call that he wanted the desserts at his party catered. But I gather he's quite a bigwig around here."

Willie nodded. "Yeah, he thought he was a pretty big cheese in these parts. And it's true he had a lot of money and employed a lot of people. But I wouldn't go as far as to say that he was well-liked or respected."

"You didn't like him," Erin stated the obvious.

"I won't be mourning him, that's for sure. Having someone like him around here, trying to scoop up all of the old mining claims and compete with the independent miners… we don't need that kind of help."

"He was your competition?"

Willie shrugged. "A little guy like me can't compete with the likes of Fontainebleau the Third. But yes, we were competitors."

Erin poured hot water into each of the cups and let everyone select their favorite teas.

"And he's been around here for a long time? I don't recognize the family name from any of the genealogy Clementine was doing."

"Not an old Tennessean family," Willie agreed. "Relative upstarts. Probably came from up north. New York types. His father, Fontainebleau the Second, he did live here. But I don't think the first Fontainebleau ever set foot in the state. It was probably the second who established the Homestead."

"That's what he calls the place where he lives," Erin acknowledged. "Is it really a homestead? Like a farm or ranch?"

"No. Never been a working homestead of any kind. It's just posturing. Pretending that he came from a gritty, hardworking background, I guess. Instead of being born with a silver spoon in his mouth."

She sipped her tea. "Have you ever been out there?"

Willie raised his brows. "Out where?"

"On the Homestead. Have you ever seen it?"

"I've seen pictures. It's quite the place. Huge mansion. I don't know how many people live there. Certainly much bigger than you need for one family, or even half a dozen. All the amenities. Staff to keep the place running and the grounds looking pristine. Even though he doesn't actually use them for anything."

"And he throws parties."

"And he throws parties," Willie agreed. He slurped his tea and put the cup down. "I wouldn't be surprised to hear that the governor was one of his guests. Wine and dine all the people who had anything to do with the mining industry or regulation. Make sure that he had everyone on his side and could pull all the political strings that he needed to."

Erin could hear the bitterness in his voice. There was no way for a small miner like Willie to have any influence on the governor or other people high up in the government. He was just a little fish, trying to stay away from predators like Fontainebleau, who would gobble him up, given half a chance.

"Do you know if he has any family?" Erin wondered if there were a wife out there, grieving for her suddenly deceased husband. Or a son or daughter grieving for a parent. Willie might enjoy seeing his competition cut down in his prime, but other people were affected. Family and friends and all of the people that he had employed.

"I don't know." Willie looked at Vic. "You've been around here long enough to know the big names. Did he have any kids? They would probably go to some big boarding school rather than public school out here, but you might still have heard of them."

"I think there is an ex-wife and a current wife. He was definitely on at least his second marriage. And some kids... yes, I think so. Maybe a son and a daughter. Maybe more. Like you say, they probably never went to school here."

Erin nodded. There would definitely be mourners. Maybe the ex-wife wouldn't be sorry to see him go, but his kids and the current wife would, she assumed.

"You think one of them killed him?" Vic suggested, leaning forward.

Erin hadn't even been thinking along those lines. "Uh… I don't know. I don't know anything about them. I guess… it's possible. When there's a lot of money involved like this, sometimes people are impatient to inherit. Or to prevent him from doing something they didn't want him to do with 'their' money."

Vic nodded eagerly. "Makes a lot more sense than some random baker who had it in for him."

"I don't imagine they will be lacking for people with motive to kill him," Willie said. "He didn't exactly endear himself to the public. Or his employees."

"Well, it's nothing to do with us." Erin sat back. She didn't want to speculate about someone else's untimely death. There was no reason for her to have anything to do with the investigation.

No one she knew was involved in it, and she was sure the police would quickly prove that her pies had nothing to do with it.

CHAPTER 7

Things were always busiest at Auntie Clem's after a murder. The townspeople came out to gossip about it and to hear the latest news. To speculate on who might have been involved. Of course they were most interested when they thought that Erin herself might have had something to do with it. She didn't want the reputation of someone who was always in the middle of crimes in and around Bald Eagle Falls. It was just because it was a small town, and she happened to be connected with a lot of people. It was just coincidences and perception.

"Is it true you made the pies for the party last night?" Cindy Prost demanded, sounding properly shocked and horrified. She was a heavyset woman and, unlike her daughter Bella, had a habitually dour expression and a sharp tongue.

Bella was on shift, so Erin knew that Cindy wouldn't dare go too far in her accusations, or Bella would jump in to set her straight.

"Yes, I did," Erin agreed calmly. "But that did not have anything to do with Mr. Fontainebleau's death. Nothing at all."

"Is that what Officer Piper said? Was that an official conclusion from the police investigation?"

Erin hadn't actually been able to talk to Terry about his investigation. He wouldn't tell her very much anyway, only what he thought was or would shortly be public knowledge. But Erin had to go to bed early to be able to get up to bake before Auntie Clem's opened in the morning, and he hadn't been back yet. He hadn't awakened her when he had returned and, when she had left that morning, he had been asleep, snoring on the couch.

"No. I'm just telling you that they had nothing to do with it."

Cindy opened her mouth to argue, then Bella came through the door from the kitchen, and she clamped her mouth shut again.

"We were shocked to hear about Mr. Fontainebleau," Bella told Erin, having overheard them talking about him. "I can't believe that he died like that."

"What did you hear?" Erin asked. "I mean... I heard that it was suspected poisoning, but..."

Of course, anything Bella had heard was probably third-hand gossip and about as far from the truth as possible. Terry was the one who had told Erin that it was suspected poisoning, so she knew that to be true.

"Yes. I heard that he was raving. Had a fit and keeled over. Of course, they're far from any hospital or medical services out there. As soon as anyone got to him, it was too late anyway; he was dead."

"He had a seizure?"

Bella shrugged. "Some kind of fit. I don't know. He wasn't right. Everyone could see he wasn't right. And then he toppled over and was just gone."

"Did this come from someone who was out there?"

Bella became suddenly reticent. "Oh. Just a rumor. You know, what's going around Bald Eagle Falls about it."

"Someone must have seen. There were a lot of people out there. The people he'd invited to the party and whoever else he'd hired to work it."

"None of the people out there were from Bald Eagle Falls," Cindy said with certainty, a snap in her tone.

Willie had said that it would be bigwigs. The governor and others in high-ranking positions, so maybe Cindy was right. Perhaps no one from town was on the guest list. But Erin was sure that he would still need some local help to run the party and keep everything going smoothly.

"I just wondered who you'd heard it from. If it was from someone who was actually there when it happened."

Bella shrugged. "Everyone is talking about it. I guess someone must have been out there to see."

The bells over the door jingled, and a couple more customers walked in. They were starting to get a bit of a crowd. "What can I get for you, Cindy?" Erin asked, hoping to move things along.

"Well, I don't think it's going to be a lemon meringue pie," Cindy said. "I'm probably going to be avoiding those for a while."

Erin rolled her eyes as a couple of the other women giggled. "I don't have any lemon meringue pies today," she pointed out, indicating the display case. "So, what *would* you like?"

Cindy picked out a loaf of bread and some chocolate caramel bars. She looked at her watch. "And then I'd better be getting on my way," she said, in a tone that suggested that Erin had been keeping her there.

Bella rang up her mother's order on the till. "Do you think maybe we should get a little more than that?" she suggested. "We might have company..." She pushed back a lock of wavy blond hair that had escaped her hat and looked at her mother.

Cindy scowled at this suggestion. "I don't suppose I have any say in the matter."

Bella just raised her brows and blinked, waiting for Cindy to make a decision.

"Yes, you'd better make it... three loaves. And... maybe a dozen cookies." She looked at Bella. "Will that be enough, do you think?"

"Maybe some rolls too? Or some pizza shells? I bet they'd like pizza."

Cindy sighed loudly at this. She indicated the pizza crusts. "Two of the large. And... I think that had better be it. We can't have them eating us out of house and home."

Bella rang up the additional items and made change for her mother. "Okay, see you later. Let me know... if anything happens."

Erin helped the next customer, again having to answer several questions about the lemon meringue pies and Mr. Fontainebleau. Erin couldn't figure out how the news of his death and the details associated with it could get around town so fast, and yet people still had to ask her over and over again if it might have been something to do with her pies or if she was worried that the police would consider her a suspect. Why didn't the news of her innocence—or at least her protestations of innocence—spread just as quickly as the news that she had made the pies for the party?

They served the rest of the customers as efficiently as possible, going over the grim news as often as necessary. As much as Erin would have preferred to discuss other things, she couldn't deny that the news of Fontainebleau's death had brought many people to the bakery, so she'd better do the best she could to satisfy their curiosity or thirst for scandal.

"So…" Erin wiped her forehead with the back of her hand as she took a deep breath, the bakery empty of customers for a few minutes. "You have company coming?"

Bella looked surprised by this question, then apparently remembered that she had been talking about it with her mother in front of Erin. "Oh. Yeah. Possibly. We've been helping out a friend. Don't know. Might have her and her kids for a little bit."

"Oh, that's great." Erin had been out to the Prost place a couple of times. They were goat farmers. "It's a nice place to let kids run around and play in."

Bella nodded. "It's good for kids to have lots of sunshine and physical activity. Much better than them having to sit at desks all day."

It was still summer break, but the kids would return to school before long. Unless they were homeschooled.

The bells jingled and Erin straightened and looked to see who it was. Another of the ladies there to ask her if she'd poisoned Mr. Fontainebleau with her lemon meringue pies, she supposed.

But it wasn't. It was a man she didn't know.

CHAPTER 8

*E*rin smiled. "Hi there. I don't think we've met before. Welcome to Auntie Clem's Bakery."

The man's eyes traveled around the bakery, taking it all in. The bakery display case, the small tables with chairs at the front of the bakery, the cold case to the side that housed their various frozen treats. His eyes returned to Erin and Bella.

He was tall and lean. His age was difficult to pin, maybe forty or fifty. His dark hair was dusted with gray specks, and his eyes crinkled with smiling wrinkles. "Is one of you Erin Price?"

Erin nodded. "That's me."

She half expected the man to hand her a long envelope and tell her she'd been served. Her mind jumped to all kinds of scenarios that might have to do with Fontainebleau's death. They couldn't file a wrongful death suit the very next day after he'd been killed, could they? That wasn't the way it was done. The police needed to investigate and find out what had happened before any charges were laid, and it wouldn't be until after a criminal trial was finished that a wrongful death suit would be filed. That was the way it worked.

But it could be something else. Could it be something to do with Brandon's death? She hoped he hadn't left her anything. She didn't want anything from his estate. She didn't want anything to do with him. If he'd left her something, she could refuse it, couldn't she?

The handsome man was reaching toward her, but he didn't have legal papers in his hand. It was something else—a small package. Erin reached out to take it from him, frowning slightly.

"What's this?"

He shrugged. "Delivery for you."

"I wasn't expecting anything."

It looked like a wrapped box of chocolates. Had Terry decided to send her something after the flower delivery? Just to show that he could match any anonymous suitor? She smiled at the thought. Having a secret admirer might not be half bad if it spiced things up a bit at home. She and Terry were not exactly in the honeymoon phase anymore, and a subtle nudge for him to do something romantic now and then wouldn't hurt.

"Well, thank you." Erin nodded and smiled at the deliveryman.

He gave a brief nod and left the bakery again. Bella raised her brows at Erin.

"What's this? Another special delivery?"

Erin shrugged, her face warming. "Must be from Terry." She shook it, but it didn't rattle like chocolates.

"Well, open it. Do I get to see?"

Erin looked at the door. There was no one else in the bakery, but she would prefer not to be in the middle of opening a gift when a customer came in.

"I'll open it in the kitchen," she decided.

Bella stayed in the front, but stood at the doorway looking into the kitchen to watch Erin unwrap the delivery.

Deciding to unwrap it methodically instead of just ripping the paper off, Erin unstuck the tape at each end of the oblong, unfolded the paper, and then slid the box out from the wrapping paper sleeve. She was right. It was not a box of chocolates. A quick peek inside the box verified what the logo stamped in foil on the outside suggested. Not chocolates, but a lacy, filmy negligee.

"What is it?" Bella prompted.

"Not for your eyes," Erin told her. Her cheeks were hot, and she was pretty sure she was turning a brilliant red.

"Oh-ho!" Bella laughed. "Officer Piper!"

Erin looked down at the wrapping paper and box. There was no card or tag. The only way she knew it was for her was that the deliveryman had asked her name. There was no address or name on the package. What delivery service didn't put some kind of label or waybill on their deliveries? She opened the box again to see if there was a card under the negligee, but there was not.

Erin felt another wave of heat, but this time it was not embarrassment. She looked around to see if there was anyone else watching her, but there was only Bella.

"Bella, did you know that deliveryman?"

"Hmm?" Bella looked back toward the door as if he might still be standing there. "No, I didn't know him. Why?"

"There's no card or label anywhere."

"Well, he said it was for you."

"Yes. Exactly. How did he know that?"

"He must have a list."

"But this is a package without any markings. How does he know this one was mine?"

"Maybe yours was the only one he had. It isn't like the big city. They don't do a lot of deliveries here."

Erin supposed that was probably true. The deliveryman might simply remember which package was which. It was distinctive, even if it wasn't labeled.

"Officer Handsome didn't write you a steamy note to go with it?" Bella teased.

"No. There isn't anything with it. I guess I'll have to ask him about it when I get home."

"Ask him what?"

Bells jingled. Bella turned around to deal with the new customer. Erin put the package into her small office next to her purse. She wouldn't be leaving *this* gift at Auntie Clem's.

Erin's mind was on the package for the rest of the workday. She tried to stay focused on her baking and her customers but couldn't help her mind going back to the lacy white and blue negligee over and over again as she sleepwalked through her day at Auntie Clem's. Everyone wanted to know about Fontainebleau and the pies, but Erin's mind was focused on this new mystery.

She wanted nothing more than to go home and talk with Terry and ensure everything was right with the world. She didn't have anything to worry about. He had just decided to counter the secret admirer's gift with one of his own. One that was blatantly more personal and intimate, showing his ownership of her. Not just flowers like anyone might give her, even little Peter Foster, with some help from his parents.

Eventually, it was time to close up shop and head home. Bella had her car there and Erin had hers, so they parted ways in the parking lot.

Terry's scheduled shifts had been amended due to the Fontainebleau investigation. He had been out late the night before, and she imagined that after he had woken up, he had probably spent most of the day at the police department offices assisting with the investigation into Fontainebleau's death. It would be "all hands on deck," and they would want the public to see that they were earnestly engaged in solving the crime. It wouldn't do to fall short on this one.

Not that they had ever been any less than diligent in solving any of the crimes that she had known of while she'd been in Bald Eagle Falls. However, she had been able to unravel some of them faster than the police department. That was just luck.

And she wasn't going to get close to the Fontainebleau murder, if that was what it was. Hopefully, it wasn't even a murder. He'd just slipped in the shower and hit his head, and a slow brain bleed had eventually over-whelmed him later in the day. It could be something as simple and innocuous as that.

She could see by the lights on in the house that Terry was home ahead of her. This probably meant that he had come home for supper, but would be returning to work after the meal for more work on the Fontainebleau case or for night patrol. Either way, she was glad he was home for a few minutes.

He was watching TV when she stepped into the house. It would have been nice if he had thought to start on supper, but she supposed he was just as tired after work as she was. Maybe more so, since he'd also been up half the night.

"Hi, hon." She bent down to kiss him briefly. She tossed the small box on the coffee table. "I got your special delivery."

He looked at the box and then at her. "What?"

"Didn't you send that?"

He stared at it. "This isn't the flowers that you said you got. What's going on?"

Erin swallowed. "I got another delivery today. Not flowers this time. I thought maybe it was from you. Trying to outdo my secret admirer."

"Well, that would have been a romantic gesture," he admitted, scratching the back of his head. "But that's been about the furthest thing from my mind today. Is that…" He stared at the box.

"You can have a look." Erin went into the kitchen to begin warming something up for them to eat. She didn't want to watch Terry open the box and examine the contents.

He was behind her almost immediately. It took only an instant to grab the box and flip the hinged top open.

"Who sent this?" he demanded.

"I don't know."

"Where's the card?"

"There wasn't one this time. No message. Just… whatever message you want to call *that*."

"Who delivered it?"

"A man. I don't know what company he was with. I'm sorry, I wasn't paying much attention and it was so quick. He gave it to me, and I thought it must be from you, and he was gone. He wasn't wearing a uniform and there wasn't any identification on the package. No name, no number, nothing."

"How was it packaged? Just like this?"

"Wrapping paper."

"What did you do with it?"

"I… threw it in the garbage at Auntie Clem's."

"We need to get it back."

"Um… okay. I think I just threw it in my office wastepaper basket. That doesn't get emptied every day."

"There might be fingerprints."

"Can you do that?"

He shook his head, brows drawing down. "Can I do what?"

"Just run random fingerprints through the system? Doesn't there have to be... a crime?"

"There is. Stalking."

"Is it?" Erin was glad to have him put a name on it. She wasn't sure how she was supposed to feel about someone sending her anonymous gifts. The flowers had been one thing; that was sweet and something anyone might do to make another person feel good. But the negligee felt very personal and intrusive if it had not come from Terry. Still, it wasn't a threat, and she wasn't sure who it had come from. Was she supposed to feel threatened? Complimented?

"Yes. This is stalking. Someone is trying to scare you. And I am going to put a stop to it. We'll find out who it is and put him behind bars."

Erin breathed out a pent-up breath. "Okay."

He looked at her, head cocked slightly. "Did you think I wouldn't?"

"I didn't know what to think. I didn't know how I should feel about it."

"You thought maybe this was just someone's idea of being... friendly?"

"Well, when it was the flowers, yes. I just thought it was a nice gesture. Something sweet. And there was nothing threatening about the note. When this came today, I was hoping it was just you..."

"Rest assured, I will not send you lingerie at work. Or send you anything anonymously. We live together. I will give you anything... *personal* here. In person. Maybe someday I'll send you flowers at work; that is kind of a nice idea and something someone who is more romantic than me might have thought to do. But I won't send you anything anonymously or anything that I think might embarrass you."

"And you don't think that this was just someone... misguided. Someone who intended to do something nice and it just came out wrong."

"If they have something wrong with them that prevents them from understanding social cues, maybe. But a normal guy would not send a woman lingerie anonymously and think it would make her feel safe and happy about herself."

"Yeah, I guess you're right."

"What did Vic say?"

"Vic wasn't on today. It was Bella. And I left her thinking... that it was from you."

"So now *she* thinks I'm the type of guy to send you lingerie at work." Terry flushed red around the collar.

"She thought it was very sweet. She's a teenager. Everything is romantic at that age. I just didn't want to tell her that it was anonymous."

"Okay... but I think you should let your employees know what is going on so they can be on the lookout for anyone or anything that is out of place. The more people there are who are aware and alert, the better."

Erin nodded. "I suppose. I'll tell them."

CHAPTER 9

It was a while before they sat down to dinner. Erin couldn't seem to keep her mind on task for long enough to get every-thing done and even simple, routine tasks took longer than usual as she kept stopping to figure out what she was supposed to be doing. Erin was beginning to regret that she hadn't just put out bread and jam and called it a day. Eventually, they sat down to a simple repast.

"So tell me about your case," she told Terry. "I haven't heard anything from you, but I've been hearing from the rest of Bald Eagle Falls all day."

"I suspect you have. Nothing like the possible murder of a mining mogul to get a small town buzzing."

Erin nodded, smiling. "They *have* been buzzing!"

"Of course, there has not been an autopsy yet. That will happen pretty quickly. They'll want to push it through because of how important Fontainebleau was. Maybe we'll have preliminary results tomorrow. But the victim did exhibit some outward signs that suggested he had been exposed to a toxin."

Erin nodded, waiting for more. Terry didn't fill her in on the details.

"Like he was foaming at the mouth, or what?"

"No. His skin. He had an unusual rash. And his behavior before he died was quite erratic. The ME's office suggested it might be mercury poisoning."

"Mercury poisoning. You mean like from fish?"

"You can get it from fish, yes. I would think that someone like Fontainebleau would know not to eat swordfish every day, and to try to source his fish from uncontaminated waters, or at least that his chef would know that. But there are other ways to get mercury poisoning too."

"You don't think someone intentionally poisoned him, do you?"

"We have to investigate that possibility. Until we know where the mercury came from, it could have come from anywhere, and intentional poisoning remains a possibility. But I'm inclined to think… maybe it was something to do with his mining operations."

"Do they mine for mercury? I don't even know where it comes from."

"Not here. But I gather it is used in processing minerals that they do mine here."

"So he might have been exposed at work? You hear about companies like that dumping toxic waste."

"I wouldn't jump right to that. In fact, that would be a good way to get my hands slapped. I'm not suggesting that Fontainebleau or his company was responsible for his death."

"No, I guess that wouldn't be a good idea."

"I'd get slapped with a slander lawsuit before I even finished talking."

Erin nodded, laughing. "Yes, you probably would. But it could be because of something that they were doing in his mines or factories? A mistake that exposed him to toxins?"

Terry shrugged. "No comment. We are investigating. You know I can't share anything about an active investigation."

He wouldn't share anything with her that wasn't already public knowledge or soon would be. Unless she managed to worm it out of him without his noticing.

"If he was exposed to mercury, then what about other people in his company? People who are working in those mines or factories every day? Aren't they at risk too?"

"There have not been any reports of other deaths or problems. If there were a leak or exposure at one of his industrial sites, you would expect some other reports. We'll have to dig down deeper, of course, but he didn't have employees dropping like flies."

That was something, at least. The police investigation would help to protect those workers if it turned out there was a contamination problem. As long as there wasn't a cover-up. With how wealthy and influential Fontainebleau had been, Erin wondered whether his family or estate would be able to hide anything they were able to discover in their investigation. It seemed like the wealthy always managed to suppress anything that showed them in a bad light.

"So you know for sure that it wasn't the pies," Erin teased.

"They're still testing all of the food, but chances are he was poisoned over a longer period of time; it wasn't something he ate for dinner that night."

"Oh." Erin had been anxious to hear that. Of course she knew that the pies had been perfectly safe, but she still had a lump in her stomach when he talked about having to test them. People would think that the police were still suspicious of the pies. Or that there was something they weren't saying. They wouldn't find anything in their testing. They couldn't. But she still didn't like it. "Of course."

"I have it on good authority that the pie was excellent," Terry told her with an encouraging smile. "Certainly no funny taste or smell."

"They were beautiful pies." Erin sighed. She thought about the perfectly peaked meringue tops, golden brown, with little dots of melted sugar. She loved making all kinds of pies, but the extra attention required to cook a meringue pie and the care it took to get them just right made them all the more special.

"I have no doubt. Don't worry about the testing. It is just routine."

"I know. And it isn't going to find anything. It's just that people will keep talking and speculating that it was something in the pies until you prove that it wasn't. And even then, maybe they'll still talk about it. Like they talk about the chocolate muffin killing Angela, even though they know that wasn't what killed her."

"Do they still say that?" Terry's brows went up.

"In a joking way. They still buy them, so they obviously don't think I'm trying to poison my customers, but they still talk about them being murder muffins." Erin rolled her eyes. "People say the silliest things."

"Yes, they do. Don't worry about the things they say or about jokes. They're at Auntie Clem's buying the 'murder muffins.' Maybe you should label them like that and see if more people will buy them with inventive names. You could come up with murderous names for all of your baked goods."

"I don't think so!"

Erin was *not* going to sell murder muffins.

CHAPTER 10

A s Erin had expected, Terry returned to the office when he
finished eating dinner. Erin defrosted a bag of cookies from the
freezer and sent them back with Terry so that the rest of the law enforcement officers in Bald Eagle Falls could enjoy a treat while they put in long
overtime hours. They needed something to boost their energy while
putting in double shifts. Sheriff Wilmot always protested that he was
trying to lose weight and that his wife had warned him off eating sweets
—but he always took some anyway.

After Terry had returned to work, Erin heard a tap on the back door
and was not surprised to see Vic. She joined Erin in the living room as
Erin worked on her planner, checking her task list and seeing what else
she needed to do to stay on top of her week. It was good to have her lists
in front of her when her mind was so scattered by all that had happened.
Everything was there in black and white—or color-coded—so she didn't
have to remember it but could work through it a little at a time.

"So… how are things going with Terry?" Vic asked. "I guess he's probably too busy with the murder investigation right now to pursue many
extra-curricular activities."

Erin looked up from her planner, puzzled. She followed Vic's eyes to
the small lingerie box on the coffee table. Her face heated.

"Oh! Uh… actually, that is evidence—another delivery from my secret admirer. I need to remember to grab the paper it was wrapped in when I get back to the bakery tomorrow. If you can remind me? In case there are any fingerprints."

"Oh." Vic nodded. "Sure. So can I see...?" She reached for the box.

"You'd better not get your fingerprints on that. Terry hasn't dusted it yet. I guess he forgot to take it with him today."

Or did he know that there weren't any prints on it?

Was it possible that Terry *was* the secret admirer? Testing to see whether Erin would be faithful to him or be distracted by another suitor? Seeing whether she would tell him everything right away or keep it from him? She thought that he had gotten over any doubts that he'd had about their relationship after finding out about Brandon, but maybe he'd just been waiting, biding his time and figuring out a way to test her.

"Erin?"

She looked at Vic, blinked, and shook her head. "Sorry, I was off somewhere else. What?"

"How did Terry react? Did he freak out?"

"No." Erin thought back. He'd been pretty calm about the whole thing. Especially if he thought this was someone trying to scare or threaten her. Shouldn't he have reacted with more emotion, even rage, if he thought someone was threatening her?

And shouldn't he have reminded her to set the burglar alarm and not open the door to anyone?

"He was pretty good about it. He already knew about the flowers, so I guess it wasn't a surprise that the guy would send something else. He wants to test the wrapping paper for prints and then run a database search to see if the sender is in the system somewhere. And then... charge him with stalking, I guess. That's what he said it was."

"There are no threats," Vic pointed out, looking down at the box. "Unless there's something inside or there was a card that came with it?"

"No. No threats. But Terry said that it could be considered stalking anyway. I don't know. I'm sure he knows all of the ins and outs of what qualifies. But you always hear about how women are told that there's nothing the police can do about actual stalkers... the ones who make threats or break into the person's house... so, I didn't think this would qualify."

"Or maybe because of all that bad press, they decided to tighten up the laws," Vic suggested. "Make it so that it was a crime they could prosecute."

"Oh. Maybe. Hadn't thought about that. Maybe they are improving the laws. There are so many ways you can stalk someone now. With all of the social media and information online, it's a lot easier to find out things about the person you want to target. So more stalkers... better laws to deal with them..."

"That's probably it," Vic agreed.

Erin nodded. She wasn't sure whether she was satisfied with the explanation or not.

"Anyway... I guess that's how things are with Terry and I right now. I mean, it isn't anything to do with our relationship, but that's what he's concerned about right now. That and the murder."

Except how concerned was he with the stalker if he hadn't remembered to take the evidence with him to work?

"Yeah, I guess that's a lot to deal with right now."

Erin shrugged. She looked toward the back of the house but, of course, could not see the parking pad from where she sat in the living room.

"And Willie's not home tonight?"

"I guess he has stuff to look after too. Seems like he's been pretty busy with business lately. I hope that whatever has been bugging him, he gets through it pretty soon. I like to be the focus when he's around."

Since he didn't live there, that made sense to Erin. Willie chose whether to be at Vic's or home or dealing with business. If he chose to be with Vic, then it would make sense for her to be his focus, for him to be able to put work aside and be with her.

Though, being undistracted when other things were going on in life was hard. She could see how it was a problem too.

"Vicky..." she said tentatively, "Have you noticed anything strange about Willie's behavior lately? I mean... anything different? Not just him being private about his own affairs, but... mood swings, confusion, irritability, anything like that?"

"You've met the man, right?" Vic asked with a laugh. "Yeah, he's been irritable lately. Like I said. Something going on with work. Distracting him. I don't know what because he doesn't share."

"And that big blow-up the other day."

"Well, it wasn't really a big blow-up, but... yeah. He did go storming out of here because of whatever was going on in his business. But that's just Willie; we're both—"

"Passionate people," Erin finished. She'd heard that line a few times before. A good excuse for their arguments and generally rocky relationship. They loved each other, but they certainly made a lot of noise about it.

Vic nodded. She shrugged with one shoulder. "Why? You're not worried about domestic abuse, are you? Because I can tell you, he's never raised a hand to me. Or me to him. We may shout and slam doors, but we're not mean and we don't hit. I had enough of that growing up. There's nothing wrong with a good air-clearing discussion, but I wouldn't let him abuse me."

Erin smiled, grateful for that. "That's good. But I wasn't really thinking about that. I was thinking about... his skin."

"His skin?" Vic blinked several times and stared at Erin, trying to understand the segue. "You're worried about the way he looks? I don't care; why should you?"

"No. I know it's from his mining and processing. And that's actually what has me worried. Terry was saying that Fontainebleau might have died from mercury poisoning, maybe from some environmental contaminant at his factories or mines. So... if Willie is doing his own processing, and he's obviously not in a lab with protective gear to keep his skin from being contaminated in the process..."

Vic nodded her understanding slowly. "Then what if he's poisoning himself, absorbing all kinds of bad stuff through his skin."

Erin nodded. "He could be, you know."

"And what does that have to do with whether he's irritable?"

Erin indicated her phone, where she had done a couple of internet searches before Vic's arrival. "I was looking at some of the common symptoms of mercury poisoning. Or other heavy metals. And mood swings and irritability are high on the list. Terry said that Fontainebleau had been behaving erratically before he died. Heavy metals affect the brain."

"He's not stupid. Stuff like lead poisoning, it causes brain damage that lowers the IQ, right? But Willie's smarter than anyone you've ever met. He might not say a lot, but he picks things up really fast. Sees things that no one else does. Understands a lot of really complex stuff that I could only hope to get someday."

"I know. And maybe that means that he's just fine and moody is just moody, not a symptom of anything else. I just think… one of us should ask the question."

"Me, you mean."

"I don't know. Someone should suggest that it's not the healthiest way for him to be living and he should maybe get tested to make sure that all of his exposure to whatever he works with hasn't affected him physically. Other than dyeing his skin."

"Huh. Well, maybe when he's in a good mood, *you* can ask him that."

Erin didn't particularly like the idea. She had a suspicion that Willie was not going to react in a positive way to such a suggestion. She would rather not be the target of his anger or get the cold shoulder. But she supposed she couldn't ask Vic to either.

"Yeah… well, we'll see if the subject comes up. Maybe we could get Terry to talk to him about it."

Vic laughed. "Yeah, that sounds like a good idea."

CHAPTER 11

*E*rin had scheduled Vic and Charley for the afternoon shift, which meant that she was free to run some errands for herself and Auntie Clem's without it eating into her evenings or weekend. She was getting better at making use of her employees and not insisting that she herself had to work every shift. They had even managed without her when she had been away with Vic or dealing with Melissa's wedding arrangements. That meant that she could put more on to them and not worry about doing it all herself.

She was just coming back from the grocery store when she saw a small group of children playing on the climbers in the school playground, and she thought that she recognized the older girl as she got closer. She pulled up to the curb and watched them play for a moment, listening to their happy shrieks and enjoying the smell of the freshly cut grass. Then she got out and approached the little family. She did not want people thinking she was some predator watching the children from a distance.

Erin nodded to the thin woman watching from the park bench beside the playground with a baby in her arms.

"Hello, Adrienne."

Adrienne stared at her for a minute before finally giving her a small smile and nod. She looked away from Erin again, down at her baby, as if to make sure that she wasn't fussing and was comfortable. Erin joined her

478

on the bench, sitting far enough away not to crowd her, but close enough that it wouldn't be awkward to visit. The baby had grown a lot over the intervening months since she had seen it last, but it still had the big eyes and thin face that Erin remembered. Not pudgy and round like a healthy baby should be. But maybe Adrienne naturally had skinnier babies. She was a thin woman. Maybe it was genetic, and not because they weren't getting as many calories as they should.

"Out enjoying the sunshine?"

The thin woman nodded. "Yes. Kids need plenty of fresh air and sunshine. But they still get bored sometimes, like to come into the playground to play somewhere new." She hesitated. "It's good for them to use their imaginations and to find things to do wherever they are. But nice if they can go somewhere designed for kids now and then."

"Sure," Erin agreed. She remembered using her imagination to turn junk into toys, a bare backyard into a more interesting setting, and long hours of unstructured time into engaging games or pastimes. She had not grown up babysat by screens and technology. Neither were Adrienne's children. "It's a nice change of pace."

Adrienne nodded, looking down to comfort the baby who was not complaining.

One of the children ran over from the climbers and stood by her mother. She put an arm around Adrienne, cuddling in close to her.

"Mama?"

"It's just Miss Erin," Adrienne told her. "You know the baker lady."

The girl was about eight, Erin thought. Her name was Hope, if she remembered correctly, but she wasn't certain enough to use it without making sure first.

"Hi," she greeted. "We've met before."

The girl nodded and buried her face into Adrienne's neck for a moment. Erin didn't remember her being so shy before. But kids went through phases.

Adrienne patted her on the back for a moment, then gave her a little nudge away. "There, now. You're a big girl. You can play with the others. Everything is fine here."

Hope didn't go back to the other children, even though they called for her to. She stayed close to her mother, holding on to her. Adrienne didn't try to shake her off, but was clearly hampered by Hope's clinginess.

"It's nice that you can come and play here," Erin tried.

"Uh-huh."

"What do you like to play best?"

Hope's shoulders raised and fell in a shrug.

"I used to like to play pirates," Erin told her.

Hope looked at her for a moment, then at Adrienne as if to ask for permission to talk. Adrienne nodded encouragingly.

"Pirate *tag* or *being* pirates?" Hope inquired.

Erin laughed. "Both, I guess. We played pirate tag while pretending to be pirates."

Hope sniffled and wiped her nose with the back of her hand. "Did you walk the plank?"

"Yes," Erin chuckled. "You can't play pirates without walking the plank, can you?"

Hope shook her head. Then, seeming to realize that Erin was intentionally drawing her out, she turned away from her and again buried her face in Adrienne's side.

"Can we go home, Mama? I want to go home."

"You and the others wanted to come to the playground. The others still need more time to play. You go play too, enjoy yourself."

Hope shook her head and didn't rejoin them.

Erin met Adrienne's eyes and saw that it was time for her to leave. Adrienne didn't like her making Hope nervous. "I'll... head back out. I'll see you later, okay? We'll talk another time."

Adrienne nodded. Erin returned to her car. Once she was gone, the girl would hopefully return to playing with her siblings.

On the seat beside Erin lay the wrapping paper from the gift from the secret admirer. Erin parked in the lot behind the town hall. She walked through the main part of the town hall to the police department offices.

Clara Jones was sitting at her desk in the reception area. Her eyes went over Erin quickly and Erin thought she detected slight disappointment in Clara's features when she saw that Erin had not brought any baked goods with her. Erin usually bribed her way in with something sweet. Or at least paved the way; it wasn't exactly a bribe.

"Miss Price?"

"Is Terry in?"

"He is... Is this regarding a case?"

Clara didn't really have any right to ask. She knew that Terry would see Erin if he were able to, and Erin didn't have to be bringing evidence on an active case for Clara to let her in. Clara was just snooping into what it was that Erin had come by to see Terry for. If it wasn't an active case, then what was so important that it could not wait until Terry was home?

Maybe Erin should have brought Terry some soup for dinner to show that she was performing a valuable service, rather than just wanting to talk to a law enforcement officer who needed to be focused on the cases at hand. Especially with such a big case on the books. Mr. Fontainebleau's people would not be happy with any reason for delays.

Not that they could see what was going on in the Bald Eagle Falls police department, to see whether they were talking to their wives or partners instead of keeping their noses to the grindstone.

"I have something he asked me to bring by."

Clara waited for more information, and when it was not forthcoming, relented and called Terry's line to advise him that Miss Price was there to see him.

There was a response from Terry. Clara clearly didn't like it. "Are you sure? I can ask her to just leave whatever it is here for you."

She knew very well that Erin could hear what she was saying.

Clara hung up the phone. "He'll see you in his office," she conceded.

"Thank you, Clara."

Erin walked down the hall to the office that was now somewhat cramped since Terry shared it with Stayner. He stood up from his chair to greet her and give her a quick hug and kiss. He stretched and rolled his shoulders before sitting down again. It was probably the first time he had gotten up in several hours.

"What can I do for you?" Terry asked, when it was clear that Erin did not have a box of cookies or thermos of soup for him.

She produced the wrapping paper, which she had slid into a plastic zip-top bag to prevent it from being contaminated by anything else.

"You wanted me to get you the wrapping paper from that second gift," she reminded him.

"That completely slipped my mind. I've been so focused on this Fontainebleau case. Thanks for bringing it by. I guess… we should start the paperwork on an official complaint. Do you mind filling in a couple of forms?"

Erin wrinkled her nose. That wasn't exactly what she'd had in mind when she had decided to bring him the wrapping paper, but she supposed that if he was going to run any fingerprints found on the paper through their database, he needed a file to record it under. They needed to do everything by the book. Random searches of fingerprints were not something that they were supposed to be doing.

"I suppose so."

"Sorry. I know it isn't any fun."

"I'm not sure it's worth it. I mean… this guy hasn't made any threats." Erin thought back to receiving the lingerie. Even if it wasn't accompanied by any kind of written warning or threat, there was a certain creep factor involved in getting such an intimate thing from a stranger or anonymous source. It was inappropriate and the sender surely knew that such an anonymous gift would not be welcomed by most women.

"Do you want to wait until he escalates?" Terry held up his hands to halt any protest. "It is extremely unlikely that this will turn into anything. Most stranger stalkers are not dangerous and never do anything to harm their target. It's the ones who are former intimate partners that are the problem, and as far as you know…"

"I don't think this is anyone I know," Erin agreed. But of course she couldn't be sure. She hadn't expected Brandon to ever show up in her life again either. She hadn't expected that anyone in Bald Eagle Falls was paying her anything more than a normal amount of attention. But she'd been wrong about that. Was there any chance that some interest from the past had shown up in Bald Eagle Falls to harass her? It didn't seem possible.

"So, chances are this will never turn into anything," Terry reassured her. "If something pops on the fingerprints, then we can give this guy a warning to knock it off, and he probably will. If nothing pops, then we know that he at least doesn't have a criminal record, and probably he'll just give up after a while. There's no reason to think that he will escalate. But we should still do what we can."

It was the opposite reaction to what women usually received when reporting a stalker. So she should be happy that her boyfriend was in the police department and wanted to take it seriously.

"Okay."

Terry took her through the forms required to be filled out to file her complaint, asking her questions and adding details as needed. When they got to the end of it, Terry produced a mobile fingerprint scanner to take her prints.

Erin stared at the scanner and shook her head. "Why? You don't need my prints."

"You touched the wrapping paper, right? We need to be able to eliminate your prints and just focus on the rest."

A lot of people were caught by "elimination prints" if Erin was to believe what she saw on crime shows on TV. The cops always said that the fingerprints were to rule someone out, just so they could get the prints that would put them at the scene of a crime. Though Erin had not committed any crime, she was still reluctant to cooperate. This was the point at which she would be telling a person of interest on TV to assert their right to remain silent or request a lawyer. They didn't have to give their fingerprints to anyone.

Terry waited for her to agree. He pointed at the wrapping paper. "Your prints are on that, right?"

"Yes."

"Then we have your prints. We can feed them all into the computer and run them against the database."

That was true.

"You're not giving me anything new by giving me your fingerprints. You are just giving me another copy of the same thing, with your name attached. So we *don't* have to run them through the database."

"You won't run my prints through the system?"

"What are you afraid we're going to find if we do?"

Erin shrugged uncomfortably. "I don't know. I haven't done anything. But... I don't know if they could be in there from somewhere else."

"Like what?"

"Like somewhere I was where a crime occurred. It does happen, you know."

"Well, yes, I do. Especially to you."

It was probably surprising that they hadn't run into this problem on any of the previous cases. But the fact was, he'd never asked for her fingerprints before.

"I think you're just going to have to trust me. I am not going to run your prints through the system. Just to compare them to what we find on the wrapping paper, so we know which ones not to put through."

But would he be left wondering where else her fingerprints might lead after that? Would he run them anyway, because he was curious about her past and what she might be trying to cover up?

"It's just that I've never had to give my prints for anything before," Erin explained. "I've never been arrested or had to give elimination prints before. It's kind of scary."

He nodded as if this were perfectly reasonable.

"Okay..." Erin looked at the scanner. "How does this work?"

CHAPTER 12

espite officially having the afternoon off, Erin was tired when evening rolled around. More exhausted than she thought she should be, she wondered if she could be coming down with something. She would have to be careful to get enough sleep and eat properly. Maybe take some vitamin C. She didn't want to get sick. That could prevent her from going to Auntie Clem's for a week or more, even if it were only a twenty-four-hour bug. People didn't want someone who had been sick near their food.

Terry was sleeping, resting up for a night shift. She didn't think he should still have been working in the afternoon if he was taking a night shift. It didn't give him a full eight hours to sleep between shifts. But he said he didn't need to; he would have a nap and then sleep after the night shift. But she wasn't sure he would. Since the initial call-out, he'd been putting most of his time into helping out with the Fontainebleau case.

Erin moved through her tai chi forms in the backyard, alone at first and then joined by Willie as he pulled the garden hose across the yard to wash off his truck while she exercised.

"I hear you think I'm going crazy." He directed a stream of water at his truck, rinsing off a layer of dust from gravel or dirt roads.

"What?" Erin frowned and looked at him, losing her place in the tai chi flow for a moment, trying to figure out what he was talking about.

"That I'm becoming unbalanced like Fontainebleau because of my exposure to toxic chemicals."

"Oh. That. Well, I didn't mean that..." She looked away from him, grimacing. "I didn't mean that you're going crazy. I was just worried when we started talking about how Fontainebleau might have been exposed to mercury or other heavy metals at his mines or plants. Because... I know your skin is exposed to whatever you do to process your minerals."

"You don't think that I'm careful? That I'm aware of the dangers?"

"Well... I just know that your skin is exposed, and you can absorb mercury through your skin. That's what I'm worried about."

"I follow traditional processing methods. There's nothing wrong with that. It's the same way that people have been processing metals for hundreds of years. People like Fontainebleau might be afraid to get their hands dirty, but I'm not. I don't care how people look at me; I know I've earned this from good, honest work."

He paused for a moment to look at the skin on the back of his hand, then shrugged. He was proud of the stained skin he had earned. Proud that he had done all of the work himself and not had some lab or plant somewhere do it for him.

"And you don't think that there's any danger to how you've been doing it? There must be all kinds of safety standards you have to follow, environmental stuff and precautions to keep from poisoning yourself..."

He continued to spray the truck, working down the length of it. "I know what I'm doing. Like I said, people have been doing this for hundreds of years. I didn't just come up with my own process. Though I've tweaked it in places, learned from experience."

"But traditional ways aren't always the best or the safest. I mean... there's a reason for the expression 'mad as a hatter.'"

"So you *do* think I'm crazy."

"No. I don't. I don't think there's anything wrong with you. Not that we can see yet. But it could poison you over time. Like with the guys who made those old felt hats. They used mercury for that, and it poisoned them over time. Not all at once. If you have been accumulating mercury, you could get treated, to reverse the process. So that you don't end up like Fontainebleau."

He shook his head. "I'll take it under advisement."

Erin didn't look at him, focusing on her tai chi forms and keeping her gaze steady on a point in the distance. "Fine."

"I'm not going to change my business practices. It's the guys like Fontainebleau who are the big polluters putting mercury into the environment. If he died from his own soil or groundwater contamination, then he got what was coming to him. The EPA should be inspecting all of his operations and finding out where the contaminants came from."

"Terry said that they are. They know the mercury could have come from one of his plants, so they're looking for it. It could be harming wildlife or his workers."

"He's probably dumping massive amounts of the stuff. I work in a very controlled environment and don't use many of these chemicals. It's just a drop in the bucket compared to an operation like Fontainebleau's empire."

"I wasn't really concerned about you contaminating all of Bald Eagle Falls's groundwater. Just about your own health."

He didn't say anything for a while, apparently focused on the complex job of washing off his truck.

"Well, I appreciate your concern," he eventually said gruffly. "But it is misplaced. There's nothing wrong with my health."

"Okay. That's great. I'm glad."

Willie finished washing off his truck in silence, rolled the hose back up to put it away neatly, and grunted an indistinct goodbye to Erin before going up to the loft to join Vic.

Erin decided to do her routine one more time, tense from her discussion with Willie rather than relaxed like she had hoped to be.

There was a movement in the woods beyond her fence, and Erin turned her head slightly to try to identify it. With a stalker on the loose, she should be aware of her environment. Terry didn't think the guy would escalate into doing something violent, but sometimes cops were wrong. Sometimes those people who were "unlikely" to escalate were the very ones who did. He wanted her to remember to set the burglar alarm when she was inside, but when she was outside, she was exposed. She had been approached in the yard before and couldn't forget that.

But the shape that she was able to make out in the trees was not a stranger to her. No stalker. It was the tall, slim redhead who lived in the summer cottage and acted as groundskeeper in Erin's woods. Running off kids who would leave behind campfires and beer cans, squatters who could end up injuring themselves and then suing Erin because it happened on her property, or anyone else who might conceivably cause Erin problems, including a secret admirer lurking around, trying to catch a peek at her while she did her tai chi at the end of a long day.

"Hi, Adele."

Adele moved closer to where she could talk to Erin without either of them having to raise their voices and be overheard or attract attention.

"Evening, Erin."

"How's everything today? All quiet?"

Adele's shotgun pointed down, gripped casually. "Well, quiet for now," Adele conceded.

Erin wasn't sure she liked the sound of that. "Has someone been hanging around? Anyone giving you problems?"

"There have been some reporters around. Think that they can set up a nest and get some telephoto shots. You or Officer Piper; I'm not sure what they think they're going to get that's interesting enough to publish, but you never know what these guys will make up."

"Reporters?" Erin repeated with dismay. She remembered Terry warning her that they might show up. Everything had been quiet, so Erin had thought that he had just been overly cautious. But maybe she just hadn't been paying close enough attention. She had expected them to jump out, bar her way, and drill her with questions. Not to lurk in the trees and see if they could get candid shots of her. "I didn't think we'd really see any. Did they leave when you asked them to?"

"So far, so good. Even those who think they have the right to be on what they think is public property are usually convinced by my arguments." Adele lifted the shotgun slightly. "They realize that they might have been mistaken."

"Well... that's good," Erin couldn't help snickering at the thought of the reporters being chased off by Adele and her shotgun. Adele could be very convincing, though as far as Erin knew, she had never fired even a warning shot. The reporters would not know enough about her to realize that she would never voluntarily hurt another creature.

Erin realized that it had been longer than usual since Adele had picked up any baked goods from her. While she herself did not eat a lot,

Adele did collect baked goods from Erin's free day-old bread program regularly, which she then distributed to a family or families who remained unknown to Erin.

"How is everything else? Everyone… okay?" Erin asked tentatively. She had a stated "no questions asked" policy for the day-old bread program, in place so that anyone could pick up baked goods from Auntie Clem's without fear of being judged for taking advantage of the offering. Erin didn't need to know anyone's circumstances or even who was the eventual recipient of the baked goods. Just that they were going to feed hungry mouths somewhere that wouldn't be filled if it weren't for her generosity.

Though Erin didn't consider it generosity to give away what would have gone in the garbage otherwise.

"Yes," Adele said neutrally. "Everything is fine."

"Good. I just… want to make sure that people are taken care of."

"Circumstances change. Fluctuate."

That could mean that one of the families Adele had been helping out was now in better circumstances, able to buy goods on their own rather than taking the day-old bread. If so, Erin was happy to hear it. She nodded.

"Good… I hope that's good news." Erin stretched and let her arms fall to her side. "As far as these reporters go…" she shook her head. "No one has approached me directly yet. It isn't like I know anything about the investigation or Terry would reveal anything to the public. I don't know how long this thing is going to go on. I guess since you don't come from here, you didn't know this Fontainebleau guy?"

Adele shook her head. "I've known men like him. But I haven't had the privilege of knowing your Mr. Fontainebleau, thankfully."

"He's not *my* Mr. Fontainebleau."

"He's your client, isn't he? Or *wasn't* he?"

"One time. And I don't even know if he ate the pie before he died. And it was his assistant who contacted me, not he himself."

"Of course not. A man like that wouldn't be making his own phone calls about catering a dinner. That would be…" Adele shook her head, rolling her eyes and searching for a word.

"Ridiculous? Beneath him? Unthinkable?"

"Any of those would do," Adele agreed. "Anyway, the sentiment is the same. It's best to stay far away from anyone like that. They will use and abuse anyone in their sphere."

CHAPTER 13

*R*eturning home after a long day at the bakery, Erin was bone tired. She picked up the mail from the floor beneath the mail slot and tossed it onto the coffee table to look at later. The house was quiet. She hadn't seen Terry's truck out front, so he was probably back at work again, working hard on the Fontainebleau case. Were they making any headway on it? She hadn't had much chance to talk to Terry about it, but was interested in hearing whether they had made any progress. Did they know the contamination had come from one of his work sites? It seemed like justice if he had ended up poisoning himself. As Willie had said, he got what he deserved if he had been dumping that stuff into the environment against the strict regulations meant to keep him from doing just that.

The mail hit the coffee table with a soft slap and spread out like a deck of cards being displayed by a dealer. There was a large, thick envelope that seemed out of place. It wasn't a bill or advertising flyer, which was about all she got in the mail these days. She bent over and picked it up.

It was stiff. Cardboard inside an envelope to keep it from being folded. Her name and address were on it written in an unfamiliar hand, but there was no return address, either in the corner or on the reverse side. Erin used her finger to slit the flap and pried apart two thin pieces of cardboard to see what was in between.

They were old newspaper articles. Not printed on copy paper. Not microfiche copies like she'd gotten when she was doing research at the library on pre-digitized copies of the Bald Eagle Falls weekly. But actual cut-out-of-the-paper newsprint copies.

Erin held the envelope open and tipped the articles out onto the coffee table.

She was still leaning over the articles when Terry got home twenty minutes later. He entered, K9 at his side as usual, and looked surprised at the papers spread out over the table.

"What's all this? More of Clementine's genealogy?"

"No. Another delivery by the... whatever he is. Secret admirer. Stalker. Whatever."

"Threats?" Terry asked sharply, stepping closer.

But they weren't single words cut out of a newspaper or magazine to form a message for her. They were actual articles.

"No. They're about Fontainebleau."

"Fontainebleau." Terry sat down on the couch beside Erin and looked at them. "These are old. Someone's been following his career for a long time."

Erin nodded. "They go back thirty years. Unless they were stolen from the library or historical society, whoever sent them to me must have collected them in some file or scrapbook."

"And why give them to you?"

"I don't know." Erin smoothed one of the articles out. "What am I supposed to do with these? How exactly is this the normal progression after flowers and lingerie? I would have thought... chocolates? But not old newspaper articles about someone I didn't even know."

"Maybe they were meant for me rather than you."

"They were addressed to me."

"But they could have been sent to you on the assumption that you would pass them on to me. Someone who was paranoid about sending them to the police department's address."

"I suppose. Whoever it is must know that I don't live alone here. If it's someone who lives in town or knows my address, they must know that, right?"

"I would expect so."

"So… if you think this was meant for you, then… why? Is this information that you don't have?"

Terry picked up one of the articles to read it. "Well, I admit that we don't know a lot about his early life. About his father and how he got his start in this business. Which it looks like is what these articles are about. The early observations on a promising career. A rising star."

Erin nodded. She had already read through each one. Nothing had jumped out at her as being out of place. "But most of it is… it's canned publicity. Stuff that came out of company press releases, not investigative journalism. It isn't a tell-all that suggests he was dishonest or got his fortune through ill-gotten gains. There's nothing… startling here."

Terry's eyes went from one yellowing article to the next, skimming over them. "No, not at a first look. It's just like you say. The story that the company would want to tell. Get some favorable press. Let people know who your new guy is. Make it all sound good."

"Why would anyone send it to us, then? It isn't anything that is going to help with the investigation."

"Maybe that's not the reason it was sent." Terry sat up, dropping the article back onto the table.

"Why else would it be sent?"

"To show you… how he got here. Maybe… humanize him, make him look like someone you could like instead of as remote as he was before he died. Rich and famous. Someone who just ordered everyone else around. The mining mogul who knew he was better than anyone else."

"That isn't what I thought about him," Erin protested. Though, truth be told, it wasn't that far from the truth. He hadn't been real to her. Just a name and a big order sheet. The money that the job would add to Auntie Clem's bank account. "I'm sure he was a good guy. I never talked to him, but just because someone is rich, that doesn't automatically make them snobby or corrupt."

She had learned from more than one source that he was corrupt or at least suspected of it. He could pay for what he wanted and do whatever he wanted without getting in hot water. Because he was who he was, a man with millions of dollars and almost as many "friends" willing to help things along.

"If you're 'sure he's a good guy,' then maybe these articles have done their job. Because that's certainly not what I have learned from my investigation." Terry looked around as if someone might have overheard them. Someone who would report to Fontainebleau's company or estate that Terry had been slandering him.

"Well… that isn't what I've heard either," Erin admitted. "But he must have had some good qualities. And maybe he was trying to change. He'd never used Auntie Clem's Bakery before. Why start now? Did he have guests that follow a gluten-free diet and he wanted to accommodate them? Or had he decided to buy local, even if it was a little more expensive than it would be to go with a big catering company further away."

Erin looked from one picture to another, showing Fontainebleau the Third as a young man, just starting out in the business. Learning the ropes by working as a laborer in his father's mines and factories. Making suggestions that showed an aptitude for making money and succeeding in the world of mines and minerals. Coming home from college to work with his father in upper management, the brilliant young man who was going to turn things around for the company.

"I've heard he wasn't well-liked," she admitted to Terry.

"That would be an understatement. Maybe 'hated by all who knew him' would be a more accurate statement."

"So, are there a lot of suspects?"

"If he was intentionally poisoned? Yes, certainly."

"Have they found any contamination at his house or where he worked? That would explain him having mercury poisoning?"

Terry pressed his lips together, considering the question. "They have found fairly high concentrations of mercury and other heavy metals at a couple of the factories. But… there is some hesitation in saying that the levels of mercury would have been high enough to kill him."

"Even exposure over a long time?"

"Different experts will give us different answers. Or if he would have spent enough time at those facilities to be affected. And we're still waiting for confirmation from the medical examiner that it was mercury that killed him. And what kind of mercury it was. I guess there are different kinds of mercury, different sources it might come from. So we also need to know what kind of mercury poisoning he had, if that's what it was."

There were still a lot of unanswered questions on the cause of death. What if the medical examiner called back and said that it was a heart attack? Or some other cause of death that was either homicide or natural causes? Would all of the investigation that the police department had done be thrown out the window?

"So, do you investigate it as if it was intentional poisoning? Or an accident?"

"Right now, we have to treat it as a suspicious death. Possible homicide. That's the best we can do right now. We can't just *not* investigate and hope that the verdict comes back that it was natural causes. We have to gather the evidence while it still exists and talk to witnesses while their memories are still fresh."

"And how many of those witnesses are suspects?"

Terry leaned back into the couch and rolled his head and shoulders, working out the muscle soreness from the time he'd been spending at his desk. While he still did foot patrol and answered trouble calls while he was on shift, Erin suspected that the majority of his time had been spent moving the investigation into Fontainebleau's death forward.

"A lot of people had reason to dislike Fontainebleau. Including people that had quite a bit of access to him. We're not talking about a mobster or leader of state with lots of bodyguards around him to protect him from all of the people who hated him. He was pretty casual about security."

"I guess he figured being out in the middle of nowhere in backwoods Tennessee was protection enough."

"I guess so. And until now… it was."

CHAPTER 14

*T*his time, it was a delivery that Erin knew about and had eagerly awaited. Not a delivery from some unknown man or woman watching her and sending her random gifts she couldn't understand the significance of.

"When is it supposed to get here?" Vic asked.

"I don't know." Erin hit the tracking number on her phone and waited for the details to come up. "Before five o'clock," she sighed.

"So it could be any time today." Vic rolled her eyes. "Sorry. You must be going crazy waiting for it."

"I am," Erin agreed. She felt like a little kid at Christmas. Back before she'd learned not to expect anything good at Christmas. Not the present she asked Santa for and not a magical Christmas miracle where she got a permanent family and the stable life she'd dreamed of. Despite all of the movies on TV and sermons at churches she attended sporadically, there was just no truth to Christmas being a magical time of wish-fulfillment. Those things only happened in movies and books. She'd never met anyone who'd actually experienced a Christmas miracle.

But she was excited. When the package finally arrived, it would be Christmas Day for her, no matter how high the Tennessee summer temperature soared.

She tried to lose herself in her work. There was plenty to be done, just like there was every day. When they finished baking the first batch of bread, it was time for opening and the morning rush, and then the customers eventually tailed off a little. She took a few minutes in her office to see if she could get a few more pieces of information entered into the computer system. She wanted to make sure she was caught up and then do a backup to ensure that she had a copy of all of her vital information in case she was ever in the position of having her computer stolen again. Or if it flooded, burned, or had some other kind of catastrophic breakdown. She never wanted to experience that heart-dropping moment of dread, thinking she had lost all of her information, again.

Charley came by for the afternoon shift. Erin had been hoping that by the time Charley got there, the delivery would have arrived, and she could test it out while Charley and Vic handled the bakery customers.

Mid-afternoon, there was a loud knock on the bakery's back door. Erin hurried out of her office to answer it.

"Someone at the door," Vic called, sticking her head into the kitchen and then grinning at Erin when she saw her running for the door. "I should have guessed you didn't have to be told twice."

Erin opened the door and greeted the deliveryman who stood waiting with several boxes on his dolly.

"Expecting a delivery?" Maurice asked. He brought in deliveries from the city regularly, one of the few delivery services that felt it was worth their while to make the trip out to Bald Eagle Falls.

"Yes!" Erin agreed.

He smiled at her excitement. "Well, then, these three boxes are yours." He looked at his clipboard and took three boxes off of his cart. Erin signed the clipboard to acknowledge her receipt. By the time she had the largest of the three boxes open, Vic was there to see. She helped Erin wrestle out the tight Styrofoam blocks that held everything firmly in place.

"There it is," she said in awe as she and Erin gazed reverently at the shiny ceramic glaze that coated the outside of the waffle maker.

"Thirty waffles at once," Erin murmured.

"Breakfast will never be the same again."

Charley was watching curiously from the doorway to the front of the bakery.

"I thought you only got runner-up in the waffle contest."

Erin and Vic exchanged looks.

"Yes," Erin admitted.

"Then how did you get the grand prize?"

Erin cleared her throat. "Well, I kind of had my heart set on it... so I had to buy my own."

Charley laughed. "Why bother entering the contest at all, then? Save yourself some time and just buy the waffle iron."

"Well, there was always the chance that I would win the contest and would be able to get it for free. Free is always better for the cash flow situation."

Vic and Charley both chuckled along with her. "Well, I guess it is at that," Charley agreed. "So why is it in three boxes? Just how big is this thing?"

"I guess there's some assembly required. And maybe some accessories, instructions, a recipe book..." Erin looked at the other boxes. "I'll get to them once I get this first box unpacked and assembled."

Vic helped her to assemble, floating between the front and the kitchen to make sure she covered both places as necessary. There were a number of accessories and manuals, as Erin had suspected. Erin nodded at the third box, which hadn't yet been opened.

"What do you think is in the last one? This looks like everything that was pictured in the assembly instructions."

"I don't know. Open it up and let's have a look."

Erin slit the packing tape on the last box and plunged her hand into the packing peanuts. "Okay, so what have we got here?"

She found the heavy, irregularly shaped object and pulled it out of the box, letting packing peanuts stream back down into the box and onto the floor.

"What's that?" Vic stared at the device, a sort of a plaque with several dials like analog clock faces on it.

"I... have no idea." Erin dug around in the box for any instructions or explanation. It didn't look like it was anything to do with the waffle iron. Maybe it had come to her in error. Maurice might have given her a box that wasn't hers. She bent down the flaps of the box to look at the address on it. It was definitely made out to her at Auntie Clem's Bakery. But someone might still have made a mistake, affixing the label to the wrong box. If there was a waybill, she might be able to get it straightened out for whoever was expecting the mutated clock.

But there wasn't even a scrap of paper in the box.

"What have you got there?" Charley asked from the doorway.

Erin turned it to show her. "I have no idea. Don't expect me to tell you the time on this thing. It looks like it came out of an airplane. Or a boat."

"Oh," Charley laughed. "My granddad had one of those. It's a barometer. Supposed to help you to tell the weather. Atmospheric pressure. It drops before a storm… or something like that."

"Huh." Erin looked at it. There were words around the big center dial like Rain, Fair, and Change. "Okay. I guess that's what all of this means. Cool, but… where did it come from and who needs to know the atmospheric pressure to make waffles?"

"That's a really cool one." Charley entered the kitchen to get a closer look at the barometer. "It looks like it's authentic. Like an antique, not just a knock-off."

Erin nodded. It was quite heavy in her hand, not just plastic parts fitted into particle board. "Yeah. Someone is going to be looking for this. I don't know how it got mixed in with my delivery." She looked at the labels on the boxes. The two that had contained waffle iron parts were clearly different from the one that had contained the barometer. "It has to be a mistake. I just hope we can figure out who it was supposed to go to."

CHAPTER 15

The next day, Erin and Vic had done the baking and opened Auntie Clem's when Erin got a call from Bella. Bella wasn't supposed to be on until the afternoon, so it was odd for her to call in unless something was wrong.

"Uh-oh," Erin intoned when she saw the caller ID. "Bella might be sick."

She slipped into the kitchen to take the call, leaving Vic to handle the customers.

"Bella, hi," she greeted.

"Oh, Erin, thanks for answering." Bella knew that Erin discouraged her employees from taking calls or even looking at their screens when serving customers, and tried to follow the same policy herself. Although she took special orders for the bakery, too, so she had to keep an eye on who was calling in case it was additional business. Bella's voice sounded different from usual. Erin figured that confirmed that she was calling in to say she was sick.

"No problem, Bella. What's up?"

"I need a favor, and... I don't really know who else to ask. I know you're working this morning, so I shouldn't, but..."

"What is it? Are you okay?"

"My car broke down."

"Oh, I see. So you won't be able to get in this afternoon."

"Well, that's one problem. But the other thing is, I'm supposed to be giving someone else a ride this morning, and now I can't, and she really needs to get in to *her* job, or she could lose it. And she has a family to look after, so… she can't afford to lose it."

"Who are you supposed to give a ride to? Just into town?"

"No." Bella sounded reluctant to go on, as if she'd decided that calling Erin was the wrong thing to do and she should try something else instead. "It's just… if it was just me, I would find a way to work it out. Or just get one of the others to cover my shift this afternoon. But she can't do that. They're very strict."

"Who?" Erin couldn't figure out who Bella would be giving a ride to. She and her mother lived alone on their goat farm. Maybe a neighbor out that way that she had offered to help?

"Well, you know Adrienne, don't you?" Bella's voice was tentative.

"Adrienne?"

"We've been helping her out. Her and her kids, so that she could go back to work. Now that the baby is bigger and can be left with someone, she needed to start working again. She lives a pretty thrifty lifestyle, but she still needs food and clothes for the kids and everything…"

"Of course. I know Adrienne; we've—" Erin cut herself off. She had been about to say that she had helped Adrienne with food from the day-old program before, but that would be breaking confidences. If Bella was helping Adrienne out, she probably already knew that, but it wasn't Erin's place to say so. "We've talked before. So you need to take Adrienne to her job?"

"Yes," Bella agreed. "And Mom's car is in the shop right now. We've got tractors, but I really can't take her to her work on a tractor. It was the worst time for my car to decide to break down. But we've done everything we could think of and can't get it started again. We'll have to get it towed into town to the shop. And *that* won't be cheap. We'll probably have Mom's back soon, but right now…"

Erin was thinking through the logistics. She could drive out to the Prost farm, take Adrienne wherever she needed to go, and bring Bella into town for her afternoon shift at the bakery, if she still wanted to do that rather than having someone else cover the shift. It would leave Vic alone for the time it took to drive Adrienne to her job, but that was probably in town and would not take long. Erin didn't like to leave just one person manning the bakery, so should she get someone to come in and help, or leave for a short time and leave Vic on her own for that long?

"Of course," she agreed. "I'd be happy to help. Where exactly does Adrienne work? In town?"

"No, at another place out here. It's kind of remote. If I was just trying to get a ride into town, I could probably find someone, but when she needs to go all the way out in the other direction…"

That probably answered the question of whether she should get someone to cover for her while she was gone. It could take a while.

"Okay. How far out is it?"

"Well, it's kind of… do you know where the Fontainebleau Homestead is?"

Erin shook her head. "The Homestead?"

"Yeah. I can give you directions. Or Adrienne can. But it's… like I said, it's remote."

And Bella said that as someone who lived in the country rather than in town herself. When someone on a farm said that a place was remote, it was remote. Erin remembered looking at the map when Fontainebleau's assistant had given her the GPS coordinates for the pie delivery. Fontainebleau liked to make people come to him. To inconvenience them and show them how important he was that he could make them leave the rest of the world behind to see him in his little kingdom.

"Yes, it is. Okay. Give me a few minutes to get the bakery covered, and I'll come out. What time is she supposed to be there?"

"Well, right now, actually, but we're doing our best to hold them off. You can't expect people to never have mechanical difficulties or run into traffic. As long as she gets out there ASAP, I think she'll be okay. She can work late to make up for it. Why don't you just head over here and, while you're on the way, I'll get Charley or someone else to come into Auntie Clem's. Vic will only be alone for a few minutes until someone can get over there."

"Okay. I'll do that. Thanks."

"No, thank you! I'll see you soon. Do you need any directions?"

"No, I remember where it is, and I'm pretty sure I marked it on my phone the last time I was out there."

"Okay, good. Just call me if you have any trouble. I can always come out on the tractor to guide you in."

Erin laughed at the image. "I think I'll be okay."

After letting Vic know what was happening, Erin got into her car and headed toward the Prost farm. She didn't mind doing a favor for Bella, an exemplary employee who never missed a shift and always offered to help Erin with other things. She wanted to get lots of business experience so that she could run her own business one day, and she had a good business mind.

And helping Adrienne to keep her job and take care of her little flock of children was important to Erin too. She had tried to befriend Adrienne in the past and to help her out in whatever ways she could. But Adrienne had remained remote most of the time and, like a number of the indigent families Erin had met in the area, didn't like to be offered "charity" by Erin or anyone else. Erin was glad that Bella had called her.

She got out to the farm as quickly as she could, *possibly* pushing her speed to slightly over the speed limit to cut down the length of time it would take to get there. Adrienne was already late, and she would be worrying over how long Erin took to arrive.

Adrienne was waiting near the gravel pad where the farm vehicles parked when Erin arrived. She stood like a wraith, her arms wrapped around her, unmoving, her clothes hanging off her skinny frame. Bella and the children were playing a game in the green field to keep them busy. When they saw the car arrive and Adrienne began to move toward it, they broke up the game and all ran to her like a little row of ducklings.

Hope grasped her mother's arm, starting to cry. "Mama, stay here with us. Please. Don't go."

"I need to go to work," Adrienne said sternly. She gave Hope a quick hug and a kiss on the top of her head, then nudged her away. "You be a big girl now, an example to the others. No tears. It's good that I have a job to go to. It means better food and new clothes for you." She smoothed the shoulder of the shirt Hope was wearing. "You're growing way too fast! You're just sprouting out of everything."

"Me too!" one of the younger children insisted. "I sprouting too!"

"Yes, you all are," Adrienne agreed, giving hugs and kisses and trying to herd the children back to Bella for her to take care of them. "Now you all be good for Bell and I'll see you tonight."

"You won't stay there tonight?" Hope sniffled.

"I hope not. But if I can't get a ride and Auntie Cindy doesn't have her car back, then I might have to. And if I do, you know the rules and go to bed for Cindy and Bella the way you're supposed to. Be good."

"I don't want you to stay!"

"If I do, it will just be one night. We'll get it sorted out. Now hush! It's time to help take care of the others, not to cause a scene. Be a big girl."

Hope wiped at her eyes and pulled the other children away from their mother, back toward the field where they had been playing. Erin didn't see the baby and suspected she was in the house, either sleeping or being cared for by Cindy.

As much as she hated Cindy's constant criticisms and innuendo, she was touched that Cindy would open up her house to Adrienne and all of the children to make sure they were cared for. She didn't think that Cindy was an actual "auntie," just a friend of the family.

Adrienne waved all of the children off and nodded to Bella. "Thanks so much. I'll let you know what happens."

Erin looked at Bella. "Aren't you coming too? You need to get to town for your shift, unless you're having it covered."

"Yeah, and if Mom's car is done, I can just drive it home from the shop. But you have to go all the way out to the Homestead and back. You can pick me up on your way back to town. I can look after the young'uns until then."

"Okay. I'll see you in an hour or so, then."

Bella nodded. "Thanks. I really appreciate you coming all the way out here to help."

Erin looked at Adrienne. She wanted to pat her on the shoulder, but restrained herself. "I'm happy to help out a friend."

Adrienne gave a stiff nod. She walked around to the passenger side of the car and climbed in.

CHAPTER 16

*A*drienne gave Erin directions for the quickest way to get to the Homestead from where they were. After Erin had driven a few miles, Adrienne sat back, her shoulders relaxing, resting her head back against the headrest.

"Thank you for coming to help," she said. "I didn't know what to do. Bella said that you would help, but… I know you are so busy. And it means you have to pay someone else to take your place at the bakery now. I'm sorry about that."

"No, it's okay. Don't worry about that. I'll just take one of her shifts another day. It won't cost me anything more."

"Except gas. And lost time."

Erin shrugged. "I think that if you can help others, you should," she said simply. "If more people did that… the world would be a kinder, gentler place."

"But most people don't see it that way. They want to know how to get ahead of everybody else. How to get more for themselves. There is so much greed and selfishness and corruption." Adrienne shook her head. "So much, Erin."

"I know," Erin agreed soberly. But there was good in the world too. She'd grown up in places where children had been prey, targeted by predators and downright evil people. And she'd lived in places where the children were ignored; they were just the means to a paycheck at the end of the month.

And she'd lived in places where she had been shown incredible kindness. There were still kind and generous people in the world, and she strove to be one of them.

But she wasn't sure how to tell all of that to Adrienne. Maybe the only way was by example.

"What's it like working at the Homestead?" she asked, rather than trying to put any of this into words. "I guess it's a pretty big place. Not like working in someone's home, not really."

"No, it's not like that. There are living quarters, but the whole place… it's run more like a hotel than a household. Lots of people, very busy all the time, trying to keep Mr. Fontainebleau and his family and favored staff happy. All the time." She nodded. "It's kind of stressful."

"I can imagine. Did you know Mr. Fontainebleau personally? Or just… you know… from a distance."

Adrienne looked out the passenger window, her face turned away from Erin. "Closer than I would like."

"Everybody I've talked to who knows him says he wasn't very likable. That he probably had a lot of enemies."

"I'm sure he did."

"You don't sound like you liked him very much."

"No. I work there. The best thing I can say about him is that he employed me. When a lot of people wouldn't. But that doesn't mean that he was good to me. I stayed as far away from him as I could, once I got to know what he was like."

"I'm glad he gave you a job, at least. That's what you needed right now, right?"

"When I came here, it wasn't just because he was offering a job. He offered residences for single moms with kids. I thought it would be so perfect, to be able to work here where my kids could stay. No commute. No worrying about finding childcare. Hope could look after Sarah while I was working, and I could still take breaks to feed her."

"But that didn't work out?"

"It isn't a good environment for kids. It wasn't at all like I had imagined it would be. I had to find somewhere else for them to stay, but I couldn't give up the job. I need the money. Even if you live as much as you can off the grid, you still need some money, raising kids, living in this world."

"Yeah, I can imagine."

"I don't know if you can."

Erin drove for a while without comment. Maybe she couldn't. Maybe she didn't really have any idea what it was like for a single mom like Adrienne, with all of those kids and no money and no partner. She thought she could understand, having been in desperate situations herself, and having been one of those kids from time to time, struggling to make it with a parent who didn't have the money or the time for children. But she hadn't been a mom. She hadn't experienced it from that perspective, with little people depending on her. Not just looking after herself but a handful of dependents.

"The entrance is up here," Adrienne pointed. "Just past the bend."

Erin slowed down as they made the wide turn. There was a split rail fence, all very old and rustic looking. Like something that might have been there a hundred years ago. There wasn't a guard booth or a security gate. No dogs or surveillance cameras. Erin was surprised. It was quite easy just to drive in. No one stopped them or demanded any identification.

Adrienne directed her to a parking lot to the side. She didn't get out immediately, and Erin waited, wondering if she were having second thoughts about returning to work. Maybe thinking of Hope and her tears, or the baby sleeping in the house at the Prost farm. It must be tough for her to keep going, to keep pushing herself despite what the children wanted. To be the parent who did what was best, even if it made them cry.

Adrienne put her hand on Erin's arm, as if stopping her from driving away. Erin waited for her next move.

"Your husband is the policeman."

"One of the policemen," Erin agreed. "But we're not married."

"Has he said anything to you about me?"

"No." Erin shook her head, wondering what Terry knew about Adrienne. Had she been caught shoplifting? Or just loitering or vagrant, the charges most often used as weapons against the homeless. "I didn't know that he even knew you. Or you knew him."

"Everybody knows who he is." Adrienne flushed a little and pushed a strand of blond hair back from her face. "Officer Handsome, with the dimple." She gave a little laugh.

Erin didn't know anyone else called Terry by that appellation, which she thought Vic had made up.

"He is a handsome man," she agreed.

"He hasn't said anything… about arresting me?"

Erin's brows went up and her mouth dropped open. "Arresting you? No, he hasn't said anything like that. Did he suggest that he might?"

"No. But I'm afraid he will. I'm afraid… they're getting closer."

"Why would he arrest you?"

"Well… here I am," Adrienne said, making a motion with her hands to indicate her place in the world or on the Homestead. "I'm pretty new here. I have access to all of the cleaning solutions and other chemicals. I don't like him. And then… he dies. They're saying it was murder. Poisoning. And who else could it be?"

"Well, literally anyone else who knew him, as I understand it," Erin pointed out. "And anyone who knew or had an idea where the Homestead is. They can just drive right in. So I don't know what would put you any higher on the list than anyone else."

Adrienne didn't explain why she might have more motive than someone else. "I didn't do it. I know that you've helped the police with other crimes. Figured them out before they could. And maybe… you could see that I didn't have anything to do with it. Maybe… spot who it really was. Figure it out before the cops decide to arrest me."

"Oh, I don't think so. This is a really big case. Fontainebleau had a lot of money and power and, from what I understand, there are a lot of suspects. They're not even sure it was murder at this point; they're still testing environmental contaminants and whether Fontainebleau was poisoned. It could have just… been accidental contamination. Nothing that anyone did to hurt him."

"I don't believe that. Someone killed him. But not me."

"How can you be sure?"

"Monsters like him don't just die. They have to be killed," Adrienne said flatly.

Erin was taken aback by this. "Well… that's not really proof of anything. You think he was killed."

"He was."

"But you don't know who did it?"

"No. It was quick... since I started, I noticed a lot of changes. The way he acted. The way he talked. How he looked. I just knew... something was happening. I wasn't surprised when he died."

"But it wasn't instantaneous," Erin looked for verification. "He'd probably been poisoned over a period of weeks or months. It wasn't just... you know, that night."

Adrienne nodded. "I know. Like I said... quick... but long enough to notice changes."

"And... you don't know who poisoned him?"

"I don't know." Adrienne looked away. "Like you said, he wasn't very well-liked. So... it could be a lot of people. But people that he would allow near his food... I don't know. I don't think many people had access to his food."

"Or drinks," Erin said. "Or toothbrush. I don't know how easy it would be to poison him from something he touched..."

"There are a lot of people in the house. But I think people would notice if someone was somewhere they weren't supposed to be, like in the kitchen or his bathroom."

Erin nodded, but she wasn't sure she agreed. So far, she hadn't seen much indication of there being security at the Homestead. But maybe it was just discreet and well-hidden.

"Do you think I could see inside?"

Adrienne's brows drew down. "Why?"

"I just want to see how things are set up. How easy it would be to get close enough access to poison him."

She wasn't supposed to be investigating the case. She wasn't supposed to have anything to do with it. But it wouldn't hurt just to look around, would it? She could reassure Adrienne that there wasn't any reason to suspect her over anyone else in the household, because they all had access. And she could satisfy her own curiosity about the way Fontainebleau lived. See where her pies had been served.

She should at least see where her pies had been served, shouldn't she?

CHAPTER 17

*I*t didn't really take any work to convince Adrienne to let Erin go along with her and have a look around the house. Maybe if Fontainebleau had still been alive, she would not have dared but, with Fontainebleau being dead, things were falling apart at the house. Adrienne wasn't really sure who her employer was anymore. The company? Fontainebleau's estate? His wife? But she was determined to keep working there and drawing a paycheck for as long as she could. Every penny she could put toward her children's expenses was important.

They entered through a side door, so there wasn't a great hall or a butler or a security desk like at a hotel or corporate building. There were just hallways and rooms for the household staff. People walked briskly like they had places to go and things to do. Erin was initially anxious, trying to put together a script to explain who she was and what she was doing in the house. But after the first few people just looked at her blankly and walked on by, she started to relax. Maybe she didn't need to give any explanation at all. People seemed to accept that if she was in those hall-ways or with Adrienne, she was supposed to be there. No one challenged her or asked for her identification.

"I do cleaning," Adrienne told Erin briefly by way of explanation. She tied on an apron and clocked in with a swipe card, then fetched a cart with a big garbage can and cleaning supplies on it and started making her rounds.

From the outside, Erin could tell that it was a big building. Lots of rooms. It took up lots of space. But she didn't really appreciate just how large it was until she started walking through the hallways. She felt like they had walked through miles of hallways before Adrienne had even begun her cleaning. Adrienne was not the only one providing maid service. There was no way one person could have kept on top of the cleaning, even working long hours every day of the week. Like a hotel, the Homestead needed a full complement of cleaning staff.

And then there were the other buildings that surrounded the main house. Garages and storage and living space like Adrienne had been given. They probably had to keep their own rooms clean, but the number of people who were needed to run the property was incredible. And all so that one man could show off his wealth. One man and his current wife, the children apparently all grown.

"You must feel like you've run a marathon by the end of the day!"

Adrienne nodded. "I get pretty sore and tired. And then I go home to the children!"

And that would take energy all its own. All of those children to corral and feed and get to bed. A baby to nurse, if Adrienne was still breastfeeding. Kids who all needed her individual attention and to roughhouse and cuddle and get all the physical attention children needed.

"It makes me tired just thinking about it. I think I'm tired when I get home from the bakery! And then I only have myself to prepare dinner for. And Officer Piper, if he's home. And the animals."

Adrienne looked amused as she started dusting the room they had landed in. "How many animals?"

"A very noisy cat. And a rabbit. And Terry's K9, a shepherd cross. And that's quite enough!"

"I guess so," Adrienne agreed. "The kids are always begging for an animal, but I don't need another mouth to feed. And it's hard enough to take care of kids without a roof over your head all the time. Animals..." She shook her head as she ran the duster over every surface. "I couldn't manage that too. Maybe someday, when we have our own place to settle down."

Would she ever actually achieve that? Erin knew how hard it was to scrape together enough money for the first and last month's rent to put down on an apartment. Even harder if you were looking for a house.

Adrienne opened the door to the next room and looked around to make sure it was empty before motioning Erin in.

"This is his private office. Or *was*, I guess. I don't know what they will do with it now." She shook her head. "I don't know how they're going to deal with anything. I guess there are ways to replace the president of a company, or the owner or shareholder. That's all legal stuff. But what do you do with a place like this? It wouldn't be dealt with under the company. Or would it, if the company owns it? Who decides what you do with a room now that he isn't in it anymore? I mean... you can't just install a new husband like you would a new president."

Erin pictured it and giggled. It was a funny thought. Interviewing a new husband, seeing if he would fit with the corporate and family climate. Dictating what he could use and what his duties would be. She followed Adrienne into the room and looked around.

As she had expected, lots of dark wood and heavy furniture. A vaguely nautical theme with ocean pictures on the wall and some complicated-looking measuring or navigating instruments on the desk and shelves. It was neat and tidy and didn't look like the place where he spent long hours working.

"Did he work out of this room a lot? Or just hang out here sometimes? Was he in some corporate office during the week?"

"He was here a lot. Liked to make other people come to him. Didn't even take meetings by video; he would tell people the internet coverage here was too spotty, even though he's got that satellite internet, which is really good. People had to come out here in person to meet with him. He would go to his other sites sometimes, but maybe... once or twice a week. And not all day."

She worked her way around the room, dusting and wiping and read-justing books or picture frames if they were not square. Fontainebleau's papers must be inside the desk drawers out of sight, or on his computer. Businesses needed paper. And it seemed like the bigger the business, the more paper it needed, even though people kept talking about achieving the paperless office one day.

The other door to the office opened, making Erin jump, and an unpleasant-looking woman looked down her long nose at Adrienne.

"When you are done in here, I need to see you in the solarium," she told Adrienne. "Since Mr. Fontainebleau is not here this week, we have some other areas that require more attention than his suite."

"Okay," Adrienne said. "I'll be just a couple of minutes."

The woman looked at Erin without blinking or smiling, then withdrew again without asking who she was or what she was doing there. Did she know? Or did she not care? Maybe with everything disrupted and Mr. Fontainebleau dead and gone, people didn't think there was any need for security.

Erin looked at Adrienne. "She's okay," Adrienne said with a shrug. "She looks sour, and she can put on a mean face for the boss when he needs a heavy, but she's pretty nice."

"Oh." Erin nodded. She had judged the woman just by her appearance without even realizing it. "What are the rest of the staff like here? Are they all pretty friendly? I've never worked for someone like this. I've worked as a caregiver for old folks. Families that really couldn't pay much, but needed someone to live in and look after grandma or grandpa. So I never worked anywhere with a staff."

"They're mostly friendly. But if something happened to upset Mr. Fontainebleau or one of the senior staff… then it sort of goes all the way down the line and everybody gets treated like it was their fault, even if it wasn't anything to do with them."

"Did that happen to you a lot?"

"Sometimes."

Maybe that was why Adrienne was afraid of being accused of the murder. Because the blame got passed down and down until it landed on the lowest person. And Adrienne was afraid that was her.

"And did you know the family? What are they like?"

"His wife is hardly ever here. They have some fancy place in New York or some such, and she mostly stays there. The ex-wife is probably here more often than the current one. There are a few kids. I could never keep straight which ones belonged to who, but they're all grown up, so it doesn't really matter. I don't think any of them could stand each other. This place is so big that they don't have to see each other if they decide to stay here for a few days."

That was kind of how Erin had imagined a place like this and a family like Fontainebleau's would work. Maybe she relied too much on TV movies, but she couldn't think of one where the rich and powerful business magnate was a good guy with a close, happy family. But she supposed that movies needed conflict and friction for the story to move forward. There wasn't really material for a movie in a family that got along together and was blissfully happy in their little chalet in the woods.

"Speak of the devil," Adrienne whispered, slowing and putting a hand out to stop Erin. Erin stopped and listened. There was a loud conversation going on somewhere close by. Too far away to hear the words clearly, but there was definitely a woman's strident voice having a conversation with one or two men. "That's Marcelle," Adrienne said. "The ex-wife. Her office is over here. Maybe... I'll dust the anteroom."

Erin was going to protest, but it was too late; Adrienne was already on the move. She opened a dark, heavy door and reached around the wall to flick on the light switch. It was empty and looked like a little reading room in a library. Books lined one wall, and there was a small antique writing desk with a reading lamp. The carpet was deep and luxurious. It was a quiet, peaceful place where Erin wouldn't have minded sitting to read through Clementine's voluminous family history books, working on her planner, or writing a letter to a friend. Except for the fact that there was an argument going on in the next room. There was a door on the opposite wall and, though it wasn't open, it allowed enough sound through to hear most of what was going on. This was where Marcelle's assistant sat while she was there, or the room that visitors were shown into before they were allowed to see Marcelle. Or maybe where an employee sat when he was kicked out of a meeting so that the board could discuss his next year's salary. A room between rooms.

Adrienne slipped into the room and started dusting shelves. Erin didn't feel comfortable going in, but Adrienne pulled her in and shut the door, leaving her cleaning cart in the hall outside. It would have been pretty crowded with the two of them and the cart all jammed in there. Adrienne resumed her dusting. Erin leaned toward the door, eavesdropping on the conversation in the next room. Not intentionally, really; they were pretty loud. She couldn't help but hear them.

"The company is half mine," Marcelle insisted. "And since Clive is dead, that makes it all mine. I want to see the financials and any deals in the works. I want to know what he's been doing and how to get my money out of it. He's been making stupid business decisions lately. Everyone said that he was losing it. Everything he touched turned bad."

"The company is not all yours," a man's voice responded, smooth and oily. "The company is only half yours, just like it has been for decades. Or rather, forty-five percent yours. The rest of the company shares are held by Mr. Fontainebleau's estate until his will has been probated and the shares distributed per his wishes. And he did not leave the shares to you."

"That's ridiculous. I put my family money into the company to rescue it and bring it back from the brink, and Clive always promised me that I would get it back. Who is running the company now? I am the largest shareholder, so I should be running it."

"You do not own a controlling interest," the oily man, who Erin deduced was a lawyer, informed Marcelle. "That is held by the estate. And until it is distributed, I am the executor and trustee, and—"

"You're running the business? You don't know anything about it! You haven't set a foot in a mine or factory in your life!"

"I am not running the day-to-day operations of the company. That is being handled by the surviving management. They know what they are doing. They know all of the ins and outs you and I don't know. And they'll continue to run the company and to select a new president and continue to do what they're doing."

"What about that merger? Clive kept talking about the merger. I don't want it to go ahead. He didn't know what he was doing lately. I know it was a bad deal."

"That is for the current management to figure out. They'll probably put it on hold until they have hired a new CEO. There's no need to rush into anything new. At a time like this, it is important to stop and take a breath—"

"I want to see the financials. Why aren't they on my desk?"

It was a different voice that answered now. "Management is reviewing the current financials. They had some questions and changes to be made, so I can't give them to anyone at this point—"

"I'm the largest shareholder. If I ask for them, you have to give them to me."

"I can give you last year's financials, if you like?"

"I don't want last year's financials. I've *seen* last year's financials. They were pretty bad, but not as bad as what I've been hearing from my inside sources. Are you cooking the books?"

"Mrs. Fontainebleau!" the accountant's voice was higher and more strident. "Are you accusing me of illegal business practices?"

"Somebody is sucking this company dry. And that's *my* money going down the crapper. My family money that I was supposed to get back with interest. It was always supposed to be an investment. I would get it back when it had doubled or tripled in size. Instead, this company is foundering, and it is because of idiots like you!"

CHAPTER 18

"*M*a'am!" the accountant protested, stung.

Adrienne was beside Erin, not moving. They were both engrossed in the discussion going on in the next room.

"Where is my money?" Marcelle demanded. "Are you telling me it's all there, my little nest egg, nicely grown in all of the time you've managed it?"

"I am not in the company management, ma'am. I only do what I am told. Keep the books. The decisions were made by Mr. Fontainebleau and the management of the company…"

"And my money is safe?"

He didn't say anything.

"And my money is all still there?" Marcelle pressed. "Sitting in the bank waiting for me?"

"Of course not. Money doesn't do any good sitting in a bank. Mr. Fontainebleau put it to work. To leverage other acquisitions and operations. New partnerships and joint ventures. He had an outstanding business mind—"

"He *used* to have an outstanding business mind," Marcelle said icily. "That's why I was comfortable leaving the money with him until now. But after what I've been hearing over the last year, I told him I wanted it out.

This company is hemorrhaging money, and I want mine out before it goes bankrupt!"

"Nothing can be done right now. Until Mr. Fontainebleau's shares are transferred to their new owners, and a new CEO has been elected, we really can't make any material changes to the way the company is operating—"

"Even though you know how badly it is doing."

There was no answer from either man.

"How bad is it?" Marcelle demanded. "Tell me it isn't as bad as I think."

"I'm sure that management will be able to stabilize—"

Marcelle gave a cry of rage, and there was a crash that made Adrienne and Erin jump.

"I will be coming back here with a court order," Marcelle told the men. "Do you understand that? I will be back, and I'll have an order that you can't touch my money until this is settled. I don't care if that means you have to fire every single employee and close the doors to every mine and factory. You need to cease operations until I get my money."

They heard a door open and then slam shut. There was a short silence.

"Continue as usual," the lawyer's oily voice said eventually. "She will not be able to get any kind of injunction against the company."

"Don't you think that we should at least—"

"No. Continue as usual. Let the management do what they like. As long as you are only taking orders, you don't have anything to worry about."

There was another period of silence.

"And if you *have* been cooking the books," the lawyer said eventually, "now would be an ideal time to disappear."

~

Adrienne looked at Erin, her eyes big and round. "Aren't you glad you're not her?"

"She must have sunk a lot of money into the company. It's huge, and she owns forty-five percent? Do you think she's going to lose it all?"

Adrienne shrugged. "What do I know about stuff like that? I just know I'm glad I'm not in her place." Adrienne ran her dust rag over a row of books. "I might not have anything, but at least I'm used to not having anything! For her to lose everything would be a lot worse. Although… she probably doesn't actually mean *everything.*"

"Yeah. Probably just that investment. It might hurt because it was her family money, but I doubt she'll lose her house or anything. She's had to have money that she's been living on since she gave Fontainebleau the investment if it happened years ago."

Adrienne worked her way around to the door they had come in, and they went back into the hallway to pick up Adrienne's cleaning cart and continue on the way. Erin was getting confused with all of the hallways and turns.

"Do you ever get lost here?"

"Not anymore. At least, not for long. But in the beginning, it was pretty confusing. It's not so bad if you're just going through the main guest areas; there are pretty obvious signs and routes. But when you're back here, going through the service hallways, you can get turned around."

"And… can anyone use them? I haven't seen much security."

"Well, anyone *could.*" Adrienne considered the matter. "But I haven't ever seen anyone but the household staff and service people back here. The family and guests, they stay out there. Why would they want to come through this rabbit's warren?"

"Maybe to hide. To get from one place to another without being seen. Get access to Mr. Fontainebleau's food or drink and then disappear before anyone knew they were here."

"Someone is more likely to see you back here than out there," Adrienne dismissed. "If I was trying to sneak around, I wouldn't use the service corridors. You could run into anyone at any time."

They reached the solarium, which was a large, open hall with floor-to-ceiling windows and lots of lush plants, with a small waterfall and pond. Erin saw fish darting through the water. She looked at the roughly broken rocks that formed the pond and other "natural" features and wondered whether they came out of the mines, and what trace minerals they might contain. Mercury? Lead? Other heavy metals that would be just as effective for poisoning Mr. Fontainebleau? Maybe his poisoner didn't have to worry about any special preparation. Just dip a cup of water out of the pond every day or two.

There were a few other workers there. The woman who had talked to Adrienne initially, asking her to come to the solarium, saw her and approached again. "Great, thank you for coming to help, Adrienne." She looked at Erin and, this time, decided not to ignore her. "And I'm sorry… are you new…?"

Erin started to say, "I'm just visiting," and was trying to figure out how to explain her presence as she snooped around the house, listening in on other peoples' conversations.

"She's my ride," Adrienne said. "My car broke down today and she drove all the way over to drop me off. She just came in to cool down for a few minutes and wanted to see the place." Adrienne made a gesture to indicate the grandeur around her. "She's not staying."

"It is quite the place," said the other woman. She then ignored Erin and proceeded to give Adrienne detailed instructions on the jobs she wanted to be done. Erin drifted away from them as they spoke, enjoying the lush surroundings in the solarium. Although it was humid from the water, the temperature was pleasant. Plenty of air conditioning to keep the glass-walled room from becoming a sauna in the Tennessee sun.

In a few minutes, the woman walked away to deal with her other duties.

"I guess I should show you back to your car," Adrienne said. She looked around. "You'll want to get back to Auntie Clem's. You've got your job and I've got mine."

"Sure." Erin would have demurred and said she could get back to her car on her own, but she was not sure she could do that. She would need someone else to walk her out, unless she went outside and walked around the perimeter until she found it. "Thanks. It was… nice to see what the place looks like."

"It's big, isn't it?" Adrienne shook her head. "Can you believe that it's all for one family? One man? I don't even know what they will do with it now that he's dead. Will anyone stay here? It's out in the middle of nowhere. Maybe the family, one of the kids?" She shrugged at her own question. "They'll probably sell it. I don't think anyone will want to live out here and look after everything."

They took a different door out of the solarium from the one they had entered through. There was what looked like a lecture hall, with a few workmen handling long coils of cable, calling each other as they worked on whatever they were wiring. Erin didn't know if it was for a sound system, network cabling, or something she hadn't even thought of.

"Pull that over here, and we'll—" The man who had just crawled out from under a table stopped talking when he saw Erin and Adrienne walking by. Erin froze.

It was Willie Andrews.

CHAPTER 19

$\mathcal{W}$illie's mouth was open and he looked as stunned to see Erin there as she was to see him. Erin walked toward him.

"What are you doing—"

He tried to wave her away before she could draw any attention to the two of them, but Erin shook her head. Willie had said that he had not been to the homestead. If he considered Fontainebleau to be an enemy, then what was he doing there, working for the guy? Or working for his estate or his company, since Fontainebleau was dead?

"Willie, what are you doing here?" Erin demanded. "What's going on?"

Willie eyed Adrienne as well, shaking his head at Erin again. "Erin, why don't you just go… back to Bald Eagle Falls. I'll talk to you tonight when I'm done. Explain all of this."

But Erin wasn't about to be put off. "I thought you couldn't stand Fontainebleau. So what are you doing here? Why would you be working for the guy?"

"I'm just doing a little subcontracting. It doesn't matter who it's for. Just a job that needs to be done. They pay their bills, so why should I care who it's for?"

"You said that he was a competitor. Why would you be working for a competitor?"

Willie opened his mouth to respond.

"And you said that you'd never been out to the Homestead, and now here you are! Why would you say that?"

"I didn't." Willie looked at Adrienne and opened his mouth, then changed course. "I didn't say that I'd never been here. I said that I'd seen pictures of it."

"You led me to believe you hadn't ever been here." Erin looked back and forth between him and Adrienne. They seemed to know each other, which was just one more confirmation that something was going on that Willie wasn't telling her about. "Are you going to tell me this is the first time you've ever been here?"

Adrienne raised one brow, interested in Willie's response to Erin's question. She wasn't going to let Willie get away with lying to Erin. She owed Erin for having driven her to work, leaving her own work at her own shop to do so. If there was a disagreement between Erin and Willie, Erin figured Adrienne would come down on her side.

"I've been here before," Willie growled. "Yes. Not that it is any of your business or anyone else's."

"Why would you tell me you hadn't been?"

"I didn't."

Erin rolled her eyes. She'd given Terry similar excuses for not having told him about Brandon Quayle. She'd said that she hadn't ever seen him around Bald Eagle Falls, implying that she had never seen him before at all. When she had not only seen him, but knew him way too well. Was Willie doing the same thing with her? Covering up because he and Fontainebleau were connected, not just by both being in mining, not just by a little subcontract cabling job that Willie had taken on, but because they knew each other?

"What was the real relationship between you and Fontainebleau? Did you know each other? I mean really know each other?"

Willie stood there looking at her. The other men he was working with had stopped what they were doing and were watching and waiting.

"Erin, I'll talk to you about this later. Right now... I have work to do here. You're holding me up."

"Are you setting up a computer network?" Erin looked around at the cables, hoping she was at least close and didn't sound like a complete idiot.

"Just some electrical." He waved off the question as if he couldn't be bothered to go into more details. "Which you already know that I do, since you asked me to help the crew at Mrs. Peach's house. But if I'm going to get it done today, I need to get back to it. So…"

"Fine." Maybe he would tell her more when she was back at home and no one was there to overhear their conversation. But she suspected he didn't intend to tell her anything. At least, nothing that got close to the truth. "I'll talk to you later, then."

Willie nodded. Erin started walking down the hall again, in the direction they had been going when she had spotted him. Adrienne pushed her cart a couple of inches, her eyes on Willie.

"You okay?" Willie asked her.

Adrienne nodded and started again to walk with Erin. They held eye contact for too long.

Not only did Willie have something to do with Fontainebleau that he wasn't talking about, but he knew Adrienne and something to do with her as well. They'd both been around Bald Eagle Falls; there was no reason they couldn't know each other. One of Adrienne's previous camps had been close to one of Willie's mining claims. Maybe they had run into each other there. Maybe he'd told her kids to stay away from the caves or had helped out when one of them got into trouble. He certainly didn't seem confrontational with Adrienne, like they'd been at odds before. Instead, he appeared to be worried about her.

And maybe he should be. Maybe Erin should be too. Adrienne was pretty sure that they were going to accuse her of Mr. Fontainebleau's murder. There was a reason for that. And maybe Willie knew what it was.

Erin and Adrienne walked together without saying anything for a few minutes. Adrienne didn't ask Erin how she knew Willie, and Erin didn't ask Adrienne about how well she knew him and how often he'd been around the house before Fontainebleau's death.

They went through a door, and Erin found herself stepping back out of the building again, to find her yellow bug parked and waiting for her. "Oh! I didn't even know this was the way out." Erin laughed.

"Sometimes what you're looking for is right in front of you."

Erin shook her head. "Yeah. You never know."

"Thanks again for helping me out. I really appreciate it."

"Of course. And… let me know if you need a drive home at the end of the day."

"Oh, I couldn't expect you to come all the way out here again. If Bella doesn't have her car back, I'll stay here overnight. There's a room for me if I need it."

"Still…" Adrienne's place was with her children, not stranded out there on the big property like she was a prisoner there.

"It's fine," Adrienne assured her. "I'll be fine. It will work out okay."

Erin put her hand on Adrienne's arm for a moment. She wasn't to the point where she felt comfortable hugging her, but she wanted some kind of physical contact to show her feelings toward the woman. To show that they were a part of a sisterhood, even if they were living very different lives.

Adrienne pulled away, nodding. "You'd better get going, then. You know the way back out?"

"Just keep taking the bigger roads until I'm out to the highway."

Adrienne nodded. "Pretty much, yeah."

Erin went to the driver's side of the car and let herself in. Adrienne stood by, waiting for her to leave. Erin rolled down the windows while she waited for the vehicle to cool. Another woman similar in age to Adrienne came out the door and saw her standing there.

"Oh, Adrienne! Hi!" She pulled out a cigarette and lit it quickly. "Just gotta get my nicotine hit while I can. How is everything?"

Adrienne shrugged. "It's been a day. My friend's car broke down this morning so I couldn't get in. Miss Erin there drove me." Adrienne nodded toward her.

"Well, you're lucky!" The other woman gave Erin a breezy wave with the hand that held the cigarette. "They'd dock you if you didn't show up."

"Yeah. I need all the money I can get."

"How are the kids?"

"Fine. Full of energy."

"I wish they were still here. They're so much fun. And Hope? How is she?"

"She'll be fine."

The woman nodded. "Kids are flexible. Isn't that what they say? They bounce back fast."

CHAPTER 20

$\mathcal{I}$t felt so good just to sit and cuddle with Terry on the couch and relax with him. It seemed like they had been missing each other all week and this was the first time they'd actually had to sit down together and have a conversation. They needed to relax together for a while before they could talk about anything meaningful, and they hadn't been able to do that, trying to fit hello and goodbye in between all of the shifts.

Erin gave Terry the highlights of the day, going to get Adrienne and taking her to the Homestead.

"And then you brought Bella into town?" Terry asked. "Did her car get fixed so she had a way to get back out to the Prost farm?"

"No, but Cindy's was fixed, so Bella grabbed it and drove it back to the farm. And then, I assume, went out to the Homestead to get Adrienne so that she could be together with her kids."

"It's nice of them to help her."

"Yeah, it is. I'm glad she's got someone to help them out. It would be really hard to have all of those kids and no home and no way to go out and get a job. I don't know if I could face that kind of hardship."

"Well, you face what you have to. You went through rough patches too."

"Yeah... but I never had kids to look after. I can't imagine doing all of that with kids to look after too. And not just one or two kids. I think she's got… five? Six?"

He laughed. "That's a lot of kids, alright. And all of them in the Prost house? That wasn't a very big farmhouse, if I remember correctly. How many bedrooms does it have?"

"I don't remember. Two or three. And they are pretty small. Maybe Cindy and Bella in one room, and Adrienne and Hope and the baby in another, and the rest of the kids in another. Or in the living room on the floor and couch. It's not a mansion like Fontainebleau's place out there."

"That place is really something, isn't it?"

"Wow." Erin sipped her tea and put it back down on the table. "Yeah, it's pretty amazing. I kept forgetting that no, it's not a hotel or convention center. It's actually one person's home. It's huge."

"Did you see the kitchen?"

"No, I didn't get that far. A few offices or meeting rooms, the solarium. And miles and miles of hallways."

"It's at least twice the size of Auntie Clem's. And I don't mean of the kitchen of Auntie Clem's. I mean twice the size of the entire place. It's very large and modern, with lots of ovens and other appliances that I don't even know the names of or what they are for."

"Oh, I wish I'd seen it. I didn't even think to ask."

"Maybe another time. You can volunteer to drive Adrienne out there again. See if she'll take you on a tour of the kitchen. Or maybe they'll ask you to cater the desserts for the funeral, and you can drive out there and take them to the kitchen. Or tell them that you'll bake them on site."

"Oh, wouldn't that be fun." Erin laughed. "I'd love to see it, but I'm not sure I'd want to use someone's kitchen other than my own for a big job like that. I wouldn't know where anything was or the eccentricities of their ovens. I'd screw something up and then I'd be in trouble."

"I'm sure you would do just fine. I've seen you at work."

"Hmm." Erin decided to take the compliment, but she wasn't sure Terry was right. He tended to see her abilities in the best light, and she often felt the need to correct him and point out the realities of the situation—which tended to just make him tense about the whole thing. She needed to take his compliments in the spirit in which they were given. "You don't think that Adrienne did it, though?"

Terry raised his brows at the change in subject. "Did what?"

527

"Poisoned Fontainebleau. She says that she's afraid she's going to be arrested for it, and she isn't the one who did it."

"Why were you talking to her about that?"

"She brought it up. I didn't. She's afraid. Especially about her kids and what would happen if she was arrested."

"Well, I don't think she needs to be worrying about that yet."

Erin leaned against Terry's shoulder and listened to his breathing. "Yet?"

"She is not in imminent danger of being arrested. We don't even know for sure that he *was* poisoned yet. Or that it was at the hand of a murderer rather than just an accidental environmental exposure."

"So you don't think that it was actually murder?"

"A determination hasn't been made yet. The medical examiner's office has done their preliminary work, but they need all of the lab tests to be interpreted before they can say for sure that it was intentional poisoning."

"Does that mean you think it was or wasn't?"

"It just means we have to wait. And while we're waiting… we have to investigate as if it were murder. We don't want evidence to be missed because of sloppiness or waiting around."

"His ex-wife thinks he was running the company into the ground, and she owns forty-five percent of it. That's a good motive."

Terry looked down at her. "Yes," he agreed, sounding amused. "That's a good motive. But I don't need you investigating over there. You need to stay out of the way and leave that to law enforcement."

"Oh, I am. I just overheard something when I was over there. And I didn't go over there to investigate," she reminded him, just in case he'd forgotten that part. "I was just helping out a friend."

"And why does she think he was running the company into the ground? He's always been a shrewd businessman."

"She said he's been making all kinds of bad decisions lately. That everything he touches turns into lead instead of gold. Like in that myth."

"The Midas touch."

"Right. Except every time he touched something lately, he made it fail."

"So his behavior has changed lately."

"Yes. She was afraid he was going to bankrupt the company, so she wanted her money out—"

"Don't you think it was probably the mercury that affected his cognitive ability and decision-making?" Terry suggested.

"Oh. Well, yes, that makes perfect sense. It *must* have been the mercury," Erin realized.

"It doesn't exactly make sense for her to poison him, causing him health and cognitive issues if she wanted him to continue to handle her investment properly, does it?"

"Uh... right." Erin had to admit that made sense. It wouldn't be smart of Marcelle to start poisoning her ex-husband while he was still managing her money. If she'd wanted him out of the way, it would make more sense to kill him quickly—being hit by a car, or in an industrial accident—so that her investment didn't lose any value. So maybe she *wasn't* the best suspect in the murder.

But there were still lots of other suspects.

Willie, among others, had said that Fontainebleau was not well-liked and there would be no shortage of suspects.

Willie among them.

CHAPTER 21

*W*ithout meaning to, Erin turned her head to look toward the back of the house, even though she couldn't see the backyard or parking pad from where she was sitting in the living room. Terry looked down at her.

"What?"

"Oh, nothing. I was just wondering if Willie is over. With Vic."

"I don't know. Why? What's up with Willie?"

Erin hesitated, not knowing whether she should say anything or not. She didn't want to get Willie in trouble, and she knew that Terry was always quick to suspect him of being involved in any crime he investigated in Bald Eagle Falls.

"Nothing. I just wanted to talk to him. Maybe I'll pop over there."

Terry raised an eyebrow, maybe doubting that she was being completely open and honest with him.

Which was fair, since she wasn't. But she didn't like it when he saw through her.

"He was over at the Homestead today," Erin admitted. "I didn't get a chance to talk to him while he was over there. We were both busy, but I wanted to talk to him tonight."

"What was he doing over at the Homestead?" Terry sat up straighter, scowling. "He said that he hadn't been there."

Erin didn't correct him. Willie hadn't lied, exactly, but he'd certainly misled them. She shrugged. "He was doing some kind of electrical. He didn't say what it was, and I guess it's none of my business exactly what he was doing. Wiring a conference room."

"Well, that's interesting, isn't it? Why don't you see if he is over there? Maybe he would like to come in for a beer."

Erin pushed herself up from the couch. She did want to see if Willie was there and to talk to him, but she didn't want there to be any trouble. "I'll see if he's there, but…"

"Ask him in for a beer. If he doesn't want to come, he won't come."

"I just don't want a big thing. The two of you don't always… see eye to eye."

"It's not an interrogation," Terry assured her. "I'll mind my manners."

Erin still wasn't so sure. But she walked into the kitchen so that she could see out the back window. Willie's truck was on the gravel pad. She texted Vic rather than Willie.

You guys want to come over for a drink?

It was a few minutes before Vic texted back an emoji confirming that they were, in fact, interested. Erin went to the fridge to get out the cold drinks and put on the tea kettle for herself. In a few minutes, she saw Willie and Vic both crossing the backyard. Vic was in first, with a cheery greeting. She grabbed one of the bottles of beer and handed another to Willie.

Willie was slower, bringing up the rear. He looked at Erin and probably read in her face that Terry already knew about his being over at the Homestead. He shook his head, looking resigned. He grabbed another beer and walked into the living room to give it to Terry and find a seat. Soon, they were all sitting around the room, looking as relaxed as possible. Vic was the only one who didn't seem to realize that there was an agenda. She made casual small talk while Terry watched Willie as if waiting for him to make a move.

Vic's chatter eventually tapered off and she looked at Terry and Willie. "What? Am I missing something here?"

Willie took her hand and squeezed it. "Erin and Terry weren't just interested in a drink."

"Well… no. I thought we'd have a visit too. It's a nice day. The temperature is dropping. We should be sitting out back instead of cooped up in here."

"Erin probably wants to follow up on a discussion we had… or didn't have… at the Fontainebleau Homestead this morning."

"What? What discussion?" Vic looked at Willie. "What were you doing over there?"

"I had a small electrical job."

Vic frowned at that, then shrugged. "Okay, then. You had an electrical job. They called Erin to do the catering and you to do some electrical. They're hiring out small locals. That's nice."

"And it wasn't the first time you'd been out there," Erin deduced.

"No. I've been there before," Willie admitted.

Terry took a long drink of his beer. "So you had a prior relationship with Fontainebleau. Even though you told me that you'd never been out there before."

"I didn't say I hadn't been out there."

"You said that you and Fontainebleau were competitors. And that you hadn't been to his place; you'd only seen pictures of it."

"I said I'd seen pictures of it. And I have."

"*And* you've been out there."

"Sure."

"How many times?"

"I haven't kept track. A few times."

"To do wiring jobs."

"I've done various jobs over there."

"I would think they would already have pretty good electrical at a place like that. And that they would already have their own guy. A live-in handyman or a general contractor they called on. A property manager."

"Or maybe they're interested in hiring small local labor. More economical and gives the local economy a bit of a boost."

"You and I both know Fontainebleau couldn't have cared less about helping the little guy in Bald Eagle Falls get ahead."

Willie chuckled. He pointed his beer bottle at Terry to acknowledge this point.

"So why not stop with the games," Terry said, "and talk about this like two adults who get what's going on. Why would you do work for someone you considered a competitor?"

"Just because we were competitors in the mining business, that doesn't mean I couldn't milk money out of him for something else. And why wouldn't I? He'd be just as happy to pick my pocket, so why not?"

"You're a savvy businessman. And you're not known for being particularly tolerant of anyone you feel is interfering with your business. That tells me there's more to it than just helping out with some small jobs that needed to be done at the Homestead."

"You have a pretty smart boyfriend, Erin." Willie brought Erin back in on the conversation, even though she was trying to stay out of it. It might be her fault that Terry knew about Willie's latest business activities, but she didn't want Willie to think that she was against him or informing on him.

She was inclined to agree with Terry. She didn't think Willie was doing work at the Homestead because it was a way to get money out of Fontainebleau, someone trying to take money from him. The little bit of money that he would get for something like that was not enough to be a motivator.

Willie tipped his beer up again and then sighed. "I guess I should have known that there are too many people in and out of that monstrosity for me to stay below the radar. I wasn't expecting Erin to show up there. But it could just as easily have been you." He nodded at Terry. "I knew it wasn't secure."

"It doesn't seem like there's any security over there," Erin said, shaking her head. "I don't understand how someone as rich as Fontainebleau and with that many enemies could live like that. Didn't he know that he was a target?"

"There is a lot of security in just being someplace as remote as the Homestead," Terry said. "That will deter ninety-nine percent of outsiders. And they'll assume that he has a lot of security. Most people won't chance it."

"And there is more than you think," Willie said. "Just because you can't see the security, that doesn't mean it isn't there."

Erin thought about what she had seen and shook her head. "Okay. Maybe there is. I didn't see a single guard, though; they don't check identification. Anyone can just walk in there. Maybe they have some electronic surveillance, but I didn't see any cameras."

"Cameras can be so small now that you won't see them. You don't know what security measures you trip when driving into the property because you don't see anything. But they don't need a guard in a booth at a security gate to get your license plate number and pictures of everyone in the car as soon as you cross the property line. By the time you get to the house, security knows exactly who you are. They don't have any reason to worry about the town baker wandering in with a maid. They're better off focusing on people who might still have evil designs against the Fontainebleaus even though the figurehead has been removed."

"So what were *you* doing there and how do you know anything about their security system?" Terry asked.

"I know the security system because I designed parts of it."

Terry gave him a half-smile. "Then why isn't it secure?"

"Because they weren't looking for a completely secure system. They don't care about something that is airtight. They just wanted something… casual. An early-warning system if some known enemy of the company or Fontainebleau himself arrived intent on committing harm. The thing about a very tight security system is that it keeps the protectee in a cage. And Fontainebleau knew that. He wanted to be free to roam without being the subject of scrutiny. To come and go on his own property as if he were free, the lord of the manor."

Erin looked at the burglar alarm panel at the front door. She appreciated that it helped to keep her safe, especially on nights when Terry might be on shift. But she hated having to disarm and rearm it all the time. She hated the feeling of being forced to live like an animal in a cage, as Willie had suggested. She could understand why someone like Fontainebleau would want to spend his money in a way that kept him safer, yet still free. So that he didn't have to deal with the bars that she did.

"And when you were there today, was it to upgrade the security system? To close up the holes that might have led to Fontainebleau being poisoned?" Terry suggested.

"No. In fact, not." Willie let the silence draw out for some time before going on. "My reason for being there today, aside from the stated purpose of the wiring I was doing, was to remove listening devices that had been previously installed."

CHAPTER 22

*H*e knew that he was stringing them along and had played his cards right. Willie sat there looking pleased with himself, enjoying their stunned expressions.

"Someone was bugging Fontainebleau's house?" Vic demanded.

Willie nodded. His face remained calm and collected, as if it should not have surprised anyone that Fontainebleau had been under surveillance. And maybe they shouldn't have been surprised by it, since they had just finished discussing the fact that the Homestead was not secure, and Fontainebleau had known that. Had made it a conscious choice.

"Who was bugging the house, and how did you find out about it?" Terry asked.

Willie shrugged. "Like I said, I designed some of the security measures."

"So you knew where the weaknesses were. Kept your eyes out for them. Maybe swept the place for bugs once every week or two. Or when you heard that Fontainebleau had died."

Willie shrugged again.

"Or," Erin said slowly, thinking it through, "you're the one who put the bugs there in the first place."

"Erin!" Vic reprimanded, sounding shocked.

Willie chuckled. At the offended expression on Vic's face, it grew into a belly laugh. It was a couple of minutes before he managed to rein in his laughter, taking another swallow of his beer and wiping at the corners of his eyes.

"No need to be offended for my sake, Vicky. Erin hit the nail on the head."

"What?" Vic demanded.

Both she and Terry looked stunned by this.

Willie nodded slowly. "Yes. I'm the one who placed the listening devices initially. So no need to spot the holes in the security system or sweep for bugs to find them. I already knew they were there. And that it was time to pull them down. Since they were not needed anymore."

"You were bugging Fontainebleau," Terry said.

"Yes."

"Why?"

"They were competitors," Erin said. "He wanted to know what Fontainebleau was up to. Industrial espionage."

"Of course," Willie agreed.

"Why would Fontainebleau hire you to work on his security system in the first place if you were competitors?" Erin asked. "Isn't that like asking the wolf to babysit the sheep?"

"I wasn't big enough to be a concern to him. He could take all of my business easily enough. Wipe me out. But I couldn't do the same to him. If we fight over a mining claim, it's my livelihood. But it's just another in a long list for him. Maybe not even a mine that he'll end up working in the next ten years. Or twenty. He just wants it in his back pocket for when he decides to exploit another area. And to have a legal way to keep little guys like me from trespassing on what he sees as his mountain. As far as he's concerned—was concerned—the whole mountain was already his. He was just wiping out some irritating little fleas."

"So he would hire you to do electrical or security work, but didn't care that you were one of those fleas?"

"No."

They all sat in silence for some time, absorbing this.

"What did you find out from bugging him?" Terry asked. "I'm sure there must be things that are relevant to the investigation of his death."

"Not very much," Willie said. "The guy was off his rocker, but I'm sure you'll find that out from other people. He was making business decisions that didn't make any sense. But his managers did what he said because they thought he was a genius. Everything had always worked out before, and they didn't seem to get that things had changed."

"And you must have heard the reactions of some of the people around him to the way he was behaving."

"They tended not to speak up around him, and the locations I had listening devices were the areas where he would tend to be conducting business. So, no, I didn't hear a lot of the doubts or concerns that must have been expressed."

"And you didn't hear anyone plotting his murder?" Vic teased.

"At this point, if he was already making rash decisions, then someone was already poisoning him," Terry said. "Or he was already being poisoned by something in his environment. Anyone planning to kill him once he had already been poisoned was late to the party. They probably didn't have time to put anything in motion."

"They could have," Erin pointed out. "They could have picked a faster-acting poison. Cyanide or belladonna. Something that would kill him right away instead of taking weeks."

Terry shrugged. "Possible, but I think that's unlikely."

"Look at how many different ways they tried to kill Rasputin before they succeeded," Erin pointed out. "I mean, the guy was poisoned multiple times, stabbed, shot, drowned…"

"It happens," Terry admitted. "Especially with longer-acting poisons. People get impatient and decide to shortcut the process."

"I didn't hear anyone plotting to kill him," Willie said, shaking his head. "People upset with him, yes. But no murder plots."

"I would hope that if things reached that point, you would call the police department and let us know what was going on," Terry suggested.

Willie tapped a finger on the side of the beer bottle he was holding. "I can't say what I would have done in different circumstances, since that's not what happened."

"Do you have a suspect?" Erin asked him. "Someone that you think might have done it?"

"I don't know anything about anyone poisoning him."

"But who do you *think* might have done it? Who had motive? Who was really likely to follow through?"

"I don't know."

She studied his face for some sign that he did have a suspect in mind. Willie was good at hiding his thoughts. "What happened to Hope?"

He wasn't *that* good. Willie betrayed surprise at the question. He blinked and looked away from Erin, focused on some distant object that wasn't visible to her.

"What do you mean, what happened to Hope? Who is Hope?"

"Adrienne's little girl. Or her biggest girl, to be more exact."

He shook his head slowly. "I don't know what you might have heard…"

"Adrienne had planned to have all of the kids there with her to start with. That's why she took the job. Because it included a room or a couple of rooms so she could board there with her kids. But something happened that made her decide it wasn't a good place for the kids, so she had to move them to the Prost farm. Where she can't be with them all the time. And Hope has been acting… I don't know. Clingy. Traumatized. And one of the other staff members asked how she was. Talked about how kids are flexible and bounce back. So… what happened to her?"

There was a long silence. Vic's expression was concerned. Willie's and Terry's faces were more carefully masked.

Erin supposed it wasn't any of her business what had happened to Hope or what Willie knew about it. But she felt bad for Adrienne and whatever she was going through. She had enough to deal with without whatever had been going on at Fontainebleau's house. And little Hope deserved to be treated like a person who had been through a trauma, not just written off as a little child who would be fine if no one acknowledged what had happened to her.

"I wasn't there," Willie said eventually. "And I never picked anything up on my bugs about it. That's something you'll have to take up with Adrienne."

"But you know," Terry said, "or you've got a pretty good idea."

"I don't have any evidence. I'm not a witness. I can only tell you that there have been rumors and whispers. And I'm not the kind of person a young woman would confide in. Someone who knows her better will need to get the story out of her," he told Erin, meeting her eyes. "Or someone with some expertise, who she would trust." He looked at Terry. "I'm not the type that inspires confidences."

"She has no reason to trust me," Terry said, shaking his head. "Her type rarely trusts officials for anything. She lives outside the law; she doesn't rely on it."

"And she thinks you're going to arrest her," Erin said.

He nodded and didn't say whether she was on his list or not. Maybe when he'd gathered enough evidence…

"I'll try to talk to her another time," Erin said finally. "See if I can get anything from her, help her out at all. But she's still pretty wary of me too. Maybe Adele can talk to her. Or Bella."

"I'm sure they probably already have," Vic contributed.

But would either of them urge Adrienne to go to the authorities? Or to seek professional help for her little girl? Erin thought there was a good possibility that Bella would. It was good that she and her mother were helping Adrienne out. Hopefully, they had a good enough relationship that Bella would be able to help them in some way.

CHAPTER 23

*W*illie shifted in his seat, stretching his muscles and arching his back. He massaged his shoulders. "Must be a weather system coming in," he groaned. "I don't think this is just from a wiring job. I don't usually stiffen up this much from something like that. Plenty of stretching and pulling, but no heavy lifting. It doesn't usually bother me."

"I think they were predicting rain," Vic agreed. "Hey Erin, this is the time to break out your glass and see if it says what kind of weather to expect."

"My glass?" Erin repeated.

"Your barometer. It should be showing a change in pressure."

"Oh, that!"

"Your barometer?" Willie asked. "When did you get a barometer?"

Erin didn't even have an outdoor thermometer to tell her the temperature outside, so she could understand Willie being surprised that she had suddenly acquired a barometer.

"It's not actually mine," she said. "It was a mistake. I'm trying to figure out who it belongs to."

"It sounds like there's a story there," Terry shook his head. "You accidentally got someone else's barometer?"

"Well, yes!" Erin laughed. "When I got the waffle iron for the bakery, you know, the new one that I've been waiting for, then it came in three boxes. Only, two of them were the waffle iron parts and manual, and one was not. It was… a barometer. We don't know how the mix-up happened. Someone must have packed the boxes wrong."

"Someone sent you a barometer."

"Yes… or no. I don't think that someone sent it to me. I think that was a mistake. They packed the deliveries wrong. The barometer was obviously to go to someone else, because it doesn't have anything to do with waffle making. But there was no packing slip or waybill, so I'm having a hard time figuring out who it was supposed to have gone to. And I'm not sure if calling the company will do any good. Some fulfillment company picked the wrong item or combined two orders. Whoever was supposed to get the barometer will probably have to order a new one."

"So are you going to keep it?" Vic asked.

"I don't know. I guess I'll call the company if I can't figure something out. Find out if they can trace who it was supposed to go to."

"You brought it home, right? We should see if it works."

"I shouldn't use it if it isn't mine…"

"You're not playing with it. You're just checking to see if it shows a pressure drop. The pressure is going to go up and down without you doing anything. You don't even have to touch it to see if the pointers are pointing in different directions than before. You can just open the box and have a peek."

Erin could see that Vic wasn't going to give up on it. For some reason, she was eager to look at the barometric pressure to see how it had changed. Was that what Willie could feel in his joints? Or had something else affected them?

She rolled her eyes. "Fine. I'll go get it and we can check, but we're not playing with it."

"There's nothing to play with. We're just going to look at the dials."

Erin went to her room, where she had stowed the box containing the barometer with some other boxes she had to deal with. Parts being returned. Some genealogical research that Naomi had thought Erin would find interesting if she could connect it up with Clementine's research. But Erin hadn't gotten around to searching for that part of the family yet. One day she would do it. Maybe she would have some time tomorrow, if the day stayed quiet.

She returned to the living room and reached to hand the box to Vic. Terry motioned for her to stop.

"Hold on. You got this delivery when?"

"Yesterday."

"And it didn't have any markings on it? No delivery address?"

"It had my address on it," Erin said, shaking her head. "And my name."

"And the name of the waffle iron company."

"No. Not the name of The Kitchen Crew. There wasn't any sender identification on it that I could see. That's why I don't know exactly how to handle it. If it was from the same company, then it should have their label and return address on it."

"So maybe it's another delivery from your secret admirer.'"

Erin had still been reaching to hand it to Vic, but now she pulled back. "Really? Why would my secret admirer send me a barometer?"

"Why did he send you newspaper clippings? We're still trying to figure out what's going on in his mind. He hasn't made a whole lot of sense up until now."

"Let me see," Vic begged, even more interested in looking at the barometer now that there was some question about where it had originated.

Erin cleared a space on the coffee table and put the box down. She opened the flaps of the box so that they could see inside. They all gazed at the instrument, brass and glass and dark wood, like it might explain itself. It looked exactly as it had the last time Erin had looked at it. How could it have changed?

But now, it gave Erin a knot in her stomach to look at it. It had been interesting before but not portentous. Now she wasn't sure what it meant, but she didn't think she would be able to look at it the same way again.

"It didn't change," Vic observed with disappointment. "It's still pointing at Fair. And the other pointers haven't changed either, as far as I can tell."

"It's just something interesting to put on your wall," Terry said. "There are a lot of pieces of junk like that. Just an executive toy. Something to attract comments. 'Oh, my grandfather used to have something like that.' You know how people are."

Erin nodded. She should be disappointed, but she wasn't. It wasn't hers anyway. She'd known that from the start.

"Like Fontainebleau had," Willie said.

"What?" Erin looked at him, not understanding.

Willie pointed to the barometer. "Fontainebleau had one in his office. You saw his place. Lots of nautical-themed nonsense. Not like he was ever on a ship or would need a barometer. Or a sextant or anything else he had in his office."

Erin tried to envision his office. There had been a number of nautical-themed items, as Willie said. But she couldn't remember a barometer. And she thought she would have noticed one, after having received one in a delivery the day before. It would have jumped right out at her. She shook her head. "I don't remember seeing one. Where was it in the room?"

It wasn't like she had searched his office. It could have been on a wall that was out of sight from the door she'd been standing in.

"What if this *is* the one in Fontainebleau's office?" Terry asked. "I remember seeing one there too. One that was... pretty similar to this one."

"But how would the restaurant supply company have ended up with it?" Erin asked, shaking her head. That didn't make any sense at all. From Fontainebleau's office to the restaurant supply company, then mispackaged and sent to Erin.

"Why would the restaurant company send you a barometer?" Terry asked, pointing out the illogic. "You just think it was from them because you got it at the same time as the waffle iron packages. Right?"

"No, it was one of three boxes. I had to sign for all three from the courier company."

"That doesn't mean they were all one delivery. Just that the total number of boxes was three. If they weren't labeled the same way, they didn't all come from the same sender. And where would it have come from? Who has been sending you strange gifts by courier lately?"

"My secret admirer."

He nodded his agreement.

"Really? You think that my secret admirer sent me a barometer?"

"Right."

"Mr. Fontainebleau's barometer?"

"I don't know. But he sent you the clippings about Fontainebleau, didn't he?"

"Well, yes. At least, we think that everything came from him. It's always possible that… they came from two different sources."

"What all did you get?" Willie asked, not having heard the details before this. Or maybe they just hadn't been of any interest before. Now that they were potentially connected to Fontainebleau's death, it was a different matter.

"Um, a small bouquet of flowers. With a note saying that I was sweet. And then…" Erin's face heated. "Lingerie. No note. Then I got an envelope in the mail here. Not at Auntie Clem's. And it was articles about Mr. Fontainebleau when he was younger. Like, real newspapers from decades ago."

"And you don't know where they came from?"

"I thought someone might have taken them from the library or historical society, but they said no, nothing was missing from their collections."

"Then maybe it came from Fontainebleau's house. Just like the barometer."

"Are you saying that it came from someone else? Not the secret admirer?"

Willie shrugged. "It's possible, isn't it?"

"I… guess so."

"The first two deliveries are personal, romantic type gifts. The other two are directly tied to Fontainebleau and are not personal or romantic in any way."

Erin thought that the barometer might be argued to be somewhat personal. Maybe significant of travel or a romantic getaway. But she let it pass. Willie had a good point.

Terry was nodding slowly. "It's possible. But it would be awfully coincidental to suddenly have two separate people sending her anonymous deliveries at the same time. Unconnected? There must be some kind of connection. I mean, you haven't gotten any other deliveries like that in the time that you've lived in Bald Eagle Falls, have you?"

"No. Nothing else."

"I'll need to take the barometer. We'll want to dust it for fingerprints. See if there is any sign that it came from Fontainebleau's office. His assistant or someone at the Homestead should be able to tell us if it was his. Or if his is missing."

"It could be his assistant. She's the one who reached out to you about catering the party, isn't she?" Vic asked.

"Yes." Erin's head was whirling. "I really don't understand how it is all connected."

"You've become known as an amateur detective. Maybe she expects you to put all the clues together to solve Fontainebleau's murder. Maybe... the romantic presents mean that it's something to do with his wife or a romantic partner. And the clippings, obviously, are connected and might have something in there to lead you to the killer or his motive. And then the barometer is meant to..." Vic shook her head, trying to find something that fit. "Tell you they're fair. I don't know. I don't know what the barometer means. It's a captain. It's someone who travels. It's a fair-weather friend. The barometer doesn't work, so maybe that means..."

"The barometer doesn't work," Willie said suddenly.

Erin nodded. "Right...?"

"Do you have any idea how an old barometer operates?"

Erin shook her head. "No."

"Like an old thermometer... some of them use mercury."

CHAPTER 24

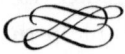

They all considered this, staring down at the barometer.

"There wouldn't be enough mercury in there to kill a person, would there?" Erin asked the obvious. "And you wouldn't be able to just put straight mercury in someone's food. You'd have to… do something with it, wouldn't you?"

Terry nodded slowly. "I would think you would notice little silver balls of liquid rolling around in your food. I don't know if eating elemental mercury would have the same effect as methyl mercury in your food. I assume you'd want to process it somehow if you were going to feed it to someone. But… if you have elemental mercury to start with, I imagine you could find out on the internet how to process it into something you could sprinkle into someone's food without it being detected. And there are enough people in his company with knowledge of chemistry who probably wouldn't need to look it up."

"Who would even know that there could be mercury in a barometer? I didn't know that. I didn't even know what a barometer was until this thing showed up."

"He had it in his office, if this is the same one," Willie pointed out. "People ask about it as a part of small talk. Or he brags that his great-grandfather was a pirate and this was his barometer. Who knows. But anyone who visited his office would probably learn what it was and could look up how it worked."

"Nobody is saying this *was* the murder weapon," Terry added. "It may have stopped working years ago. It may or may not have mercury in it or ever have had. The police lab will have to check. But maybe it was supposed to make you *think* about mercury being used to poison Fontainebleau. That whoever sent it to you knows something about how he was killed."

"So now my secret admirer is the killer?" Erin asked. "Is that what you think?"

"I think that someone wants you to know what is going on. Or to get involved."

"Or they want to make you look guilty," Vic said, pointing to the barometer. "Put the weapon into your hands."

And Erin had blithely played into his hands, taking the barometer home with her. Putting it under her bed. What if she hadn't said anything about it and Terry had found it there? Would he have suspected her? Would he have known that it had come from Fontainebleau's office?

"Did you see it there?" Erin asked him. "At the Homestead when you went up after Mr. Fontainebleau died? Was it in his office then?"

Terry nodded. "I told you I saw it there."

"Then you know I didn't have anything to do with it. I hadn't ever been to the Homestead before today. I didn't... I don't know, bring it home with me after visiting him a few months ago, get the mercury out of it, mix it with something that I could put in his food, and then give it to him a little at a time."

Terry blinked at her. "I never would have thought that you did. That's ridiculous."

"Yeah, it is," Erin agreed, the muscles in her stomach relaxing a little. "So if he's trying to make me look like a suspect, he failed."

"I don't think that was ever his intention," Terry said, looking at Vic and shaking his head.

Vic shrugged. "We're just brainstorming here. Coming up with ideas. No one knows what's actually going on in this weirdo's mind."

"No." Terry nodded. "I think that we can all agree on that. Whoever this guy is... none of us really knows what it is that he has in mind. What he wants Erin to do, or if he is taunting us, or thinks he's being clever. We don't know if he had anything to do with Fontainebleau's death, or if he knows who did, or is just a prankster. We don't know if this is the barometer that came from Fontainebleau's office. Just that it looks like it. And a lot of people could know that."

"Was it in the pictures?" Erin asked.

"What pictures?"

"The newspaper clippings. There were pictures of Fontainebleau at the Homestead. Was the barometer in any of those?" Erin took out her phone and tapped through to her photos.

Terry raised an eyebrow. "You took pictures of them?" He had, of course, taken them as evidence in the investigation. But Erin had taken photos of them first. They had been sent to her. Why shouldn't she have copies?

"I wanted to be able to look at them later. Read through them. See if there was any clue about who it was that did this. Who sent them, or who killed Mr. Fontainebleau. I haven't had a chance to read through them yet." Or, more accurately, she couldn't bring herself to read through all of that crap about the up-and-coming businessman and his family history and where everyone thought he was going. The densely written newsprint was daunting, especially to read through on her phone, and she hadn't been able to make herself go through it when she'd had the chance.

She flicked through the articles and zoomed in on a couple of photos taken in an office in the Homestead. She couldn't tell whether it was the same office or not, but there *was* a barometer on the wall.

Of course, Terry took the barometer into evidence to be examined and disassembled at the police lab in the city, and Erin had to make a lengthy report on how it had come into her possession. She felt a little silly that she had thought that it had been part of the waffle maker delivery. It had not been packaged or labeled the same way. And, of course, there was no packing slip because it wasn't some mass-produced decoration ordered through a fulfillment company. She had made assumptions at the time because she had been excited about the arrival of the waffle maker and getting it assembled. She hadn't been thinking about the secret admirer or the murder.

She was pretty sure by now that it *was* a murder. There was no way that it had just been accidental exposure to mercury, even if there was mercury contamination at some of Fontainebleau's work sites. Maybe that was why someone had decided that mercury would be an appropriate murder weapon. Maybe they thought that because of the contamination, it would be seen as accidental causes rather than murder. Or perhaps they thought that was what Fontainebleau deserved after exposing his workers to a dangerous toxin.

Erin had a restless night, her brain constantly going over what Willie had said. How much of what he said was the truth? And how much of the truth was he sharing? He knew more than he was prepared to share. It had been difficult to even get the little bit they had. Did he know who had plotted to murder Fontainebleau? Had he heard something on one of his bugs or through other people working at the Homestead? It was a big place; a person could work there all day and never even see Fontainebleau. Just because Willie had been there and planted listening devices, that didn't mean he knew anything more than anyone else.

And Adrienne. What exactly had she and her children been through while they had been there? Surely Adrienne wouldn't still be working there if it had been anything too bad. She knew that there were other jobs, and that she was at least taken care of if she didn't find something right away. Bella and Cindy would help her with the children and provide shelter. Erin could help with food. It wouldn't be ideal, but if things were too bad at the Homestead, she could choose to leave.

Erin tossed and turned. She tried to stay still so that she didn't keep Terry up. He needed his sleep if he was to be any help in cracking the case. But she was so restless, and her brain so busy with all of the ideas she had gathered the day before, that it was late into the night before she managed to get to sleep.

CHAPTER 25

The next day was Sunday, which was good, because Erin could have one of her employees manage ladies' tea and she could rest and relax after her long night. Maybe even get in a nap during the day if she needed it.

But, of course, she knew it was hopeless. She wouldn't have a nap during the day. And if she did, she would end up with a headache, and she wouldn't be able to fall asleep at bedtime because she'd slept during the day. It was better to just push through the day and be sure to be good and tired when bedtime rolled around.

So when she started to get drowsy in the afternoon, she decided it was time to get out and go for a walk. Getting out of the house would wake her up and ensure she didn't give in and have a nap.

It was a lovely day out. It was nice to have a break in the weather where it wasn't quite so hot. A little cloudy, but it didn't look like it was actually going to rain. She should be safe going out. She would go on a walk through her woods. Maybe see Adele and make sure that everything was going okay with her. It had been a long time since they'd had a good chat. Then she could decide whether to go any farther or return home. Maybe make some nice iced tea and relax with Vic if she were around, or work on her plan for the next week if Vic and Willie had gone to the city.

Then Terry should be back for an early supper and a relaxing, sleep-inducing evening.

She had it all planned out.

The woods were warm but shaded, dappled light filtering through the treetops to the ground below the canopy. Birds sang, squirrels ran across branches, and there was no one else around. She had the whole woods to herself.

She didn't run across Adele as she had expected to. She even stopped at the little summer cottage and knocked on the door to see if Adele was home, but there was no answer. Erin wasn't as bold as Vic would have been, so she didn't try the handle and poke her head in to call a yoo-hoo to Adele before entering. If Adele didn't answer the door, Erin didn't think going further was necessary.

Maybe Adele had caught a ride into the city and was doing some shopping or other errands. She didn't spend much time or money on food or worldly goods, but even someone like her needed to buy something now and then. A new cast iron frying pan or big soup pot.

Erin chose a trail she didn't normally use, because she knew it eventually ran out on a paved sidewalk, and she usually didn't want to walk through the neighborhood on the street when she had the option of walking in the woods. It was just so much more relaxing.

She saw a shape through the trees and squinted, trying to make out the figure.

"Adele? Is that you?"

The figure paused and turned toward her. Erin saw immediately that it wasn't her gamekeeper, but a man. She opened her mouth to apologize and then slink off in the other direction in embarrassment, when she thought she recognized the man.

"Uh, hi." She took a few steps along the path to get a better look. "I don't think I've seen you around here before."

He looked like he would flee, but then his body relaxed and he gave Erin a shy, slow smile. "No, I haven't been around here before. I've driven by and always thought it looked like a fine place to explore, so..."

As Erin got closer to the man, she knew it was him. "This is actually private property," she told him. He should have seen the Private Property sign at some point, no matter which direction he came from. The perimeter was well-marked so that Adele could more easily get trespassers to leave or call the police if they refused.

"Oh. Well, I'm sure the owner probably doesn't mind people taking a walk through as long as they don't mess anything up. There are a lot of pathways, so people use it often enough."

"It's *my* private property. A lot of the pathways are actually game trails. I can't exactly keep the deer and other animals from trespassing."

"Oh." He looked at her, now that they were close enough to see each other's features. "You're Erin Price."

"Yes. And I think… you delivered a package to me last week."

"Well, that's what I do," he admitted, smiling.

Erin gazed up into his friendly brown eyes. "It was strange, though; there was no address on the package."

"Sometimes there isn't."

"How can you deliver something if it doesn't have an address on it?"

"When they call it in, they give the address. If it isn't on the package when I get there, that doesn't really matter."

"How do you keep them straight? Most courier companies would put their own label on it."

"Nah. Never bothered to get one of those mobile label-makers. Not enough business here to worry about it. I just put a sticky note on it. Put the order number on it. Then there's no danger of mixing them up. Everything is marked."

"But what if the sticky notes fell off?"

He shrugged and shook his head, bemused. "I haven't ever had any trouble with my system. Don't see why it should matter to you."

"Well, I'm not sure that the package I received was actually meant for me. There was no packing slip or waybill, and it wasn't anything I was expecting…"

"You think I gave you the wrong package?"

"Well… maybe. There was no note, and… no one I know would send me…" Erin shrugged, her face burning. Even though the deliveryman had not seen what was inside the package, she was still embarrassed. It was clear from the packaging that it was a gift. And it was small enough that he could guess at the contents. It hadn't been heavy enough for a book or a box of chocolates. There were other possibilities, but she was afraid he had probably guessed what the package was without being told.

"If you didn't think it was for you, then why didn't you call to let me know there had been a mix-up?"

"Call where? I don't know your name or your company name. I'd never seen you before. There's no waybill. So how, exactly, am I supposed to get ahold of you to find out where it came from?"

He nodded slowly. "Well, that is a puzzler," he admitted.

"So I'm talking to you now. Who was it that sent me that package?"

"I don't recall."

"But you have records, right? You can look it up and find out."

"I don't keep anything for short-term deliveries. If it had come all the way across the country, that would be different..."

"But it was local, and you don't keep records for local deliveries?" That didn't sound right to Erin. "What about taxes? Don't you have to prove to them what work you have done? Where your income came from?"

"I keep what I need to."

"But you have no idea who sent me that package."

"No, sorry. A friend or family member. It shouldn't be hard to figure out."

"It didn't come from a friend or family member. That's just the problem. It came from a..." Erin paused, trying to decide on the right word. She didn't want to scare this guy off if he did remember who had sent the package or if he was the one who had been sending her things himself. "A secret admirer. I'd really like to know who it is and to talk to him."

"Oh, that sounds exciting. How interesting." The man looked at a watch on his wrist. "I have to get going. There's somewhere I'm supposed to be. It was nice chatting with you, Erin Price. Enjoy your day."

"No, wait." Erin stepped forward and tried to block his way. "I need to know who is sending me things. If it is you, then I need to talk to you about... what you sent and what it means. Because I'm not getting it all. The messages that I'm supposed to get from each thing."

He held her gaze for an instant, then shook his head and raised his hand in farewell. "Sorry, I can't help you."

"What's your name?"

He turned and walked away. Erin followed after him a few steps, but then stopped. What was she going to do? Lay hold on him and pull him back? Even if she had the physical ability to control him, he had already said that he didn't know who the sender of the packages had been. He wouldn't change his tune just because she said she really *really* wanted to know. Even if it was related to the Fontainebleau murder, she didn't see him having anything else to say to her about it.

CHAPTER 26

*E*rin called Terry to tell him about the man in the woods. He drove over and tried to spot him but was unsuccessful. She called Adele and left a message about him, hoping that he might come back to walk in the woods again. But she suspected that he hadn't been there just to take in the wilderness, but had been looking for her. And even if he had been there to enjoy nature, she had told him that it was private property and he was trespassing, so what were the chances he would return?

Monday, she was back on shift at Auntie Clem's as usual. The gossip surrounding Fontainebleau's murder seemed to have quieted down without any new information having come out. Erin was mostly thinking of her brand-new waffle iron and what she would do with it first. Probably a couple of batches of her pumpkin spice waffles, something people could keep in their freezers and pop in the toaster in the morning. Like the mass-produced commercial stuff, only better. Suitable for sweet or savory toppings. And the family restaurant might want some of them too, so they had another offering for those who came to the restaurant hoping for a gluten-free meal.

And then she could branch out and start making blueberry waffles. And chocolate chip. And whatever else she thought people might enjoy. She was really looking forward to putting the new waffle iron to good use.

"Your phone, Erin," Vic pointed out.

Erin noticed the vibrating in her apron pocket. "Oh, thanks. I'll get it when I take a break. They can leave a message."

But it kept ringing and ringing after it should have gone to voicemail. Eventually, Erin ducked into the kitchen to see who it was and why they either kept calling her back or the phone had decided not to go to voicemail. Whoever it was, they were being very persistent.

Adrienne.

Erin looked at the name on the face of the phone and tried to decide what to do. She had already decided to call back, of course, but she was in a quandary. She always told her employees to deal with personal calls later, when they weren't on shift. And whatever Adrienne wanted Erin for was undoubtedly personal. She wasn't calling with a catering order or special birthday cake request.

But Erin had truly meant it when she told Adrienne to call her if she ever needed anything. It wasn't just an empty, trite offer for Adrienne to get in touch with her.

And Adrienne had taken her up on it.

She owed it to Adrienne and the children to see what was going on and to help if something was wrong.

Sighing, Erin swiped to call Adrienne back and brought the phone up to her ear. "Adrienne? Is something wrong?"

"I need to get back to the farm. I need to see what's going on. Bella can't come out to get me because she's looking after the kids. And they've only got one operating vehicle right now. It isn't big enough for everyone."

"Okay. Okay, well, what's going on?" Erin asked, hoping for more information. It sounded like Adrienne was already at the Homestead, and she usually would work there until late afternoon or evening, so she shouldn't need a ride until the end of the day.

"Our camp. Someone was there and messed things up. I have to see how bad it is and what's salvageable. All of our stuff is there! Who would go all the way out to the Prost farm to mess with my stuff?"

"Your camp?" Erin repeated.

"My tent and the whole set-up. We moved out to the Prost farm so I could be closer to the kids, and Bella and Cindy could help out when I wasn't there. My camp. My house."

Understanding washed through Erin. She had seen Adrienne's camp a couple of times before. Once when it was set up in Erin's woods when they had been squatting on her property without her knowledge. A big army-surplus tent and another canopy with her kitchen things under it. Coolers for food and various cookery implements and pots. A smaller tent that was probably for the older children. And there were probably other necessities out of sight. An outdoor shower and a latrine. Everything the family needed to survive in the wild, as independent from other people as they could be.

Erin had assumed that Bella and Cindy were putting them up in the house, but it sounded like they had instead allowed Adrienne to set up her usual camp on their property, where she could be independent, at least while she was there to look after the children.

"Okay. Um, when do you need me? When do you want to go back—"

"Now. I need to go now. I need to see how bad it is."

Erin looked toward the front of the bakery. She would need to arrange for someone else to come in and help Vic. Erin didn't like to leave any of the employees on their own. It was safer if they worked in pairs, and a lot easier to keep track of additional baking in the ovens and make sure that nothing burned while managing the customers in the front.

"Okay. I'll be out as soon as I can. It will take me a little while to get there."

"I know." Adrienne let out an audible sigh. "Thank you. I didn't know who else to call. I didn't know what else to do."

"I'll be there as soon as I can."

"Thank you."

Erin puzzled over who could have a grudge against Adrienne and be so angry that they would go to all of the effort of driving out to the Prost farm to wreck what little Adrienne had. It wasn't like she was taking anything away from anyone.

She crossed the property line onto the Homestead and remembered Willie talking about her license plate and picture being logged as she did so. She looked around, but couldn't see any sign of surveillance cameras. Wherever they were, they were well hidden.

When she reached the parking lot she had previously used to drop Adrienne off, she pulled out her phone to let Adrienne know that she had arrived, but didn't need to. Adrienne opened the door and exited the building, making a beeline for Erin's car.

"Thank you so much," she said breathlessly as she climbed in. "I don't know what I would have done if you hadn't come. I don't know who else I could have called."

"I'm glad I could help," Erin told her. "I'm sorry that it had to be under these circumstances, though. I hope… that everything is okay."

"It's everything I have," Adrienne said. "I can't believe that anyone would want to destroy my life like that. How screwed up is that?"

Erin shook her head. She had found, when in dire circumstances herself, that people didn't really see the homeless and indigent as people. People acted as though they were animals, another species. They wouldn't treat someone in their own social strata that way. But someone who was homeless? Who had no friends and no resources? Someone who wouldn't go to the police with her problems? That was different.

She followed the road back out to the highway and toward the Prost property. Adrienne was texting on her phone. Probably telling Bella that they were on their way. That she would be home in just a few more minutes.

It seemed to take twice as long as it should to get to the Prost farm. Erin knew it was just because she was in a hurry, and kept looking at her speedometer, thinking that she couldn't be going fast enough. But she was over the speed limit, not under it.

CHAPTER 27

Finally, they reached the familiar farm. By the time she stopped on the gravel parking pad, the children were all running toward their mother, Bella trying to keep up behind them with the baby in her arms.

"Mama, you have to see," one of the smaller girls insisted. "Somebody wrecked everything! Our camp! Why would they do that?"

"I don't know, honey." Adrienne gave them all hugs and kisses, trying to comfort them. Her expression was one of dread. How could she face losing everything she had tried so hard to build? She looked at Bella and took a deep breath.

Erin expected her to ask how bad it was, but she apparently couldn't bring herself to do so. She just climbed out of the car and headed toward the dense woods. Erin wasn't sure whether she should follow but, eventually, she did. It wouldn't make sense for her to sit in her car waiting to be told how bad it was. Or to turn around and return to Auntie Clem's without waiting to hear the news.

She had to move quickly to keep up. The children were running, Adrienne close behind them.

Eventually, they got to the clearing where their camp had been set up. The tents were flattened. Clothing and cooking implements were scattered around. The coolers that had held their food had been kicked open and dumped—maybe trampled. Adrienne looked around, her face stricken. She went to the main tent and lifted it, examining it to see how bad the damage was. A couple of the children were crying, snot running down their faces. Bella jiggled the baby and didn't say anything, waiting for a report on the disaster. Adrienne looked around and then inside the tent.

"I don't think any of the poles have been broken, and the canvas is intact," she said, her voice devoid of emotion. "It just needs to be set up again." She dropped it to the ground. She looked around at the other items that had been scattered. "It's a mess. But I don't think anything has been destroyed. Some of the food. But most of our stuff is either in cans or in the house in the fridge."

"So… it isn't so bad?" Bella asked tentatively.

"No." Adrienne sat on the ground and looked at the chaos around her. "I think… everything is actually okay. It will take some work to whip it into shape, but the kids can help. They know what to do."

Hope, rubbing red eyes, perked up at this. "We can help, Mama."

"Yes." Adrienne rubbed the head of one of the children closest to her. "You guys are good workers and you know how to set up camp. You can help."

She produced a crumpled tissue from her pocket and wiped noses. "Enough tears. That's not how we get things done."

"Samuel Andrew," Hope said with authority, "you get the food and put it back in the coolers. If it is still good. If it is mashed but still okay, put it in a pile on the picnic table. We will make a casserole. Jeffey and Samantha, you get all the clothes and sort whose they are. I'll help fold later. Mama and me will get the tents back up." She looked at her mother for approval.

Adrienne nodded. "That's my big girl."

"Wow, you're a really good organizer," Erin told Hope sincerely. "What can I help with? I don't want just to stand around and watch."

Hope considered. "You're the baker, so you can help Samuel Andrew with the food."

Erin nodded. She picked up one of the overturned coolers and snapped the lid back onto the box where the hinge had popped. One of the young boys wandered over and picked up another cooler.

"You need to tell me what to do," Erin told him. "Do certain things go in each cooler?"

He considered her, sucking on his finger, and she didn't think he was going to say anything at first. "Fruits and veg'tables go there," he told her finally, indicating the cooler she had readied. "Carrots and potatoes. Most fruit you have to eat the first day. The cans don't go in a cooler. They go over there." He indicated a pile of striped canvas. "The pantry. When Mama puts it back up."

"Okay." Erin went to work, picking up what food was salvageable and putting it either in the coolers or on the picnic table, wondering what kind of casserole they would make with the motley assortment of ingredients. But she was sure they would manage it somehow. It was clear that the family was well-practiced in how to manage their camp. It was probably not the first time they'd had to deal with wanton destruction. And certainly, they had to move around often to avoid trouble, so they knew how to take everything down and put it up again with the minimum amount of fuss.

"What about me?" Bella asked. "I could help too."

"You take care of Sarah," Hope told her, looking at the baby in Bella's arms. "If she settles, you can fold clothes."

"I can put her down on a blanket. She can help me with socks."

Hope laughed. "Babies can't sort socks!"

"Maybe not, but she'll be interested enough in them if I give her some to hold and play with."

"Don't let her put my socks in her mouth," Hope shook her head at this thought. "Wet socks are bad. They give you blisters. And baby drool socks are gross!"

Bella laughed. She found a blanket, spread it out on a flat, unused spot on the ground, and sat down to help fold clothes as the young children sorted them into piles.

~

"You've got really good kids," Erin told Adrienne as they all worked together to get the camp whipped back into shape. "They're very smart and know how to work together."

Adrienne nodded. "We depend on each other. They know how to do lots of things, even the little ones. We can't depend on people like Bella or you to provide for us and do things for us. We want to be self-sufficient."

She rolled her eyes. "I know it might not look like it right now, 'cause the car doesn't work, so I need help getting around, and we're using the Prost land, but we try to do for ourselves. Don't rely on government or programs to help us out. One day that will all be gone, and anyone who relies on them is going to be out in the cold."

Erin wasn't sure if she believed in the eventual collapse of the government and social programs, but she nodded anyway. She could understand Adrienne's desire not to depend on anyone else, and knew that those who relied on social programs were often left in the lurch when there were cutbacks or they no longer qualified for services. It was best for Adrienne to do for herself if she could.

Adrienne and Hope worked together efficiently to sort out the tents and shelters that had been knocked down. It could have been a lot worse. If the vandal had broken the tent poles or slashed the canvas, it would have been difficult for Adrienne to recover but, as it was, within an hour, things were looking pretty good again.

Chairs and stumps had been set up for seating, and Adrienne ordered everyone to sit down and have a drink of cold water after working hard in the heat of the day. The water bottles the children handed out before sitting down to drink had obviously been reused. Erin wondered whether they had been filled in the house or in a nearby stream. The water was cool, but not cold, having been dumped out of the cooler and left scattered across the ground by the vandal.

"It's safe," Adrienne told Erin, catching her hesitation about drinking water from an unknown source. "They bottle water from mountain streams and sell it for hugely inflated prices. This here is 'artisan' water." She took a long swallow to show that it was safe to drink and wiped her mouth with the back of her hand. "It's been certified as free of dangerous bacteria or environmental contaminants, and we've been drinking it for a few weeks. Nobody's gotten sick."

Erin forced herself to open the water bottle and drink to show that she took Adrienne at her word. It was very refreshing and not flat and stale like water that had been sitting on shelves in bottles for months before purchase.

"What about heavy metals?" she asked. "I know some of these mountain streams can contain high levels of arsenic or lead..." Or mercury, but Erin didn't want to suggest that. Adrienne was already worried enough about being accused of poisoning Fontainebleau without bringing that up.

Adrienne rolled her eyes and shook her head. "It's perfectly safe," she repeated, but didn't answer whether it had been tested for any heavy metals.

The children seemed healthy enough after drinking it for several weeks, but Erin didn't know how long it might take for them to show effects from lead or mercury. She planned to only have a few sips of the water until she could leave. Maybe she would take it home and get it tested herself. Though she wasn't sure Adrienne would let her take one of her bottles away with her.

Once the children had rehydrated, Adrienne sent them off to play. She didn't give Erin any sign that she hoped to be taken back to the Homestead to finish her shift.

"Do you have any idea who would have done this?" Erin asked, once the children were out of earshot. "Vandalized your camp, I mean? It seems like such a random thing to do, and you're all the way out here; someone actually had to come here intending to mess things up. They didn't just stumble across your camp like they might if it was in the woods in town."

Adrienne didn't say anything, but she smoothed out a couple of crumpled papers that had been in her pocket and handed them to Erin. Erin looked at the block letters on the two notes in disbelief.

KEEP YOUR MOUTH SHUT AND GET YOUR CHILDREN OUT OF HERE

LEAVE BEFORE SOMEONE GETS HURT

Erin shook her head. "Who would do this? You're not hurting anyone by camping out here. Why would someone want to run you off?" She looked around her uneasily for any sign that someone was watching them. She had assumed that the vandal would be long gone but, if he wanted to drive Adrienne off the property, maybe he was watching to see if he had succeeded.

"I don't know," Adrienne admitted. "We've run into this before, when we were squatting on a property without permission or too close to town. But out here...? Who cares that we're here?"

"You're not camped anywhere near anyone's property line? And the kids aren't playing on someone else's land?"

"No. This is all the Prosts'. And if Cindy didn't want us here anymore, she isn't one to mince words. She wouldn't do something like this. She'd just tell us we'd worn out our welcome."

Bella nodded her agreement. "We actually like having you here. Mom loves hearing the kids play and helping to look after Sarah. She likes getting to play 'grandma.'"

It was hard for Erin to picture critical, sour Cindy doting on the little children. But everyone had good and bad points. Maybe a love for children was a good thing about Cindy that Erin had not previously known about.

CHAPTER 28

"*H*ow is Hope doing?" Erin asked Adrienne. "She seems happier when she has a job to do."

Adrienne looked at Erin, frowning. "Hope is fine."

"What happened to her?"

"I don't see how it's any of your business."

"It's not," Erin admitted. "I just wondered what it had to do with Mr. Fontainebleau. If it did. And how… it might come up in the investigation."

Adrienne scowled and shook her head. "It won't come up in the investigation if everyone keeps their mouths shut. But that isn't going to happen if you are asking questions. You should just leave it alone."

"Did he hurt her? Or did he just scare her? Or did she see something that upset her?"

Adrienne didn't answer. Erin looked at Bella, wondering if she knew the details. Not that she would share them with Erin with Adrienne sitting right there telling Erin it was none of her business. Erin just wanted to make sure that someone knew. That Adrienne had support from someone. Maybe she wouldn't ever willingly deal with the police or a social worker, but Erin hoped she at least had the support of her friend.

"You can trust Erin," Bella said, which was not what Erin had been expecting. "She's a good listener and she wouldn't do anything that would hurt Hope."

"But your boyfriend is a cop," Adrienne addressed Erin directly. "And you'll talk to him about it. I don't want cops involved. I promised not to involve the police."

"I won't talk to him about it if you don't want me to. But he needs to know what was happening in that house if he's going to solve Mr. Fontainebleau's murder."

"I don't care if they ever solve his murder. Whoever killed him did the rest of the world a favor. They should get a prize, not go to prison."

"Well, maybe they'll get off if there were mitigating circumstances. If they did it to protect children like Hope..."

Adrienne chewed on her lip. "I don't really care why they did it. I'm just glad they did."

Erin shook her head. She didn't know what had happened at the Homestead, but Adrienne was clearly pretty bitter toward Fontainebleau, even though he was already dead.

"You don't know," Adrienne said. "So don't judge."

"I'm not."

She couldn't know what she wasn't told. It was up to Adrienne to decide whether to tell her about it or not.

Adrienne took a few long swallows of her water. "It's a big house. You saw that. And you might expect it to be wired like an airport, with microphones and cameras everywhere, so that no one could get away with anything. Walking off with a Tiffany lamp or some Monet. But it's not. Mr. Fontainebleau didn't like all of that monitoring. Not because he trusts people and thinks the best of them. That's not the way it was."

Erin nodded. She was already aware of some of this because of her discussion with Willie. She knew that Fontainebleau had only done the minimum necessary to protect himself and his property. Maybe he *did* think that people were inherently good, no matter how Adrienne perceived it.

"I'll tell you why he didn't want any electronic monitoring," Adrienne said darkly. "It was so that no one could prove what *he* was doing."

A knot of dread formed in Erin's stomach. She hadn't anticipated that perspective. There were a lot of shady things that someone rich and powerful like Clive William Fontainebleau III could get away with. But the fact that it was something that had traumatized Hope made Erin's chest hurt, like she'd actually been stabbed in the heart. She was having trouble catching her breath.

"I thought that it was so nice that they would let me bring all of the kids and move in there. To have our own little place and make it easier for me to work and still be close to my kids. He and his assistant talked about how important it was for them to be able to employ single moms and people who couldn't get jobs in other places because they weren't able to accommodate children or parents with responsibilities." She stopped for a moment and cleared her throat. "He was friendly with the kids and told them to call him Uncle Gus and gave them little treats or acted like they were important. He knew their names. I told the kids that they had to stay out of the way. That they weren't supposed to be around the big house when I was working, but had to stay in our rooms in one of the small houses. I didn't want them getting underfoot and wrecking things for us."

Erin nodded. It was a windfall for Adrienne to land a job like that, where she could take care of her kids the way that she wanted to. Erin could see how enticing that would be. To be able to be independent and work to build up the savings to get a place of her own eventually. Not having to worry about shelters or trespassing or other people wandering into their camp.

Adrienne went on, "But Hope said that she'd been in the house. Helping Uncle Gus. That he gave her money to do things for him, so she was working like Mama."

"What was she doing for him?"

"I thought just following him around, helping to tidy his desk, things that little kids do to try to be grown up. Maybe he gave Hope her own duster. I told her I wanted her to stay in our rooms, that I would do the work and it was her job to do her schoolwork and help look after the other kids." Adrienne swallowed. Her jaw worked, clenching and unclenching. "I went back the next day partway through my shift to check on them. The baby had been fussy and I wanted to make sure she was okay and that Hope was where she was supposed to be. But she wasn't. One of the other women, one who works in the kitchen, said that Fontainebleau had come looking for her. He had told her that Mama needed her, and she needed to come with him."

Erin cleared her throat but didn't know what to say. She could barely breathe, anticipating the story. She didn't need to be told. She had lived around enough predators to know how the story went. How it always went.

"It's such a big house." Adrienne's eyes welled up with tears.

Erin could see her frantically searching through the house, looking for her daughter and the man who had taken her. Asking people desperately if they had seen either one of them, where they might be.

"It took forever to find them. Everyone just looked the other way. They knew what was going on, and they just looked the other way! I found them together. My poor baby. You know that what she was doing for him had nothing to do with dusting the shelves or straightening his desk."

Erin shook her head, her own eyes burning. "Adrienne... I'm so sorry." She couldn't help adding, "Why wouldn't you go to the police? Why not have him arrested for what he did? He couldn't be allowed to just go on doing that."

And Adrienne had kept working there. Why would she work for someone who she knew had assaulted her daughter? Erin could see why Adrienne was afraid this would leak out and she would be accused of murdering Fontainebleau. Anyone with a heart would have wanted to kill Fontainebleau after that. And a mother! She must have wanted to cut out his throat. Slow poisoning by mercury would be too easy for him.

"I wanted to. I was going to. But..." Adrienne swallowed, fighting back the tears and outrage, "they said that he would never be charged. No one would believe me. They would say that I was just trying to embarrass him, or that I was trying to extort money out of him. It *wasn't* the money. It was never about the money."

It was Bella who leaned forward, her brows knotted, and asked, "What money?"

"I could stay there. I could keep working there, with nothing changed, and if I didn't say anything, didn't do anything to blacken his good name, then I would get a bonus. Enough for a stake. To buy our own land." Adrienne sobbed and couldn't go on for a minute. "Our own land, where we could build, where we could live without anyone bothering us or ever being kicked out again. He'd make sure that we were looked after. That the kids never had to go hungry. That I could have a running car. The nightmare would be over and I could live like anyone else. Like *you*," she looked at Erin, "with your own house in town, and a car and a business. Respectable. With friends and everything you need." She scrubbed at her eyes with the palms of her hands. "He had the money to do it. He had millions. Kicking a few dollars in my direction would be nothing for him. Just a drop in the bucket. All I had to do was keep working there and keep my mouth shut."

Bella moved closer to Adrienne and rubbed her back soothingly. "Adrienne, honey... you never said. You never told me all of that."

"I didn't want to tell anyone. I'm ashamed of myself. What a terrible thing to do to my baby. To say that what happened to her doesn't matter, if it means that I can get the money to start us out on our own. She matters more than a piece of land and a few dollars."

"Of course she does," Erin agreed. "You want to give them all the stable life they need. You want all of them, not just Hope, to feel safe and secure and have their own place in the world." What Erin would have done for a family who loved and protected her and kept her forever when she was a little girl. It had been a dream that she knew she would never achieve.

Adrienne nodded. "I want the best for her. Kids recover and they bounce back. I'm giving her memories and a life that will wipe out all of that other stuff. She won't remember any of it. Going to the police would just keep stirring that all up. She'd have to talk about it. To keep telling about it over and over. A court case would just destroy her. To have them say that she was lying and just making things up, just doing something I told her to go get money out of him. This way... it's over and done. She doesn't have to think about it or talk about it anymore. She has her family and a safe place to sleep, and she can grow up to be healthy and strong and just forget about Uncle Gus and what he was doing. She won't even remember it when she's older."

Erin wanted to hug Adrienne, or to pat her shoulder and rub her back like Bella was doing. She wanted to go find Hope and assure her that everything would be okay and squeeze her hard to let her know that she was safe and that wouldn't ever happen again.

Though the truth was that there was no guarantee it wouldn't happen again. Children who were abused were often re-abused over and over again throughout their lives. They ended up in bad situations and relationships and gave off a "vulnerable" vibe that attracted predators like bees to honey. At least Hope wasn't in foster care, where predators loved to lurk, seeking out the most vulnerable. At least she was home with her mother and siblings and had been removed from the Homestead.

And Fontainebleau was dead, and would never again be allowed to molest another child.

CHAPTER 29

*A*drienne sighed and drained the remainder of her bottle. "I know you think I made the wrong choice. I know you think that you would choose something different if it happened to you. But you don't know that. You don't know how you would have reacted when they presented you with the two choices, and you saw how it would rip your child's life apart if you went to the police. It wasn't the money. It wasn't the land and the house and the car. It was Hope. Giving her a better life. Protecting her from what would happen."

"I can't say. It wasn't me," Erin agreed. She might think she would have gone to the police, but she knew that in the past she had avoided talking to them, even when her own boyfriend was a cop. Even when she knew and respected every cop in town and knew that they would treat her as fairly as they could.

"Well, it's over now," Bella said. "This is what happened, and now it's over."

"Of course... Hope wasn't the first," Adrienne said, her voice tight with barely controlled emotion. "This scumbag had been able to do whatever he wanted to for years. Preying on single moms. Their children. The wives of employees. People he had promised to keep safe and take care of for decades." She shook her head. "Decades! Do you know how many victims that means? Some of them never told their parents or spouses, just suffered in silence because he was so rich and powerful and could make anyone shut up and do what he wanted them to. Because his people would keep writing checks, making threats, and doing whatever it took to keep everyone quiet. Leaving a trail of victims behind him…"

"Did you talk to other people that it had happened to?" Erin asked. "Other victims?"

Adrienne shook her head. "Everyone keeps quiet. They all get paid to keep their mouths shut and not say anything about it, even to each other. Even if they all know what kind of a person he is—was."

"That's really too bad," Erin commented. "It's an environment like that that lets him keep abusing people." She looked away, not wanting to put too sharp a point on it, because Adrienne had joined the ranks of those who had agreed to stay quiet about it. Even after his death, she was still keeping it quiet, refusing to come forward and tell what had been going on. She was still part of the problem instead of the solution. Erin could understand that she didn't want Hope to be traumatized more by the system than she already had been at the hands of Uncle Gus. But that wasn't a solution and didn't help the next child.

"I heard them talking," Adrienne said, following some segue that her own mental processes had led her to. "Matthew, one of the guys who had been working with him for years. Decades. He'd been loyal, one of Fontainebleau's biggest supporters. He had just found out… his son did one of those DNA tests. The ones that give you stuff about your ancestry and who you're related to. Only, none of Matthew's family showed up as being related to him."

Erin's eyes widened. "What?"

"It shows his cousins, aunts, uncles, and anyone who has done one of those DNA tests. But it didn't. Instead, whose family do you think it showed?"

Erin tried to clamp her jaw shut, but it sagged open again in disbelief. "Fontainebleau? It showed his family?"

Adrienne nodded. "So all along, this boy he thought was his son, turns out he isn't. Not biologically. It was Fontainebleau. He slept with Matthew's wife and no one ever told him. Never gave him a clue that the baby might not be his."

"What did his wife say about it? He must have confronted her?"

"His wife is dead," Adrienne explained. "Been dead for years. Depression. Suicide, as far as I can guess."

"Oh, my. Oh, that poor man. And his son!"

"Yeah. Imagine finding it out now, twenty years later. Finding that he put in however many decades for this guy, loyal to him to the end, just to find out that he had forced his wife."

"Did he know the circumstances? Whether it was… you know… she didn't just have an affair?"

"After working for this guy for that long, do you really think he had any doubt? He must have heard all of the stories about Fontainebleau. He knew it wasn't just an affair."

"What did Fontainebleau do about it? What did he say?"

"What he always says. Money talks. He sends them to the purser and lets her take care of them. Money if he'll keep his mouth shut about it. And do you really think he wants to have his dead wife's name dragged through the mud? Or his son's parentage broadcast all over the state? Best thing to do is to hold out for as much money as he can get… and keep his mouth shut."

"I can't believe that he wouldn't talk about it. If he was one of Fontainebleau's top guys, he must have already made a lot of money. I wouldn't think…"

"That it would be as easy to talk him into it as it was to shut me up?" Adrienne finished bitterly. "Yeah, he probably had to pay Matthew a whole lot more. Give him early retirement, so he never has to work again. He's a nice-looking guy. Tall, distinguished, dreamy-looking eyes. He could easily get married again. Settle down with another family. He's still young enough."

Erin blinked, a face popping into her mind at the description. "Wait —what did he look like?"

Adrienne looked surprised. She tried to describe him in more detail. Erin thought she recognized him from the description.

"And who's this person he was supposed to go see? Mrs. Purser?"

"The purser. Like on a ship. The person who pays the bills, looks after the financial stuff, and ensures everyone is comfortable and happy. She's supposed to keep all the discontents quiet. Pay them off and make them sign nondisclosure agreements."

"Is that all she does?"

"No, she does other stuff around the Homestead, too. Keeping everything running smoothly. Like the head of the household staff." Adrienne shook her head. "She told me... that he'd never gone after a child before. Only young women. She promised me... she said she'd make sure it didn't happen again. That I should sign the agreement, but she would make sure that he was dealt with. I guess I should have realized that it was all just talk. She was never going to go to the authorities with what she knew. She was just telling me that to make sure that I signed the agreement, so I was legally bound. So I couldn't... do what I'm doing now and tell you or anyone else. But he's dead and gone now and I don't care if people know what a terrible person he was. They can come after me for slander or whatever they want to. If the cops arrest me for murder—I'm going to spill the beans. I'm going to tell them everything I know."

A person could be pushed only so far, and it would seem that Adrienne had reached her limit.

CHAPTER 30

*E*rin had promised not to tell anyone about what had happened to Hope, especially not the police, so she couldn't go to Terry and use him as a sounding board. She couldn't point him in the right direction and hope that he just figured it out himself.

Back at her office at Auntie Clem's, she wrote notes in her planner, trying to map out a path that would allow her to find out more and, hopefully, find something that she could give to Terry and the Bald Eagle Falls police department. She couldn't prove who had killed Fontainebleau, but if she could find some proof… then she could give it to the police, and they could make an arrest, and Adrienne would be safe. She wouldn't have to worry about being arrested for the murder herself. What would happen to all her kids when they took her to prison? Even if she was found not guilty, the children would have to be in someone else's care for years if she were charged. Jury trials didn't go that quickly and, if Adrienne made a plea, who knows how many years she would get? As much as Erin would like to think that the law was just and the sentence she received would be appropriate, she didn't believe it.

But would Erin want the real killer to end up in prison? The person who had decided that Fontainebleau deserved to die for all of the damage he had done? For all of the broken hearts and broken lives? Would that really be justice? After all Fontainebleau had been allowed to do because his money and power could silence anyone who got in his way?

~

"How did things go with Adrienne today?" Vic asked as she and Erin worked together on clean-up and closing at Auntie Clem's. "Is she okay? What happened?"

Erin tried to focus on the question. Vic knew nothing about what had happened at Adrienne's camp or the revelations about Hope and Fontainebleau's history. Erin knew Vic could keep a secret, but Adrienne had asked her not to talk to anyone about the attack.

But Vic didn't need the details about Hope. She was just wondering about Erin's trip to the Homestead to rescue Adrienne and take her home to the Prost farm to see what had been done there.

"It looked pretty bad to begin with, all of Adrienne's tents and their belongings scattered all over the place. Everything knocked down and destroyed. But it wasn't actually as bad as all of that. Some of the food was wrecked, but the clothes, tents, and everything were okay. If someone had really wanted to wreck everything, they could have broken up the tent poles and slashed the tents and the clothes. Poured bleach on them or lit them on fire. But they didn't do any of that. Just scattered everything around. It took work to clean it up and get everything organized and set up again, but there wasn't any permanent damage. Her kids are smart and good at working together and getting their camp set up."

"That's a relief," Vic said, blowing out her breath. "I don't understand how anyone could do that to someone already down on their luck. To anyone, I mean, but especially to someone like Adrienne, who is struggling so hard to keep her head above water. I feel awful for her. How could someone be that cruel, just throwing everything around for no reason?"

"I know," Erin agreed. "It burned me up. I'm glad it wasn't as bad as it looked at first, but I still think it was nasty. It isn't like Adrienne is doing anything to bother anyone. She is living where she has permission to; it isn't on public property or trespassing on private property. She looks after her kids, works hard, and keeps her mouth shut. So I don't understand why someone would try to run her off like that."

"Run her off?"

"Yeah. There were a couple of notes… telling her that she should clear out. But where do they think she's going to go? She doesn't have a working car. Doesn't have a permanent home. It isn't like there is a shelter to go to in Bald Eagle Falls even if she *would* agree to go to one. And she won't go anywhere like that because she says it isn't safe for the kids. Where exactly do they think she's going to go?"

Vic shook her head as she poured out the batters that were to soak overnight. "Why would anyone want to run her off? She's such a hard worker. She's not some drunk or deadbeat."

"I don't know. People don't like to have to look at the poor and the homeless. They don't want them anywhere near their properties. They're fine with social programs that help people out, as long as it doesn't mean the homeless people are in their backyards. Try to help addicts or single-parent families by actually giving them a home in your neighborhood…" Erin shook her head. She'd seen too much of that kind of self-right-eousness. "Where exactly are they supposed to go? You can only have shel-ters and halfway houses in the slums? How does that help get people away from that life?"

"If you have an answer, I'd love to hear it."

Erin just shook her head. "But I can't even figure out who doesn't want them there. They couldn't be much more out of sight. It isn't like anyone has to see them out there. And they had to seek out Adrienne's camp and target her. It's in the middle of nowhere!"

"People can be really cruel."

"Yeah."

They worked in silence for a while, used to the routine. It was rare that any of the employees needed to refer to the procedural checklists anymore. Erin kept them all up to date so that it was easy to open and close Auntie Clem's, and that all of the recipes and till codes and other procedures were all in one reference binder.

"Do you think…" Vic started and then broke off.

Erin waited, then, after a moment, turned and looked at Vic, whose brow was furrowed as she wiped down counters and started running through the last few checks before leaving.

"Do I think what?"

"You've been over at the Homestead and probably heard things from Terry. About what things were like over there, what kind of person Fontainebleau was and everything. I mean, everybody says how much he was disliked. He was rich and arrogant. But I mean… I just wonder what kinds of things he was involved in."

Thinking back to what Erin had discovered about Fontainebleau, she wondered if there was anything she could reveal to Vic without breaking confidences.

"What do you mean?" If Vic was already halfway there, Erin couldn't be blamed for confirming her suspicions.

"I mean… organized crime."

"Oh." That took a turn in a far different direction from what Erin had been expecting. She didn't know what to say. "Well… I don't know. I haven't really heard anything about that."

"A lot of big businesses, they're involved with organized crime. Directly or indirectly. You know how you always hear about the construction industry, how it's so intertwined with the mob? Maybe that's just on TV. I don't know."

"I don't either," Erin admitted. "It makes for good TV, but it's probably exaggerated. Not *all* construction companies are involved with the mob. Or protection rackets. Money laundering or hiding bodies in the foundations of new buildings. I don't think much of that happens in real life."

"No," Vic agreed. "But on the other hand… I know how the clans are. They mean business. And they *do* get involved with other industries. Not just drugs or money laundering. Around here… it could be things like mining. Lots of money in it. Big industry."

"You're thinking… that the Jackson clan might be involved with Fontainebleau's business? They might have some kind of claim on it?"

Vic bit her lip, pausing in her work. "I was thinking about the Dysons, actually."

Erin was startled. She had thought that maybe Vic had heard something about Fontainebleau or his business through her family connection with the Jackson clan, even though she had nothing to do with anyone in her family but Jeremy anymore.

But her only connection with the Dyson clan was…
Willie.

CHAPTER 31

$\mathcal{E}$rin looked at Vic. "What makes you think Fontainebleau might have been involved with the Dysons?"

Vic looked away, shaking her head. "I just... wondered what was going on with him. Like I said, everyone keeps saying what a terrible guy Fontainebleau was... and... is it really just that he's competitive? Buying out claims that the independent miners think should be theirs?"

"You'd have to ask Willie about that." After saying it, Erin clamped her mouth shut and tried to figure out how to take the conversation in another direction. She hadn't meant to throw it back at Willie, who Vic was obviously already worried about. And not just Willie himself, but the possibility that the Dyson clan might be involved.

It was a long time since Willie had been a soldier for them, and he now lived and worked independently of them, except for doing supposedly legitimate work for Nelson Dyson, who had split off from the main part of the clan. This might be worse than working for the main clan, putting Willie between two warring factions as well as at risk from the law.

"I mean about the mining," she said. "Not about the clan."

"You think he is involved with the Dysons, though, don't you?"

"Well, with Nelson." Erin shook her head. "But I don't know anything about it. Doing computer work for him doesn't necessarily mean that he's doing anything to break the law or anything that would involve money laundering through Fontainebleau's company. It could be completely innocent, like he says."

"Yeah. Or it could be a complete lie and he's up to his eyeballs in clan stuff." Vic made an angry noise in her throat. "I thought that when I left my family I was done with anything to do with the clans. And then I find out that Willie is still… I don't know what he's doing. But he's had some blow-ups lately. I thought it was just stress over some mine or claim jumper. But it seems like he was more than just a competitor to Fontainebleau. I think it goes a lot deeper than that."

"Going into Fontainebleau's home and planting bugs?"

Vic rolled her eyes and nodded. "Yeah. That's pretty hard to stomach. If he was afraid that Fontainebleau was sniffing around his mines, then why not just protect his mines? Like he's always done? Why go into Fontainebleau's Homestead and plant bugs there? He just wants to keep one step ahead of the guy? Make sure that he's not doing anything against Willie's interests?" She shook her head, sighing in frustration.

"Well, at least he was open about that. Admitted to what he'd been doing."

"Don't count on it. That's what he confessed to when you had him in a corner, because you'd seen him out there. Is it really the truth? I mean, did you see him removing listening devices?"

"No… I saw him pulling wire. With other workers."

"Right. *Not* covert surveillance. Willie out there in the open with other people."

"Then…" Erin was confused. "That doesn't sound like anything too bad. What's the big deal if he was just doing an electrical job? Something Fontainebleau hired him for?"

"Because he's covering something up. Something worse than planting or collecting bugs. He's trying to distract everyone from what he was really there for."

"What do you think he was there for?"

Vic didn't say anything. She went to Erin's tiny office to grab her purse and get ready to go.

"Something worse like poisoning Fontainebleau?" Erin demanded. "I don't think Willie had anything to do with that. Not for a minute."

"No?" Vic sounded slightly relieved at Erin's vehemence. "You don't think he would do something like that? No matter what the reason?"

"Not because of work. Not because he thought that Fontainebleau was acting against his interests. No."

But would Willie do it if he knew what had happened to Hope? He hadn't answered her when she had asked for information on what had happened, but that didn't mean that he didn't know. She suspected he knew a lot more about it than he had let on, but he was leaving it to Adrienne to manage the information. Giving her privacy.

But that didn't preclude his deciding to do something to end the problem permanently. Erin knew how protective he was of her and Vic. She could only imagine how protective he would be toward a little girl like Hope, who had been harmed.

"So I'm probably just blowing things out of proportion," Vic said. "It isn't anything to do with the Dysons."

"What made you think that it was?" She couldn't see Vic jumping right from the impression that Willie wasn't telling her something to assuming it was because it was the Dysons. That might be their biggest moral conflict, but that didn't mean that every one of Willie's secrets had to do with the Dysons.

"Well, just... every now and then, something that I hear him say on the phone. Or that comes up on his screen. I don't think that he's doing anything *really* bad. I mean, up until now, I just figured... it's his business. How he manages his business and what he chooses to do with Nelson Dyson, whether honest or shady, is up to him. And if he doesn't want to talk to me about it, then fine. I'd rather not know if it is something that could potentially get him in trouble."

But if it was something to do with a murder, that was different.

Vic and Erin headed for the back door. "I don't think Willie would poison Fontainebleau over a business deal," Erin assured her. "He's not that kind of guy. He finds other ways to deal with his problems. Like bugging the Homestead."

"Somebody was asking him, I think, about what he found out at the Homestead. He kept saying that he would deal with it later. That there wasn't anything to report."

"And you think that was Nelson or someone from the clan? Then you *do* think that Willie was planting bugs? Or retrieving them?"

"I don't know. I wish I did. I think… that's the kind of thing that he would do for Nelson. Think about it. If he was setting up networks and security for Nelson, then it's not a stretch that he might set something up at the Homestead under orders from Nelson. And then Nelson wants to know what he's found, demands to know what Willie's discovered so far…"

"You know, I think there was something in those newspaper articles."

"What?" Vic looked at Erin as they got into the yellow VW. "You think there was *what* in those newspaper articles?"

"I don't know. I have to look at them again. I just have…" Erin shook her head, frowning and trying to catch the fleeting impression that had just tugged at the back of her brain. "Sorry, I didn't read the articles carefully, just glanced over them, and then looked at them again when I was looking to see if the barometer showed up in any of the pictures. I just think… there's something I should have seen."

"That has something to do with Nelson?"

"I don't know."

Even without looking at Vic, Erin could tell that the younger woman was rolling her eyes. And she couldn't blame her. She wasn't sure what it was she was trying to say or what her brain had caught hold of. But she knew she needed to read through the puff-piece news articles about Clive William Fontainebleau III to tease out what she had missed. The key was there.

Vic was there to offer moral support, since they couldn't read the articles on Erin's photo roll simultaneously. Even zooming in and scrolling down each column without losing her place in the articles was difficult. It was not exactly how newspaper articles were meant to be read. But it would have to do because they were the only copies she had.

The articles were from decades before, when Fontainebleau was entering the family business as a young man, having gotten whatever business degrees his family's money had bought him. He was joining his father in the industry, acclaimed as the golden boy who could turn the company around and put it back on the track to success.

Erin read a few articles this way, then leaned back on the couch and closed her eyes, relaxing her shoulders and trying to process what she had read and whether there was anything there. She reached out to hand her phone to Vic.

"Why did he need to turn the company around?" she asked.

Vic took the phone from her hand and started flicking through the articles. Her reading speed was much faster than Erin's, or maybe she was just focused on answering that one question instead of absorbing everything the articles had to say.

"Yeah, they allude to it a few times," she confirmed. "Turn the company around. Return it to its former glory. Taking over the reins of the family fortune from his father. I guess... his father didn't have the same business acumen as he and his grandfather had?"

"It sure doesn't sound like it."

"They were expecting Fontainebleau the Third to be a business genius. When he hadn't actually had anything to do with business yet, he had just finished school. But everyone figured he was the answer."

"So his father must have been really bad. And the company was in pretty poor shape."

"Maybe business just wasn't his father's thing. Maybe he was the artistic type and had never wanted to be part of something like that."

"Maybe," Erin agreed. "Or maybe he had a specific vice. He was a drinker or a gambler."

"Oooh..." Vic drew the word out in realization. "If he was a gambler and got in with the wrong people..."

"Or tried to cover up by taking out a loan from a... less legitimate source. Someone who charged a high lending rate, say."

Erin opened her eyes. Vic was nodding vigorously. "And if Fontainebleau the Third had to run the business the way that the Dyson clan said to, because they were hugely in debt to them..."

"I mean, it was decades ago," Erin said, pointing to her phone to indicate the articles. "But if he had to work hand in hand with them to get out from under... once you've been in business with organized crime, it's pretty hard to get out."

"And then, more recently, Fontainebleau the Third starts making questionable or unwise business decisions. The clan starts to get concerned. Wants to know that he's still the right guy to run the company..."

"But that would be the clan, not Nelson. Nelson has split off. He doesn't have anything to do with the historical business of the clan, right? He wouldn't have anything to do with an old debt by Fontainebleau's company."

"I don't know. He could have bought that debt. Or maybe since he was a Dyson, Fontainebleau went to him when things started to falter again. Figured that he just needed a little cash, and things will turn back around again. Because he'd done it before. He had all of these other plans and something was bound to work out."

"It could be." Erin took her phone back from Vic. "But of course… this is all speculation."

"But it would explain Nelson Dyson wanting to know what's going on. He needs ears on the inside and knows Willie is good at this kind of thing. And Willie's interests are aligned, because he wants to know what Fontainebleau is doing too, wants to make sure he is staying away from Willie's mines."

CHAPTER 32

*E*rin tapped through the photos again, but wasn't reading them this time. She was just skimming over the headlines and the titles. And there was more she hadn't read yet. Her secret admirer/stalker/informant had picked each one carefully and sent it to her for a reason. What information did he want to give her that she hadn't figured out yet? The barometer. Fontainebleau the Third coming back from school to save the company from the hole his father had put it in, whether that had involved deals with the local leg-breakers or not. And what else? Were there clues there as to the young Fontainebleau's skirt-chasing?

"If we can figure this out from the articles, then the police can too," she reminded Vic. "They have the originals of these articles."

"But they don't know Willie has been getting calls from Nelson. And there's not actually anything in there that says that Fontainebleau the Second had anything to do with the Dyson clan. That's just our speculation. There's no proof of anything. Not in those newspaper articles, anyway."

"Are there clues in the other things that he sent?" Erin cast her mind back over the other gifts. "If the newspaper articles and barometer were to tell us about Fontainebleau and his killer and maybe something about why Fontainebleau was killed, then do the other gifts mean something too? I thought that they were just… romantic gifts from a secret admirer when I got them. But what if they were supposed to tell me something right from the beginning, only I missed the significance?"

"Well, I guess they could be," Vic agreed. "Flowers and lingerie. Could be something to do with a wife or girlfriend. Someone he had an intimate relationship with. They could point toward a suspect. If the newspaper articles and barometer are the why and the how, then maybe the flowers and lingerie are the who. His wife or ex-wife. Someone else he's seeing. It shouldn't be too hard to narrow down who he's been seeing, even if it is a mistress on the side."

Erin grimaced. She didn't want to tell Vic everything she had learned from Adrienne. But finding out everyone that Fontainebleau had been intimate with, even just going back a few months, might be more challenging than Vic expected. "Actually… from what I gather, Fontainebleau was… very active. That might be a pretty wide pool."

"Oh." Vic gave a little laugh. "I didn't know. I guess that's part of why he isn't very well-liked. Maybe the details of the flowers and lingerie are important clues? They might point to someone specific?"

Erin pictured the flowers. Just a small bouquet of colorful flowers. They had not been ultra-romantic. Not a dozen red roses. But also not black roses. Or white lilies that might be more funereal. When she had seen them, she had thought that they might come from Peter or the Foster family as a thank-you for helping get Mr. Foster the job at the bookstore. They could even have been from Naomi, for that matter. There hadn't been anything creepy or stalkerish about them. But nothing that she could see that would point to a specific person. Unless they were someone's favorite flower, a particular gift that Fontainebleau had sent to her, or they were code for someone's name. Daisy or Susan or Iris. Erin knew few flower names. She couldn't have named most of the flowers that had been in the bouquet.

"I don't know much about flowers, do you?"

"I know there's a whole 'language of flowers' thing, where different flowers and colors represent different messages, but I don't know anything about it. Other than red roses being love and yellow roses being friendship."

"You know more than I do. Maybe we can look them up online. But

I'm not sure what flowers were in the bouquet, and I didn't take a picture."

"They must have been ordered from somewhere close by. We might be able to find out more from the flower shop they were ordered from."

"Yeah. Though we'll have to come up with a good story, because I don't think they'll give us any information like they would to the police."

"I guess they'll already have been around asking who ordered them and if they were charged to a credit card."

"Maybe," Erin said doubtfully. "Terry never said he was going to, and we didn't know at the time that they were anything other than... an anonymous gift. It wasn't until later that things started to get weird."

"He must have after, though. When you got the lingerie and then the newspaper articles. He must have looked into it."

"I guess. Probably."

"And then there's the lingerie..."

Erin nodded. She immediately started blushing. Why should a little lace negligee be so embarrassing? Especially if it was a clue as to the identity of the murderer rather than a romantic gift from Terry or a secret admirer? It wasn't anything to do with Erin. Certainly not a statement about how the man who had sent it felt about her. It might not even have been sent by a man. There was no reason it couldn't have been sent by one of the women at the Homestead who knew what was going on and wanted to point Erin in the right direction.

Vic giggled at Erin's blush, which just made her more embarrassed.

"So what kind of clues could the lingerie give you?" Vic asked. "I never saw it, so you'll have to describe it in detail for me."

Erin opened her mouth, sure that her face was lobster red.

"And I mean in detail," Vic reiterated.

Erin put both hands over her face. "I didn't really look closely. I mean... it was a negligee. Lacy, sheer. Not like something I'd wear around the house."

Vic laughed at the thought. Erin didn't usually even wear a nightgown, like Vic. A t-shirt and shorts were more her speed. Maybe yoga pants on a cooler night.

"What color?" Vic asked.

"White, with some baby blue trim."

Did the blue mean something? A clue to point them toward Fontainebleau's illegitimate son?

"And what about the cut? Was it… slim? Busty? Like it was bought for you, or someone else?"

Erin thought about it. She hadn't tried the negligee on. From the time she had first seen the foil stamp on the box, she had known in her gut that it was not from Terry. She had not taken it out of the box when she'd received it at Auntie Clem's. She had taken it out of the box only once at home, to hold it up and get the full effect when Terry was not in the room to see. It had been longer than a camisole or baby doll, but not floor length. Somewhere around knee level on Erin's short frame. Mid-thigh for someone taller like Vic. And the cut? Had she noticed? Had she held it up to herself to see how it would fit?

"I don't really know. I guess… It was maybe bustier than I could wear. Maybe for someone a little taller and better endowed than me."

Vic nodded.

And what did that tell them? They didn't know anyone at the Homestead other than Adrienne. It would not have fit her thin frame. But it wasn't a glass slipper that would be a perfect fit for one woman who worked at the Homestead. Or that Fontainebleau might have had contact with at some other location.

"There's nothing that says that the secret admirer—or whatever he is —picked out the size to represent a particular woman specifically. Or that he was any good at eyeballing a woman and knowing what size of negligee to get," Erin pointed out. "In my experience… men can be pretty ignorant of things like cup sizes."

Vic started to giggle. "I haven't had much experience with sexy lingerie myself," she said, "but yeah… I don't think most guys are much more advanced than 'big or small.' Maybe if he's a lingerie designer or salesman. But not Joe Blow off the street."

"Or Willie?" Erin guessed.

Vic giggled even louder, and this time she was the one turning red. "I have to admit, my situation is a little more confusing, since I have a variety of… *options* and may change from one day to the next. But yeah. The man is hopeless."

Neither one of them could speak for some time. Erin had to get herself a glass of cold water when she started hiccuping. Every time she tried to get back on track with a serious study of what clues the secret admirer might have been giving her that they might have missed, she just started laughing again.

Poor Willie.

CHAPTER 33

$\mathcal{E}$rin had not told Vic about the woman Adrienne had referred to as the purser, who handed out the checks to keep people quiet. And she hadn't told Adrienne that she had recognized her description of Matthew, the man who had been talking to Fontainebleau about his son.

She wondered what kind of payment that warranted. Not only had Fontainebleau assaulted Matthew's wife, but he had fathered a child who might have some claim on his estate. The boy could come forward at some point and demand to be acknowledged. Fontainebleau had another son, but there was plenty of money to go around. However much the purser had given Matthew, it probably wasn't as much as he would have gotten in court for all of those years of parental support. Or enough to even touch what Matthew's son would receive if he were to inherit after Fontainebleau's death. There wasn't any amount that would compensate him for the loss of his wife to depression, which would certainly have been exacerbated by the assault, the birth of her son, and keeping the secret from Matthew, who continued to work for Fontainebleau for years after.

Erin waited until Charley came in to take the afternoon shift, and then once more drove out to the Homestead. Not to see Adrienne this time, but Freda Jones, the woman known as the purser.

What if Jones refused to see her? She didn't have any reason to talk to

Erin. And probably a hundred reasons not to. She had enough work without having to deal with a nosy baker from town who wanted to know all of her secrets.

Or at least, one of them.

And not only did Jones not have any reason to see Erin, but she also had no reason to reveal the identity of the man Adrienne had seen. She had paid him to be quiet, so why would she disclose the information to Erin? Erin would need to be smart about it. To prise the name out of Jones without her knowing why or that it had any real importance to Erin.

But she didn't know how she was going to manage that. Jones would know she hadn't driven all the way to the Homestead to gossip over a cup of tea and reminisce about the various people she had paid off over the last year.

Erin hesitated at whether to park in the same place as she had when she had dropped off and picked up Adrienne. Maybe she should park out front like she was an expected guest instead of sneaking in a side door like one of the staff. But she didn't know the protocols, who was allowed to park there and how to convince the receptionist to let her talk to the purser. Her chances were better if she worked her way in from the back.

Erin let herself in the door, which was not locked. She was amazed every time she got there at the lack of security. Or visible security. She looked around the entryway for cameras. There should at least be cameras at the outside doors, even if Fontainebleau did not like them in the inner rooms. She couldn't imagine how the security staff could keep track of who was coming and going without them. But Willie had said that they could be hidden, that she wouldn't even see them. Maybe someone was watching her arrival.

She walked into the Homestead with no idea how she would even find the purser. She didn't know her way around in the rabbit's warren of back hallways. And she had no idea whether the purser's office was conveniently beside Mr. Fontainebleau's office or buried somewhere else in the maze.

She didn't have far to go before she came across a couple of women chatting as they walked down the hallway. They stopped talking at looked at Erin curiously, apparently knowing she didn't belong there.

"I got turned around," Erin told them, smiling warmly. "Can you tell me which way to go to find Mrs. Jones?"

The two women exchanged glances, then directed Erin down an adjoining hallway, with a series of turns she should take to find the purser. Erin nodded as if this all made sense and went down the hall they had indicated. The process was repeated several times, Erin getting closer to Freda Jones's office each time, until she finally arrived.

She knocked tentatively on the door, unsure whether Jones would be on the phone or with a visitor, and if people normally walked in or had to be called upon and have an appointment set ahead of time. There was a "Yes?" from within. Erin opened the door and poked her head in uncertainly.

"Uh—Mrs. Jones?"

A woman sat at the large, heavy desk. Perhaps fifty years old, with red hair bobbed at her shoulders, graying around the roots. She wore glasses and was dressed in conservative business attire, a modest gray dress with a classic cut. "Come in. Can I help you?"

She set aside the file she had been looking at and gave Erin her attention. Erin entered the room, hesitated, and pulled the door closed behind her.

"I'm sorry to disturb you without an appointment. My name is Erin Price, and I work in town—"

"At the bakery."

"Yes." Erin nodded. "Auntie Clem's. I don't think I've ever seen you there…"

The woman did not look familiar. She knew most of her regular customers, but wouldn't necessarily remember if Jones had been there only once or twice in the time that the bakery had been open.

"No, I haven't had the pleasure," Jones agreed. "Although I have had the pleasure of eating some of your baked goods. They are very good."

"Oh, thank you. I didn't know if… I thought you probably get your groceries for the Homestead delivered from the city."

"Yes, usually. But we occasionally have other goods brought in from Bald Eagle Falls or other towns close by. For a while, we were able to get these locally crafted jams." She smacked her lips. "Jam Lady. Did you ever have those?"

Erin laughed. "Yes, I know the Jam Lady. Both the brand and the person. It's too bad that they aren't able to make them anymore. They were really good. Though maybe… there's always the possibility they could take it up again." Erin knew the secret identity of the Jam Lady, though she would never reveal it.

"That would be wonderful. You'll have to tell me if they do. They were very good." Jones motioned for Erin to take a seat in one of the large leather chairs in front of her desk. "Please. Have a seat." She adjusted her glasses. "What can I do for you today?"

"I'm looking for some information on a man who works here. Or used to work here; I think he has retired now. I don't know his last name, only his first name. And maybe he didn't even work out of the Homestead. He might have worked at one of the company's other locations."

"Yes…?"

"His name is Matthew? Around fifty years old, I think. Graying hair. Rimless glasses. Pleasant looking."

Jones nodded. "Matthew Harris," she offered.

And Erin had his name. She hadn't had to be sneaky about it at all.

"What do you want Matthew for?" Jones asked.

"He has some information that I need. I ran into him the other day but forgot that I needed something else…"

"What would you need someone with his expertise for? I know that bakers need a certain amount of understanding of basic chemistry, but I wouldn't think that there would be a lot of overlap between the chemical processing that Matthew is an expert in and the chemistry of rising dough and protein structures."

Erin's heart quickened at the revelation that Matthew was knowledgeable in chemistry. He could probably transform elemental mercury into something that could be hidden in Fontainebleau's food without a second thought.

"Well, no, it wasn't actually anything to do with chemistry, more with… history. He's been around these parts for a while. He has a lot of knowledge about… the history of the area."

Jones's eyes were quick and discerning. Did she know more than she was letting on? Were Erin's answers more revealing than she had meant them to be?

"Well, I hope Matthew can give you the information you need. He was always a very good employee. I was sorry to see him go."

"Do you know what he's doing now that he retired from the company? Is he just fishing and enjoying life? I know he has a son..."

"Yes, I think he's planning on spending more time with his family. After putting in so many years with the company, he deserves it. But I wonder how he will enjoy retirement. Some people are never really able to slow down and adjust to it."

Matthew might be forced to slow down more than he expected to.

"Does he live in the city now? I don't have his address."

"Actually, he's in Bald Eagle Falls. The two of you are practically neighbors."

"I don't suppose you have his address?" She might be pushing her luck asking for it. And she was sure that Terry would have access to Matthew Harris's address through DMV records or other government sources.

"Well, let's see..." Jones tapped her computer keys and clicked busily on her screen. "You're Adrienne's friend."

Erin swallowed. She nodded slowly. She hoped that her being there would not cause Adrienne problems. She didn't want Jones to associate the nosy baker with the hard worker who really needed to keep her job at the Homestead.

"I know Adrienne, yes. Helped her out by giving her a ride a couple of times lately. She's... very appreciative of her job here. I'm not here because of anything to do with her."

Jones looked away from her computer to meet Erin's eyes for a moment, then looked back at the computer again. "Yes. The job seems to be very important to her."

"It's hard for a single mom to find something stable. And Adrienne... faces a lot of challenges."

"It's too bad that she's run into problems."

That was too subtle for Erin to know whether Jones was hinting at the assault on Hope, or Adrienne being homeless and a mom, or a gentle warning for Erin to stay out of the way and not cause any more problems for her.

"I hope that... nothing will change with Mr. Fontainebleau's death. That she'll still be able to work here like she has been."

"Maybe things will be better now."

That was reassuring. They at least weren't planning on booting Adrienne out the door with the change in management.

"If she abides by the terms of her agreement," Jones added, still looking at her computer screen.

Her employment agreement? Or the nondisclosure agreement that kept her from talking to anyone about what Fontainebleau had done? Adrienne would have to take better care. If she had been overheard talking to someone about what had happened, even someone in the Homestead who already knew, she could be in trouble. Erin made a mental note to give Adrienne a heads-up. She didn't want to lose her job or the money she had been promised that would allow her to move into a place of her own.

"Of course," Erin agreed.

Jones looked away from the screen and made eye contact again. She gave a nod. "Good. Matthew's address…"

Erin dug her planner out of her purse and flipped to a fresh page to take down the address. Jones read it out.

"I enjoyed working with Matthew," she said. "We were both here for a long time. I enjoyed getting to know him and his family over the years. Give him my regards…"

"Sure, of course. I'll let him know that you were thinking of him."

CHAPTER 34

*E*rin's thoughts were whirling as she drove home. Matthew was living in Bald Eagle Falls and she knew where to find him. Jones knew who Erin was and that she was friends with Adrienne. She still wanted Adrienne to keep working there but Adrienne had to abide by the terms of her NDA. Jones and Matthew were friends. Jones knew things would be better for Adrienne with Fontainebleau out of the way. She had known Matthew's family, saw what Fontainebleau had done to them. Yet she had stood by and let Fontainebleau destroy the family.

And Adrienne? Had Jones made the same false promises to others as she had to Adrienne? Said that she would take care of things and see that no one else was put in danger, and then let the same thing happen again time after time, family after family?

Erin knew that Terry would not be home yet, and called to see whether he was at the police department offices or out on street patrol. He liked to be out and about so, if there weren't anything pressing on the Fontainebleau investigation, he would probably be out with K9.

"Erin. How are you doing?"

"Good. Are you in the office? I have some information for you."

"Uh, no. But I'm not far. I can meet you there. What's this about?" He was using his *have-you-been-poking-your-nose-where-it-doesn't-belong* tone of voice.

"I'll tell you about it when I get there."

"Hmm. Okay. See you in a few minutes."

By the time she got to the police department, Terry was standing in the reception area, talking to Clara while he waited for Erin to arrive. She appreciated not having to get past the gatekeeper to see him. He just ushered her into his office and cleared space for her to sit down. He sat behind his desk and K9 lay down on the floor beside him with a sigh.

"So... what have you got?"

"I think I have the name and address of my secret admirer." She didn't know why she was still calling Matthew her secret admirer when she knew that his reason for contacting her had nothing to do with how he felt about her, but only to pass on clues about Fontainebleau and his killer.

"Really. Where did you get that information?"

Erin pulled out her planner and passed it to him so he could copy Matthew's information. "I just... Adrienne had heard him talking to someone at the Homestead, and when she described him, it sounded like the man who delivered the lingerie. And I talked to him when I ran into him in the woods. I just... I suspected that he was the one who had sent it, not that he was just the deliveryman."

"But you don't know for sure. He might just be a courier."

"Maybe. But the man that Adrienne saw at the Homestead... well, obviously he had access to Fontainebleau. And if he worked at the Homestead, then why would he be a courier? If it's the same guy, he retired from Fontainebleau's company, but I don't see a scientist like him rushing out to get a job as a courier. If he did want to work, I would think it would be in... academics or as a consultant in the mining industry. Not delivering parcels around Bald Eagle Falls."

Terry nodded. "You seem to know a lot about him for someone Adrienne just happened to mention that she saw at the Homestead that sounded like someone you had seen here in town."

"Adrienne knew a little bit about him. That he had just retired, and some other stuff. And when I talked to the woman who's in charge over there, she was the one who said that he was a chemist."

Terry's eyebrows went up. "A chemist?"

"Yeah. I figured... someone like that would know how to mix up the kind of mercury you could add to food."

"Yes, he probably would. And exactly when did he retire?"

"I'm not sure exactly when. And... if he took the barometer from the Homestead, he could get in and out, even if he doesn't have a legitimate reason to be there. You know that their security is... not very good."

"Who is this woman you talked to who is in charge?"

"Her name is Freda Jones. I don't know all of her duties, but she knew Matthew's last name and where he lived. They've both worked there for a long time, so she knew him quite well."

"And didn't have a problem with giving you his personal information?"

"Well... I was a little surprised at that too. I figured she'd turn me away, or I'd have to find a good reason why I should have access to it. But all I had to do was ask. She seemed happy to give it to me."

"Maybe she suspects him of having had something to do with the poisoning. Although, you would think that if she knew something, she might want to talk to the police investigating it."

"Maybe she doesn't know anything, so she didn't want to throw accusations around, but she still has her suspicions." Erin shrugged. "I don't know. It seems like a lot of people just don't want to talk to the police."

Terry nodded. "Welcome to my world. 'We want you to keep the peace and arrest all of the criminals in the area, but we don't want to give you any information that will allow you to do so.'"

Erin chuckled. "Yeah. That sounds frustrating."

She knew that she should probably leave. She'd given Terry the information that she had come to give him. It was up to him to follow up on it.

"How are you going to... you know..." Erin motioned to the address he had written down, "make contact with him?"

"Knock on his door. Tell him that we have some questions for him. Follow up on the anonymous deliveries. Hope that it leads us to something about Fontainebleau's death."

"I was thinking... wouldn't it be better if *I* contacted him? I mean... he picked me out as the person to send his deliveries to. He obviously wanted to tell me about it, for me to figure it out."

"You are not a law enforcement officer."

"Well, I know that."

"We can't involve a civilian in an investigation."

"But you have before. I've helped before. Answered questions. Helped work through possibilities."

"Not the same as sending you in as an agent of the police."

"Well then, maybe… it will take you a while to get your stuff together, and I could just happen to go over there first."

"Erin."

"You use informants. You do that all the time."

He raised his brows.

"Well, okay, maybe not all the time. But they do on TV. And you use information that civilians bring you."

"I'm not sending you in to talk to this guy by yourself. There's every likelihood that he is a killer. Now he may have done the world a favor by getting rid of someone like Fontainebleau, but someone who has killed once is that much more likely to kill again. And people who are trapped tend to fight back."

"I just think… he'll talk to me. He's been trying to give me clues as to what happened. So let him. Let him give me the final clues so that you know who it was and can make an arrest."

"Clues are not the same as proof. I need proof before I can arrest someone."

"Maybe he'll have it. He had the barometer."

"And we don't know whether the barometer actually had anything to do with the poisoning of Fontainebleau. The medical examiner says he was not poisoned with elemental mercury. It had to be made into a compound and sprinkled or stirred into his food or drinks."

"But Matthew is a chemist. He could have done that."

"We'll need proof. Not just talking to him. A search warrant for his home or workshop, wherever he might have mixed it. Witnesses who can put him in proximity with Fontainebleau. Motive."

Erin opened her mouth and closed it again. Terry looked at her, waiting.

"Motive?" Terry suggested again.

"I… this is unverified."

"As is everything else at this point. Don't hold back on me."

"Fontainebleau assaulted Matthew's wife. Years ago, without Matthew realizing it. Matthew just recently discovered that his son is not his biological son, but Fontainebleau's."

"Well… yes, that would certainly be a motive. What is the wife's story? Does she confirm this? That it was an assault rather than an affair?"

"I think that either way, it gives him motive to kill Fontainebleau. But the wife is dead. Suicide some years ago."

"Ouch."

"So Fontainebleau really screwed up Matthew's family. And was never punished for it. That's a pretty good motive."

"Yes, it is," Terry agreed. He leaned back in his chair, staring at his computer screen. "I'm going to have to discuss this with the others. Work out a plan. Make sure we've got all of our ducks in a row before approaching him."

"And tell them that I should be the one to talk to him. Because I'm the one he reached out to."

Terry scowled. "I'll talk to the others."

CHAPTER 35

"Stand back and to the side until I tell you otherwise," Terry reminded Erin. He was not standing directly in front of the door himself as he reached over and rang the doorbell. He formed a fist to knock on the door loudly, as cops did, then relaxed it and just waited. The point was to keep it as informal as possible so that Matthew would feel comfortable talking to them instead of clamming up because Terry was a law enforcement officer. Things had taken longer to arrange than Erin had expected but, after the many hours it took for the police department to formulate a plan that everyone could live with and make all of the arrangements, they were finally standing on Matthew's front step.

The door opened slowly, and the familiar face peered out. The man looked at Terry, K9 standing beside him, and then his eyes slid to Erin and he smiled.

"Erin Price," he greeted pleasantly.

"Matthew?"

He nodded. He opened the door the rest of the way and motioned them in. Terry stepped forward and glanced around inside, then made a slight motion for Erin to follow him. He was the first one in the house and was keeping a close eye on Matthew and for any other sign of danger in their surroundings.

There didn't seem to be anyone else in the house. If Matthew's son lived there, it would seem he was out. The house was quiet and still.

Matthew ushered them into a comfortable-looking living room, one that had seen use and was not just preserved in pristine condition for someday in the future when somebody important might visit.

"Have a seat, please," Matthew invited, motioning to the couch in the living room. He swept several magazines off the surface, stacked them, squared the edges, and put them down on the coffee table, which was already thick with reading material. "Sorry. Just getting caught up on some reading."

They sat down and K9 lay at Terry's side.

Erin looked over the magazine titles. They all seemed to be professional magazines. Chemistry, engineering, mining, mineralogy. Way over Erin's head. Was there anything in there on the latest methods of processing with mercury? Erin had done a couple of internet searches and found that mercury was used in processing gold. She had always thought of the mines in Tennessee as being mostly coal, as attested to by Willie's darkly stained skin, but there were other precious minerals mined in the area.

Erin looked at Terry. He gave a little nod. "I should introduce myself. I'm Terry Piper from the Bald Eagle Falls police department. We haven't met before, I don't think."

He wanted to be sure that Matthew could not claim that he had been tricked or coerced into giving a confession to a police officer if it turned out that he said something they wanted to use in court. It was not an undercover operation.

Matthew nodded his understanding, not appearing to be put off by this information. "Yes. Nice to meet you."

It was Erin's turn. She was a little tongue-tied facing her secret admirer, and uncertain how to start the conversation. She hoped to be able to get a lot of information from him and, if she goofed up, they might be kicked out with nothing but denials. Matthew knew something, and it might take some delicacy to get all that information from him.

"So, you know who I am," Erin said with a little laugh. "But you have the advantage over me because we've never been introduced. You're Matthew Harris."

"Yes."

"And you're my secret admirer. The person who has been sending me packages."

"I've been delivering them."

Erin gazed at him steadily. "I think you're more than the deliveryman."

He looked away after a few seconds. "What makes you think that?"

"You used to work with Fontainebleau. At the Homestead. You had access to the newspaper clippings and the barometer. Those couldn't come from just anyone."

"A lot of people might have had access to those things. And I don't work there anymore. I'm retired."

"It's pretty easy to get in and out of there. There isn't any security guard or gate. Maybe if they thought you were a threat, they would do something about it, but people walk in and out of there all day. I've been in a few times, and no one has ever challenged my right to be there. I've never had to talk to any security personnel."

"There is plenty of security that you don't see. They would get rid of you fairly quickly if they didn't want you to be there."

"But they didn't. Someone was able to poison Mr. Fontainebleau without getting caught. And you were able to get the newspaper clippings and barometer out of there without being stopped."

He shrugged. "So you say."

"I think… you want to tell me about what happened. You want someone to know what you did, and you picked me out to be the one to tell. That's why you've been sending me these gifts. Because you want to tell me what happened."

"Someone should know. But there are certain… barriers to telling anyone the full story of what has been happening at the Homestead."

"Well… I'm here. So why don't you tell me about it?"

He sat back and looked at Erin with an expression of consternation. "I said that there were barriers."

Erin nodded. Until he said what those barriers were—whether he was afraid to talk in front of the police or had some ethical dilemma, she couldn't do anything to encourage him to tell the story. She could maybe prompt him, talk about what it was that they knew so far, but Matthew needed to break through a few of those barriers before they were going to get anywhere.

Matthew looked at Terry, and back at Erin again. "I'd like to be able to talk to you about what I know… but I can't. I'm sorry."

Erin hadn't expected a flat-out no. "You sent me those things for a reason."

"Yes, obviously," he agreed.

"And it wasn't just because… you admired me and wanted to give me a barometer."

"No."

"I think that you gave me the barometer to point out that mercury was involved."

Matthew said nothing.

"You know that Fontainebleau was killed with mercury poisoning," Erin said.

"I imagine the symptoms line up," he said mildly. "I'm not a medical examiner, and I can't tell you what they found in the autopsy."

"The medical examiner has determined that mercury toxicity is the cause of death. And since there wasn't enough mercury at his work sites to cause death by casual exposure—and his employees who are there every day would succumb to it first—the manner of death was homicide."

Matthew spread his hands. "Then you already know that," he summarized.

"The paramedics and medical examiner immediately noticed the rashes. And the descriptions of his behavior in the weeks before his death suggest heavy metal poisoning."

Matthew nodded.

"You're familiar with mercury, aren't you, Mr. Harris?" Terry asked. "Handling it, toxicity, compounding it."

"Sure. It was my job to know all of that stuff."

"Why don't you tell us what led you to poison him? I suspect you would really like to get it off your chest. What Fontainebleau did that deserved death."

"I can't do that. For one thing, I did not poison him."

"You had good reason to hate him."

Matthew shrugged, not disagreeing.

"You gave him years of your life. Decades. And he had betrayed your trust. The impacts on your family were catastrophic."

Matthew swallowed. He looked around. "Can I get you something to drink? I didn't offer you a drink."

Even though both Terry and Erin immediately shook their heads, he got up and headed to the kitchen. Terry made to get up and go after him, but Erin put a hand on his knee to encourage him to stay there. He looked at her and stayed. But he gazed toward the kitchen as if he could see through the walls and waited for Matthew to make a wrong move. K9 was his mirror image, ears pointed toward the kitchen.

CHAPTER 36

They could hear the familiar sounds of a kettle being put on and the clinking of cups. No indication that Matthew was leaving through the back door or getting a weapon. Erin hadn't felt unsafe with him from the moment they'd walked into the house. Maybe part of that was Terry being there. She knew that he wouldn't let anything happen to her. But she didn't think Matthew would do anything violent. If he were the murderer, he had killed with good reason, and he hadn't shot Mr. Fontainebleau, but had poisoned him. Murder from a distance, over time, patient and waiting.

Eventually, Matthew returned with a tea tray. He set it down and poured water into each of their cups, motioning for them to help themselves to the tea bags, cream, and sugar. Erin reached for one, and Terry touched her arm, warning her. She looked at him. He gave his head a slight shake.

Taking tea with a poisoner? Maybe not the brightest possible move. While Erin felt sure there was nothing wrong with the teabags, commercial teas she'd used her whole life, there was the possibility of tampering. That they had been soaked in some poison, injected, or opened and closed again. Matthew looked from one of them to the other.

"They're perfectly safe. I told you I didn't poison Fontainebleau."

"You could have more mercury around here," Terry pointed out. "You could have prepared these ahead of time for just an occasion like this. We would be fools to drink them."

Matthew shook his head. "Hand me any one of them."

Terry selected a teabag and handed it to him. Without any apparent concern, Matthew plopped it into his cup to steep. That was a pretty good indicator that there wasn't any poison in the bag or any of the others that awaited them on the tray. Erin looked at Terry to see if this had convinced him.

Terry didn't take one. "They could all be poisoned. You might not care if you die. That might be your plan. If cornered, you take the coward's way out."

"You have a high opinion of me," Matthew said sarcastically. "I can assure you I have no intention of dying. Or of being arrested." He turned abruptly to a side table and picked up a photo frame. He turned the picture toward them. "My children," he explained, showing them the photo of the three of them standing together, arms around each other, smiling at the camera. Matthew, a daughter, and a son. The daughter a little shorter than he was, and the son almost a head taller, a gangly teen. "My daughter just had a baby. My first grandchild." He got out his phone and fiddled with it for a few minutes, finally turning it around to show his daughter, older in this picture, with a swaddled newborn in her arms. Swiping the picture, he showed them another, with proud grandpa holding up the baby for the camera. "Do you think I could leave them now? They need me. And I didn't raise them by myself just to abandon them for something like this. Their mother committed suicide. I could never do that to them."

He used his spoon to squeeze the teabag against the cup a few times and then lifted the teabag out and set it on his saucer. He took a sip of the tea and exhaled a long sigh.

"But he's not your son," Terry said. "You recently found out that he isn't actually biologically yours."

Matthew looked surprised that he knew this. "That doesn't make him any less my son. I raised him from infancy. I was there for the ultrasounds and doctor's appointments before he was born. I was at my wife's side and held him first." He swallowed hard, eyes shining. "Of course he's my son."

"And you wanted to punish Fontainebleau for what he had done. For what he did to your wife. For his complicity in your wife's death."

"Of course I wanted to. But what good would that do? How would it change anything? I wouldn't risk my life with my children and grandchildren for that despicable man. I should have turned him in. But after this long, I didn't think there was any chance of him being charged. Not after this many years, and with his power and wealth. His influence would keep him safe, just like it always had."

"You knew about other cases?"

He looked away. "Of course I'd heard the rumors. We all had. I never saw any proof of it, and I was happy to keep it that way. Better that it was an unfounded rumor than that I knew the truth." He snorted and shook his head at himself, sounding disgusted. "All of us should have been more interested in the truth and stopping a predator than in preserving our own jobs and reputations. Letting him operate in the dark like that, year after year, was tacit approval of what he did. We were all complicit in those assaults on those young women."

"Then why are you keeping quiet?" Erin asked. "Even after his death? Why would you keep protecting him and his reputation?"

"What difference would it make now? He has been stopped. He won't ever do that again. There's no reason for me to give up my... security to talk about what kind of a monster he was."

"You'd rather have the money," Terry said.

"I would rather be able to give my children and grandchildren the things that they need. To make sure that they never want. I took early retirement. I was owed every penny. I worked for him for years and earned every cent."

"You let him buy your silence."

Matthew shook his head, his jaw clenching and unclenching. "I haven't said a word. And I'm not going to. But there were things I *could* do." He made a motion toward Erin. "Ways that I could communicate without words."

"So you started sending me the anonymous deliveries," Erin said. "That was your way of telling the story."

He shrugged and sipped his tea.

"But you haven't told us anything," Terry pointed out. "Was the lingerie supposed to symbolize his sexual assaults? Or is that just the spin we're supposed to put on it when you realized that you didn't have any chance of courting Erin? The flowers? Were they supposed to symbolize something? Innocence and purity? And there's nothing in the news articles to indicate what he had done. Just puff pieces about the golden son coming back to save the company from ruin. There was nothing there about his predatory behavior or what he did once he took over the company. You didn't even pick any modern pieces that talked about what he had done over the years. You picked old articles that said nothing."

"Anything modern, the police could get off the internet, and I assumed you were already doing that. The old articles... you'd have to go to archives to find. And why would you, since all of his history was included in the current press? Or a version of it, anyway."

"I thought you picked those articles to show his father's involvement with the Dyson clan," Erin said. "How his father got the company into debt and what Fontainebleau the Third had to pull the company out of. Or his ongoing involvement with them."

Matthew raised his brows. He had another sip of tea and wet his lips. "There were always rumors of his involvement with organized crime. But I never saw any proof of it. I wasn't involved in the financial stuff. Just in the operations of the mines and the chemical processing. Anything on financing and debt and how he got his money... that wasn't anything to do with me."

CHAPTER 37

"So you won't talk about what Fontainebleau did to your wife or how she was involved with him," Terry stated.

"I can't. I signed an agreement."

"You would have to if called to testify in court."

"But that isn't going to happen. I'm not going to court."

"If we find evidence that you were involved in poisoning Fontainebleau, you certainly are."

Matthew set his teacup down and folded his hands. "I was not. You won't find anything to prove that I was. In the weeks before Fontainebleau's death, I wasn't even here. I was visiting my daughter. Helping her to get settled with the new baby. Making sure they had everything they needed."

"We have a warrant to search this house."

Erin's secret admirer looked a little surprised by this, but raised his shoulders in a shrug. "You won't find anything."

Terry stood up. He reached out a hand to give Erin a hand up as well. "This is your exit cue," he told her. "And I call the others in to do the search."

Erin nodded. She had been expecting this, though she hadn't expected the interview to end so quickly or that she would be left confused about whether Matthew had really had anything to do with the poisoning. She had thought that by the time she left, Matthew would be under arrest, and she would know for sure that he had been the one to kill Fontainebleau. If it had been a TV show, he would have confessed his involvement, and there would be plenty of evidence to back his story up. As it was… maybe Terry and the other law enforcement officers would find something in the search.

Matthew stood, putting his teacup down carefully. "I have one more delivery for you, Miss Price."

Erin's eyes went to Terry to gauge his response. He shook his head. "No more games. If you have something to say, then say it."

"This isn't from me. As I said… I can't say anything. I can't afford to lose my retirement funds."

Terry didn't look happy about this. But what were they going to do? Refuse to accept a piece of evidence that was offered to them? If it was like the rest of Matthew's gifts, it probably wouldn't solve the case, but it was possible that it would at least push them in the right direction.

"Just wait here," Matthew instructed, and headed for the hallway.

Terry's hand shot out, and he grabbed Matthew by the shoulder. "You're not going anywhere." K9 growled a warning.

Erin's heart was in her throat. She couldn't help thinking of the TV shows she had seen where the perpetrator of a crime walked out of the room to get a wallet or some other possession, followed by an off-screen gunshot as they committed suicide.

"Matthew," she protested.

He looked back at her. "I just want to get that delivery for you."

"You can tell us where it is and we'll grab it during our search," Terry told him sternly. "You sit back down there and stay put. We don't like suspects walking around a scene while we are conducting a search. Things get damaged, destroyed, flushed down the toilet. I would tell you to leave until we are finished, only I don't want you out of sight."

Matthew sighed and pulled gently away from Terry. He sat back down in his chair. Terry nodded at Erin.

"Out you go. Send the sheriff in."

Erin walked out of Matthew's house and nodded to Sheriff Wilmot, waiting at the edge of the property line. "He's ready for you."

Wilmot and the others walked up to the door, Wilmot flourishing a sheet of paper folded lengthwise at the door. "Search warrant," he announced, and then was inside the house and Erin couldn't see or hear any more of what happened. The law enforcement officers entered and shut the door behind them.

Erin waited outside of the house.

This hadn't been part of her agreement with Terry, who expected her to go home once her role in the investigation was completed. But she wanted to be there when they retrieved the item Matthew had intended to deliver to her. Or when they found traces of mercury or lab equipment in the house. Or maybe a written confession of what he had done.

Though she wasn't sure now that he had actually done anything.

Murderers lied all of the time, of course. Matthew still wanted to be able to see his children and grandchildren, so he didn't want to be arrested. He would say he hadn't done it even if he had. And if they could verify that he had, in fact, been visiting his daughter and new grandbaby, and couldn't have gotten back to the Homestead to poison Fontainebleau during that time, then they would have to admit that he was not the poisoner.

They didn't come out again within a few minutes like Erin had hoped. It couldn't take them very long to find whatever Matthew wanted to give her, but Terry also wouldn't know that she was still waiting outside for him to bring it to her. They had arrived in Terry's truck, so she returned to it and sat waiting.

Eventually, the Bald Eagle Falls police department exited Matthew Harris's house. They didn't carry very much with them. A few items to be tested for mercury residue, Erin assumed. Maybe some personal correspondence or a journal that they wanted to examine at length. And whatever it was that Matthew had planned to give her, if that hadn't been a ruse to get out of the room before the search was performed.

The law enforcement officers clustered together outside the house to discuss proceedings. Maybe they needed to search the backyard and whatever garage or shed Matthew had, if they hadn't already.

Looking away from the others as he talked, Terry's eyes focused on his truck, and he saw Erin inside. He shook his head and walked over to her.

"You didn't need to wait around. You should have gone home."

She couldn't exactly complain that she hadn't had her own vehicle to get home in, since everything in the town was within walking distance.

"I wanted to see what you found out. And what Matthew had for me."

He held up an envelope with Erin's name hand-printed neatly on it. "That is apparently the last delivery."

"Did Matthew write it?"

He looked at the printing and shrugged. "I don't know. He won't say a word about it, of course. Keeping his agreement not to say anything to anyone about the whole affair." He rolled his eyes heavenward. "If he was so concerned about justice being done, he could break his NDA and speak to us."

"But then he would lose the money he has to live on for the next few years. He's too young to start drawing on a 401K or pension."

"What is more important? Seeing justice done or having money? I thought that he was concerned with right and wrong."

"I think the most important thing for him in all of this is family. And he needs to take care of his children. Does his son still live with him?"

Terry nodded. "Searched his room. Nothing of concern there."

Erin let out a breath. "Good. I was afraid that he might be protecting someone in his family."

"That doesn't mean that it *wasn't* his son who poisoned Fontainebleau. But he would have needed access to the man at the Homestead. And I think that the staff out there would at least be able to tell us whether his son ever came out for visits in the past few weeks. Even if they aren't in the habit of kicking out anyone who doesn't belong."

"But how old is he? Eighteen? I doubt if he would plan out a crime like that. Mercury poisoning isn't something an eighteen-year-old would necessarily think of or have the patience to carry out. Teenagers are impulsive. A shooting or stabbing, maybe. Not something that took place over a period of weeks."

Terry made a gesture that was half nod, half shrug. "I don't think the son had anything to do with it. I'm just saying that there isn't any evidence one way or the other right now. I want to interview him to see what he has to say about his father's behavior over the last few weeks. If he's noticed any changes. Any odd smells coming from behind closed doors. Talk of getting back at Fontainebleau or someone who has done him wrong."

"You don't think he would tell you anything, do you?"

"No, probably not. But you never know. Maybe he's had some concerns. Sometimes kids need someone to talk to…"

She didn't like the idea of his acting sensitive and empathetic toward the young man just to get incriminating statements about his father out of him.

Erin reached for the envelope. "So, can I see it?"

"We need to take any fingerprints or trace evidence, and then open and read it. After that…"

Erin rolled her eyes. "*Then* I can see the note that was intended for me?"

He shrugged, having the grace to look slightly embarrassed. "Maybe. You know that we're not able to release evidence in an active investigation."

"Without me, you wouldn't have that evidence. I can't even see it? You can open it now. Let me read it. Or take a picture and send me when you open it at the police department offices. You can't just push me out of my own…" She trailed off, realizing that she was going to claim it was her own investigation. But she was a baker. Not a police officer or private investigator. She didn't have an investigation. Just curiosity about what had happened to Mr. Fontainebleau. It wasn't *really* any of her business, even if Matthew had tried to bring her in on it.

The corner of Terry's mouth quirked up, and the dimple appeared on his cheek. "It's not your investigation."

"I know. But I really want to know. I think I deserve to see what's in a letter that's addressed to me. I didn't have to bring you into any of this. I could have just gone to see Matthew on my own without telling you. Then he would have given that to me and I could have read it. And *maybe* shared it with you, if I felt like it." She gave him an impish smile, teasing him.

"I will *try* to get you a copy. I can't open it here, but at the police department offices… I'll share it when I can. If I can."

"You've got a camera. Someone has to take pictures of it."

"You are relentless."

"But that's what you love about me, right?"

Terry shook his head. "Do you want me to drive you home on the way back to the office? Or do you want to walk?"

K9 gave a little whine at the word "walk." Erin laughed and scratched his ears. "Sorry, boy, I think you're going to be sitting in the office for the rest of the day." She looked around. It had been hot sitting in the truck. She hadn't wanted to run the air conditioner the whole time Terry was in the house, idling the engine, so she had only turned it on for a minute or two every now and then to take the edge off. But out in the open air, it actually wasn't too bad.

She would go for a walk and think about what she had learned about the case so far. Maybe she wouldn't need the final delivery. Maybe she'd be able to figure it out herself if she put her mind to work while she walked.

CHAPTER 38

$\mathcal{E}$rin didn't have any brilliant insights on the way home. Matthew Harris could be the poisoner. Maybe. Even if he had an alibi for the weeks that Fontainebleau had been suffering from mercury poisoning, he might have poisoned the man before he left, and it just took him that long to die. Mercury was a slow killer.

Or Matthew might have put it into something that Fontainebleau would continue to consume while Matthew was gone. Teabags, coffee grounds, a daily vitamin, cigars or some other indulgence that he would take dose by dose the entire time that Matthew was away, slowly poisoning himself until he succumbed.

Maybe he was supposed to die while Matthew was still out of town instead of waiting until he came back so that Matthew could declare with authority that he hadn't even been there when Fontainebleau had died. That he was totally in the clear.

But so many other people had just as much or more opportunity to poison Fontainebleau. And just as much motive as Matthew did. Fontainebleau had hurt a lot of people, broken a lot of lives.

There was nothing else Erin could do about it. She didn't have anyone else to ask questions of or any other avenues to pursue. She had exhausted all of her leads. Terry held the final piece of evidence. He and the rest of the police department would be examining it as Erin worked on the next day's plans and made herself supper. Sorting out all of the clues and coming to a landing on it without any input from Erin.

She was surprised to hear Terry come home as she was putting her supper dishes in the dishwasher. She looked around, realizing that she would have to get everything out again to dish up dinner for Terry. He would be tired and hungry after a long day of investigating.

Terry didn't relax and release K9 from duty when he walked in the door. He didn't even glance toward the kitchen or sniff at the air and say that something smelled good. He looked at Erin and gave her a nod of acknowledgment.

"I need your help."

Erin laughed. "You need my help? Well, that's the last thing I expected to hear from you. Was the last clue a recipe that I need to make? Some mercury-containing ingredient that you need me to identify?"

"No. I need to know if you can identify the author of the note."

"It wasn't Matthew?"

He shook his head. "No, not as far as we can tell. We're at a loss as to the author, but since you are the intended recipient, we assume you will know who the sender is."

Erin nodded. She sat down on the couch to get comfortable and waited for him to give her or read her the note. Terry sat on one of the chairs, perched on the edge as if ready to jump up the instant she told him what he wanted to know. He reached into the zippered portfolio that he held against his body under one arm and withdrew a plastic document holder with a single sheet of notepaper in it.

Blank white paper, nothing identifiable about it. As far as she could see, no name, address, or watermark for the company. Torn from a tablet on someone's desk rather than taken from a ream of copy paper. Erin focused on the words on the page.

I told A that I would take care of it, and I did.

I have watched the man ruin so many lives and helped him to do it. But I couldn't let it go this time.

I couldn't let him attack a child and just cover it up.

It was in the fish that Fontainebleau ate at least once a week for his health. I didn't poison it. He did that himself by dumping wastewater into bodies of water that he hoped would not be tested. He knew that it was not safe and would poison the wildlife and anyone who depended on the lake for their water source.

He knew it would poison someone. It seemed only fitting that it should be himself. All I did was provide the kitchen with the fish he had contaminated.

Erin stared at the words on the paper in perfectly formed cursive handwriting. Something that the younger generation could barely read or write anymore. But for the older generations, it was natural, and it looked like the author had practiced until her formation was perfect, all with regular slant, size, and spacing, even though there were no lines on the page.

"Do you know who wrote that?" Terry asked.

"I... don't know the handwriting. Sorry."

Erin hoped that he would leave it at that. She couldn't help him. He would have to figure it out himself, and he wouldn't be able to because everyone had agreed not to talk.

"Erin."

She raised her brows and shook her head. She handed it back to him.

"Don't try to put me off by not answering the question directly."

Erin cleared her throat. "Would I do that?"

He chuckled. "Of course you would. You're a master at deflection."

Erin couldn't help the embarrassed smile that spread across her face. She had done it to him too many times lately. He was on to her. She wasn't going to be able to distract him from the fact that she hadn't actually answered the question he had asked.

"We can go to the Homestead and ask questions about who provided the kitchen with fish, if that is really how he was poisoned. But that will tip everyone off, and we'd rather go in there knowing who our target is. So," Terry's voice was stern and all business. "Who wrote that note?"

Erin sighed. "They call her the purser. She's the one who is in charge of writing the checks to pay off Fontainebleau's victims to ensure their silence. She's the one who... would know where all the bodies were buried, so to speak."

"What's her name?"

"Freda Jones."

"She's the woman you said gave you Matthew's information. His name and address."

Erin nodded. "Yes."

He frowned. "Why would she give you that information? Especially if Matthew was the one who had this note? Why would she send it or give it to him and then send you to talk to him?"

"I don't know. I'm... a bit lost."

"She's confessed. It wasn't signed, but she knew you would understand where it came from."

Erin nodded. Her heart started beating faster. Earlier in the day, she had been worried about Matthew's intentions, afraid he would harm himself either by self-poisoning or by walking out of the room and shooting himself. But he wasn't the poisoner. At least, not according to this note. And if Jones was confessing, what were the chances that she was just sitting at the Homestead waiting for Terry or one of the other cops to go out there and arrest her?

"You don't think... Do you think that she's done something? She must have written this right after I went out to see her, and then asked Matthew to give it to me. You don't think...?"

"I don't know. You stay here, and I'll head out there and find out. Hopefully..."

Did he hope that he would find her and be able to arrest her? Or did he hope that she would have dealt justice to herself as well as to Clive William Fontainebleau III?

"I'm not staying here," Erin objected. "I'm coming with you."

"This is a police action, Erin. You can't."

"I'll follow you out, then. You can't stop me from coming."

"Why would you want to go out there? The news isn't going to be good. You know that. Either this woman is arrested for killing a truly despicable character and saving countless other people harm, or she's already dead. Neither scenario is one you want to be a part of."

"I'm already a part of this. She sent me the letter, and I told you who wrote it. I'm already all mixed up in this."

"There's no need for you to go out there. I can tell you what happens after it is all over. You don't want to see anything. And you wouldn't be allowed to. All that you'd be able to do is sit outside the house waiting for me to tell you what we find."

"That's all I want. I need to be there. I know I won't see anything and wouldn't want to. But you can't stop me from being a part of this."

"Apparently not," he agreed dryly.

"Do you want something to eat on the way?"

"What?" Terry looked distracted.

"A sandwich. Have you had anything for supper?"

"We ordered in at the office. Thank you, though." He met her eyes for a moment and nodded his thanks. "You're always looking out for me."

"No more than you do for me."

He reached out a hand to her to help her to her feet. Erin handed him the note in its plastic envelope instead of giving him her hand.

"That's not what I—"

"I know," Erin agreed. "Let's go."

Terry shook his head and led the way back out to his truck. K9 stuck close to his side, though he looked back at Erin once or twice to ensure she was following.

CHAPTER 39

They didn't have much conversation on the way out to the Homestead. Terry was busy on his phone, talking to the other law enforcement officers and ensuring everyone was on the same page. The Homestead was a big place and not secure. They would all head out there and try to cover the exits to ensure that Freda Jones couldn't slip out of their grasp, but they all knew there was no way they could cover every escape route. They didn't know what roads might run from the back of the property, through narrow country trails, before eventually coming out onto the highway. They could block the main road, but there were too many other possibilities.

"You need to stay in the truck," Terry told Erin again. "I mean it. No coming to check on me or anything else. You stay there until I tell you otherwise, which means you're going to be there for a while."

"I will."

Would she be able to see Freda one last time? Or had her last meeting been the only opportunity she would have to see the woman?

Eventually, they reached the Homestead. Terry parked in the more public lot at the front of the building. Other police vehicles passed them to cover other parts of the building. Erin watched Terry walk in with K9 at his side and wondered what he would find. Was Freda waiting to turn herself in? Or had she taken her own life? Would she try to run?

It was hard to picture Terry's progress, since Erin had never walked in through the front doors herself. She could only imagine what the grand hall looked like, whether it was bustling with activity or quiet and still. Whether there was a receptionist that would greet Terry and take him around to Jones's office, or a security guard or other staff member who would escort him.

She pictured Jones's office as she had seen it. Neat and tidy. A big, heavy desk. Not something made of particle board and assembled there. A real solid, antique desk. Bookshelves, a computer on the desk, sparsely decorated considering that she had worked there for decades. There wouldn't be any sign of the poison in her office. Not if she had seen to it that Fontainebleau was fed fish contaminated by his own plants. She didn't have to have a chemistry degree like Matthew to compound raw elemental mercury into something that could be sprinkled on Fontainebleau's food or dissolved in his drink. They wouldn't be looking for any evidence of chemistry projects in her office.

It was an interminably long time. Jones did not come sprinting out of the building or race by in a little compact car with the police in hot pursuit. Eventually, Terry walked out, talking on his phone, with K9 keeping pace at his side. He hung up the call before approaching the truck. He swung himself up into the driver's seat to talk to Erin.

"Your Mrs. Jones has flown the coop. No sign of her."

"She's not *my* Mrs.—"

"I know. But she's not there. Looks like she cleaned everything up, packed her bags, and left. No one knows where she was headed or if she has any relatives that she might have gone to. She worked with Fontainebleau for a long time. People didn't really go to her unless there was trouble, so she didn't have a lot of friends in the company."

A lonely life, only ever dealing with the people Fontainebleau may have harmed. But she'd had other duties as well. Administrative stuff that didn't involve paying people off.

"Where does she live? In town or in the city? On a farm?"

"Here on the Homestead. We've already checked out her rooms, and there's nothing there that gives any clue as to where she might have gone. I don't know how much she had to pack, but with what I have experienced in moving apartments or houses… she must have been planning this for some time. She didn't just pack an overnight bag and make a run for it. Everything personal has been cleared out. We'll have to ask around, see whether anyone saw a moving truck or rented trailer around here the last day or two."

"Well, she was poisoning Fontainebleau for weeks, so she had plenty of time to plan her... exit," Erin observed.

"Yes. She's a cool customer, watching Fontainebleau dying over the past few months. A sociopath."

Erin grimaced and shook her head. "I don't think so. I think she had feelings, empathy for the people that Fontainebleau had hurt. The lives that he had ruined. She said that she couldn't stand by and watch it anymore. It got to be too much for her."

"That's what she says. But she'd stood by for years, so what had changed? She might have been on the verge of losing her job, being fired or forced into retirement. This could just as easily have been about getting back at him, emptying a bank account or two, and setting up a new life somewhere else as about protecting his future victims."

"It was because of—" Erin cut herself off. She couldn't give away Adrienne's secret. Couldn't tell him about what had happened to Hope or that Adrienne had refused to come forward to the police afterward. He could call in social services, saying that Adrienne had harmed Hope by not seeking treatment for her. It wouldn't help Hope to be taken away from her family. That would just be another blow to all of them.

Terry waited, then shook his head, scowling. "You need to tell me, Erin. Holding things back isn't going to help anyone. If you know what's going on, you need to come out with it."

"No. It's just... in the letter. She said that it was something to do with a child. That she couldn't just sit back and watch when he had attacked a child."

Terry nodded slowly. "Yes. Someone around here must know what she's talking about. Something like that, they wouldn't be able to cover up."

Erin nodded. Hopefully, he was wrong and people would stay quiet, as they had been doing for years. They had been conditioned to keep quiet about what they saw and heard, about all of the rumors of Fontainebleau's behavior. She hoped that they would protect Hope, just as Jones had done. Erin wasn't going to be the one to reveal the incident to the police.

Terry studied her, and Erin knew he suspected she knew more than she was saying.

"Do you have any idea where she would go? Did she say anything to you about somewhere she would like to go, family members, anything like that?"

"No. Our conversation was pretty short. She didn't say anything personal like that."

"You just asked her for Matthew's information, and she gave it to you."

Erin shrugged and nodded. "Yes."

"I guess the two of them were in collusion... she knew he was sending you clues. And she had sent him the letter or was planning to. Maybe he had told her it was okay to give you his information if you went looking for him. It doesn't seem like he was making much effort to keep his identity a secret."

"No. I think that he wanted me to find him, in the end. Even if he couldn't tell me anything, he wanted me to know that he had done his best to reveal the truth."

"Only the truth that he wanted to reveal was about what Fontainebleau had been doing, not who had killed him," Terry pointed out. "He never sent you anything that pointed to Freda Jones until she gave him the letter to give to you."

"Maybe that had been the plan all along."

Terry shook his head slowly. "You think she always planned to confess? Not just when she thought we were closing in on her?"

"We never really had anything that pointed to her... other than her promise that she would make things right. And I never thought..." Erin trailed off.

"What promise?" Terry demanded.

Erin scrambled to repair her mistake. "Like she said in her letter. That she promised someone she would make things right. I thought that meant that she would go to the police about Fontainebleau, but maybe she meant that she would make sure it never happened again by getting rid of him."

"When did you know that she promised to make things right?" Terry countered.

"I... don't know. When I read the letter."

"You didn't think she was going to the police when she said that in the letter. You had her confession right in front of you. You knew that when she said she was going to make things right, she meant that she had killed him. *Unless* you found out about this promise before today."

Erin breathed slowly in and out, trying not to let anything in her face give away the truth to Terry.

"Who did she make this promise to? You know more than you're letting on, Erin. Who was the child that was attacked? Who did she promise that she would make things right?"

"I… can't say."

"You never signed a non-disclosure agreement. You can't withhold evidence from the police."

"I'm not. It's just… hearsay. I heard something from someone who heard it from someone else… It isn't evidence."

"You still need to tell us what you know."

"I don't *know* anything. And what I was told, I promised not to share."

"Crimes need to be reported to the police. Especially crimes against children, who need to be protected. You have a duty to report that."

"No, I don't."

He looked for some argument to persuade her that she needed to tell him. But Erin kept her mouth shut. She wasn't a nurse or a teacher or someone else who was required by law to report any suspicions about child abuse. She was just a regular citizen. And a regular citizen wasn't required to report rumors to the police. What Adrienne said Jones had said was not evidence.

Terry scowled. He climbed out of the truck without another word and returned to the Homestead to continue his investigation. Erin would have a long evening sitting in the truck waiting for him. But she was the one who had insisted she had to ride along.

CHAPTER 40

"Special order came in," Bella informed Erin as they switched places, Erin entering the kitchen and Bella going out to the front to serve customers. There was a green special-order sheet on the counter.

Erin picked it up and looked at it before putting the additional cookie sheets in the ovens. Not a birthday cake order, but a request for two lemon meringue pies. She had not made any since the day Mr. Fontainebleau had died. Even though everyone knew she'd had nothing to do with poisoning him, she still wanted to avoid any whispers behind her back or jokes about it. But apparently, someone had decided they weren't willing to wait until she felt like making them again. She looked up at the top of the order slip to see who it was for.

Matthew Harris.

Was he serious?

It seemed like poor taste for him to ask for the dessert she had made for his employer's last meal. Like he was celebrating Fontainebleau's demise.

Of course—many people *were* silently celebrating his demise.

Despite all of the non-disclosure agreements that had been signed, people were talking. The public funeral that had originally been planned had been canceled, with the announcement that the family had decided just to have a private memorial. Erin assumed they didn't want to deal with the possibility of victims showing up at the funeral and throwing eggs or shouting about what Fontainebleau had done to their families. A public funeral would probably have been only sparsely attended, now that the word was out about what kind of person he had been. Public figures were distancing themselves from Fontainebleau like rats fleeing a sinking ship.

Erin hesitated, then pulled out her phone and dialed the number beside Matthew's name.

"Hello?" his voice was cautious, uncertain. He didn't know her number.

"Mr. Harris, it's Erin Price from Auntie Clem's Bakery."

"Oh," his tone warmed. "Hello, Miss Price. You got my order."

"Yes, I did. Are you serious, though? You really want lemon meringue pies? You don't think that's too… morbid?"

"Of course not. There's nothing wrong with your lemon meringue pies, and I wouldn't want anyone to think there is. I *want* to be seen eating a pie from Auntie Clem's Bakery, to shake people off of this idea that it's something to whisper about once and for all."

"Well… that's very kind of you. I certainly wasn't expecting you to act as my PR agent."

He chuckled. "Your assistant wasn't sure when they would be ready. If you can let me know, I will be happy to come pick them up."

"If you're not in a rush, how would tomorrow afternoon be?"

"That would be just fine. Do you want to call me when they are ready, or should I just pop by?"

"I'll have them ready by mid-afternoon. Any time after two." Erin could work that into her schedule and it would give the pies enough time to chill before he picked them up. "And I'm assuming you'll be taking them straight home to the fridge? They can't be left in the vehicle while you shop, or they'll melt in this heat."

"I will take them straight home," he promised.

"Okay… I'll see you tomorrow."

∼

Erin heard the crunch of gravel behind the house and got up from the couch to look into the kitchen and out the back window to confirm that Vic and Willie had returned. She knew that they had been to the city to see some kind of specialist, but she hadn't pried to find out which one of them needed to see a medical professional or what for. She just hoped it wasn't anything serious.

Their body language was stiff and they didn't look at each other, like they had been arguing on the way home.

Erin put the kettle on. She didn't know whether Vic would come to talk to her or not, but she was in need of a nice calming tea herself. She didn't like to see them fighting. She looked studiously away from the window, not watching them return to the loft. She waited until she had heard the loft door shut before turning to look out the window again. Vic was making her way to the back door.

Erin turned back to the tea kettle and prepared the tea things. Maybe a few defrosted cookies to go with it... a little sugar went a long way to easing hurt feelings.

Vic tapped on the back door and entered. "Whew, these dogs are barking," she told Erin. "We must have walked twenty miles today." She sat down at the kitchen table and pried off her shoes. "Sorry for being so rude, but I really can't wear these another instant!"

Erin chuckled and continued to get their tea ready. The kettle began to sing. In a few minutes, she took everything over to the table and sat down. Vic immediately reached for a cookie.

"You always know just what to do," she complimented. "Tea and cookies are perfect."

"Good. Sounds like you had a long day."

"Long doesn't even begin to cover it. And Mr. Cranky-pants over there," she indicated the loft apartment with her eyes, "has not been the best of company."

"Well, you can relax now." Erin was determined not to ask where they had been and what the results of their consultation with the specialist had been.

"It's all your fault, you know," Vic told her. "Asking about Willie and whether his work could be causing health problems. Heavy metal poisoning and all that."

"Oh." Erin put her hand over her heart. "I'm sorry! I didn't mean to cause problems."

"Well, somebody needed to say it. What sense would it make just to let him keep poisoning himself?"

"I hope... well, did everything go okay? Is he...?"

"The doctor was pretty shocked by his condition. Said that people hadn't been working in conditions like that for a hundred years, and what made him think that exposing himself to those kinds of toxins was a good idea?" Vic rolled her eyes. "She didn't mince words. Which is good, because you and I both know that nothing is going to get into that hard head of Willie's if she held back."

"What does that mean for him?"

"He needs to detox immediately. And I'm not talking about wheatgrass shots for a week. I mean real medical intervention. They did his first chelation therapy today, and his calendar is booked up for some time to come. No alcohol, to give his liver the best chance possible to do its job. A special diet to give him all of the extra vitamins and minerals he needs to deal with the chelation and support liver and kidney function. She said he'll probably feel like he's got the flu for a few weeks and be restless and irritable. He'll want to stop. But he has to keep going and complete the protocol if he wants to clear all of the heavy metals and other toxins that he's been exposed to since he started mining and doing his own processing, however many years that's been. It's apparently a miracle that he's even functional right now."

Erin shook her head in amazement. "Wow. I'm glad they caught it now. Do you think you'll be able to keep him on the program?"

"I can't force him. I'll do my best, but it's gotta come from him. And he's going to have to upgrade to modern processing methods and protective gear and all of the proper precautions. To keep from poisoning himself more."

"Poor Willie. I feel bad about it... but I'm glad he saw someone and is doing something about it. We don't want him just dropping dead one day!"

"That's what I told him," Vic agreed, nodding. "He says that he'll live his life how he wants to and doesn't buy into all of this stuff, but... I can tell it scared him. She showed him all of his levels, and everything is in the red 'danger' zone. If he wants to live to be an old man, he's got to change."

Erin looked toward the loft apartment. "Is he pretty mad at me?"

"At you? No. At life. At the doctors. At everything. Maybe even me, because I pushed him so hard to get this testing done. But not at you. You saved his life."

"He's saved mine more than once." Erin's eyes burned with tears as she thought about how important Willie had been in her life, how gentle he was toward her, and how he always looked out for her and Vic. "I'm glad to return the favor."

Vic took another cookie and munched on it. There was a yip at the back door, and she got up and padded across the kitchen barefoot to open it and let Nilla in. Nilla ran around for a while, seeing where everyone was, including the animals, before finally lying down by the kitchen table to watch Vic and Erin.

"Things are going to change around here," Vic said. "Things are due for a change."

CHAPTER 41

*E*rin had Matthew's two lemon meringue pies ready for him at the front of the store. He had refused to pick them up in the back, insisting again that he wanted people to see him with the lemon meringue pies to reassure everyone that they were safe. He stood in line while Erin served other customers and, when he got to the counter, she handed him the two boxes.

"Don't go over any bumps. You don't want the meringue getting stuck to the inside of the box."

"I'll be careful," he assured her.

Erin moved to the till to ring up the total. When she reached out to take his money, he put an envelope in her hand. Erin looked down at it, then at his face.

"One last delivery," Matthew told her.

"That's what you said about the last one."

"Well… it was. This one isn't about Fontainebleau. It's just… to say thank you."

Erin opened the envelope, which contained a photograph. Funny how few actual photographs she saw anymore. Everything was electronic, on people's computers, phones, or fancy digital photo displays. In the photo were Matthew, his son, his daughter, and the new baby. They were all smiling. Matthew looked happy and peaceful in the picture.

"Thank you," Matthew said.

"I didn't really do anything. It was a police case."

He nodded and handed her the money for the pies. "Put the change in the tips jar. And I guess I'll see you around town."

Erin nodded. "Take care, Matthew."

"You too."

He left with his pies. Erin tucked the photograph into her apron pocket. The bakery was quiet. Bella had left to deal with a personal issue, but promised to be back in time for the after-school rush and to help close. Erin busied herself with straightening up, restocking a couple of things in the display case, and wiping down the counters in the kitchen.

She heard the bells at the front door and returned to the counter to deal with her next customer. Bella had come through the front door instead of the back. Not only that, but Adrienne was behind her. She had Sarah in her arms, but the rest of the children were not in evidence.

"She did it!" Bella announced. "Before Mrs. Jones left, she saw that everyone who was owed received the money they had been promised, deposited directly into their bank accounts."

Erin studied Adrienne, who looked rather shy. She had always faced Erin with some level of defensiveness before. She tended to come off as angry and confrontational, but Erin knew that a lot of it was vulnerability. Like an animal that puffed out its fur to make itself look bigger. Pretending to be confident and tough when she felt anything but. This time, though, the barriers were down.

"That means I have enough money to buy a property," Adrienne told her with teary eyes. "And to fix the car and look into building a house. A house instead of a tent!"

"That's wonderful," Erin told her. "You won't have to keep moving. You can settle down and have a stable life. The kids can go to school. That's so nice. It must be a big relief."

"I'm still going to homeschool the kids," Adrienne told her, hugging the baby closer, possessively. "But no one will be able to kick us out. We'll be able to live on our own property, and no one can complain that we're trespassing or squatting."

Erin nodded. "I'm really glad that it worked out for you. And... how is Hope doing?"

She wasn't there clinging to her mother, which was a good sign.

Adrienne looked toward the door. "She's watching the other kids in the park. I didn't want them all going to the bank with me." She rolled her eyes. "All of that paperwork and restless children!" She hesitated for a moment. "Maybe I'll have her see someone," she said. "I don't know yet. I know that's what everyone thinks I should do, but I don't know if it is right for her. We'll see."

"Terry might be able to recommend someone. He had to see a therapist after his head injury. He didn't like having to do it, but he said the doctor was pretty good."

Adrienne looked off into the distance, nodding to herself. "Maybe," she agreed. She might be imagining the home she would build for her and her kids; a safe place free of the evil man. Maybe just coming to terms with it all and finally feeling at peace. She and her kids would finally have a home of their own. The rest could be worked out.

"So…" Erin frowned. "It wasn't Freda who was trying to scare you off. She wasn't trying to get you to leave because she was afraid you were going to talk about what Fontainebleau had done or that she had promised you she would make things right."

Adrienne shook her head. "I wondered… obviously someone didn't want me and my kids around, and I could have made trouble for her."

"Then who was it? I guess we'll never know."

"Actually… I just ran into Marcelle in the bank, and…" Adrienne looked back in the direction of the bank.

"Marcelle? Fontainebleau's ex-wife?"

"Yeah. I guess she's lost a lot of money."

Erin nodded. "When Fontainebleau was sick and started to make bad decisions and run the company into the ground."

"And then all of the money Freda paid out… what everyone was owed. I don't know how much it was, but Marcelle was as mad as a spitting cat."

Bella shook her head. "She lit into Adrienne like she'd stolen all that money from her personally. Screaming about how she was supposed to leave town so that the people who really deserved the money would get it."

Erin rolled her eyes. "She's probably still got more than you've ever had in your life," she told Adrienne.

Adrienne nodded. "Ain't that the truth." She sighed. "But I don't need it all. Just one little corner under the trees, where the kids can run free and we can have our own roof over our heads. That would be heavenly."

"Will be," Bella amended.

Adrienne nodded, that shy smile spreading across her face again.

"Will be."

CHAPTER 42

The bells rang, and Erin looked up from the price label she had been writing for goods in the display case. Usually, she had Vic do them because she had much more attractive printing than Erin. Erin's numbers or letters never seemed to stay a consistent size, no matter how much she practiced. But Vic and Willie were off on a retreat, and Erin needed a few more labels written.

She didn't know the man who had walked into the store. He looked a little rough and down on his luck. Or maybe he'd just been traveling and was in need of refreshment. Erin gave him a pleasant smile, hoping to lift his spirits.

"Hi. Welcome to Auntie Clem's."

He nodded at her and looked around. Besides the bakery display case, there wasn't much to see, so his eyes soon returned to her.

"I was told that Adrienne's friend worked here. Would that be you?"

"I know Adrienne," Erin admitted. "But they were probably referring to Bella. She's not here at the moment."

"Well, if you know Adrienne, then maybe you can tell me where I can find her."

Erin was cautious. She didn't know who this guy was or why he would be trying to find Adrienne. Adrienne was a private person and would not want Erin giving out her personal details without permission.

"I could maybe get her a message. Would that help?"

"You have her phone number?"

"I have Bella's phone number. Bella will be able to get ahold of her."

"I don't want to be sent around in circles," he growled. "Do you know where Adrienne is or how to get her?"

"No. Sorry, I don't."

"You know where she lives? Someone said she was outside the town limits. Out in the sticks."

"Yes. I don't know exactly where. I haven't been out there myself. Sorry."

He scowled and shook his head. "If you can get a message to her, tell her that Simon is looking for her." He gave her a hard look. "Her husband."

Did you enjoy this book? Reviews and recommendations are vital to making a book successful.

Please leave a review at your favorite book store or review site and share it with your friends.

Don't miss the following bonus material:
Sign up for mailing list to get a free ebook
Read a sneak preview chapter
Other books by P.D. Workman
Learn more about the author

DON'T MISS A THING! GET THE LATEST NEWS AND A FREE EBOOK

PDWORKMAN.COM/SIGNUP

PREVIEW OF CINN-FULL SECRETS

PREVIEW CHAPTER 1

*A*ll you need to do is tell me where she is," Simon growled. "Come on, you can help a guy out."

Erin shook her head. She continued to line up portions of cream cheese icing samples in tiny paper cups along the tray, deliberately avoiding eye contact with him. The rich, spicy smell of the freshly baked cinnamon rolls filled the bakery.

"Sorry, can't help you," she told Simon. As if she hadn't already told him a dozen times. She would just keep repeating it calmly as if he were a child, and sooner or later, he would leave. At least, that was the theory she was operating under. She hoped that it would unfold the way she planned. She didn't want there to be any trouble.

"You know where she lives," Simon insisted. "Where she works. You know where in town she might be."

Erin shook her head. "I don't keep track of Adrienne, sorry."

"Where's the other one? Bella? She would tell me where Adrienne is. She knows that we're back together again. You think you're protecting Adrienne from something, but you're not. We're together; I'm just wondering where she is right now. I need to talk to her."

Bella came out of the kitchen and stood back behind the counter with Erin. She was an older teen, still in high school. She had a brilliant business mind and wanted to own her own business after college. She was one of Erin's most dependable workers and always came up with good ideas. She was slightly heavy, with wavy blond hair and a ready smile.

At least, she usually had a smile on her face. Today, she was obviously not entertaining friendly thoughts about Simon.

"You and Adrienne are *not* together again," she told him icily, "and Erin and I are not helping you find her or talk to her, or pass a message to her, or anything else. Why don't you go back to Las Vegas or wherever you were? Adrienne doesn't want anything to do with you."

"My wife is in Bald Eagle Falls, Tennessee, so I am in Bald Eagle Falls, Tennessee," Simon said in a sharp, flinty tone. "And I'm not leaving here unless she and the kids are with me."

"That's not going to happen," Bella told him flatly.

Erin would never have had that kind of confidence as a teenager. She hated confrontation and would do just about anything to avoid it. But Bella was a dragon, standing up to a man twice her age, protecting Adrienne and her children.

Erin had been worried that Adrienne would get back together with Simon. Despite their efforts to keep Simon from tracking her down over the past few weeks, he had met up with Adrienne in town a couple of times. Bald Eagle Falls was not a big place; it wasn't that hard to find her if she was in town instead of at Bella's family farm, or wherever else she and her children might be squatting now. Erin wouldn't be surprised if Adrienne had moved her family deeper into the bush. Simon could find out from anyone in town where the Prost farm was if he knew that was where his wife and children were. People were always trying to be helpful and put families back together, even when you told them there was good reason to keep them apart. Friends and family members were notorious for feeling sorry for a wrongly done husband and father who just wanted to make things right.

They had looked pretty cozy when Erin had seen them together. Erin worried that Adrienne would take him back and put the children at risk. Adrienne had told Erin that she didn't want anything to do with Simon, but her actions didn't bear that out. It was obvious that she was attracted to him. They had been together long enough to produce several children —Erin didn't know if all of the children were his or not, but at least a few of them were—so the relationship it was a comfortable place for Adrienne to return to. Being with Simon would feel natural. It would be easy to be seduced by his lies and believe that he was now going to support her. He was a changed man.

Only he wasn't. A leopard didn't change its spots.

Adrienne wanted to believe Simon would support her and her children now. That he wouldn't abandon them again, or do whatever other stupid stuff he'd done in the past. Adrienne admitted they had already broken up and gotten back together more than once. Erin was reminded of Adele, the gamekeeper who lived in the woods behind Erin's house and helped to keep them free of trespassers. Despite saying that she never wanted to see her husband again—and hadn't even told anyone she was married when she had first moved into town—Erin had seen how Rudolph Windsor had still persuaded her to take him in. He was bad for her and had a criminal past, but that had not stopped her from allowing him into her life again. Though, of course, it hadn't lasted.

Erin had her own history too. Would she have fallen back in with Brandon if he had shown up unexpectedly in Bald Eagle Falls and tried to woo her instead of stalking her? She would like to think that she would not have been tempted. She had lived with him out of desperation when she hadn't had anywhere else to go. It hadn't been a matter of loving him. She supposed that was the difference between her and Adrienne or Adele. It was a lot harder to resist a man you loved.

As far as Erin knew, Simon wasn't a criminal, just a lowlife. Someone who had abandoned his wife and kids one too many times. Gathering what she could from Simon's and Bella's words, Adrienne had finally decided to be tough and kick Simon to the curb.

And he was desperate to get back together with her now that she had money.

PREVIEW CHAPTER 2

*I*f you're not going to buy something," Erin told Simon, "please move on. Other people are waiting to be served."

Simon's small, black eyes flashed. He wasn't going to be put off that easily.

"Buy something? All of these empty carbs?" He looked over the items on display in the bakery case.

It wasn't like he was an athlete, keeping his body in pristine condition. He was on the short side for a man, with skinny arms and a gut. Not someone who worked out or watched what he ate.

Erin didn't bother to explain or excuse the preponderance of carbs in the display case. It *was* a bakery. Simon had known that when he had shoved his way through the front door.

"What are these?" Simon pointed to the sample cups Erin was preparing.

"Cream cheese icing for the cinnamon rolls. These ones are dairy," Erin pointed, "and these are vegan. Non-dairy."

"Non-dairy cream cheese?" he scoffed.

"Not everyone has the benefit of being able to eat dairy," Erin said evenly. "There are a lot of people who are allergic or intolerant. And they would still like to be able to enjoy their cinnamon rolls."

"They are cinn-fully delicious," Vic intoned from where she stood at the register.

Simon barely spared the pretty blond a glance. Most men would have at least given tall, slim, Vic a look of admiration. But maybe Simon had learned from Adrienne that Vic was trans, so he ignored her.

"All this stuff about everybody being intolerant or allergic to everything these days is just a crock," Simon asserted. "Sure, there are a few people who have celiac disease or will actually die if they eat something, but that's just a few people out of thousands. Everybody else," he shook his head in disapproval, "they're just being trendy. Pretending they are doing it to be healthy when they're just being difficult."

Wasn't he the one who had just complained about all the carbs?

"This is a gluten-free and specialty bakery," Erin pointed out. "If you don't want gluten-free, dairy-free, or another special diet, then there isn't anything here for you." Erin looked at the clock on the wall. "And I think it is time for you to go." Erin leaned to the side to see who was behind Simon, even though knew very well who was behind Simon and didn't need to be so dramatic about it. "Mary Lou, what can I get you today?"

Mary Lou stepped forward, so she was beside Simon rather than behind him. She looked into the display case, smoothing her pantsuit over her hips.

"I'm sure Joshua would like to try some cinnamon rolls," she said. "The regular icing will be fine."

"Great," Erin agreed. "Do you want just a couple?" She knew that Mary Lou was on a budget. She wished she could do more to assist the family, but they wouldn't accept any "charity." Mary Lou also didn't usually eat any desserts and was very careful of the number of calories she ate to avoid putting extra pounds on her slim figure. Joshua, Mary Lou's son and Roger, her husband, would eat one. But six or a dozen was not in their budget.

"Yes, two should do it," Mary Lou agreed. "And a loaf of bread," she pointed to the multi-grain-crusted loaf she wanted. "And... maybe a pizza shell. The herb one."

Erin proceeded to serve Mary Lou, ignoring Simon, who didn't move out of the way.

"Do *you* know Adrienne?" Simon asked Mary Lou.

Mary Lou looked at Erin, raising her brows as if she didn't know how to respond to his question. Erin gave an infinitesimal shake of her head. Of course Mary Lou already knew not to tell him anything. Erin was confident that she wouldn't.

"I'm sorry, no," Mary Lou told him coolly.

"You don't know who Adrienne is?"

"I'm afraid not."

Simon didn't believe it for a minute. "In this small town? Everybody in Bald Eagle Falls knows everyone else," he insisted. "If they're not actually related to each other. I know who you are. You're the wife of the man who tried to—"

"Simon," Erin interrupted, trying to avoid a painful topic of conversation. "Did you want a cinnamon roll? You really need to buy whatever you're going to and get out."

Erin hated to be rude. She didn't routinely tell people to leave Auntie Clem's Bakery, but she was tired of Simon and his antics and didn't want him harassing all of her customers.

"You're the only one new here," Simon told Erin. "I know everyone else."

"I'm not exactly new," Erin pointed out. She had been there for a couple of years now, longer than she had lived in most places.

"You're new," Simon told her flatly, shaking his head. "Families like mine and Adrienne's have lived on the mountain for generations. We are real Tennesseans. Living here for a year or two doesn't qualify you to make any judgments about me or my family."

"I'm not making any judgments about you or your family," Erin told him, bemused. "And my family has lived here for generations; I'm the only one who has not. I don't see what that has to do with anything. You're in a bakery. Buy something and move on."

"You can't talk to me like that."

There were increasingly restless movements from the other customers. No one had come to get in the middle of some domestic situation. Mary Lou gave Simon a disapproving look and walked past him to the register to pay for her purchases.

Erin took her phone from her apron pocket, tired of dealing with Simon. She tapped the screen a couple of times to call Terry.

That is, Officer Terry Piper.

He and K9 would be happy to get Simon on his way. They were probably bored with a quiet patrol day and could use some excitement.

"Erin," Terry's voice was warm, but also concerned. She didn't normally call him when she was on shift at Auntie Clem's. "What's up?"

"I have a trespasser at Auntie Clem's who is causing some problems, Officer Piper," Erin told him, her eyes on Simon. "I could use some help."

"I'll be right there," Terry growled. He terminated the call.

Erin slid her phone back into her pocket. She looked past Simon again.

"Betty, what can I get you?"

Betty Thompson was a senior who usually came in with her husband and was notoriously slow in choosing what she wanted to buy. Best to get her up to the counter so she could start pondering her choices. At least now that she had been coming to Auntie Clem's for a couple of years, she didn't have to ask for the ingredients in each item or to ask Erin where each had come from or to debate the benefits and drawbacks of each.

Betty shuffled up to the display case to have a look, giving Simon a wide berth.

"Okay, give me a cinnamon roll," Simon snapped. "You see? I'm a legitimate customer. I'm not trespassing."

He'd been back in town for long enough to know that Terry Piper was, in fact, law enforcement and that he would be on Erin's favorite contacts list. It wasn't just a bluff.

Erin got a single cinnamon roll for him and put it in a sleeve. She did not ask him, as she would have asked any other customer, if he wanted her to warm it in the microwave for a few seconds so that the icing would soften and run into the spiral layers.

"Did you want the cream cheese or non-dairy icing?" she asked him politely, as if she hadn't heard his earlier diatribe.

Simon choked, swore under his breath, and then apparently decided that if he were trying to be a legitimate customer, he'd better watch himself. "Cream cheese," he snarled.

Erin nodded and added a plastic knife and a little container of cream cheese icing to his bag. She briefly entertained the idea of giving him the non-dairy icing to see if he noticed the difference. But she had seen enough people cause harm by restaurant employees "testing" to see if someone really would react to a small bit of a food they claimed to be allergic or intolerant to. She would never give someone anything other than what they had ordered. It just wasn't in her make-up.

She put the bag on the counter next to the cash register for Vic to ring up.

The bells on the door jingled as it was pushed open, and Terry came in, devastatingly handsome in his police uniform, a bit of a five o'clock shadow on his jaw after a long patrol. K9 walked briskly at his side; ears pointed alertly forward as he looked for any sign of trouble.

"You're having a problem?" Terry asked Erin, not seeing any immediate issues.

Erin indicated Simon. "Mr. Simpson is ready to leave."

Simon glared at Erin. "I'm a customer," he said, holding up the bag containing the cinnamon roll. "I have a legitimate reason to be here."

Erin folded her arms. "And now that you've completed your transaction, you're ready to leave."

He opened his mouth to argue. But where was that going to get him? If he had already purchased what he needed, then there was no need for him to stay around. If he was there for another reason, like to threaten Erin into revealing where he could find Adrienne or to cause problems with the other customers, he obviously couldn't do that in front of local law enforcement.

And even if he didn't happen to think that Terry Piper was a formidable force, he had to consider whether he would win or lose in an argument with K9. And most people Erin knew would choose not to be on the receiving end of a German shepherd bite.

"You're ready to go?" Terry asked.

Simon looked at Erin and Bella, then back at Terry and K9. There wasn't any way for him to save face or to stay there any longer, so he gave up.

"Yeah, I'm leaving," he agreed. He shook his head and departed the bakery.

A collective sigh went up from the remaining customers. And staff.

"That guy is trouble," Terry observed.

Erin nodded. "That won't be the last we see of him."

"Just keep calling me. Or the dispatcher if I'm not available. Don't try to argue with him or convince him to go. Just call me the second he walks in the door. It shouldn't take too long to discourage him from showing up here."

"Okay. I'll let everyone else know," Erin agreed.

But Erin was wrong, because it *was* the last time that Simon would set foot inside Auntie Clem's Bakery.

~

Cinn-full Secrets, Book #22 of the *Auntie Clem's Bakery* series by P.D. Workman
can be purchased at pdworkman.com

~

ABOUT THE AUTHOR

P.D. Workman is a USA Today Bestselling author, winner of several awards from Library Services for Youth in Custody and the InD'tale Magazine's Crowned Heart award, and has published over 100 mystery/suspense/thriller and young adult books, including stand alones and these series: Auntie Clem's Bakery cozy mysteries, Reg Rawlins Psychic Investigator paranormal mysteries, Zachary Goldman Mysteries (PI), Kenzie Kirsch Medical Thrillers, Parks Pat Mysteries (police procedural), and YA series: Tamara's Teardrops, Between the Cracks, and Breaking the Pattern.

Workman loves writing about the underdog, who the reader may love or hate. She has been praised for her realistic details, deep characterization, and sensitive handling of the serious social issues that appear in all of her stories, from light cozy mysteries through to darker, grittier young adult and mystery/suspense books.

> P. D. Workman, does not shy from probing the deep psychological scars of childhood trauma, mental illness, and addiction. Also characteristic of this author, these extremely sensitive issues are explored with extensive empathy, described with incredible clarity, and portrayed with profound insight.
>
> ——KIM, GOODREADS REVIEWER

Some of Workman's titles have been translated into Spanish, French, Portuguese, German, and Italian.

Workman began writing at an early age and is a prolific reader as well as writer. She is also passionate about teaching and learning, expresses her creativity through art and cooking, and loves exploring the Calgary parks and green spaces where the Parks Pat Mysteries are set. She was a legal assistant for many years and has done extensive charitable work.

Workman was born and raised in Alberta, Canada, and is married with one adult son.

~

Please visit P.D. Workman at pdworkman.com to see what else she is working on, to join her mailing list, and to link to her social networks.

~

If you enjoyed this book, please take the time to recommend it to other purchasers with a review or star rating and share it with your friends!

tiktok.com/@pdworkmanauthor

facebook.com/pdworkmanauthor

x.com/pdworkmanauthor

instagram.com/pdworkmanauthor

amazon.com/author/pdworkman

bookbub.com/authors/p-d-workman

goodreads.com/pdworkman

linkedin.com/in/pdworkman

pinterest.com/pdworkmanauthor

youtube.com/pdworkman

patreon.com/pdworkmanauthor

reamstories.com/pdworkmanauthor

Find P.D. Workman's books at

PDWORKMAN.COM

Scan the QR code below

www.ingramcontent.com/pod-product-compliance
Lightning Source LLC
Chambersburg PA
CBHW070342030726
47504CB00001B/38

* 9 7 8 1 7 7 4 6 8 7 5 8 1 *